DEATH MATCH

BY CHRIS BUNCH AND ALLAN COLE

Sten
Sten 2: The Wolf Worlds
Sten 3: The Court of a Thousand Suns
Sten 4: Fleet of the Damned
Sten 5: Revenge of the Damned
Sten 6: The Return of the Emperor
Sten 7: Vortex
Sten 8: Empire's End

Battlecry: Sten Omnibus 1
Juggernaut: Sten Omnibus 2
Death Match: Sten Omnibus 3

BY CHRIS BUNCH

The Seer King
The Demon King
The Warrior King

The Empire Stone

Corsair

Dragonmaster 1: Storm of Wings

DEATH MATCH

STEN OMNIBUS 3

Chris Bunch *and* Allan Cole

This omnibus edition includes
Sten 7: Vortex
Sten 8: Empire's End

www.orbitbooks.net

ORBIT

First published in Great Britain in 2012 by Orbit

Sten 7: Vortex
First published in Great Britain in 2001 by Orbit

Sten 8: Empire's End
First published in Great Britain in 2001 by Orbit

A CIP catalogue record for this book
is available from the British Library.

ISBN 978-1-84149-495-1

Typeset in Sabon LT Std by Palimpsest Book Production Limited,
Falkirk, Stirlingshire

Printed and bound by CPI Group (UK) Ltd, Croydon CR0 4YY

Papers used by Orbit are from well-managed forests
and other responsible sources.

MIX
Paper from
responsible sources
FSC® C104740
www.fsc.org

Orbit
An imprint of
Little, Brown Book Group
100 Victoria Embankment
London EC4Y 0DY

An Hachette UK Company
www.hachette.co.uk

www.orbitbooks.net

Contents

STEN 7: VORTEX

To
Andy AFFA Anderson
and
Harry Harrison

A pair of Stainless Steel Rats

'When your fear cometh as desolation,
and your destruction cometh as a whirlwind;
when destruction and anguish cometh upon you.'
—PROVERBS 1:27

BOOK ONE

CONVECTION

Chapter One

The Square of the Khaqans brooded under storm clouds knuckled black in the sky. A weak sun crept through those clouds, picking out flashes of gold, green, and red from the towering buildings and domes.

The square was immense: twenty-five square kilometers solid with gaudy buildings, the official heartbeat of the Altaic Cluster. On the western edge was the lace-pattern fan of the Palace of the Khaqans – home to the old and angry Jochian who had ruled over the cluster for a hundred and fifty years. For seventy-five of those years the man had labored on this square, lavishing billions of credits and being-hours. It was a monument to himself and his deeds – both real and imagined. Almost as an afterthought there was a small shrine park in a forgotten corner of the square in memory of his father, the first Khaqan.

The square sat in the center of Jochi's capital, Rurik. Everything in this city was huge; the inhabitants were forever scurrying about, reduced in scale and spirit by the size of the Khaqan's vision.

Rurik was quiet this day. Humid streets emptied. Beings huddled in their tenements for mandatory viewing of the events about to unfold on their livie screens. All across the planet Jochi it was the same.

In fact, on all the habitable worlds of the Altaic Cluster humans and ETs alike had been cleared from the streets by loudspeaker vehicles and ordered into their dwellings to punch up the livie cast. Small red eyes at the bottom of the screens monitored their required rapt attention. Security squads were posted in every neighborhood, ready to kick in the door and haul away any being whose attention flagged.

At the Square of the Khaqans itself, three hundred thousand beings had been ordered in for public witness. Their bodies formed a black smear around the edges of the square. The heat from the living mass rose in waves of steam and drifted up into the menacing clouds. The only movement was a constant nervous shifting. There was not one sound from the crowd. Not the cry of a child or a cough from an Old One.

Heat lightning branched over the four gilded pillars that marked each end of the square and the enormous statues honoring Altaic heroes and deeds hunched over it. Thunder boomed and echoed under the clouds. Still the crowd held its silence.

Troops were formed up in the center of the square, weapons at ready, eyes scanning the crowd for any sign of danger.

At their backs loomed the Killing Wall.

A sergeant barked orders, and the execution squad clanked forward, walking heavily under the burden of twin tanks strapped to each being's back. Flex hose ran from the tanks to a two-meter-long tube held by each squad member.

Another order, and hands sheathed in thick fireproof gloves flexed the triggers of the flamethrowers. Molten fire dripped from the ends of the tubes. Gloved fingers tightened, and a howl rent the air as flame exploded out and against the Killing Wall.

The squad held the triggers back for a terrible moment of heat and acrid smoke. The flames hammered at the wall in heavy waves. At the sergeant's signal, the fire stopped.

The Killing Wall was unmarked, except for the deep red glow of superheated metal. The sergeant spat. The spittle exploded as it touched the wall. He turned and smiled.

The execution squad was ready.

A sudden squall erupted, drenching the crowd and sending up hissing clouds of steam from the wall. It stopped as quickly as it had begun, leaving the crowd miserable in the humid atmosphere.

There was a nervous buzz here and there. Among so many beings, fear can keep the silence only so long.

'This is the fourth time in as many cycles,' a young Suzdal yipped to his pack mate. 'Every time the Jochi police come hammering on the door to call us out to the square, I think, this time they're coming for us.' His little snout was wrinkled back with fear, exposing sharp, chattering teeth.

'It's nothing to do with us, dear,' his pack mate said. She rubbed the thick furred hump that protruded above her muzzle against the adolescent male, spreading soothing hormone. 'They only want the black marketeers.'

'But all of us do it,' the frightened Suzdal yipped. 'There's no other way to live. We'd all starve without the black market.'

'Hush, someone will hear,' his pack mate warned. 'This is human doings. As long as they're killing Jochians or Torks, we mind our own business.'

'I can't help it. It feels like what some humans call Judgment Day. Like we're all doomed. Look at the weather. Everybody's talking about it. No one's seen anything like it. Even the Old Ones say it's never been like this on Jochi. Freezing cold one day. Blistering hot the next. Snow storms. Then floods and cyclones. When I woke this morning, I thought it smelled like spring outside. Now look.' He pointed at the heavy black storm clouds overhead.

'Now, don't get yourself overwrought,' his pack mate said. 'Not even the Khaqan can control the weather.'

'He's going to get to us eventually. And then . . .' The young Suzdal shuddered. 'Do you know one being who has been executed yet who was *really* guilty? Of anything . . . big?'

'Of course not, dear. Now, be quiet. It'll be over with . . . soon.' And she rubbed more hormone into his fur. Soon the chattering teeth were still.

There was a crash and a boom and howl of music over the great loudspeakers, so loud that the foliage in the scattered parks of the square shivered with the beat. The gold-robed Khaqan Guard trotted, spear formation, out of the palace. At the apex of the spear was a floating platform bearing the Khaqan on his high-back, gilded throne.

The whole group quick-marched to a position just near the Killing Wall. The platform settled to the ground.

The old Khaqan peered about him with suspicious, rheumy eyes. He wrinkled his nose at the close smell of the crowd. An ever-attentive privy aide caught the gesture and sprayed the Khaqan with his favorite sweet-scented incense. The old man pulled a decorated flask of methquill from his belt, uncorked it, and took a long drink. It quick-fired through his veins. His heart raced and his eyes cleared along with his enthusiasm.

'Bring them out,' he barked. It was an old, shrill sound, but it put the fear of the cowardly gods who tended this place into his servants.

Orders were whispered down the line. In front of the Killing

Wall, metal hissed on oiled bearings, and a dark hole yawned. There was a hum of machinery, and a wide platform rose up to fill the hole.

There was a long, audible shudder from the crowd when they saw the prisoners standing there in their chains, blinking in the dim light. Soldiers hustled forward and prodded the forty-five men and women to the wall. Metal bands emerged from the wall and clamped them into place.

The prisoners looked at the Khaqan with stunned eyes. He took another pull on his flask and giggled with the heat of the methquill.

'Get on with it,' he said.

The black-robed inquisitor stepped forward and began reading the names and confessions of each of the assembled felons. Their list of crimes boomed over the loudspeakers: Conspiracy to profit . . . Hoarding of rationed goods . . . Theft from the markets of the Jochi elite . . . Abuse of office to profit . . . On and on it went.

The old Khaqan frowned at each charge, then nodded and smiled at each disposition of guilt.

Finally it was done. The Inquisitor slid the charge fiche into its sleeve and turned to await the Khaqan's decision.

The old man sipped at his flask, then keyed his throat mike. His shrill, raspy voice filled the square and buzzed on the livies in the billions of homes in the Altaic Cluster.

'As I look at your faces, my heart is moved with pity,' he said. 'But I am also ashamed. All of you are Jochians . . . like myself. As the majority race in the Altaics, it is for the Jochians to point the way. By good example. What are our fellow humans, the Tork, to think when they hear of your evil deeds? Much less our ET subjects, with their looser grip of morality. Yes . . . What do the Suzdal and the Bogazi think when you Jochians – my most prized subjects – flaunt the law and endanger our society by your greed?

'These are terrible times, I know. All those long years of war with the filthy Tahn. We suffered and sacrificed – and, yes, died – in that war. But no matter how heavy our burden, we stood by the Eternal Emperor.

'And later – when we believed him slain by his enemies – we struggled on, despite the unfair burdens placed on us by the beings who conspired to assassinate him and rule in his place.

'During each of these emergencies, I asked your help and your sacrifice to keep our lovely cluster safe and secure until the Emperor's return. As I believed he would, all the time.

'Finally, he came. He disposed of the evil privy council. Then he looked around to see who had remained steadfast in his absence. He found me – your Khaqan. As strong and loyal a servant as I have been for nearly two centuries. And he saw you – my children. And he smiled. From that moment on, the Anti-Matter Two flowed again. Our factories were alight once more. Our starships soared to the great market places of the Empire.

'But all is still not well. The Tahn wars and the actions of the traitorous privy council have sorely tested the Eternal Emperor's resources. And ours as well. We have years of hard work ahead of us before life can be normal and prosperous.

'Until that time comes, we must all continue to sacrifice the comforts of the present for the glorious life of the future. All of us are hungry now. But at least there is food enough to sustain. Our AM2 allotment is more than most, thanks to my close friendship with the Emperor. But it is only enough to keep commerce alive.'

The Khaqan paused to wet his throat with methquill. 'Greed is the greatest crime in our small kingdom now. For in these times, isn't greed nothing more than murder on a mass scale?

'Every grain you steal, every drop of drink you sell on the black market, comes from the mouths of children, who will certainly starve if greed is left unchecked. The same for our precious AM2 supplies. Or the minerals for tools to rebuild our industry, and the synthcloth that keeps us from the elements.

'So it is with a heavy heart that I sentence you. I have read the letters from your friends and loved ones, begging my mercy. I wept over each one. I really did. They told a sad tale of beings gone wrong. Beings who have listened to the lies of our enemies, or fell into callous company.'

The Khaqan wiped a nonexistent tear from rimless eyelids. 'I have mercy enough for all of you. But it is a mercy I must withhold. To do otherwise would be criminally selfish of me.

'Therefore I am forced to sentence you to the most disgraceful death known, as an example to any others who are foolish enough to be tempted by greed.

'I can allow only one small concession to self-weakness. And I hope my subjects forgive me this, for I am very old and easily moved to pity.'

He leaned forward in his chair as the livie camera dollied in until his face filled one side of the screen for the viewers at home. It was a mask of compassion. On the other side of the screen were the forty-five doomed beings.

The Khaqan's voice whispered harshly. 'To each and every one of you . . . I'm sorry.'

He cut the throat mike and turned to his privy aide. 'Now, get this over with quick. I don't want to be out here when the storm breaks.' And he eased his old bones back into the throne to watch.

Orders were shouted, and the execution squad took up position. Flamethrower barrels were raised. The crowd drew a long breath. The prisoners hung dully against their bonds. Thunder crashed overhead from the clouds.

'Do it,' the Khaqan snarled.

The flamethrowers roared into life. Solid sheets of fire burst out at the Killing Wall.

In the crowd some beings turned away.

A Suzdal pack leader named Youtang barked in disgust. 'It's the smell that gets me most,' she yipped. 'Puts me off my rations. Everything tastes like cooked Jochians.'

'Humans smell bad enough without being parboiled,' her assistant leader agreed.

'When the Khaqan started these purges,' Youtang said, 'I thought, so what? There's so many Jochians, maybe it'll thin their ranks some. Leave more for us Suzdal. But he kept at it. And I got worried. Pretty soon, he's going to have to start looking elsewhere for his examples.'

'He thinks the Bogazi are stupidest, so they'll probably be last,' her assistant said. 'We'll be purged just before them. The Torks are human, so if he sticks to whatever it is he calls logic, they're probably next.'

'Speaking of Torks,' Youtang said, 'I see one worried-looking friend of ours over there.' She said 'friend of ours' with disgust. 'Look. It's Baron Menynder. Jabbering at some other human. Jochian, by the cut of his clothes.'

'It's General Douw,' her assistant yipped, excited.

The Suzdal pack leader pondered for a moment. The human she was looking at was a short, squat being with a pure bald head. The beefy face was ugly enough to belong to a thug, but Baron Menynder affected spectacles that made his brown eyes large, wide, and innocent.

'Now, what would the Khaqan's defense secretary be doing talking with Menynder? Couldn't be professional advice, even though Menynder had the same job once. But he's past it now. His time was four or five defense secretaries back. The Khaqan fired or killed all the rest. Clot, that Menynder is a canny old being,' Youtang mused almost to herself. 'Got out just in time. And he sticks to his own business and keeps his head low.'

She studied the situation a little longer, getting a closer look at General Douw. The Jochian appeared an ideal general, well over two and a half meters high. He was sleek and athletic, at least next to the tubby Menynder. His silver-gray locks fitted his head like a tight helmet, in stark contrast to Menynder's bald pate.

'Douw must be liking what he's hearing,' the Suzdal pack leader finally said. 'Menynder's been going nonstop since we started watching.'

'Maybe the old Tork is feeling extra mortal these days,' her assistant said. 'Maybe he has a plan. Maybe that's what the discussion is all about.'

The work at the Killing Wall was done. There were only ashes where the condemned had once stood. At the western edge of the square, the Suzdals could see the Khaqan and his guards disappearing into the lacy palace. In the center, the soldiers were being formed up and marched off a platoon at a time.

Youtang watched the two humans in deep discussion. An idea stirred. 'I think we should join them,' she said. 'One thing about Menynder is that he's a clotting great survivor. Come on. If there's a way out of this alive, I don't want the Suzdal to be left behind.'

The two beings edged through the crowd.

The storm broke. Shouts of pain and terror echoed across the square as hailstones hammered out of the clouds, bursting like shrapnel.

The loudspeakers blared dismissal, and the crowd erupted out of the square.

Menynder and General Douw hurried away together. But by the time they reached the main gate, the two Suzdals had caught up with them. The four paused in the shelter of an enormous statue of the Khaqan at the edge of the gate. A few words were exchanged. Then nods of agreement. A moment later the four hurried off together.

The conspiracy had been launched.

Chapter Two

'An aperitif, m' lord?' a voice purred in Sten's ear. Sten brought himself back to reality, realized he'd been preening like an Earth peacock in front of the oak-framed mirror on the wall, and covered a blush.

The owner of the voice was female, black-haired, invitingly constructed and costumed, and was holding a tray of fluted glasses. The flutes contained a black, slightly bubbling liquid. 'Black Velvet,' she said. Indeed you are, Sten thought. But he said nothing, merely lifted an inquiring eyebrow.

'A combination of two Old Earth spirits,' she continued. 'Earth champagne – Taittinger Blanc de Blancs – and a rare brewed stout from the island of Eire. Guinness, it is named.'

She paused and smiled – a most personal smile. 'You should enjoy your stay here on Prime, Sr Ambassador Sten. As a member of the household staff, it would be my disappointment were you to leave . . . dissatisfied.'

Sten took one glass, sipped, and said his thanks. The woman waited, found nothing further, smiled once more – a more formal smile – and passed on.

You are growing old, Sten thought. Once upon a time you would have admired, asked, and gotten either a turndown or an acceptance for later. Then you would have downed six glasses to stagger you through this idiotic ceremony. But you are now an adult. You do not get drunk because you think parades are foolishness. Nor do you leap for the first beautiful woman who presents herself.

Besides . . . that smiling servitor was certainly an Intelligence – Mercury Corps – operative who quite possibly outranked Admiral (Inactive-Reserve) Sten (NI).

Finally, at the moment he was not in the mood for a fling. Why not? While part of his brain puzzled, he tasted. Odd combination. He had tasted fermented and augmented effervescent grape juice before, although it had seldom been this dry. The other liquid – Guinness? – added a sharp, solid bash to the taste, not unlike a pugil stick to the head. Before he left Prime he would drink more of these, he resolved.

Sten moved back until his shoulders touched the wall – old habits as an Imperial assassin died hard – and looked about the monstrous chamber.

Arundel Castle rose triumphant over its own ruins. Built as the Eternal Emperor's grandiose living quarters on the Imperial world of Prime, it had been destroyed by a tacnuke as part of the Tahn's unique way of beginning a war *sans* preliminaries. During the ensuing Empire-wide battle, Arundel had remained in symbolic ruins, the Eternal Emperor headquartered in the vast warren under the desolation.

When the Emperor had been assassinated, Arundel had been left as a memorial by his killers. It had been rebuilt upon the Emperor's return – even more lofty and looming than before.

Sten was in one of the castle's antechambers. A waiting room. A waiting room that could have served handily as a hangar for a fleet destroyer.

The room was packed with fat cats, military and civilian, humanoid and otherwise. Sten glanced once more in the mirror and winced. 'Fat cats' was slightly too apt a phrase. Now that you have finished the Emperor's latest bidding, he thought, you need to get back in shape. That sash you were admiring but a minute before with all its decorations *does* accentuate a bit of a paunch, does it not? And the wingtip collar serves to give you another chin. Don't you hope it's the collar?

The hell with you, Sten told his backbrain. I am happy at the moment. Happy with me, happy with the world, happy with where I am.

He looked yet a third time in the mirror, returning to the train of thought interrupted by the servitor. Damn. I am still not used to seeing myself in diplomatic drag. Instead of some kind of uniform, or at least a disguise. This outfit, this archaic shirt, coat with a forked tail that stretches nearly to my ankles, these pants that reach down to shiny low-top boots . . . this is still strange.

He wondered what would happen if the Sten who *was* – that poor clottin' orphan from that slave company world who was lucky and quick with a knife – looked into that mirror and it became that fictional favorite, a timescreen? What would that young Sten think as he peered into it, knowing he was looking at himself in years to come?

Years? Many more than he'd like to total.

What an odd wonderment. Especially here. Waiting on the pleasure of the Eternal Emperor, to be congratulated and awarded for service at the highest level.

Yes. What would that younger Sten think? Or say?

Sten grinned. Probably – other than 'Why the clot didn't you follow up with Black Velvet?' – a grunt of relief. So. We're clottin' alive. Never thought we'd make it. Without thinking, his right hand moved over and touched the rich silk of his coat.

Under that – and under his diamond-studded shirtsleeve – was still the knife. Surgically hidden *in* his arm. Sten had built it – had grown it and then 'machined' it on a biomill – as a slave laborer on Vulcan. It had been his first possession. The knife was a tiny, double-edged dart, contoured to fit no other hand but his. Needle-pointed, it could cut an Earth-diamond in half with only blade pressure. It may have been the most deadly knife that man, with his infinite fascination with destruction, had ever built. It was kept in place by a surgically rerouted muscle.

But it had been more than a year, no, almost two years since it had been drawn in anger. Four wonderful years of peace, after a lifetime at war. Peace . . . and a growing sense in Sten that he was finally doing the task he was suited for. Something that did not involve—

'How correct,' a voice said in a flat, lethal monotone. 'You always *did* remind me a bit of a pimp. I see you have become one. Or at least dress like one.'

Sten growled back to reality, arm dropping, fingers curling, the knife reflexing down into its killing slot; stepping away from the wall, left foot coming back, poised on toe, weight centered, slight crouch . . .

Clotting Mason.

Correction. Clotting Fleet Admiral Rohber Mason. In full dress whites, his chest a blaze of decorations, all of them well earned and probably no more than one-third of the hero buttons Mason deserved. He had never bothered to get that livid scar that ripped across his face removed. Sten figured he probably felt it added to his charm.

'Admiral,' Sten said. 'How is the baby-slaughtering trade?'

'It goes well,' Mason retorted. 'Once you learn to shorten your lead and range, it's simple.'

Mason and Sten hated each other for no known reason. Mason had been one of Sten's instructors back during flight school and had done his best to make sure Sten never graduated. Mason was considered by his students as an unmitigated bastard. The students were correct. And, unlike the livies, after graduation Mason's heart of stone was not revealed as a pose. Under the granite was ten-point steel.

During the Tahn war Mason had risen to admiral. He had many qualities: He was brilliant. A tyrant. A master strategist. A killer. A brutal disciplinarian. A leader who backed his subordinates to the grave and beyond. For instance, when he was unable to find just cause to wash Sten out of flight school, he graduated him with the highest marks. Mason was possibly the best tac pilot in the Imperial Forces. Second best, Sten's pilotego growled.

Fiercely loyal to the Emperor, he had survived the privy council's purges through luck and meanness. Now he was no doubt carrying out Imperial orders as he had in the past – efficiently and savagely. Yes, Sten thought, there had been peace. But only compared to the nightmare of the Tahn war. Beings still died.

'I heard you'd become the Emperor's messenger boy,' Mason said. 'Never could understand how a *real* being could stand living in a world where everything's gray and there's no truth.'

'I've gotten to like the color,' Sten said. 'It doesn't stain the hands as much as red. And it washes off.'

A booming voice broke the mutual glower. 'Gentlebeings, your attention, please.' The buzz of polite diplomatic chatter died away.

'I am Grand Chamberlain Bleick.' The speaker was a ridiculously costumed, undersized being, speaking in the loudest smarmy twitter Sten had ever heard. Of course. He had a throat mike and porta boomer.

'We want to ensure that all of you noble ones receive the correct recognition, and that this ceremony proceeds as planned. Therefore, we must adhere to the following rules. The awards will be presented in descending order of merit. A subordinate will announce each category.

'When your award is called, you will form a single line here, at the entrance. When the annunciator' – Bleick indicated a being in red flummoxry – 'announces your name, you will enter the main chamber. You will walk directly forward approximately seventeen steps, where you will see a line graven on the floor.

'The Emperor will be standing on the far side of that line.

'If you are the only recipient of an award, stop directly in front of the Eternal Emperor. If you are one of a group, proceed directly to the line and stop next to the nearest being on your left.

'Please stand at attention.

'An Imperial aide will read the citation for your award. A second aide will physically give you the award, either on a sash or she will pin it directly to your uniform. If there is an error, please try to cover any pained reaction. The ceremonies are, of course, being taped for subsequent broadcast to your home worlds.

'Additional copies, I might add, may be secured through my office at a reasonable fee.

'There are no scheduled recipients for any of the Imperial Privy Household Orders. The next ranking are hereditary awards: dukedoms, baronetcies, and the like. Those who are receiving one of those . . .'

'Hereditary,' Sten breathed in surprise. His lips did not move, nor did his voice reach beyond Mason's ears. It was a talent learned in military formations and prisons.

Mason, too, had the talent: 'The Eternal Emperor has seen fit to find many new and unique patterns to reward those who serve him well.' His voice was quite devoid of irony.

'But—'

'Not only does it please the red-tape bastards,' Mason said, 'but their bureaucratic bosses, as well.'

The disapproval both men felt never showed on either's face. But strong sentiments *did* materialize a few meters away.

The man was huge and very white – from his flowing mane to his sweeping muttonchop whiskers and formal court dress. He also looked to be slightly drunk.

'Right lot of mad idiots,' he said in a voice that rolled like thunder. 'Clottin' titles make a yearlin' think he's automatic blood stock. Give unproven whelps ideas, that does! First time I heard of such drakh!

'By haveen, th' Emp's slippin', allowin' all this formal dancin' by this crew of scrotumless ijiots! B'dam' if I'll take part in any such monkey dancin'. Tell th' Emp, if he wants—'

Whatever Whiskers was about to suggest for the Emperor was swiftly broken off as four very, very large humans slid out of nowhere and formed a mini-cordon around the man.

Sten heard more protests, but most smoothly the man was

brought under control and guided – he was too large to be frog-marched – out a nearby exit.

The four men were wearing a new, police-type gray uniform that Sten could not recollect having seen around Prime or the palace before. He saw one of their shoulder tabs, a round black and gold patch with a gold *I*, and the letter *S* scrolled around it.

'Who were the eighty-sixers?' he wondered in that monotone to Mason.

'New security element. Internal Security. The limit of my knowledge or curiosity.'

'Who are they organized under? Mercury? Mantis?' Sten's natural curiosity sprang from his former – at least officially – membership in both organizations.

'I say again my last . . .' Mason's voice was louder, frostier. 'Goons, gestapos, and guessers have never been my province.'

Sten found it polite to follow the ebb as awardees formed up, walked through the door, and vanished.

Hereditary orders . . . Meritorious orders . . . Decorations (military) . . . Decorations (civil) . . .

Sten stopped in front of the chamberlain, who consulted his list. 'Sr Plenipotentiary Sten, you will be the only being honored with this award today. You may enter.'

Sten walked toward the high gaping doors, and two beings in those red suits – and, Sten thought, some kind of whitish artificial hair – opened the doors.

A voice blared: 'The Most Honorable Sten . . . of Smallbridge.'

The yawning Award Chamber was now filled with those who had already gone. Sten smoothed forward, at that slightly slower-than-normal pacing every diplomat learns that shows best on the livies. He formed a dignified expression on his face.

Most Honorable, he thought. Very interesting. As I recall, I was only Very Honorable the last time I was at court. Does Most Honorable give me a bigger paycheck?

'Ambassador Plenipotentiary Sten fulfilled the highest standards of the Imperial Service, at considerable risk to his own personal safety, in a recent mission to mediate between the Thorvaldians and the inhabitants of Markel Bat. Not only was peace preserved, but a new era of tranquillity was brought to the cluster. He is to be honored by being named to a new ranking, A Companion of the Emperor.'

Which meant, Sten thought, whatever the Eternal Emperor wanted it to. Which was anything except an Imperial Privy

Household Order – whatever *they* were. At least those obnoxious clots hadn't actually gotten around to killing each other. Nor had he found it necessary to kill any of them, tempting as it had been at times.

None of these thoughts appeared on Sten's face. Nor did his expression change as he walked toward that line, his eyes sweeping the huge chamber.

Up there . . . the iris in the chandelier . . . a tracking gun turret. That huge portrait – a one-way screen with a riot squad behind it, most likely. There, and there. At belt level. To either side of that line . . . hidden laser projectors.

On each side of the Awards Chamber's doors were paired Gurkhas. Quiet, small, brown men, faces blank, in dress uniform, their slouch hats' chin straps held just below their lower lips. And, holstered on one hip, each had a miniwillygun. On the other hip the lethal, slashing kukris that helped make the Gurkha the most feared and respected soldier in the Empire. Plus there were about ten more of those gray-clad Internal Security types scattered through the room.

So? Wouldn't you put on a little bit more security if some clot had gone and killed you a few years earlier?

A man stood alone just beyond that line.

The Eternal Emperor.

Dark hair. Blue eyes. Well muscled. He looked to be, at the oldest, in his mid-thirties. No, Sten corrected, his eyes made him out to be a bit older.

But certainly not old enough to be what he was – the man who for over a millennium had single-handedly built this Empire, the Empire that stretched beyond any beings' visualizations, the Empire that had almost been destroyed and now was being reassembled.

Sten came to rigid attention. The Emperor looked his personal envoy up and down, then nodded in formal approval.

The two Imperial aides – the one who had recited the citation, and the other, who was holding some kind of medal in an open, velvet case – stepped forward.

Then the Emperor broke tradition. He turned to the aide and took the award from its case.

He stepped close, looping the decoration over Sten's neck. 'Forty-five minutes,' the Eternal Emperor monotoned, in a prison whisper just as skilled as Sten's. 'Backstairs . . . my chambers . . . we need a drink.'

Chapter Three

Sten stepped onto the security grid. At the Internal Security officer's signal he offered his palm to the identification beam. The grid hummed into life, and Sten was bathed in a glow of colors. Somewhere in the bowels of Arundel a whole host of facts was collected: Sten was being analyzed by the most sophisticated snooping equipment in the Empire.

The first level was ID. As soon as Sten's palm print was checked and rechecked, his bio was being scanned for any potential animosity to the Emperor. That information was checked a third time against the latest Mercury Corps records, up to date within the past twenty-four hours.

The second was organic. His system was analyzed for any possible bacterial or viral threat to Sten's boss. It had been possible for a long time to build a living germ warfare bomb.

The final level was for weapons, from the obvious hide-out gun or blade, to the not so obvious surgically implanted explosive. Or, in Sten's case, the knife in his arm. He knew that when the scanners caught it, his authorization for bearing such a weapon in the Emperor's presence would override any alarm.

Sten got the okay, stepped off the grid, and headed along the corridor for the Emperor's quarters. He was feeling edgy about the upcoming conference with his boss. It had been a long time since the two of them had had a face-to-face. Something extra-important must be up.

But that wasn't what was bothering him. It was the supertight security that made him nervous – an odd thought from the man who had once headed up the Emperor's personal bodyguard. Then he had fretted at any lapse, worried at the Emperor's tendency to plunge off into crowds, or sneak away for a private adventure.

Sten didn't blame the Eternal Emperor for clamping down hard after what had happened. But now that he had gained a great deal of experience as a public man himself, Sten also knew it was dangerous for any being in authority to adopt a bunker mentality. The tighter the screen, the harder the job of the villain, admittedly. But it also could make it tough for the guys in the white hats.

And as for the Internal Security beings he had seen so far, Sten had picked up a bit of a skin crawl. Why, he couldn't say. The closer he got to the Emperor's presence, the more the IS personnel bothered him. They were all so . . . vaguely familiar.

When he saw the tall, fair young man at the door, Sten got it. The man was a twin of the Emperor – as were all the men he had seen since he had entered the Emperor's private apartments. The main physical difference was that they were taller.

He grudgingly admitted that this arrangement made good sense. Individually, the IS guards resembled the Emperor enough to draw any assassin's fire. And in a group around him, they were a living shield.

The IS officer clicked his boot heels together as Sten approached. 'You are expected, Ambassador Sten,' he said in soothing tones that were in odd contrast to his stone face. Suspicious eyes measured Sten. Compared. Sten was a little hurt to see the suspicion replaced with self-satisfaction. The clot thought he could take Sten with ease.

'You can go right in,' the IS officer said.

Sten's muscles and reflexes tingled with memory, as he played his own measuring game. The man's eyes narrowed. He *knew* what was going on.

Sten laughed. 'Thanks,' was all he said. The door whisked open and he entered. He saw the startled look on the man's face as he realized his worth had been found sadly lacking. Sten could take him with ease. Sure, he was a little slower. Out of practice. But it would be no problem at all.

The stregg hit the Black Velvet, thought about making trouble, then was seduced by all that smoothness. Sten felt his belly warm to a cheery glow.

The Eternal Emperor beamed at him, then refilled the shot glasses with the fiery drink the Bhor had named after an ancient enemy. 'As our old Irish friend Ian Mahoney says, "This one's just to let the Good Lord know we're serious."' The Emperor downed another shot.

Sten followed his lead. If the boss wanted the meeting to be boozy, then Sten had little choice but to participate – with feeling. Besides, the Eternal Emperor had been right. As usual. Sten really had needed a drink.

'Now, let's see about that dinner I promised you,' the Emperor said. 'Until further notice, Ambassador, you are in charge of keeping the glasses full.'

He began bustling about that marvel of low-tech goodness married to high-tech speed he called his kitchen.

'A difficult duty, sir,' Sten said, 'but I will do my very best.' He laughed, refilled their glasses, and carried them to the counter. He took his usual position perched on one of the tall stools.

Sten sniffed the air appreciatively. It was a mixture of vaguely familiar smells but with a tantalizing mystery to them. The Eternal Emperor could give a master chef lessons. Even Marr and Senn, the greatest banqueters in the Empire, grudged this.

The Emperor favoured re-creating the recipes of ancient Earth. Though from the Emperor's perspective, the recipes weren't so ancient, Sten thought. He had ruled for three thousand years.

Sten sniffed the air again. 'Asian?' he guessed. He was no mean cook himself. He had picked up the hobby – inspired by his boss, perhaps – whiling away long hours at dreary military posts where the food was even duller than the company.

'You're only thinking that because it's complex,' the Emperor said. 'Although there are some influences, I guess. But the other way around. The Chinese *were* the best cooks. These folks, however, gave them a run for the money. Some people say they were even better. I go back and forth.'

He palmed a spot at the counter's edge and a refrigerated shelf slid out, revealing an array of jars and pots of good stuff. He stacked them on the counter.

'The theme tonight is India,' the Eternal Emperor said. 'Sort of goes along with the job I've got in mind for you.'

He smiled. Sten had seen his boss in friendly moods before, but never quite so downright jolly. Uh-oh. Another impossible task. Sten was only mildly bothered. The potential difficulty intrigued him. But he couldn't fold up too easily.

'Not to be contrary, sir,' Sten said, sipping at his stregg, 'but I was hoping for a little leave time.' He saw a flicker of irritation on his boss's face. Good.

'Don't push it,' the Eternal Emperor snapped. Sten was alarmed to see the irritation building to quick fury. 'I'm sick and tired of negatives. Don't you people get it? I'm holding this thing together with spit and baling wire and . . .' The Emperor's voice trailed off.

Sten watched him bring the anger under control. It was a definite fight. The Emperor shook his head and gave Sten a sheepish grin.

'Sorry,' he said. 'Pressures of the job and all. Sometimes it makes me forget who my old friends are. My *real* friends.' He toasted Sten and sipped his stregg.

'It was my fault, sir,' Sten said. His instincts told him it was important to take the blame. 'The smell of all that good food got to the lazy side of me.'

The Emperor liked that. He gave a sharp, too-right nod, and went back to work – and the subject.

'My current pain in the ass,' the Emperor said, 'resembles the place this food comes from. Within the borders of India there were more people of more different opinions than just about any place on Earth. It was one mass of hate groups who had been at each other's throats so long they had forgotten about what pissed them off in the first place. I take that back. Actually, they remembered all too well.

'A Hindu or a Sikh could tell you to the day and the color of the sky what atrocity the other guy's great great-grandfather had committed.'

He slid over a bowl filled with a greenish-looking mass. 'It's dhal,' the Emperor said. 'A kind of a bean – or in this case, pea – dish. It's deliberately bland. To give balance to the rest. Clear the palate every bite or so. I made it up yesterday. All we have to do is reheat.'

'About this problem child,' Sten prodded.

'Right.' The Emperor took a hit off his stregg. 'I could have used another example besides India. But their food was mostly potatoes – and pig when they could get it. They made a helluva sausage, though. Wrapped in flour and fried. But I didn't feel like sausage.'

Sten sniffed the ingredients the Emperor was assembling into some kind of order. 'India will do just fine, sir,' he said.

'The place I'm sending you is the Altaic Cluster,' the Emperor said.

Sten frowned. He was only slightly familiar with the cluster. 'The Jochians, among others, right? But, I thought they were among the best allies we have on board.'

'They are,' the Emperor said firmly. 'And I want them to stay that way. Trouble is, the Khaqan – which is what the fellow who runs the joint calls himself – is up to his ass in alligators.'

The Emperor held up a mound of cubed meat. About two pounds worth, Sten noted. 'This is goat,' the Emperor said. 'I had a field constructed for him and his brothers and sisters. Had the field planted with the same stuff his ancestors ate in India – mint, wild onion, you name it.' He plunked the mass into an ovenproof casserole.

'The Khaqan is getting old and a little past it,' the Emperor went on in his typical veer back and forth between subjects. Except that over the years Sten had noted there really was no veer at all: Each topic always had something to do with the other.

'Anyway,' the Emperor continued, 'the trouble is mostly his fault . . . Still, I can't afford to lose him.'

Sten nodded agreement. Whoever this Khaqan was, the Altaic Cluster was an important ally. Worse: It was damned close to Prime. 'What's threatening him, sir?'

'Just about everything and everybody,' the Emperor said. He started shaking out spices over the goat. 'A little ginger,' he said, shifting to the recipe again. 'Ground cloves, cardamom, chili, cumin . . . heavier than the others . . . couple of squeezes of garlic, and ye olde salt and pepper.'

He dumped in some yogurt and lemon juice, and stirred up the whole mess, then set it to the side. He started frying onions in peanut oil.

'There are three separate species in the Altaics,' the Emperor said. 'Split four ways. And all of them are sons of bitches. First, there's the Jochians. Human. The majority race. The Khaqan is a Jochian, natch.'

'Right,' Sten said. That was the way things usually worked under one-being rule. Present company excepted. There were far fewer humans than other species in the Empire.

'Their top world is Jochi, which is where the Khaqan hangs his head. It's the center of the cluster. Anyway . . . to the other villains in this piece . . .'

He dumped half the fried onions on the lamb and mixed it up. He pulled the rice off the range. The water had been boiling for about five minutes. He drained the rice, stirred it up with the onions, and spread it out over the goat.

'A little butter drizzled on the top,' the Emperor said, 'and . . . voila! I call this Bombay Birani, but basically it's an old goat stew.' He slammed on a tight-fitting lid, popped the casserole into the oven, and set it for bake.

'Now, I'm going to cheat,' the Emperor said. 'The way this is supposed to go is, you set it at 380 degrees. Bake one hour. Then cut it to 325 and go for an hour more.'

Sten tucked those figures away, along with the rest of the recipe.

'But Marr and Senn, bless their souls, have come up with a new oven. Cuts real time half or more. And I can't tell the difference.'

'About those other villains, sir?'

'Oh, right. Okay, we've got the Jochians. Human, as I said. Besides being the majority race, they've got one of my old trading charters. I gave it to them maybe five hundred years ago. It was a wild and woolly frontier area then.

'Which brings me to the Tork. Human, as well. Old boom-town types.'

Sten didn't know exactly what the Emperor meant, but he got the drift.

'The Torks hit the cluster earlier when Imperium X was discovered in the region,' the Emperor went on. 'Miners. Ship jumpers. Storekeeps. Joyboys and joygirls. That sort. Except, when the Imperium X played out, they stayed on instead of drifting to the next glory hole.'

Imperium X was the only element that could shield the Anti-Matter Two particle. AM2 was the fuel that had built the Empire. And it was under the rigid control of the Eternal Emperor. So much so, that when the privy council had assassinated him, all AM2 supplies had automatically stopped. For six years the privy council had searched fruitlessly for its source. In the meantime, the Empire had plunged toward ruin – a state Sten was currently engaged in helping to turn around. Although sometimes he wasn't sure he would see it happen in his lifetime.

'Of course, the Torks objected when the Jochians showed up. These merchant adventures smacked some heads together, showed them my charter – and that was that.

'Time passed, and the Jochians fell apart a little. Turned into not much more than separate worlds – city-states. The current Khaqan's father pulled things back together a couple three hundred years ago.'

Sten made no comment. It was frontier justice. He had used a little of those old ways to bring the privy council to bay. 'What about the other two species? Natives of the cluster, I assume?'

'Correct. They break down into the Suzdal and the Bogazi.

Don't know much about them. They probably have the same touchy points as any other beings. Apparently when the Torks arrived, they were just climbing off their own home worlds and had discovered one another.

'They had pitiful spaceships. But they were doing a good job of knocking each other off when the Torks came along. Didn't have to do too much ass-kicking. Star drive has a way of putting any backward being in awe.'

Sten could imagine the shock. Here you had just managed to struggle up the tech ladder from stone to space. You look around at the waiting stars, feeling pretty good about yourself. You're standing at the top of your history, right? No one who has ever gone before has accomplished as much.

Then, wham! Aliens – in this case, human – show up with all their fancy gadgets, plus weapons, all of which can blow you back to flaking stone chips. Plus, marvel of all marvels, they can jump from one star to the next, from system to system. Even cruise the galaxies with ease. AM2 drive. The greatest achievement in history.

For the first time, Sten imagined what it must have been like when the Emperor arrived on scene many centuries before with AM2 under his arm. It would have rocked any civilization that existed, put them on their knees begging to see the light.

The Eternal Emperor was musing over some half-remembered ingredient. 'Cilantro,' he said. 'That's the ticket.' He crumbled some leaves into a dish of chopped up cucumber and yogurt.

Yes, Sten thought. AM2 plus the secret to eternal life . . . It must have really been something.

It was an incredible dinner. Unforgettable. As usual.

There were mounds of food all over the table. Dhal and cucumber cooler. Three kinds of chutney: green mango, Bengal, and hot lime. Real hot lime. Little dishes of extra hot sauces and tiny red peppers. And fresh griddled flat bread – chapatis, the Emperor called it. Plus the Bombay Birani. Fragrant steam rose from the casserole.

'Dig in,' the Emperor said.

Sten dug.

For long minutes they just ate, savoring each bite and washing it down with what the Emperor swore was Thai beer.

When starvation was no longer threatening, the Emperor speared a hunk of goat with his fork and held it up to examine it.

'About my old buddy, the Khaqan,' he said. He popped the goat into his mouth and chewed. 'He's a tyrant of the first order. And I won't deny it. Trouble with being a tyrant is you can never lose your moves. You can't let the lid up a little to allow the steam to escape. If you do, your enemies take it as a sign of weakness. And you've got trouble.

'You also can't get sloppy. Or senile. The Khaqan, I'm afraid, is getting sloppy. He may even be getting senile, for all I know. I *do* know he has every life-support system available close by. Constant blood and organ purging, hormone implants, that sort of thing. With luck, he can live long enough for me to take the time to figure out what happens next. Right now, I'm too busy.'

Sten nodded. He could only begin to imagine just how busy the Emperor was. Sten wasn't privy to the big picture. But from his assignments – diplomatic brushfires all – and his circle of knowledgeable friends, he had a hazy idea.

The Empire had been crumbling when the Emperor returned. Whole regions had been without any AM2 for a long time. With the cheap power gone, industries collapsed. Rebellions erupted. Beings were forced to fend for themselves in all sorts of ways.

The Eternal Emperor had been scrambling ever since, plugging up leaks where he could. Abandoning some areas entirely. Pulling in his sphere and clamping on rigid economic and military controls. And there were many new faces among his allies. Beings with whom he had no past history. Questioning beings. Frightened beings who looked at their miserable populations and shored themselves up against constant conspiracies and coups.

'I've given the Khaqan a lot more AM2 than he deserves,' the Emperor said. 'But he's been squandering it. Putting it to building big monuments to himself, instead of using it to feed his people. They're getting sick of it.

'I even warned him about his behavior. A year or so ago our ambassador to the Altaics rotated out. It was routine. What wasn't routine is that I haven't named a replacement yet.'

That was a fairly heavy-duty gig against the Khaqan, Sten thought. 'I'm surprised he didn't wake up,' he said.

'So am I. Like I said, he's old. Set in his ways. But if he goes under, all the doubting Thomases among my allies will get the jitters. Demand more AM2. Which would blow the clot out of the economy.'

Sten understood. All money was pegged to the value of the basic power unit of the Empire. Produce more, inflate the money.

Produce less, and it deflates. Here there was a double whammy: since there was less power, fewer goods would show up at market. So all prices would shoot up, leading to more scarcity. Black markets. And finally, restive populations.

The Emperor was walking a helluva tightwire.

'Who's the Khaqan's likely successor?' Sten asked.

The Emperor sighed. 'No one. He has no living heirs. And he's also a micromanager. Decides on every detail, from how much water there should be in the main palace pool to the rates the gravcabs can charge. He discourages any initiative. As a capitalist, the Khaqan is so-so. As a CEO, he stinks.'

The Emperor swilled more beer. 'However, he's getting pretty desperate, now. He's been begging me for some sign of support. Show his people I'm in his camp. Along with the AM2, of course.'

'And you want me to be that support?' Sten said.

'Right. Put on a big show for him. You're one of my top heroes. Medals. Honors. Victories. In the field of battle and the halls of diplomacy and all that hogwash. I'll have my media people make a big deal of it. Not that you'll need much of a buildup.' He looked at Sten. But instead of smiling, he looked thoughtful. Sten decided he didn't want to know what his boss was thinking.

The Emperor broke off and grinned. 'Take anybody you want – your pals the Bhor, some crack troops, your usual crew of experts, whatever. Just make sure everybody sparkles. And to make this a real show-the-flag exercise, I want you to take my personal ship. The *Victory*.'

Now *that* brought a grin to Sten's face.

The Emperor laughed. 'I thought you'd like that.'

The *Victory* was purportedly a dream ship. A new class battle-wagon/tacship carrier built to the Emperor's specifications. Regal as all clot. To impress the natives, he said. Everything about it was ultraluxury, from private crew quarters to the Emperor's personal suite.

'Now, this is what I call a great job description,' Sten said, toasting his boss. 'Now. If you want kisses and hugs for the Khaqan in public, what's my attitude when we're alone?'

'Chilly politeness,' the Emperor said. 'Real reserved. Scary as you can make it. I want him to see my eyes in yours. Tell him I've promised to put in a new ambassador right away. However . . . I also want some progress on who his successor is going to be when he kicks. That way, I can start some private discussions with *that* fellow. See if we can't make life a little more pleasant – and stable – in the Altaics when the old boy is gone.'

Sten nodded that he understood the drill. He also realized that the Emperor would be wanting his opinion on who that successor ought to be.

'One more thing,' the Emperor said. 'Tell him I'm putting him on my personal invitation list. The short list. I'll expect his visit in a year or so.'

'He'll like that,' Sten said. 'More propaganda for the home folks.'

'Yeah, he will,' the Eternal Emperor said. 'But he's not going to like what I have to say. In private.'

And he speared the last hunk of goat. He snipped it from the fork with sharp white teeth.

Sten didn't feel sorry for the Khaqan a bit. He sounded – in Kilgour's words – like a 'right bastard.'

Chapter Four

'Ah'll gie th' poss'bil'ty y' may hae saved me,' Alex grudged. 'Nae, lad. Tis m' shout this round.'

He got up, walked to the bar, paid the barman, and brought back the tray. Four mugs of beer and four single shot glasses of clear liquid. Sten indicated the shot glasses with a questioning finger.

'Quill. Nae stregg. Thae's none ae that off the Bhor Worlds or away frae th' Emp's palace, so this'll hae t' cure the dog.'

Sten was still a little skull-fried from his marathon dinner-drunk-orders group-plotting session with the Emperor some days earlier. Obediently, he dumped one shot down his throat, gagged politely, and chased it with a beer.

'Y'll note, Ah'm but bein't civil an' keepin't y' company,' Alex said as he did the same. 'Dinnae be haein' th' thought Ah'm still a wee alky. Gie it all up, Ah did.'

The two of them sat, anonymous in gray shipsuits, near the back of a spaceport bar near Soward City's vast spacefields. The bar was a businesslike hum of sailors getting drunk enough to transship, or drunk enough to realize they had finally ported, and the whores and hustlers were helping both sets toward their missions.

'I really did save you?'

'Oh, aye,' Alex said. 'She was wee, she was wily, she was gorgeous, and she e'en had her own money.'

'Maybe you *should* have married her.'

'Ah clottin' near did. Th' banns were read. Th' hall wae hired. Ah found a sky pilot thae'd go through the ceremony wi'oot gigglin'. Ah'd e'en introduced her t' m' wee mum.'

'What did *she* think?'

'She consider't, an' said thae i' Ah hadda marry, still so young an' barely beyont th' cradle as Ah am, she c'd live wi' th' lass.'

'I say again my last: maybe you should settle down. Start thinking about the next Laird Kilgour of Kilgour.'

Alex shuddered gently. 'Ah dunno, lad. Thae wae a moment . . . but then Ah thought a' myself, years gone, brain gone i' Ah e'er had one t' begin wi', teeth gone, chewin' on pap, puttin' milk i' th' brandy, wi' bairns bouncin' around an' all. Cacklin' on aboot how th' old days are gone, an' modern clots dinnae lift a candle t' th' mighty ones thae're gone, men frae the old days, when men were men an' th' sheep ran like hell.

'Disgustin'. Clottin' disgustin'. So Ah considers . . . looks at your signal . . . writes oot a well-reasoned arg'ment an' slips out th' back afore dawn.'

'Mr Kilgour,' Sten said. 'An act of cowardice! You at least should have stayed and explained.'

'Rotate around it, lad. Th' way th' lass impress't m' mum was by beatin't her ae arm wrestlin.' Ah'm mad, but Ah'm noo daft.'

Sten checked the time. 'We're due at the *Victory* in ten minutes. Let's drink and get.'

Kilgour blurred into motion, old battle reflexes reappearing. The beer and alk on the table vanished. He burped politely, rose, and started toward the exit, threading his way between tables, Sten in his wake.

Alex's way was blocked by a very large quadruped, whose

gray hide looked as if it would make an acceptable suit of armor. The being emptied the large plas balloon he had been sniffing and bounced it away into a corner. All three of his – her? its? – eyes glared around separately, then settled on Kilgour. The being's twin manipulating arms flexed.

'Men! Don't like men!'

'Ah dinnae either,' Alex said equably.

'You man.'

'No.'

'What you?'

'Ah'm a penguin. Frae Earth. A wee slickit cowerin't birdie thae lives on herring.'

Sten ran through various ET handbooks, trying to ID the being. Nothing in his memory had four legs, three eyes, two arms, a dim brain – last undetermined for certain, given probability said being was blitzed – stood two and a half meters tall, weighed several squillion kilos, and had a terrible attitude.

Oh, yeah. Not very vestigal claws on the arms.

Sten felt mildly sorry for the being.

'You not penguin.'

'An' how d'ye know, lad? Y' dinnae hae th' look ae a passionate penguin pervert aboot y'.'

'You man.'

'Look, son. Y're tired. Y'hae a bit t' . . . snuff, snort, swill, or suck. Hae y'self ae sitdown, an' Ah'll buy y' a wee new balloon.'

'Don't like men! I hurt men! First I hurt you, then hurt him.'

'Ah well,' Kilgour said. 'Sten, y' bear witness t' m' wee mum Ah'm noo goin't out an' gettin' in th' bloody frae like Ah wae a cub again.'

'I'll tell her.'

'Ah knew Ah c'd rely on you.'

The being was reaching for Kilgour's neck – what little neck the tubby man had.

Kilgour's hands circled the being's arms, just where a wrist would be on a humanoid. And he levered down. The being scrawked in pain and collapsed down on what were maybe knees, just as gracelessly as an Earth camel. Kilgour, still holding the being's 'wrists,' stepped forward – and the quadruped collapsed back into a sprawled, seated position.

'Noo,' Alex said. 'Y' see how easy pacifism is, when y' put y'r mind t' it?'

'If you're through playing, Mr Kilgour?'

'Ah'm through, Admiral. But Ah hae t' buy m' friend his round. As Ah promis't.'

Kilgour, an upright and honorable man from the high-gee world of Edinburgh, Sten's long-time aide and accomplice and one of the Empire's most highly trained elite commandos, *did* keep his word – and bought the now quiescent monster a balloon before they left for their inspection tour of the Imperial battle cruiser *Victory*.

''Tis all i' th' the leverage,' was his only explanation to Sten. 'Like tearin' a phone book apart.'

'What's a phone book?'

''Tis quite a ship,' Alex said, three hours later.

'Aye,' Sten agreed. He took off the sensor hood he had been wearing and stopped his run-through of the *Victory*'s tertiary and redundant TA systems.

Alex's eyes swept the room before he spoke. There weren't any crewmen within earshot, and the com box wasn't picking up. 'Perhaps Ah'm gettin' old,' he went on, still tentatively, 'but the way this scow's set up's noo like it would have been back in the – the old days.'

'You mean before the Emperor's assassination.'

'Aye,' Kilgour said. 'Thae's a bit too much flash ae filigree f'r this to suit th' *old* Emp. Or am I rememberin't th' past ae better'n it wae?'

'I've been thinking the same thing,' Sten said. He touched keys, and the computer obediently threw a three-meter hologram of the *Victory* into the air over the mess table they were sitting at. Another key combination, and the computer began peeling the hologram, displaying the new battle cruiser from all angles and deck by deck.

'Ah'd heard this wae t' be a 'maphrodite,' Alex said. 'But it looks more like a three-way or four-way arrangement t' me.'

Sten nodded agreement. He wasn't happy, on a number of levels. First was the entirely pragmatic consideration of the *Victory* as a warship. Sten had experience with tools, vehicles, and ships that were ostensibly dual- or multiple-purpose. Almost without exception that meant that the tool did quite a number of things badly, and nothing well.

Battle cruisers, for instance, were based on aeons-old designs of ships that had enough muscle to beat up almost anything – except battleships or monitors – and enough power to run away from the biggies. Quite frequently, though, it worked out that the class was too slow to be able to catch and destroy smaller ships, and played hell getting away from the monsters. Plus, once the ship was caught, its armament, quite capable of bashing a stray destroyer or such, was too light to damage a battleship, and its defensive systems, active or passive, were too weak.

Sten had gone through the builder-promised specs on the *Victory*, cross-correlating them with the actual performance the battle cruiser produced during its trials. Unless the Imperial procurement people were on the take – not an impossibility, but not very likely – it looked as if the *Victory* might be an effective weapon.

The problem was this tacship capability the Emperor had evidently decided was vital. The *Victory*'s rear third was dedicated to hangar/weapons/quarters for a complete tacship flotilla – three squadrons of four ships each. The tacships were Bulkeley-II class ships, developed and refined during the Tahn war. They were just-over-hundred-meter-long needles of destruction. They were built to get in at speed, hit hard, and get out. Anything else – crew comfort, defensive capabilities, armor – was secondary or nonexistent. Sane pilots hated the tacships – they required constant hands-on pilot response and were unforgiving, as in kill you, if the slightest error. Sten loved them.

So on one hand the *Victory*'s added capability was something Sten appreciated. But it also meant that the rear spaces were flying time bombs, packed with sensitive explosives, fuels, and weaponry. The large hangar and maintenance areas meant any hit in those spaces might destroy the battle cruiser. Plus the *Victory* was more than a bit blind and defenseless around the stern. 'Thae'll be a problem,' Kilgour had observed. 'Means thae i' we cannae break an' run, we'll hae t' retreat backwards, clutchin' our bustle an' flailin' wi' our wee ladylike brolly.'

That image of Earth Victorian times brought up the *Victory*'s final oddity: complete luxury. Sten already knew the ship had been outfitted for luxury – even the lowest-rank wiper had his own tiny compartment. Paneling appeared to be wood and stone on many of the passageways. The kitchens could efficiently prepare and serve Imperial conference banquets with no strain.

Sten appreciated this to a degree. A lean, clean fighting machine might sound good in the livies, but Sten knew from his tacship experience that after three or four weeks into a mission, one thing *not* appreciated was a fresher one had to squeeze oneself into to degrease the body. Especially if that fresher just happened to have a sharp corner cleverly located where elbows and knees went.

But then there was the Imperial Suite, which included living quarters large enough, it seemed, for an entire Imperial court, plus guest area and troop support sectors, including armories and gymnasiums. Sten was glad to see the latter – he was still aware of the smallish handles he had previously noted in the Imperial mirror.

The Imperial Suite – if that was the correct label for such a large area – covered the upper quarter of the *Victory* between the tacship decks to the forward command spaces for the *Victory*'s own crew. A frontal cross-section would show the Imperial area as a T, the figure's leg extending deep into the ship's center. Like all flagships, the *Victory* was designed and built so the Imperial – or flag – quarters were independent of the warship's own areas. For thousands of years every admiral had known he was a better captain than the flagship's own captain, and would frequently drop the larger concerns he was paid to worry about and play skipper-for-a-day.

Yes. Sten agreed with Alex that this Imperial Suite was a bit much. The heads had gold fixtures. The basins were real marble. The bedchambers were richly upholstered. As for the beds themselves, particularly the ones – plural correct – in the Imperial private quarters, Sten wondered how they would be described in the inventory:

BED, Mark 24, perhaps. *Multiple-user-capable. Structurally reinforced to allow occupants limitless creativity. Bed fitted for hydraulic modification while in use, which includes adjustment overall area from polyhedron to circular to conventional; vertical adjustment of any portion of bed for height. Internal and external multiple capabilities, including, but not limited to, internal illumination, external illumination, holographic projection, holographic recording. Includes refrigeration and snack area. Includes full communication capability. Overhead rack (can be hidden) capable of supporting as many as three beings. Fitted for light array to include, but not limited to, stroboscopic or holographic imaging.*

The owner of such a bed, Sten summarized, would be listed as orgy-qualified and -experienced.

The Emperor?

Sten did not give a damn – but it was odd that during his time as captain of the Emperor's Gurkha bodyguard, he hadn't noticed that the Eternal Emperor seemed particularly sex-driven. He hadn't thought much about it, but sort of guessed that after a few thousand years maybe the possibilities had been completely explored.

But now?

Hell, he was not even sure he was right – it wasn't as if Sten had personally explored every inch of Arundel Castle to ensure that what was listed as a storeroom might not, in fact, have been an Imperial bordello.

The problem was going to be, Sten thought, sleeping in that bed himself. Why you puritanical little clot, his mind jeered. There have been times, he prodded himself, that he'd been known to roll about in a big pile with friends. And speaking of which, his thought went on, who's going to see you sleeping in that humongous great bed, anyway? You might as well have been a clottin' castrato of late.

Sten brought himself back to the issues at hand. 'Mr Kilgour,' he said, 'I'm not at all sure what this goatrope they call the Altaic Cluster is going to be. But I'm getting the idea our boss isn't giving us all these goodies just because he likes my legs.'

'Prog: ninety percent,' Alex agreed.

'Which means I'll be needing all my assets. So, uh, do you think it'd be a proper utilization of your talents, Laird Kilgour, for you to skipper this solid-gold whorehouse?'

Kilgour appeared taken aback. 'Me? But thae's an admiral rank. Twa-star, Ah'd hazard. An' th' highest rank Ah e'er held, last time Ah meter-metered the matter, wae but wee warrant.'

'I don't think that would present a problem,' Sten said. 'And it wasn't what I asked.'

Alex considered. Then slowly shook his head. 'Ah dinnae think so, lad. But Ah'm touched ae the thought. T' now, thae's nae been a Kilgour been an admiral. 'Ceptin' the pirates, a' course.

'M' mum'd be pleased, an a'.

'But . . . nae. Marchin' swabs here an' bye, pushin' all this steel aroun' th' sky . . . thae dinnae tweak m' testes. Ah'm more int'rested in all thae clots we're goin' out to straighten oot – Ah think thae's m' main talent, skipper.'

Sten was very damned elated. Beyond the value he placed on Kilgour's friendship and quite literal back-guarding ability, he knew that the man whom the Emperor called Sten's personal thug had real talents at diplomacy, situation analysis, and solution breakdown.

Then a notion crossed his mind. Sten grinned – it was just a shade farcical. But it would bear consideration.

He shut down the computer and stood up. 'Come on, Laird Kilgour. Let's go back to the bar and see if that rhino's ready to buy us a round.'

Alex came to his feet, then frowned and checked the wallchrom. 'Nice thought, boss. But we cannae. We'll be haein' vis'tors back ae our quarters.'

'Visitors? Kilgour, are you running another number on me?'

'Noo, lad. Hae y' e'r, e'er known me to stick ae match under y'r breeks jus' t' see how high y'll jump?'

Sten didn't even trouble with an answer, nor with kicking his 'diplomatic adviser' in the slats.

'I shall be entirely gotohell,' Sten said.

'Is that all you're going to say? No "Clottin' Kilgour did it to me again?" No "But duty calleth, m' lady, and I must away?"'

'Nope.'

Sten crossed from the entrance to his suite in Arundel Castle to the sideboard. 'Best I can do,' he said, 'is I just came from a room I'd like to show you, someday.'

'Do I get an explanation?'

'Nope.'

'Do I get to see that room?'

Sten did not reply. He picked up a decanter and eyed its contents.

'Stregg?'

'Yes . . . stregg.'

'It's early – but I'll have one if *you're* drinking.'

Sten found two corrosion-proof shot glasses, poured them full, and took one across to Cind. She half sat, half lay on one of the room's couches.

Sten had met Cind many years earlier under circumstances both would have preferred to be different. Cind was a human woman, a descendant of the warrior elite who had once defended the religious fanatics of the Lupus Cluster, known as the Wolf Worlds. Sten had overturned that corrupt and militant church government during his days as an undercover Mantis Section operative.

When the bodies stopped bouncing, Sten had decided – with the Eternal Emperor's ex post facto grudging approval – that the victors and new champions of the Wolf Worlds were the Bhor, the excessively nonhuman, obsessively barbaric, insistently alcoholic gorillas who were native to the cluster.

Cind grew up in a failed warrior culture – and studied war. Studied war until it became her love and her obsession. She joined the Bhor and became a warrior – sniping and ship-to-ship boardings among her specialties.

Part of her youthful obsession was the superstalwart that had destroyed her own Jannissar culture. A man of myth named Sten. Then she met him. And found he was not the bearded ancient she had envisioned, but a still-young, still-vibrant soldier.

In hero worship, she found her way to his bed. Sten, however, was in shock after a combat mission had led to the death of his entire team and had no interest in romance, especially from a seventeen-year-old naïf. Yet somehow he had managed, entirely accidently, not to make Cind feel like a fool or himself like a complete idiot.

During the fight to destroy the privy council, they met again and again – but always professionally. Somehow, they became friends.

Then, when the Emperor returned and the privy council was destroyed, Cind traveled with Sten to her home worlds, the Lupus Cluster. Their perceptions of each other had changed during this time. Still . . . nothing happened between them.

And when Sten left to assume his new tasks as Imperial ambassador plenipotentiary, Cind soldiered on, but with less of an interest in hands-on slaughter than in studying the causes and results of war.

Now both soldiers sipped stregg, shuddered, and sipped again.

'I assume,' Sten said, 'that you've arrived as part of my Imperial circus and diplomatic mission to the Altaic Cluster.'

'Is that where we're going? Alex said the AOR was classified.'

'It is. You can draw the area briefing fiche from Mr Kilgour.'

Silence in the room. The old sexual tension between them warmed that silence.

'You look well,' Sten said.

'Thank you. Since the last time I saw you, I decided I should become more familiar with civilian dress.'

Sten admired – she had done her homework. Cind, just past twenty, trim in the conservative four-piece suit, hair close-cropped, makeup just enough to enhance without being seen, would have been taken by most as a CEO of a top multi-world corporation. No one could have seen – and few besides Sten would have theorized – that the heel on her dress flat was the haft to a hideout knife, that her pouch contained a miniwillygun, and that her necklace could do double duty as a garrote.

Cind eyed him. 'Do you remember the first time we met?'

Sten gurgled stregg through his nostrils, a distinctly unpleasant sensation.

Cind laughed at his reaction. 'No, not that time. Before . . . at the banquet. I was in the receiving line.'

'Uh . . .' Sten thought back. The woman – then girl – had worn . . . seemed to him she had just been wearing a uniform of some sort. But he felt he would be an utter ass if he so said.

'I wore walking-out semidress,' she said. 'But that wasn't what I first chose.'

It was now Cind's turn to look away, as she blushingly described the sleek sex-outfit she had paid nearly a campaign's bonus for, put on, and then ripped off and thrown away.

'I looked like a clottin' joygirl,' she said. 'And . . . and later, I figured out all I really knew how to look like – how to be – was a soldier. Which also meant a soldier's whore, I guess.'

And there it was again, Sten thought. For some reason Cind was able to say astonishing things to him, things that other women had only said deep in intimacy and after long knowledge. And it was the same for himself as well, Sten realized.

He also realized that he wanted to change the subject. 'May I be formal?' he asked.

'You may, Admiral.'

'Not Admiral. This time around, I'm a civilian.'

'Very good.'

'Why so?'

Cind smiled once more. Oh, Sten thought. No chain-of-command drakh. No 'It's not military kosher to want to hold hands with a lower (higher) ranking soldier.'

'I am in a most uncomfortable position,' Cind said, stretching into a more comfortable position and thus placing Sten in a slightly *un*comfortable position. 'I am a major now.'

'Congratulations.'

'Perhaps. Would you like to meet my ranking private?'

Sten waited. Cind rose, went to an adjoining door, and opened it. 'Private? Post!'

There was a sudden clashing of leather, and a creature lumbered into the chamber. Just 150 centimeters tall, it must have weighed around 150 kilograms – twenty more than the last time Sten had seen the horror. The creature's knobbed hairy paws brushed against the ground, as did its enormous brush-tail beard, as the monster pushed its great trunk semierect and bellowed.

'By my mother's beard,' came the shout. 'Here are you two, ambassador and major, drinking all of the stregg, and leaving a poor, thirsty private, who loves you like a brother, to die of thirst, forlorn, abandoned in the outer darkness.'

'What,' Sten said, 'in the name of my father's – your father's, hell, Cind's father's – frozen buttocks are *you* doing here, Otho?'

'I am but a simple soldier, following in the way of a warrior, as the great gods Sarla, Laraz, and – who the clot's that other worthless godling? oh yes – Kholeric have told me.'

'He's been into the stregg,' Sten said.

'He's been into the stregg,' Cind agreed.

'Bring in the rest of the motley crew,' Sten said. 'Buzz down for Kilgour. Tell him to have the kitchen stand by for a buffet in-chamber. Tell him to order up more stregg, some of that horrible stuff the Emperor calls Scotch, and, oh yes, indeed, a case of – hell, whatever goes into a Black Velvet. And get his butt in here with a good thirst. Now, Otho. How many goddamned Bhor do I have?'

'Only a hundred and fifty.'

'Oh, Lord,' Sten said. 'And we're still weeks from departure. Major Cind, have you arranged billets for your beings?'

'I have. There's an entire wing set aside on a new officers' quarters, just inside the Imperial grounds here. Set up for clean and black work.'

'So the Bhor won't be able to get out and maim, pillage, and loot Prime?'

'With luck.'

'Good. Now, Private Otho. Pour us all a drink, and explain. Quickly.'

Sten needed an explanation, because when he had last been in Otho's brawling company the being had been a chieftain, the ruler – if a Bhor could be said to rule anything save by acclamation – of the entire Lupus Cluster.

Now here he was as a rear-rank warrior, as if he were a young Bhor whose beard was yet to sprout.

'I didn't know,' Sten said, after the third stregg, but before Kilgour and the rest of the Bhor had descended on him and sobriety vanished into the night, 'you beings had second childhoods.'

'Don't be a scrote,' Otho growled, refilling his horn. 'First – the Lupus Worlds are at peace. Clotting well better be, if they don't want to get killed.

'Which is good – I guess. But it is a meatless plate, my friend. Back then, back when we were being exterminated by the Jann, I never dreamed how *boring* peace can be. So I ran away to join the circus.'

He sighed – or Sten arbitrarily assigned the value of 'sigh' to the alk- and stregg-laden gas blast that erupted from Otho's bowels to typhoon across the table. 'And I am becoming civilized.'

'Say clottin' what?' Alex said as he entered, and Otho's tale was interrupted by the obligatory roars, shouts, embraces, liquid kisses, and toasts that made a Bhor greeting synonymous with second-degree assault.

Then the Taittinger and Guinness arrived. Sten was forced to demonstrate Black Velvets to his guests. Otho said the stuff was weak mix for suckling babes. Alex preferred his Guinness straight from the pump and drunk in Eire. Cind touched her flute to Sten's. They drank, and their eyes held the moment.

Then Sten brought the conversation back to some kind of a track. 'Otho, you said being here had something to do with your becoming civilized.'

'By my father's icy arse, so it does. Using human standards, even. If I am civilized . . . and a great leader – which, considering my beard is yet uncut, I may be – then I am now spending my wilderness years. Which I understand must be spent among primitive beings.

'I found a fiche recently, the biography of what, evidently, you humans consider a great being. His name was Illchurch, or some such. Now, when he had done his first stint as a leader, where did he spend his wilderness years?'

Otho gestured with his glass, sloshing drink over the edge. 'I'll tell you where. Among a primitive Earth tribe he called Americans. Since I could find no remnants of such a tribe, I decided to settle for what must be the second best primitives . . .' Otho raised his glass in toast. 'To the human race.'

Chapter Five

'I would like,' Sten said formally, 'to request the pleasure of your company this evening.'

'The pleasure is mine, sir. How many troopies do I bring for backup?'

'One more time. May I buy you dinner, m' lady?'

'Oh. Just a moment, I've got to check the 'dex . . . yes. I'd be delighted, Sten. How formal is this place?'

'Sidearms should be unobtrusive, but color-coordinated. At . . . 1930?'

'*Seven*-thirty it is,' Cind said, and broke the connection.

'And dinnae we look pretty, lad. Are we wooin' or spookin' t'night?'

'A little of both.'

'Ah.' Alex brushed nonexistent lint from Sten's raw silk shirtjac. 'Well, y're set up on th' far end. Sh'd Ah hae extraction set up, or will y' RON?'

'My God,' Sten said. 'I never realized the joys of being an orphan before. Mother Kilgour, I don't have any idea of whether I'm remaining overnight anywhere, whether I'm even going to get kissed, and what concern is it of yours, anyway?'

'Ah'm mere remindin' you y' hae a 1115 wi' th' Emp tomorrow, f'r final briefin'.'

'And I'll be there. Anything else?'

'Noo . . . yes. Y'r scarf's all crookedy.' Kilgour straightened it. 'An' as m' mum useta advise, dinna be doin' aught you cannae stand up in church an' tell th' deac aboot.'

'She really said that?'

'Aye. An' now y' ken why th' Kilgours are nae a church-goin't clan.'

Kilgour slid out. Sten made a fast final check – damn, but I seem to be spending a lot of time in front of mirrors lately – and he was ready. He tucked a hideout willygun into a chamois ankle holster, curled his fingers twice – the knife came out of its armsheath easily – and he was ready for a night on the town.

There was a tap on the door.

'It's open.' He wondered what new, last-minute harassment Kilgour had come up with. But no one entered. Instead, again came the tap.

Sten frowned, crossed to the door, and opened it.

Three small, well-muscled young men stood there. They wore civilian clothes – but their suits all looked as if they had been issued by some central authority.

They were Gurkhas. They snapped to attention and saluted. Sten started to return the salute, then caught himself.

'Forgive me, honored soldiers. But I am no longer a soldier.'

'You are still a soldier. You are Sten. You are still Subadar.'

'I thank you once more,' Sten said. 'Would you come in? I have but a few moments.'

Sten ushered them inside. The three stood in uncomfortable silence.

'Shall I send for tea?' Sten asked. 'Or whiskey, if you are off duty? I must apologize for my bad Gurkhali. But my tongue is rusty.'

'We will have nothing,' one said. The other two looked at him and nodded. He was now their appointed spokesperson.

'I am Lalbahadur Thapa,' he said. 'This man is Chittahang Limbu. And this one here is Mahkhajiri Gurung. He thinks he is of a superior caste, but do not let his arrogance trouble you. He is still a good soldier. All of us carry the rank of Naik.'

'Lalbahadur . . . Chittahang . . . you bear honorable names.'

'They are – were our fathers. This Mahkhajiri's father runs the recruiting depot on Earth. At Pokhara.'

Havildar-Major Lalbahadur Thapa had fallen saving the Emperor's life from assassins years before. Long ago, Subadar-Major Chittahang Limbu had replaced Sten as commander of the Gurkhas – at Sten's request. Chittahang had been the first Gurkha to command the unit, establishing a tradition.

Gurkhas, in addition to their other virtues, had very long memories, at least as regards their friends and enemies.

'How may I serve you?' Sten asked.

'A notice was posted in the Administration Office, saying that you desired volunteers for a special mission, and any member of the Imperial household was invited to apply.'

'You?'

'There are twenty-four more of us.'

'But . . .' Sten sat down. He felt as if somebody had sucker-punched him in the psychic diaphragm. He regained equilibrium. 'Gurkhas serve only the Emperor.'

'That was true.'

'Was?'

'Only cows and mountains never change. We discussed this matter with our captain. He agreed that serving the Emperor by helping you with your mission, whatever it is, would be *sabash* – well done.'

'This volunteering was done,' Sten said carefully, 'with Imperial permission?'

'How could it be otherwise? The notice ended with "In the Name of the Emperor."'

Gurkhas could be very naive on occasion. Sometimes it was theorized they were deliberately so, using blankness as a device so they could do exactly as they had previously decided.

Sten thought that if the Emperor did not know – and approve – of their request, all hell might break loose. After all, one of the most impressive Imperial boasts was that after the assassination the Gurkhas had refused service under the privy council, returned to Earth, and waited for the Imperial return.

Sten didn't let this potential ego problem show on his face or in his words. Instead, he beamed. 'I am most honored, gentlemen. I shall speak to your commanding officer and to your *bahun*, and begin the proper ceremonies.'

Fortunately the Gurkhas were not obsessed with long ceremonials, so Sten was able to usher the three men out in a few moments without offending anyone's dignity. Then he allowed himself a few minutes of ponderment and one stregg.

Damn, he thought. Why me? Why this? I think I'd better walk very small when I bring this up to the Emperor. Then the thought leapt:

But if it works out – and I go in with some Gurkhas – the Emperor is sure going to get the flash he said he wanted. Plus, his backbrain chortled, I won't have any trouble keeping my back covered . . .

*

Cind had no idea what was going on.

First Sten had asked her out – socially. Then he had made that strange remark about sidearms being unobtrusive but color-coordinated.

She had chanced a fast call to Kilgour, a man she felt was on 'her' side. Maybe. And whatever 'her' side was anyway, which she was none too sure of.

Of course, the Scotsman had been less than no help.

'You remember, Mr Kilgour, a conversation we had some time ago,' Cind began. 'When you said I was, uh, too young and striking to play spy?'

Alex thought back. Vaguely. 'Ah do.'

'Sten invited me to dinner this evening. I have the idea that . . . this is about half professional.'

'Thae's a good startin't point, lass. Th' puir waif canna do naught thae's not work-related. 'Twill lead him t' an early grave, Ah'm fearit.'

'Where are we going?'

'Y'mean morally, collectively, or historically?'

'I mean where is Sten taking me for dinner? And how should I dress?'

'Ah. I misunderstood. Th' place is secure, an' y' should dress cazz. Cazz dressy. Carry heat i' y' wish. Ah would. But y're safe.'

'You'll not tell me any more.'

'A course not, Cind. Dinnae Ah think – an' Ah'm tellin't th' truth – y' hae moves aboot y', giein' thae y' did some growin't since th' last we've seen y'? Dinnae Ah think, were y' noo so young, an' you an' Sten in love, Ah'd take y' home m'self to meet m' mum? So why sh'd Ah denigrate y' an' start tellin' y' wha's goin't on, when deep down, y' ken already?'

Without waiting for a response, Kilgour blanked the screen.

Clotting men, Cind thought.

Clotting . . . and then she deciphered Kilgour's brogue. Love? You an' Sten, emphasis Sten? Of course she probably was in love with him, assuming love was something that made you not sleep well at night, build entire castle complexes in the clouds and then move into them, and behave generally, if you didn't watch yourself, as if you had just injected an opiate.

But . . .

But Sten? Love?

Clot men, she decided, was a safer and more productive way to think.

At least now she knew how to dress.

Cind's outfit was a whisper of sensuality, a simple collarless garment with a deep V dip on the neckline, a close-fitting waist, and a slight flare just above the knees. There were no buttons, zips, or velk to suggest how it stayed together. The waist had a plain belt-tie. Of course, like all 'plain, simple, well tailored' garments, it had cost Cind a quarter of her last proficiency bonus.

What made it special, besides the cutting, was the fabric itself. Mantis Section – the ultraelite operational section of Imperial Intelligence – wore the ultimate in camouflage uniforms. They were phototropic, changing colors to match the background the soldier was next to.

A civilian had bought marketing rights to this fabric and then modified it. The material remained phototropic – but it reflected the background of five minutes earlier. The color recorder and time delay were part of the garment – the belt, on Cind's dress. It also held a strip computer with a simpleminded color wheel that could override the phototropic commands so the wearer would not suddenly find herself wearing a pink dress against an orange background. The belt further contained sensors that muted or increased the color response to match the current light level. On a random factor, it sent strobe images to certain panels and, just to make sure the garment's audience stayed interested, occasional real-time flashes of what lay beneath, when panels would go transparent for eye-blink flashes. Those transparencies could be programmed to match the wearer's modesty. Or, in Cind's case, to never show the knife sheathed down her backbone or the mini-willygun in the small of her back.

Cind met Sten dressed to kill, in several ways.

And for once the male animal didn't screw up. Sten not only noticed and complimented her outfit, but asked intelligent questions – as if he were really interested – about how the cloth worked.

Still better, he brought a complementary flower.

Flower was not quite the right word. Aeons earlier, an Earth-orchid grower, exiled from his native tropics, had developed the ultimate *oncidium* orchid – many, many tiny little blossoms on a single stem, crossbred with a native chameleonlike and highly adaptable plant form. The result produced a living bouquet – a necklace – that exactly matched its wearer's garb.

She gave Sten a moderate kiss and a hug in thanks. And, as she pulled away, she allowed her little fingernail to trail across his neck and down his chestline.

She did not want him to think, after all, that she was a *total* virgin . . .

The bar-restaurant was secreted in an industrial cul-de-sac not far from Prime World's Embassy Row. Sten missed the turnoff and had to bring his rented gravsled – he had politely rejected the garish official transport he'd been offered – back for another approach. The building sat by itself, isolated in gloom, almost impossible to see. But as the gravsled grounded, bright lights flared.

Cind blinked in the glare. The lights seemed less intended to illuminate the path than to allow those inside to see approaching visitors. There was a very small sign halfway up the curving walk:

The Western Eating-Parlor. Number Two.

'Not a very exotic name,' she observed.

Sten grinned. 'There are wheels within wheels here. Supposedly this joint started back on old Earth, way, way back. Like pre-Empire back. Outside a city called Langley. It catered to an exclusive clientele, the story goes. Which hasn't changed in all these centuries.'

'Okay, I'll bite. Who're the customers?' She raised a hand before Sten could answer. 'Don't tell me. But give me a hint.'

'Okay. Take the first letter of each word in the name: *T-W-E-P.*'

'Twep,' Cind sounded.

'Long *E*,' Sten said.

Oh. Like in the old archaic term 'Terminate With Extreme Prejudice.' Cind had heard the term used by elderly intelligence types. Officially sanctioned murder.

Inside, the restaurant was a hush of real leather, murmured conversation, and skillful service.

The maître d' was a horror.

Half of his face was gone, replaced by a plas mask. Cind wondered how long he must have been without medhelp – it was very rare to see, at least in what passed for civilization, someone whom reconstructive surgery did not take on. He didn't notice Sten and Cind for a moment. He was supervising two busboys, who were covering a large blast hole in the paneling. Then he greeted the newcomers as if they were strangers. 'May I help you, sir?'

'She's clean, Delaney.'

Delaney grinned with the half that remained of his face. 'Indeed she is. I have an upstairs snug, Cap'n. An' your friend's at the far bar. I'll bring her up.'

'You've been here before?' Cind whispered as Delaney led them through quiet luxury.

'No. Delaney and I go back a ways.'

Delaney's hearing was very sharp. He paused. 'FYI, the captain lugged me off a mountain once. A real big mountain. During a bad time. When I wasn't computin' real well.' His fingers touched where his face was.

'I had to,' Sten said. 'You owed me money.' A bit embarrassed, he changed the subject. 'What happened to the wall?'

'You ever operate with an octopots with a service name Quebec Niner Three Mike? Called herself Crazy Daisy? Kinda cute if you go for cephalopods.'

Sten thought, then shook his head.

'She retired as OC, outa Mantis 365,' Delaney added helpfully. 'Mostly out of NGC 1300 Central?'

'Must've been before my time – wait a minute. Was three-six-five the guys who stole the sports arena?'

'That's them.'

'Okay. Know the team. Never met her. But isn't she on some renegade list?'

'You must be thinking of somebody else.' Delaney shrugged. 'She's clean-up with anybody here.'

'Sorry. Didn't mean to interrupt.'

'Anyway, she was in this afternoon. Celebrating something. Kept climbing out of her tank and floppin' up and down the bar. Gettin' nasty. Pourin' down shots of jenever cut with dry ice. Anyway, she'd bought herself a toy. Old projectile weapon she'd had made up. Called it a goose gun. Anyway, she decided she wanted to show it around. I maybe shoulda said something, but—

'At any rate, she showed off how it loads – she'd had some special rounds built up for it – and then she says it'd put a hole in the wall you could throw a human through.

'Guy down at the end – ex-Mercury REMF Analysis, shoulda stayed quiet – says drakh. So Daisy blew a hole in the wall 'n' started throwing the guy at the hole. He was right, and the hole wasn't big enough. But Daisy kept trying. I had to tell her to knock it off and go home after three, four tries.'

Cind hid her giggle. Delaney led them into a small room and seated them.

'You'll have what, skipper? Scotch, or are you streggin' tonight?'

Sten decided to be reasonable. 'Scotch. It's early.'

'Do you pour Black Velvet?' Cind asked.

'We pour *anything*. Or if it doesn't pour, we'll get you the needle, the inhaler, or a suppository blank. And I'll tell Aretha – that's the name she prefers to use – to come on up.' He left.

'This,' Cind said, 'is a spook bar? Correct?'

'It is. Mostly Mantis.'

Every profession had its own watering holes, from politicians to pederasts. And each had its own requirements. The Western Eating Parlor was an almost perfect intelligence operative's bar. Situated in a capital – *the* capital, in fact – it was unobtrusive. It would serve its retired or active clients any of the exotics they had become fond of on a hundred hundred worlds. All of the help had some degree of intelligence background, from Delaney the maître d' to the barman who was the son of a recently deceased planning type who was waiting his appointment to the appropriate university, to the busbeings who might just have done some contract wet work in the past. The Parlor was unbugged; it was kept that way with frequent, sophisticated sweeps. The press were discouraged, except for those journalists who needed deep background and would never blow a source.

The Parlor, like the dozens of other spook bars, gave its clients not only a chance to get radically unwound, but a chance to pick up on new information or what a new assignment *really* might bring down on the hapless operative whose control had been less than generous with the facts.

That was why Sten had asked Alex to book dinner at the Parlor. The Eternal Emperor was being entirely too generous with things for this to be anything other than a nightmare assignment.

Aretha sleeked into the room and curled onto an oversize ottoman, hooves tucked underneath her. She – question mark – might have been taken for a sextuple-legged herbivore, considering the swept-back, needle-sharp horns, the brown-white-striped fur coat, and the hooves on the first and rearmost set of legs. But when she put her head back and bayed amusement, the prominent canines and cutting premolars and molars said otherwise. She ordered mineral water to drink – Sten and Cind immediately put their drink intake at 'nurse' – and a slab of animal tissue, pounded and raw. Sten had charbroiled Earth salmon, a relatively new addiction, with butter and dill sauce. Cind also sampled Earth salmon. Raw.

Aretha briefed them – as only a Mantis field operative could. Sten was grateful that she spoke through a synthbox after the initial, polite greetings. Translating someone else's speech, even when it was in one's own tongue, could get wearisome, especially if the speaker had a dual diaphragm and evidently was at home in a language with glottal stops and sibilants.

She knew of Sten and his reputation and said she would help as much as she could. She assumed this woman had a need to know. Helping, she went on, would best be done by her kicking Sten in the genitalia, ensuring that he could not take this posting.

Three years earlier, Aretha had been deputy military attache at the Imperial Embassy on Jochi, she said. She was recovering from a minor case of zagging when zigging was indicated. Sten estimated her rank at lieutenant colonel.

'Nightmare,' she went on. 'A nightmare indeed.

'First let me tell you about the humans, my dear ambassador-to-be. Horrible. Horrible. Horrible. Former miners, with all of the forethought and logic that means. Go to any length to prevent regulation, then howl like a spavined pup when the material being mined runs out.

'As a culture, the Torks have enough imagination to want everything, but not nearly enough brains to achieve it. So that means they will willingly deny anyone else possession of these same mostly imagined treasures. Because the Altaic Cluster can only be considered a treasure if you have a way to package and export hatred and ethnocentrism.

'Consider the Jochians. Perhaps you did not know they were once a self-named Society of Adventurers. Given a charter to plunder by our own Eternal Emperor, long may he wave.'

'I know that.' Sten did not feel it necessary to tell Aretha that the information had come from the Emperor himself.

'Adventurers – pirates at one time. Then their culture swash-buckled itself down into anarchy and city-world solar systems until the oncoming of the Khaqan. The first. There have only been two.

'The Khaqan was also a liar and a thief and a back-stabber.

The thing was, he could do it faster and better than any other Jochian. So he rose to the top. Like scum on a pond.

'He either died or was murdered by his son, the present Khaqan. Who has all of his father's talents at chicanery, and a fondness for building monuments to himself to the exclusion of all logic, needed public works, or continuing the social umbrella. And the Empire did nothing about his excesses while I was there. Possibly the Emperor had larger problems. Certainly, he would have heard almost nothing about how severe the problems really were.

'Unfortunately, our beloved Emperor had appointed an ambassador whose talents – I should not think anything less than complimentary, but allow me to say that in two E-years of intense observation I thought Ambassador Nallas's primary talent was lunch.'

'What about the cluster's other beings?' Sten asked.

'Merciful clouds, they manage to fit in very well with the humans. First we have the Bogazi. Have you ever seen a livie on the planet Earth?'

'I've been there.'

'That is right. I forgot. Think chickens.'

'What?' Sten said.

'Mean chickens.'

Sten chortled, almost spraying Cind with Scotch.

'I am not even beginning to jest. Fowllike. Large. Two and a half meters tall. Bipedal. Hammer beaks. Beaks lined with teeth. Two arms – hands most capable of weapons use or strangulation. Retractable spurs. Not chicken temperament, however. Except under times of extreme duress, when panic seems to be the correct measure, and they rush back and forth and to and fro, flailing about with all these wonderful evolution-provided weapons.

'They seem to have evolved from an aquatic bird. I understand, however, that in common with chickens their drumsticks are most tasty. We were not, unfortunately, in a position where a little sedate galluspophagism could be accomplished.

'They group like feline carnivores – one male, five or six females. The grouping is called – I am not making this up, either – a coop.

'The male is smaller, weaker, and marsupial – their young are born alive, by the by. Extremely colorful. The females hunt, so they have natural camouflage – not phototropic, such as your quiet assistant, but nearly as effective. They're highly democratic – but you should hear the discussions before a decision is reached. A rookery. You will enjoy them.'

Sten *was* enjoying Aretha's descriptions and company. The food came. They ate.

'Sten has given me all the fiche,' Cind said, halfway through her sushi inhalation. 'What about the fourth set of beings – the Suzdal?'

'You could – I could, at any rate – almost get used to them. Think of a protomammal that evolved. Originally a pack carnivore. Small. A meter and a half to two meters. Six beings to a group. Attractive beings – quite gold in color.'

'Why'd you have a problem with them?'

'If I believed in racial memory, which I do not, or if my home planet has fossils of small, pack-hunting carrion eaters, which it does not, I would offer that as an explanation.

'I cannot. Perhaps their language – an incessant yapping – is what is bothersome. For certain what *is* loathsome is their violence. The Suzdal like to kill. A prime social pleasure is turning an animal loose on open terrain and hunting it down. In packs. It would almost seem that *they* have an Ur-memory.

'Whatever it is, the Suzdal fit in perfectly with everyone else in the Altaic Cluster – beings who hate each other, and have hated each other for so long they forget why. But that does not stop them from a little considered genocide whenever possible.'

'Wonderful,' Sten said. He worded his next question very carefully. 'I have heard reports that suggest that the Imperial energy shipments are . . . being diverted.'

'You mean someone is stealing the AM2,' Aretha said. 'They are. Or rather, the Khaqan is.'

'Where's it going?'

'Not sure. I attempted to learn – and found my esteemed ambassadorial leader a stumbling block. Some of it, I think, is going to the Khaqan's cronies within the cluster. Some of it is being outshipped, and the profits used to build his monuments. More is just disappearing.'

Aretha finished her dinner and had a final sip of mineral water. 'You have no doubt been told of the Khaqan's infatuation with large, ornate structures. But until you see for yourself just how massive an edifice complex he has, you will not believe it.'

'I thank you, Aretha. It would seem to me – and this must stay QT – that the most logical way to keep the lid on the Altaic Cluster is to quarantine all four races to their own sectors. At least, kept at arm's length, they can't manage a pogrom a week.'

Aretha whinnied laughter. 'You were not told.'

'I evidently have not been told several things,' Sten said.

'Many, many years ago, the Khaqan decided to settle this terrible problem. So he intermingled these beings.'

'What?'

'He arbitrarily chose resettlement. A nation of Suzdal, for instance, that rose against him would be moved, once the rising was suppressed. Frequently their new home would be in the middle of Bogazi worlds.'

'Oh, drakh,' Sten said. He poured himself a drink – straight. He started to drain it, then offered the decanter to Cind. She shook her head.

'Even more amusing,' Aretha went on, 'the Khaqan formed various militias. Each of a single group of beings.'

'That makes no sense,' Cind said.

'Oh, but it does. If you use each group of militia only against their traditional enemies, it keeps the anger focused everywhere except on you – the Khaqan. Another advantage is that these militia forces, stationed worlds and light-years away from their native sectors, are not only potential hostages, but keep the home worlds from being able to easily mount a revolution or civil war.'

There was a loud crash, what sounded like gunshots from downstairs, and then whooping laughter. Aretha looked longingly at the door to the snug.

Sten smiled. 'Thank you, Colonel. I owe you one. Now, if you'd ask Delaney to bring up the bill?'

'Would you permit me to buy you a drink downstairs?'

'I don't think so,' Sten said. 'I've got an early morning, and the . . . gentleman I'm seeing might not appreciate his favorite ambassador sporting a mouse.'

With a whicker of pleasure, Aretha was out the door and headed down the stairs. In a second, Sten and Cind heard an even louder crash.

'I hope this place has a back door,' Cind said.

'It does,' Sten said. 'Have you ever heard of a spookery that didn't?'

Sten's tongue caressed down Cind's neck, following the cleavage of the dress. Cind sighed . . . deep in her throat . . . near a growl. His hand moved along the inside of her thigh.

Their rented gravsled was on autopilot, holding a westering speed of barely fifty kph, and an altitude of nearly six thousand meters, out of any traffic lanes. Sten had managed to turn on all coll-sensors before the two of them tumbled, locked together, into the wide back.

Sten's hand found her belt buckle and fumbled. Nothing happened. 'I feel like a teener,' he said.

'You should,' Cind murmured. 'You tell me all about that enormous Imperial bed – and then hurl me into a rentawreck's backseat like we were flashing pubescents. Serve you right if a cop overflew. I can see it now,' she murmured into his ear. 'Hero Ambassador Found With Nude Bodyguard.'

'But you're not . . .'

His fingers suddenly became capable.

'Yes, I am,' Cind said throatily, as the dress came away and the nipples of her small breasts shone dark in the moonlight.

Their lips came together, tongues moving smoothly as if this were long-rehearsed and never the first time, and then her warmth caught him and drew him down and in for the eternity.

Chapter Six

The atmosphere in the Imperial study was autumnal. There was no alk or stregg in sight. Sten felt himself very definitely in the V-ring as he came to the end of his Altaic mission briefing and sped through the last few items.

'Coding . . . SOI . . . emergency procedures . . . all that's here in the fiche. We're ready. The *Victory* can lift within three E-days when victuals and ordnance are boarded.'

Sten put two copies of his fiche on the Emperor's desk. They were coded and marked for the highest security access. The Emperor ignored them.

'You seem,' he said, 'to have also done an excellent job of picking your personnel for this mission. Your longtime aide – the heavyworlder. The Bhor. Their commander. Most photogenic. And an excellent way to avoid . . . foreign entanglements.'

Whoever had had the meeting before Sten's must *really* have crapped in the Emp's mess kit. But Sten was used to vile temper from his superiors and paid no mind. 'One more thing, sir. Also regarding personnel.'

'What else do you want?'

'A skipper for the *Victory*. I think you've arranged it so that I'm going to be very busy on Jochi.'

'Is there somebody you want?'

'Fleet Admiral Rohber Mason. He's currently awaiting reassignment here on Prime.'

At first the idea had come to Sten as almost a joke. Then, on further consideration, it seemed a better and better idea. Mason might run a tyrannical ship, but the morale of the *Victory*'s crew was not especially of concern to Sten. Keeping himself alive was – and Sten knew that Mason the martinet was as capable of that as anyone. Besides, he knew that the admiral would follow orders. He was mildly curious to see whether it would bother Mason to serve under a man he disliked. Probably not – Mason almost certainly had the same feeling for all sentient beings. Sten himself had learned as a Delinq and then a soldier that one did not have to be friends with someone to task with them.

'Mmm. Very well. But you have a habit of wanting my best.'

So the Emperor had heard of Sten's prospective Gurkha recruits. 'Yessir. And that brings up something else. I've had twenty-seven of your Gurkhas volunteer for this mission.'

'And you told them?'

'I told them that if this was in accordance with Imperial policy, they would be welcome. They seemed to feel your approval had been tacitly granted.'

The Emperor swung his chair around and stared out the window at the sprawling castle grounds. He said something that Sten could not make out.

'Pardon, sir?'

'Nothing.'

Silence. Then the Emperor swung around again. He was smiling. He chuckled once.

'Having a few Nepalese along,' he said, 'would certainly suggest to the Altaic beings that your mission is taken very seriously – and that you have access to the very highest levels, wouldn't it?'

Sten did not answer.

'Take them,' the Eternal Emperor said. 'It will do them good. We probably should start a program of rotating the Gurkhas into temporary outside field duties. Give them experience – and keep them from getting stale.'

'Yessir.'

'I think,' the Emperor said, 'you have done an excellent job of preparing yourself and your team for this mission. I wish you success . . . and luck.'

He stood and held out a hand. Sten shook it, then came to attention and saluted – even though he was in mufti. Very smartly he about-faced and headed for the exit. No parting glass, he thought absently. But he was more intent on what his mind suggested the Emperor had said, when his back was turned: 'So everything changes . . .'

The Emperor held his ceremonial smile until the doors closed behind him. Then he dropped it. He stood for a long moment looking at the door Sten had gone through before reseating himself and keying the chamberlain to allow the next catastrophe to enter.

Sten stopped at Arundel's Admin Office long enough to have them issue orders transferring Mason to the *Victory*, and to tell the Gurkhas' CO that the volunteers' request had been approved and that they should pack their kit and report aboard the next day. Then he headed for his gravsled in a truly sour mood. Hell. He should have told Lalbahadur Thapa to go sit on one of Nepal's eight-thousand-meter peaks until his pubes froze, and take his twenty-six friends with him.

And having somebody slither around and find out that he and Cind were not sleeping solo – not that they'd kept their building relationship particularly secret – he didn't like that, either.

Sten *knew* that the Emperor had survived as long as he had by keeping his Intelligence the best available. He knew that every retainer in the Imperial household had had at least some intelligence training, and most of them were ex-specialists. And he guessed it made sense to know whether your ambassador plenipotentiary was available, booked, or in area-wide lust.

But he did not like it.

As he went down the broad steps to the parade ground, he automatically touched his forehead, returning the salutes of the posted sentries. Too many goddamned nosy people in this world, he thought resentfully. He suddenly snickered. He guessed spooks never did like it when somebody looked under *their* sheets.

There was another gravsled waiting beside his, a nearly exact duplicate. That was strange . . . Sten's transport was a sleek, stretched, blazingly white luxury item that reeked official muckety, from its assigned driver and guard – one of Cind's Bhor – to the small ambassadorial flags mounted on each corner of the vehicle, to the phototropic bubble roof. Not uncommon on Prime. But Sten's diplo-yacht was emblazoned with the Imperial crest on a solid red slash on either side of the vehicle's doors.

The other gravsled lacked only ambassadorial markings to be a clone of Sten's. The door came open . . . and Ian Mahoney stepped out.

Mahoney was ex-head of Mercury Corps, ex-head of Mantis Section, the man who had plucked Sten off the factory world of Vulcan and recruited him into Imperial Service. Mahoney had gone on to command the elite First Imperial Guards Division, then to become overall commander for the final assault on the Tahn. Then, when the Emperor had been killed, Mahoney had begun the drive to destroy his assassins, the privy council.

The Empire regained, Mahoney had been given an assignment much like Sten's: to be one of the Emperor's roving trouble-shooters, with ultimate authority.

The task of trying to piece the ravaged Empire back together was enormous. So Sten and Mahoney had only seen each other twice during the intervening years, and even those two occasions had been briefly seized moments.

Mahoney mock-scrutinized Sten's shoulders. 'I can't make out the epaulettes,' he said. 'This time, do I outrank you, or do you kiss *my* ring?'

Sten laughed, and wondered why he suddenly felt so good. He realized there were very few people he could talk to openly, let alone consider a bit of a mentor, even though he had pulled Mahoney's butt out of a crack as many times as Ian had saved him.

'Damfino,' Sten said. 'I'm not sure what pay grade I'm getting this time around. Let's stick with me calling you "sir" – that way I won't have to be apologizing for old habits. Time for a drink?'

Mahoney shook his head. 'Unfortunately, the path of duty calls, and it is a stony path indeed. I am due to make a rather more meaningless than usual speech before Parliament shortly. And much as I'd love to stomp to the podium, belch stregg, and start by damning all politicians' nonexistent souls to the Pit, I think the boss' – Mahoney jerked a thumb up at the Emperor's apartment – 'would have words with me.'

'Clot,' Sten said. 'You and I fought the war to end wars, and they *still* won't let us do any malingering.'

Mahoney frowned, seemingly deep in thought. 'Why don't we kill a few minutes before my speech? It'll give us a chance to talk, plus get a little exercise, which we both could use. Have these poor excuses for politicians' hearses meet us over there – if you have the time.'

'I have the time.'

'Wasn't it around here,' Mahoney said, 'where the Emperor had his workshop? Building . . . what were they?'

'Guitars,' Sten said.

'Wonder why he never rebuilt the shop, after . . . his return?' Mahoney asked.

Sten shrugged. He had really wanted to blow some steam off, but so far Mahoney had kept the conversation relentlessly trivial.

'Those were some days, weren't they . . .' Then Mahoney's casual tone changed. 'Damn, but you take hell's own time tracking down, boy. Keep the smile on the face. We're just beyond parabolic mikes now, but there's a long-range eye that's up on one of the battlements. It can read lips.'

Sten's bobble lasted for only a microsecond. Then he became the total professional. 'How do you know we're clean?'

'I have a copy of all security plans – and changes – to Arundel. Woman in the tech department owes me a small favor.'

'What's going on?'

'Damn, Sten, but I wish I could answer that straight on. Or that we had more than two minutes before we're in range of the next pickup. Because I'm not all that sure. But things . . . just aren't right. Haven't been, as far as I can see, since he came back.' Mahoney grunted. 'Or maybe I'm just becoming a senile, paranoiac old man. But the fault, from my seeing, is the Emperor.'

Sten almost slumped in relief. There it was – somebody else saw something.

'And if I try to give you specifics, you'll think I'm past it,' Mahoney went on. 'Because . . . It's all little things. Little things that lead to big things.'

'Like the new Guys in Gray,' Sten wondered. 'This Internal Security?'

'That's a bigger thing. Still bigger is that they don't answer to Mercury or Mantis. And it's strange that the closer they get to the Emperor himself, the more they look like they're his damned sons or something. Time!'

'Right. Just getting tired. But lately, retiring back to Smallbridge has sounded better and better,' Sten picked up smoothly. 'Let the world go by and all that.'

'I always said you lack ambition,' Mahoney said.

'And lacking it more the older I get.'

'Clear,' Mahoney said. 'Have you spent any time around court?'

'Not really.'

'It's being taken pretty seriously these days,' Ian said. 'It used to be a place the Emperor had to stash obnoxious or stupid people with money or clout. Give them a title, tuck them here on Prime, and they can't stir up any trouble back home. Most of them now are still prancing peacocks. But it seems that the Eternal Emperor spends more time in their company. Plus there's starting to be some people here who aren't popinjays.'

'What does that mean?'

'I don't know,' Mahoney said.

'Have you noticed the Emperor's temper's on a short fuse these days?' Sten asked.

'You see,' Mahoney answered, starting to spread his hands helplessly and then changing his mind, 'drakh like this – like whether he's being cranky – I don't even know if it's important. Maybe he was always like this. Maybe he's just pushing too hard, trying to put this crumble of an Empire back together. I . . . I truly do not know,' Mahoney said once more.

'That's the other question,' Sten said. 'Maybe the real question, and what's been eating at me. *Can* this clottin' Empire be saved? Or did the combination of the Tahn war and the privy council batter it too much?'

'Clean it up . . . three, two, now . . . Again, Sten, the only answer I have is DNC – insufficient data.'

They walked on, as the path wound toward the artificial mountain the Emperor had built with the ostensible reason of keeping him from having to look at the clots in Parliament, talking of this, and that. At last Mahoney announced that they were outside any bugs, and asked about Sten's current assignment.

'We've got ten minutes now, so give me the full details.'

Sten did. Mahoney mostly kept silent, except for an occasional shake of his head or grunt.

'Now, there's a fine example of what I've been groping at,' Mahoney said. 'The Altaic Cluster. Good analysis by the boss, yet you wonder why he let it go on for so long. Blame it on being busy with bigger catastrophes.

'What's bad is that he told you to go out there and lay sacred hands on the Khaqan and bless his hustle. He could just as well, and possibly more wisely, have sent you out to get a feel for the problem and *then* reach a solution as to whether to reinforce the old thief or just send in Mantis to cut his throat.

'Now there's a point that just occurred to me, thinking out loud as I am. It's as if he doesn't quite have the same patience or depth.

'Oh well,' he said. 'Oh well.'

'The problem is,' Sten said, smiling a bit ruefully, 'is that the Emp is, as far as I can see, the only game in town.'

Mahoney did not answer him. 'I'm sure it'll all straighten out,' he said obliquely. 'Now. We're coming up on range of more bigears. Let me take care of *my* business. I didn't go to all this clottin' trouble because I particularly care about your pissant personal problems. There's chaplains for trash like that.'

Sten laughed, feeling a great deal more cheery. Mahoney was using the old Mantis 'sorry you're bleeding to death but could you do it in another color, since I always hated red' hard-edged sympathy.

'First, here.' Mahoney's hand brushed Sten's, and a square of plas passed between them. 'That's body-temp sensitive. Keep it close. If you drop it it'll char.'

'What's on it?'

'A very elaborate, very complicated computer program, and its two brothers. Get to any Imperial computer terminal that's cleared for ALL/UN input, and key the codes in. The first one will wipe *all* references, anywhere in the Imperial records, including Mantis and Imperial Eyes Only, to one Ian Mahoney. The second does the same for Sten, No Initial; the third for that thug Kilgour. After wiping, it then mutates in all directions, destroying as it goes.'

'Why the hell would I need *that*?' Sten said in complete shock.

Mahoney didn't answer. 'One other thing. And listen close, because I am only going to say it once, and I want you to bury it in your backbrain.

'If the drakh comes down – *really* comes down, and you will absolutely know what I mean if it does – start by going home. There's something waiting.'

'Small—'

'Think, goddamn it,' Mahoney snarled. 'You've got your head up like you were a straight-leg trainee. That's it. Four tools, maybe. Or four parts of an old man's degenerating into senility?'

Mahoney chortled suddenly. '. . . said, "You clot, the line was there's *hope* in her *soul*."'

Mahoney laughed. Sten, more than familiar with situations when sudden merriment *sans* joke was required, also laughed. 'Fine, Ian. If we're telling old stinkers, here's one of Kilgour's, which I won't even begin to try in dialect.'

As his mouth began the words to the half-remembered joke, Sten forbade himself a guilty look back over his shoulder at Arundel Castle . . . and concentrated on jokes, obscene, Scots, stupid.

Days later, Ian Mahoney stood in the shadows near a spaceport hangar. Far across the field a violet flame plumed into the night.

The *Victory* lifted smoothly on its Yukawa drive until it was a thousand meters above Prime. Then its captain shifted to stardrive, and suddenly there was nothing but silence and night sky.

Mahoney stood for a long time looking up at that nothing.

Luck, lad. Better than mine. Because I'm starting to think mine's running thin.

And I hope you learn it may be time for this town to hunt up another game – and find out just what exactly it could be.

Chapter Seven

There were about twenty beings cloistered in the room. The atmosphere was conspiratorial. Thick with talk – and smells. The sweet musk of the Suzdal, the mint/fish odor of the Bogazi. And the methane and ammonia aroma of humans.

'Like privies smell,' the Bogazi male clicked. 'Own privies.'

'Shush. Might hear,' one of his wives warned. She fussed over him, tucking a stray feather back into his fabulous tail display. His name was Hoatzin.

He tapped the big hammer of his beak against hers, showing pleasure. 'Humans I study in books only,' Hoatzin said. 'Some in school I see. But not close.'

He waved a delicate grasping limb at the humans in the room. 'This *very* close. Like it. Not smell. Like study close.' Hoatzin was a teacher, as were most males in his society. They reared the young. Their domain was the nest and the book. For the wives, it was the hunt.

Hoatzin looked over at the main table with pride. This is where the leaders of each group held forth, seeking a way, or, at least, agreement to agree. His chief wife, Diatry, was one of the four. She was speaking now.

'In circles we talk,' she said. 'Big egg circles. But big nothing in egg. Could all night stay. Talk and talk. Still egg not hatch.' She peered down the hammer beak at the much smaller forms around her. Even by Bogazi standards she was tall: nearly three meters.

The Suzdal pack leader made a tooth display. The dim light glittered all along the sharp edges. 'Summed up like a true Bogazi,' Youtang said. 'Forget the flesh. Get to the bone of the thing.' The flattery to a former enemy was not intended. Youtang was getting weary of all the fencing. She would probably be surprised to learn that she had one other thing in common with the Bogazi: In their hatred of the smell of humans, they were sisters.

The general sighed. He wasn't sure how he had let himself be talked into this meeting. Except that the Tork, Menynder, was notoriously persuasive. Douw was frightened. What had started as an information-only probe had developed into a full-scale engagement. The current griping irritated him. As the Jochian secretary of defense, he certainly had the most to lose.

'What *more* am I supposed to say?' Douw gave his shoulders a helpless shrug. 'That conditions are intolerable? Of course they are.' He looked nervously around. 'I mean . . . *some* conditions are bad. On the other hand . . .'

'There's a foot,' Menynder broke in.

'What?' Douw's face was a blank.

Like a cow, Menynder thought. A silver-haired cow. 'This isn't a staff meeting, General,' he said. 'Every being here has a life on the line. We gotta start talking plain. Otherwise the risk isn't worth it.'

He motioned around the room. 'I told you the place was clean. I had it scoured for bugs stone by stone. Now, so far I have provided a safe place to meet. Right in the middle of the squeakiest clean Tork neighborhood on Jochi.' He ticked the rest off on his fingers. 'Youtang stuck her neck out contacting the Bogazi. And Diatry, here, is probably on the Khaqan's *Most Suspicious* list, so she risked it even coming out of her roost.'

The Tork shifted his heavy weight in the chair. 'Face it, General, if he knows we're here we are already dead. Now, let's go.'

Douw soaked this up, slowly churning it through his conservative military mind. Menynder was right.

'After close observation of the Khaqan,' he said quite formally, 'I have come to the conclusion that he is insane.'

No one laughed. Every being in the room realized the step Douw had just taken. It was almost as if the words had been delivered in a courtroom.

'Furthermore, I believe he has become a danger not only to himself, but to all the beings living in the Altaic Cluster.' The general sucked in breath and let it out in a great whoosh. There. It was done.

The room erupted.

'I'll say he's insane,' Youtang said. 'Killed every one of his own cubs, didn't he?'

'One hatchling was trouble,' Diatry said. 'With rebels he plotted.'

'Sure. But what about the others? Three daughters and a son. He killed them all. Afraid they wouldn't wait until he died for them to try to take over.' Youtang was especially outraged by this sin. The Suzdal were highly protective of their young.

'In gluttony he lives,' Diatry said. 'Food. Drink. Sex. Money. Power. Too much of all he has. All over Altaics, roosts are cold. Markets they are empty. Stores outside we line. For hours and hours. What a life is this?'

'Drakh. That's what,' Youtang snarled.

'What do we do about it?' Menynder pressed.

'Do? What's to be done?' Douw asked.

Menynder boomed laughter. 'Well, from the looks of things in this room, we're all pretty much in agreement that the old buzzard has to go.'

'Three questions we must decide,' Diatry said. 'One: Do we kill? Two: If kill, how? Three: Once gone, who rules? In these I am correct, yes?'

There were no arguments.

'Let's start with the last part,' Menynder said. 'Speaking as a Tork, I'm tired of us getting short-ended because we're a minority.

Whoever takes the Khaqan's place is going to have to deal with that.'

'I agree,' Youtang said.

'Same for Bogazi,' Diatry said.

'What if we felt out Dr Iskra?' Menynder wondered. 'He's respected all over the cluster. And he has a rep for seeing all sides of a problem.'

Iskra was a member of the Jochian majority. But he was a famous professor who had made his mark in Imperial circles. Another plus was that he was currently the Emperor's territorial governor of one of the conquered Tahn regions.

There was a long silence, as the beings in the room pondered the suggestion.

'I don't know,' Youtang said finally. 'Lots of smoke. Not a lot of substance. I mean, who knows how he really thinks?'

They all turned to see what General Douw had to say about the proposal. The general's brow was furrowed with thought. 'Do you really think we need to kill the Khaqan?' he asked.

There was a frustrated murmur around the room, but before anyone could speak, the door crashed open.

Every being in the room lost a lifespan as they looked up to see their worst nightmare: the Khaqan. Standing in the doorway. Flanked by gold-robed soldiers. Riotguns leveled.

'Traitors!' the Khaqan roared. 'Plotting my murder!'

He strode forward, face a bloodless mask of death, bony finger jabbing like a specter to pierce each heart, emptying lungs and defecating organs.

'I'll roast you alive,' the Khaqan shrieked. He was at the table now, his fury pouring over them. 'But first, I'll take you apart – small piece by small piece. And I'll feed the pieces to your children. And I'll feed them to your friends. And they'll be the ones who stand at the Killing Wall.'

He gathered up the fury into a chest-bursting balloon and shouted: 'Take them to my—'

Sudden silence. Everyone stared at the Khaqan. His mouth was a wide O. His eyes bulged. The death face had turned swollen red. Even the soldiers were gaping at him.

The Khaqan plunged face forward on the table. Small bones cracked. Blood gouted from his mouth. Then the body slowly slid to the floor.

Menynder squatted beside him and put a practiced hand to the Khaqan's throat.

He stood. Removed his spectacles. Cleaned them. Put them back on.

'Well?' Oddly, the question came from the captain of the guard.

'He's dead,' Menynder announced.

'Thank God,' the soldier said, lowering his weapon. 'The old son of a bitch had gone looners.'

Chapter Eight

The ambassador and the warrior lay entwined in bed asleep. Naked limbs had curled around each other until the two bodies resembled an ancient Chinese puzzle knot, of the erotic variety. The ambassador's groin was covered with the warrior's barracks cap.

Through the thick insulated walls of the ambassador's suite the distant sounds of a shift change could be heard. Somewhere in the bowels of the *Victory* a pump shuddered into life and began filtering the fluids in the hydroponic tanks.

The blond curls of the warrior stirred first. Long lashes fluttered open. The warrior peered into the face of the sleeping ambassador. The warrior's eyes roamed downward to the barracks cap, then lit with mischief. Little teeth flashed in a crooked grin.

Cind carefully untied her portion of the knot. Sliding her lovely limbs out of Sten's embrace, she knelt on the Eternal Emperor's yawning bed. There was room for a whole division of lovers on its silky smoothness. But for what Cind had in mind, the vast playing field was a waste.

She gently lifted the cap away. Her slender fingers reached for their target. Blond head and soft lips dipped downward.

Sten was dreaming about Smallbridge. He had been roaming the snowfields that spread from the forest to his cabin by the lake. For some reason he had been dressed in battle harness

– tight battle harness. Odder still, the harness was cinched over his naked flesh. It wasn't uncomfortable or anything. Just odd.

Suddenly, he was inside his cabin, lying by a crackling fire. The harness was gone. But he was still naked – and something wonderful was going on. Then he realized he was asleep. And dreaming. Well, it wasn't all a dream. Not the naked part. Or the wonderful goings on. Then the fire crackled louder.

'Ambassador, your presence is requested on the bridge!' The fire was talking.

'What?' This a murmur.

'Ambassador! Do you hear me?'

'Go away, fire. I'm busy.'

'Ambassador Sten. This is Admiral Mason. If you please, I need you on the bridge.'

The wonderfulness abruptly stopped. Sten opened his eyes, suddenly in a sour mood. His mood curdled more when he saw Cind's rounded curves and disappointed face. Her lips formed the word 'Sorry.' She shrugged.

Sten palmed the switch of the com unit on the built-in bedside stand. 'Okay, Mason,' he said, doing his best not to snarl, with little success. 'Be right there.'

Cind started laughing. Sten's frown deepened. Clottin' Mason.

'Give me the order,' Cind said, 'and I'll trot out a firing squad and have him shot.'

Sten finally saw the humor and joined her laughter. 'Do I get to torture him first?' he snarled. 'I know just where I want to start.' He clambered off the bed and started to get dressed.

'I'm off shift for another two hours,' Cind said. 'So if you're back before I have to shower . . .' She let the rest trail off suggestively.

'I'll hurry,' Sten said.

Two hours later, he checked the clock, thought wistfully of Cind, and turned back to Mason.

'Maybe we're drowning our own sensors,' Sten suggested tentatively. 'The *Victory* is pretty new. Not much time on the engines. Leaky baffles, perhaps?'

The scar on Mason's face purpled. He had personally checked the scans on every flex nut and seam. No way would he allow some slipup to embarrass him in front of this son of a Xypaca. He would rather eat drakh for rations.

'I had it happen on my first tacship,' Sten lied smoothly,

knowing what Mason was thinking. He wasn't needling the man. After all, Mason was in charge. Sten just wanted the problem solved. 'It was brand new and barely broken in when Mr Kilgour and I got it.'

Sten indicated his heavyworld friend, whose technical knowledge had been commandeered by Mason's com officer. The two were conferring, hands flying over the com center panel. Buzzwords thickened the air.

'The designer hadn't factored the effect broken-in engines would have on the baffling,' Sten said. 'Blew clot out of our reception. Transmissions, too.'

Mason's scar returned to normal color. 'Good thought,' he said. 'I'll check it.' He gave orders to his chief engineer, mentally kicking himself for not thinking of it first.

A few minutes later word came back. 'That was no good,' Mason said. He was too professional to gloat. The admiral wanted the problem solved, too. 'You were right about the leakage. But it's minor. Not enough to foul things up.'

Sten nodded. He had only been hoping. He looked over at Kilgour and the com officer, wanting to ask how they were doing. But he kept his lips buttoned. Not his place.

'Anything to report?' Sten heard Mason ask his com officer.

The com officer and Kilgour exchanged looks. 'He'd better tell you, sir,' the officer said.

'Ah wae puzzlin't i' it twere th' bafflin' myself, sir,' Kilgour said. 'But thae'd on'y mess wi' transmission. The talkin'. Nae the hearin'.'

'Except for some stray old radio echoes, sir,' the com officer told Mason, 'there's not one thing being broadcast on the whole planet. Jochi is silent, sir. Not even any livie feed. And you know how broad *those* bands are? I've tried every kind of transmission I could think of to rouse someone, sir. Sr Kilgour threw in a few ideas of his own. I double-identified the *Victory*. I even pointed out that his majesty's personal emissary was on board.' He gave Sten a worried nod. 'Still no answer.'

'Anything from the other worlds in the system?' Mason asked.

'Negative, sir. As silent as Jochi. But the funny thing is . . .' His voice faded.

'Yes? Speak up, man.'

The com officer looked at Kilgour and licked his lips. Kilgour gave him a reassuring nod.

'It's real spooky, if you don't mind, sir. There are no broadcasts, as I said. But every scanner we've got going is just showing a flicker of life. As if everybody on Jochi was tuned in at the same time. Listening. But not talking.'

'Th' silence hae a wee echo t' it, sir,' Alex said. 'Like a specter m' ol' gran conjured t' frighten us bairns wi'.'

Mason gave Alex a withering look, then turned to his com officer. 'Keep transmitting,' he said.

'Yes, sir.'

The com officer keyed the mike. 'This is His Imperial Majesty's battleship *Victory* calling. All receiving stations are requested to respond.'

Keyed off. Waited. Got silence. Tried again. 'This is His Imperial . . .'

Mason motioned to Sten and strolled to a quiet corner of the bridge.

'I don't understand what's going on,' Mason said. 'I've carpet-bombed half a planet, and even out of the smoking ruins some poor bassid managed to get on the air. Spotty transmission, yes. Silence, never.'

'There's only one way that I can think of to answer the question,' Sten said.

'You mean, land anyway?'

'That's what I was thinking.'

'But the Emperor wanted a big show. Honor guard. Me in dress whites, you in tux and tails, and the whole band playing to idolizing crowds as you and the Khaqan greeted one another.'

'I'll arrange something later,' Sten said. 'The Emperor is worried about this place. I'd rather forget the show and find out what's happening.' He shook his head for effect. 'Can't imagine what he'd say if I came back and said, Sorry, sir. Mission abandoned. Seems the inhabitants of Jochi got the throat plague, or something.'

'I'll land,' Mason said. 'But I'm going to full alert. And clear for action.'

'I am in your capable hands, Admiral,' Sten said.

Mason snorted and went back to the com center. Sten slipped quietly off the bridge.

'Some ghost, Kilgour,' Sten said. He wiped the sweat from his brow and pulled his collar up to protect his neck from the fierce Jochi sun.

'Mayhap' th' wee specter hae a bomb aboot him,' Alex said.

Sten took another look around the Rurik spaceport. Except

for his party, there wasn't a being in sight. No one living, anyway.
He thought he saw a charred stump lying in the rubble about a
large bomb crater. Or maybe it was just an optical trick of the
heat and the lung-drowning humidity.

There were similar craters all over the spaceport, as well as
the fire-blackened outlines of what must once have been a few
parked tacships and a lot of combat cars.

There was a sudden howl of air, and a small whirlwind touched
down, sucking up bits of rubble as it cut across the ground. In
the odd behavior of cyclones, large and small, it ran around the
edge of the immense crater in the center of the field. Another
bomb hole. A big clottin' bomb. The hole was where the control
tower had once stood.

The twister lifted off and was gone.

'Now we know the answer to why no one was talking,' Sten
said. 'Everybody's too scared. Didn't want to be noticed.'

'But they're all a listenin', though,' Alex said.

Sten nodded. 'They're waiting to hear who wins.'

Heat lightning flashed. Then there was a heavy roll of thunder.

His Gurkhas suddenly lifted their willyguns. Something – or
someone – was coming. Sten could make out a small figure edging
around the ruins of the control tower. Cind and her scouts? No.
They had reconned off in the other direction.

'Still on'y one ae them,' Kilgour said.

'Maybe it's the band,' Sten said dryly.

Gradually the small figure got larger. Sten could make out a squat,
barrel-chested human, sweating copiously in the heat. Picking
distastefully at his sodden clothing, the man tromped steadily onward.
In his left hand he was tiredly waving a kerchief-size white flag.

'Let him past,' Sten told the Gurkhas.

They parted ranks, and the man lumbered gratefully to a halt
in front of Sten. He took off a pair of antique spectacles. Blew
on the lenses. Wiped with the flag. Put them back on. Looked at
Sten with his oddly magnified brown eyes.

'I hope you're Ambassador Sten,' he said. 'And if you are, I'm
real sorry about the lousy reception.' He looked around at the
bomb craters. 'Ouch. I guess they really went at it.'

He turned back. 'You *are* Ambassador Sten, aren't you?'

'I am.' Sten waited.

'Oh. Forgive me. The heat's getting to my old Tork head. I'm
Menynder. About the only one you'll find around here to speak
for my people.'

He wiped a sweaty hand on damp clothing and with an embarrassed grimace held out his hand.

Sten shook. Then he pointed around at the signs of destruction. 'What happened?'

Menynder sighed. 'I hate to be the one to break the news, but . . . the Khaqan is dead.'

Sten had to yank fast into his diplomatic bag of tricks to turn the gape that was growing onto his face into professional surprise.

'Clottin' what?' Kilgour said. 'An' who kill't th' ol'—'

'Natural causes,' Menynder assured them. He eased his collar away from his neck. 'I was there myself. Saw the whole thing.

'It was a terrible experience. We were all just about to sit down to . . . dinner, and the Khaqan keeled over on the table. Dead. Just like that.' He snapped his fingers.

'There was an autopsy?' Sten asked coolly.

'Lord, did we have an autopsy,' Menynder said. 'Nobody wanted to . . . I mean, under the circumstances, we thought it wise. Two teams worked on him. And we really pored over those reports. Just to make double clottin' sure.' He fingered the collar again. 'It was natural causes all right.'

'When is the funeral?' Sten asked. This had torn the whole thing. The Emperor would not be pleased.

'Uh . . . kind of hard to say. You see, we all agreed to agree until the final coroner's report. Things sort of fell apart before we got to talking about a funeral.' Menynder indicated the bomb craters. 'If you see what I mean.'

Sten did.

'I don't want to point fingers,' Menynder said, 'but the Jochians started it. Squabbling among themselves over who was to be the new Khaqan. The rest of us weren't consulted. Although we told them plainly, *before* the shooting, that we had some ideas of our own.'

'Naturally,' Sten said.

'Anyway, when the Jochians ran out of hot words, they started fighting. We all hunkered down. Then a stray shell landed right in the middle of a Tork neighborhood. It was . . . pretty bad. My home world thought it best to send a militia.'

'Oh?' Sten said.

'Just to protect my people. Not to get into anything with the Jochians.'

'How did that work out?'

'Not well.' Menynder sighed. 'I didn't think it would. There have been some . . . ahem . . . sharp exchanges, if you know what I mean.'

Sten could see just fine.

'Of course, once our militia showed up, well the Bogazi and the Suzdal militias decided their folks needed protecting, too.'

'I figured that,' Sten said. It was getting worse and worse.

'Okay, you've got the picture. Now, I've got some real bad news for you,' Menynder said, checking his timepiece and looking nervously around the spaceport.

'Och, so thae's th' braw news, i' it?' Kilgour growled, liking it even less than Sten, if that was possible.

'See, everyone's been glued to the emergency bands, praying for the cavalry to show up. We *all* heard your broadcasts. Folks probably overloaded the *Jane's* fiche, checking out the *Victory.*' He pointed at the sleek craft behind Sten that was the Emperor's ship. 'Personally, I already knew. Pride myself in keeping up at my old trade. But I had only vaguely heard of you.' He nodded at Sten.

Sten cursed under his breath, remembering the com officer saying he had tried everything.

'So . . . I'm the cavalry,' Sten said.

'You got it, Ambassador,' Menynder said. 'I checked the Imperial *Who's Who.* Pretty impressive. Hero soldier. Hero diplomat. The Eternal Emperor's main man. At least, that's how it's playing on Jochi.'

Sten could imagine. This was not good. Definitely not how he had planned this miserable day.

'Everybody's on the way now,' Menynder said. 'I hustled like clot to beat them. And they're going to want your ear. They'll kick reptile snot out of each other trying to rip it off your corpse, if they have to.'

Menynder let this sink in a second before going on. 'See, whoever has you, is top dog.' He winced. 'Gotta watch myself. Some of my best friends are Suzdals.'

'I assume you had some sort of a plan,' Sten said. 'Otherwise you wouldn't be here.'

'I sure did,' Menynder said. 'Although I might have trouble convincing you of my good intentions.'

'Ah. I see,' Sten said. 'You were thinking we could go have a nice quiet word in some safe Tork neighborhood. Am I right?'

Menynder grinned. 'What the clot? It was worth a try. If not, maybe you better get out of here. Fast.'

Sten ignored this. Thinking. He got a glimmer.

'How far to the embassy?' Neutral turf. No one would dare fire on or even near the Emperor's embassy.

'Clear across town,' Menynder said. 'You'd never make it.'

There was a grind and heavy clank of tracks. Sten jolted up to see an armored ground vehicle push its way through rubble. A small flag flew from a standard next to the tank's chain guns. Sten didn't have to ask. It was Jochian.

There was a cry from the other side of the field. Sten turned to see Cind running like the wind, her Bhor scouts right behind her. She was yelling some kind of warning and gesturing at a low building behind her.

Mortar dust suddenly sprayed out from the building. The entire front collapsed. Another track emerged under a rain of metal and brickwork. The track was also armored. It had chain guns and flew a flag – Jochian, as well.

Cind panted up to Sten. 'And that's not all,' she said, pointing at the track. 'There's more of them. Plus soldiers. And from the sound of things, a great big mob on its way.'

The tracks' main gun turrets suddenly swung around. They had spotted each other. Simultaneously, their guns opened up, hurling spent uranium AP shells.

Admiral Mason's voice crackled over the *Victory*'s outside speakers. 'I suggest we leave, Ambassador,' he said.

Sten agreed. He turned to Menynder. 'You better make yourself scarce,' he said. 'Good luck.'

'We're going to need a lot more than luck,' Menynder said. And he puffed away for cover. Sten and his group sprinted to the ship and thundered up the ramp.

Behind them, first one track exploded, then the other. A mortar round slammed in. More tracks appeared. Guns blazing.

Braced against the gees exerted by the *Victory*'s fast take-off, Sten watched the battle scene shrink away from him on the bridge's main screen.

Some welcome, he thought. Now, how the clot was he going to unravel this muck-up?

Sten huddled with Mason in the admiral's cabin, trying to figure out what to do next. As they worried over several possibilities – ranging from poor to plain stupid – the reports kept flooding in. Jochi was no longer silent.

Sten's eyes swept over a sheaf of transcriptions the com officer had handed to him. 'They've gone mad,' he summarized. 'Everybody's calling everybody else all kinds of obscenities. Prodding the other guy to come out and fight like beings.' He read on, then gave a low whistle and lifted his eyes. 'Which they are doing.' He tapped one report. 'A Jochi militia caught some Torks in a building. They wouldn't come out to be slaughtered. So the Jochians burned it around their ears.'

'Wonderful,' Mason said. 'Plus we have so many riots going on that the algo computer has scorched its wires running progs on how fast this thing can spread.' He snorted. 'So much for diplomacy. Proves my own private theories on the behavior of the average citizen. The only thing any of them understand is a good shot up alongside the head.'

'I don't think that would work here,' Sten said dryly. 'The Emperor wants their hearts and minds. Their scalps won't do him a clottin' bit of good.'

'Still . . .' Mason said.

'I know,' Sten said. 'With these folks it's damned tempting. Unfortunately, what's happening right now was triggered by our arrival.'

'I'm not taking the blame for this,' Mason said, a little hotly.

Sten sighed. 'No one's asking you to, Admiral. It's my ass the Emperor will want on toast. Although, if it gets much worse, he may not be satisfied with *just* mine.'

Mason opened his mouth to retort. Sten raised his hand, silencing him. He'd had a sudden thought. 'My father used to tell me about this beast,' Sten said. 'A mule, I think he called it. It was a sport. A mean and stubborn sport. Said the only way to get its attention was to hit it with a board, first.'

'I already suggested something along those lines,' Mason said.

'Yeah. I know. But for these beings, a hit on the head may be too subtle . . . Okay. Try this idea on for size . . .'

Mason leaned closer as Sten sketched in the broad outlines of his plan.

The Jochi mob was pressing close on the Bogazi barricade, showering rocks, debris, and taunts on the small group of neighborhood defenders. The shops on either side of the broad main street of Rurik were blank eyes of shattered glass. Many of them were gouting flames.

Overhead, the midday sky was black with threatening storms.

Heavy clouds jostled one another, triggering thick blue arcs of electrical fire.

A tall Jochian rushed the heap of furniture and scrap timber that made up the barricade. He hurled a grenade, turned, and ran for safety.

A burst of fire cut him down. At the same instant, the grenade went off. The explosion shrapneled through the Bogazi. There were screams of pain and anger.

A big female Bogazi hurtled through the gap cut by the grenade. Spurs jutting out from her forearms, she snagged two Jochians. She brought the big hammer beak down once. Twice. Skulls cracked like pollution-thinned eggshells.

She dropped the corpses on the ground and turned for another victim. A heavy bar swung against her throat. The Bogazi flopped beside the two corpses.

More Bogazi came pouring out. In a moment, the main street's storm drains would be awash in blood.

There was a sudden banshee howl from overhead. A heavy wind blasted along the street, battering the crowd with dust and small debris. The mob stopped in midriot – and gaped upward.

The gleaming white body of the *Victory* swept down the boulevard toward them. Not high in the sky, but just below the roofs of the high-rise buildings that lined the street, a looming bulk never meant for the heart of a city.

Close to the barricades the howl grew louder, and the warship went into a hover on McLean Drive, close enough for the mob to get a good long look at the Imperial emblem on its sides.

This was the Imperial presence – mailed fist and looming overlord in one.

'My God, would you look at that,' a Jochi chemical worker breathed.

'Maybe now, justice we get,' a Bogazi said.

'Wait up! What's he doing?' another awe-stricken Jochian said, absently tugging at a Bogazi's sleeve.

The *Victory* settled still closer, until it was no more than twenty meters overhead. The crowd huddled under the dark cloud of its body. Engines stirred, then the ship slowly began to move forward, straight down the broad avenue.

The two sides of the conflict gaped after it for a moment or two. Then they turned to stare at one another. Makeshift weapons tumbled to the ground from hands and grasping limbs.

Above them, the black sky was suddenly bright blue. Sun

painted lacy clouds a multitude of colors. The air was fresh and tasted of spring.

'We've been saved,' a Jochian said.

'I knew the Emperor wouldn't abandon us,' said another.

Someone shouted from a rooftop: 'The ship's heading for the Imperial embassy.'

The spell broke and the mob, laughing and shouting in relief, rushed after the ship.

The *Victory* sailed slowly along just above the pavement. Below it, the street was suddenly jammed from side to side with a sea of beings. Bogazi and Jochians and Suzdal and Torks, all mingled together, joking and slapping one another on the back.

Thousands of other beings leaned from the windows of the tall buildings, cheering the *Victory* and its majestic flight.

All over Jochi – in fact, all over the entire cluster – beings stopped what they were doing and rushed to witness the arrival of the Emperor's man.

By the time the ship reached the Imperial embassy, there were literally millions of beings surrounding its broad, gated grounds. And there were billions more watching on their livies.

All hostilities had ceased.

Inside the *Victory*, Sten quick-brushed his clothes. Cind ran her fingers through his hair, pushing strands into place.

Alex looked at a livie screen and the enormous crowd waiting outside. 'You're a bleedin' Pied Piper, young Sten,' he said.

'Don't say that,' Sten said. 'He got paid off in rats. Or house apes, and I don't know which is worse.'

A crew member tickled the port controls. The port swung open. Sten felt the fresh breeze on his face. He heard the thump of the ramp settling to the ground.

'Okay,' he said. 'Now let the bastards come to me.'

He stepped out into a torrent of cheers.

BOOK TWO

CAT'S CLAW

Chapter Nine

'I've never been one to kill the messenger bearing bad news,' the Eternal Emperor said.

'Yessir,' Sten said.

'In this case, however,' the Emperor continued, 'it's a good thing I've known you such a long time.'

'Yessir,' Sten said.

'You get the point that I am not pleased?'

'I do, Your Majesty,' Sten said. 'Absolutely . . . sir.'

The holo image of the Emperor wavered as Sten's boss crossed to the antique drinks tray in his study and poured himself two fingers of Scotch.

'You have something to drink there?' the Emperor asked a bit absently.

'Yessir,' Sten said. 'I thought it best to haul along my own supplies.' He took the hint, hooked a bottle of Scotch off the desk of the previous ambassador, and poured himself a drink.

The Emperor mock-toasted: 'I'd say confusion to my enemies – but if they get any more confused we'll all go into the drakh head first.'

He drank anyway. Sten followed suit.

'You know there's no way I can keep this from getting out?' the Emperor said. Sten didn't answer. It had not really been a question.

'There's already reports in the media hinting at a building crisis in the Altaics. Wait'll they find out how bad things really are.' The Emperor refilled his glass, thinking. 'What really hurts is I've got some crucial agreements in the works. Agreements hinging on strong confidence in the Empire. The slightest sign of a hole in the structure I've rebuilt is going to put those agreements into decaying orbits. And . . . when one fails . . . then a lot of other things come into doubt.'

Sten sighed. 'I wish there were some way I could paint a more hopeful picture, Your Majesty,' he said, 'but this is probably the stickiest assignment I've ever handled for you. And it's not really begun.'

'I'm sensible of that, Sten,' the Emperor said. 'The Khaqan just picked a lousy time to die.' He sipped his drink. 'You *are* sure someone didn't help him along?'

'I've gone over all the reports,' Sten said. 'And it's pretty clear how and why he died. It was an aneurysm. An artery blew a cork. The only thing I'm not sure of is the circumstances.' Sten was thinking of Menynder's claim about a dinner party honoring the Khaqan. 'Personally, I don't think it matters that much. If there was some kind of conspiracy in the works . . . well, from what I've seen it wouldn't be all that unusual.'

'I agree,' the Emperor said. 'In fact, if there was no sign of a conspiracy, I'd be damned suspicious. Fine. Let's leave the circumstances alone – for the time being.'

'Yessir,' Sten said.

'What we have to do,' the Emperor said, 'is get this thing under control fast. If the whole Empire is going to be watching, I don't want anyone to think I'm going to be less than firm about this. There are going to be some who'll say I screwed up. There are going to be others who'll say I've lost my moves . . . since I got back. And then there'll be those who are just hoping I've gotten soft so they can stir up trouble. So, with that in mind, I want to set the tone of how to handle things right from the start . . .

'Which is this: If anybody moves we don't like, smack them down. We install a new government. Immediately. With my *full* support. Once this is done, there will be *no* objections. Not in my earshot, anyway. And, if there are loud or violent quarrels with my decision in the Altaics, then I want them silenced. Fast. With whatever it takes. I will suffer no humiliation in this!' Slam went the Emperor's hand on his desk. Even through the holo speakers it sounded like a shot.

Abruptly the Emperor stopped steaming and gave Sten a thin, unfelt smile. 'I want to be damned sure both my enemies *and* my friends know I will not be fooled with.'

'Yessir. I . . . agree, sir . . .'

'Do I hear a silent "but" in your agreement?'

'Not with your overall point, Your Majesty. Not at all. This is no time to show hesitancy. However, when you briefed me on this place, you weren't exaggerating about how contrary these people are. Even if we use a big hammer to nail this together, I think we'll still need to be real careful how it *goes* together.'

Sten hesitated, trying to read the Emperor's face. It was blank. But not necessarily angry blank.

'Go ahead,' the Emperor said.

'As you know, sir, I've talked to all the leaders – at least the beings who *say* they are the leaders. Until I get some better analyses, based on immediate HUMINT, I'll just trust in my instincts: This thing can split a lot more than four ways. Clot, it already has. When I arrived two Jochi factions were firing on each other at the spaceport.'

'Listen to those instincts,' the Emperor said.

'Soon as I showed up,' Sten continued, 'all of these faction leaders, human and ET, clawed their way to the embassy, each one begging to be made the new honcho. I made them wait for official invitations. Called them in one by one.'

'And took your good time about it, too,' the Emperor said. 'Made them cool their heels and ponder their sins against me. I like how that was handled.'

'Thank you, sir,' Sten said. 'Frankly, now that this place has come apart once, I'm real doubtful it can be put back together again. Not the way it was before.

'They're all sitting in their neighborhoods now, sir. And on their home worlds, as well – with nothing to distract them but their personal problems. Picking over wounds. Thinking things can somehow be different. And in this case, sir, just the thinking might make it so. Of course, each of these beings sees some kind of personal vision of paradise for his own group. Personally, I think it's going to be sheer hell around here for a long, long time.'

'Unless we fix it,' the Emperor said.

'Unless we fix it, sir,' Sten agreed.

'To begin with,' the Emperor said, 'I'm giving you a battalion of Imperial Guards. That ought to help make the glue stick.'

Sten jolted. 'So much . . . sir? I was hoping for maybe one Mantis Section. If we stay a little lower profile, and if things don't work out . . . we take less blame. Besides, sir, I really believe I can do better with scalpels than a hammer.'

'I can't take that chance,' the Emperor said. 'You're getting a battalion. I'm already a target of ridicule. Fine. I'll be a big damned one. Also, I have another reason.'

'Yessir,' Sten said.

'Any other thoughts?' the Emperor asked.

'Yessir. Out of this whole sorry lot, I *do* have one pretty good candidate to take over. If only temporarily.'

'Who?' The single word had a guarded edge to it. Sten didn't realize this, however, until later.

'Menynder, sir. The Tork. He's a tricky old buzzard. But he's the one being everybody seems to respect. His enemies list is real short. And I think he could get people to listen long enough for things to take hold. Pick up their own momentum.'

'Good choice,' the Emperor said. 'Except . . . like you said, he's probably just a temporary solution. I have a permanent fix in mind.' He took a casual sip of scotch. 'The man's name is Iskra. Dr Iskra. He's a Jochian.'

Sten furrowed his brow. He'd heard it. Vaguely. Enough to know Iskra commanded a great deal of respect. But Sten was so new on the ground that he would just have to take the Emperor's word on Dr Iskra's sterling qualities.

'I've already spoken to him,' the Emperor said. 'One of my ships is picking him up now. He should be with you in a few cycles. He's the other reason I'm sending a battalion of Guards. Dr Iskra asked for them. He'll use them as personal security. At first.'

'Very good, sir,' Sten said. His antennae for trouble gave a bit of quiver over Iskra's request for the troops before he'd even seen the Altaics and evaluated the current situation. He pushed the worry to the back. But he didn't lock it away.

Also, the only thing that mattered was that this whole thing worked. Sten had picked up exactly none of the Imperial Foreign Office's traditional bad habits, such as placing ego in front of solution.

'Anything else?' the Emperor asked. He seemed restless, anxious to be on to other things.

'No sir.'

'Then . . . until your next report . . .' The Emperor leaned forward to touch a button on his desk.

But as the holo image of Sten in the Jochi embassy chamber thinned, the Emperor quickly checked the expression on Sten's face. It was properly respectful. And then Sten was gone.

The Eternal Emperor absently picked up his drink and sipped, deep in thought. Total concentration was one of the many abilities he had fine-tuned over his many centuries. He gave the subject of Sten a full five seconds of that concentration.

Was he loyal? Without question. In the Emperor's absence, Sten had been the architect of the plan to depose the privy council. The keystone of the alliance he had created was absolute commitment to the Emperor's memory.

Yes, Sten was loyal. And the Emperor had given him many honors. But few beings realized just how great a hero Sten was.

For perhaps the first time, the Emperor was aware that he was fortunate Sten was on his side. For some reason, the thought was not entirely comforting.

The Emperor tucked that nugget of discomfort away. Later, he would fit it into the larger puzzle. He pulled his mind back from its task.

There was another man whose assistance he required. Of the very silent – and deadly – variety. Yes. He must take no chances in this Altaic matter. No chances at all.

Chapter Ten

The livie casts were filled with reports of Sten's razzle-dazzle with the *Victory*. The Emperor's spin experts flooded the media with dramatic pictures of the ship's progress over awed Jochi crowds and the hero's welcome Sten received when he landed at the embassy.

Much was made of the calming influence the Emperor's flag had on the poor hysterical beings of the Altaic Cluster. The death of the Khaqan came almost as an afterthought, with appropriate sad words from the Emperor, mourning the demise of 'a dear friend and trusted ally.'

There were the usual assurances from key aides that order had been restored, and that the Emperor's people were 'Working closely with local leaders to assure an orderly transition of government.'

Sten sighed as he palmed the switch cutting off the livie anchor in mid-toothy charm. He had expected the Emperor's damage-control campaign. Which – no surprise – was highly effective. Unfortunately, the spin the Emperor's teams were putting on events was so optimistic that Sten feared that a minor hiccup might be viewed as total disaster.

A situation he was doing his damnedest to prevent. Sten bent his head to his task, ignoring the buzz of techs in the embassy com room working under Alex's directions. For the tenth time he struggled with the diplomatic note. The problem was, how was he going to tell General Douw, Menynder, Youtang, Diatry, and the other Jochi leaders that they had been cut out of the loop? That the new Khaqan had been chosen – without consulting them?

Dr Iskra was on his way. And Sten would have to tell the group soon, or he would be in an especially embarrassing situation.

He could see it right now: 'Good afternoon, gentlebeings,' Sten would say. 'I'd like you to meet your new despot. Comes highly recommended. In fact, I think you may all even know the gentleman. Sorry I didn't mention it sooner. But the Emperor doesn't trust a single one of you. And could give a clot if you live or die. Just so long as you do it quietly. Now . . . If you'll excuse me . . . I'll repair to the barricades whilst you good beings fight it out amongst yourselves.' And he would take off as fast as a Jochi twister.

Oh, boy. This was going to be near impossible to put a good face on. However, there was no getting around it. The note would have to be written, yes. But the real deed must be done in person.

Sten's mind started to cramp. He looked up to see how Alex was coming along with his little spy mission. Not for the first time, Sten marveled at how many of their old nasty skills the work of peace involved.

His eyes swept the bank of screens filling one wall of the embassy com room. 'Coom on, y' wee Frick 'n' Frack,' Alex coaxed, tickling some controls. 'Be't ae good bat.'

Kilgour had made a preliminary scavenging survey of the embassy to see what goodies the previous ambassador had left behind. The first pass was immediately useful. Stashed in the basement storerooms, he found hundreds of tiny robotic monitors. They were winged – and looked a lot like bats. Alex dubbed them Frick and Frack One through One Thousand or so, in honor of the live batlike beings who snooped for Mantis operations. He had recharged the monitors' powerpaks, consulted with his team of techs and experts on the Jochi culture, programmed in patrol sectors, and sent the bats aloft to spy.

They were broadcasting pictures right now of scores of scenes all over Rurik. And those pictures told a different story than the Emperor's livie casts.

Yes, calm had been restored. But only compared to the mess Sten encountered when he first arrived. The screen in the upper left-hand corner showed the scene outside a Jochi military compound. Peaceful . . . on the surface.

But as Alex coaxed his little snooper closer, Sten could see several armored tracks. Idle, but ready to go in an instant. Maintenance crews were hard at work on others. He could see gravlifts hauling in ammunition and supplies.

The screen below it displayed a rebel Jochi force undergoing intense drilling and training. Another, a Tork encampment, bristling with arms and hot talk.

There were similar scenes on other monitors: Suzdal and Bogazi barricades being rebuilt and strengthened; militias patrolling neighborhood streets, in one case pointedly ignoring a group of adolescents filling glass jars with pilfered flammable fuel.

The main market district of Rurik was empty. Shops were buttoned up tight, some with hired thugs as guards. Sten saw gangs of young beings swaggering through the streets looking for trouble and loot. One of Alex's bats swooped past a blasted-out store-front. Figures hauled out valuables by the armload. In this case the looters were soldiers, with a few police sprinkled in.

'Aha, wee Sten,' Kilgour said. 'Here's th' lass Ah wae blatherin' aboot.' He threw the projection to one of the larger, center wall-screens. Sten saw a joygirl exiting an alley. The screen's map inset showed she was near a Jochi military compound. A wolf whistle shrilling through a speaker told him just how close.

The view shifted, and Sten could see several soldiers reacting to the scantily clad woman. The joygirl stopped and posed with hand on hip, bosom and other goodies jutting. A soldier called to her. The joygirl gave a pouty flip of her head, swiveled on shapely heels, and ankled back into the alley.

The soldiers looked at each other and laughed. Two split away to follow.

'Now watch this lass at work,' Alex said, tugging at a tiny joystick as he sent the bat soaring over the alley. The soldiers had caught up to the girl. Bargaining was in progress. Finally, price agreed on, the joygirl leaned against the alley wall. Fumbling with his clothing, and joking with his buddy over his shoulder, the first soldier advanced.

As he was lifting the joygirl off her feet, there was sudden motion, so quick that Sten almost missed it.

The joygirl had some hefty friends. They clubbed the soldiers down. By the time the joygirl had finished straightening her scant tunic, the soldiers' unconscious bodies were being stripped of weapons, uniforms, and IDs.

Sten watched the joygirl and her group head off to set up another trap. 'How many does this make?'

'A score or so. But on'y since Ah've been countin'. She's verra quick. Got a few more lads jus' t' haul th' stuff t' the rebels.'

'Jackrollers for a Free Jochi, huh?' Sten said. 'It'd almost be funny, if I didn't think any minute now the lid was going to blow off the pot.

'The big pain is that there isn't much we can do. Except sit tight, hope for the best, and jawbone the locals to be patient. And wait for Dr Iskra to show up.'

'When first we met, young Sten,' Kilgour said, 'you were nae such a honey-tongued liar. Ah'm pleased a' y'r progress.'

'Thanks . . . I think,' Sten said. 'Trouble is, now I've got to be really creative.' He tapped the diplomatic note he was composing. 'When Iskra arrives there's going to be some pretty pissed off beings.'

'Y'll do fine, lad. Liars like us'r made, nae born. Otherwise, our dear mums'd ice us when we were bairns.'

Sten groaned in agreement. But what choice did he have? He knew that just as long as relative calm lasted on Jochi, so the rest of the cluster would stay at 'peace.'

The joyous enthusiasm that had greeted his arrival had lasted about as long as the sudden spring weather – which had almost immediately turned foul. Tempers rose with humidity. Black clouds bunched under that humidity. Moods bounced from euphoria to headache gloom. Which, Sten was already learning, pretty much described the nature of all the beings on Jochi.

A few hours before dusk on the second day, a whole snake's nest of cyclones appeared above the Rurik skyline. The twisters roared around in the strange nonlogic of the inanimate. Dashing for the city. Scaring clot out of everyone. Then retreating. All the while, sucking up trees and topsoil and outbuildings – which did nothing to lessen the fear. Suddenly, they sped off and were gone.

Ever since then the citizens of Rurik had been casting nervous looks at the horizon. And at one another.

Then, just the previous day, winter had returned with a cold snap as if the spring and then the humidity and heat had never been. Another part of the wonders of Jochi.

Sten went back to his lying scribbles. '. . . Whereas the Eternal Emperor . . . in his deep affection for all the beings of the Altaic Cluster . . .'

'Holy clot! Look't thae!'

Sten's head bounced back up. He looked where Alex was pointing. The center monitor screen was complete confusion. Sten strode over to get a closer look.

A whole mass of beings was parading in front of some institutionlike structures; evidently built by the late Khaqan, the structures were heroic in size and drabness. To Sten, they looked like giant beehives tied together with sky-high walkways and beltways.

'It's the Pooshkan University,' an earnest young tech said. Sten recalled that her name was Naomi.

He groaned. 'Students? Oh, no.'

'Aye. W' hae hormone trouble, lad,' Alex said. He twiddled with controls and suddenly a dozen views of the university leapt up on the main screen.

Here, uniformed campus cops were being hauled out by young beings and dumped through the main archway. In another section of the campus, Sten could see students smashing through what appeared to be a glass-fronted cafeteria. In half a second a wild food fight erupted.

Teachers were fleeing for cover, not too successfully ducking hurled food and other debris. Bonfires were being set all over the campus. Fed, Sten was sure, with the records of any students who happened to be failing.

He also caught glimpses of naked flesh through bushes and trees and heard squeals of joy as some of the students protested in a more passionate manner.

A huge barricade was being erected at the main gate of Pooshkan University. There was enough logic to the tumble of junk that Sten was sure engineering students had to have been involved. Which took planning.

Further proof of this was the sudden unfurling of carefully

printed banners. The banners demanded many things. But mostly they demanded: 'Democracy Now!'

'Wonderful,' Sten said. 'The one thing nobody in this place is going to get.'

He peered closer at one of the views of the students – and he realized just how odd these students were. To begin with, it was a mixed group. As many Suzdal and Bogazi youths as there were Jochians and Torks. Second, they were all working – rioting, actually – together. This almost never happened on Jochi, much less in the rest of the cluster, where segregation was a prized fact of society's status quo.

'What kind of a place is this?' Sten asked, noting as he did, just how well fed – and clothed – these young beings appeared.

'Gie us a reading, lass,' Alex said to the young tech.

Naomi shook her head. 'I don't have to look it up. Pooshkan is *the* premier university of the cluster. That's where all the top beings in the Altaics send their sons, daughters, chicks, and pups.'

'Rich kids,' Sten groaned. 'Double wonderful.' Then he shrugged. 'Oh, well. Sounds like a local problem to me. The cops will handle it.'

'Oh-oh,' Kilgour said.

'What's with the oh-oh?' Sten hated to ask.

'Wish't an' y'll receive't,' Alex said. 'Th' wee pigs are comin' out. An' spritely.'

Sten saw a phalanx of cops moving toward the main gate, complete with helmets, riot shields, electric prods, and – he saw a small track moving in – tear gas.

'Clot!' was all Sten said.

'An' here come the Lookie Lous,' Kilgour said, pointing at crowds of adults gathering at the edge of the campus. Some were shouting at the cops. Some at the students. Some at one another. The onlookers were definitely segregated into tight knots of angry ethnics.

'Hell with it,' Sten said. 'Still a local problem. No way are we getting involved.'

As he spoke, the com board lit up with incoming calls. Alex's people started fielding them. '. . . Imperial embassy. Yes, we've heard of the disturbance at the university. No, the ambassador has no comment . . . Imperial embassy . . . the Pooshkan riot? Yes, sir. No, sir . . . Imperial embassy . . .'

Totally disgusted, Sten grabbed his scribblings and started for the door. 'Don't call me unless it gets worse,' he yelled over his shoulder. 'In fact . . . don't even call me—'

'You best take this one, lad,' Alex said, proffering a com set.

'Who is it?' Sten asked, almost snarling.

'A wee bairn frae Pooshkan,' Alex said. 'In fact, it's thae one.' He pointed at a monitor screen, which showed a close-up of an imperious young Jochian. A handsome boy despite a tendency to lard about the jowls. Sten could see him talking into a com set that apparently was connected to the embassy board.

'Th' ringleader, methinks,' Alex continued. 'Milhouz i' th' name he gives.'

Naomi whistled. 'Student president,' she said. 'His parents are on the board of the Bank of Jochi.'

It dawned on Sten just how dicey this Pooshkan place was. A bloodied nose would be viewed as pure murder in some quarters.

'Yes, Sr Milhouz,' Sten said into the com unit, smooth as glass. 'This is Ambassador Sten speaking. How may I help you?'

As he listened to the young voice jabbering away in his ear and saw the flushed, excited features on the monitor screen, Sten knew he would have to break the first rule he had set himself in Phase One of this operation. Which was: Do not leave the embassy. Make them come to you.

'You may expect us in a few minutes, young man,' he said, and broke connection. As he turned back to the board, he saw that Cind had entered the room. From the look on her face, he could see she had a pretty good idea of what was going on.

One of the monitor screens showed students hurling a shower of debris at the cops.

'This damned thing could be the spark that sets off the big kabang,' he told Cind. 'So, here's the drill. I'll need about ten Gurkhas. Maybe fifty Bhor. But we want to go at this real low profile. Concealed weapons. No uniforms. We don't want to act like storm troopers.'

'Pretty tall order for the Bhor,' Cind said. 'Especially Otho.'

'If this works right,' Sten said, 'everybody will be so curious about Otho and the others, they'll be too busy gaping to cause trouble. Alex?'

'Ready ae you are, lad,' Kilgour said.

'Okay, boys and girls,' Sten said. 'We're going back to school.'

Chapter Eleven

The day was bright and bitterly cold as Sten and his crew moved through the Square of the Khaqans. He gawked along with the others at the monuments towering over them. He felt like an insect marching through a land of giants.

'I keep waiting for one of them to step on me,' Cind said, in an odd echo of his own thoughts.

'By my mother's long and knotty beard,' Otho rumbled, 'the man had ego enough for a fleet of us.'

Otho lifted a hairy paw to shield his eyes from the glittering domes and brooded at a particularly awesome display of bad taste. It amounted to a platform resting on the shoulders of a dozen statues. The statues – easily twenty meters high – were of perfectly formed male and female humans, probably Jochians. They were stark naked. Posed on top of the platform was an idealized statue of the Khaqan swathed in golden robes. He held a torch aloft, complete with eternally licking flames.

'I could understand the man if he built drinking halls,' Otho finally said. 'It's much more useful to a boasting being. Besides, if you set a good table and are not stingy with the stregg, no one minds a braggart.' He peered at Sten with his bloodshot eyes. 'Not that I am one to follow this practice. I prefer my guests to extol my deeds.'

Sten pointed at the legend inscribed in one corner of the display. It read: TO HE WHO LIT THE ALTAICS WITH HIS GLORY. Under it, in smaller letters: From A Grateful People.

'Maybe he had a similar idea,' Sten said. 'Except he dispensed with the good times for one and all.'

Otho's massive brow beetled at him. 'This is why I said a drinking hall would make better sense. For a being who ruled so long, this Khaqan knew nothing of leadership.'

Sten laughed agreement and motioned his group onward. He had decided it would be better to walk to Pooshkan University. It wasn't far from the embassy, and walking would certainly be lower profile than a phalanx of armored gravcars.

Besides, the first rule Sten had adopted as he learned the ropes of diplomacy was that it was important not to become isolated. He knew many ambassadors whose feet had never touched real ground. They were whisked from the steps of the embassy to state chambers to banquet and back again, for their entire tour of duty. He had also noted that their advice was invariably wrong.

In this case, he had found the scene on the street to be no different from what he had seen on the com room vid screens. Except, emptier. But the *feel* was different, there in the bright sunlight and sharp cold. His breath steamed. Shadowy figures ducked out of sight as his team tromped along, wary hands and paws near weapons belts.

Everywhere Sten looked there was a gigantic portrait or statue of the Khaqan, peering down on the mere mortals who must tread the avenues to their inconsequential appointments.

Especially unnerving was the low sound of thunder that rumbled continually behind the distant mountains. It definitely added an edge to one's mood.

Sten kept that in mind as he mentally prepared himself for young Milhouz and the other student agitators.

All those thoughts had vanished, however, when they entered the Square of the Khaqans. The sheer size of it would stagger any normal being's imagination. Just as the blinding colors fuddled the senses. It was a difficult place to get any kind of perspective. Turning away from a garish pillar, the eyes would clear, only to be confronted by a monument so large it made one dizzy.

Despite the sheer size of the square, Sten felt frighteningly closed in. With good reason. His professional eye noted that the square was built for maximum crowd control. Then he saw the Killing Wall. He didn't have to ask what it was as he looked over its black smoothness. A monument of hatred. Of power gone mad.

A sudden helplessness gripped him. He felt far too small for the task. His mind told him that was silly. The square had been designed to elicit exactly that response. Still, the feeling was difficult to shake.

At last they reached the far exit. Pooshkan University was just beyond. As Sten heard the low chanting of angry students, his mood instantly lifted and spring returned to his step. At least this was something he could confront. And maybe even solve.

'Th' cops're stokin' up their wee courage,' Alex said. He had gone on ahead with a Gurkha squad to scout the situation. 'Th' gravlighters're pourin' in by th' minute. Wi' reinforcements. An' the brass're well back oot a harm's way i' th' mob should break through.'

'Worthy warriors all,' Otho snorted. 'They lead from the rear. Even to attack children. I tell you, my friend, there is no honor in this place. I swear to you I will feel no joy when I break their heads.'

'Now, Otho,' Sten soothed. 'Breaking heads is not your job description. This is a diplomatic mission, remember?'

Down the street they could all see and hear the squalling confrontation that was their mission. Sten professionally estimated that there were about a squillion beings about to go at it, tooth, nail, tear gas, and guns. There came a thunderous shower of rocks falling on the cops' riot shields. Oh, yes – and rocks as well.

'I promise I will use no more than this, my friend,' Otho said, shaking a clenched ham of a paw. The other Bhor rumbled in agreement.

'Your orders,' Cind snapped at Otho, 'are to use nothing but open hands. Or elbows and knees. Light kicking is also permissible.'

There was a long silence as Otho peered at this small thing issuing orders. Cind stared back. 'Is that understood . . . Private?' she said.

Laughter boomed from Otho. 'By my father's frozen arse cheeks,' he said, 'open hands it is.' He glanced at Sten and wiped moisture from the edge of one bloodshot eye. 'She makes me proud,' he said. 'She proves the worth of Bhor training and ideals.'

As Otho struggled with his emotions, there were more loud shouts down the street. A police bullhorn rumbled a warning. And there was another rock shower.

'Dinna be bawlin't, m' great hairy beast ae a friend,' Alex said. 'W' hae a riot to tend to. Remember?'

'We're going to have to get to it first,' Cind said, indicating the confused mass of beings jamming the street and the arched entrance to the university.

Then Sten heard a familiar voice. 'Beings of Jochi,' it thundered over a porta boomer, 'listen to the pleas of your children . . .'

It was young Milhouz. Sten spotted him standing high off the ground, on the base of yet another heroic statue of the late, not so great Khaqan.

'We bring you a message of hope and lo—' And the voice cut off as a group of shielded cops charged the students. There were screams of pain and anger, which were overridden instantly by a roar from the crowd of adult onlookers.

Then there were cheers and some laughter as the charging cops abruptly changed course and beat a hasty retreat. Milhouz flashed a victory sign.

But Sten could see that the victory would be short-lived. The cops were humiliated now – and even more scared than before. He could see that they were about to renew the assault, this time in massed and deadly force.

He nodded to Cind. 'You know the drill.'

They moved forward. Alex took a flanker's role, moving with the Gurkhas around the cops. Cind took some Bhor to cut between Alex and the angry crowd of adult civilians. Sten, Otho, and about twenty Bhor went straight up the middle, through the cops.

'Ooops! Pardon me,' Cind said, as she jabbed an elbow into a burly Tork dockworker. 'How rude of me,' she apologized, neatly clipping a Suzdal in the jaw.

'So very sorry,' Lalbahadur Thapa said, as a sharp toe made contact with the shins of a towering Bogazi. He squeezed his slim figure past two more and trod heavily on the toe of a mammoth Jochian, blocking his path.

'My fault,' Alex said as he leaned a shoulder into a cop and sent him tumbling against his mates. His arm swept back in awed reaction to his own clumsiness. Another cop went sailing. 'Och! Thae must've smarted. F'rgive me, lad.'

'Coming through,' Sten shouted. A knee lifted and caught a crouching cop in the behind. The cop went mask first into the ground. 'Sorry about that. Imperial business, you know.'

A thick cop arm circled Otho's neck. Two more came at him, riot sticks raised to strike. 'By my mother's beard,' he said, 'my boot wants tying again.' He leaned forward to do the deed, and the cop went sailing over his head – right into his charging colleagues.

Someone had Cind by the shirt. A big someone. She jabbed him in the eye with a finger. The big someone howled in pain and let loose. 'I don't know what's wrong with me today,' Cind said. 'I'm so clumsy.'

A Suzdal snapped at Chittahang Limbu. The little Gurkha grabbed it by the ear just as the jaws reached his throat. He twisted. The Suzdal went with the twist, tumbling over into his pack sisters. 'I am such a silly man today,' Chittahang mourned. Then, under his breath, he muttered, 'Yak pube.'

'Make way! Imperial business! Make way!' Sten shouted. Remarkably, it was working. Most of the cops parted to let them through. Those that didn't got an elbow or a heavy Bhor slap.

Alex came upon two cops beating the bejabbers out of a small student. Without pause, he lifted them from the ground and slammed them together. He let go. They fell to the ground. Unconscious.

'Och, no. Ah hope Ah dinnae go an' break y'r wee heads. Sten'll hae m' hide f'r it.' He moved on.

Otho and four Bhor broke through to the statue. They turned – like living armored tracks – sweeping a wide, clear space around them. A few seconds later, Sten was in the center of the clear space. A few seconds more, and the whole group had taken up formation around him.

Sten looked up at Milhouz. The young Jochian's jowls were flushed with astonishment.

'Sorry I'm a little late,' Sten said. 'Now. If you'll give me that thing, I'll have a little chat with these good people.'

He indicated the porta boom in Milhouz's hand. The young Jochian stared at him, mouth open. Then he nodded and handed Sten the boomer.

'I can't believe you did that,' he said.

'Neither can I,' Sten said. And he turned to face his public.

'First . . . we demand respect for the dignity of all species of the Altaic Cluster,' Milhouz said, stabbing a finger at the document that he and his fellow students had drawn up.

'I don't think anyone would argue with that,' Sten said. He glanced around the cafeteria table at the other student leaders. They were all very young, all very solemn.

Strange, Sten thought, how much youthful beings looked alike. Whether Suzdal, Bogazi, or human, they had those great wide innocent eyes and round helpless faces. Terminally cute, Sten thought. Which, come to think of it, was an odd bit of universal genetic programming. The probable reason parents didn't kill their young at birth.

'Second,' Milhouz continued, jowls flapping like a small, burrowing rodent, 'the equality of all species must be the cornerstone of the future government.'

'The Emperor's record is pretty clear on that,' Sten said dryly. 'He's a noted champion of equality.'

'Still must be said,' the Bogazi student broke in. Her name, Sten remembered, was Nirsky. From the way the other Bogazi males fawned on her, he assumed she was pretty.

'Then, say away,' Sten said.

Milhouz cleared his throat for attention. 'Third. All militias must return to their home worlds. Forthwith.'

'I suspect that will be high on the agenda of any new authority,' Sten said.

'You're patronizing us,' Milhouz complained.

'Not at all,' Sten said. 'I'm merely underscoring a fact.' He kept his features bland.

'No one ever listens,' the Suzdal yipped. He had been introduced to Sten as Tehrand.

'Yes. That's right. We stayed up all night hammering out these demands.' The speaker was a Tork. A very lovely Tork, who obviously doted on young Milhouz. Her name was Riehl.

'I'm listening,' Sten said. 'I went to some trouble to get here, remember? Now, why don't you go on?'

'Fourth,' Milhouz continued, 'we demand amnesty for all students at Pooshkan who participated in this blow for freedom. And this must include us – the members of the Action Committee.'

'I'll do my best,' Sten said, meaning it.

'Not good enough,' Nirsky said. 'Promise, you must.'

'Promises are easy to make,' Sten said, 'but hard to secure. Once again – I'll do my best.'

Milhouz's face took on a look of saintly purity. 'I'm willing to take my chances,' he said. 'I'd gladly lay down my life for my ideals.'

'Let's not get carried away,' Sten said. 'No one's life is at issue here. All I'm saying is when the new government is in place, some people might not take too kindly to the damage you've caused.

'There may be charges. Fines. A little jail time at the most. Which, by the way, I'll do my damnedest to prevent. But they may not listen to me. So, be prepared.'

Squabbling erupted. Sten leaned back in his chair as the students tossed his comments back and forth. Tehrand shot him a threatening look, Suzdal teeth gleaming. Sten paid him no mind, just as he ignored the thirty or more other students in the room, many of whom were also giving him the evil eye.

Although he had elected to meet with the group alone, he doubted there was much they could do that he couldn't handle, should the situation turn nasty.

'I'm sorry,' Milhouz finally said, 'but that demand is not negotiable.'

'What if it's refused?' Sten asked.

'We'll burn the university to the ground,' Riehl said, her pretty features flushed with resolve.

'I wouldn't advise that,' Sten said. 'In fact, I really wish you'd consider making no threats at all. It'll give me more leeway to negotiate with the police.'

'One week only,' Nirsky said. 'Then burn we must.'

'We all agreed,' Tehrand said. 'We voted on it.'

'So have another vote,' Sten said. 'You can say it's in light of new factors Sr Sten has brought to your attention.'

'Democracy doesn't work that way. All votes are final,' Milhouz said pompously. 'Which brings us to the next and most important demand . . .

'The rule of the Khaqans must end. In fact, the rule of any form of tyranny must end. We demand a new order. Only through democracy can the problems of the Altaics be finally resolved!'

'To further this end,' Riehl said, 'we have drawn up a list of candidates acceptable to the Pooshkan Action Committee.'

'Hold on,' Sten said. 'Tell me more about this "approved" list. Doesn't sound too democratic to me.'

'Oh, but it is,' Milhouz said. 'In its purest sense.'

'And he doesn't mean that primitive theory where *every* being gets to vote, no matter how . . . undeserving.' Riehl gave Milhouz a melting look. Sten figured Milhouz for the list of the 'deserving.'

'I see,' Sten said. He made diplomatic *hmmm* noises. 'How interesting you should think that way.'

'Good. You understand my point,' Milhouz said, taking this for acceptance. 'Let's be frank. Most beings – meaning the, well, uneducated classes – want to be told what to do.' He leaned forward, impassioned. 'They feel . . . uncomfortable with weighty decisions. They want structure in their lives. It makes them . . .'

'Comfortable,' Sten helped.

'How astute of you, Sr Ambassador. Yes. That's the word exactly. Comfortable. And happy, as well.'

'Educated ones know best,' Nirsky said.

'A long-known fact,' Tehrand yipped.

'There can be no tyranny if you have an educated elite, is what Milhouz says. Isn't that right, de – ahhh. Isn't that right?' Riehl blushed at almost revealing her feelings.

Milhouz gave her a warm pat on the thigh, letting his hand linger. 'Yes. I did say . . . something like that. But, I'm no genius. Others mine the same field.' He gave Sten a very solemn look. 'So the thought isn't entirely original.'

'How very modest of you,' Sten said.

'Thank you, Ambassador. Anyway . . . back to the point of our . . . manifesto. We believe the new leaders of the Altaics should be chosen from all the great families of the cluster. The most educated Suzdals, Torks, Bogazi, and Jochians – like myself.'

'Would success at this university help in their . . . qualifications?' Sten ventured.

'There is no greater laboratory of learning than Pooshkan University. So . . . that goes without saying.'

'I should have guessed. How foolish of me,' Sten said.

'Although we do see a great need for improvements here,' Riehl said. 'Many of the courses are . . . incorrect in their thinking.'

'I assume the overhaul of the university is also among your demands?' Sten asked.

'Absolutely.'

'And you'll burn the university if they don't?'

'Yes. Who to stop us?' the Bogazi said. 'My brood most important. If someone hurt me – much trouble.'

'The same with all of us,' Riehl said. 'It's a good thing for those cops that you came along. If they had done something stupid . . . why, our families would have destroyed them all. Believe me.'

Milhouz handed Sten the sheaf of paper that was the Action Committee's manifesto. 'Those are our demands. Take them . . . or leave them.'

Sten drew the moment out very long. 'Then . . . I'm leaving,' he finally said. And he rose to go.

The room erupted in total panic.

'Wait,' Milhouz said. 'Where are you going?'

'Back to the embassy,' Sten told him. 'I'm no good here. Besides, this is really none of my business. It's definitely a local problem. So . . . if you'll forgive me . . . I'll go watch what happens to you next on my livie screen. With a nice stiff drink to warm my belly.'

'But you can't leave!' Riehl shouted, nearly in tears.

'Watch me,' Sten said.

'But police will—'

'Kill all of you,' Sten said. 'They're pretty mad. I don't think it'll take much to set them off. Your pedigree will probably just make them madder. You know how cops get? Touchy. Very touchy.

'Funny, isn't it? You people think you're rioting. But the cops riot instead. Happens every time.'

'What do you want from us?' Milhouz wailed. His jowls were white with fear.

Sten turned at the door. 'Better question. What do you really want? And don't give me that manifesto business.'

There was total silence.

'I'll tell you what,' Sten said. 'I'll see if somebody will talk to you. Give your views a fair hearing.'

'Someone . . . important?' Milhouz asked.

'Yeah. Someone important.'

'A public hearing?'

'I don't know. Maybe.'

'We want witnesses,' Tehrand yipped.

'I'll ask,' Sten said. 'Now . . . will that do? A fair hearing of all your views. To be taken into account by decision-making people. Okay?'

Milhouz glanced around and saw slight nods of heads. 'It's agreed,' he said.

'Good.' Sten headed for the door.

'But . . . if they don't at least listen . . .' Milhouz was trying to pull some pride in for the group.

'You'll burn the university to the ground,' Sten finished for him.

'In one week!' Milhouz snapped.

'I'll keep that in mind.' And Sten was gone.

Chapter Twelve

Sten returned to the embassy in a mood that could only be livened by a few ax murders.

He took one look at that lying diplomatic note still only half-written and sent the burn pad spinning across the room.

Juvenile as all hell. Also, not nearly satisfying enough.

He thought about kicking the desk over but caught himself in time, considering the mass of that enormous wooden block big enough for the Khaqan's tastes and noting, also, that its legs already were scarred, trophies of previous ambassadorial self-mutilations undoubtedly resulting from dealing with the charming, altruistic, visionary residents of the Altaic Cluster.

Sten next thought of ordering Admiral Mason to his quarters in hopes of provoking an off-the-record punchup but settled instead for a loud feral growl, aimed out the sealed window at the slamming rain from the storm that had settled in over Rurik.

There was a chortle.

And a giggle.

Sten did not turn.

'An' dinnae y' hae pity ae th' lad,' Alex's voice crooned. 'Discoverin't he's th' wee one whae hae Imperial custody ae an entire *cluster* ae Campbells?'

'And this,' Cind said, her voice equally sincere, 'is the brave Sten. The great warrior I grew up worshiping. The man, legend had it, that led all of the beings in the Lupus Cluster to peace and plentitude, never losing the smile on his lips or the song in his heart.'

Sten still did not turn.

'Is there one clottin' being in this whole clottin' cluster who isn't out to clottin' murder every other clottin' being?' he demanded. 'Is there clottin' *anybody*, from these pampered apparatchik fools who think they're innalekchuls and students to those clots running around with their clotting private armies to these clotting imbeciles who're trying to play button, button, who's going to wear the clotting throne to this clotting imbecile Iskra that our Eternal Clotting—' He broke off, found out that his lungs were pumped airless, inhaled, then went on, a bit more carefully, considering Cind's presence: '—that we're supposed to hand the clotting keys to the clotting kingdom to, is there *anybody* who has one lousy cc of the milk of human kindness hidden somewhere about his/her/whoever's person?'

'Tsk,' Alex mourned. 'Th' clottin' language. In frae of a clottin' laird an' all.'

'Somebody pour me a drink.'

'Not yet, skipper. P'raps y' dinnae want alk runnin' aroun' y'r system.'

Sten finally turned around. Both Cind and Kilgour were wearing Jochi civilian clothes. Poor-people-type civilian clothes. Dark colored.

They had Jochi cloaks over their arms.

Even more interesting, both of them were wearing combat vests. Each vest held a small com link, a cut-barreled, collapsing-stock willygun in an underarm sling, two spare magazines of the ultra-lethal AM2 rounds, and a sheathed combat knife. The vests would be invisible under the cloaks.

Even better, Kilgour had a bulky parcel under one arm, a parcel that was wrapped in a third cloak.

> 'Atween th' dark an' th' twilight
> Whae th' night's beginnin't t' glower,
> Com't a pause in thae day's occupations.
> Thae's know't ae th' Thuggee's Hour.'

As he recited, Alex unrolled the parcel, revealing it was, as Sten had hoped, a set of indigene civilian clothes, a weapons-equipped combat vest, and a pair of phototropic coveralls.

Kilgour continued:

> 'Ah ken i' th' close below me
> Th' clatter ae tippie-toed feet
> Th' thunk ae a dagger thae's buried
> An' deathrattles soft an' sweet.'

'You two clowns are going out and play Sally-Down-the-Alley spook games, and leave me here with the paperwork.'

'A noble ambassador,' Cind said, 'can't be out in the cold and wet dealing with common turncoats.'

'You are right. I've got to keep track of my new station. Kilgour, did you remember my kukri?' Feeling slightly more gleeful than he had in some time, Sten doffed his ambassadorial tunic.

'Y'll be wantin' th' Mantis cammies underneath, boss. I' th' event we're blown.'

'What do you have?'

'Y' ken one ae the Emp's complaints, or so y' relayed to me, wae that the Khaqan wae black-marketin' the AM2. Sellin' it outsystem t' pay f'r his edifice complex, aye?'

'So?'

'Assumin't thae villainy ne'er changes, the villains mere look f'r new bosses, Ah had th' notion it might be braw an' productive t' find a wee bit aboot how thae black-market conduit work't.'

'Very good. Very clottin' good,' Sten approved. 'At least somebody around here's thinking. Lord knows it isn't me. So who's this lovable citizen who suddenly wants to sell his cluster's leadership down the pike?'

Alex explained. The Mercury Corps station chief for the Altaic Cluster, a relatively junior and inexperienced operative named Hynds, holding the usual cover slot of cultural attache, had put one of his better Jochi agents in motion.

How good, Sten wanted to know. Kilgour shrugged.

'Our wee spook thinkit A Level. But frae his reports, an' th' one debriefing I sat in on, th' agent's nae better'n B. Howe'er, we're dealin't, boss, wi' whae tools're on hand. Ah dinnae hae time yet t' be doin't m' walshingham.

"T any rate, Hynds' agent claim't he's got one ae th' schemin't smugglers who's doin't his nut frae gettin' cut out ae th' pie.'

'Do you have any verification or any second source that this canary who wants to come in and sing is anything better than somebody who wants to pick up a few Imperial credits for a creative lie?'

Kilgour looked injured that Sten could suspect him of credulity, but continued his explanation.

The man they were supposed to meet claimed to have been the owner/captain of a small shipping line that had been used by the Khaqan to move AM2. Hynds' agent had obtained a fiche of one of the line's ship logs and two lading fiche from the man.

'A course, th' cargo wae listed ae pears, plums, poppies, or some such, but th' destination wae int'restin'. It went t' th' Honjo, who're ne'er backward t' buy AM2, wi'oot askin't too close whae th' home ae origin was.'

'Thin,' Sten evaluated.

'No drakh,' Kilgour agreed. 'Plus meetin' ae night. In ae t'r'ble part ae town. Wi' nae heavy backup allowed. Thae's why Ah hae guns. An Ah hae th' notion Cind might be a braw part ae th' discussion. An' y'self, assumin't y' still hae wind enow t' keep up.'

'Let's go.' Sten grinned. The prospect of a little action, even though it would almost certainly be meeting some lying sort in a back alley who'd try to sell them wolf tickets, was energizing.

'You realize, Captain Cind,' he said, 'that a certain Private Otho's going to make us cut our beards off just for general principle for excluding him from a situation that might include a bit of mayhem?'

Then he thought of something else. 'Just how *do* we go? Suddenly remembering that I'm an ambassador and can't just go slithering stage right without someone noticing.'

Cind looked smug. 'While you've been out playing Diplomacy with the Bumf Brigade, I thought it might be appropriate to see how secure our bedroom is. And I would suspect the former ambassador of a slight taste for the strange.'

Cind crossed to the light controls and forced one up-down toggle sideways. A panel hissed open.

'Ah,' Sten said. 'What's life without a secret passage?'

'Running from here past our bedroom,' Cind explained. 'Then down back along the wing the clericals and junior staffers are quartered in. It goes underground just next to where the kitchen is, I think, and then surfaces as part of the rear wall.'

'Wi' peepyholes an' doors into th' maidservant's bed. Th' lad wae a romantic,' Kilgour said.

'A pervert,' Cind corrected.

'An' whae's th' difference?' Kilgour wondered. 'A'ter you, skip. Cap'n, if y'll go next, Ah'll walk drag. Y' dinnae hae t' worry, by th' bye, aboot bugs. Thae's no one knows aboot th' passage 'cept Cind an' myself.'

Kilgour was very wrong . . .

The meet was almost four klicks from the embassy. The streets were nearly deserted except for an occasional gravsled moving very slowly through the blinding storm, and once or twice a being scurrying along on some no-doubt-cursed errand.

Their route led them to and through Rurik's enormous public transport terminal. As they approached the terminal, Sten wondered why all transport terminals were situated in slums. Which came first? Or did transiency encourage transients?

The paired cops just inside the entrance glanced at them, identified the trio as an urban peasant, his wife, and a friend or distant relative and of no interest. Kilgour led Sten and Cind on a circuitous route through the huge building. Benches were filled with beings who, it appeared, had been waiting endlessly. Some slept. Some ate. Some read. Some stared at the blurry entertainment or transport-status screens. More just stared. On Rurik, being able to wait in line without going mad from screaming boredom was more than an art form. It was a necessity.

They stopped beside a refreshment stand. There were no hot drinks available, but three varieties of summer ices could be purchased. The only food for sale that Sten could see was a thin broth made from tubers, and the tureens were filthy. Rancid fat floated on top of the soup.

Cind, still considering herself a student in espionage, studied the other two as they, in turn, studied the people around them without seeming to pay attention.

So far, the run appeared clean, although Sten knew there was little possibility of detecting a full-scale effort to track them, with each tracker following only momentarily before passing them along to the next agent.

Finally Kilgour shrugged hopelessly, pointing up at one line on a transport status screen that was blinking: SERVICE SUSPENDED INDEFINITELY DUE TO WEATHER. Muttering inaudibly like a proper peasant who had just been told he could not go home again, he led them toward an exit.

They were passing a door marked OFFICIAL ONLY when Alex's head jerked a signal and he darted sideways through the door. Cind was caught by surprise, but Sten had her by the shoulder, and they were following Kilgour. The door closed behind them, Alex booted a jamming wedge into the jamb, and they were in an echoing dank stairwell with an open gate and rain below.

Hand signals from Kilgour. You, Cind. On point. Down the stairs, outside, secure the exit.

Cind flowed silently down the stairs like mercury, cloak opening slightly, gun hand on her weapon's grip, finger carefully near but not on trigger, ready to pull the gun into firing position. She slipped out into the night and went instantly flat against the wall.

She found a moment to admire Sten and Kilgour. Again, she was learning from these two. She had never been around combat teams where the order-giver was the one most familiar with the conditions and immediate problem, not the one with the highest rank.

Sten came out the door and was flat against the wall on the other side. Alex followed.

He, too, found spare brain for a personnel evaluation: Th' lass fits, dinnae she? She dinnae ken, but she'd fit wi' th' best ae Mantis noo. Ah reck Ah'll hae t' tell Sten Ah gie m' blessing.

Then he, too, was out in the pelt of rain, and they were moving at the double down a maintenance access road and into the slum streets behind the terminal. A block away they took cover in a doorway and held, waiting to see if they were pursued.

The street stayed rain-dark and empty. Kilgour nodded with satisfaction. He took a bug sensor from his vest and quickly swept all three of them. Nobody had planted them as they went through the terminal.

'How did you know that terminal door would be unlocked?' Cind asked.

'Ah, lass,' Kilgour said. 'Ah thought brighter ae y'. Who d' y' think unlocked it? Who do y' think hung that "official" sign? Dinnae y' gie me credit f'r m' craft?'

He didn't wait for an answer. 'Noo. Straight t' meet our new friend.'

They moved on, staying close to the buildings. They went unnoticed – in this area, everyone moved as if he either had a secret or a stash, or was a footpad.

The slum they were moving through was a vertical desolation row, monstrously huge, as was everything else on Jochi. The buildings had been constructed over a hundred E-years earlier as high-rise flats for administration workers, fitted with enough conveniences and luxuries to prevent those who greased the Khaqan's wheels from being too unhappy. Time had passed. The buildings deteriorated. The government workers found cleaner, safer, newer quarters. The poor moved in. The McLean lifts stopped, and there were many, many flights of stairs to climb. The building supervisors were afraid or venal. And one of the curses of Jochi struck – Jochians were good at building things, but never seemed to consider that buildings, roads, or monuments needed maintenance.

Now, windows were shattered or boarded. The upper stories of the buildings were mostly dark. There was only the occasional flicker of light from a squatter's fatlamp or a thieves' lair.

The buildings' facings had been intended to look like stone. Now they hung, peeling, or lay in great slippery sheets across the cracked paving. Garbage littered the streets and was piled high in the buildings' service lanes.

Their route led them near one of the rivers that ran through Rurik. It was less a river than a moving slough, shallow and filled with junk and abandoned vehicles that had been pushed off the high bridge that spidered overhead.

Probably years earlier the embankment had been a nice place to stroll on holidays or on summer evenings. Not now. Sten decided he was not fond of this situation whatsoever – assuming this was where the meet with the agent had been set. If it was on that bridge, that was an excellent place for a trap. And *under* the bridge, next to the river? Sten shuddered. Not even Alex, with his supreme and usually justified confidence in his cunning, his heavyworld muscles and his experience, would go into that midnight nightmare.

Or so Sten hoped.

'Here's the drill,' Kilgour explained. 'Ah tol' this wee agent Ah was noo a dumber, an' was bringin't backup. Thae's you, Cind. Ah dinnae say where y'd be, so Ah'd be apprec'tive i' y'd vanish into yon shadows, an track wi' me as Ah hike.

'Ah'm to stroll doon th' bank, an' th' finkette's t' make the meet. Ah dinnae like th' plan, but th' lad wae skitterish. Boss, i' y' agree, y'll be th' invisible fly i' th' haggis. Hie y' doon noo o'er th' retain't wall, an' gie me cover. Frae in front, i' y' please.'

'Thanks, Kilgour. I flog it through river mud, and I've got to move faster than you?'

'Aye. An' quieter. Thae's whae y're a wee admiral, an' Ah'm noo but a puir agent-runner.'

Sten checked his gun. It was ready.

'I' y' feel aroon i' th' vest, y'll find a wee corn'copia ae grenades. Bester, flare, frag, blast.'

'What's the prog for trouble?' Cind whispered.

'Nae bad. Or Ah'd hae wee Sten carry a howitzer. Nae more'n seventy percent. Enow talk. Go.'

Watching the embankment closely, one might have seen a shadow. A shadow that moved. But it was a trick of the light

from the bridge, light dimly seen through the slashing rain. The
shadow that was Sten oozed over the retaining wall onto
the river's 'beach.'

Pure mire. Sten's foot sank into something that probably had
been sentient a bit more recently than the muck. His nose wrinkled. Getting soft, son. Remember, back in Mantis training when
they had you low-crawl for half a kilometer through an open
sewer line – and then announced the freshers were off limits when
your training patrol returned to base? A sickener, it was correctly
termed in Mantis slang.

Sten realized he was a bit stiff, a bit out of practice at snoopery,
as he lurked on, a wharf rat looking for carrion. Behind him,
through the hiss of the rain, he dimly heard Alex's deliberately
slammed boot heels on the embankment's paving.

Cind held close in to the shuttered buildings across from the
embankment, flitting from shadow to shadow, about fifty meters
behind Alex the Target.

Kilgour shivered, but not from the cold rain sheeting down.
How many times had he skulked toward a meeting with some
local agent? Scores, Laird Kilgour, he thought. An' hae y' e'er not
felt th' chill crawl 'tween y'r shoulder blades, waitin' for the
sights to cross an' th' round t' slam home?

Ahead of him was a tiny building, next to a shattered lamppost.
The building might have been a transport stop or a policeman's
watch box.

Movement. Alex's fingers considered the cutdown gun slung
in his vest, but found the miniwillygun holstered in the small of
his back more subtle. He edged the pistol's safety off, even though
no one could have heard the click through the storm noise. Ball
of finger touching the trigger, he held it ready, the weapon's muzzle
just inside his cloak. Without realizing it Alex centered himself,
legs slightly crouched as he moved on, foot coming clear of the
ground sweeping in, almost touching his other ankle, then out,
weight coming down on the ball of his foot, then the other leg
moving forward.

The shadow was man-sized. It moved once more. Lightning
shattered behind him, and Kilgour's finger tightened on the trigger.
Then he relaxed. The shadow became a man, wearing a hooded
ankle-length raincoat. In the flash, Kilgour had seen the man's
empty hands outside the coat's sleeves.

Contact.

'An' thae sun break't through th' darkest clouds,' he said,

cursing himself for his imbecile choice of passwords that had seemed quite clever back in his warm, dry office.

The waiting source – the shipper – *should* have responded with 'So honor peereth in the meanest habit.'

Nothing but storm howl.

Over the wall, some meters beyond the watch box, Sten went to Condition Red. The cloak's frogs ripped away, and the cloak dropped away into the muck, as his hand pulled the stubby gun off its harness and his thumb spun the selector down off SAFE past FIRE, past BURST, to AUTO, other hand yanking the stock full open, tucked under arm, down on one knee in the slime, eyes moving, moving, for targets.

Perhaps he had seen something. Perhaps there had been a momentary flicker of reflection from above the man, a shiny wire, or perhaps there was nothing.

Kilgour hissed shock, mind snapping orders to his reflexes. Nae, nae, dinnae go doon an' flat, body. Y're i' th' death zone.

Y' hae a couple seconds, lad. More'n enow time.

Contact had not answered, because Contact was very dead. It was somewhat close to normal, in Kilgour and Sten's shadow world, to learn that the oppos were on to your agent by finding him with an extra smile. And hanging by a wire noose from a lamppost wasn't all that uncommon a form of execution. But when the body was propped up, waiting for you at a meet . . .

Ambush.

Alex snapped the grenade out of his vest pocket, thumbed the impact fuse on, and sidearmed the tiny bomb overhead, to the right, just as he spun into motion, three leaping steps coming for a high jump. He dove forward, airborne, then slammed down on the rain-slick pavement, skating forward a meter, an' Ah need more time i' th' gym, because Ah'll hae bruises ae th' squeeze box t'morrow.

I' there *is* a t'morrow, he thought, as projectile fire shattered toward the watch box.

Triangulation, Sten analyzed. They've got us from three sides. This is a serious hit . . . as his finger came back on the trigger and he blew one potential assassin in half.

Cind had gaped for a microsecond at the space where Kilgour had been.

Then Kilgour's grenade, mortared high into the air with heavy-world muscles, hit the brownstone sixty meters above and some meters ahead of her – and detonated.

The front of the building peeled off, bricks cascading over the second murderer, just as Cind's AM2 round made the cascade a decent burial instead of self-defense.

The third member of the team was just bringing the trigger back for his second shot when Kilgour had him in his sights and snapped a round. The round whip-cracked past the third man; Kilgour's mind muttered about clottin' pistols beyond arm's reach, and his left hand had the pistol butt cupped for stability and two rounds double-tapped out – and the third man was dead, as well.

The team was moving – Sten up toward the retaining wall, Kilgour rolling like a beachball across the street toward some rubble, and Cind crouching first in one doorway and then in another. Kilgour jammed the pistol back in its holster and snapped his willygun into firing position.

The thunder from that lightning blast crashed across them, and Sten realized he had been counting in his mind: The lightning burst was only two kilometers away, and a bit more than six seconds have passed since we saw the shadow was a man.

Ambush. Why? Just to tell Kilgour that another intelligence group was watching him? Melodramatic way to announce the info – this contact, even if he had been a genuine smuggler, had given them nothing. Not a very professional organization, either. Pros never hit each other. It wasn't necessary once one had closed off the leak or potential leak.

Whatever. They could analyze who, what, and why later. Now it was time to extract. Run like hell. Sten wasn't worried about Jochi cops showing up – he doubted their dedication to real police work at best and knew damned well they wouldn't patrol this district except in watch-size formation. But it would be embarassing for the Imperial ambassador to be seen in a vulgar brawl like this.

Sten started up, instinctively taking command even though the run had been Kilgour's thus far.

His mind had time to absorb the *klang*, his eyes time to see a flicker from behind and above them, on that bridge, and the mortar round *blapped* into the river mud, muck spraying, but killing shrapnel damped.

Then the automatic weapons opened up. High-rate projectile as bullets sheeted in a *wheep* into the mire just beyond him, and Sten wriggled back over the wall, rolling, landing on a shoulder; then he saw the muzzle flashes from the third-story window across from him. Willygun up, swearing at the short barrel, lousy accuracy, no time for the sights, he skeet-gunned a long burst through the muzzle flashes, and the weapon kept firing, dead hand on the triggers, as the gunner fell, pulling the gun over with him, the rest of the gun's magazine emptying itself in the sky. Gunfire shattered on from two other guns.

Sten found himself next to Kilgour, both of them trying to marry that wonderful sheltering pile of rubble, a pile that was getting smaller as the mortar's gunner corrected his aim, and a second bomb blew against the pavement.

'Th' bastards're serious, boss.'

They were – this went far beyond an acceptable if extreme attempt to remove a problematical intelligence specialist. When the first hit failed, the cover should have disengaged and withdrawn. Whoever these beings were, this was a full-blown military ambush, eager for some Imperial corpses, regardless of the expense.

The army, Sten wondered. No. They weren't players – at least he didn't think so. Not yet, anyway.

Where the clot was Cind? His question was answered as a grenade blew a long-boarded window open, and she shouted, 'Covering! Move!'

Sten slammed Alex's butt, and Kilgour was on his feet, hurtling forward and diving into the abandoned shop. Sten sprayed a burst in the general direction of death; infantry muscles took over, and he was dashing forward, coming in as Alex blasted covering fire, and he was through the window, recovering, to one side. Cind came through the window like a bounding Earth marten in the snow, a spatter of rounds accompanying her.

Their momentary shelter would soon become a death trap, Sten knew. At least, he thought, they didn't have to worry about running out of ammunition. Not for a day, anyway – each willygun's tube magazine held 1400 one-millimeter balls of shielded AM2.

Again, the mortar's gunner corrected his aim, and another bomb *klanged* out of the tube and arced toward them, and Sten gnawed drakh-smelling carpet just like so many rats had before him.

The gunner's range was long – the bomb exploded above them, against the building's face. Bricks avalanched down, just as they had from Kilgour's grenade.

'By the beard of my mother,' Cind said absently, 'but that's the first good thing that's happened since the party started.'

She was right – the opposition had just given them an adequate breastwork to fight behind. But Sten was chortling. 'Your mother's what?'

'Clot off,' Cind said. 'You see what happens when you run away and get raised by Bhor?'

'Speakin't ae which,' Kilgour said, 'Ah could but wish f'r a few ae thae gorillers ae th' moment, aye?'

'Yeah. Right. You wish for Bhor, and I'll wish for a back door. Guess which one we'll get,' Sten said.

They were up and sliding toward the back of the building, barely able to see in the gloom, stumbling through overturned refuse.

'Any idea who doesn't like the way we comb our hair?' Cind asked. Neither man had an answer. The way this Cluster thought, it might be almost anyone.

At the rear of the shop, Sten found the back door. It had been closed off with heavy timber X-ed over the door and spiked down. Not a problem, Sten thought, with Kilgour's proven grunt-and-groan talent.

About one second later, their enemies also found the back door, and a grenade shattered against it, punching holes in the panel. Sten saw movement outside through the blast holes and sent a burst and then a bester grenade after it. There were screams, which were chopped off as the grenade exploded. The bester grenade blanked time for anyone caught in its radius – two hours worth of unconsciousness, and the victim had no knowledge that even a second had passed.

'Y're bein't merciful, skip.'

'Like hell,' Sten snarled. 'I got the wrong clottin' bomb. You just rip and tear, since you got us in this sorry mess in the first place.'

'Ah,' Kilgour said. 'Thae's days – an' nights – th' magic dinnae seem to work.'

He grabbed, one-handed, one of the X-braces and pulled. The heavy plank – and the rest of the door – came away.

'You can leave the rest of the building,' Sten said.

The three edged out through the hole. Sten looked at the four men scattered around the door. Human – which meant Tork or Jochian. Douw's faction? Or maybe that other group of Jochians whose goals and leaders Sten was still to hear from? Insufficient data. All four of them wore coveralls without insignia.

'Noo. Le's roll this up. Thae's no more pleasure or sport t' be gain't, an' thae's still baddies left.'

Sten took point, and they doubled away, down the alley, moving as fast as they could and still keep complete silence.

Their luck ran out in two separate catastrophes. The storm quite suddenly stopped, just as suddenly as it had broken. Worse, the sky cleared, and two of Jochi's moons three-quartered at them.

'Cind, do the Bhor have a weather god?' Sten wondered.

'Schind. He rules ice storms.'

'Drakh.'

Then their second ruin struck. A searchlight beam pinned the team like insects. Sten imagined the three of them silhouetted like an old photo negative, then all three of their weapons chattered and the light blew, hissed, died, and was dark, and they were flat behind the stripped, torched, and abandoned wreck of a gravsled.

'I saw 'um,' came a surprised shout. 'Thet bit one. Hez that Imperial we'b seed in livie!'

Sten swore. This would take some explaining.

First to these provisional power-grabbers on Jochi. Sten also thought his Eternal Emperor might hear of the incident and have some questions as to why his ambassador plenipotentiary had been out farting around on a completely unnecessary bit of cowboy intelligence.

Oh well. At least they wouldn't get killed now. And maybe Sten could figure a way out of the Imperial flaying.

Then: 'Th' gamclotting ambassador?'

'Yah.'

'Kill the scrote! Now!'

'Ah dinnae ken who's daft enow t' wan' to ice th' Emp's lad,' Alex said, 'but w' kin sort th' villain out later. Back. Th' way we came.'

A small infantry rocket round crashed against the wall above them – and that way too was sealed.

'We're sandwiched,' Cind announced. 'Anybody know how to levitate?'

'Be serious. Ah dinnae hae e'en a wee chuckle noo, let alone lev'ty.'

They were well and truly trapped.

Solid rounds chewed up the gravsled above them.

'How come,' Sten wondered, 'when you see the livies, and the hero ducks behind a stupid gravsled, all the slugs ricochet instead of punching right on through like in real life?'

Nobody answered.

The return fire stopped. They heard the shuffle of feet coming in.

Cind lifted her gun. Sten shook his head, and she saw the kukri blade gleaming in the moonlight.

Cind's combat knife slid out of its sheath.

There were four attackers.

Number One saw nothing – Cind's knife was anodized flat-black, and there was no reflection as the blade went home under his rib cage, into his heart, and the man's momentum sagged him forward.

Number Two heard nothing as the two minikegs Kilgour called fists slammed against the side of his head, and his skull eggshelled.

Number Three had a moment to blink, then that curved short-sword of the Gurkhas clove him, slashing his shoulder blade apart, snapping ribs, and burying itself in his stomach.

Number Four had too much time. He had time to shove his rifle sideways, into Sten, sending him stumbling back, hand coming off the gore-slick kukri handle, and then the gun's barrel was aiming.

Sten let himself fall back into a crouch, right hand dropping, fingers curled, death sliver coming out of his armsheath.

Left hand braced, he slashed near-blindly – in a knife fight do anything but think about things.

Too much time . . . and Four saw his gun barrel cut in half.

Too much time . . . and Sten recovered, blade coming down and then flashing up into Four's solar plexus, flashing up, intestines spilling as he gutted the man like a fish.

Sten's knife was reflexively bravo-wiped on the corpse's coveralls, then went back into his arm.

He ripped the kukri free from Three's body, avoiding looking at the man he had so neatly eviscerated. Another one, Sten. Another one on the long list.

Cind and Alex were awaiting orders.

Sten picked up his gun and tapped its stock. The other two nodded. It took ten minutes for the enemy to realize that even though there had been no shrieks or gunfire, the four they had sent in would not be coming back.

They sent seven men in next.

Sten let them get within four meters of the gravsled before he signaled. Fire spat – and seven bodies were shattered on the paving.

The third wave came less than two minutes later.

Grenades paved their way, blasts crashing against the alley walls.

'Thae're no playin' fair,' Alex said.

'I'm not planning to let them take me,' Cind said.

'Nor I,' Sten said. 'But there's no gain in suicide.'

'We're waitin', lad. F'r a wee idea.'

Sten considered . . . and as he did, thunder drumrolled and the storm smashed in again. He swore. Five minutes earlier and . . .

Very well, he thought. Use what you have. Add some confusion. 'Kilgour. Can you get a grenade among 'em?'

Alex considered. 'Close.'

'When it blasts . . . we go. Fifteen meters, go flat, grenade again, and we'll go in on them.'

Cind and Alex looked at him. There was no expression on either of their faces.

'With no one to drink our souls to hell,' Cind sighed, unclipping a grenade from her harness and coming to a crouch.

'Ah well, ah well,' Alex sighed. 'A' least we're noo dyin't in bed.'

He set his gun down, readied a grenade, and came half-up, into classic throw position. A braw cast, he thought, thumbed the button, and threw.

The grenade hit, bounced, and exploded, barely a meter short of the enemy position, and the three were up, as lightning opened hell's gates for them and thunder tympanied and Cind ululated a Bhor war cry and they were charging, three against – against who knew how many.

Sten, pure bluff, pure rage, bellowed: 'Ayo . . . Gurkhali!' As good a battle shout as any to die with.

The ululation echoed against the brownstones.

And the Gurkhas heard him.

And attacked.

A brown wave of men came out of the night, guns spattering fire, and then they were closed with the enemy. The men spun in sudden confusion at the attack from their rear, and the Gurkhas gave up their guns and slashed in with the kukri.

Two Gurkha fire teams ran past Sten and the others, each with a light crew-served automatic weapon. Moving in pure drill, they went down and opened up, fire roaring down the alley and unsealing that end.

By the time Sten realized he was alive and would stay alive

– or, at least, make it out of this stinking alley – none of his attackers could say the same.

The rain felt wonderful on his face. Cind's shoulders as he squeezed them were the most comforting thing he had known. Alex's beam was the friendliest expression he had seen.

Portable torches gleamed from where the enemy's position had been. The three stumbled toward them.

Mahkhajiri Gurung was waiting for him. 'Sir, you were very hard to find. This district we found very confusing. I wish you would have summoned us sooner. And when you go out next, would you wear a locator?'

'How,' Sten realized, 'did you even know I'd left the embassy?'

Mahkhajiri shrugged. 'After Mr Kilgour find secret passage, we did, too. Even though he did not bug passage, we did.

'You see, we are not as good as Mr Kilgour, and cannot sense in our deepest sleep if some assassin came to attack you in that passage. We Gurkhas need all the help we can get.'

Sten, Cind, and Alex looked at each other.

'All right,' Sten said finally. 'So you know everything. I guess the only question I could have is where are the Bhor?'

'Up on the bridge. Out on the embankment. There were many people with guns we thought should be dealt with.

'The Bhor wanted that honor. We agreed, since they are far more capable of diplomacy than we are.'

That would mean no prisoners out there, either.

'I want,' Sten said, 'a gravsled and back to the embassy and a drink.'

'Waiting,' Mahkhajiri Gurung said. 'In the street.'

With a nod, Kilgour pulled Sten aside as they walked down the alley. 'Lad, thae was a bit closer'n Ah'm comfortable wi'. Dinnae it be time to be noo studyin't war no more?'

'It is.'

'Y' ken, Ah know, th' mos' interestin' thing aboot this evening?'

Sten did. Someone had knowingly tried to kill the Eternal Emperor's ambassador plenipotentiary. Not in the heat of battle, but by direct order.

Any rational being would know that such a murder would produce the most immediate and most lethal response from the Emperor.

Sten realized that there were people – factions – here on Jochi that made the lunatics he had been dealing with appear to be sane, peaceful beings.

And so the question would be, who did this semiarmy belong to? Mortars . . . automatic weapons . . . men attacking like trained, or at least semitrained, soldiers.

They belonged to somebody.

Sten would wait for the howls of outrage, wondering what conceivable cover story someone would find for the bloody death of one or two companies of gunmen.

But over the days that came, there was never any mention of the incident.

Not from anyone.

Including Rurik's police force.

Chapter Thirteen

The proposal was very brief. It was handwritten on three pages of what appeared to be antique paper. The bloodless man sitting across from the Eternal Emperor finished reading it and replaced the pages on the desk.

'Your comments,' the Emperor asked.

'Interesting, sir.' A neutral tone.

Unsurprising, since everything about Poyndex was neutral. He had formerly been head of Mercury Corps – Imperial Intelligence – in the final days of the Tahn war. An efficient, passionless soldier, he had continued serving under the privy council. Later, in a piece of internal politicking, he had been made the junior member of that council.

But when the Emperor returned, Poyndex betrayed the council to the Empire. All he asked – he knew all he *could* ask – was for his life. He had had nothing whatsoever to do with the assassination of the Emperor. Nor had he publicly had any part in the various purges and atrocities ordered by the council.

The Emperor took his offer – and the privy council's back was appropriately poniarded, and Poyndex disappeared into the hinterlands of the Empire.

'You show no surprise,' the Emperor said.

'Sir . . . May I speak frankly?'

It was the Emperor's turn for silence. Poyndex chose to interpret that as permission.

'I am only surprised that I am still alive, Your Majesty. When you ordered my return here to Prime World, I was sure—'

'No,' the Emperor said. 'If I had wanted your corpse, it would have been done silently and at the time of maximum ire. I decided the interregnum would not be memorialized by show trials. Besides, I remember you as being a most efficient chief of Intelligence.

'Now I have need of your services. I want you to take over this newly created entity, Internal Security. It is to be run somewhat differently than Mercury. Its operatives have been and will continue to be recruited from nonmilitary channels. They are required to swear an oath of fealty to me, personally, rather than to the Empire. Their tasks and duties will be known to me alone. The only duty they have been tasked for, in public or classified records, is my protection. Which I plan to give the widest possible interpretation to.

'All IS missions will be assigned by me, and their accomplishment will be reported to me. There will be no other elements in the chain of command. The unit will have the highest priorities in its missions. All reports will be single-copy Eyes Only or orally delivered. There will be no records kept in Imperial Archives. Now . . . your response?'

'There is not much of a choice, Your Majesty,' Poyndex said. 'Just knowledge of the existence of this unit could be . . . embarrassing. And . . .' He tapped the proposal on the desk. 'This plan, and the problem it is intended to solve, is certainly something that must never be common knowledge.'

'Your reasoning is correct. You are, in fact, the only being besides myself privy to both the problem and my projected solution,' the Emperor said. 'But before you accept, I have a single question.

'What is to keep you from betraying me, as you betrayed the council?'

There was a very long silence. Poyndex stood and paced.

'I will answer that, sir,' he said, 'even though I prefer not to ever discuss my own personality quirks. I find the subject . . .

embarrassing. Perhaps, if you will allow me, a story – a parable – will help.'

Poyndex took a breath. 'In Spyschool One, they tell the story about a famous spymaster. Serving an ancient Earth imperator. He is credited with creating modern espionage, in fact – where each man spies on his brother and is spied upon. His ruler, impressed, wanted to reward him. The man wanted but one thing – the baton of a field marshal.

'His emperor was shocked at the request, and refused. Spies are not given the rewards of honest soldiers. Nor – he did not add – should they be given public fame.'

'The man's name was Fouché, and the dictator's name was First Napoleon,' the Emperor said.

'You know the incident, sir. Well, it is told to discourage the budding young intelligence specialist from wanting fame or public glory. And I thought I had taken it to heart and learned to suppress whatever need I had to appear in the public prints, together with other feelings that lessen a reasoning being's efficiency. But when the late Sr Kyes made his offer to elevate me to the privy council, an offer made very much to serve his own interests I learned, I discovered I was still ambitious. After the privy council's – and my own – downfall I corrected this weakness.'

'Did you?' the Emperor wondered. 'Ambition is a hydra.'

'Does it matter, sir?' Poyndex asked. 'Because unlike those dunders on the privy council, I doubt if you would ever expose your back to me.'

The Emperor nodded. Enlightened – or fearful – self-interest was an acceptable motivation. Especially for the tasks he planned to set Poyndex.

'I accept your assignment, Your Majesty. Of course I do. In fact, I am honored.'

'Good. There will be other people assigned to you. Some of them will come from . . . equally gray backgrounds. And some of them will be given missions you will have no need to know about.'

'I understand, sir.'

'Just like that one.' The Emperor indicated the proposal. 'I have three questions on my proposal,' he went on. 'Do you need to know any more about this device?'

'No, sir. And I would refuse to listen if I did. Just knowledge of this is risky enough to endanger my continued survival.'

'Do you think the task can be accomplished?'

'Yes,' Poyndex said flatly. 'We've had far more elaborate work done on doubles, triples, and defectors, Your Majesty.'

'Good. Very good,' the Emperor said.

'We will need about a month to assemble the personnel, sir. Probably two cycles for the work itself, and of course, complete seclusion,' Poyndex said.

'I have already thought of that.' The Emperor reached across the desk and picked up the proposal. He took a firestick from his desk, ignited it, and held it to the paper. The papers instantly flamed into sheets, and then were gray ashes.

'The site will be ancient Earth.'

Poyndex rose, saluted, and was gone.

The Emperor stared after him. It was a pity he would never offer Poyndex a celebratory drink, or make him dinner when a plan was complete, as he had done with Ian Mahoney or Sten.

But that had been long ago, and this was another time.

Chapter Fourteen

'Y'r mug's screw't up like a basset, young Sten. And Ah dinna ken y'r worry,' Alex said. 'Th' hae no choice in th' matter. 'Tis th' Emperor's command.'

'That doesn't make it any easier,' Sten said.

'I agree with Alex,' Cind said, a Bhor fascist at heart. 'I know you don't like just flat out announcing to these people their fate has been determined. A new leader is on the way and they'll just have to like it or choke on it. But I don't see any way to sugar-coat it. Those *are* the facts, and they'll just have to live with them.'

'It wasn't sugarcoating I was looking for,' Sten said.

'Make up your mind fast, lad,' Alex said. 'Our friendly four will be here any minute.'

'Here's how I see it,' Sten said. 'When Dr Iskra arrives – and I still don't know exactly *when* he is going to arrive, damn it – anyway, when he arrives and takes command, things can go into the drakh in a hurry. What if everyone tells the Emperor to put his new fearless leader where the sun is mortified to go?'

'The Emperor would crush them,' Cind said flatly.

'Probably,' Sten said. 'Still. Beings have done stranger things. Up to and including mass suicide. I guess they don't quite believe it will really happen to them.'

Sten reflected on the millions of dead and the awful destruction the Tahn had caused themselves.

'I want to do this right,' he said. 'Otherwise, we'll end up with a six-way civil war on our hands. I want the Emperor's choice to stick. Make them worry about refusing to go along with Dr Iskra.'

Cind didn't get it. 'If they're all *that* crazy – and from what I've seen, all the species in this Sarla-forsaken cluster are certifiably insane – wouldn't worry just aggravate the problem?'

Alex was thoughtful. 'Nae s' fast, lass. Our Sten i' sharpenin' his Mantis wits.' He turned to Sten. 'C'd we no make't personal, lad? Fear alone c'n make a man braw. But, add guilt t' fear and y' oft find a lurkin' coward.'

Sten looked up at Alex. And the light bulb dawned. 'Why kiss me, Dr Rykor,' he laughed.

'Ah'm no so blubbery,' Alex sniffed.

But Sten wasn't paying any attention. He was hastily drawing up a game plan. Just as the outline took shape, the com line buzzed.

It was time.

'Before we begin, Sr Ambassador,' General Douw said, 'the four of us would like to express our –' The silver-haired Jochian glanced nervously around the sterile room Sten had chosen for the meeting. '– our appreciation for your . . . ahem . . . hospitality.'

Sten ostentatiously glanced at the time display ticking away on the far wall. It was the only decoration. 'My pleasure,' he said, sounding bored. He drummed his fingers on the table.

'We know you're a busy man, Sr Sten,' Menynder said, peering at him amiably through his antique spectacles. 'So, as soon as we got word you wanted to see us, we got together to hammer out a little presentation.'

'Oh?' was all Sten said.

'We're extremely proud of this effort,' the general broke in. 'In fact, I personally view this as an historic moment.' He pushed over a sheaf of documents. 'Herewith is our plan for a new government. All four of us have signed on. I think you'll be impressed with our efforts.'

'Must only clear with home worlds,' Diatry, the Bogazi leader, said.

'I can guarantee the Suzdal,' Youtang barked.

Sten frowned at the documents and prodded at them with a suspicious finger.

'Something wrong?' Menynder asked. The old Tork's alarm bells were going off. They had ting-a-linged a bit when he had walked into this white-on-white room. It was decidedly unfriendly. Reminded him of an interrogation room. He also noted the walls were thick enough to be scream-proof. The only furniture was the long, bare table they were seated at. And five hard chairs.

'Are you *sure* you want to give this to me?' Sten asked, poking at the offending documents.

'Of course we're sure,' General Douw said. 'This is the blueprint, I tell you, the blueprint of our future.'

Sten just stared at him.

The general got a little panicky under the stare. He turned to Menynder. 'That's what *you* said, isn't it?'

'Quiet, General,' Menynder warned.

'Why should I be quiet? We're here to air our views, correct? To be firm, but fair. We agreed, right?'

'You talk, talk, talk,' Diatry said, picking up which way the wind was blowing. And it was definitely smelling.

But Douw was still on his self-destructive course. 'I'm not going to take all the blame,' he whined. 'It's not my fault! Sr Ambassador, please . . .'

'You want to remove these?' Sten asked, shifting to a gentle tone and pushing the documents back toward the general. 'I'll pretend I never saw them.'

'Sure. No trouble. Lot of drakh, anyway,' Douw babbled, hauling the sheaf of papers back.

'What is your pleasure, Sr Ambassador?' Menynder said. 'How can we make your mission easier?'

'Two things. The first is a mere matter of curiosity. The Eternal Emperor's curiosity, I might add.'

'Which is?' Menynder asked.

'The dinner party you had for the Khaqan. On that tragic night.'

Stone silence in the room. Gotcha, Sten thought. He let the silence lay there for a long time.

'You four were among those in attendance, correct?' he asked at last.

'Uh . . . well . . . I arrived awfully late,' General Douw said.

'Then you were there,' Sten said. A statement.

'Certainly, I was. Nothing suspicious about that, is there?'

'Who said anything about suspicion?' Sten asked. He gave Douw a quizzical 'Why are you acting so guilty?' look.

'Quite right,' Douw said. 'I mean, you didn't. I mean—'

'Yes, Sr Sten. We were all in attendance,' Menynder broke in.

'Odd,' Sten said.

'Friendly gathering only,' Diatry said. 'Is strange to have friendly gathering only where you come from?'

Sten ignored this. 'And the Khaqan gave no sign he was ill?' he asked. 'A little pale and weak, perhaps? Or . . . maybe a show of temper?'

'Why'd he be angry?' Youtang yapped. 'It was merely a social evening.'

'I think he very happy before he die,' Diatry said. 'Not angry. Tell big joke. We laugh. Ha. Ha. Then he die. We all very sad this happen. Cry boo hoo.'

Sten shifted course again. 'I've gone through his appointments calendar,' he said. 'And the dinner wasn't listed.'

'It was, uh, a last-minute thing,' Menynder said quickly.

'I guess that explains that little mystery, then,' Sten said.

'That's what was bothering you?' Menynder asked. 'The appointments calendar?'

'Not me,' Sten said. 'The Eternal Emperor. Remember?'

'Yes. Of course,' Menynder said. He took his glasses off and wiped them with the kerchief from his pocket. 'Any other little mysteries we can clear up?'

'No. I don't think so. Oh. Yes. One more thing. The place where this famous dinner occurred? Who'd it belong to?'

'A friend of mine,' Menynder said. 'The Khaqan wanted privacy. I arranged it.'

'In a Tork neighborhood?' Sten asked.

'Why not?'

Sten stared at Menynder. He let that stare linger until Menynder began to sweat. Then he moved his gaze from face to face, studying each being closely. He wound up the tension until it was a supertight ball of kinetic energy just waiting to be released.

Then he let it go. 'Why not, indeed,' Sten said.

He pretended not to notice as four very worried beings whooshed out air.

'Now, for the main reason I've called you all together,' Sten said.

Douw, Menynder, and the two others bent close to hear Sten's words. He had their complete attention.

'After careful study and long consideration, the Emperor has found a solution to your dilemma. And I think you will all agree it's pure genius on his part.'

'I'm quite sure it is,' Douw said, not giving a damn at that second.

Menynder was wiping sweat from his brow while Diatry and Youtang were busy mentally ticking off the sins Sten had failed to sniff out.

'Gentlebeings,' Sten said, 'I'm pleased to announce the Emperor has handpicked the being who will lead you into a new era of good fortune . . .

'His name, gentlebeings, is Iskra. Dr Iskra.' Sten looked mildly around the room. His game plan had worked. There was not the slightest sign of objection.

'Good choice,' Menynder said. 'In fact, I remember his name being mentioned the night of that dinner we were discussing earlier. Isn't that so, General Douw?'

Douw shuddered. That clottin' dinner again! 'Yes, quite so. And, we're honored the Emperor took a personal interest in our small affairs.'

'When is he expected?' Menynder wanted to know.

At that moment, a big ship smashed overhead and plunged for the spaceport. The crack of a shattered sound barrier rocked the embassy. Oh, clot, Sten thought. Just in time. He continued, however, without missing a beat.

'As we speak, gentlebeings. As we speak.'

Chapter Fifteen

Dr Iskra arrived with an impressive amount of pomp, even if the circumstance was a bit premature. Sten would have preferred that this construct of the Eternal Emperor, this dictator-in-waiting, would have arrived a few cycles after the various in-place schemers had figured out that none of them were about to be the nominated replacement – and had time to decide how they would play the new hand.

But Sten had learned eons before, early in his Imperial Service, that it was a valuable lesson in real life to wish in one hand, crap in the other, and then watch to see which one filled up first.

That rumble portending Dr Iskra's arrival was fortunately an overflight. Sten had time to scrag Alex and the Gurkhas and have Cind find enough nonstregged Bhor to present an Impressive Package at the spaceport. He also made sure to bring two livie operators from the embassy, in case no one else remembered to document this historic event.

Two heavy cruisers hung over the landing field, McLean generators hissing, their destroyer screens and picket tacships darting around them. Four fleet transports settled down on the field. Ramps dropped and gravlighters flitted out, scattering a rim of security troops as they went. Other troops formed an inner shield within the square formed by the transports.

Sten, Alex, and Cind watched with a critical eye.

'Th' Guards,' Alex said, '*still* dinnae hae recov'rd frae th' war an' th' priv'tations ae th' privy council.'

'Alex,' Sten observed mildly, 'did it ever occur to you that *no* unit we've ever been assigned to is now qualified to hold the bullocks of the lowliest private we knew? At least the way we remember it?'

'An' whae's th' matter wi' thae?' Kilgour asked in injury. 'Tis nae but th' truth, aye?'

'Aaargh.' Sten stalked forward – flanked by an Impressive of Gurkhas and Bhor – as the largest of the cruisers landed in the middle of the square formed by the transports.

A rigid color guard had doubled out of the cruiser and was drawn up, in line, by the time Sten arrived at the cruiser's ramp. The cruiser's commander and the commander of the Imperial Guard battalion saluted Sten. The battalion came from the Third Guards, a unit Sten had never operated with, nor knew much about. Once, a long time before, his cover on a Mantis operation had been as a dishonorably discharged officer of the Third Guards, and he wondered, amused, if that cashiering was somewhere in the unit's records. Imperial Intelligence tended to set up cover stories very carefully. Sten hoped not – he never wanted to explain to this Guards colonel, an efficient-sounding if somewhat thick individual named T'm Jerety, why the Imperial ambassador plenipotentiary had in the dim past been cashiered for atrocities, ambiguity, and angst, or whatever crimes his cover identity had required.

A dry, hot wind swept across the field as Dr Iskra walked down the cruiser's forward ramp.

No one's expression changed. On the part of the newly arrived Imperial forces it came from familiarity. Sten was impressed, however, with the professionalism of his own crew. All he heard was a low sigh from Kilgour, a suppressed sinusoidal squeal from Otho, and a *sotto voce* comment from Cind, who was going to *have* to relearn her Bhor-taught freebooting ways and dreadnought tongue:

'Clot,' came the whisper. 'He looks a hanging judge who wears rubber panties under his robes. Rubber and pink lace.'

Her description was apt.

Dr Iskra at twenty meters was very unimpressive. He was not tall. He was thin. He wore nondescript, baggy civilian attire that any zee-grade livie would have costumed its absentminded professor in. A professor, Sten decided, of Undercurrents of Subconscious Thought and Priapic Imagery in Agrarian Nonrhyming Poets You Never Heard Of. Balding, in an age when natural body hair was an easily added or subtracted cosmetic item. What hair he had was combed or slicked over his pate as if to hide it.

At twenty meters, a figure of fun or pity.

At three, the image changed, Sten thought.

Dr Iskra menaced. Sten could not tell why. It might have been the hard gray glare from eyes that never seemed to blink or look anywhere but into your guts. Or it might have been the tiny pinch marks around Iskra's lipless mouth. Or that none of the lines on his face would fit a smile.

Iskra was flanked by the usual civilian aides/disciples that any politician-in-exile collects.

Sten bowed a salute. Iskra did not return it.

'You are Sten, yes? Very well. Enough of this ceremony. There is much work to be done. I want immediate transportation to the palace, yes?'

'I have embassy gravsleds standing by,' Sten said.

'No. No.' Iskra turned to Colonel Jerety. 'I want six heavy gravlighters. I will ride in the second. The first should have flags mounted as decoy. One company of your battalion should secure the route. I want a second company on zone security awaiting my arrival at the Square of the Khaqans. I want a third company to secure the palace itself. My chambers, of course, will be those used by the late usurper. See that they are cleared. And I want one guardsman per servitor, until I have had a chance to have my servants screened.'

Colonel Jerety saluted and shouted orders, apparently unaware that most statesmen either knew nothing about security, or wanted the least amount between them and their adoring populace. Or, perhaps Jerety was used to such demands from Iskra by now. Sten wondered if Iskra also had a food taster on his staff.

Iskra turned back to Sten. 'As I said, there is much work ahead of us. Please accompany me to the palace, so that we may discuss the proper manner of implementing my assumption of authority, so the minimum of order is lost.'

Sten bowed once more. His face was as blank as Alex's, Otho's, or Cind's.

Awaiting them in the Square of the Khaqans was a claque. Since all of them were human, it must have been assembled by either Douw or Menynder. Most likely, considering how long it usually took the secretary of defense to come to full drive on anything, it was one of Menynder's cheering sections.

Iskra went slowly, knowing he was being recorded by the livie crews, up the sweeping steps to the palace's main terrace. He turned and looked down at the cheering minicrowd. Sten wondered if he would make a speech. But Iskra just nodded jerkily, as if accepting no more than his due, and turned to the waiting officialdom, which included the full gaggle of Jochi leaders, plus the Bogazi and Suzdal representatives.

His eyes swept them as thoroughly as any camera. And as emotionlessly. Again, he nodded.

'Thank you for welcoming me home,' he said. 'Tomorrow we shall meet to discuss how those of you who are qualified will help me implement our New Order for the cluster.

'Now, I am tired. I will eat, rest, and go over my notes. Someone from my staff will contact you as to the exact time and place of our conference.'

Without waiting for a response, he swept through the open two-story-high doors that led into the palace. Sten followed.

Several Guards officers and one scared Jochi palace flunky were inside.

'I am—' the flunky began.

'You are Nullimer,' Iskra interrupted. 'You were majordomo to the Khaqan. As was your father. And your father's father served the pig that bred the Khaqan.'

Nullimer looked ready to faint.

'You also,' Iskra went on, 'once warned *my* father at a court function that the Khaqan was speaking ill of him.'

Nullimer blanked, obviously not remembering the incident, then covered.

'Yes,' Iskra went on. 'And you will be rewarded for that, even though your warning was not taken with sufficient gravity. I can only hope that you will serve me as faithfully as you did that evil one.'

Nullimer started to his knees. Instantly Iskra was beside him, lifting him up. 'No, man. There shall be no kneeling in this New Order.'

Iskra turned, as if now addressing the claque outside, or the dignitaries still milling about out on the terrace. 'You see? Everything is known. And everything shall be rewarded.' His voice lowered. 'Or punished.'

Then, more strongly: 'Everything!'

He spun back to the majordomo. 'You have heard. Now, go. Tell the kitchen I will eat. I will give this officer here my weekly menu.'

Nullimer, alternately flushing and beaming, managed to stumble from the chamber.

Iskra spoke to one of his aides. 'After that, he will serve me well. But have his quarters fine-combed – in the event my assessment was in error.'

The aide nodded and passed Iskra a printed list. Iskra handed it to one of the Guards officers.

'This is what I eat,' he said. 'Please have the kitchen made aware. And inform them that this diet, of course, shall not apply for banquets or special occasions.'

Iskra pinned an expression that could be considered a smile on his face for an instant, then swept on.

Sten couldn't resist. He stopped beside the Imperial soldier and glanced at the list. It was one cycle's worth of menus, with the note that at the end of a cycle the menu was to be repeated. He had time to see one day's offerings:

Morning
Black bread
Herbal tea

Midday
Vegetable soup
Mineral water

Dusk
Lung soup
Nut cutlet
Garden salad, undressed
Cream torte
One glass, nonvintage Rurikdoktor white wine

Before Bed
Digestive crackers
Herbal tea

Sten hoped that any conferences with the Imperial ambassador around mealtime would be considered a special occasion. Especially the evening feeding. Sten hoped that the lung soup was to remind Iskra of his poverty-stricken days in exile. Gods forbid he actually *liked* it.

But that cream torte? Perhaps that was Iskra's one allowed indulgence? Sten, if someone had made him dictator-elect, would have thought in terms of concubines, strong drink, hallucinatory substances, or bad company. But each tyrant to his tastes.

Iskra was waiting, looking impatient. Sten hurried to catch up.

'This, I assume, was the Khaqan's bedchamber?'

'It was,' one of Iskra's hovering aides said.

'Then it shall be mine. However, I shall wish some changes.'

'Of course, Doctor.'

Iskra looked thoughtfully around the huge chamber. 'First, get rid of that obscenity of a bed. I will not be succumbing to the sexual practices of that worm. You know what I sleep on. Those pictures. Have them removed. Give them to a museum, or have them burnt. It doesn't matter. We will have little time for gross representations of the miserable past.

'Have them replaced with a wallscreen on that wall; a map projector on that one. Fiche storage and book cases on the other walls. We shall have that fireplace punched out, into the next room, which shall be my battlechamber.

'Now. Leave. You, J'Dean. Return to the Imperial ship. Inform the rest of my staff they may relocate to this palace. Have the Imperials provide security for their passage.'

The aide nodded – just as jerkily as Iskra. Perhaps it was their own version of a salute. He withdrew. Doors closed, and Iskra and Sten were alone.

There was no preamble. 'You have been in communication with the Eternal Emperor?'

'I have,' Sten said.

'He has given you instructions? That I am to be given your fullest and most complete support, without questions?'

'I must correct you, Doctor. To prevent a future misunderstanding. I was ordered to provide full support by the Emperor. However, I am not, nor is any member of my embassy, under your command. We are here in the Altaic Cluster representing the Emperor, the Empire, and its interests and its citizenry. We are also here, under Imperial instructions, to ensure that the peace is kept and a stable government is in power.'

'Different words,' Iskra said. 'The same meaning.'

Sten chose not to participate in the debating society. 'May I ask your immediate intentions?'

'I intend that this cluster shall live in peace, as you said moments ago. I further intend that the brutalities, injustices, and evils of the Khaqan and his lickspittle underlings shall end immediately.'

'Admirable intent,' Sten said, forcing some warmth into his voice.

'Thank you.'

'You have used the phrase New Order twice in my hearing,' Sten went on. 'What, precisely, does that mean?'

'You are not familiar with my writings? With my analyses?'

'Apologies. But I have been busy of late, trying to keep small points of light from becoming firestorms. And I learned of your imminent arrival only recently.'

'You *must* read them,' Iskra said earnestly. 'Otherwise, it is impossible to understand the Altaic Cluster, let alone to help me rule it.'

'Then I shall. Immediately. But – what you just said. You intend to rule this cluster. Forgive my ignorance. But what form will that take? To be exact, how representative will your government be?'

'Very,' Iskra said firmly. 'It shall bear no resemblance whatsoever to the Khaqan's tyranny. But one thing, Ambassador Sten.

'Since you are from a civilized world, do not make the mistake of becoming anthropomorphic about the beings of my cluster.'

Civilized world, Sten thought. Vulcan? A man-made planet of slave labor and sudden death? He kept his face blank as Iskra continued.

'Understand that none of us, Torks, Jochians, Suzdal, or Bogazi, have ever known democracy. Beings here may rave about it, but it is an inconceivable idea in reality to them. Much like expecting someone who is blind from birth to envision a sunset, yes?

'So my New Order means a certain amount of direction. Guidance. That is the only way for us to find eventual freedom. Not in my time, of course, nor probably that of my sons yet unborn.

'But it will come.

'That is the oath I swore on my father's grave, and reconsecrated myself to, when the Khaqan murdered my brother.

'The Altaic Cluster will be at peace. And my sacred trust will be fulfilled – no matter the cost to this generation! There can be *no* true heroism or godhood without sacrifice along the path!'

Dr Iskra's eyes glittered red, reflecting the sun setting outside.

Chapter Sixteen

'Why,' Alex Kilgour wondered, 'do Ah hae th' feelin' ae a' thae an' ae a thae's a roarin't crock?'

He gestured at the wallscreen, which showed the terrace of the Khaqan's palace. I must learn to change the labels, Sten told himself. Iskra now wears the crown.

On the terrace stood Dr Iskra, hands raised, a slight smile on his face as below him the packed square boomed with cheers.

Behind him stood the Altaic power structure. The humans, at least, all showed the same expression of pleased relief on hearing of the assumption. Sten was not familiar enough with either the Bogazi or Suzdal to understand their emotional projections. So that big meeting, he thought, must have been just the obligatory change of command speech, as when one took over a new unit and was required to meet the unit's lower-ranking officers and make nice. Then, later, one announced the terror and that heads were to roll.

The cheering stopped, and Iskra resumed his speech.

'. . . a time of healing. A time for all of us to abandon the past, the dark shadows of vengeance, and strike out boldly together to secure the future for ourselves and for generations to come.

'We are all Altaics. We share the same systems. The same planets. But instead of realizing our common destiny we waste our substance in feuds begun for forgotten reasons. We hate our neighbor because his genetic code differs from ours. But we all came from the same universal plasm, no matter our species, race, or home planet.

'You know me.

'You know the justice and honor I represent.

'You know I have spent years in exile, fighting in every way I knew to bring down the abhorrence that was the Khaqan. And I succeeded.'

'Aye. Jus' you an' a wee attack ae apoopoplexy. Next he'll be claimin't t' hae created AM2 an' Scotch, as well.'

'Now it is time for our next task. Now it is time, and past time for all of us—'

Sten palmed the mute switch, leaving Iskra to gesticulate in silence. He and Alex were alone in the embassy apartments assigned to Sten, apartments that were security-sealed and constantly checked for bugs.

'You think it's a crock,' he told Alex, 'because it is.' He indicated a large pile of fiches and abstracts.

'Y' hae dredged throo all ae th' doc's natterin's, a'ready?'

'Read a couple. Had the rest abstracted. Iskra isn't exactly clear like crystal when he writes. And he's supposed to be such a brilliant speaker.'

'Th' clot dinnae do aught t' make my adrenaline adren,' Alex agreed.

'Nor mine. As far as I can tell, and I'm surely not a political philosopher, his main theory seems to be first we obliterate anything that the Khaqan did, then figure out what's to come next. This New Order, he says somewhere, "must remain supple and sensitive to change and challenge." He's in love with assonance.'

'Aye, he is an ass. Ah dinnae ken aboot whether it belongs to wee Nancy or no. An' of course, th' one thae's most supple t' this change is th' good Dr Iskra?'

'Of course. He's traveled. He's studied. He's done comparative analysis on every political theory going, including the Emperor. I didn't know the Emp picked him as one of the territorial governors of a Tahn solar system after the war. He did well – at least according to him.'

'Ah dinnae wonder,' Alex said. 'Th' Tahn dinnae understand aught but a boot ae' their neck a'ter the rules they grew up wi'. Doc Iskra – clot, e'en a Campbell – would'a likely been deemed liberal.

'Whae about th' real problem? All these races who're nae happy wi'out they're slittin' another one's weasan? Hae Iskra got a plan to end that?'

Sten shook his head. 'He talks a lot about equality. But it sort of works out that some people in the Altaic Cluster are a bit more superior than others.'

'An' lemme guess. Iskra, bein' a Jochian, somehow hae th' notion thae Jochians are th' most superior ae all.'

'Correct.'

'Clottin' wonderful. "Ware ye ae th' new boss. Same ae th' old boss." An wee Iskra's th' Emp's han'-picked golden boy. Ah dinnae mind he's bein' a dictator, lord knowin' you an' I o'er th' years hae installed a few dozen ae them. But Ah'm nae taken wi' th' wee lad haein' nae th' slightest bit ae subtlety or patience. Ah'll wager he's a lad thae wan's th' world, an' he wants it yesterday.'

'I'll live with that call,' Sten said. He stared back at the screen and the appropriately enthusiastic beings behind Iskra. 'I wonder just what – besides general make-nice – Iskra said to his rump parliament . . . Anybody there you think we can corrupt?'

Kilgour thought. 'All ae 'em, in time,' he said. 'But i' y' want a fly on th' wall yest'day, Ah'd start wi' Menynder. He appears t' hae his eye on th' main chance more'n most. An' a wee bit ae follow-through.'

'Agreed,' Sten said. 'See if we can't make him into a nice reliable source.'

'No puh-roblem.' Kilgour was silent for a minute. Then, seemingly irrelevantly, he asked, 'Did y' e'er gie y'self th' fearful luxury ae wonderin' i' our Fearless Leader's gettin' a wee touch senile?'

Sten flinched, as if an icy blast had touched him. He didn't answer, but went to the bar and poured two large drinks. Not of Scotch; not of stregg. But pure quill alk, as he had grown used to drinking as a field soldier. He handed one to Kilgour.

'If he is,' Sten said, after sipping his drink, 'and Dr Iskra is an example, the future's going to start looking like that.' He gestured outside the double-paned security window at the huge, building thunderheads that were bringing yet another slashing summer storm down on the capital.

'Dinnae fash, lad,' Kilgour said, knocking back his drink, waiting for Sten to do the same, and going for more. 'We're th' Emp's spearheaders, aye? So i' this harbinger's a busto, we'll nae survive t' see th' rest.'

Sten did not feel reassured. 'Now,' he said, taking Alex's example and slugging his drink down, 'we'll have the fun of seeing just how Dr Iskra shows his firm hand – and what happens to anybody who disagrees with him.'

'Ah hae th' answer t' that one, too,' Kilgour said. 'Th' clot's an idealist. Which means we'll be wadin't in blood t' our scrotes. Six months an' thae'll be lookin't back an' talkin' aboot how kind, gentle, an' silky th' late Khaqan was. Hide an' watch. Or do you hae th' desire t' take my bet Isky's nae but a timit, slickit lambiepie?'

Sten shook his head. 'Like you say. I'm mad, but I don't think I'm clottin' daft. Other than being here in the first place. No. I don't think Dr Iskra is going to end up being remembered for his sweetness and light.'

'To you gentlebeings,' Dr Iskra said, 'I know that I can present the future without need of equivocation. You are professionals, students of the inevitable historical process, and concerned as I about ensuring the glory of the Altaic Cluster.'

There was a murmur. It could be taken as the listener chose, up to and including agreement.

There were only fifteen beings in the huge auditorium. It was part of the barracks complex belonging to the unit that had formerly been known as the Khaqan's Own, the purportedly elite unit whose prime function was guarding the late Khaqan's life, possessions, relatives, and friends. The walls were freshly repainted with new murals showing soldiers of the Own serving an offstage master, waiting, chins thrust forward nobly, on barricades against an offstage foe. Helping innocent citizens against offstage disasters. All of the soldiers, and all of the civilians on the mural, were Jochians.

The fifteen beings were among the highest-ranking officers of the Khaqan's military. Not *the* highest-ranking flag officers. Iskra had selected carefully.

Each of them had received verbal orders to stand by for a special assignment. One by one, *sans* staff or aides, they had been picked up by a representative of Iskra and taken to the secure complex.

All of them were career military. All of them came from long-serving families of what the Khaqan had called 'the State.' And all of them were Jochians. Iskra had not wanted the presence of the few Torks, Suzdal, and Bogazi who had gotten their stars.

Among them was a tall, silver-haired man. General Douw. He was doing his best to remain unnoticed – until he could see which way the wind was blowing.

'We Altaics,' Iskra went on, 'are beings that genetically wish for rocks we can cling to as the tides of change wash about us.

'One of those traditions should be – but never was under the Khaqan or his father – the military. The beings who are prepared to defend the state with their lives, unquestioningly. And not just the soldiers in the field, but those who dedicate and sacrifice their entire lives to that service in the services that support them.

'These are the beings whom I, as a babe, grew up somehow, instinctively, loving and respecting. I must confess, and I do not wish it spread beyond this room, that I cried when I discovered that my health would not permit me to serve as a soldier.'

Iskra paused, eyes moving over the faces before him. They held on Douw for a moment. Just long enough to frighten the general. Douw nodded and tried to make his expression sympathetic.

Iskra continued. 'Of course, when I grew a few more years, and realized the monstrous crimes a soldier was required to commit under the Khaqan, and my father and my revered brother found me mature enough to tell me the truth, knowing I would not chatter it forth in childish gossip, I was very grateful for my illnesses.

'But I have skewed.

'We do not have much time. You fifteen are the men and women I must have for my New Order. You represent the military. Not the rabble the Khaqan called his army and navy.

'And you are all Jochians.'

Iskra stopped and let the silence build and become uncomfortable.

No one who had reached flag rank in any military would miss a cue like that.

'I noticed that,' a hard-faced woman whose uniform dripped medals said. 'Should we draw the conclusions we would like?'

'Which are, General F'lahn?' Iskra led her on, as he would encourage a prize pupil.

'I have read your writings, Doctor. And they spoke to me of a cluster where all of us, Torks, Suzdal, and Bogazi are united toward a common goal. A goal that the best, the Jochians, lead, carrying the banner. Or do I misunderstand?'

'You misunderstand nothing,' Iskra said. 'Which is why I said I can speak honestly.

'This is a new day. A New Order.

'But that is yet to be. What must happen now is a return to peace. We must start from a position where all beings know safety. Security for themselves, their homes, their jobs, and their children.'

There was another murmur – this one of definite agreement. General F'lahn would be rewarded for her bravery in walking point.

'Never happen,' an admiral growled. 'Not so long as we have these pocket armies, these militias, running about, calling themselves soldiers.'

'That shall be dealt with, I promise you, Admiral Nel. Either they shall be dissolved, or brought under the command of properly trained officers, or . . .'

He did not finish. Nor did he need to. And the fifteen officers were now beaming openly.

'Yes,' Iskra went on. 'Just as the eventual New Order will give other beings a sense of place . . . This nonsense at Pooshkan University, for instance.'

'Dr Iskra. The Khaqan committed some terrible crimes. And some members of our military, even to my infinite shame some Jochians, were the assassins. Have you considered this?'

The questioner was the lowest-ranking flag officer present, Brigadier S!Kt. She was also a disciple of Iskra's, who had been driven into retirement. All that had saved her from being murdered by the Khaqan was that she came from an incredibly rich family who had traditionally supported the Khaqan. One of Dr Iskra's first actions on arriving on Rurik was to 'request' that she return to public service.

'I have. And these rapes and murders were monstrous. Against my fellow Jochians, against the Torks, against the Suzdal, and against the Bogazi. Orders are even now being issued for any military people involved to be picked up and questioned closely.'

The meeting froze. Douw shrank down in his seat.

But Iskra pasted on his smile. 'Of course, if any of you here today happened to be in charge of units involved in these crimes, I fully understand how much deadly pressure you were put under by the Khaqan. None of you, to speak bluntly, are considered anything other than the honorable soldiers you are. Anyone who thinks otherwise shall encounter my severest judgment.

'And I would appreciate your assistance in this matter. Fiches will be provided to you when you leave of the units and officers I propose to investigate.

'If you know any of them to be innocent, and my informants are in error, please advise a member of my staff immediately. And, if there are any criminal individuals or units *not* on the fiche, I would appreciate your including them.'

Silence. A few officers – especially General Douw – chanced smiles. The *lettres de cachet* would be open.

'I think we have an understanding, yes?'

Nods. Larger smiles.

'A final question.'

'Yes, General F'lahn.'

'Your own family . . . was treated most shamefully.'

Iskra's face was stone. 'That is another matter. Of no concern to you. Of no concern to the state. Blood is blood. Blood must be answered.

'Those who helped the nightmare worm that called itself the Khaqan persecute and destroy my father, my family, and my brother will be destroyed.

'I know them.

'I have known them for years.

'Lying awake, on my pallet, dreaming of the homeland I thought I would never see, I saw their faces, and I swore that if I was offered the chance, there would be a reckoning.

'This reckoning is now at hand.'

Complete silence in the hall. Then the silence was broken by the applause of the Altaic Cluster – a forearm slammed hard against the body. Applauding the loudest was General Douw.

After all, each of them, and each of their families, had enemies. Blood, indeed, *had* to be answered.

'. . . there would be a reckoning. This reckoning is now at—' and the man palmed the recorder off.

'And what will your Imperial master think of that?' Dr Iskra asked, a note of challenge in his voice.

'The matter should not concern him,' the man answered. 'The Emperor chose you to rule the Altaic Cluster, after having decided you were the most qualified being. In what manner you choose to consolidate your power is not important, especially when it comes to minor trivia like a purge of the military hierarchy.'

Dr Iskra visibly relaxed. The man allowed him to relax while he went to a table and poured two cups of Iskra's night-time herbal tea.

'That is assuming,' he suddenly said, 'that this action is handled as it should be. Which means you should be cautious as to how many private enemies you let these generals add to your list . . . And the matter must be handled immediately.'

'It will be,' Iskra said. 'In the way you outlined as being the most effective. Of course, I have had to provide slight modifications, given the social characteristics of my people.'

The man looked at Iskra and decided not to ask further.

The man was the Eternal Emperor's liaison to Dr Iskra, ordered to operate under deep cover. No one beyond the Emperor himself was to know of his existence – especially not any of the Imperial mission on Rurik. That exclusion specifically indicated Sten, the Imperial ambassador.

Sten knew the man.

He was the consummate spymaster, a man who served no one but himself and his employers of the moment, who had best be the highest bidders.

His name was Venloe.

The man responsible for the assassination of the Eternal Emperor.

Chapter Seventeen

The forest was far north of Rurik. It began where an equally huge swamp ended, and it stretched for many kilometers, almost to the shore of a nearly tideless inland sea.

In the local peasant dialect, the forest was called 'The Place of Smokes.' In summer, windstorms swept through the forest, lifting huge clouds of debris high into the atmosphere. In spring and fall, dank fog crawled over the dry, silent land. In winter, polar storms made the 'smoke' white.

Near that inland sea, many years earlier, the Khaqan had

determined to build himself a retreat! Since everything on Rurik was big, and since the Khaqan thought even more grandiosely than his world encouraged, this retreat was to have included buildings sufficient for his entire court.

The property was surveyed.

Here and there one could still see colored markers that had been injected into tree trunks or stumps.

Roadways had been cleared, but never paved.

The Khaqan lost interest before any construction had been done, and the Place of Smokes returned to its desolation. Now, the forest's only visitors were illegal charcoal burners in summer and fall, and fur hunters in the winter.

They did not stay long. The forest was too huge. Too silent. Too uncaring.

The long line of gravlighters crept along the remains of a road, deep in the forest heart.

Each gravlighter's cargo area was packed with beings, human and ET. Some of them wore uniforms, hastily pulled on in summons to angry door-knocks and now ripped and torn. Others wore only what garments they had been able to grab as they were rushed from their homes or places of duty.

They were closely guarded by beings who wore the same uniform. But all of these guards were human.

The prisoners were silent. Some of them nursed wounds.

The gravlighters turned onto a narrower lane, then again, onto a track. The track opened onto what had been a meadow.

The lighters grounded.

Orders were shouted. The prisoners dismounted.

There were other prisoners still in the gravlighters. They lay, unmoving and trampled, on the lighters' decks. For the moment, these dead or near-dead were ignored by the guards.

Further orders brought the surviving prisoners into line.

Among the prisoners were Acinhow and N'ern. One was a minor prison officer, the other a tax official. Both of them had had time, when being arrested, to grab a few rationpaks, which had kept them alive on the long trip north.

'And now,' N'ern whispered. 'I see no sign of a prison. Are we to build our own from this forest?'

Acinhow shook her head slightly and indicated with a nod.

Halfway across the meadow were long, open trenches. Earth-moving equipment waited nearby.

Other trenches had been dug beyond them. But these had been filled in. Earth mounded above them in rows.

N'ern's face became gray.

There were whispers as other prisoners saw the trenches. Shouts from the guards for silence.

It took N'ern two attempts before she could speak.

'The children will never—' She broke off.

Acinhow shivered.

N'ern tried once more.

'At least . . . at least,' she murmured, 'it will be honorable.'

Chapter Eighteen

Sten was up to his ass in R-O-U-T-I-N-E. Which on Jochi meant a permanent state of borderline panic. Two thirds of the lights on the com board were winking yellow alert. The remainder were red.

His com techs – all schooled as diplomatic ombudsmen – hustled the board. Whittling away at the drakh. Soothing when mere calm words would do. Referring callers to appropriate agencies – knowing it would be some time before *any* Jochi governmental department would be operational. Dispensing small Imperial embassy favors where they could.

Anything worthwhile was boiled into an intelligence monograph and sent on to Sten. So many such reports had been pouring in that Sten had wound up spending his whole morning in the com room, poring over the reports, as well as fielding a stream of calls only an ambassador could deal with.

The first call of the day had been from young Milhouz, urgently wanting to talk to the ambassador. Sten put this at the bottom of the mental stack of things he had to do. Yes, he had promised the Pooshkan students a hearing with someone in authority. After meeting Dr Iskra, Sten wasn't real sure how to make his promise good.

Later with that. He would figure out something – just as soon as he made sense of all these reports of scattered disturbances all over Jochi. Especially in the neighborhoods and ghettos of Rurik.

There were a few more blood feuds being settled than usual. But no rioting. Some small-scale street maneuvering by the militias. But no shots fired – in anger, at least. A slight increase in looting. Also family violence.

Sten scrolled on. He came to another urgent call from Milhouz. The com officer had boiled the message down to the following: 'Have successfully won delay in ultimatum,' it read. 'Committee has agreed to extend deadline by one more week.' Sten noted the com officer was Freston, his most senior and trusted dial-twiddler. Unfortunately, the man was far too efficient, and it had taken Sten to rescue him from a seemingly inevitable and murderously dull career running high-ranking REMF com staffs.

Under *Observations*, Freston had written: 'Subject's manner outwardly calm. Voice box tension, however, indicates instability of individual. Sees Ambassador Sten as father figure. *Suggested handling*: Continue firm line. Softer approach will further feed instability.'

Clottin' great, Sten thought. A father figure to a spoiled rich kid. He didn't even *like* Milhouz, thought of him as a shrill-voiced toady taking advantage of a group of equally useless individuals. Clot him! He would call back when he was good and ready. Father figure, my clottin' . . .

Sten skipped ahead, musing over other reports. Then he hit another warning. Panic buying had erupted. As well as hoarding. All over the planet, shops that stocked nonperishable food and drink were selling out. Fuel and cooking-oil stocks also were being depleted.

He did not like this. It meant that it was going to take a great deal more than fine-minded speeches for Iskra to convince people that some kind of normal life lay ahead.

Sten gazed at the drakh heaping higher and higher in his bowl. This defied Kilgour's law of drakh hitting the fan. Alex insisted that trouble came in threes. Sten disagreed, even if the axiom came from Kilgour's sainted 'mum.' It was Sten's opinion that trouble kept coming until you could take no more. Then you got hit twice more.

The com room door hissed open and Cind boiled in. He was glad to see her. But he was not glad to see the look on her face.

'I get the idea you're not here to tell me Iskra's idea of paradise has dawned on the streets of Rurik,' Sten said.

'Not unless paradise includes storm troopers and mass arrests,' Cind said.

Sten reacted in his best diplomatic manner. 'Say clottin' what?'

'I've been checking up on those rumors of people going missing,' she said. 'They aren't rumors. I've got eyewitnesses. Heads of families – whole families, sometimes – are being grabbed right and left. By Iskra's soldiers.'

'What kind of game is that man playing?' Sten asked. 'He'll have the whole thing down around his ears before he barely gets started.'

One of the com officers signaled him. 'I've got another call from young Milhouz,' he said. 'He's holding right now. He says it's real important he talk to you. An emergency, he claims.'

'Sure it is,' Sten said. 'Lie to him. Tell him I've been stricken with beriberi, or some such. Then get Dr Iskra on the line. I want to talk to him. Now!'

A few minutes later, the thin-lipped face of Iskra appeared on the center vid screen.

'I understand you have a matter of some urgency,' Iskra said.

'I'd like an explanation, is what I'd like, Doctor.'

'I don't appreciate your tone, Sr Ambassador.'

'I tend to sing in that key,' Sten said, 'when I hear a leader I am supporting is perilously close to embarrassing the man I answer to. The Eternal Emperor.'

'In what manner am I doing this?'

'I have *confirmed* reports, Dr Iskra, that your soldiers are engaged in mass arrests.'

'If you would have asked me first,' Iskra said smoothly, 'I would have confirmed that fact for you. Save you a great deal of trouble – and misunderstanding.'

'Fine. I'm asking.'

'Yes, there have been some arrests,' Iskra said. 'Although, I *do* think referring to them as mass arrests exaggerates the circumstances. For convenience's sake, the accused ones were arrested at much the same time, just as they were transported to and are being held in a single prison – Gatchin Fortress, which is the traditional site on Jochi for those beings in the public eye who have been indicted. I assure you, however, these are merely routine matters involving restoring stability to the cluster. My people want assurances that justice has returned to the Altaics.

'The individuals in question have been accused of various crimes. Some serious. However, to be absolutely frank, I fully expect many of these accusations to prove false. That they are victims of petty beings seeking revenge.

'But, as I indicated, people are demanding trials. Therefore, I shall give them those trials. Fair trials. So that anyone falsely accused can publicly clear his or her name.'

This is a great load of drakh, Sten thought. 'What about the guilty ones?' he asked.

'Aren't you treading heavily in places you shouldn't go?' Iskra asked. 'What business is the justice system of the Altaics to the Imperial ambassador?'

'None at all,' Sten admitted. 'But I am determined to see the Emperor's orders carried out. Which means he expects a return to stability in the Altaics. Creating new blood feuds, Doctor, is not a good way to accomplish this.'

'I promise you, Sr Ambassador,' Iskra said, 'the trials will be completely fair. And I will be as merciful as possible to the guilty. Does that satisfy you?'

Sten had to say it did. Of course, Iskra was lying. But Sten couldn't afford an open break with the man. He would lose all control, and the mission would be doomed.

'It was a pleasure talking to you, Sr Sten,' Iskra said when they were done. And the screen went blank.

'We'd better increase surveillance,' Sten told Cind. 'Get more of Kilgour's bats in the sky.'

'You'll be needin' more'n Frick 'n' Frack,' Alex said. Sten jumped. He hadn't heard Kilgour enter. ''Less m' ears're waxed tight, they're shootin' oop th' univers'ty.'

Sten was astounded. 'The students? Where'd they get the guns?'

'Ah dinnae think it wae kids doin' th' shootin',' Alex said.

'Clot!' was all Sten said. He raced for the door, Alex and Cind tearing after him.

As he sprinted through the embassy, shouting for the duty company of Bhor and the Gurkhas, and stormed out the door and across the broad grounds, the specter of complete disaster choked his mind. The little twerp Milhouz had been right about at least one thing. If something happened to the coddled young beings of Pooshkan, pure hell would break loose over the Altaics.

Sten could hear the sound of gunfire coming from the university as he reached the embassy gates.

Then he was brought up short. The boulevard outside was barred by many Jochi soldiers. Iskra's men. The soldiers were backed by two armored tracks.

A burly major loomed up at him.

'Get out of my way,' Sten rasped.

'I'm sorry, Sr Ambassador,' the major said, 'but I can't permit you to leave.'

'By whose orders?'

'Dr Iskra's orders, sir. But please don't misunderstand. It's for your own safety. I have also been instructed to apologize for any inconvenience. You'll be permitted to leave once the emergency has passed.'

Sten heard more shots coming from Pooshkan. 'Is that the emergency?' he said.

The major shrugged. 'Young hooligans are rioting. Committing terrible deeds. Destroying public property. Murder. Looting. Sexual atrocities. It's a terrible, terrible thing.'

'Lying clot!' he heard Cind mutter.

'I must see for myself,' Sten said.

The major stayed professionally calm. But Sten could see the soldiers tense around him. Someone whispered, and there came the hum of turrets turning toward the embassy.

'I honestly can't permit it, sir,' the major said. 'Really. It's for your own safety. Please don't press the point and force me to do my duty.'

Sten was hollow inside as he turned away. He heard another burst of gunfire and what sounded like distant screams.

What the hell could he do? He thought about Milhouz and those other poor damned rich kids. Sure, he had no use for them. Would have wished them away and out of his life if he could.

If only he had returned Milhouz's calls sooner. If only he had . . .

Aw, clot!

Alex and Cind tried to soothe him as he headed back inside. There was nothing left to do now – except brace for the backlash.

Chapter Nineteen

The children of the Altaics didn't die without a fight.

More than twenty-five thousand students had packed the campus when Iskra's forces struck. It started as a feint at the barricade. Sixty club-wielding cops charged the ten-meter-high jumble of rubble.

Caught unaware, the students were rocked back. A squad of cops burst over the side and hammered around them, cracking skulls and breaking limbs.

A pair of young Suzdal broke in among them. Bodies slithering under the blows, sharp teeth ripping at tendons. The cops were driven back. They pretended to regroup for another charge.

The young barricade defenders screamed for help. Hundreds came rushing to the rescue.

At the Pooshkan Action Committee headquarters, Milhouz and the other young leaders heard the screams.

'We've been betrayed,' he shouted.

'Come on. We have to help!' Riehl said, voice breaking with alarm. She headed for the door along with Tehrand and Nirsky.

Milhouz didn't respond. He had just caught a glimpse of something out the window. Through a long alleyway between the Language and the Cultural Arts buildings, he spotted the silhouette of a tank, moving down the road that paralleled Pooshkan.

'Milhouz!' Riehl shouted again. 'Come on. We've got to stop them!'

Milhouz saw the blur of another armored track go by at speed. He calmed himself and turned to Riehl. She was hovering at the door along with Tehrand and Nirsky.

'I'm going to try Ambassador Sten one more time,' he said. 'Threaten pure hell if he doesn't stop this.'

He moved toward the com line the engineering students had installed and shot a look over his shoulder at his companions. 'Go ahead,' he said. 'I'll be right with you.'

The three rushed out.

Milhouz stopped. He turned his head to study the open door, head tilted like a feral animal. He waited a moment, listening to more screams of help from the barricades.

Then he ran to the window and opened it, flung a leg over the sill – and jumped.

At the barricades, the cops were retreating again – this time under a heavy cascade of rocks and timber and pieces of rebar.

Riehl and the two other student leaders raced onto the scene. There were cries of recognition.

At the top of the barricade, young beings were waving for them, calling their names, urging them to help rally the students for the next assault.

Riehl looked wildly back for Milhouz. Leadership was demanded, now, dammit!

'Must go to top,' Nirsky chirped.

'Up. Up. Up,' Tehrand snarled.

Still hoping her lover would show up at any minute, Riehl ran forward. Young hands grabbed her, hoisted her high, and passed her from hand to hand. Up. And up. Tehrand and Nirsky followed behind her.

She was set on her feet. Riehl peered down at the massed cop force. She turned to face the students and lifted an arm high, fist clenched.

'Freedom for the Altaics!' she screamed.

The students took up the cry. 'Freedom! Freedom!'

Above the melee Riehl heard the sound of heavy engines. She turned to see the cops parting ranks, revealing first one armored track. Then another.

The big vehicles lumbered forward. Double-timing behind them came soldiers. Weapons at ready.

The first track stopped. Turret clanked up.

An explosion . . . then another.

Canisters of tear gas arced high and plunged into the mass of students. There were shouts of pain and terror.

Eyes streaming with tears, Riehl held her ground. She shook her fists at the tracks.

Almost on cue, both tracks charged – hitting the barricade full force and cracking through it as if it were paper.

Debris burst upward.

Riehl saw the sharp piece of rebar coming at her, tumbling through the air in slow motion.

'Milhouz!' she screamed.

The rebar took her through the throat. She did a slow doll's fall off the crumbling barricade.

The soldiers opened fire.

Tehrand and Nirsky died where they stood.

Some students fled the onslaught. Others held their ground, only to be chewed apart by the soldiers' fire, or to be crushed under the tracks. Still . . . many apparachniks did their parents proud.

But in the end the soldiers flung them aside and poured onto the campus, firing magazine after magazine into the crowd. The last of the student holdouts finally broke and ran wildly for cover.

The soldiers followed.

As night fell there were still sounds of gunfire coming from Pooshkan. But not concentrated fire. Only single reports – as the soldiers hunted down the children of Jochi and shot them.

One by one.

Chapter Twenty

Poyndex felt one moment of incredible power.

He had given the Eternal Emperor orders – and the man had obeyed.

Then he caught himself. *You are a clotting fool – and worse. I thought you had changed yourself, cut that blind ambition out of your soul like it was a tumor.*

With all his strength, Poyndex closed his hand on the rusting barbed wire in front of him. The jagged metal knifed into his finger and palm. After a minute, he released his grip and examined his bloody hand. Let it infect if it is going to, he thought fiercely. Let it swell and fester. Because this crude hunger for real power you feel has almost destroyed you once. And there will not be a second chance.

Poyndex told his body he felt no pain from his hand, and shut off that nerve center's screaming. He looked across the wire, down at the Umpqua River, swirling in spring flood.

This is, he thought, the second time I have been on Manhome, the planet Earth. The first was serving the privy council, which I did well. Especially here, short-stopping that assassination team Sten led. What would have happened, what would have been different, if I had been more alert to the changewinds, and not stopped him? If I had let the privy council die?

You would not have been doing your duty.

True. But might that not have prevented . . . other events?

Who could tell, he thought. Then I would have remained just a colonel, just head of Mercury Corps. Perhaps I would never have come to the attention of the Eternal Emperor when he returned, even though that spotlight hardly showed me in the best light. Perhaps I would have been purged into retirement after the Emperor took power, as so many others have been.

Do not allow yourself to second-guess the past. Learn from it . . . but do not think it could be or should be changed. The present and the future are more important – especially this return to Earth. This comes close to the moment of triumph.

That proposal the Emperor had given him had been very thorough, for all its brevity:

It was necessary for a certain surgical operation to be performed on the Eternal Emperor. Something artificial was to be removed from deep inside his body. But the operation must be planned and conducted without the Emperor ever realizing what was going on.

To Poyndex, that was simple. He had, as he had told the Emperor, dealt fairly frequently with enemy agents who had suicide orders conditioned into them – from physical devices to programmed deathtrauma to the hardest to defuse, psychological bombs that ordered the agent's personality to self-destruct.

He had warned the Emperor that the plan would be initiated without the Emperor knowing the exact moment it began, given the suspected nature of the device in his body. Certain events would occur. The Emperor must not question them, or allow his mind to feel alarmed. He must accept whatever happened as if it were common and natural.

The Eternal Emperor had taken a long moment before agreeing.

Stage One was assembling the surgical team. Years earlier, when Poyndex had graduated from field agent through agent runner to planner, he learned he had held three major myths about the medical profession:

A) A doctor had ethics or a code requiring him to believe in and maintain the sanctity of life. The truth was that a doctor was no more or less idealistic than any other member of society. Which to Poyndex meant without any morality beyond self-interest, profit, or the drooling current beliefs of that doctor's society. It was quite easy to involve doctors in projects on the phsyiology of torture, mass euthanasia, or involuntary sterilization of society's misfits, to name only a few areas that Poyndex had been involved with over the years.

B) The only doctors who would perform 'illegal' actions were less than competent. The fact was that he had never found it difficult to recruit the highest level professionals – provided they were given the appropriate sop of 'patriotism,' or 'duty to the Empire,' or even, in extreme cases, 'duty to life.'

C) That after performing the required deed, a doctor might be stricken with guilt or even just a desire to discuss what happened. The fact was that the only guilt Poyndex had ever seen a medico evince was when the mores of the society changed without the doctor being aware of the change, the fee had not been paid, or his malpractice insurance did not cover the deed. And every doctor seemed to hate every other doctor, which kept shoptalk from ever being worrisome.

For this operation, it had taken no more than two hours for Poyndex to find his surgical team. Among them were the best and the brightest of the Empire's doctors. And all of them had been on Poyndex's payroll for years.

The cover story – which Poyndex had planted no more heavily than a casual mention to an OR nurse who was a Mercury operative – was that the operation would be performed on one of the Emperor's doubles. Everyone 'knew' the Emperor had doubles, who were sent into high-risk or high-boredom assignments. In fact, there were none and never had been, a blatant stupidity that Poyndex meant to bring up with the Emperor at an early date.

Once assembled, the team was sent to Earth. The Emperor had been right: the site was perfect.

Aeons earlier, the Emperor had decided he liked salmon fishing. He had bought from Earth's government, and from the local government of the province of Oregon, the entire Umpqua River, from its headwaters to its mouth at the Pacific Ocean. Over the decades he had also bought out everyone who lived or worked on or near the river. A few locals were permitted to live and work near the Umpqua – after all, provisions, guides, game wardens, and so forth were necessary. The Emperor then went fishing, using sites that were no more than level ground that a few tents could be pitched upon.

But on that river an industrialist, Tanz Sullamora, had also built a camp. Sullamora, however, had found he couldn't stand either the wilderness or fishing, so his camp had been turned into a luxurious retreat. Sullamora, once the Emperor's most loyal supporter/groupie, became a bitter enemy and the leader of the assassination plot. But he died when that bomb destroyed the Emperor, as well.

His secluded resort became a place where the rest of the conspirators, the self-named privy council, went for consultations.

Now . . .

Now it was where the Emperor went to take a long-needed – as the livies praised – rest from his onerous duties.

This time the Emperor never knew that he had traveled to Earth.

Days before the departure date, his food had been gently drugged with sopors. The Emperor didn't realize he was receding into a fog. He continued to perform his duties and consult with his aides on important issues.

He did not realize that these aides – none of whom he recognized – were carefully trained Mercury Corps operatives, presenting him with problems that grew simpler and simpler. Eventually they were so easy a one-celled protozoa, *Amoeba quaylus*, could have solved them. The entire scenario was a traditional operation, called a reagan/baker, devised to maintain a senile ruler in power as long as possible.

Poyndex and his technicians took the Emperor down and down, until he was unconscious. But they continued the slow dosage, now in an intravenous solution that everyone nursing the comatose being thought was just nourishment.

Poyndex was taking no chances.

Eventually his technicians reported that the Emperor was one stage above the suspended animation the early longliners had used, the animation that had killed most of the passengers and crew on those monster ships that had stumbled out from Earth for the nearest stars before stardrive had been devised, and before AM2 had been discovered to make that drive a practicality.

Poyndex then ordered the Emperor stabilized and transferred to the *Normandie*, the Emperor's yacht-battleship that officially did not even exist.

The Emperor held, very comfortably and safely, in that state. Poyndex felt a bit of pride.

Next, the nature of the device – or devices – hidden inside the Emperor's body should have been examined electronically. Poyndex could not. He was fairly sure there were no anti-examination booby traps on them. The Emperor, after all, could stride through security screens without anything happening.

But he was only fairly sure.

Therefore, feeling as if he were living in the Dark Ages, he ordered his chief surgeon to begin exploratory surgery. The surgeon was further told that the operation must be done at speed, as if he were in a trauma center, with only seconds to keep the patient from dying.

It was well that Poyndex gave those instructions. He had scrubbed and gowned and gone into the operating theater, an arena he was quite familiar with. The first incision opened the body cavity, and Poyndex saw the device. He brushed the surgeon's hand aside and held the back of his fingers against the plas ovoid. It was growing warm.

'Excise it,' he snapped.

'But—'

The surgeon's scalpel lased twice, and the device was free. Bastard, Poyndex thought. Got you before you could detonate.

'There. Another one.'

'But there's hemorrhaging!'

'Screw that! Cut!'

A second device.

'What are the vital signs?' Poyndex asked hoarsely.

'Stable.'

'Good. Doctor, open the rib cage.'

The heavy bone-cutting laser made the cut.

'There. Another one. Take it out.'

The cuts were made. Poyndex was sweating. There could be one more. But he couldn't just send in the machete team.

'Survey. Scan the medulla oblongata area.'

'Yes, sir.'

Time stopped.

'There appears to be . . . some kind of short-range transmitting device. Very short-range – one third of a meter. If you wanted an opinion, I'd say it was a very sophisticated encephalograph. But that's all it is.'

Poyndex almost sagged.

'Then that's all. You can slow down. Stabilize him. Stop the bleeding. And button him up.'

'What about these?' The second surgeon indicated the three man-made devices that had been cut out of the Emperor's body.

'Mine. You did not see them.'

The three plas objects went to immediate tech analysis.

The first devise was a sophisticated bomb, using conventional matter for the detonator and Anti-Matter Two for the explosive. It would have been enough to create a one-eighth-kilometer parking lot with the OR as ground zero. Poyndex grinned tightly. Now he knew where that mysterious blast had come from that went off microseconds after the privy council's assassin had shot the Emperor. The bomb was intended to prevent autopsies, at the very least.

The second device was a combination receiver and booby trap set to detonate if the Emperor was ever cut open. It further contained certain programmed circumstances. It took Poyndex some hours to puzzle out the purpose of the device. The electroencephalograph still in the Imperial skull would continually transmit the Emperor's thoughts. If those thoughts deviated beyond the programmed circumstances, the bomb would detonate.

Interesting, he thought. One way to keep yourself from going insane. Or . . . And he decided not to ponder further possibilities.

The third device was the most interesting. It was a very high-powered transmitter. Its activating mechanism was linked to the Emperor's vital organs. So, Poyndex thought. If the Emperor is killed, the transmitter transmits. Or, he theorized, if the Emperor is tortured into doing something he should not, or drug-conditioned into a certain pattern, or if he becomes neurotic/psychotic beyond the allowable profile – the bomb goes off and the transmitter transmits.

To whom?

To where?

And sometime later, the Eternal Emperor returns.

Poyndex was tempted to continue his investigation.

Then he caught himself.

What were the chances of the Eternal Emperor, when he recovered consciousness from this operation, ordering the death of everyone involved with this project?

Excellent.

What were the chances, even if everyone involved with this wasn't disappeared, of the Eternal Emperor ordering everyone connected with this operation brainscanned to see what they knew about this incredible secret?

Better than excellent.

Poyndex suddenly knew, with an absolute knowledge beyond experience, paranoia, or amorality, that his chances of living, if he investigated where this mysterious signal was beamed at, were far less than zero. Hating this loss of knowledge, but wanting to live even more, he personally destroyed all three devices.

He was not sure of what he had just done. Nor why the Emperor had this bomb in his body, or why he wanted it removed. It made sense for the Emperor to protect himself against kidnappers.

But . . . if he were eternal, as he most provably was, what happened when the bomb went off? How did the Emperor survive the blast?

Psychic projection?

Clot that. Next he would be accepting the wacko beliefs of the Cult of the Eternal Emperor, who thought that their ruler periodically went out to commune with Holy Spheres.

The hell with it. Now was the time to be nothing more than a supremely loyal servant.

'Sir. You are bleeding.'

Poyndex came out of his kaleidoscoping thoughts and returned the Mantis soldiers' salute. 'Thank you. I must have cut myself. I'll get it treated.'

The soldier nodded and continued her patrol, eyes sweeping the wilderness, alert for any signs that an enemy of the Empire lurked out there.

Grateful for the pain, his decision, and the interruption, Poyndex walked toward the infirmary.

He allowed himself one second of pride.

From this moment, the Emperor – aided by his servant – would no longer be controlled by the past.

*

The Eternal Emperor's eyes opened.

He found himself in a cold, sterile place. Naked.

Was he once more back on that ship? A flash of panic. Had mistakes been made? Was he now that mewling waffler he had grown to hate?

No. He felt some pain. And not the sullen muscles of rebirth.

He remembered . . .

Yes.

He must be on Earth. And Poyndex, as he had promised, had performed his duty.

The Emperor yet lived.

He allowed his mind to wander, still half-anesthetized. But even stuporous, he realized that he no longer felt watched. He no longer felt he had to guard his every thought.

The link was broken.

The eyes of the warden, the assassin, the Voice on the ship, were closed.

Now he was alive.

Now he could rule as his fate, his weird, intended.

Now he was free.

The Eternal Emperor smiled.

BOOK THREE

WALL CLOUD

Chapter Twenty-One

The massacre at Pooshkan University backblasted across the Altaics. Rumors of the tragedy burst on the streets of Rurik *as the troops were opening fire*. Sten filed this anomaly away as significant while he tried to make sense of the chaos erupting all around him.

Surrounded by Jochi troops whose purported orders were to protect the Imperial embassy, Sten sat in the eye of the storm watching events unfold, filing a blizzard of 'Eyes Only' reports.

The massacre itself he had witnessed via two teams of Frick and Fracks, which had swooped over the soldiers as they opened fire on the students. There was no question in his mind that Iskra had ordered the attack. Proof, however, would be difficult. The soldiers wore no identifying insignia on their uniforms. They were clearly human. But they could just as easily have been a rebel Jochi militia. Or even Tork.

Sten also noted that the first rumor claimed the attack was the work of a Suzdal militia unit.

This tidbit of disinformation came *as* he watched Riehl tumble off the barricade. The rumor was followed by its opposite a beat and a half later: It was the Bogazi who had committed the atrocity.

Sten, who had witnessed a great deal of blood spilled in his life, had to force himself to watch the gory drama that unfolded. He heard several young com officers retch at the sight. Even Freston, the chief of the com unit, turned away.

'Th' man's no daft . . .' Alex muttered as he watched the butcher's work on the vid screen. 'He's clottin' insane.'

Sten ignored him, as he attempted for the tenth time to get Iskra on the embassy line to demand that he call off the dogs.

For the tenth time, his call was repulsed by a low-level functionary, who said that Iskra was 'meditating' and had left strict instructions not to be disturbed.

'I'll meditate *him*,' Sten snarled. Then, to Alex: 'Get me some eyes on the palace.'

Seconds later he was patched into a pair of Frick and Fracks soaring over the Square of the Khaqans.

The news there was just as bad. A group of protesters, spurred on by the rumors of the Pooshkan massacre, was advancing on the Khaqan's palace.

His stomach churned as, instead of the expected confrontation between the mob and Jochi troops, he saw a contingent of Imperial Guards sweep out of the palace and down the steps.

They charged into the crowd, hitting like shock troops. The confrontation was violent – and brief. In moments the crowd was hammered and put to flight. As the frightened beings fled, he saw many civilian bodies heaped on the ground.

To make matters worse, many of the Imperial Guard soldiers chased after the fleeing protesters, flailing at them with riot sticks.

Cind swore. 'They're acting like clottin' cops, instead of soldiers. And bad cops at that.'

Sten made no comment. He had his emotions under an iron lid now, but there was a backbrain crawl that wouldn't go away. When this was over many fingers of blame were going to be pointing in many directions. And the Imperial Guard had just made itself a potential target.

'I want the whole station on red alert,' Sten told Kilgour. 'Notify the kitchen to keep the caff coming. And tell housekeeping to haul in some cots. Until further notice, we all work until we drop.'

Alex hustled off to kick the staff into overdrive. Sten turned back to the monitors. His eyes were already red-rimmed and scratchy. He felt Cind's soft hand touch the back of his neck.

She didn't say a word. But the light pressure gave him strength. Sten buckled down to a decidedly ugly task.

As the hours passed, tragedy mounted on tragedy.

A Suzdal militia, hatred stoked white hot by rumor, caught a Bogazi neighborhood napping. They torched it. Then they stood back and slaughtered the frightened Bogazi as they poured out of their hutches.

Revenge came almost immediately. As three Suzdal adults shepherded twenty or more cubs from their homes to a feeding hall, a group of Bogazi burst out of hiding. The Suzdal adults were dead in moments. Then the cubs. One Bogazi lifted a small cub high in the air. She split it with her beak, then swallowed it whole.

'Grandmother was correct,' she chortled to her friends. 'Suzdal good for nothing. Except eat.'

The incident was sure to kick more fuel on the fire. The Suzdal were among the most protective parents in the Empire, genetically predisposed to slaughter anything threatening their young.

More incident reports flooded in.

That evening a small Tork militia unit attacked a Jochi market-place. But the Jochians were ready. Troops leapt out to confront the Torks, who howled in surprised terror, turned, and fled. The Jochians followed. No sooner had they broken ranks, however, than a much larger Tork force burst onto the scene, striking from the rear. Two hundred plus died at the market. Most of them civilians.

On and on it went. Rurik was one enormous blood feud. Sten could barely keep up with the events. Numbly, he kept filing the reports, putting in calls to Iskra, and getting no answer. He had similar luck with the Eternal Emperor. His boss was indisposed. Sten was mildly surprised. He had never known the Emperor to be sick.

The following day, Sten stared bleary-eyed at the monitor screen as – marvel of all marvels – a *peaceful* group of citizens marched on Pooshkan. It was a mixed crowd, equally composed of the four races of the Altaics. They were carrying wreaths to lay at the site in memory of the slain students.

The group carried large, hand-lettered banners pleading for a return to peace and order in the Altaics. Some of the banners even had nice things to say about Iskra.

Sten was not surprised at what happened next. He chopped the volume and turned away from the screen as soldiers guarding the site opened fire. He looked at Cind. She stood soldier straight, jawline set firm. But her eyes were smudged dark. She gave an involuntary shudder as they both dimly heard screams of terror coming from the university.

Her mouth opened, as if she were about to speak. Then it closed again, with a sharp snap.

She wants me to make it stop, he thought. But she knows there's nothing I can do.

Sten had never felt so low. So unheroic. Not that he believed in such things. And if there were any fantasies of that sort in Cind, they had been thoroughly ground out in the course of the last few hours.

He heard Freston call his name. Sten turned.

'It's Dr Iskra, sir,' the com officer said. 'He wonders if it would be convenient to meet?'

Sten went loaded for *Ursus horribilis*. In fact, forget the grizzly. Packed in a blunderbuss, his diplomatic note to Iskra would peel the hide of *Ursus articis*, as well.

Although he didn't directly charge Iskra with ordering the massacre at Pooshkan, he did some heavy denting around the edges. He also lumped in the attack on the wreath-layers, as well as the unauthorized use of Imperial troops on civilian populations.

The wadding he had tamped the charge with was a clear threat that he would recommend that the Emperor rethink his support of Iskra.

Unfortunately, Sten knew he was creeping out on two-mil-thick ice. The importance of the Altaic Cluster was such that the three cardinal rules of diplomacy absolutely applied. A: Check with the boss first. B: Check with the boss first. And, most important of all . . . C: Check with the boss first.

Still, although he was hamstrung by his failure to reach the Emperor, Sten tromped into his meeting determined to carry off his bluff.

Iskra leapt to his feet as soon as Sten entered the room. 'Sr Ambassador,' he said, 'I protest your failure to support my government!'

Sten buried an unprofessional gape. He buttoned his lip. Raised an eyebrow. Chilly.

'Furthermore, I am going to ask the Emperor that you be withdrawn from service in the Altaics.'

'How kind of you to tell me in person,' Sten said dryly. 'I suppose your request—'

'Demand, sir. Not request.'

'Demand, then. Although I suggest you eliminate that word from your vocabulary when you address the Emperor. Back to my question. Does this . . . demand . . . have anything to do with the chaos raging outside your doors? Or is it just you don't like the cut of my formal wear?'

'I blame you for the agony my poor people are experiencing,

yes. Can you deny you and your . . . staff . . . have shown a definite lack of enthusiasm in my appointment?'

'I can. Easily. Enthusiasm is for amateurs. My professional duty is to support you. But – and this is a serious *but*, sir – my mission is to restore order to the Altaic Cluster. A mission, I must add, that is sadly in danger – if not doomed as we speak. And you, sir, must take full responsibility for this. As I so intend to inform the Emperor.'

'Then I was right,' Iskra hissed. 'You do oppose me.'

'After what happened at Pooshkan, you expect plaudits? A military band to trumpet your accomplishments?'

'You blame that – abominable action on me? Me!' Iskra made his best face of outrage. Sten would have laughed if the dispute had not been over blood.

'I'll have you know I'm sickened over the incident. I've ordered a complete investigation. Headed by a man whose reputation is above reproach: General Douw.'

Ho-ho, Sten thought. So that's the way of the land, is it? Douw had been seduced into Iskra's sphere.

'I'll inform the Emperor,' Sten said. 'He'll be . . . interested. Which is not the word I'd use, Doctor, to describe his reaction to the mess you've stepped in.'

'Bah! A stronger hand is all they need. These are my people, Sr Ambassador. You don't understand them. Blood feuds are an integral part of our history. It's a fact of our nature, and always bubbling under the surface. This is why, when your support of me is so lackluster, it only takes a small incident – such as the tragedy at Pooshkan – to threaten chaos.'

'Chaos is what you've got all right,' Sten said. 'What do you propose to do about it?'

'That is *my* concern,' Iskra snapped. 'The private business of this cluster. Remember that.'

'I'll do my best,' Sten said.

He thought about the note in his pocket, the one tearing Iskra a new defecating orifice. If he delivered it as planned, it wouldn't make his future relations with Iskra any easier.

He thought about the young people dying at the barricades of Pooshkan. Clot future relations. Sten determined at that moment to rid himself of this man. He would gather every molecule of evidence. Build a stone bucket. So when he did speak to the Emperor, he would have proof enough to hammer Iskra out of the Altaics.

Besides, the man had already declared himself an enemy. At

this point, most diplomatic rule books suggested a body blow – to the gut.

Sten pulled out the note and gave it to Iskra. 'A little bedtime reading,' he said. 'Now, if you'll excuse me . . .' He exited the room, leaving Iskra gobbling after him.

As soon as he was gone, Venloe stalked in.

'That was unnecessary,' he snapped. 'You've just made yourself a very serious enemy.'

'Him? Sten is a mere functionary.'

'Another mistake, Doctor. Believe me, he's no functionary.' With a chill, Venloe remembered his encounter with Sten and Mahoney. He was alive this moment only because they had needed him. 'He was also right about the university,' Venloe said.

'It was necessary,' Iskra said. 'As I told that fool of an ambassador, my people need a hard hand to rule them. It's all they understand. The incident at the university gave me a perfect excuse to use that hard hand. My name will be blessed for generations when this is over. Believe me. I know my place in history.'

He peered at Venloe with a slight sneer on his lips. 'You surprise me. I didn't think you'd be so squeamish over a little blood spilled for good purpose. Strange how you think you know a being.'

Venloe just grunted noncommittally. The thought crossed his mind that if his assignment were of the usual nature, just how easy it would be to kill Iskra. Right now. Without raising a sweat or leaving a sign of foul play.

'I guess you don't,' he said.

Iskra stared at him, trying to engage him in a childish battle of stare-down. Venloe's fingers itched to put them both out. Instead, he lowered his gaze.

'Good,' Iskra muttered. 'Now, I have some things I need. Desperately. I want to go over these requests thoroughly. So the Emperor will understand my requirements.'

He began detailing a massive shopping list that Venloe was sure would not be looked at kindly by the Eternal Emperor.

'I'm all ears,' Venloe said.

Sten leaned back in the seat of the gravcar. A heavy rainstorm sheeted the windows.

He was damned if he knew how to proceed next. Iskra was one of those beings that all diplomats met at least once in their careers, but were never the wiser afterward.

How did one deal with a ruler bent on his own ruin? The easy solution would be to just walk away. Unfortunately that was almost never a logical alternative.

Difficulty number one: In situations such as this, there is almost never an obvious successor. If the ruler is ruined, so is the kingdom. Which might be just ducky for all parties outside the kingdom, except for:

Difficulty number two: Suicidal rulers are always propped up by outsiders, whose own fate rests on the well-being of the threatened kingdom. In other words, nature is not allowed to take its course. If lightning strikes moral dry brush, many nationalities rush in with a fire brigade.

Sten realized that he was getting a major lesson through Iskra. The Altaics, he realized, had been doomed to their present unpleasantness the moment the first Jochians arrived in the cluster, clutching the Emperor's charter.

The charter – a fancy word for a business relationship between the Jochians and the Emperor – made them special, favored above all others. Their right to rule became as God-given as any ancient monarch. The charter eventually created the Khaqans, who forced themselves on an unwilling populace.

Without the external support of the Emperor, the beings of the Altaics would have been forced to find some other solution. There would have been bloodshed, but eventually the Jochians, the Torks, the Suzdal, and the Bogazi would have hammered out some kind of a consensus.

When he took the assignment, Sten had envisioned working out a situation that would have led to such a consensus government. He had hoped at least to build a scaffold others could stand on to hammer up a building.

Instead . . . Instead, Sten had clottin' Iskra to deal with. What kind of drakh was in his boss's mind?

Sten pulled himself back from irritation. No good to beat up on the boss's decisions. The Emperor might be eternal, but he had never claimed to be perfect. If Sten wanted him to choose a wiser course, Sten would have to help.

The driver signaled. They were approaching the Suzdal embassy, Sten's first stop. It was the first step in his plan to build an outside consensus.

As he looked out the window, one third of that plan went into the crapper.

The Suzdal embassy was empty. Some young Tork ruffians were combing through piles of hastily abandoned personal articles.

Sten slid out of the gravcar. The young beings spotted him and tensed, ready to flee. Sten waved away his security force, which had quickly piled out of its own vehicles. He walked casually up to the kids.

'Good pickings?' he asked the taller one, guessing that size might have something to do with leadership.

'Whotsit to ya?' the smallest of the Torks snarled. So much for guessing. This was not one of Sten's better days.

'Better question,' Sten said. 'What's it to you?'

He fished out some credits and flashed them before glittering little eyes. The little Tork snatched. Sten yanked his hand back.

He nodded, indicating the embassy. 'Where'd they go?'

'Clottin' home is where they went. Whaddya think?' The kid glared at the money, lips compressed. Sten crossed the young Tork's palm with a few credits.

'Tell me more,' Sten said. 'Start with when they left.'

'Three, four hours ago,' the kid said. 'We was playin' down the street, when all of a sudden there's this big clottin' bust-up. Suzdal yappin' and yippin' way they do. Gravlighters and Suzdal soldiers all over. 'Fore we knew it, they had the whole place packed up and they was gone.'

Sten fed the kitty with a few more credits. 'Anybody after them?'

'Nope. And nobody showed up later, either. Suzdal left on their ownsome all right. And they weren't talkin' scared, neither.'

'What *were* they talking about?' Sten asked, handing over more filthy lucre.

'Killin' Bogazi, whoddya think?' The young Tork was clearly astonished at Sten's woeful ignorance. 'We snuck in close, see? Checkin' drakh out for anything valuable they might be leavin' behind.

'We heard the pack leader talkin' to the crooked leg whot runs the militia. Said there was a big fight comin'. With the Bogazi. That's why they was goin' home. To help with the fight.'

The kid looked up at Sten. His eyes were old. 'I figure the Suzdal ain't got a chance,' he said. 'They're mean. But the chickens are meaner. Whatcha think? Suzdal or Bogazi?'

Sten handed over the rest of the credits. 'Do you care?'

'Clot no! Just tryin' to figure the odds. The money's on the Bogazi in our neighborhood. Ten to one. Thought maybe you'd tell me somethin' so I could shave 'em some. Get down some serious action.'

He waved the fistful of bribe money in Sten's face. 'Way I figure,' the kid said, 'guy's just gotta get a bet down any chance he gets. I mean, a person could be runnin' around lucky all day and never know it. If you know what I mean.'

'I certainly do,' Sten said. He left, thinking even less of his chances than before.

'My vision is a simple one, General,' Iskra said. 'But I think you'll agree that simplicity of concept is the first definition.'

'Without question,' General Douw said. 'This is one of your attributes I have admired from afar for years. You see a thing, a complex thing, and then with a little rearranging it is no longer complex. It is simple. It is real. It is genius.' Douw didn't have the faintest idea what he was saying. It didn't matter. The general was an expert at flattery. He sipped at the water Iskra had given him as refreshment – pretended to savor it as if it were wine.

'It's like the glass of water,' he said, grabbing for any kind of analogy at all. 'I see water, but you see . . .' His brain slipped a cog. What the clot did Iskra see? Maybe he just saw water. Personally, Douw could see a green-skinned amphibian. One that went croak, croak, croak.

'Yes. Go on,' Iskra said. 'What do I see, General?'

'A symbol,' Douw gasped out. 'That's it! Symbolism. Now who but a genius could see symbolism in a simple glass of water?' He quickly checked Iskra's face to see how this bit of verbal dancing had gone down. The doctor was beaming and nodding. Whew. Thank God.

'You strike for the heart of the matter, as always,' Iskra said. 'This is why I felt I needed you. I knew I would find a kindred spirit.'

'Absolutely,' Douw said, brushing back his silver locks with a nervous hand. 'No question about it.'

What an old fool, Iskra thought. 'You are perhaps the most respected individual in the military, General,' he said.

'Why, thank you.'

'It is only the truth. You have a reputation for loyalty. And as a fierce defender of Jochi tradition.'

'The old ways were best,' Douw said. This was a subject he could warm to quickly. 'Sometimes I think the old values have been put aside too hastily.'

'That is *exactly* my vision,' Iskra said.

'It is?'

'Of course. But it will take harsh measures to return us to the glory days of our Jochi forefathers.'

'True. How true. Unfortunate. But true.'

'However, I certainly do not wish you to become involved in the *real* unpleasantness. There are things that need to be done that I fear would tarnish the reputation of a true Jochi soldier. I will have . . . Special Duty units trained and outfitted for these tasks, and they will be responsible directly to me, and outside the military's usual chain of command.'

Douw beamed. 'How perceptive of you, sir.'

'However, I wish you to command my conventional forces in the struggle to bring peace to our glorious cluster. It will require cool thinking, and unshakable purpose.'

'Then I am your man,' Douw said. 'And thank you for the honor.'

'When our people first came to this cluster,' Iskra continued, 'they were faced with a hostile territory filled with ignorant species and a barbarian breed of humans.'

'Terrible times. Terrible,' Douw babbled.

'There were not so many of us, then.'

'How true. I've always said that myself. Not many of us in those days. But we made up for numbers with bravery.'

'And one other thing,' Iskra said.

'Right. That other thing. It was – uh—'

'Wit,' Iskra said.

'That's it. Wit. Was on the tip of my tongue.'

'To suppress those beasts – I'm sorry, I'm not with the modernists. They are beasts. Nothing more. To suppress those beasts, our ancestors adopted a tactic summed up by a simple, elegant phrase. The phrase and all it stands for, I believe, is a vital part of Jochi heritage.'

'I know the answer,' Douw said, 'but your words are much finer than mine. Please say it for both of us.'

'Divide and conquer,' Iskra said. 'We brought the beasts to their knees by that simple ploy. Our forefathers inflamed the Suzdal and Bogazi. And the Torks, as well. And we put them at each other's throats.

'We even made a tidy profit selling arms to all sides. We let them kill each other. And then we stepped in to rule.'

'By God, we should do the same thing now!' Douw smacked fist into palm, his patriotic heart aflutter. 'Divide and conquer. A return to hallowed tradition.'

'Then . . . you'll accept the post I'm offering?'

'With pride, sir,' Douw boomed. 'With pride.' He wiped a manly tear from the corner of an eye.

Menynder had a shabby little walled estate in the center of a Tork neighborhood.

Sten's professional eye noted that the shabby look was carefully cultured. The walls were chipped and vine-covered. The big entry gate was old and sagging. The garden just inside the gates was overgrown. But the security wire circling the walls was bright and new. The gate was reinforced with steel. And the garden invasion was proofed with thorny hedges or saw-toothed ferns.

Menynder's intelligence profile showed that he had money. Heaps of it, for a Tork. But he was careful not to flaunt it. Just as he had been careful to quickly make himself scarce the moment the drakh hit the fan.

'I'm in mourning,' Menynder explained as he cast the fishing line into the green waters of the pool.

Sten sat beside him on the banks of the pond. The rain had turned to baking hot sunshine. But it was cool here under the tree that shaded the old Tork's favorite fishing spot. Menynder reeled in the line, checked the bait and lure, and made another cast.

'A death in the family? I'm very sorry to hear that,' Sten said.

Menynder removed his glasses, dabbed at nonexistent tears, and replaced the glasses. 'It was a young cousin . . . He died at Pooshkan.'

Sten started to say he was sorry again, but caught a cynical glint in Menynder's eye. 'How close was this cousin?' he asked instead.

Menynder grinned. 'I don't know – seventh, eight removed. We weren't very close. Still, it was a shock.'

'I can only imagine,' Sten said.

'I'm so shaken,' Menynder continued, 'that I fear it will be at least a year before I can show my face in public again.'

'Do you really think the Altaics will calm down by then?' Sten asked.

'If it doesn't,' Menynder said, 'I'll have a relapse. Grief is a sneaky disease. It comes and goes. Comes and goes.' He reeled in his line, then cast it out.

'Like a fever,' Sten said.

'Yeah. Without the trouble of symptoms. A man can grieve and fish at the same time.'

'Funny thing about fishing,' Sten said, 'is that you look

wonderfully purposeful. No one ever bothers a person when he's fishing.'

'I get the idea I'm not the only one fishing here, Sr Ambassador,' Menynder said. He tried another spot in the pond.

'I guess I'm just trying to think of the right bait,' Sten said.

Menynder gave a firm shake of his head. 'Forget it. There aren't enough credits and honors to draw me out. I've lived a long life. I'd like to finish it out naturally.'

'Hard thing to accomplish these days,' Sten said.

'Isn't that the truth.' Menynder's line tangled in debris. He gave a flip of the rod and shook it loose. 'Frankly, I don't see that it will get better. Not in my lifetime.'

'It'll be solved,' Sten said firmly. 'One way or the other.'

'I assume you have plans for me being involved in the solution?'

'Yes, I do.'

'You're probably thinking that because I was fool enough to stick my neck out.'

'You got some beings talking together whose normal reactions are to fight instead.'

'I used to think I was good at that sort of thing,' Menynder said. He reeled in the line three clicks.

'You still are. From where I sit.'

'Rotten, useless talent. If a talent it even is. Personally, I think I'm just a clottin' good liar.'

'Some big things are going to be coming down,' Sten said. 'A long time ago – under similar circumstances – I advised a being like you to get out of the line of fire. I told him the best thing to do was develop a good hacking cough.'

'Did he take your advice?'

'He did.'

'Did he live?'

'He did. He also prospered.'

'But – you want *me* to do just the opposite?'

'Yeah.'

'You gave the other guy better advice.'

'That was then. This is now.'

'No offense, Sr Sten, but I don't have the awesome majesty of an Imperial appointment to protect me. I've got squat for security. Even if I did, this is the first place the good doctor would send the battalions with the jackboots and clubs.'

'You don't think Iskra is going to work out either?'

'Clot, no! What really slays me is that I once mentioned his name myself. Favorably. Tell your boss he fouled this one up good. But don't quote me. I'd rather skip the attention, if it's okay with you.'

'I won't lie and say you're the only hope,' Sten said. 'But you could be an important one.'

'You think I should risk my life – and my family – for some noble tilting at windmills? To save the Altaic Cluster?'

'Isn't it worth it?'

Menynder reeled in his line, thinking. Then he sighed. 'I don't know.'

'Will you help me?'

'Maybe some other time,' Menynder said.

Sten got to his feet. He looked out at the green waters of the pond, wondering why he hadn't seen even the dim shape of a fish.

'Is there anything in there?' he asked.

'Used to be,' Menynder said. 'I used to stock it every year. Then the weather got real wonky. Case you hadn't noticed. Did something to the water. Changed the balance, or whatever. All the fish died.'

'But you're still fishing.'

Menynder laughed and cast his line out again. 'Sure. You never know when you might catch something.'

Sten found Kaebak, the Bogazi foreign minister, in the embassy compound. She was lowering the flag. Kaebak was alone except for her security force. Everyone else had already departed for the spaceport. Kaebak planned to join them. Hastily.

'There's no need for this,' Sten said. 'I can guarantee the security of your embassy.'

'Bogazi not need security,' Kaebak said. 'Fear is not in us. Anger is. Suzdal forget Bogazi anger. We make them sorry they forget.'

'Why are you blaming the Suzdal for what's happening? Their pups died at Pooshkan, as well.'

'Bah. This is lie. Suzdal make propaganda. Blame Bogazi for own bad deed. This is excuse. They want war. Fine. We give them all they want.'

As far as Kaebak was concerned, the interview was over. She stepped up into her transport. Sten made one last effort.

'Come to the Imperial embassy with me,' he said. 'Let me open my intelligence files. You'll see that the Suzdal are dupes as much as the Bogazi.'

The transport lurched into life. Sten stepped back. Kaebak poked her beak out the window.

'They fool you, too. Not need to look at Suzdal lies. I go home. Help hutchmates make doggy stew.'

Sten's rotten luck persisted throughout the day and into the early hours of the next. He put in call after call for the Eternal Emperor.

But each time he was turned away with the tiresome message that the Emperor was indisposed – and no one would tell him how long this sickly state was going to last.

Sten was flying blind and in desperate need of guidance. The situation was getting worse by the hour.

Iskra, he was certain, had to go.

But there was only one being who could make that decision. The fate of the Altaics hung in the balance.

He took one last stab at it.

'I am so very sorry, Sr Ambassador,' came the soothing tones of the Imperial secretary. 'I am sure the Emperor will return your call as soon as he is able. Yes, I gave him your messages. Yes, I indicated their extreme urgency. So sorry for the inconvenience, Sr Ambassador. But I'm sure you'll understand.'

Sten ground his teeth. Where the clot was the Emperor?

Chapter Twenty-Two

'I've been meaning to have this little session with you for some time,' the Emperor said. 'The delay is unforgivable, really. I owe you and your organization a great deal.'

The old woman chortled her response. 'It is ours (giggle) to serve, Your (giggle) Eminence. After all, isn't that what the (giggle) Cult of The Eternal Emperor is all about?'

'Still. You stood by my . . . memory . . . in difficult times.'

'How could any (giggle) time be difficult,' Zoran asked, 'when you are with us (giggle) *always*?'

The Emperor made no attempt to answer. He let the silence lie there, dark as the room he had had the old woman ushered into. He had wanted to create a certain atmosphere for his task: a gloomy majesty. But Zoran's infernal giggling kept lightening the gloom. It was making him angry.

Which was a rotten way to start. She was such an odd old bird. One hundred and fifty plus years, but with the wellformed body of a young woman under her orange robes. As the high priestess (elected) of a cult, she should have been – or so he had expected – a buzz-brain. That had been confirmed by the constant giggling – until he realized that the giggling was an artifice to throw a questioner off. And her eyes blazed with more intelligence than rapture from being in his exalted presence.

'Is it true,' he finally said, 'that your, ah, organization believes I am a god?'

'A representation of the (giggle) Holy Spheres, is a better description of our (giggle) beliefs, Your Majesty,' Zoran said.

'Then . . . you *don't* worship me as a god.'

'Worship is such a (giggle) nondescriptive word, Your (giggle) Eminence. We don't sacrifice (giggle) fat lambs, or our first (giggle) born. But we do (giggle) honor you.'

'As a god?'

'As an eternal (giggle) being.'

'Dammit, woman! Am I a god, or am I not?'

The giggling ceased. Zoran sucked in her breath. The Emperor was spooking her. She hadn't expected a halo to be surrounding his exalted presence when she entered the room. Actually, she had expected a sort of ordinary-looking human. Which he was – although he was even better-looking and taller in person than on the livies.

What was upsetting her – besides the darkness of the room, which she assumed was for her benefit – was the Emperor's eyes. They never looked at her directly, but shifted from side to side. Endlessly. It was almost . . . pathological. Thinking this bothered here even more.

'Excuse my irritation,' the Emperor said. 'Heavy matters of state and all.' He leaned toward her, smiling his most charming smile. Zoran noticed, however, that his eyes still didn't rest. 'Will you forgive my rudeness?'

'Oh, Your Majesty,' Zoran said, returning his charm with her best gush, 'it is I who must beg you for forgiveness. I'm just a silly old woman. And you are being so very patient with me.'

The Eternal Emperor grunted. This was better. He noticed the giggling had stopped. Better still.

'Now, perhaps you would be so kind as to explain this god business to me?'

'Oh, certainly, sir. If I sounded obscure, it is only habit. There are so many different types of beings in the order. The word *god* doesn't translate the same to every manner of person.'

'This is true,' the Emperor said. He prided himself on his knowledge of obscure lore.

'In human terms, however,' Zoran continued, 'I suppose god is an accurate description of your holy self.'

The Emperor laughed. 'Imagine. Me – a god.'

'Oh, but we imagine it all the time, Your Eminence,' Zoran said. 'In fact, all members of the Cult of the Eternal Emperor are *required* to imagine this twice a day. In our prayers. To you.'

'How very interesting,' the Emperor said, eyes narrowing into a smile . . . but shifting, shifting. Back and forth. Back and forth. 'In fact this is one of the more interesting conversations I've had in some time.'

'So happy to be able to amuse you, Your Highness,' Zoran said.

'Tell me, how many beings actually believe in – ha-ha – me?'

'Thousands upon thousands, Your Highness. Possibly even millions.'

'Millions, mmh?'

'Accurate figures are difficult at the moment, Your Majesty. But I can say our membership reached record numbers during your, uh, absence. They soared even more upon your return. For a time.'

The Emperor's lips tightened. 'You mean there's been a falloff?'

'Yes, Your Highness. I'm so sorry to report. But it was only to be expected. Beings are so weak. And they got used to you being back.'

'So soon?' the Emperor hissed.

'It is only being nature, Your Majesty. Also, our treasury isn't what it used to be.'

The Emperor knew about her past funding. It had secretly come from Kyes, the only intelligent member of the Council of Five. Zoran had not been aware of Kyes's real purpose. The Emperor intended to keep it that way.

'What would it take to, uh, increase enthusiasm among your congregation?'

'Very little, Your Highness. I tell all potential donors that members of the cult are the most dedicated in the Empire. They are ordinary beings, who live useful, productive lives by day. In their spare time they shed their worldly costumes for robes and spread word of your glory to all who will listen.'

'In other words, no middle-beings skimming the donations,' the Emperor said.

'Exactly, Your Highness. Ninety percent of every credit donated goes directly to the cause. Only ten percent goes for administration, transportation, mail, that sort of thing.'

'Remarkable,' the Emperor said. He meant it. He had also had his agents confirm this as part of an intensive investigation of the cult.

He pulled a fiche out of his desk and handed it to Zoran. 'I've had my people do a little . . . research. You'll find the results here. There's a breakdown – region by region – of my entire Empire. As well as a profile of my most, shall we say, *appreciative* subjects.'

Zoran found her hands shaking as she took the fiche. She quickly covered the reaction. 'How can we ever thank you, Your Majesty?'

'Oh, it's nothing. Merely a little assistance for your good works. Now . . . to the matter of funding. There can be no connection between us, you understand?'

'Yes, Your Majesty. It would be . . . unseemly.'

'Quite. You'll be contacted shortly. A large donation will be made available. Put it to good use. There will be more, later. When it's needed.'

'Yes, Your Highness.'

'I'm glad we understand one another,' the Eternal Emperor said.

Zoran was not so glad. This was proof, she thought, that it is not always wise to pray so hard for a thing. Because there was a great danger your prayers might be answered.

And now she didn't dare reject it.

Chapter Twenty-Three

'Ah hae observed,' Alex observed, 'a wee miracle.'

'You're learning to talk right?'

'Hae Ah ripped y' smeller away, recent?'

Sten ostentatiously protruded his tongue, felt his nose's continued presence, and shook his head. Kilgour was a brightener, as always – one of the reasons he had been such a prized member of Mantis.

Besides his seemingly innate capabilities as a murderer . . .

Alex handed Sten a fiche. Sten dropped the fiche into a viewer. It was the Eyes Only weekly report that Jochi police commanders received. He saw nothing beyond the usual crop of homicides, brutalities, and greeds.

'Y' c'n scan i' y' wish, but Ah'm noo a walkin't breathin't abstract.'

'GA.'

'Thae's arsenals all o'er Jochi bein' ripped, wee Sten. Some copshops, but mostly military. Thae's tearaways beyon't count oot there.'

'Somehow, I'm not surprised,' Sten said dryly. 'Given what we're in the middle of, if I were a resident of this sorry-ass land, I'd be looking to acquire a small equalizer. Such as,' he went on, 'a *Perry*-class battlewagon. And that'd be for a backup gun.'

'Hae a drink, skip. Cind, pour the wee lad a dram. He's wanderin't. He's discons'late an' forlorn, nay, fivelorn, 'cause th' braw Emp dinnae call him back.

'Y' ken, lass, th' problems thae command bring't. Ah reck thae wae a time when Sten wae happy, dancin't i' thae streets, celebratin' nae but a full belly, a empty bowel, a pint backed up ae th' barman an' ae warm blankie t' pass out in.

'Noo, he's bein't cynical an' takin't th' long-range view. He's plain forgot thae'll be no t'morrow unless Ah will it.'

'*You*, Alex?' Cind wondered pointedly, as she slid the decanter over. 'You mean you're really the Prime Being?'

'A' course,' Alex said, pouring rounds of stregg. 'An' Ah can prove it. I' this stregg's poison't, an Ah go int' convulsions, writhin' aboot like Ah'm Nessie, an' croak, thae'll be no t'morrow. Right?'

'Not for you, anyway.'

'Ah. Th' stregg's nae poison't, so you lightarses c'n drink an' keep up. An thae's th' proof. If thae's no t'morrow f'r me, an' Ah'm th' most important one, thae's no t'morrow f'r anyone, right?'

Sten and Cind looked at each other. Obviously Kilgour was at least two streggs up on them.

'Noo,' Kilgour continued, 'back t' thae armories bein't thieved. All report'd i' th' class'fied sum'ry ae events th' topper coppers hae, which Ae 'mediately arranged f'r us to get, just after Ah guineapigged thae' local brew an' found it nae fit f'r man, beast, nor Campbell.

'Y' ken an oddity aboot thae thefts, boss. Weapons bein't ripped right, left an' straight clottin' up, but thae's no report ae kill't security.'

'Oh.'

'What is this "oh,"' Cind wondered.

'It's real hard,' Sten explained, 'to break into an armory that's supposedly guarded by the army or the national reservists or whatever, without some patriotic sod objecting to said breaking into, which should have produced some old semiretired sergeant type playing hero and either gunning down or getting gunned down.'

'Aye. Th' clottin' army's in on the deal.'

'Hell,' Cind said. 'Maybe I better stick to straight soldiering. This special operations drakh like you two specialize in makes you cynical.'

'Ah mentioned thae,' Alex said, 'aeons ago, back ae Newton, when y' wanted t' be Sten's handholder when he wae slippin' onto Prime.'

'You did. I should have listened.'

Sten himself wasn't listening to their back-chat. 'I would not mind a little independent action,' he said. 'First, it'd be good for my morale. Second, it'd be nice to advise these local clots the world isn't marching to their particular jodie; and third, I don't like the idea that this local goddamned military thinks they can set up a private terrorist organization – or anyway have one at their beck and call. Let's find out where these guns are going.'

Cind looked skeptical. 'What do we do? Frick and Frack every arsenal that's still unraided? Takes a lot of sensors.'

'Nope. They've got the motive, we'll give them the opportunity. We'll use the gambit that I, hem, hem, call the Ploy of the Singing Gun.'

'Zeegrade livie,' Cind said.

'Not at all. All we need—'

'Is this,' Kilgour finished, sliding a willygun onto Sten's desk. 'I' th' clots are lookin' f'r any gun, Ah suspec' thae'll be hemorrhagin' their wee hearts oot frae a bonnie official Imp-issue bang-stick, aye? Ah hae th' thought Ah'm right, since thae's been three villains lurkin't 'crost frae th' side gate's guard post frae a couple nights, noo.'

'You never let me be clever, Mr Kilgour.'

'Och, boss. Ah dinnae ken thae's what y' were doing. 'Sides, y' still hae furlongs ae room t' be clever. Such ae, who's goin' t' bell th' cat?'

'We'll just – hellfire and damnation.'

'Aye. Ah dinnae trust th' embassy security staff. Colonel Jerety's Guards dinnae hae th' brains t' understand whae's intended. Th' Bhor'd most likely cut their beards off i' y' suggested th' idea to them. An' Ah *know* the Gurkhas'd flat tell you to pack your bum wi' salt an' piddle up a rope.'

Sten nodded. Kilgour was right. 'I would pay good money for two lousy sneaky, evil Mantis types who'd plant this for me.'

'I'm not sure what's intended,' Cind said, 'but I'll go.'

'Nae. Th' oppo's got y' pegged too close, Ah reck.'

'Mr Kilgour. They'd *never* think the ambassador's ace boon would be out on a night like this, would they? Especially wearing soldier-type gear.'

'Ah, boss, Ah tried that one, too. But 'twill nae play. E'en in disguise, thae'll see m' comfortable bulk,' and Alex patted his solid midsection proudly, 'think Ah'm an ol' soldier, an' nae fall frae such a gimmick. E'en on a night thae's as blust'ry ae this one.

'But now, i' thae peer oot, an' see a young so'jer, a wee lad, who's taken on a dram too much a' th' canteen, an' somehow's walkin't his post i' a military manner or so . . .'

'Kilgour, planting a weapon's something they give you when you're still a Mantis trainee. You want me, Ambassador-type Sten, to—'

'It's braw, lad, t' rediscover an' redefine y'r roots. Teaches humility.'

'Bastard.'

'Y' been talkin't t' m' mum again.'

'Don't wait up. Just leave me some stregg.'

'Maybe,' Cind said. 'I'm going to need a couple three more while Kilgour tells me I really do know what's going on.'

'On wi' y' lad. 'Tis late, th' relief's goin't oot in a few minutes, an' Ah suspect th' sincer'ty ae the boyos 'crost th' street. Ah'll put a Frick ae y'. Sure th' next Mantis reunion th' tape'll be a big hit.'

Sten gestured obscenely, wanted another stregg, but decided not. It was hard to play drunk if you really were brain-burned. Besides, he had to find a security guard's uniform that fit.

Less than an hour later, the Imperial security platoon walked its rounds in a formal manner. The platoon was brought to a halt at each post. An order was bellowed by the watch commander. The relieved guard saluted, came to port arms, and doubled to the rear of the formation. The new guard also saluted and went to his post. Then the platoon moved on.

The new guard walked his post in a military manner for a while, then stopped to relieve himself. Across the wide avenue, the two watchers noted that he set his weapon down and steadied himself against a wall with one hand before he did.

The guard secured his fly and turned. Then he remembered the willygun, hastily turned back, and brought it back to shoulder arms. He walked a few paces, then the weapon evidently became uncomfortable. Against standing orders, he loosened the sling and carried the weapon over his shoulder.

He walked his rounds twice more. One of the watchers thought he saw the glint of a container at the man's lips, and certainly his pace seemed to get a bit more erratic. The guard returned to the gate and hunched into an alcove against the wind, a few meters away from the post's sentry box. The guard was motionless for a few minutes.

The two men exchanged glances. The first started to whisper

something, and the sentry box's com buzzed. And buzzed. And buzzed. The guard roused himself, stumbled hurriedly to the box, and answered the com.

The willygun sat, momentarily forgotten, in the alcove – and the sentry had his back to it. By the time the guard finished his loud and laborious explanation and shut the com off, the willygun had vanished.

Kilgour, watching a Frick-screen from dry, warm, and semi-drunken comfort in Sten's office, waited a few more minutes before activating Phase Two, which was the sergeant of the guard finding the sentry drunk and the weapon missing and ordering him to durance vile.

He poured Sten a double when he heard the sentry coming down the passageway.

Now for Phase Three, which could take place at any time. Buried in the butt of the willygun was a small transmitter. It was in RECEIVE mode at present. In an hour or two, after it had been moved to wherever the thieves were dumping the stolen arms, Kilgour would activate that transmitter for a directional signal. And, whether the gun had been stolen by profit-oriented thieves or by one or another of the private army members, it would end up in an interesting place.

At that point Sten and Alex could decide what Phase Four might be.

'Clean, lad. Clean like the old days,' he congratulated Sten as he entered the office and sank into a chair.

'Clot the old days. Damned wind goes straight to the bone. Where's Cind?'

'Th' lass said she c'd do a better lush'n both of us workin' tandem. An' she muttered some'at aboot some old warrior needin't his bones warmed.'

Sten grinned and slid the untouched stregg over to Kilgour. 'Then I'll be saying good night, Laird Kilgour. I'm retiring to meditate on the sudden benefits of old warrior-hood.'

'Aye. An' Ah'll be thinkin't, i' m' celibate mis'ry, ae whae nastiness com't next.'

The next nastiness, not surprisingly, was provided by the charming beings of the Altaics and was far bigger than a bugged weapon in some death squad's possession.

Admiral Mason, even more grim-faced than usual, informed Sten of the events. There had been little for him or the *Victory* to do of late – praise some benevolent godlet who must have gotten lost and passed through the Altaic Cluster – and so Sten had ordered Mason to assign his ships out to various ELINT duties through the cluster.

Mason had objected, mostly because it was Sten doing the ordering, but had shut up when Sten pointed out that he trusted absolutely no one here in the Altaics including the embassy's own intelligence sources and staff – who, if they had been efficient, certainly should have filed earlier warnings on what had happened.

Mason reported formally, requesting permission to speak to Sten alone. Sten ran a secretary, a code clerk, and his protocol chief out, and sealed the office from all electronic surveillance. This sealing automatically alerted Kilgour to eavesdrop from his office next door.

Mason, without preamble, set up a small viewer and keyed it on. A holograph formed on Sten's desk. It showed the barricades set up at the main entrance to Pooshkan University, the students manning them, and then the students being attacked. The livie, blurry and short, purportedly had been made by a tourist from another world whose cab had gotten lost and ended in the middle of the melee. The livie was a forgery, of course – it did not show the armor that the military had used in smashing the students, and the attackers now wore plain coveralls rather than issue army uniforms.

'You have seen this?' Mason said.

'I have. Once an hour for the last week on every pirate broadcast around.'

'Version B,' Mason said, and dropped in another fiche.

The same scene, except this time there weren't many humanoids at the university. Now, the barricades were manned by Suzdal pups – and the attackers were Bogazi.

'Wonderful,' Sten said. 'Where'd you get this version?'

'As per your orders, I punted the *San Jacinto* out to run a bigear between the Suzdal and Bogazi. They picked this up on an open broadbeam that any of the Bogazi worlds could pick up.'

'Would you care to bet,' Sten said, 'that if the *San Jacinto* had waited around for a while it could've snared the same livie, but with the Bogazi as victims?'

'No bet. Sir.' The *San Jacinto* was another of Sten's secret advantages – the destroyer was brand new, named after the spy ship that had been the first Imperial warship officially destroyed by the Tahn. The DD consisted of weapons, engines, and sensors, and in fact was only a marginally more liveable if vastly larger version of a tacship.

'So everybody's propaganda machine has turbochargers on,' Sten said. 'How long until the crusade starts will be – oh. You have more.'

Mason did – but this was far too touchy for anything other than verbal from the *San Jacinto*'s captain to Mason and thence to Sten.

The jihad was already under way. Two full Suzdal fleets – one the official fleet that the Khaqan had permitted for 'local security,' the second a ragtag of armed transports, smugglers, and perimeter patrols – were assembling.

Amid the intership and -system raving, the Imperial ship's analysts had determined the target. The Suzdal proposed nothing less than a full destruction raid on the Bogazi's capital world. The cancer must be excised to its roots, no matter the cost on either side. The Bogazi had, for far too long, been allowed to . . .

'Allowed to attack, burn, chop, destroy, eviscerate, et cetera, et cetera, et cetera,' Sten said. 'And of course the equally level-headed and pragmatic Bogazi are massing to defend their realm.

'The defense, once it is successful, will become a to-the-last-fowl attack on the vile hounds of Suzdal, correct?'

'Yes, sir.'

'This job gets more and more pleasurable by the minute. Kilgour. In with you.'

Alex, without bothering to explain, was through the door.

'You've got the fort. Mason and I are going to wander out and prevent a pogrom.'

'Yessir.' Kilgour was at attention. If he was angry at being excluded, Alex was too consummate a professional to show it around an outsider.

Mason's expression was incredulous for one beat before it, too, froze into military attention. 'Are you assuming command?'

'I am, Admiral.'

'Very well. I must caution you there is an inadequate amount of time for any Imperial reinforcements to reach us before the Suzdal and Bogazi will be in contact. I already ran the progs.'

'So I figured, as well,' Sten said. 'Not that we'd be authorized backup anyway – our Empire is spread fairly thin these days if you hadn't noticed.

'So we'll just pick up some indigenous junk, and you, me, and the *Victory* will clean some clocks.

'Shall we saddle up, Admiral?'

*

'Am I right, Alex, in not getting pissed that Sten left you, me, the Gurkhas, and the Bhor in place because he's officially still here in residence?'

'See, Major Cind? Y're learnin't t' think. Another lifetime a three, an' y'll actually be allowed t' hae an idea.'

'Clot off, Kilgour.'

'Thae's clot off, *Mister* Kilgour t' you. Dinnae y' ken, Ah'm noo th' ambass'dor designate, an' deservin' wee respect.'

'Exactly what you're getting. Very wee respect . . .'

Boredom has killed more soldiers than bayonets.

It was what killed the Tukungbasi brothers. Not just their own boredom, but their section sergeant had grown a little careless, as had the platoon leader and company commander, up through Colonel Jerety. Providing security for Dr Iskra and the palace of the Khaquans had become a routine task.

The Tukungbasi brothers, in their first posting to a combat unit, were not happy. They had not joined the Guard to be used as honor guards or riot policemen. They never knew that no one in that Third Guards' battalion liked the assignment, especially the careerists. But, being professionals in a professional outfit, no matter that infantrymen *never* made good peacekeepers, they kept their mouths shut and soldiered.

Soldiered, kept their barracks and equipment spotless, drank the barely palatable local beer in the on-base canteen, and bitched.

Especially about the restrictions, which made no sense to the soldiers. They had been welcomed to Jochi, had they not? So why were they quarantined in their assigned quarters and recreation areas, which were sealed and closely guarded?

Maybe Jochi was a little rough, but they were combat troopies, weren't they? They were in no jeopardy, so long as they watched themselves.

The soldiers didn't realize that there had been too many livie minutes shown of them exerting the minimum-but-necessary force to keep Dr Iskra safe, and also of them being used to prevent street fights from building into full riots. And they certainly weren't aware of the commentary that frequently accompanied that footage, let alone the stories that were created, built, and spread in the alksoaks and caff shops of Rurik.

Boredom . . .

Fortunately, the Tukungbasi brothers had a friend. One of the old women who worked in the canteen always greeted them with a smile and a bad joke. She said she was sorry they couldn't get out and meet the people of Jochi. Especially her granddaughter.

She showed them a holograph.

Both brothers agreed that the restrictions were more than a pity – they were terrible injustices. That woman in the holograph was very beautiful. The old woman asked if they would like to write her a note. One of them did. The note was returned. The young woman really wanted to meet the brother – and mentioned, in passing, that she had a girl friend who felt the same. Both of them were sorry they were natives of such a stupid world like Jochi, and wished they could have a chance to meet some real men from the outside. From worlds where things happened.

The brothers Tukungbasi, coming from a very rural backwater planetoid, were flattered.

The notes from the young woman and her friend grew more interesting. The Tukungbasi brothers lost all interest in any romance/lust with fellow soldiers. None of the women in the battalion – at any rate none who weren't already attached – could compare in beauty, let alone in suggested areas of romantic expertise.

One off-shift day, a note told them to walk near the perimeter wire. On the other side, tantalizingly close, within one hundred meters, were the two young women. Very beautiful, indeed. The young women waved, and it nearly killed the Tukungbasis not to acknowledge those waves.

They determined to get beyond the wire.

They could be out at dusk and back before dawn, their fantasies fulfilled. They started looking for mouse holes.

And since the Guards unit was infantry, not security specialists, and the perimeter was set to keep outsiders from getting in, not the obverse, they found one.

All that was necessary was to wire across one of the robot sniffers and slip out after the roving patrol passed. Of course that patrol had become routine, as well.

Beyond the wire they slipped out of their night-cammies and stashed them in an entryway. They admired each other, resplendent in full walking-out uniform. Everybody loves a man in uniform . . .

The Tukungbasis, inexpert in seduction, had at least decided to bring a bit of a present. They had bought two bottles of alk in the commissary, a brand neither had been able to afford. But since they had nowhere to spend their pay, both men were flush. Besides, this evening would be special.

The old woman in the canteen had given them a map to her granddaughter's apartment. Neither Tukungbasi thought it a bit odd that the old woman was actively conniving in the seduction of her granddaughter – the barracks rumors had already determined that anybody in the Altaics would do anything to anybody.

Not far from the truth – but not at all what the rumors intended.

The woman lived in an upper story of one of those vertical slum apartments. The Tukungbasis should have found it odd that the building was the only one in the row with a clearly marked address sign and an entryway light that wasn't shattered.

They found the apartment and tapped on the door.

They heard a feminine giggle and a sultry voice. 'It's not locked.'

The older brother turned the handle. The door swung open. He saw a shabby couch, a table, and two flickering candles. Then two shadows loomed on either side of the doorway, a filthy blanket was over his head, his arms were pinned at his side, and he heard a choked gurgle from his brother.

That was all he saw.

They burned his eyes out as a start.

The three sentries walking their post at the main entrance to Iskra's palace found the Tukungbasi brothers.

Their bodies were suspended from two hastily erected tripods about fifty meters outside the perimeter.

They were identified by their absence at a shouted emergency muster.

Their torturers had left them otherwise unrecognizable.

There was no sane reason, a grim Colonel Jerety growled to his staff, for these young soldiers to be killed.

Which was exactly the reason they had been slaughtered.

They were the first.

'I have a question, Mr Kilgour.'

'GA, Major.' For some reason Cind was being formal, and Alex followed her lead.

'When someone is arrested, and held for trial, isn't it customary for them to be allowed some kind of representation? Even if the trial's going to be rigged? Even here on Jochi?'

'Ah'd so think.'

'And isn't it normal for a prisoner to be allowed some kind of communication with his people? Even here on Jochi?'

'Thae's a leap in logic Ah'll no make, gie'n thae nature ae these charmin't folk we're dealin' with.

'Stop playin' riddle-me, Major.

'Wha hae y' come up wi?'

Before Cind could continue, Alex started swearing. He had figured it out.

Cind had become curious as to what had happened to those beings purged by Dr Iskra in time past. Beings Iskra had guaranteed would be brought to trial.

She had heard nothing – and a quick subject scan through the logged media in the embassy records had also produced nothing. Nor did Sten's own highly experienced com officer, Freston, remember hearing anything.

She then checked with Hynds, the already-in-place Mercury Corps station chief. After the ambush in the slums, Hynds had lost complete faith in what little analytical abilities he had and now rated all his sources either Grade III: unreliable; IV: possibly doubled by the opposition; or V: double agent.

He did have three assets in the military, all low-grade and all out of the main circuits. Hynds contacted them. All of them were terrified, none of them would volunteer to find out any data, and none of them had heard anything about what had happened to the soldiers and bureaucrats who had been arrested.

Save one thing: They were, just as Dr Iskra had told Sten, being held in Gatchin Fortress, far north of Rurik.

Kilgour rolled Cind's data around his mind. 'Umm.'

'You real busy?'

'Aye. Y' checked th' weather?'

'I did. Pack a parka.'

Chapter Twenty-Four

'We have the full projection – prog sixty-five percent accurate – in the battlechamber, if you wish to see it, sir.'

'Negative, Admiral,' Sten said. 'I sure as hell don't have your skill at deciphering blinking dots of light – and the digest box tells me just how shafted we are.'

'I await your orders.'

Sten had had about enough of Mason's behavior. 'Admiral? If I may speak to you privately?'

Mason nodded for the officer of the deck to take the con and followed Sten into the admiral's day cabin.

'Admiral,' Sten began, 'I directly requested you for this assignment believing you were enough of a professional to follow orders and leave personalities out of it.

'I was wrong. From the time that we arrived on Jochi, you've behaved like a sulking bratling who's just got his bars and who thinks that makes him God.'

'Ambassador—'

'We'll start with that. My civilian rank is meaningless. I have never resigned my military rank, nor asked to be placed on reserve status.

'On Jochi, you asked if I was assuming command. I said I was. Therefore, referring to me by my military rank is perfectly acceptable.

'You will remain silent, Admiral Mason. And I would appreciate your coming to attention. I have neither the time nor the energy to get into a testes-measuring contest with you, nor is it necessary. If you wish, we will step out of this cabin, and I will relieve you of your command in front of your staff and the officers of the

Victory. You will find that order will be considered quite legal, and will be considered admissible procedure at your court martial.

'Do you wish that?'

Mason remained silent.

'You will, until advised otherwise, refer to me as Admiral. I, in turn, respect your rank, and will continue to channel my orders through you as suggestions. I have no intentions of undermining your authority. Nor do I think it admirable for you to continue to behave in such a childish manner. You lessen yourself and your rank in the eyes of your subordinates.'

That got the clot. Mason flushed, stiffened, and took a moment to bring himself back to corpselike control.

'That is all I have to say. Do you have any comments or suggestions?'

'No. No, sir.'

'Good. This problem will not repeat itself. Now. Shall we go out there and start keeping the peace?'

Mason's salute sonic-snapped; he about-faced and stalked back out onto the bridge.

Sten allowed himself a grin. Hell, all those absurd cliches that had been snarled at him as he rose through the ranks still worked, given that the person on the receiving end really believed all that drakh.

Oh, well.

He followed Mason – promising himself that when this was all over he *would* decoy the bastard into a dark alley and black-jack him for a week and a half.

Sten's next action was to 'request' that Admiral Mason assemble his top four staffers and the *Victory*'s XO in a conference chamber and link, on secure screen, the skippers of the escort ships.

'Gentlebeings,' Sten said without preamble, 'the situation is pretty obvious.'

There were nods from the officers.

The *Victory* was plunging through a rift between two rich open clusters. On a screen corrected for human eyes, human spatial prejudices, and human conditioning, the tiny fleet was flashing into darkest night, with high-banked lightclouds on either side. A more detailed screen would show tiny subsidiary splotches of light to the left and right of the *Victory*'s projected orbit. These were, respectively, the Bogazi hastily assembled fleet(s?) ready to defend their capital world and cluster on the left; and, to the right, in the middle of the darkness that was the rift, the attacking

Suzdal fleets. The battlechamber, of course, would show each and every world and ship, to the limits of its preset range.

The *Victory* would go hey-diddle-diddle, straight up the middle between the two fleets, in—

'Contact timetick,' Sten requested.

'Rough estimate, two ship-days, sir. Exact—'

'Not necessary. Thank you, Commander. Is there any data suggesting they know we're inbound?'

'Negative, sir.'

That was unsurprising – one continuing advantage Imperial ships had was vastly superior sensory systems. And one very secret gimmick: before any AM2 was released to non-Imperial sources it was given a 'coating' made from a derivative of Imperium X. Any non-Empire ship on stardrive would produce a slight purple flare on Imperial screens, a flare that could be picked up at a far greater range than the unaltered Imperial drive signature. It wasn't much – just enough of an edge to win a war every now and then.

'The object of our little game,' Sten began, 'is obviously to keep our Suzdal and Bogazi allies from slaughtering each other. And, incidentally, to keep either or both of them from deciding that anybody who breaks up a bar brawl between friends deserves a good one upside the head.'

There were suppressed smiles. Admiral Mason did not give briefings like this.

'Right,' Sten continued. 'Obviously the only way that we can accomplish this is with pure guano. Fortunately, Admiral Mason is, as you all know, one of the most skilled Imperial leaders in deception.'

Sten really wanted to phrase it differently and say that Mason was fuller of drakh and therefore more guano-qualified than almost any admiral he knew, but he refrained.

'He and I discussed our problem, and he had some interesting plans. I had a couple of ideas that might be worth considering. There will be five stages to our plan. Stage One is appropriately evil; Stage Two is honorable; and Stage Four might give someone here a medal or two. Stage Five will be pure naked dishonesty, which I shall implement.'

'Stage Three, sir?' The question came from the captain of the destroyer *Princeton*.

'That's my own cheap idea,' Sten said. 'All hands aboard the *Victory* have been spending their off-shifts working on it.'

Sten flexed his fingers unconsciously. 'All hands' was no exaggeration – his own itched from metal fragments and real wood splinters embedded in fingers and palms.

'We'll get to that in time. Stage One we will begin immediately, while the briefing continues. Order all weapons officers and all Kali crews to action stations.'

The Kali missiles, now on their fifth generation, were monster ship-killers. The Kali V class were nearly thirty meters long by now, having grown not only in expense but in size as each generation was given newer and more sophisticated tracking, homing, ECM, and 'perception' suites. Power was from AM2 – the Kalis were, in fact, miniature starships. All that had not been necessary to improve from generation to generation was the payload. Sixty megatons was still enough to shatter any ship on any military register. Even the *Forez*, the Tahn battleship that remained the mightiest warship ever 'launched,' had been rendered hors de combat by Kalis.

The Kali was 'flown' into its target under direct control by weapons officers. The control system was helmet-mounted and used direct induction to the brain. Actual control had progressed from the old manual joystick and tiny throttle to involuntary or voluntary neural reaction from the 'pilot.' The Kali could also be set to use other, automatic homing systems. But those were only used under special circumstances – weapons officers were chosen for their killer instincts, second only to potential tacship pilots, and they preferred playing cheater kamikaze.

Stage One was a launch of all available Kalis.

They burst out from their launch tubes on the *Victory* and its destroyers at full drive for thirty seconds, and then power was shut down. The missiles lanced ahead of the Imperial squadron.

Right behind them came the *Victory*'s tacships, under the same full power/cut power/run silent orders.

This was Stage One – Sten's hole cards.

Stage Two waited for some time, until watch officers reported alarums from the Bogazi fleet. They had 'seen' the oncoming unidentified ship that was the *Victory*. Since they were waiting for the Suzdal, their sensors were slightly more efficient, not masked by their own drive emissions. Sten waited a couple of ship-hours, having ordered that no response be made to any challenges from either Suzdal or Bogazi, then assembled his human actors for the next part of the plan.

All Bogazi and Suzdal com channels were blanketed by the *Victory*'s powerful transmitters.

All receiving vid screens showed:

The well-known Imperial Ambassador Sten. Standing on the bridge of a warship, in full and formal garb. He was flanked by two equally grim-faced officers, Mason and his XO, also in full dress uniform.

The broadcast was very short and to the point. Sten informed both sides they were in violation of Imperial and Altaic treaties of long standing, as well as civilization's common agreements of interplanetary rights. They were ordered to return immediately to their home worlds and make no further aggressive moves.

Failure to respond would be met with the severest measures.

The broadcast was not meant to convince, or even to threaten. It was merely a pin in the map to legitimize the real bludgeon Sten had prepared.

The one he hoped nobody figured out was made of metal foil and lathes – quite literally.

The response was as expected.

The Suzdal did not answer the cast, either from their fleets or from their home worlds. The Bogazi, slightly more sophisticated, broadcast a warning that all neutral ships should stand clear of given coordinates. Any intrusion into this area would be met with armed response. Any errors might be regretted but would be considered within the acceptable parameters of self-defense.

There was no response from the *Victory*.

Sten hoped this would worry both sides.

Another timetick. It would be four ship-hours until the *Victory* would be directly 'between' the two enemies.

And they, in turn, would be in range of the *Victory* in five hours, and each other in twelve.

The situation was developing in an interesting manner.

'Three hours, sir. And the Bogazi fleet is now under drive.'

Sten rose from the weapons couch he had asked to borrow for a nap. This was calculated bravado, intended to prove to all the young troopies that Sten was so confident that he could doze before action.

Of course, he had not slept.

What bothered him was that in the old days he actually had nodded off every three or four times he tried the ploy.

Mason came out of his day cabin. 'We're ready, sir.'

'Very well.'

Mason came quite close to Sten. 'You didn't sleep, either, did you?'

Sten's eyes widened. Was Mason actually trying to be friendly? Had that absurd reaming-out caused the admiral to make an attitude check?

Naah. Mason was just setting Sten up so, come another time, he would be the one waiting in that dark alley with the sap.

'Perhaps we might begin Stage Three,' he said.

'I shall give the orders.'

Stage Three was a truly monstrous bluff.

Back on Jochi, Sten had run a fast list of ways to make people unhappy. He dimly remembered one, told as a joke but also as a mind-jog, back in Mantis training. The story went that aeons earlier, a young guerrilla officer was trying to delay a military convoy. It must've been in the dark ages, because the vehicles were evidently ground-bound, and there was no mention of air cover. The convoy had armor and heavy weapons. The guerrilla officer had twenty men, only half of them armed.

The guerrilla could have thermopylaed nobly and slowed the convoy for five minutes at the cost of his entire band. Instead, he looted a nearby farmhouse. He took all of the dinnerware in the house and carefully positioned each plate, facedown, in the roadway.

Land mines. Sten had objected – the armor's commander must have been a complete clot, since it was unlikely that land mines *ever* looked like mess tins, even in those medieval times.

After Sten had finished doing the push-ups that every military school seemed to award its trainees at regular intervals for sins ranging from breathing to buggery, the instructor had pointed out that of course the track commander would not have mistaken them for any land mines *he* was familiar with. They could be something new. They could be booby traps. And if they were real, and he drove over them, and started losing vehicles, it would be his butt in front of the firing squad.

So slowly, laboriously, he had to send forward clearing teams to lift each plate, determine it was a plate, and move on to the next. The guerrilla leader further slowed progress down by regular sniping, in spite of the convoy's counter-fire.

'The convoy was delayed by two full E-hours, so the story goes, with no loss to the guerrilla force. Think on that, troops. Mr Sten, you can stop doing push-ups now.'

Land mines . . . space mines. Yes, that was it. Mines – those lethal devices that just sat waiting for a target and then blew it up or, worse, lurked until the target came within range and then went hunting – were never popular weapons. In spite of the fact they were the most efficient, least expensive killers of expensive machinery and beings known. They seemed somehow slimy to 'honest' soldiers. Or, anyway, not especially glamorous.

Sten had never imagined that killing one's fellow beings was glamorous. And if he'd had one iota, Mantis Section would have burned it out of him. He had also seen how effective the Tahn use of mines had been. The Tahn operated under the valid if uncivilized principle that killing was killing and needed no particular moral justification.

The Empire's conventional military, being 'honorable,' knew little and cared naught about mines – therefore, anyone they armed and equipped, such as the Altaic Cluster, would be unlikely to be expert, either.

So, during the flight out from Jochi, the hangar deck of the *Victory* had become a carpentry shop. The lathing Sten had ordered up was wire-tied into rough hedgehog-looking configurations and wrapped with metal foil.

There were several hundred of these blivets stacked on the hangar deck.

On command, these were dumped, a few at a time, into space. They formed a stream, a divider of sorts, between the two fleets. Of course, they were still traveling at the same velocity as the *Victory*, but Sten planned to wreak his next move before his 'mines' cleared the field of operations.

They had the immediate and desired effect.

The oncoming fleets went into modified panic mode as the Suzdal and Bogazi sensors picked up the 'mines,' and their commanders tried to figure out what these strange objects were that were emerging from the Imperial ship like so many bits of candy tossed to the crowds in a parade. On their screens they would have seen the *Victory*, its accompanying destroyer screen, possibly some tacships, and then the mines streaming across their screens.

Very good, very good, Sten thought. They're worried. Now we wait . . .

Shortly both fleets ordered destroyer squadrons forward to investigate.

Now we show them our dinner plates have bangs in them.

'Admiral Mason?'

'Yessir. All ships . . . all weapons stations,' Mason ordered.

'Targets . . . the destroyers. Mind your discriminators. One target per weapon. Any young officer disobeying that order will be relieved, court-martialed, and cashiered.'

Mason, the gentle father figure.

Kalis homed at half speed, or else were told by their discriminators that another missile was swifter on the pickup. Close in, just before the Suzdal and Bogazi destroyers picked them up on their screens, the missiles went to full drive.

Screens on the *Victory*'s bridge flared as the Kalis hit, then cleared to show open space where a destroyer had once been.

Three destroyers from the Suzdal and two from the Bogazi survived to return to their parent fleets.

Any analysis would have shown that these missiles were being launched by those strange-appearing 'mines.'

Sten nodded to Mason once more – and the tacships smashed in from the high elliptic they had held. Get in, launch, and get back out were their orders.

Two cruisers and five destroyers were killed.

Very good, Sten thought. I am sorry beings are dying, but they are not Imperial beings. And fewer are being killed than if battle were joined between the two fleets. Let alone if the Suzdal fleet was allowed to complete its attack on the Bogazi home world.

Now for the *coup de grâce*, Sten thought. Again, we start by setting the stage.

Ambassador Sten made another broadcast, once more ordering both fleets to break action and return to their home worlds.

But evidently his 'cast was poorly shielded from other com links. These were being made by the *Victory*, and tight-beamed 'back' in the direction the *Victory* had come from.

They were coded, of course. But both computer and staff analysis determined that the *Victory* was linked to other ships, ships out of detector range. And it appeared as if it were an entire Imperial fleet, and the *Victory* was but the scout – a monstrously large and well-armed scout, but still a scout – for the real heavies. Minutes later their prog must have worsened, as the *Victory* changed frequencies and code and began broadcasting to *another*, equally 'unseen' war fleet.

The Bogazi and Suzdal may have been less than sane in their approach to civil rights, but in military matters they were quite capable.

Without acknowledging Sten's orders, both fleets broke contact and, at full power, fled home.

Sten whoofed air and plumped down into a chair. 'Damn,' he said honestly, probably blowing his command-cool façade, 'I really didn't think that would work.'

'It will only work once,' Mason said softly, so that his officers could not hear.

'Once is more than enough. We'll blanket their butts with every straight-fact 'cast we can come up with and hope they come to what passes in the Altaics for senses. And if they try again, we'll come up with something stinkier and whomp them again! Hell, Admiral, a clot like you should *always* be able to think of something.

'Now. Return course. For once we're ahead of their clottin' schemes. Let's see if we can stay that way.'

Gatchin Fortress had been built to be both impregnable and terrifying. It had never been intended for use as a real fortress, but as a final prison for anyone opposing the Khaqan. It sat, solitary, on a tiny islet nearly a kilometer out at sea. Great stone walls rose straight up from the tiny island's cliffs. There were no beaches, no flat ground outside those walls. And there was no ground access to the island.

Alex and Cind sprawled near the cliff face on the mainland, watching.

They had prepped for their mission far more thoroughly than just throwing a set of warm undies into a ditty bag. They lay under a carefully positioned phototropic camouflage sheet that now shone a white that matched the snowbanks and dirty rocks around them. Each of them had a tripod-mounted high-power set of amplified-light binocs, plus passive heat sensors and motion detectors focused on Gatchin's ramparts and the causeway.

'Damn, but I'm cold,' Cind swore.

'Woman, dinnae be complainin't. Ah been on y' world, an' thae's a summer place compared t' it.'

'No kidding,' Cind said. 'And now you know why so many of us live *off*-world. Besides, didn't you tell me your home world was ice, snow, and such?'

'Aye, but th' ice's gentler, somehow. An' th' snoo comi't driftin' doon like flower petals.'

'You see anything?'

'Negative. Which is beginnin't t' make me think you're right.'

'We'll know for sure before nightfall. I hope.'

'Aye. An' while y're waitin', Ah'll narrate a wee story, thae's got an obvious bearin't ae our present, froze-arsed predic'ment.

'Hae Ah e'er told y' ae th' time Ah entered a limerick contest? Y' ken whae lim'ricks are, aye?'

'We're not totally uncivilized.'

'Thae's bonnie. 'Twas whae Ah was a wee striplin't, assigned t' a honor guard on Earth. Th' tabs announc'd thae contest. Large credits f'r th' prize. Who c'd come up wi' thae dirtiest, filthiest, lim'rick?

'Well, Ah hae braw experience when it com't t' dirty, filthy lim'ricks.'

'I've never questioned that.'

'Ah'm payin't nae heed nor reck t' thae cheap one, Major. So Ah ship't m' filthy poem away, an aye, 'twas so filthy e'en a striplin't like m'self blushed a bit, thinkin't m' name wae attach't.

'But thae credits wae bonny, as Ah've said. An' lord know't a puir wee ranker needs a' th' coin he can secure. So time pass't an' time pass't, an' then one day Ah sees th' tab, an' Ah'm thunderstrick!

'Ah'm noo th' winner! Ah hae nothin'! Th' winner's some clot nam'd McGuire. D. M. McGuire, ae th' wee isle ae Eire, they name't it, frae th' city ae Dublin. An' th' lim'rick's so dirty thae cannae e'en run thae own prizewinner!

'An a'ter Ah recover frae m' heartbroke, it starts gnawin't ae me. I mean, thae *cannae* be a filthier lim'rick thae whae Ah submitt'd.

'So Ah taki't a wee bit ae leave, an Ah moseys t' Eire, an' thae cap'tal ae Dublin, an' Ah begins lookin't frae D. M. McGuire. Days an' weeks pass, aye, but finally Ah trackit doon th' last McGuire i' Dublin.

'She's a wee gran lady. Sweet, wi' a twinkle i' her eye, an' a smile ae her lips, an' y' jus' *know* she's goin't t' church ever' day, twice't, an' thae's nae been a foul word cross her lips.

'This cannae be th' D. M. McGuire ae the contest, but Ah'm des'prate. So I screws m' courage t' th' stickity point, an' asks.

'Dam't near crap m' kilt, when she says, "Aye. Ah am."

'Ah begs her f'r whae it was.

'I's noo her turn t' blush, an' she say't "Ah'm a respect'ble widow. Ah cannae use language like thae around a man."

'She talk't funny, she did. 'Twae hard t' understand her, sometime.

'Ah ask't her to write it doon, e'en. But she cannae do thae, e'er. Thae *must* be the scummiest poem e'er wrote. So Ah argue, an' argue, an' plea, an' finally she say't, "Cannae Ah tell it, but wi' blankety frae th' vile words?"

'A course, Ah says. Ah'll hae nae grief figurin't it oot frae there.

'An' she tak't ae deep breath, an' recites:

> 'Blankety-blankety blank
> Blankety-blankety blank
> Blankety-blank
> Blankety-blank
> Blankety river of shit.'

After a long silence . . . a giggle. Alex beamed. 'Ah knoo frae th' first thae wae someat aboot y' Ah admired. Noo thae's three.'

'Three what?'

'Three bein's whae admir't m' stories. One's a walrus, one's a lemur, an' y're the third.'

'Exalted company indeed,' Cind said. 'Now, what's the moral that pertains to our present situation?'

'As wi' any braw preacher,' Alex said, 'Ah dinnae think m' sermons need further explication.'

And silence hung down about them.

In fact, the nothing they had seen so far was grimly productive. Cind and Alex had been in their hidey-hole for two full days. They had seen no aircraft approach Gatchin, nor had they seen any sign of sentries atop its walls. At night, only a few lights gleamed from the ominous citadel.

Two hours later, just before dusk, Alex grunted. 'Ah hae some'at. Comint frae th' south. Twa gravsleds. Cargo lighters, Ah reck . . . Whae's th' castle doin't?'

'Nothing,' Cind said. 'None of those cupolas – I think they're AA launchers – are moving.'

'Bad,' Alex said. 'Worse. Thae's no sign ae guns or guards ae th' lighters, either. An' Ah can make out th' cargo ae th' deck. Clot. Rations. Rations enow frae noo more'n a platoon, Ah'd guess. Y' hae them i' your eyeballs noo?'

'I do,' Cind said. She watched as the lighters settled down onto an overhead landing deck. After a moment, she saw a couple of uniformed men come out to meet the lighter. Neither of them was visibly armed, unless they were carrying pistols.

'No security at all,' she said.

'No food, no security, no guards, which mean't no prisoners, aye?'

'Right.'

'So where'd Doc Isky stash th' usual suspects?'

Cind shook her head. No clues.

'Shall we start lookin't? Knowin't we dinnae want to find?'

And at full dark, they bundled up the surveillance post in silence. Both of them had a pretty good idea where the purged soldiers and officials were. All they had to do was confirm their suspicions.

'Rejected,' Iskra stormed. 'Rejected. Unable to meet requested quota at this time. Personnel not available. All patrol elements available for client governments are committed for foreseeable future. What the hell is going on?'

'The Empire is still recovering, sir,' Venloe said, his voice most neutral. 'There's not exactly the cornucopia available that there was before the war.'

'I am not concerned with the Empire,' Iskra said. 'What I am concerned about is the absolute failure of the Imperial system to support its ruler. The Emperor chose me to bring the Altaic Cluster back to stability and order. Yet I am denied the tools I must have to accomplish my task.'

Venloe thought of saying something – Iskra's massive shopping list had been either arrogant, ignorant, or insane. Among other items Iskra had requested – demanded – were a full division of Imperial Guards for his security, two first-line battle squadrons from the Imperial Navy, and a flat doubling of the AM2 quota for the Altaics, with no justification given on any item other than 'to continue the reestablishment of a legal government and public order.'

'Do these bastards want me to fail?'

'I doubt that, Doctor.'

'The Emperor had best make these bureaucrats aware of one thing. I am certainly the only one who can bring peace to this cluster. My continued success is vital. Not only for my people, but for the Empire, as well. So far, I have been a loyal supporter of Prime World's policies. I doubt if anyone involved with the highest levels of Imperial authority would be happy if I should choose to consider other alternatives.'

Venloe, by now, was getting better at covering his reactions to Iskra's pronouncements. This last, however, forced him to suddenly turn his attention to a com screen that was showing nothing particularly important. By the time he turned back to Dr Iskra, his expression was again bland, pleasing.

He decided, however, that he would not ask Iskra to elaborate. Other alternatives? Such as what? The shattered Tahn? The ghosts of the dead privy council?

Did the good doctor now think the Emperor needed him more than he needed the Emperor?

That information, once relayed, would certainly produce an interesting reaction. Venloe did not, however, look forward to relaying it.

Sten had expected to return to mountains of problems and whirl-pools of disaster. Instead:

'Nae problem, boss. Ah did th' important stuff, Cind took th' normal tasks, an' Otho ignored th' dross. Y' c'd a' stayed on y'r wee vacation another year wi'oot bein't missed.'

'Shall we kill him, Cind?' the Bhor rumbled.

'Later.'

'You'll have to stand in line,' Sten said. 'I outrank both of you.'

'Why are we not drinking?' Otho said. 'To celebrate the return of our warrior-king Sten. Or to celebrate it is the first day of the week, whichever feels more important.'

'Because, lad, we're workin't t'night.'

Alex, looking smug, indicated that Sten should make the explanation. Sten grinned – the heavyworlder was more than a bit better at keeping Sten's feet buried in firm loam than that slave who was supposed to whisper 'This too shall pass' in an imperator's ear during his triumphs. Or whatever the phrase had been.

'That rifle we bugged and let the baddies steal seems to have settled in for the winter,' he said. 'I think we should exercise visitation rights.'

'Hah,' Otho said. 'Good. I do not truck with these Imperial soldiers. But those two brothers they butchered – they need a blessing sent to hell for them. I hope that rifle is not all alone, concealed in the closet of some pimple-faced alley shooter.'

'I don't think so. It's hidden somewhere in the back of a takeout food store.'

Otho grunted in pleasure. 'Good. Probably not just a single villain. Snack place, hmm. That's a good cover for lots of people going in, coming out. I will remember that.

'So, this is a group, most likely. Does anyone have a clue who they are murdering for?'

'Not yet. That's one of the things we want.'

'How hard do we hit them?'

'I want intelligence,' Sten said. 'Body count is all right if the place is guarded, but it's distinctly secondary. Cind?'

'Ummm . . . do you have an overhead on the area? Thanks. Open access to the rear, we'll need one squad. We'll go in with – let's see, another squad for the front, one platoon backup, four in the door. Keep a company in reserve, I guess.'

'We will nae' be beggin't assistance frae Colonel Jeraty ae his Guardsmen.' It was not even a question.

'Absolute negative,' Sten said. 'I'm assuming there could be a leak from them and sure as hell a leak if we transmit it through the embassy and into Iskra's com link. And if we start pumping secure signals direct to the Guards, somebody might smell something.'

'Are you thinking, my Sten, that scrote Iskra has his own private terrorists?'

'Right now, Otho,' Sten said, suddenly feeling tired, 'I suspect everyone in this clotting cluster of joining or heading up death squads. Except you two.'

'An' whae aboot me, boss?'

'Hah. I say again my last. Hah. I *know* you. Now. Enough frigging about. We'll go in with the Bhor for the terror factor. The Gurkhas stay in reserve.'

'They won't like that,' Cind said.

'Good. I intend for them to not like it. The way things are going, I think I'm going to need me some *very* angry young men in the very near future.

'Major Cind, write the ops order. We've got complete dark of the moons by 0245. We'll move then.'

There was only a single light on in the restaurant, in back of the pay counter. Behind the heavy gratings Sten could see that the interior was deserted, as was the street.

'Who'e'er this place is a cover for,' Alex whispered, 'hae confidence. Nae e'en a watchman. Or else thae found m' bug an' left it i' th' grease trap f'r a wee joke.'

'Confidence – or else they've paid for cover. Look.' Sten pointed up as a police gravsled hissed slowly over the rooftops.

'Whae about them? Or are we irk't enow t' start killin' cops?'

'Otho has orders to put up some flares and airburst some grenades if there's interference,' Cind said. 'That should suggest the big boys are playing and they'll stay away. But if they escalate, so do we.' The com clipped to a loop on the shoulder of her combat vest clicked. 'Rear squad's in position. We're ready.'

'Then shall we?'

Blur:

Kilgour was up; at waist level, he swung a solid-steel battering ram with two handgrips, as if it were a pumice fake. Impact – and grating and door and jamb pinwheeled into the building. Alex let go, and momentum sent the battering ram with the debris as he ducked out of the way . . .

Cind thumbed a bester grenade inside . . .

Eyecover and purpleflash . . .

Sten spun through the door, back against solid cover, gun sweeping . . .

Cind rolled in, going flat . . .

Sten ducked forward, toward the kitchen's entrance . . .

Kilgour in the shop, covering; Cind up, leapfrogging Sten into the kitchen; Sten moving, Kilgour providing cover . . .

Back room deserted . . .

Kilgour up with the battering ram . . .

'Laraz,' Sten shouted. A password to keep them from getting shot . . .

The door crashing down and dark night outside . . .

Gun barrels . . . hairy Bhor faces peering over sights . . .

'Clear,' Sten shouted. 'Close up your units, Cind. Keep the reserve platoon across the street.

'Otho. Three troopies.'

'Sir.'

'It's o'er here, Skip. Under th' stove.'

'Need a hand?'

'Hah.'

Kilgour put his weapon down and, seemingly without strain, lifted the huge kitchen range to one side. Stove power lines screeched but did not rupture.

'A wee hidey-hole,' he observed, reaching down and pulling up on a small metal ring, inset into the concrete floor. The ring – and floor – lifted smoothly, a counterbalanced trapdoor.

'Y'reka,' he observed. 'An' Y-not-reka. Boss?'

'Hang on a shake. You three,' Sten said to the waiting three gorilla-substitutes. 'I want you to tear the place apart. Make it look like somebody's done a rip-away-the-walls search before they found the hiding place. There's no point in giving away all our secrets.'

The three Bhor looked at each other. It wasn't as good as killing someone – but at least it was destruction. They went to work happily, smashing and crashing.

'And what do we have?' Sten had to lift his voice over the shatter.

'W' hae a typ'cal terrorist's arsenal,' Kilgour observed.

Alex was correct – but it was a very large typical terrorist's stash – a basement room nearly three meters on a side, packed with weaponry. The guns were what Sten expected – just what any private thuggery, or, depending whose side they were on, freedom fighter, would secrete: stolen, bought, or purchased sporting arms in a dizzy array of calibers. Military armament, stolen from or contributed by the Jochi army. Two very elderly crew-served support weapons. Six or seven home-built mortars. A few bombs for same. A half case of grenades. Not enough ammunition for all of the guns. Some knives. Sten thought he even saw a clotting sword. Three or four pistols on a shelf. And two Imperial-issue willyguns.

'Noo, one ae' them's ours,' Kilgour said. 'But where'd th' other lad come frae?'

'Who knows? Willyguns've been around for a long time,' Sten said. 'Maybe somebody at the embassy had one before us. Maybe the Third Guards lost one and hasn't realized it yet.'

Kilgour tossed one of the sporting rifles up for Sten to examine. Sten then gave it to Cind, who ran a fast, professional eye over it.

'Most of my experience is with real soldiers,' she said. 'This clot is filthy.'

'Nae as bad ae most,' Kilgour observed. 'Most terrs ae m' acquaintance hae more time f'r rhetoric thae bore-cleanin't. Boss, w' hae th' cheese noo. Are we haein' public ootcry or whae?'

'We'll blow it in place,' Sten decided. 'You see anything down there that'd link this to anyone?'

'Negative, skip. Thae's professional enow t' no leave callin't cards. Hello. Whae's *this*?'

He passed it up to Sten. *This* was a pistol – but a pistol that fired AM2 rounds. Sten lifted an eyebrow. The Empire, for obvious reasons, tried to keep as tight a hold on the super-lethal willyguns as possible. That held doubly true for pistols, even though that weapon, in fact, was suited only for robberies, last stands, plinking, and parades. For such an arm to be in private hands was most unusual.

And this pistol was even more special. It was anodized with what appeared to be both silver and gold. The grips were some kind of translucent white horn. And the entire weapon had been engraved with scrollwork.

Sten examined the engraving closely – no hunting scenes or beings that might give a clue as to what world this surprise had come from.

'Is there a holster?' he asked.

'Aye. An' ae th' finest. Real leather, Ah'd hazard. No initials, no maker's marks, no nothing.'

'This,' Cind observed, after she had examined the gun closely, 'is something an ambassador might give a ruler. Or the other way around. I wonder if we ran the serial numbers, would we find that the late Imperial ambassador happened to be on the sales roster? Or its recipient – intended, anyway – someone like the Khaqan?'

'Y' hae th' ball,' Kilgour cautioned. 'Dinnae be runnin't wi' it, no matter how good th' sup'sition might be. All we hae's a muckety's toy f'r sure. Seems a pity t' destroy somethin' like thae.'

'It does,' Sten said. 'It's fitting for a laird. Keep it, Alex – no. Wait.'

Alex grinned, most evilly. He was not even slightly disappointed at the evident loss of his souvenir. 'Y' hae a dream?'

'You'll get it next time around,' Sten said. 'When we recover it again. I'd like for that pistol to maybe give us something else. Pull that bug out of the willygun. See if you can plant it in this little beauty.'

'Nae problemo, boss.'

'Now, when you planted the charges to destroy this assemblage of death,' Sten went on, 'what happened is that only two of them went off. A third one just burned – but make sure it burned up and the detonator's gone. We don't want to make the scenario so realistic the baddies get some real bangs.

'Since the blast wasn't complete, it destroyed all of the long arms, but blew the pistols up – over there.'

'Why,' Kilgour complained, 'd' all th' schemes start wi' me, th' great powder monk ae th' ages, bein't inept?'

Sten extended his hand, all fingers in a fist except the middle one, which was rigidly extended. 'That, Mr Kilgour, is the only response a drunken, relieved, and stockaded sentry can come up with. Now let's blow this joint before the local yokels hear something or get forced to pay attention.'

Kilgour called for a demo pack and started wiring the place. Cind pulled the Bhor outside into a perimeter. Sten left his demo man alone. This wasn't the hardest job Kilgour had ever rigged – among other things, he had once defused a nuclear device under close-range hostile fire and boody-trapped a camel – but it required a bit of concentration.

'How do you know,' Cind asked, 'that somebody will pick up that pistol and we can track it to another arsenal?'

'I don't – not for sure. But people who make their living around things that go bang seem to get a little wiggy if you show them a trick knife or handgun.

'But I'm hoping for it leading us to something more than just another safe box. I'd be very happy if that lovely, ornate piece ends up in the hands of someone with the authority to appreciate it.'

'Like who?'

'Like whoever's running this organization. Which would give us somebody to deal with in the open.'

'Sten, you are an evil man.'

'You're just saying that to get in my pants.'

'This is true. And I'd kiss you, except it'd be bad for discipline.'

'Mine or the Bhor?'

'Yours, of course.'

But she kissed him anyway.

Venloe tried to read the face on the screen. He could not.

'Is that everything?' the man asked.

'It is, sir.'

It was so silent that Venloe could hear the carrier wave hum.

'Do you have any suggestions?'

After a pause, Venloe said, 'No.'

'Go ahead. We must consider all possibilities.' The man on the screen touched, as if unconsciously, the center of his chest.

Venloe chose his words carefully. 'When you briefed me for this assignment, I asked . . . about a fallback option.'

'And I said I was not prepared to discuss that eventuality. I was not then, and I am not now. My policy is quite firm. Dr Iskra is to be given the fullest support.'

'Yes, sir. I apologize.'

Again, silence.

'An apology is not necessary. I do not mean for my servants to be slaves. I want one thing very clear. Dr Iskra is to be ruler of the Altaic Cluster. That is the primary objective. However . . . however, what you referred to as a fallback option cannot be ignored. Explore its possibilities and ramifications.'

The screen went blank.

Venloe nodded in automatic obedience. And, even though there was no one to hear him, he replied, 'Yes, Your Majesty.'

Chapter Twenty-Five

The Eternal Emperor listened thoughtfully to Sten's report on Dr Iskra. He made no comment as Sten took each stone from the bucket and stacked it upon its miserable brother.

Sten told him about the student massacre. The proof that it was Iskra's work. The deliberate disinformation campaign to stir up war among the inhabitants of the Altaic Cluster. The lies Iskra had told to cover his campaign of terror. The mysterious attacks of Imperial personnel. The empty fortress. And much more.

Finally, he was done. Sten waited, hoping to see which way the wind was blowing.

'I assume,' the Emperor said, 'that your recommendation in this matter does not come down on the side of Dr Iskra.'

'I'm sorry, sir,' Sten said, 'but it's my job to tell you things you're not especially going to like.'

'Quite right,' the Emperor said. 'Otherwise, you'd be as useless as all these fools I've got around me. One thing I do know, Sten, is that I can always trust you to tell me the truth – no matter how unpleasant.'

'Thank you, sir. Now . . . if you'll allow me—'

'Hold on,' the Emperor said. 'No need to go further.'

'I beg your pardon, sir?' Sten was truly bewildered. He was also unsettled by this new habit the Emperor had adopted of never looking him in the face. And those damned eyes. Moving back and forth as if they were active ball bearings.

'I said, no need to say more. I know what your recommendation is going to be. Unfortunately, I have to reject it.

'Iskra stays. You will continue to support him.'

'I'm very sorry to hear that, sir. And I hope you won't take this the wrong way – but I'd like to be relieved of my post.'

The Emperor's eyes ceased their restless moving. Just for a moment. They bored into him like cold steel. Then the Emperor laughed. 'I can see why you'd say that, Sten,' he said. 'You think I've lost confidence in you.'

'Possibly, sir. But that's not for me to judge. It's just that . . . well, you need someone you can trust to carry out your orders.'

'I've already said I trust you, Sten.'

'Yessir. But I've already made it plain I disagree.'

'True. However, agreement has nothing to do with it. These are my orders. You should also know that Dr Iskra has asked me to have you replaced. I firmly rejected his request.'

'Yes, sir.' Sten couldn't think of anything else to say.

'And I told him the same thing I'm going to tell you. You're too close to the situation, Sten. Can't see the forest for the trees, as they say.'

Sten knew there was probably truth to this. He was not privy to the big picture. Unlike the Emperor.

'I still don't think I'm the best man for the job, sir. Although, I thank you for your faith in me.'

'We've been through a lot together, Sten,' the Emperor said. 'I know what you can do. And what you can't do. In fact, I believe I'm the better judge of your capabilities.

'Also, the matter with the Altaics has grown even more critical. If I were to pull you out, the bad publicity would be devastating. Now, maybe I was hasty bringing in Iskra. Although I still think he's the best of the poor lot of options I was looking at. Regardless. I've hung myself out with this man. It's vital that I am not embarrassed.'

'Yes, sir.'

'I'm counting on you, Sten,' the Eternal Emperor said. 'Perhaps more than I ever have before. Make it work. Do whatever you have to – but, make it work.

'Those are your orders.'

'Yes, sir.'

'And Sten?'

'Yes, sir?'

'Smile. Be happy. It's all going to come out just fine.'

'Yes, sir,' Sten said. He made his best salute, as the Emperor's image vanished.

Chapter Twenty-Six

Sten couldn't sleep. Every time he drifted off, the Emperor's face floated into view. He was haunted by those eyes. Eyes that were never still. Eyes that swept the edges of his conscience, netting Sten's secret doubts and hauling them in as evidence.

In Sten's nightmare the Emperor would pile up all those doubts into a writhing, eel-like mass. He would turn to Sten, face dark with anger. And those eyes would swivel for him. Sten knew if they ever came to rest, he was through.

Here they came now. Turning. Turning. Cutting a smoking path along the floor. Then they rose up, searching for his own eyes – to burn them out.

Sten gasped awake. His body was sheeted in cold sweat. He stumbled into the lavatory and dry-heaved into the toilet. He knelt there for a long time, feeling stupid for having such a silly nightmare – but frightened of returning to bed for another bout with the dream.

A soft rustle and the perfumed warmth of Cind.

'I'm okay,' he said.

'Sure, you are. I frequently find perfectly healthy and happy people crouched on the bathroom floor choking up their guts.'

'I'll be fine . . . in a minute.'

'I know you will. Now, don't argue, bub. Or you'll be in for some real trouble.'

She hauled him up, stripped him, and shoved him into the shower. Cold spray needled down, shocking him into full awareness. The film of sweat came off like old grease. Then the cold water turned to hot, steam billowing in clouds. Cind's naked form came through the clouds. She was armed with soap and a rough-surfaced sponge.

'Turn around,' she said. 'I'm going to start with your back.'

'I can do it,' Sten said, reaching for the soap.

'I *said*, turn around.' She rasped the sponge across his chest.

'Ouch! Okay, okay. You win!' He turned around.

'In case you haven't noticed,' Cind said, 'I always win.'

She wet down the sponge, soaped it up good, and started scrubbing away.

It felt good. He forgot the eyes.

Later, propped up on pillows and tucked into fresh bed-clothing, Sten sipped at the hot spicy tea Cind had ordered up from the embassy kitchen. Outside, he could hear wind howling through the streets of Rurik. Oddly, he felt peaceful. Cozy.

Cind perched on the bed next to him, a soft, colorful robe pulled around her. Her normally smooth brow was furrowed as she considered Sten's dream.

'Did you ever wonder,' she asked, 'what it would have been like if the Emperor had never come back?'

Sten shook his head. 'Sounds like a worse nightmare to me,' he said. 'Things were pretty messed up, if you recall.'

'I remember all right. And, yeah, it was messy. But the point is, we were *doing* something about it. Everybody had a lot of hopes. Some idea of a future.'

'Don't you think we have a future now? Things are tough, I agree. But, once we get over this hump—'

'We'll be back to normal?' Cind broke in. 'Tell me what normal is, Sten. I'm young. I don't know about all those wonderful days before the Tahn war.'

'Don't be sarcastic.'

'You're evading my question.'

'Okay. So, it wasn't a paradise.'

'What was it, then?'

Sten made a rueful face. 'Pretty much like now, I admit. Except . . . there was more of everything.'

'Everybody was happier then, huh? The people here on Jochi, for instance, were happier, right? Sure, they had the Khaqan hammering on them, but they had more in their bellies. Which made it all very nice. A veritable heaven for the oppressed.'

'You're being cynical again.'

'You're evading again.'

'It's just the way things work,' Sten said. 'Somebody has to be in charge. Make things go. Unfortunately, once in a while that somebody is a bastard. A tyrant.'

'Like the Khaqan?'

'Yeah. Like the Khaqan.'

'Like Dr Iskra?'

'Especially Dr Iskra. At least the Khaqan had the excuse of being a senile old fool.'

'But we're under orders to shove Iskra down these people's throats,' Cind said, 'even though we know he's probably worse than the Khaqan. Does that make sense?'

'Not unless you look at the big picture,' Sten said. 'In the best of times, the Empire is a delicate balance of some pretty hard-case personalities. And these, you will agree, are not the best of times.'

'No argument there.'

'Good. Anyway, Iskra may be a son of a bitch. But, he's the Emperor's son of a bitch. And he helps the Emperor keep things from going to hell.'

'In other words, it's expedient? It's right, even though we're going to make all these people miserable for many generations to come?'

'I wouldn't quite put it that way. But, yeah. It's expedient. Besides, there are billions of other beings in the Empire to think about.'

'And how many of them are run by someone like Dr Iskra?'

Sten opened his mouth to answer. The answer stuck. His jaw snapped shut.

Cind pressed on, not sure herself what she was getting at. 'What makes a good tyrant, Sten? A good dictator? A perfect supreme ruler? Or is there such a thing?'

'Probably. For a while, at least. A lot of times people desperately want to be commanded what to do. And they'll squabble and kill each other until a Man on a White Horse comes along to save them. And they'll gladly hand over all their rights to this person.

'If they're lucky, the new ruler will be young, a person with a strong vision. It doesn't really matter what that vision is, just as long as everyone agrees it's worth going after. The actual doing tends to put the rest of the house in order.

'The problem is, I've never heard or read of a case where entropy doesn't apply. Like the Khaqan.'

'Explain, please.'

'When the dictator is on the job too long, he gets sloppy. Distant from his people. Starts assuming his powers come straight from God on high. He gathers a group of sycophants about him. Jackals who will do his bidding, in return for a share of the carrion.

'Finally, all rulers – absolute rulers, that is – reach a point where they depend on the jackals more than the people. And that is the beginning of the end. Because they lose sight of who *really* gives them power. Which is, simply, the people they rule.'

'Nice lecture, Professor Sten.'

'Didn't mean to lecture.'

Cind was quiet for a moment. She fussed with the tie of her robe. Then, real low: 'Sounds like a pretty good description of the Emperor, to me.'

Sten didn't answer. But, he gave a small nod.

'You didn't answer my first question,' Cind said. 'What do you think would have happened if the Emperor hadn't returned?'

'No point in thinking about it,' Sten said. 'The crude fact of the matter is, without AM2 we'd all be barbarians. There'd be almost no communication beyond the smallest planetary system. Interstellar travel would either be with the old killer longliners or, if it was under stardrive without AM2 power, would bankrupt a system's resources. No progress. Clot, progress! We'd all regress. To complete ignorance. And the Eternal Emperor – those jokers on the privy council learned to their dismay – is the only one who controls the AM2.'

'What happened to it?' Cind asked. 'I never really did understand.'

'It just stopped,' Sten said. 'Near as anyone can figure – and the council did a damned great heap of figuring – the AM2 supply stopped the moment the Emperor was killed . . . or whatever it was that happened to him.'

'Where *does* the AM2 come from?' Cind asked.

'What?' Sten was truly puzzled. But it was the kind of puzzlement that made a being feel as if IQ had been sadly lacking for a long time. A stunned-ox kind of sensation.

'If it stopped, it has to start from some place,' Cind said. 'I don't mean a great big secret depot of AM2, or anything. Because even that would eventually be emptied. And have to be filled up again. Which means, somebody – or thing – has to go fetch it. Where is it fetched from? Or is that a stupid question?'

'Not stupid at all,' Sten said.

'I didn't think so. It just suddenly occurred to me. Then I figured, someone must have asked that question before.'

'Not very loudly,' Sten said. 'The Emperor does not like people messing about with his AM2.'

'Still. AM2 must exist someplace. In great quantities. Mountains and mountains of it. Sitting there for the taking. And whoever finds it—'

'Somebody did,' Sten said as a great light dawned. And he wasn't sure the discovery made him happy.

'That's what made him Emperor, right?' Cind said.

'Only partly right,' Sten said. 'But you're forgetting something. It took more than just the AM2.'

'How so?'

'He's also figured out a way to live forever. Or near enough as dammit.'

'Oh, that!' Cind said. 'Big deal. Who wants to live forever? After a while, everything would be boring. You'd never get a kick out of doing things like—'

'Ouch!' Sten yelped as Cind nipped his nipple with sharp teeth.

'And there'd be no thrill anymore when you—'

'I'll give you . . . a couple of hours to stop that,' Sten said.

'Also,' Cind said, 'you probably wouldn't care a bit if—'

She wriggled her hips and pulled at his head. Sten went where she was pulling, dimly thinking that the woman had a wonderful way of proving her point.

Chapter Twenty-Seven

It was still on the meadow's floor. But the Place of Smokes was not silent. The wind whipped the tops of the conifers in a steady roar.

Sten, Alex, Cind, and Otho stood near one of the embassy gravsleds. Their Gurkha security element had deployed smoothly from the accompanying gravlighter into a perimeter.

The poacher discovered by Alex's bottomless purse had given them nervous instructions from the rutted road down the track into the clearing. When he had seen Cind unload recording gear, he had wanted his credits on the spot. Alex had paid and asked the man if he would wait: when they were finished, they would return him to his village.

No. The man insisted he would walk home. Thirty kilometers? It did not matter. The poacher walked backward into the trees, turned, and pelted away with devils on his heels.

Sten did not know whether the man had been more afraid of someone recording his face, or of the long, shallow furrows that stretched across the meadow.

'City beings dug those,' Otho said. 'Rustics would have known earth subsides once it's put back. And they'd have mounded the trench when they covered it over.'

No one commented.

'How many?'

Sten shook his head. He had little background as an undertaker.

'There's five thousand that people have had the guts to report missing,' Cind said.

'Square thae,' Alex said absently, his eyes fixed on the covered trenches. 'Which'll mean thae'll be – other places yet t' find.' He turned to Sten. 'How d' we play th' card, boss?'

Sten thought, then walked to the gravsled and opened an equipment locker. He removed two shovels and gave one to Kilgour.

'I guess,' he said, 'we'll treat it like an archaeologist's dig. We'll cut a slit one meter wide across one trench. Cind, I want you recording. Make sure the film shows the ground has not been disturbed for some time. There's little plants—'

'Lichen,' Alex said.

'Lichen, then, grown up. No footprints except those we'll make approaching the . . .' He let his voice trail off.

'Sir,' Otho said. 'The soldiers can do the digging.'

Sten shook his head and motioned to Cind to start the recorder. Then he walked to the nearest trench and marked the limits of the exploratory slot with his shovel's blade. He started digging carefully. The sandy loam took little effort to dislodge. Alex dug with equal care on the other side of the trench.

Sten was down less than a meter when he suddenly stopped. 'Otho. There's a trowel in the locker.' He knelt and dug still more gently with the tool. He grunted. Then he coughed hard and threw up to one side of the trench.

Otho brought him a canteen and a breathing mask. He gave a second mask to Alex. 'It is a smell you never become used to.'

Sten rinsed his mouth out and put the mask on. He was glad it concealed his expression. 'Two . . . maybe three months?'

'Thae's aboot th' right time, boss. Cind? I' y' c'd gie us a shot, straight doon int' th' crypt?'

Cind moved closer.

Through the finder, she could see a woman's back. Her hands had been tied behind her with plas cuffs. Next to it, was a man's face. The remains of his eyes were wide, and his mouth was open, the scream silenced with dirt.

Cind told her eyes to stop recording – the machine would do the work. They did not obey.

'Why,' Otho wondered, 'did Iskra not dump these bodies into the sea? Or burn them with his fire?'

'Being buried alive,' Sten said, 'is an honorable death here on Jochi.'

Otho growled. 'And how can murder ever be honorable?'

Sten gave Alex a hand out of the grave.

'Y' dinnae answer m' question, boss, on whae use w' put this atrocity to? Ah cannae say Ah think thae'll be aught good i' we call in th' penny dreadfuls, an' let th' deed be howl't 'crost th' Altaics. Thae'll be more tinder f'r th' firestorm i' we do.'

'You're right. We'll cover the hole back up. And all we'll do – at least at first – is ship a copy of Cind's record to Prime.'

'Eyes Only frae th' Emp? Sten, this isn't th' first, it's just th' worst ae what we've been tellin't th' boss. Whae makes y' think he'll pay this any more heed – Ah ken he's seen more gashly sights o'er th' aeons.'

'I don't know,' Sten said. 'But he'd damned well better start – because you had it when you said there's a firestorm building. And we're right in the middle.'

Then they fell silent.

And there was no sound but the shovels scraping dirt back into the mass grave . . . and the high roar of the wind as it built up force overhead.

Chapter Twenty-Eight

The question of whether the revelation at the Place of the Smokes would change the Emperor's course would not be answered.

Her family was not rich, not poor. Or at least not what the citizens of Rurik called poor – on many other worlds she would have been thought a slummer. But she knew both her father and mother, and only two of her brothers had died as babes. She had always eaten at least once a day, and her clothes were clean, if restyled and resewn garments her older sister had owned.

She was a Jochian. But she did not remember, as a child – at sixteen E-years, she of course considered herself adult – having any particular hatred for Suzdal or Bogazi. Even though she seldom saw either of the ET species in her sector. And she never felt anything more than pity for the few Tork families she encountered.

Some years before she had heard stories that her world would change, change for the better. Once that tyrant the Khaqan was gone – she had never thought of him one way or another before – a new day would dawn.

It would be brought by a man named Iskra. Some of her friends gave her pamphlets that talked about how this noble man had always believed in the Altaics, had believed they were to be civilization's center, and that the new fire would be sparked by Jochians.

She did not, of course, actually read any of this doctor's writings. She had been told they were far too complex for someone of her sex and education, and she did not need to waste the time. She joined a small organization, a secret organization, of course, and was oath-sworn to help bring that new day in whatever way she could.

And then Iskra returned to his home world. She had been part of the roaring throng that welcomed him. She thought she had actually seen him – a dot far away on a balcony of the palace that had belonged to the Khaqan.

Then the stories had started. The new day was not dawning fast enough. The Torks still paraded and showed off their riches, riches that had been ill-gotten from Jochians. And worse, Jochi was still polluted by the presence of Suzdal and Bogazi.

Even when the 'aliens' left, there were still evils plaguing Dr Iskra's attempts to bring a firm hand to the madness. And of course, once her cell leader explained, she saw the real villains clearly: those Imperials who were trying to use Dr Iskra as their cat's-paw, just as they had used the Khaqan. Now she realized Dr Iskra was being held as a near-captive in that palace – not ruling freely as she once believed.

She wanted to do something. Something that would bring the change even faster.

Somehow, some way, she could help.

On the livies she saw what others had done. Two young men and a woman – a woman even younger than herself – had doused their bodies with flame, willingly shaming themselves with this dishonorable death, because only by such a stroke would all of Jochi realize *they* were the ones who were shamed.

She told her cell leader of her willingness to die. He said he would ask *his* counselor if such an act would be good.

Two days later, he told her that this was not to be her fate. Instead, she would be allowed to perform an even greater task, a task that would drive the Imperials from their worlds like a great wind from the north.

She was delighted and humbled.

She studied and rehearsed carefully.

Two days after Sten found the bodies buried in the forest, she was told it was time.

'The clots never listen,' the sentry said to the other two Imperial soldiers assigned to the guard post. 'Y' can tell them a hundred times this is closed off, you can't get a back way to the market stalls this direction, and they'll nod, smile, and try again next time they come to town. When the Maker asked the Jochians if they wanted brains, they thought he said drains and said "Go ahead and flush."'

The sentry post was at one of the entry streets that opened on the Square of the Khaqans. It was now secured, because the part of the palace that had been given to the battalion from the Third Imperial Guards for barracks/offices/mess was about a hundred meters away.

He yawned – less than an hour after dawn, which meant less than another hour until the post was relieved and he could eat – picked up his willygun, slung it, and walked out of the sentry shack. He watched as the gravlighter floated toward him. A clottin' antique, he thought. Damned thing actually travels at a cant.

Its cargo compartment was full of what looked like half-ripe, half-rotten tree fruit that no one but a Jochian would have bought, let alone considered eating.

He shook his head. He resolved that when his hitch was up he would *never* bitch about anything on his home world, having seen just how little these Jochians actually had. You would almost feel sorry for them, if they weren't such hate-shoutin' bastards, he thought.

He couldn't see who was behind the controls of the lighter through the cracked, dirty plas shield. The sentry held both hands flat – universal language for 'Ground it.'

The lighter stopped – but didn't land. It moved back and forth in the gusting wind that came across the wide Square of the Khaqans.

The sentry swore. He moved to one side. Maybe the driver

couldn't see him. Then he half smiled in approval. Pretty one, she was. He motioned again – just as the gravlighter went to full power and drove toward and over him.

It may have looked battered, but the lighter's McLean generators were freshly rebuilt and tuned for maximum power. The sentry had one second to think the young woman had misunderstood, then he rolled out of the way as the lighter drove forward at speed.

Imperial – and commonsense – security: the entrance to any secured compound should always be laid out so any entering vehicle, ground or aerial, would be forced to slow to minimum speed. But this particular gateway had but one V-turn in it.

Solid blocks, heavy-duty fencing, or even rolled razor wire had to be stacked to at least three meters above the ground. This gateway had only three rolls of razor wire, the third piled between the second.

The gravlighter snagged wire – but kept on moving.

It was imperative, Imperial security directives continued, that any compound include a secondary vehicle block, in case the outer barrier was breached.

No such block had been constructed.

Under no circumstances, the directives went on, even more sternly, was a troop barracks ever to be vulnerable to a suicide assault. Minimum precautions in hostile areas included monitors, AA posts, ground obstacles, roving patrols with heavy antiarmor weapons, etcetera, etcetera.

The gravlighter was only ten meters from the steps leading into the Imperial Guards' barracks when the young woman pilot – that friendly smile she had forced to the sentry now a rictus – reached down to a small control box that had been hastily welded to the floor.

There were two pull-levers, one sprayed red, the other blue. She had been instructed that the blue lever would start the timer, and she would have thirty seconds to clear the area.

The red . . .

The red was to be used in the event of emergencies.

She never knew that both knobs were the same, because she had determined that there would be no mistakes made. This would be the shot – the blast – heard far beyond Jochi or the Altaics.

It would be heard on Prime World, where that evil puppet master, the Eternal Emperor, would be forced to listen and realize what his machinations had produced.

She pulled the red knob straight up.

She died first as the three tons of conventional explosives that was the gravlighter's real cargo detonated.

The blastwave crashed through the wall of the barracks. Of the 650 beings carried on the Guard battalion's TO&E, more than half of them were still asleep, or being shouted awake by noncoms. Five hundred and eighty total Guardsmen were in the palace building.

Colonel Jerety, caff pot in hand, was about to ask his executive officer and battalion sergeant major if they needed refills when the blast rolled over him.

The explosion smashed down the barracks.

The lucky ones died in the blast.

The slightly less lucky ones never recovered consciousness or were crushed as the building fell about them.

But there were others.

The screams started even before the shock wave died, and while the dust was still boiling.

Halfway across the city the shock wave hit the embassy.

Sten, still abed, was brooding, and Cind was trying to convince him that his day would be vastly improved if he would lie back and let her tongue continue its wanderings, and he felt the rumble and the building shake, and he was on his feet, naked, sure for an instant that the bastards had hit the embassy itself.

He was at a window, ignoring Cind's shout to get down, and staring out as that great pillar of smoke and flame began building.

Deep in his guts he knew this was the turning point.

What would happen next, he had no real idea.

But he had a skincrawl/soulcrawl that it would be something to make all the murder and treachery that had gone before seem like nothing.

Chapter Twenty-Nine

'I knew things were going to be pretty bleak when I got back,' the Eternal Emperor said, 'but, like most of my subjects, I thought all I needed to do was tighten the Imperial belt and slog onward.'

The Emperor topped up Mahoney's glass with Scotch and refilled his own. 'I was stupid enough to think that with a little imagination and a lot of hard work the crisis would pass.' He let his gaze rest briefly on Mahoney, then moved onward.

Mahoney had the sudden flash of a lizard searching for a fly. He shoved the disloyal image aside. 'I'm sure it will work out eventually, sir. We all have complete faith in you.'

The Emperor gave a hollow laugh. 'Faith is an overvalued commodity, Ian. And, yes, it *is* a commodity. I should know. I just purchased some for extra insurance.'

Mahoney let that go by. He didn't want to know what the Emperor was talking about. 'How can I help, sir?'

'That's one of your most admirable traits, old friend,' the Eternal Emperor said. 'When I call, you're always ready to volunteer.'

In other times, Mahoney would have flushed warmly at the compliment of being called the Emperor's friend. Now the words sounded cold, insincere. 'Thank you, sir,' he said. He sipped his drink to cover confused emotion.

'First, let me tell you what has come to pass,' the Emperor said. 'I've got a desk full of fiches from my experts' – he thumped the side of his antique desk for emphasis – 'which contradict each other on just about every point except one.' The Emperor turned a thumb downward. 'And that's the direction my Empire is heading.

'The optimists say we're going downhill slowly. They've got progs of complete collapse within twenty E-years. The boys in the middle say five or six.

'The pessimists tell me it has already happened. They say we're being carried along by economic inertia. That the sheer size of my Empire covers up the hard, cold fact that we are dead, dead, dead.'

'Surely they're all in error, sir,' Mahoney said. 'Experts make their fortunes on gloom. Not good news.'

'No error. Except, possibly, my own. I've been simply ignoring what's staring me in the face.'

'But . . . I don't see how this can be.' A bit shaken, Mahoney gasped back his drink, then reached for the decanter to refill their glasses. It was empty. He rose and went to the sideboard to fetch another. Mahoney started to pick up another decanter of Scotch, then changed his mind, seeing a flask of stregg. He lifted it up. 'Maybe we need something stronger, boss,' he said.

The Emperor's face paled with anger. 'What's *that* doing there?' he barked. 'I don't drink that anymore.' Alarmed, Mahoney watched the rage build.

'Dammit,' the Emperor snarled. 'I told Bleick I don't even want that drakh in my presence.' Then he caught himself and gave Mahoney a weak attempt at a smile. 'Sorry,' he said. 'Little things get to me these days.'

Mahoney just nodded and walked back to his seat with a decanter of Scotch. What the clot was going on here? Why the sudden hate for such an innocuous thing? For the first time, Mahoney felt he was in the presence of a stranger. A dangerous stranger.

The Emperor continued as if nothing unusual had happened, as Mahoney refilled the glasses with Scotch.

'When the Tahn war was over,' the Emperor said, 'the debt we had taken on was astonishing. But I had a firm, workable plan to whittle it away without causing too much discomfort. Unfortunately . . .'

He didn't have to fill in the rest. Mahoney knew quite well that the Emperor had never had the chance to put that plan into motion.

'I could still have pulled it off,' the Emperor said, 'if it weren't for the actions of the privy council. My God, did they spend. But not for one thing worthwhile. Not a thing that could eventually put credits back in the treasury, or even spur a little mini-boom in the economy.'

The Emperor leaned back in his chair and propped his feet on the desk. 'The Tahn war debt,' he said, 'now equals only about one tenth of our current deficit. I reckon that same deficit – at current cut-to-the-bone spending – will double again within one E-year.'

Mahoney was not a money man. It did not interest him. Large amounts offended his sense of morality. And he certainly didn't understand it. But, *this* he understood.

'The Empire's problems hit critical mass about four years into the privy council's reign,' the Emperor continued. 'At that time the impact of the AM2 shortage hit the point of no return. It's put everything into a helluva spin. A big, clotting vortex, sucking us into the hole. And each time a system's economy collapsed and fell in, it tipped another into the funnel. Now the mess has taken on a life and logic of its own. Unless I take drastic action – real quick – even the healthiest parts of my Empire are going to get pulled in.'

The Emperor drained his glass, slapped it down on his desk, and turned those scary eyes on Mahoney. A slight flicker . . . and then they swept on.

Mahoney had the sudden feeling that he was being set up. The Emperor's facts were too pat. Too glib: x times y must absolutely equal what I am going to tell you next.

'Not only that,' the Emperor said, 'but I am personally strapped. Just about broke. As you know, Ian, in the past I have sometimes used my personal resources to help the Empire over some rough spots. But the privy council looted those resources, as well. Now we don't even have my money to fall back on.'

'What do you plan to do, sir?' Mahoney asked. His tone was neutral.

'I have to rein everybody in, Ian,' the Emperor said. 'All over the Empire, we've got thousands of different leaders doing things a thousand different ways.' He casually filled his glass and sipped. 'So, to start with, we need uniformity. Second – and most important – we have to put an instant end to all areas of conflict. Look what's happening over in the Altaic Cluster, for example. Our good and highly competent friend, Ambassador Sten, is going out of his mind with the trouble those beings are causing. It's those sort of unstable regions and situations that led to the Tahn disaster to begin with.'

The Eternal Emperor shook his head. 'I'll tell you Ian, the only way I can see out of these woods is if everybody follows one being's lead. And from where I sit, I've got to be that guide.

'I want to cut out the middle men, Ian. From here on out, I need to be the only one in charge.' He shrugged. 'Else, we might as well all give up and go home. Unfortunately, there's no other home to go to.'

'How do I fit into this, sir?' Mahoney asked.

'I want you to run the whole show,' the Emperor said. 'I want you to be in charge of putting together my recovery plan.'

'Which is, Your Highness?'

'My pet pols will announce the first stage of my plan in Parliament next week. I'm going to make a one-time offer to all the provinces. I'm going to encourage them to give up independent rule. They'll be offered the chance to become dominions – of my Empire.'

'Excuse me, sir,' Mahoney broke in, 'but why would they do this? Why would they give up all that power? As you've taught me, that goes against the nature of most beings.'

'Certainly it does. So does the carrot I'm going to offer. As well as the stick. But, to greed first. As provinces they are paying full price for AM2. Plus, they are under strict rationing. As dominions, they will not only pay less for the AM2, but will pay lower overall taxes, as well.'

'What if they refuse, sir? What's the stick?'

The Eternal Emperor smiled. A nasty smile. 'Oh . . . to begin with, I'm also announcing a tenth of a credit tax hike on AM2 for all provinces. That's on top of increased rationing. Which – since economic nature will then take its course – will push the price of AM2 on the spot market into double digits.'

Low laughter. Mahoney shuddered.

'That's just for starters,' the Emperor said. 'I've got a few other thumbscrews in mind. As a long-time kingmaker, I've gotten pretty skilled at unmaking them, as well.'

'Back to my original question, sir. How do I fit in?' Mahoney did not forget that his *real* first question had been 'How can I help, sir?'

'I want you to be point man with the provinces. I want to heap more glory into your honors chest. As thanks, as well as to boost your prestige in the eyes of the fools you will be visiting.

'And I want you to visit every major province leader. Cajole them. Irish charm them. As well as twist the right arms if you have to. Just be firm, Ian. Make nice promises. But make sure they see the weight in the stick I'm handing you.'

'I am deeply honored, sir,' Mahoney said quickly. 'But I am the worst man for that job. I would be disloyal not to refuse this honor. Such an appointment would not be in your best interests . . . sir.'

The Emperor turned a cold face to Mahoney. 'Why, Ian?' The question was soft, the eyes looking blankly over Mahoney's shoulder.

'Because I think it's a terrible idea, sir,' Mahoney burst out. 'You've always asked honesty of me. I've always given it to you. So . . . there it is, sir. I don't want the job, sir. Because I don't believe in it.'

'What's there not to believe in? It's a plan. Not a . . . religion.'

'First off, sir, in my estimation, the stick will be needed more than the carrot. You'll have to force dominion status on most of them, sir. And they will resent the clot out of it. Which means, your orders will be followed grudgingly at best. Which automatically sets all your actions up for failure. And that, sir, is my humble opinion.'

It was also Mahoney's professional opinion that anything micromanaged was doomed. If no one had anything to gain, why chance failure? A 'let the big man do it' attitude develops fast. It also offended his democratic, Irish soul.

In Mahoney's view, beings were best left in charge of their own destiny. In the past that had been what he had always loved about the Empire. It had problems, to be sure. But, mostly there was room for all sorts of ways of doing things. Room for genius, as well as for fools.

Now he was even beginning to wonder about his previous view. How much room was there? Really?

'In normal times, I would agree with you, Ian,' the Emperor said. 'I could list many examples from history.'

'The British Crown's takeover of Earth's old East India Company comes to mind, sir,' Mahoney said. 'One of your favorite examples, sir. As a lesson in failure, I believe.'

The Emperor laughed. Mahoney thought the laugh had a little bit of the old spark to it. It made him feel a little better.

'Go ahead, Ian. Throw my own logic back at me. Not too many people would have the nerve. That's the kind of thing that keeps the mental juices going. Keeps me from getting stale.'

He leaned over his desk, lowering his voice slightly. 'I tell you, Ian, the crew of beings I've got around me are gross incompetents. I miss the old days. When you and I and a few other talented beings – like Sten, for example – kept things going on the fly. I love that old kind of political freebooting.'

The Emperor sat back and sipped his drink. Coldness shrouded back over him. 'Unfortunately . . . that is no longer possible. And I'm not just speaking of the current crisis.

'Things have become too big. Too complicated. Governing by pure consensus is ideally suited to a tribe. Twenty or thirty beings, maximum. Any number after that weakens the effectiveness of the ideal.

'It's time for a new order, my friend. A universal order. New thinking by right-minded individuals is called for.'

Mahoney couldn't help himself. 'I'm not sure that rule by an *enlightened monarchy* fits the definition of "new thinking," sir,' he blurted.

The Emperor shook his head. 'You're right, but you're wrong, Ian. You're forgetting I'm . . . immortal.'

He settled his gaze on Mahoney. His eyes were like mirrored glass, reflecting Mahoney's image back at him. 'I can think of nothing more perfect in the social art of governing than to have a single-purposed, benevolent ruler, who will keep the course until the end of history.'

The Emperor kept those eyes riveted on Mahoney, boring in at him. 'Can you see it, now, Ian? Now, that I've explained? Can you see the sheer beauty of it?'

The com buzzed. Mahoney was temporarily saved from answering. Then, as the Emperor spoke to the individual on the other side the reprieve became permanent. He was rescued by the worst kind of news.

The Emperor snarled orders and angrily cut the line. He turned to Mahoney. 'There's been a disaster in the Altaic Cluster, Ian,' he said. 'I mean, Imperial-troops-dead-in-the-most-humiliating-circumstances-type disaster.'

He turned his face to the window and looked out at the idyllic grounds of Arundel. He was silent for a long time, thinking.

Finally, he turned back. 'Forget the previous job offer, Mahoney,' he said. 'We'll argue that matter later. I've got something much more important for you to do.'

'Yes, sir,' Mahoney said. This time, he knew there was no way he could refuse.

Chapter Thirty

Digging out the Guards' barracks was three days of grimness. Five hundred and eighty soldiers had been inside when the monster bomb of the gravlighter had detonated.

Four hundred and thirty-seven dead. One hundred and twenty-one injured – most with major traumatic injuries requiring amputation so severe that the embassy's surgical team doubted if more than half would accept limb regeneration. Twenty-three uninjured – physically uninjured.

There had been twenty-six, at first. Three soldiers had been dug out of the rubble seemingly unscathed. One of them had stood up, grinned, said 'Thanks, clots, now, who's pourin'?' taken five steps, and dropped dead. The others just died quietly in their hospital beds. And the twenty-three survivors were all psychological casualties, of course. No one ever knew – or reported, at any rate – how many Jochi civilian workers had also died in the blast.

But it was three days before the last screamer, lost in the maze that had been a palace building, rasped into silence and death.

This battalion of the Third Guards had ceased to exist. Otho found the battalion flag buried near Jerety's body and had it cased for shipment to the division's home depot. The battalion might be reconstituted after an appropriate interval. Or it might never exist again.

The wounded, and the injured Guardsmen who had been outside their barracks, were loaded on the *Victory* and evacked.

Sten had put Mason in charge of the rescue operation, and he himself had spent as much time as he could digging with the rest of the Imperials. Then he had ordered Mason to take the *Victory* to Prime and unload the casualties. He had sent Prime a copy of Mason's orders, but had not much cared whether they would be met with Imperial approval or not. He was slightly surprised to receive that approval – and a brief, coded addendum that further support would be provided immediately.

The next communiqué from Prime had been announcing medals. Some were given to Gurkhas or Bhor that Sten had commended. Others went to Colonel Jerety and the top-ranked officers of the Guards battalion. If these officers had survived the blast, of course, they would have been relieved and at the very least shot for criminal incompetence.

Sten, Kilgour, and Mason were also gonged. To them the awards were meaningless medals to be tossed in a drawer and forgotten. The disaster should have been studied for its lessons – not memorialized with tin and ribbon. But that is the nature of any military unit.

By then, Sten had other problems.

The blast that destroyed the Guards unit seemed to be the catalyst. Jochi went somewhat berserk.

Suddenly, the Empire was the enemy of the Altaic Cluster. The Empire must be taught a lesson. The Empire must not meddle.

Sten admired – slightly – the campaign. To a degree it *was* spontaneous – peasants never seemed to need much direction for their latest pogrom – but mostly it was carefully choreographed.

At first, Sten had been in a reactive position: filing the correct protests with Dr Iskra and what Iskra laughingly called a government; filing the appropriate responses, trying to keep the livie reporters off his ass . . . and incidentally keeping the embassy functioning and his staff alive.

He had immediately declared Jochi a high-threat world and informed all Imperial worlds that any citizen visiting the Altaic Cluster did so at extreme personal risk. He insisted that Prime require a visa for anyone coming to the cluster.

He sent out teams of well-armed Gurkhas and Bhor to find all Imperial citizens and escort them to the safety of the embassy.

Most Imperial visitors – thank some non-Altaic god – had been professional businessbeings, who were skilled at sensing trouble and scooting out of its way. But there were always the exceptions: the elderly couple who were determined to see a part of the universe they had never visited; the honeymooners who, it seemed, had picked Jochi out of an archaic travel fiche. Sten rescued the old people. He wasn't in time for the newly married beings.

And then the embassy itself came under siege.

At first it was just small groups of Jochians, and any person or vehicle attempting to enter or exit the embassy was stoned. Sten consulted with Kilgour. Yes, Alex agreed. The situation looked to be worsening.

'Then we'll show them how to throw a real riot.'

'Aye, boss.'

And Kilgour set to work, readying the response. He could have done it in his sleep by now. This was hardly the first time he and Sten had been besieged by 'civilian mobs' on a 'peaceful world.' They had a very effective standard defusing order prepared.

The crowds grew bigger. Instead of rocks, they were throwing firebombs and nail-wrapped improvised grenades built out of lowgrade explosives.

According to Dr Iskra's flunky, J'Dean, these people represented the righteous wrath of Jochi. Wrath about what, Sten did not bother to ask. J'Dean told him that Dr Iskra, who was quite busy at the moment, would happily send out troops to clear the area, if Sten so requested it. Right, Sten thought. Another massacre, which will be clearly and positively laid at my hands, since I know this conversation is being recorded.

'No,' Sten said politely. 'The Empire will not harm innocent Jochians freely expressing their political opinions as is their right.' He broke the connection. He didn't think even Iskra's tape doctors could butcher that into a statement of slaughter.

Then the sniping started. Projectile weapons, being fired by marksmen who had seen at least some training. One secretary was shot in the leg, and one clerk was temporarily blinded when a near miss shrapnelled rock from a wall into her face.

That was enough. Sten ordered everyone nonmilitary inside, and only essential movement to be made during daylight hours even by troops.

Naturally, the next stage would be a direct attack.

Sten put all nonessential personnel into the many levels of sub-basements under the embassy building. He stationed anyone with any military training or weapons familiarity near the entrances and exits to the compound buildings.

The Bhor had been quite busy following Kilgour's blueprints. The somewhat monstrous beings may have been thought of as barbaric killers – which they were, of course – but they were also sophisticated traders and pilots. Which meant that each of them had, by now almost at a genetically transmitted level, talents as shade-tree mechanics. Any of them could, for instance, weld anything, up to and including radioactive materials, by hand, safely, and with minimum shielding. Or rebuild a broken engine never seen before – given no more than hobbyist's machine tools and an hour to puzzle it out.

The embassy already had two elderly riot-control armored vehicles. The guns were stripped off, and Alex rearmed the clunkers with his own choice of devices. Four embassy vehicles, including the stretched luxury ceremonial gravlighter that Sten had inherited from his predecessor, were stripped, given improvised armor, and equipped with the same weaponry as the riot vehicles.

Four of the Gurkha trooplighters were also modified, with heavy iron vee-blades welded to their prows. These four were stationed near one of the embassy compound's sally ports.

Sten and Alex were building and camouflaging bombs, then planting them at ground level on the compound's outer walls.

That night, Lalbahadur Thapa, who Sten had commissioned Jemedar, took two unmodified lighters and a platoon of Gurkhas out a side gate on a smash and grab on a central hardware depot. He returned having taken zero casualties and having accomplished his mission, although, he told Sten, he had never seen a mongery so large but with so little stock in trade. 'How can these Jochians find so much time to be killing their neighbor and have so little time to be taking care of their own food and shelter?'

Sten didn't know, either.

Kilgour took off twelve members of the embassy's own security staff for special duties. They would be armed with the stolen 'weaponry' and were dubbed, with Alex's archaic sense of humor, Tomcat Teams.

By dawn, the embassy was ready. Sten thought the assault would come sometime between noon and dusk – it takes time to organize, fuel, oil, and motivate any mob.

The Gurkhas and the Bhor were put on standby for reaction forces, in the event the mob made it through the gates or over the wall, or if a charge became necessary.

That left two tasks.

Alex took care of the first – he ran a last-minute, complete check on the embassy's security, concentrating on any structures outside the embassy grounds that had line of sight on the compound and could be used as command centers. These included two buildings – one a new office structure, the other one of the near-abandoned vertical slums. Each had a new com antenna on the roof.

They were marked.

Cind had her best riflemen in the embassy courtyard, and targets set up. The range was subminiature, of course, and was intended only to let the snipers make sure the sights of their weaponry hadn't been jarred or shifted since fired last.

Cind was grateful that the rounds to be fired were AM2 and not projectile-type, so she did not have to calculate at what centimetric range a target would give the same zero as the desired thousand-meter flat zero or any other stone-age nonsense. The AM2 went, without deflection and with a straight-line trajectory, straight for its target.

Their weapons were Imperial sniper rifles. These ultra-lethal devices were modified-issue willyguns, using the standard AM2 round. But the 'propellant' was not a laser, as on the standard infantry rifles, but modified linear accelerators hung around the barrels. A conventional-looking sight automatically found the range to the target. If the target had moved out of sight – behind a wall, perhaps – the scope was twisted until its cross hairs were where the sniper imagined the target to be, invisible on the other side of the wall. A touch of the trigger, and the weapon shot around corners.

Cind had her own personally modified sniper rifle, fitted with every comfort known, from thumbhole stock to set trigger to heavy barrel. One of the Gurkhas, Naik Ganjabahadur Rai, spotted for her.

Sten hoped the crash of gunfire from behind the embassy walls might deter some of the prospective rioters' enthusiasm, but he doubted it.

They waited.

The day built, with shouts, rocks, bottles, and chants coming over the embassy walls. It was midafternoon before Sten felt the mob was all frenzied up and ready to be dealt with. It probably took so long since the day was raw and windy – not exactly perfect weather to destroy an embassy.

He moved Cind's snipers to the roof of the embassy. One floor below, lurking in an office with the windows removed, Alex waited with two Bhor antimissile teams.

All of Sten's assault troops were on a single command freek, which normally would produce instant com babble. But since he was using the superexperienced Gurkha and Bhor soldiery, Sten thought he could keep the gabble within reasonable limits. Their coms were also set for an instant-override section band.

'All sections, all troops,' he opened. 'On standby, this band. Section leaders, make your com check, both freeks, and report. Sten, out.'

He was broadcasting *en clair*, since there was no time for codes, and no particular need, either. If whoever was masterminding this 'spontaneous demonstration' wanted to listen in and try to react, that was fine with Sten.

All elements checked in five-by and zed probs, except that one section leader had to replace two com units. One of these centuries, Sten thought, they will actually come up with an infantry radio that is reliable five meters beyond the manufacturer's bench. But not this one.

Sten moved a tripod-mounted high-power set of binocs into position and decided it was time to check the street scene outside.

Shouts. Banners. Horn blasts. Screaming rabble-rousers. Barricades blocking the side streets. The dull crack of a couple of small-caliber weapons, aimed at he knew not what. The embassy was completely surrounded by a sea of madness. The mob swayed, roaring.

Roaring like that wind in the Place of Smokes, he thought, and then turned that part of his mind off.

Quite a crowd, he estimated. Nearly . . . let's see. He guessed over a hundred thousand beings.

'How do you know there's that many?' Cind wondered, from her sprawl two meters away from him.

'Easy,' he said. 'I just count their legs and divide by two. Hang on. Cind. Targets. Alpha. Thirteen thirty. Five hundred meters. Bravo. Fifteen hundred. Four – correction, three hundred seventy-five. Charlie. Sixteen hundred, four hundred. One more – Delta. Zero nine hundred, six hundred meters. Looks like he might be the big Limburger. Monitor, please. Sten, clear.'

He was using a clock locator, with twelve hundred being the central boulevard that ran from the embassy to the palace, and ranges in meters.

The spotters reported promptly. All targets that he had suggested were beyond the crowd swirl. He had looked for beings who were standing on top of things, speechifying, organizing, rabble-rousing.

Crowd roar was getting louder. Now, Sten thought, if these

speech makers are just angry citizenry, concerned about injustice, in a few moments they'll shout their way to the front of the mob.

But they were not moving.

Professional-type rabble-rousers, then. Ones that whoever's throwing this masked ball would rather not sacrifice if bullets start zipping about. Or else they're just cowards, in which case I'm almost sorry for what's about to happen.

'Alex.'

'Aye, lad.'

'When you take your two, we'll take the windbags.'

'Aye, skip. Hae y' a mo' f'r some incidental intelligence?'

'No . . . yes.'

'Ah hae m' wee ticky ticky wi' me. Th' one thae's th' twig f'r thae flashy popper w' hae oot there?'

Sten thought . . . oh. Alex was talking about the detector that was linked to the bug in that elaborate pistol they had bugged in that back-alley arsenal.

'GA.'

'As y' said. Th' whoppin' Camembert hae i'.'

Son of a bitch, Sten thought. So. As he had thought, this 'mob' was being created, built, and driven. And whoever was running this operation was also involved with a little private terrorism. And, he was morally willing to believe, even if it wasn't justified enough for an intelligence summary, willing to send a suicide bomber in to kill over four hundred Imperial Guardsmen.

'You're detached, Alex. Don't lose that ticker.'

'Ah thought y'd say thae, boss. An' Ah' wish't y' t' be impress't, an' owe me one, frae bein't so self-sacrificing. Ah'm off th' net, an'll be mon'trin' frae com central. Alex, clear.'

'Cind?' Sten had his hand over the com mouthpiece.

'I heard.' She spoke into her open mike to her sniper section. 'This is Sniper Six Actual. Delta is a negative target. I say again, Delta is a negative. Over.'

That target – that being – that Sten had spotted far beyond the mob's reach and surmised to be the horde-officer-in-charge was carrying the bugged pistol. As much as he wanted to hit Delta now, the target must be taken later.

'Here they come!'

'Unknown unit! ID yourself!'

'Sorry. Main Central.'

Sten swung his binocs. Indeed, here came a thrust of people toward the main gate.

A stumble, really. Sten gave an order.

Irritant gas hissed from projectors atop the embassy walls. A very thin spray, and the gas was cut ten-to-one. It was dyed yellow and would stain anyone it touched. This was in case Sten or anyone else needed to ID any rioters at a later date, since the dye would take at least seven baths to scrub off.

The gas was intended to be no more than an annoyance, but was also intended to be a suggestion that worse things could happen.

The first wave fell back, blinking. Then the now-tawny trouble-makers surged forward. This time they were brandishing knives, improvised spears, and firebombs.

Sten touched buttons on the det panel in front of him, and his and Alex's bombs went off. They were not bombs so much as high-pressure spray cans. They had been disguised as trash bins, streetlight bases, and anything else that would have been part of a believable street scene. Each bomb contained at least twenty liters of lubricant.

It became quite hard to walk on the slick streets just around the Imperial embassy.

Then the Tomcat Teams hit, darting out from the embassy's quickly opened and shut sally ports.

They were two-man units, one man with a willygun and orders not to use it unless the team was trapped, the other with a great pack full of what had been looted from that warehouse. Ball bearings. Many, many ball bearings, grabbed by the handful and scattered underhand.

Ball bearing mousetrap.

Tomcat.

It got *much* harder to be a raving rebel and not be in a seated or prone position.

The mob hesitated. The front rank was suddenly unsure of what was going on, and the rear ranks wanted to find out what was going on and get in on the looting that could be no more than seconds away.

The embassy sally ports opened again, and the two riot-control vehicles, along with the four others Sten had modified, lifted out and opened fire.

Water.

Under medium pressure. Not even at a firehose blast.

The first several ranks of the crowd decided they wanted to go home. It was cold out.

Sten would oblige them, as his second wave of gravlighters boomed out of the embassy. Screams, and people dove out of the way as the dozer blades closed on them before they realized that the gravlighters were deliberately attacking at three meters above the ground.

The lighters weren't intended as weapons – they drove on at speed, toward the barricades down the side streets. They shattered against them once, spun back, and hit again, piled debris and civilian gravsleds spinning out of the way. Now the streets were clear.

The lighters turned and sped back into the embassy grounds. No casualties. Sten sighed in relief – this had been the most dangerous part of his plan, the most likely to produce Imperial casualties.

The mob was swaying, indeterminate.

That gravlighter attack was Sten's bit of humanitarianism, planned to give 'his' mob a back door when the next part of the plan was implemented. He, too, wanted them to go home.

'Now!'

And now people died.

Bhor fingers touched firing switches, and missiles spat out of launch tubes. They were fire-and-forget, but even a guided or unaimed missile could not have missed. Both impacted at point of aim: one on the top floor of that slum, the other in the penthouse of the office building.

Beings who had had no intention of involving themselves in real physical violence, let alone in real jeopardy, had bare seconds to blink, as two fiery lines homed, and the missiles blew.

Blastwaves curled out . . . and other fingers touched triggers. Alpha . . . Bravo . . . Charlie . . .

The street speakers were dead, too, even before they had time to look up to see the plume of death smoke from their superiors' lairs.

The mob was frozen.

And the gates of the embassy swung open.

The yammers, shouts, and screams stopped.

There was utter silence.

And then there came the even crunch of boots on rubble.

Sten, flanked by twenty Gurkhas, strode out the embassy gate. All of them held kukris, the half-meter-long curved-blade knives, held at a forty-five degree angle to their chests, at the ready.

They came forward ten paces. And stopped, without orders.

Ten Bhor, willyguns leveled, came out, veed back for flank security. They, too, crashed to a halt.

There was a murmur from the crowd. These were the killers. The little brown men who took no prisoners, men who, the wild stories had said, killed and ate their own children if they were not murderous enough. All of the slanders the most skilled propagandists on Jochi had spread on the Nepalese warriors, slanders that the Gurkhas had paid no mind, now back-blasted. These men were even more terrible than the tales said. These were not men, even, but killers, who went in with the long knife, and came out leaving nothing but blood and silence behind them.

Again with no orders, Sten and the Gurkhas took one measured pace forward, then stopped.

Another pace.

Another.

In five more paces, they would close on the rabble.

The crowd broke. That mob, intent moments before on obliterating the embassy and tearing apart every being within it, became a scatter of frightened souls, interested only in getting tender behinds out of harm's way.

Howling, screaming, they pelted away, away from the knives, away from the terror.

There was not a flicker from Sten or the Gurkhas.

Sten barely nodded, and the Gurkhas, in unison, about-faced. With equally measured pace, they walked back inside the embassy grounds. The Bhor waited until the Gurkhas were inside, then port-armed and doubled after them.

The gates clanged shut.

Sten moved to a wall, made sure that he could not be seen outside, and sagged against it. A little close, he thought.

Jemedar Lalbahadur Thapa marched to him, came to attention, and saluted.

Sten returned the salute. 'Very good.'

'Not very good,' the Gurkha said. 'Anyone can frighten sheep. Or children. The dead of the Imperial Guard are unavenged.'

Sten, too, turned grim. 'Tonight,' he promised. 'Tonight, or the next night. And then we will not be playing child's games, nor with children.'

It took, in fact, three nights before that moving dot that was the telltale pistol came to rest.

Sten's operation order was verbal, with no record being made, and very short.

Twenty Gurkhas. Volunteers. Standby for special duties at 2300 hours. Sidearms only. Barracks dress.

Alex had lifted an eyebrow at that last: Why not the phototropic cammies?

'I'll want no one to wonder about this later,' Sten said shortly. 'This is authorized slaughter, not private revenge.'

The entire Gurkha detachment volunteered, of course.

Eight Bhor. All master-pilot rated. Four gravlighters. Basic weapons.

Again, Cind told him her entire team wanted to go in. Starting with her, she added.

Sten had said nothing about the nature of the special duties. Evidently he did not have to.

The soldiers assembled at 2200 hours. Outside, the sky was partially overcast, black clouds racing across the face of the four currently visible moons.

There was none of the Gurkha's usual prebattle barracking. They knew. As did, somehow, everyone in the embassy. The canteens and hallways were deserted.

Sten and Alex blackened their faces, put on cammies, and checked their weapons. Sten had his kukri, the knife, and a pistol. Alex had a handgun and a meter-long solid-steel bar he had wrapped with ordnance nonslip tape.

Alex went to the com room for a final look at the target – they had not only the pistol's beeper broadcasting, but four Frick and Fracks orbiting the area, and eight more grounded for area intelligence.

The Gurkhas and their eight Bhor pilots were drawn up in an embassy garage. Cind was in front of the formation.

Sten returned her salute and ordered the troops to open ranks for inspection. The Gurkhas had their kukris drawn. The chin straps of their slouch hats were tight under their lower lips – and their eyes were fixed on infinity.

Sten passed down the ranks. Merely as a formality, he checked one or two of their blades. They were, of course, hand-honed into razors.

He turned the formation back to Cind, and she ordered the weapons sheathed and ranks closed. Alex hurried out of a stairwell, a most grim smile on his face.

'W' hae a feast a' friends,' he said. 'Alive-o, alive-o she cried.

Th' sensors hae fifteen vultures gatherin't. Thae'll be havin't a conference or p'raps a party, but i' looks like th' whole clottin' cell's i' place.'

Sten's acknowledging smile was equally humorless.

He gave the mission orders:

Four-man teams. After grounding, move to the target zone. Wait for the assault command. No guns to be used unless in complete emergency.

And:

No wounded. No prisoners.

They doubled out into the courtyard, where the gravlighters waited. The Bhor slid behind the controls, the Gurkhas boarded the first two – the others would be used for cleanup – and the lighters lifted, flying nap of the city toward the attack zone.

The target was less than twenty minutes flight time away. No one spoke. Sten, hanging over the pilot's right seat, saw the large-projection map on-screen and the blinking dot that represented that pistol and their objective.

It had come to rest two days earlier in a large mansion, surrounded by extended grounds, on a riverbank just outside and upstream from Rurik. A headquarters? A safe house?

Sten did not much care. He and Alex would shake the place – afterward.

The lighters grounded a few hundred meters from the sprawling house.

There was a half-alert sentry at the front and another at the rear. They were silenced.

Alex checked the main entrance for sensors or alarms. There were none.

Sten drew his kukri, and in a ripple, twenty-one other knives flashed in moonlight.

Then the corpse-glow vanished, obscured by clouds.

They went in.

The task took five minutes. There had been no outcry. When it was over, the bodies of fifteen butchered terrorists, and the two sentries, were lined up on the overgrown lawn. Cind searched the bodies for identification and anything intelligence-worthy. There was very little.

Sten and Alex took porta lights from one gravlighter and searched the mansion, in the high-speed, fine-tooth manner they had learned in basic intelligence. Neither of them spoke.

Alex broke the silence. 'Ah hae indicators. Th' mob wae big fans ae Iskra. Look't all th' prop'ganda. All th' same. Jochi for Jochians an' thae. But Ah noo hae aught thae'll link th' quack solid.'

'Nor do I.'

'Clot. Whyn't the bassid happen t' slip oot ae th' evenin', t' hae a brew wi' his thugs, an' we'd find him here.'

'That only happens in the livies.'

'Ah know thae too. But a lad can dream, canna he? C'mon, Sten. Thae's nae f'r us here. Do Ah fire th' place?'

'Yes.'

The bodies had already been loaded onto the two spare gravlighters. Sten waited until he could see flames build inside the mansion, then he ordered withdrawal.

The seventeen bodies would be weighted and dumped far out at sea.

Terrorism, properly implemented, was a double-edged sword. Dr Iskra's people might have a bit of trouble recruiting more action cells after this one vanished into the night and fog.

Then the killers departed, having gone in with the long knife, and come out leaving nothing but blood and silence behind them.

Chapter Thirty-One

Few socio-historians would argue that at the height of his reign the Eternal Emperor held more raw power than any being who had come before him.

His admirers – and they had always been legion – wrote that for most of that reign he chose not to exercise that power. The cynics say that was the key reason he held it for so long: The Emperor was the ideal third-party solution to many heated and bloody disputes.

In short, power was conferred because it was the safest place to put it.

So, when the Emperor set out to win more power still and to wield it against his enemies, he faced a formidable task. As soon as his intentions became clear he knew he would be opposed by despot and democrat alike.

He also knew that the first target his opponents would choose was his competency to rule. The Emperor was too much of a political fox not to understand that all his pluses had a flip-side negative.

The Emperor's triumphant return from death had thrilled his billions of subjects. Grand parades and public spectacles were staged for nearly two years. He was a hero beyond heroism.

But parades all have an end – usually in a back alley where the colorful bunting is revealed to be dull tatters. The thrill of victory soon turns to boredom with mundane daily life. Finally, the victory itself raises problem-solving to an impossible standard. Average beings become frustrated that their own personal problems persist.

They usually lay this to a gut belief that their leaders simply don't care. Socio-historians like to dodge this point. It's one of those basic truths that kick the pins from under their science. Which is why there's nothing a historian distrusts more than the truth.

To counter this political prime negative, the Emperor had to show success. In normal times, he could have pumped up the volume of any number of his efforts. Now, there was nothing but ruins and suffering all about him. To be sure, he had the Tahn war to blame for the ruins; suffering was laid to the excesses of the privy council.

Unfortunately both of those causes had become – in the words of that mythical pol, Lanslidejons'n – pretty old dogs to whup.

The Emperor didn't need excuses. He needed positive action.

When the Khaqan died he saw his opportunity. Here was an entire cluster in shambles. But it was a fixable shambles. Once it was repaired, the cluster would be portrayed as a mini portrait of his Empire: Humans and ETs living and working happily together in the warm glow of Imperial benefice.

This is why he chose Dr Iskra. The being had performed dully but well as a territorial governor. His books were politically correct, his passions tempered. And he surveyed well in the Altaic Cluster. When his name was added to a list of potential rulers, it was viewed favorably by all.

In the survey of Jochians, he came in first. With the Torks, he placed second – after Menynder. Just as he placed second after the favorite sons – an archaic political phrase, no longer implying gender or species – of the Bogazi and Suzdal.

Iskra seemed the safest of bets. The Emperor got into trouble by coppering that bet, then publicizing it Empire-wide.

Sten wasn't sent to the Altaics just because of his undisputed skills of turning ascorbic acid into a tasty, hot-weather drink. His accomplishments were so high-profile that his name guaranteed the attention of the media, hacks as well as pros.

Next, the Emperor launched a sophisticated, although purposely blunt, public relations campaign on Iskra's behalf.

There were thoughtful front-page think pieces planted in scholarly publications, discussing the plight of the citizens of the Altaic, pointing up the gulf between species in the past, and laying that division at the feet of the senile Khaqan. Praise was lavished on Professor Iskra in these pieces. There were frequent mentions of Iskra's abilities as a 'healer of wounds.'

The yellow press was fed the common touch. Iskra was portrayed as an intellect with a heart, a being sworn to live a Spartan existence as an example to his people. His dietary oddities were turned into sidebar recipes and columns on sure-fire ways to health and long life.

The PR clamor over Iskra was so loud that only a fool – and that fool a hermit – wouldn't know the Emperor's prestige was hung out to dry in the Altaics.

So when the bomb blew at the Imperial barracks on Rurik, more than the lives of the Emperor's troops were destroyed. His own plans were in danger of going up in the same smoke.

Sure, he had that big dog Mahoney waiting in the wings. But he couldn't unleash him yet. There was much political groundwork to prepare.

The Emperor needed a momentary, stopgap solution.

He acted swiftly. The solution was a news blackout.

Ranett was an old-fashioned see-for-herself newsbeing. She was also a legendary combat reporter who had covered the Tahn war from the front lines. She had kept her head low during the murderous years of the privy council. But she had kept on scribbling notes during those years. When the Emperor returned she had turned those notes into a stunning series of livie documentaries detailing the atrocities and stupidities of the privy council.

The last installment ran just as Iskra was assuming power in the Altaics. The broadcast was viewed by billions. It would be cynical to say that this was the reason the Eternal Emperor had insisted on personally thanking her in a tag to that final broadcast.

Ranett took this praise from on high in typical stride. When the vid camera shut off she turned to the Emperor and asked, 'Your Majesty, what's with this clown, Iskra?'

The Emperor's smiling face went blank. He pretended he hadn't heard. His attention suddenly shifted to important matters of state. Before Ranett could repeat the question, the Emperor's front men had hustled him out the door.

So Ranett decided to learn the answer to the question herself. Her editor was not pleased.

'I got Altaic Cluster stories and Iskra beeswax comin' out my clottin' ears, Ranett. Who needs more? Besides, good news does not sell vid casts.'

'I don't think it's all that good,' Ranett answered. 'Otherwise I wouldn't ask.'

'That's a lotta drakh, Ranett. Anything happens in that cluster is good news. They been down so long, everything looks up to them. No, what we need is for you to go find some nice little war to cover. With lots of blood.'

'If I go to the Altaics,' Ranett said, 'I think I'll find all the blood you want.'

'Whatcha got besides reporter's instinct?'

Ranett just stared at her editor in eloquent silence. Then she shrugged, meaning: *instinct was all she had, but it was by-god bankable instinct*. The editor stared back at her. Hard. His silence was equally eloquent in this routine battle of the wills. Then he lifted an eyebrow, meaning: *are you really, really sure?* Ranett shrugged again.

The editor sighed. 'You clottin' win. Go, already.'

Ranett went low profile. She got a spare berth on a freighter bound for the Altaics. The only beings aware of her journey were her editor, the company clerk who made out the expense chits, and the freighter captain, a reliable drunk.

Ranett was one of those individuals who habitually find themselves in the right place at the right time. 'I'm just lucky that way,' she would tell her colleagues at the press club bar. They never believed it. They attributed her good work and fortune to 'lies, bribes, and looks.' Ranett didn't lie, would rather skip a story than grease a palm, and her looks were merely adequate.

Her luck struck again two E-days out of the Altaic Cluster,

when she caught word of the disaster on Rurik. As she listened to the confused broadcasts on the ship's communicator, Ranett chortled. She would be the *only* major-league newsbeing in place to report on the incident and its certain nasty aftermath.

Ranett hustled off to her cabin to double up on her homework. She had hauled along a big case of fiches on the cluster's dirty little history.

Eighteen E-hours out of Jochi, the captain came sober and shamefaced to her door. 'Got some bad news, lady,' he said. 'We gotta go back.'

Ranett pierced him with that look famous for buckling knees far sturdier than his. 'Explain, please.'

The captain shook his head. 'I can't. Company veep wouldn't say why. Just said, do not deliver cargo to Jochi. And to get my butt back to Soward.'

'So, forget the cargo,' Ranett said. 'You can still deliver me.'

'No way, lady. Sorry.'

'I'll pay extra. Double fare. Hell, I'll charter your whole damned ship!'

The captain sighed. This was wounding his mercenary soul. 'I was ordered not to set down on Jochi. In any circumstances.'

Ranett came to her feet. 'You people have a contract with my company,' she snapped. 'And I expect it to be carried out – in full!'

She racked the captain up against the wall. 'Now, get that buttwipe veep on the line. You hear?'

The captain heard.

She started with the veep and worked her way up to the president of the shipping line, scorching space from the Altaics to Prime in the process.

It was hopeless.

As the freighter turned maddeningly around and set off on its return journey, Ranett learned two things: The shipping line was as upset as she was at the action – there was an expensive and perishable cargo aboard the freighter. And the order had been initiated outside the company.

Meaning it was political.

Meaning the action could only be aimed at her.

Someone real important wanted to stop Ranett from getting the story on Jochi.

And there was nothing she could do.

Her editor was equally irked. 'Nobody will admit it, but this has Imperial interference written all over it,' he fumed on the deep-space hookup. 'I jerked chains all the way up to Arundel, but it's no good. Everybody's scared.'

'How'd they find out I was on the way?' Ranett asked.

'Snoops. Bugs. What else? I'm having our offices swept by security right now.'

'What's our competition doing?' Ranett wanted to know.

'That's the only good news,' the editor said. 'It's not just us. Nobody but nobody with press credentials gets to the Altaics.'

Enough details did leak out, however, to put the Emperor into a high rage.

BARRACKS BOMB TOLL SOARS, read one vid screamer. SHAME ON THE ALTAICS, read another. And there were many more: GUARDSMEN'S FAMILIES IN SHOCK ... TRAGIC IMPERIAL FOUL-UP ON RURIK ... The more thoughtful vid casts weighed in with: ALTAIC TURMOIL TIED TO ISKRA ... QUESTIONS RAISED ON EMPEROR'S CHOICE OF OBSCURE PROFESSOR ... ISKRA: THE SCHOLAR TYRANT.

'Next time I write a constitution,' the Emperor railed, 'I want an Official Secrets Act with *real* damned teeth in it. I want prison terms. I want firing squads – I want clottin' torture chambers, dammit!'

The woman with the lush young figure and old pol eyes applauded. 'No problem with that drakh,' Avri said. 'Last polls I ran on the media showed the rubes are with ya, boss. Ten percent think a free press is important. Sixty-five percent say kick those rabble-rousers off the sleigh. And the other twenty-five percent were so dumb they thought the Evening News was a livie sitcom.'

The Emperor's rage turned to booming laughter. 'That's what I liked about you from the start, Avri,' he said. 'You always cut to the chase.'

'I got my masters in scalp hunting on Dusable,' she said. 'But I got my Ph.D. watching you in action ... sir.' Avri looked the Emperor up and down in frank admiration. 'I never met or heard of a politician living or dead who coulda pulled what you pulled.'

The Emperor made humble noises. 'I didn't invent anything. I just stole from the masters.' He gave Avri a wolfish grin. 'Of course, I put a few new twists on the rules.'

'I'll say you clottin' did, uh, sir.'

'Knock off the sir,' the Emperor said. 'When we're in private, of course. There's no room for respect in a business that votes graveyards.'

The Emperor had met Avri on his long road back from death to the Imperial crown. He had needed to fix an election on Dusable, and she was handling the perfect candidate for the job: an empty-headed pretty boy who would sit and heel and fetch in those votes like a good little political doggy.

At the time, he had mainly appreciated Avri's crooked brain. But as he looked at her now, poured into a black body suit, other areas of interest came to mind. Avri caught the look. She gave him a 'don't mind at all' smile and stretched back in her seat to give him a better view. The Emperor felt a stir. He put it aside for a while. Let it age in the cooler.

'How are things lining up in Parliament?' he asked.

'Real nice,' Avri said, a bit disappointed. But she brightened quickly as she took up her favorite game: counting yeas and nays. 'Tyrenne Walsh has been practicing that speech we worked up for him. The dumb clot doesn't understand a word he's saying – but he *sounds* positively yummy.' Walsh was the pretty boy Avri and the Emperor had put into the top job on Dusable – toppling one of the canniest and dirtiest old political bosses in the Empire, while they were at it.

Now the Emperor had called in Avri to launch his plan to turn the independent Imperial provinces into under-his-thumb dominions.

'Here's how I have it mapped,' Avri said. 'Walsh gives the lead-off speech, just like you said. He makes with the high-minded buzzwords to start: duty, loyalty, patriotism . . . all those words that hit the symbolism buzzer hard.'

The Emperor nodded. 'Fine. Fine. Then he makes the big statement, right?'

'That's what you wanted,' Avri said, 'but I think you're moving for the bottom line too fast. I mean, we don't want him to sound like your stooge.'

The Emperor chuckled. 'Heaven forbid.'

'Well, that's how it'll sound,' Avri said. 'What we want him to do is announce that he's going to be the first big boss to turn over his system to you.'

'You mean, to become one of my dominions,' the Emperor said.

'Sameo, sameo,' Avri said. 'Of course, in Walsh's case it don't matter. He's already being run. By yours truly. But some of the other types are used to calling their own shots. They're not gonna go that easy.'

The Emperor saw her point. 'What did you have in mind?'

'A hero sandwich,' Avri said. 'If we put enough garbage in this bun, nobody'll notice how thin the slices of ham and cheese are. And they'll have voted and be halfway home before the heart-burn cuts in.'

'Go on,' the Emperor said.

'Okay, so we wave the flag like you said.' Avri made a crude pumping gesture with a closed fist. 'Then we lay on some personal suffering biz. You know: the letter from the little old lady who's sending in her last credit to help bail out the Empire. And I did a vid layout on some starving infants. Good creepy drakh. Orange hair. Swollen bellies. Real neato heart tuggers.'

'Blood, sweat, and baby urine,' the Emperor said. 'It always works.'

'Sure. With your left hand. Okay, now get this. While they're still gaggin' on the screwed up kids, I wanna smack 'em good with an old soldier's routine I worked up.'

'This is getting pretty interesting,' the Emperor said. 'I might vote for this thing four or five times myself.'

'You better,' Avri said. 'You need *margin* on this sucker . . . Now. I dug up some old general of yours. Been retired thirty some years. More dirt in his head than brains. I got him all worked up about the quote 'plight of the Empire' end quote. Got him good and weepy. At the end, he struggles to his feet – I put him on crutches – and calls on all the beings in your Empire to pull together.

'He does a terrific unity whine. Says this is the greatest emergency in his lifetime. And that no sacrifice is too great to ratchetaratcheta – it'll work like a charm. I guarantee it. Laid it on a test group last night. Not a dry eye in the house. Best of all, the audience emptied its pockets for the Imperial relief fund. Best bucks per capita those frauds have ever seen.'

'Then Walsh makes the announcement?' the Emperor asked.

'Then Walsh makes the announcement.'

'Great job,' the Emperor said. 'But I have one wrinkle to add to your problem.'

'What's that?'

'That boost I'm planning in the AM2 tax?'

Avri nodded. 'Yeah. Good idea. Scare clot out of the holdouts. What about it?'

'I want to make it retroactive. To all the AM2 since the end of the Tahn war.'

Avri whistled. 'Might scare 'em too much.'

'Sorry. You're going to have to work around it, somehow.'

Avri's eyes suddenly brightened. 'Maybe if the general died at the end. On-camera collapse type of thing. So we're leading with quote "dying last words" end quote. He's pretty feeble. I imagine the techs can give him a stroke for the retake.'

'Bad idea,' the Emperor said.

'Yeah. Somebody might find out. Leak it.'

'I'm not worried about that,' the Emperor said. 'It's just his dying words will upstage Walsh. And he's the boy carrying this thing.'

Avri caught his logic. 'That's why you're the boss,' she said. 'I'll figure something. It'll be easy.'

The interview over, Avri was giving the Emperor 'the look' again – eyes misting over, squirming in her seat. 'Anyway,' she husked, 'that's the plan.'

'No quarrels from me,' the Emperor said. 'Put it into action.'

He returned the look. Let his gaze run across her body. Starting from the toes . . . working slowly up.

'Will there be anything . . . else?' Avri asked.

The Emperor let it wait. Then: 'Maybe . . . later.'

'Did I mention my secretary?' Avri asked. She licked her lips. 'She's been a lot of . . . help on this thing.'

'I'll have to thank her some time,' the Emperor said.

'I could call her . . . now.'

'Make it personal?' the Emperor said, voice low.

'Real personal. Just the . . . three of us.'

'Call her,' the Eternal Emperor said.

Chapter Thirty-Two

Poyndex screened the report yet again. It had not changed since he had last read it, three minutes ago. If it had not come from a long-trusted – as much as any spymaster ever trusts a source – field agent, he would have thought either someone was trying to shuck him, or else the report was on a loop from years before in the days of the privy council.

Poyndex had promised himself, back on Earth, that he would be 'good,' that he would quit running agents and trying to figure out what was 'really' happening. Of course, he could not. No one who had ever walked in the shadow world ever believed that the truth was what was in the spotlight.

According to the report, someone was putting large credits behind the Cult of the Emperor. Just as Kyes of the council had years earlier. And this someone was not an easily findable 'anonymous benefactor.' The credits were coming in through multiple sources, all of which could be traced just so far, and then hit a stone wall.

Poyndex idly ran the cult through an open-search function to see if anything else of interest was going on.

In a few minutes he had an answer.

A great deal was occurring. High-ranking cult members that a file had automatically been opened on, back in Poyndex's Mercury Corps days, were realizing their dreams. They were being promoted – frequently over the heads of their former superiors – quite rapidly.

Hair lifted suddenly on the back of Poyndex's neck. His fingers slashed keys, and he bailed out of the search. His forehead beaded sweat.

Poyndex considered, then grimaced.

He was probably being paranoiac. But the same sense of danger shrilled that had howled through his system after that bomb in the Imperial guts had been removed.

He was grateful he had programmed his computer to work with cutouts. The search, for instance, could be traced by a sufficiently skilled expert. But the trace would lead to an open library terminal on a faraway frontier world.

The Cult of the Emperor was active . . .

He slid open a hidden cover on the side of the keyboard and forced two tabs together, activating an OVERRIDE command and breaking a fingernail in the process.

There was but one being Poyndex could think of who could play that many cultists like puppets on a string, and who would also have that many sterile channels to pour money down . . .

His computer instantly wiped itself sterile and was overwritten, just as standard military procedure dictated. Then it was automatically wiped yet again . . . and again overwritten.

The Eternal Emperor himself . . .

Poyndex's computer clicked, and the third, final program was added, files and a program that excluded any action that Poyndex had taken within the last E-week.

But what benefit could the Emperor gain from the Cult of the Eternal Emperor?

Poyndex felt a little safer.

Did he want to have himself made a god, for pity's sake?

And now there was a chill beyond zero Kelvin, and Poyndex felt that never again would he be safe, never again could he not look over his shoulder knowing what he now believed true.

Sr Ecu, the universe's diplomat emeritus, banked, nearly spun out, and wished that his race understood the unquestionably leavening benefits of profanity and obscenity.

Below him was arctic desolation.

Gray seas crashed high against a solitary rock pinnacle to his right. To his left a monstrous iceberg floated. It was bright blue on the slate seas – the only primary color as far as the eye could see. An achingly lonely color.

Ecu did not wish to judge this world, but he found it had all the charm of the Christian religion's hell, with the fires out.

On an ice floe far below, a dot moved. He focused on the dot, and the dot became a huge, obese aquatic creature, a creature whose blubbery hide, tusks, and skin suited it for this frozen hell, who probably thought the weather a pleasant spring freshet.

It made little sense that the unknown being on that ice cube below appeared to be a primitive fish-eater – but in fact could well be one of this world's premier philosophers. Or poets.

A shearing gust caught him, and Ecu almost lost control once more. His three-meter-long tail thrashed air, trying to stabilize, as his great white wings curled, reconfiguring lift areas to the blast – their red-tipped winglets trying to damp Ecu's overcontrolling.

He was too old and too dignified for this nonsense, solo-flying through a polar storm as if he were a spratling who had just discovered flight.

He also thought that everything to do with this self-appointed project of his smacked of the low-grade melodramas that children and bumpkins appreciated, with clearly marked heroes and villains – One Being against the Forces of Evil, and so forth.

Let alone that Sr Ecu actually believed, and winced from the belief, that he was the only being who seemed to be aware of this great evil, an evil that could bring everything shattering down. This, his thoughts continued, was absurdity, and he prided himself on being someone who had learned that there was seldom truth and almost never light. Everything was shades of gray, to be analyzed and interpreted most carefully.

Perhaps Rykor would have attendants waiting, who would skillfully sedate the Manabi and escort him to a padded room where he could spend the rest of his days babbling about the Eternal Emperor.

Perhaps that was why he had sent the material ahead of him, material that he had laboriously transferred into an exotic code they'd used back during the days of the tribunal – when the members of the privy council were to be brought to trial for their crimes.

Sr Ecu tried to bring his thoughts under control, just as he wished, with equal lack of success, that he could cause this williwaw to subside into a calm. He thought, ruefully, that one reason his mind was so undisciplined was that he was frankly terrified. Fear was a feeling that always prevented logical analysis.

Not that he was irrational to feel it.

Sr Ecu might have served the Eternal Emperor on many occasions, and even convinced his race to ignore their long-held neutrality and clandestinely back the Empire during the Tahn war, but he was under no illusions as to what the Emperor would most likely do if he was aware of Sr Ecu's thoughts, beliefs, and mission.

Which was one reason he had vanished from his own world, telling no one his mission or destination. His passage to Rykor's home world had been made on one of the Romany free-trading ships. Another relationship, he realized, that had come from the tribunal days, and had originally been created by that man who had wanted anyone to be able to fly: Sten.

Sten had drawn Ecu into his involvement with the tribunal with a simple gift: a kit-built holographic display of an ancient Earth 'air circus,' where ground-bound humans jeopardized their lives by riding in twin-wing combustion-powered aircraft any self-respecting *archaeopteryx* would have sneered at.

Seeing the model, Sr Ecu had marveled:

'*Did they really do that . . . I've never really appreciated before what it was like to be permanently grounded by an accident of genes. My God, how desperately they wanted to fly.*'

'*Beings will risk a great deal,*' Sten had said, '*for a little freedom.*'

He wondered how the human was doing in his assignment in the Altaic Cluster. He hoped well – but he suspected, especially considering the recent news blackout on the area, that the situation, already bad, was growing worse.

He considered if Rykor somehow thought his mad theory to be correct, whether Sten would be brought in. How? In what capacity? he jeered at himself. And to do what?

Are you starting to do what these humans do, and think that any time a seemingly irresolvable problem appears, the solution is to collectively throw up your hands and turn everything over to a ruler in shining armor, who, of course, turns out to be a tyrant?

That was what had created the present situation.

That, Ecu corrected himself, and AM2.

AM2. That was the stumbling block. Without AM2 everything in the Empire, its triumphs as well as its crimes, would be lost.

And AM2 was what would prevent, Ecu finished morosely, finding any real solution to this problem.

The horizon cleared, and he saw an island ahead. It was as grim and uninviting as the rest of this world, jagged rocky spires jutting up from bouldered shallows. Desolate – but his white sensing whiskers told him there was life down there.

Then his eyes confirmed his other sense, as he saw movement

on one of the island's rocky 'beaches.' More beings, like the one who had waved to him, were sprawled on the icy wave-washed slabs as if they were humans basking in a tropic sun.

He heard a bellow over the wind-howl as one of those beings stretched to its full height on rear flippers, and *hoonked* a greeting. Rykor . . . it must be.

The being humped a few awkward meters on land, dove, and became eely grace into a breaking wave, then vanished.

Now, Sr Ecu thought in irritation, how am I supposed to emulate her behavior? Am I supposed to follow her underwater like I'm triphibious?

Then black rock moved aside and there was the entrance to a wide tunnel yawning in the middle of one of the island's cliffs. Around it and above, on the cliff top, antennae bristled.

Ecu tucked and plummeted, reflexively curling his winglets even though the tunnel was more than wide enough to allow a medium-size starfreighter entry.

This was Rykor's home – and her office.

Ian Mahoney frequently compared Rykor to a walrus in jest. But in fact, the similarities were only physical – to a degree – and Rykor's species was also aquatic by evolution and preference. The physical resemblance wasn't that great – Rykor was a third again as big as the biggest Earth *Odobenus*, with a body length of over five meters and weight of more than two thousand kilos.

Her species, however, was known for its intellect, particularly in areas requiring intuitive analysis and the ability to draw extrapolative conclusions from fixed data. Therefore, they were poets. Philosophers. City- and world-planners. And, as in the case of Rykor, psychologists.

When she retired, she was the highest-ranked psychologist in Imperial Service. She also had been used, *sub rosa*, by Ian Mahoney – then head of Mercury Corps and Mantis – as his specialist in the headworkings of spies, saboteurs, assassins, and traitors, Imperial and unfriendly.

She had been convinced to come out of safety and seclusion by Sten, when he had set up the tribunal. She had then, like everyone else involved in what had seemed triumph at the time, been offered anything and everything. But after the Emperor's return, she had realized why she had retired in the first place: there were volumes to be written on human and other species' behavior patterns that she and no one else had experienced and could possibly explain.

Plus Rykor had a surfeit of what was, truthfully, bending her skills into the service of someone else to convince the analyzed person/culture to behave in a certain manner.

Now she was being asked to use her talents once more. But for a far greater purpose – this time by Ecu.

'This is most unusual,' Rykor apologized. 'I had this chamber constructed to deal with my land-bound friends and clients. And also as a personal joke, since I spent so many years serving the Empire from either a saltwater tank or a gravchair.'

Sr Ecu waggled his sensing whiskers, politely indicating amusement – his species needed no ego reinforcement for being clever.

This chamber *was* fitting revenge. It was a high-ceilinged, wide-mouthed tidal cave, whose above-water entrance had been closed with a transparent wall. Ecu thought the wall was probably mobile and would rise and fall with the tide. Looking out to sea, there appeared to be nothing between the crashing surf and the viewer except those spray-drenched boulders that formed a partially sheltering lagoon outside. Wind and sea sounds were miked and their level controlled by a mixboard. Entrance to this cave was by diving under the wall for Rykor and her fellows, or by solid passageways for land beings.

Ecu hovered just above the artificial shelf Rykor had built for land-bound visitors. It, too, was tide-responsive and would rise and fall so that it always was a few centimeters above the gentle waves inside this cave.

The shelf was fitted with all sorts of comforts and devices, from viewers to coms to computers. Above this conference room were apartments and dining areas.

Rykor's own quarters and work areas were reached by underwater tunnels that led from chamber to chamber. The equipment Rykor used in her normal course of work was either environmentally insensitive or sealed.

'I am,' Rykor said, 'somewhat unfamiliar with the . . . etiquette, let alone the practicalities, of entertaining an aerial being. Do you, well . . .'

'Roost?' Ecu's whiskers twitched once more, and, after a moment of slight embarrassment, Rykor's own face bristles ruffled and her sonic-blast laughter echoed around the chamber until the active acoustic system damped it.

'No,' he said. 'My race lands but seldom. And then for specific purposes.' He did not explain; Rykor did not ask.

'May I offer you refreshment? Since the Manabi are not the most commonly entertained race in this Empire, it was most hard to learn what you preferred to ingest. But I gather the following, in spray form, is considered pleasurable. Even though these microorganisms aren't exactly duplicated on this world, we have synthesized the mixture.'

Her flippers stretched and touched keys on a floating panel beside her. An overhead screen flashed a chemical formula. Ecu scanned it. Again, he 'laughed.'

'Your source was correct, Rykor. We do enjoy that organic compote. But it also renders us hors de flight, and we become "pissed as newts," as our mutual friend Kilgour puts it. Perhaps later. Perhaps when we have begun our discussions I will feel less like a fool, less worried, and more able to relax.

'Or you may wish to sedate me with that formula, since I fear my basic neural reactions are becoming unpredictable.'

'Manabi,' Rykor said flatly, 'don't go insane.'

'I may be the first.'

The cave was still, except for the sound of the sea and the wind, dimly in the background. Rykor floated motionlessly for a while.

'No,' she said, firmly. 'You are not insane. I have gone through your material. Analyzed it both intellectually and electronically. Further, I allowed my most trusted aide – do not start: he is, in fact, one of my sister's pups and is to be trusted, since the corruptions of the Empire don't interest us, and thus far nobody has attempted to subvert us with fishing rights on an Imperial river on Earth.'

She laughed again and Ecu felt himself relax.

'First, though,' she said, 'let me express my thanks for that parcel you sent. It's the first real "book' from ancient Earth I've owned. A question: Was the volume originally waterproofed?'

'I had that done.'

'Ah. I surmised. I found it most interesting, and charming, in a sad sort of way. I imagined this primitive human, writing in the darkest of dark ages, sitting there and staring out at what must have been terrible times.

'In those days, there would have been nobody but witchfreuds, I think they were called, who cast spells and made vile potions in cooking pots, their couches spread around the great tribal fire that kept out the real and imagined monsters of the dark.' She whuffled sympathy. 'And so this poor man imagined that one day there would be rules for psychology. That it would become a science. Except that – what did he call it? Psychohistory? It was a fascinating conceit.

'I, myself, find that dream fascinating. Although I realize that if we can't solve the n-body problem in astronomy, the tera-cubed-tera-plus bodies that constitute intelligent life will never be fitted into a computation.

'I must say, however, I found the scribe's hero, that Selden human, rather repellant. Far too reminiscent of some of my creche tutors, full of false truth, wretched prejudice, and themselves.

'But I digress.

'I see why you sent me that present, however, and how this fictional, fumbling attempt to find order in an entropic universe and equally entropic Empire pertains to the data you provided.

'A question. Were you selective in the material – choosing only data that supported your theory?'

'I was not,' Ecu said. 'I attempted to provide as complete an assemblage as I knew how.'

'Your experience in diplomacy suggests that you do know how to be fair,' Rykor said. 'I took the liberty of reducing your raw data into symbolic logic.'

Again, she touched keys, and several screens lit. Ecu, even though he did not use symbology a great deal in his art, knew the discipline.

It took almost an hour for the data, even crunched into computer language, to screen.

As gibberish to most people, it may have been a little less depressing. But not to the two experienced beings in the sea cave. Finally the last screen blanked.

'Is my reduction approximately correct?' Rykor asked.

'Not approximately. Exactly.' Ecu's wings sagged. The situation was as bad as he had thought it was.

'Summarizing your theses verbally,' Rykor went on, coldly, clinically, 'it's evident that the Empire is in the direst straits. Not cause for total panic, though, since this isn't the first or the fiftieth time that Imperial catastrophe has loomed. However, you have further theorized that this economic, social, and political decline is being accelerated by the Empire itself. Specifically, by the actions the Eternal Emperor has taken since his . . . return.'

Sr Ecu said, 'That was where I feared I was becoming less than competent in my thinking.'

'Not at all. Since I've reassured you as to your sanity, would you now care for that refreshment? Because it's now my turn to reason, and to add some interesting data that I have gotten on my own, since your package arrived.'

'Thank you. I shall indulge.'

'It is in a pressure container, just to your right. Activated – yes, with that rather large lever.'

Moisture hissed into the air. Sr Ecu felt himself lifted and momentarily was reminded of the time, once on Earth, when he had seen simple avians frolicking in a spray of water.

Rykor treated herself to what appeared to be a slab of flamedried peat. 'Piscean leather,' she explained. 'Hung just beyond the highest reaches of the ocean spray, and wind-dried. It's as close to a narcotic as my sometimes simplistic race has managed. Although research goes on.

'Continuing. I noticed that you included in your data the disaster our young crusader, Sten, is trying to solve. The Altaic Cluster. He's sustaining a madman, as you're aware. A Dr Iskra. Did you know that this Iskra is a being who's been supported in exile for years by the Emperor? To control the former ruler.

'I further found that Sten is under direct orders from the Emperor that Iskra must be kept in office, regardless of cost.'

Ecu's body rocked in a nonexistent blast of wind. 'What is your source on this?' he asked.

'I cannot say. My colleague remains in the system, and therefore in danger.'

Rykor stopped and her tail flippers crashed down against the water's surface. 'How odd,' she mused. 'To hear myself say a friend's life is in danger because that friend is close to our respected ruler, and because this friend speaks a bit of the truth.'

'I, myself, have felt potentially in physical jeopardy,' Ecu confessed.

Rykor did not answer that, but went on. 'A second fact. I don't recall when I stumbled upon it. But I assure you it was in the course of some legitimate field of inquiry. As I said, I disremember the circumstances, but I found myself wondering just what the Emperor gained – directly, monetarily – from his rule. Or was the mere exercise of power adequate recompense? So I investigated.

'Obviously I was most careful in my curiosity. But I found that, indeed, the Emperor had rather incredible funds, invested in various arenas where his governing policies would also prove financially rewarding. The investments were made with multiple cutouts that could never be traced back to the Emperor. I found such an action neither moral nor immoral. These investments, I further learned, had been used during times of disaster to support the economy . . . as well as his policies. Which would suggest these profits would be considered "moral" by most. I think they're called a slushy fund by humans.'

'Slush.'

'Is the spray affecting – oh. Yes. Slush would be correct. A few days ago, I very carefully rechecked a couple of those funds.

'The Emperor's personal wealth is increasing at a monstrous rate, second by second. In these times, which most would call depressed, our own ruler is vastly profiting from his own Empire's poverty.'

'That's insane,' Ecu said, his normal smoothness broken.

'For the first time, I agree with your application of the word, even though it is clinically without meaning. By the way – some support for what you just said. Have you been watching the Eternal Emperor when he appears on livie casts lately? More and more rarely, of course, and when he does the angles are favorable and remote. But look closely at the way his eyes shift, like a whipped Earth canine waiting for another beating – or else someone who is slipping further and further into what used to be called a manic-depressive psychosis.'

Again, Sr Ecu wished that profanity provided a meaningful form of expression to his race. Rykor was suggesting that the Empire was now ruled by a madman, and the thought was monstrously inconceivable. Yet, his backbrain reminded him how many times had he dealt with insane rulers and felt vague, impersonal sympathy for the poor beings they tyrannized.

'Another piece of the puzzle,' Rykor continued. 'The Emperor has ordered large increases in military development. The Cairenes, for instance, were desolated when the Tahn war ended. Military shipbuilding was no longer necessary, and their patron, Sullamora, was killed.

'Then, and I do not understand this, the Cairenes somehow became AM2-fat during the course of the Imperial return. You'll recall that the Emperor's physical return was on a ship from the Cairenes' central system of Dusable. Very well, somehow the Emperor was helped, and the beings of Dusable were rewarded.

'That is the way politics has worked. So ignore the original Golden Calf and his Eggs, or whatever creature it was.

'But their prosperity has continued. Within the last E-year, I've learned, nearly a hundred contracts have been placed with the shipyards of the Cairenes. None of them were put out for open bids. In these times, when there is peace, why build warships? There are more than enough left from the wars. In fact, the scrap yards are full of never-commissioned hulks.'

'Could it be,' Ecu theorized, deliberately playing devil's advocate, 'what I have heard the Emperor call pork-barreling?'

'It could. But I dislike using anything nonsentient to reason from. It's my discipline's prejudice, of course.

'But here is another part of that same puzzle piece. A colleague of mine – actually she was one of the humans I attempted to train into logical paths – had an interesting assignment. She's an expert at the psychology of military recruiting. She prepared a campaign, under very exact orders, for the Tahn worlds.'

'What?'

'Yes. Our former enemy, now even further depressed than the Empire. Nothing is being done to improve their economic lot, by the way. But recruiting officers are blanketing these worlds and signing up recruits.'

'It's evil,' Ecu said, 'but it happens that the military, historically, offers its shilling most loudly where poverty is the worst.'

'Correct. But if you remember, the Emperor was determined, at war's end, that the old military ravings that the Tahn called their homicidal/suicidal "culture" would be destroyed. But today these Imperial recruiters are using a campaign that rings every change on the idea that it's time for the warrior Tahn to rise up and redeem themselves. Prove they still have the thews of their elders, even though those elders fought in an evil cause. Now it is time for you to help defend the Empire. And so on and so forth.'

Ecu drifted high up, near the cave's apex, while he thought on this. 'It might make sense, to an economic babe, to spend your way out of a depression by purchasing unneeded weaponry,' he said. 'But you do not hire soldiers or sailors. They are simply too expensive and too troublesome in time of peace. Simple welfare and breadlines are more cost efficient, if you are one who can think that cold-bloodedly. Why look for soldiers,' he finished, 'if there is no enemy?'

'Possibly the Emperor *does* see an enemy,' Rykor said softly.

'Consider the nature of kings,' she said in a near-whisper. 'Consider what they become.'

'But the Emperor is Eternal,' Ecu said, his normal equanimity shattered. 'This has never happened before.'

'No. It has not. Something has changed. But that is not my concern.' She tapped keys again. 'It's deceptive, and very easy, for each generation, as it ages, to whine about Armageddon. But computers do not become irascible and curmudgeonly.

'I ran progs. Predictions.

'We'll go through this later, after we have both rested, to make sure that there is no error. But the conclusions I've ended with are these: The Empire is finally proving that it is no genetic sport. Like all Empires before it, it is following the path of hardening, corruption, decay, and is now doomed to destruction. Not from any historical process, or from any external enemy. But because of one being: The Eternal Emperor.'

That had been Sr Ecu's final judgment exactly.

'I assume,' Rykor said, after some time and thought had passed, 'that you came here for more than confirmation of your sanity. You are far too rational a being to travel this far, at this risk to your race and person, just to want reinforcement.'

'Yes,' Ecu said. And suddenly the thought flashed through him: Here he was, master diplomat. Consultant. Expert adviser. Gray eminence for half a thousand rulers, and a being who had even proffered advice to the Eternal Emperor himself, and whose advice had been accepted. Here he was, needing Rykor's advice, as if he were an emotionally troubled spratling.

He understood just why Rykor was held in the respect she was.

'You want to know,' Rykor said, 'what we must do to prevent this.'

'Yes,' Ecu said once more.

'I do not know. I have considered, and will consider again. But I have no answer.

'However, I will offer you one thought, since everything I've said is slightly bleaker than midnight. Consider this. What would have happened if the Emperor had not returned? I mean, returned at all, not returned at a later date.'

'We would have had chaos,' Ecu said. 'A collapse into barbarism.'

'I agree. But it would've stemmed from one reason only – the loss of AM2, correct? The presence or absence of the Emperor is not a significant enough factor to bring everything crashing down.'

'Yes,' Sr Ecu said cautiously. 'I agree with that.'

'Thank you. Now, isn't it true that every race, every culture, has had dark ages? Sometimes many of them?'

Sr Ecu's body ducked – an assenting nod.

'And they are always recovered from?'

'I cannot say always,' Ecu said. 'Races might well have slipped into total barbarism, and we have not encountered them. Or degenerated into complete anarchy and race-suicide.'

'Eliminate the always, then,' Rykor went on. 'But it is true, generally. Isn't it also true that once the blight of savagery is thrown off, the next stage is a renaissance?'

'Yes. And you cheer me, even if I don't believe that would apply to the Empire. Its presence is too large, too ancient, and too omnipotent.'

'Not if AM2 is taken out of the equation.'

'But the Emperor is the only being who knows where AM2 exists in its raw state, or how it is synthesized.'

'Sr Ecu,' Rykor reprimanded gently, 'you're far too educated and sophisticated to allow yourself to think there is but one inventor who can produce a particular invention. One painter who can produce that picture. Or one philosopher who is capable of producing a social system.'

Sr Ecu said, 'Again, you have cheered me. But I'm afraid I don't believe that putting together some sort of Manhattan Project to look for AM2 would be successful. The privy council seemed to have tried hard enough.'

'The privy council was, and again I've got to use semantically loaded words, evil. A less charged word would be self-oriented. But I'll use evil. Evil, being the opposite of good – both words are in quotes – is, by definition, short-sighted, self-serving, lazy, and dishonest. Therefore their search could only be limited and doomed to failure.'

'Rykor, how can you remain such an optimist, after all your experience?' Ecu wondered, amused. 'I have seen evil triumph at least as frequently as good.'

'As Kilgour would say in that primitive dialect he believes to be an understandable language, a clean mind, a clean body. Take your pick.

'Now,' she said, heaving her bulk out of the water, onto the shelf, and into a gravchair, 'shall we move to an upper chamber, where food and more of your spray awaits? We needn't panic tonight. Even entropy moves at a measured, slow pace.'

Ecu floated above her gravchair as they moved up, deeper into the crag's depths, still considering their ultimate problem. He realized that somehow both of them had rather casually accepted the fact that the Emperor must be removed, or at least rendered harmless. Putting aside the matter of AM2, the next question would be, who could conceivably, in the human phrase, bell this colossal cat?

A name passed through his brain once more:

That man who wanted anyone to fly.

Sten.

Chapter Thirty-Three

The echoes of the barracks bombing were still reverberating when Iskra moved to consolidate and extend his power. The Eternal Emperor's news blackout played right into his hands.

Iskra hit the airways with a blistering attack on those (unnamed) traitors who had humiliated the Altaic Cluster by their cowardly attack on the Emperor's peacekeeping forces. He declared martial law. Set a one-hour-after-dawn and one-hour-before-dusk curfew. Banned all demonstrations, public protests, and strikes. He also hinted darkly at 'other measures' that would be 'revealed at the appropriate time.' He ended with an impassioned plea that all citizens search their 'souls and their neighbors' souls' for any sign of disloyalty.

After generations of violent repression, people knew what was going to happen next. Some dug into mattresses and gardens for bribe money. Some made lists of enemies they could nark on. Most cowered in their homes and waited for the crash of bootheels and rifle butts thundering on doors.

But experienced as they were in the politics of fear, the beings of the Altaic Cluster were not braced for what followed.

*

Milhouz was lean and proud in his new black uniform with its rakish beret and silver 'Students for Iskra' badge. He had a captain's tab on one shoulder and a Purity Corps patch on the other.

He hoisted his pistol and snarled orders to his eager, youthful forces. 'I want this timed perfectly. Get into position – quietly, dammit! And when I give the signal, we all rush at once. Got it?'

There was a hushed chorus of 'yessirs.'

Milhouz made imperious go-for-it motions with his hands. The Purity Corps sprang into action.

His battering ram squad took point. Milhouz and the main force followed behind. They all trotted down the dark, tree-lined lane that led to the central Rurik library. Jochi's moons dimly lit the scene.

The lights were burning late at the library that night. The head librarian – an elderly Tork named Poray – had lobbied hard for a permit to ignore the curfew and work late that night. His official reason: to comb through the stacks for seditious material banned under Iskra's emergency decrees.

The librarian's real intent was to rescue as much of this material as possible. Poray and his staff put out a call to all like-minded intellectuals. It was a drill they had performed many times during the rule of the Khaqans. In the past, this tradition had saved the most valued texts in the library system.

As the dark shapes of Milhouz's Purity Corps fanned out around the building, Poray was once more mourning his choices. He couldn't save everything. Enough seditious material had to be turned over to make a large display of the intellectual community's loyal intentions.

He eyed the trolleys of fiches and books being rushed to the secret vaults in the library's basement. To one side was a mound of material he was planning to give to Iskra's book burners.

It was a very small mound.

Poray sighed. He was not doing well. He had to cut harder. He hefted two elderly volumes. They were real books – the library's sole copies of the works.

One was a much-thumbed *Fahrenheit 451*, by Ray Bradbury. The other was a pristine copy of *Common Sense*, by the ancient thinker Thomas Paine.

Poray hated playing intellectual god. It tormented him that his tastes were the sole judge of what should stay and what should be destroyed.

He looked at *Common Sense* again. Then at *Fahrenheit 451*. He shrugged.

Bradbury went on a trolley of books to be saved.

Common Sense was for the burning. Forgive me, Sr Paine, Poray thought.

There was a smash of glass and wrench of metal as Milhouz struck.

Poray gaped as black-uniformed youths thundered into the library. There were screams of terror from his staff and volunteers.

'Down with the intelligentsia!' someone bellowed.

Milhouz thundered toward Poray, pistol coming up. Poray instinctively raised Thomas Paine as a shield.

Milhouz fired.

Poray fell to the ground.

As dead as *Common Sense*.

The line from the grocer's stretched half a kilometer. Hundreds upon hundreds of hungry beings were lined up, ration cards ready for the moment the doors opened.

They had been waiting since the morning curfew lifted, which meant seven hours for the first being in line. All under a sun that had dawned a scorcher.

'It gets later and later every day,' grumbled one elderly woman.

'And less and less food to buy,' muttered another.

'All garbage,' said a third. 'Dr Iskra should come down here and look at this slop. He'd have the storekeep's head for being such a thief.'

Before anyone could answer, the line surged forward. 'They're opening!' someone shouted. Then the line came to a jolting halt. There were shocked gasps. People in the back craned their necks to see what was happening at the front.

The grocer's was not opening.

Instead, a line of troops was trotting out from the alley, weapons ready.

An officer's voice bullhorned over the crowd: 'No one will move. This is an inspection of papers. You will have ration cards displayed in the left hand. Citizenship papers in the other.'

The crowd grumbled, yet moved quickly to do the officer's bidding.

But the old woman who had complained about the long wait for food had other ideas. She stepped out of the crowd and hobbled up to the officer.

'You should be ashamed of yourself, young man,' she said. 'We are all hungry. And we have waited hours and hours to buy food for our families.'

The officer shot her where she stood. He kicked her still-twitching corpse. 'There you go, grandmother. Now, you don't have to wait.'

The Bogazi neighborhood watch commander picked her way along the barricade, checking for gaps in the protective jumble and inspecting the guards at their posts. The barricade proved as sound as her last inspection, her guards alert as when they first came on duty.

She looked over the sleeping neighborhood. Not a light in a window, a stir in a hutch. This is good, she thought. This is very good. Then she heard a low sound from behind her. She whirled around. The sound was gone. Imagination only, she thought. I am silly being.

The gunship popped up above the barricade, chain guns yammering.

The watch commander was cut in half before she had time to gurgle a warning.

Two more gunships jumped into view, opening fire on the neighborhood. Within minutes the hutches were burning and Bogazi were streaming out. Some were wounded. Some were carrying wounded. All were paralyzed with fear.

Jochi troops smashed through the barricade. They were followed by a long line of gravlighters.

One hour later the trucks were loaded with the Bogazi survivors and heading out into the night.

The next day, dozers scooped up the dead along with smoking rubble. By nightfall the neighborhood was bare ground.

The following evening the Jochi vid casts announced the availability of new home sites for 'qualified citizens.' They were snapped up by morning.

A letter from Sapper-Major Shase Marl, to Direktor-Leader S!Kt, Seventh Military Front commander:

> . . . and while I realize sending this letter violates the military chain of command, I felt I had no one else who would have the authority and distinction to solve this problem, as you will see.

I write you not only as my supreme commander, but also because I remember, years past, before that evil one who used to rule (cursed be his memory) forced you into retirement. You spoke before my firster class at Kuishev Academy, and I never forgot your words. How an officer has a duty beyond his written orders, a duty to his honor and his race. This letter is my last chance to fulfill that duty.

The problem arose when my unit was ordered to lead a clearing operation on Ochio IX, one of the Disputed Worlds, Sector Seven of your front. Only partially pacified, there were still Suzdal combat elements on the world who were insisting by force of arms their right to possess this planet which, of course, is rightfully Jochi. I was briefed, assigned an area to quiet, given certain supporting units, the names and duties of which do not matter, except for one. This unit was Third Strike Company, Second Saber, Special Duties Corps, led by a Captain L'merding.

I inspected the unit prior to deployment, and formed the impression this soldiery appeared to be adequate in their parade-ground bearing, and particularly well equipped in their weaponry for antipartisan operations. This was in spite of the fact I did not feel they were sufficiently trained, nor were their noncommissioned and commissioned leaders particularly impressive. I made no criticism, of course, to Captain L'merding, but merely welcomed his unit and said I would attempt to give them special opportunity to excel and prove their new corps worthy of belonging to the Jochian Army and serving Dr Iskra.

Captain L'merding's only response was they had their orders and would fulfill them.

At this point I should have approached my superior, Colonel Ellman, and requested a clarification of command. I did not. The troops were landed, and we moved out into the rural areas, which were inhabited by a mixed population of Torks, Jochians, and Suzdal, where the Suzdal bandits had their strongholds. As usual, the Suzdal resisted bitterly (see OpRept 12–341–651–06, three month, weeks one, two, and three), and inflicted casualties on my force. Very few prisoners were taken, since, as you know, the Suzdal prefer death to surrender. The first problem I encountered with Third Company was that Captain L'merding refused to deploy his unit into the countryside, answering my orders with a flat statement that the real enemy was not bogtrotters – those were his exact words – but rather the evil conspirators behind them in the towns and cities. I chose not to examine this odd statement, being a soldier, not a political person.

My attention was primarily focused on combat, of course, and it was not until the third week of the clearing operation that I was given information I found impossible to believe at first, but knew I must investigate to protect the honor of Jochi. This report accused 3/2, Special Duties Corps, of the most appalling atrocities. I personally went to the area Captain L'merding's company was responsible for and found that these accusations were true. The Special Duties unit *was* killing Suzdal civilians in violation of accepted standards of war. Their targets were, in particular, any educated Suzdal, particularly those who were teachers or lawgivers. They also seemed to pay particular attention to any Suzdal with wealth. These beings were removed from their homes and vanished. Captain L'merding refused to specifically say what had happened to them, but their fate was obvious.

There were confirmed reports of children being slaughtered, rapes of Jochi civilians, and buildings being looted. In addition, murders of unarmed Suzdal civilians had been committed in broad daylight and their bodies left in the street. Clearly, this so-called strike company was composed of nothing but gangsters and hooligans. Captain L'merding had posted directives throughout the area, under his own signature, saying use of the Suzdal language, written or spoken, was banned and all Suzdal were forbidden to gather together in groups of more than two. Immediate execution was the penalty for violating any of his commands.

He had posted other orders that were equally as illegal, but the worst by far was his announcement that any criminal act committed by any Suzdal would be responded to with the most extreme measures, which would include razing of that Suzdal's home warren, extirpation of that Suzdal's breeding line, and the execution of one hundred Suzdal, to be chosen at random, as retribution. I told Captain L'merding he was relieved. He laughed. I attempted to place him under close arrest. My aides and myself were disarmed, beaten, and told to leave the area or face the ultimate consequences. I returned to my own unit and notified my battalion commander of Captain L'merding's actions, and requested a combat unit be sent to seize this shameful being and his murderous thugs. I was first told by Colonel Ellman to mind my own affairs. I argued, and was given a direct order to leave L'merding's monsters alone. In fact, Colonel Ellman informed me, this company and the other elements of the Special Duties Corps were obeying orders given from the very highest – orders that might be disagreeable to hear, but orders that must be obeyed to accomplish their vital mission. I refused to accept this and went over Colonel Ellman's head and appealed first to my brigade commander and then, when nothing happened, to the division leader.

I was told I was guilty of insubordination and behavior shameful to Jochi. When I persisted, I was quite illegally reduced one hundred numbers on the promotion list, without hearing or trial. I am now desperate, direktor-leader, and am appealing to you.

Is there no honor left in the Altaics? Is there no dignity left in our noble race? Has our own army, the army that I dedicated my life to serve, become nothing more than back-alley assassins?

The letter was never answered.

Six weeks later, Sapper-Major Shase Marl was shot to death in a rear area. His unit's day-report said that there had been an accidental discharge of weaponry, and that the culprit could not be identified.

Sapper-Major Marl was promoted one rank, posthumously, awarded a campaign ribbon and one star, and honorably interred on the Disputed World of Ochio IX.

The main road leading into Rurik's spaceport was a solid sea of miserable life. Thousands upon thousands of beings slogged through a heavy downpour, pushed, prodded, and flogged onward by Jochi troops.

There was no species division in this forced march. Suzdal was jammed into Bogazi into human.

The crowd of refugees was so thick that if a being fell the body would be carried along by the mass. People cried out mournfully for family members, or for simple pity.

Waiting for the refugees at the spaceport were scores of ancient freighters Iskra had pressed into service. More troops manned the gangways of these freighters, shoving beings into the holds until they were packed beyond reason.

At the signal, the hold doors were slammed shut, and the freighters blasted off their pads. They had barely reached orbit before the next ships took their places.

Professor Iskra watched the scene with intense interest. He palmed controls for a variety of vidscreen views: wide shots of the jammed avenue; close shots of hopeless faces; another long shot showing the spectacle at the spaceport. As one freighter lifted off, he leaned back in his chair and allowed himself a long, pleasurable swallow of his herb tea.

Iskra looked over at Venloe, a rare thin smear on his lips that Venloe supposed was a smile.

'I hope you realize that we are watching history unfold before us,' Iskra said. 'Who could imagine such an exodus? Such a vast cleansing of our world?'

Venloe just grunted.

'Come now,' Iskra pressed. 'Surely I deserve at least a small compliment for my handling of this crisis?'

'Not my job description, Professor,' Venloe said. 'Besides, you've got a big enough cheering section.'

Iskra was enjoying himself too much to be angry. 'That's all right. I don't expect compliments from the ignorant.'

Venloe thumbed at the vidscreen. 'You think that's genius?'

'What do you call it, my uneducated friend?'

'Crazy,' Venloe snapped. 'Or just plain stupid.'

'My, my. Humanity bleeds in that cold heart.'

'Don't mistake professional opinion for a warm and cuddly nature, Professor,' Venloe said. 'It should be obvious to anyone other than a pedantic fool that you're just making things worse. This is all not only unnecessary, but dangerous. Every time you do something like that' – he jabbed a finger at a picture of a soldier hammering a lagging refugee – 'you make yourself five or six more enemies.'

'This isn't a popularity contest,' Iskra said with a laugh. 'Besides, I would think you'd be pleased. After what happened at the barracks, I'd think you'd be delighted that I'm revenging your poor, dead Guardsmen.'

'Don't put it on us,' Venloe warned. 'You were never requested to take this kind of action. Don't drag the Emperor into this thing.'

'But he already is,' Iskra purred. 'And quite vocally. Why, the entire Empire knows how important I am to him.' He gestured at the vidscreen. 'Just as everyone in the Altaics will soon know that it is in his name all these sacrifices are being made.'

Venloe's eyes narrowed. 'What are you talking about?'

'This is just the beginning.' Iskra laughed. 'Oh, it will take much more work to purify the Altaics.'

'Meaning?'

'Watch my next vid cast,' Iskra said. 'I think even you will be impressed at my new emergency decrees.'

Venloe looked away from Iskra's sneer. On the vidscreen he saw a refugee break out of the crowd. The being quickly unfurled a handmade banner.

He had just time to make out the words on the banner before the man was hammered down by soldiers: WHERE IS THE EMPEROR?

Chapter Thirty-Four

'There's no way, Your Highness, anyone could have foreseen what Iskra has become,' Venloe said, adding one milliliter of concerned sympathy to his tone, 'let alone yourself. The last time I checked, you had to worry about an entire Empire.'

To Venloe's concealed astonishment, a flickered expression crossed the Eternal Emperor's face. Surprise that anyone should care? Venloe could not – would not – interpret what he had seen on the screen. The Emperor's countenance swiftly reverted to calm authority.

'Yes,' the Emperor said. 'You're right, Venloe. You understand a bit of the reality of ruling. I can see why Mahoney thought highly of you, even though you were on opposite sides.'

It was now Venloe's turn to poker-face. Ian Mahoney had, in fact, not only refused to touch palms with him as a gentleman should have when the game was over, but had said he would like to kill Venloe. Slowly. Venloe had believed him. Absolutely.

The Emperor didn't appear to have noticed Venloe's studied lack of reaction.

'These latest actions of Dr Iskra and his regime that you, Sten, and . . . other agents have reported are completely psychopathic,' the Emperor continued. 'So we must deal with the problem directly and immediately.'

'Yes, Your Majesty. Thank you for clarifying the situation. I'm afraid I was confused about which option should be used,' Venloe lied, deliberately laying it on a trifle thick, trying to see at what point the Emperor's famous antisycophant snarl would cut in.

The Emperor, however, was looking off at another screen Venloe could not make out. 'I've called up,' the Emperor said, 'the fiche you prepared on what we called the fallback option. A thorough job, Venloe. My compliments.'

'Thank you, sir.'

'I will tell you which option I want implemented shortly. One thing, though. There'll be a change to the one I'll order. I wish you to be directly involved. It isn't enough to control the exercise at long range. There must not be – cannot be – the slightest error.'

Venloe bristled a bit. 'Your Highness, my operations have been uniformly successful, and I've always kept one thing foremost in my planning.'

'Which is, that if the drakh comes down, you're safely on a stage headed out of town.'

'I've never before been accused of being a coward, sir. The reason I prefer to work by remote control is to keep my client's hands clean. If the operative is caught and then plays true confessions, it doesn't matter, because no one beyond a field agent or two, who's been deliberately given misinformation, will be caught in the net.' Venloe thought, but certainly didn't say, that his clotting plans worked well enough to have speared the biggest fish of all: the clotting Eternal Emperor himself. But he was hardly suicidal.

'That's not a concern here,' the Emperor said. 'And that was an order. I want you on-scene and capable of personally rectifying any error, if an error is made.'

'Yes. Sir.'

'Very well. I've told you that Mahoney has been assigned to the Altaics, and in what capacity. He knows nothing of this plan, by the way. And I want you to extract yourself from the Altaics as soon as possible – after the operation has been completed. Now, adding Mahoney to the equation, your option must accomplish several things.

'First. Dr Iskra is to be killed. Instantly. He must not be allowed to suspect anything before the moment of removal.'

'Obviously, sir.'

'Second. In view of Mahoney's orders, his task will be made much easier if some of these lightweights who've been flocking around Iskra, those ineffectual power-seekers Sten has mentioned in his reports – it would be well if some of them ceased to exist. The confusion of their replacement is desirable, in the eyes of the Empire.'

'That would suggest that Your Highness will order either Option C or R.'

'Correct. And you will know which of the two when I give you the final condition.

'The Empire cannot be implicated in this matter. Not even in whispers or the vaguest of paranoiac rumors. And the best way I can see for us to remain beyond suspicion is if one of our most highly respected and honored servants is unfortunately killed in the debacle.'

'The – ambassador? Sir?'

'Yes,' the Eternal Emperor said. 'We all exist but to serve. And this will be his greatest service to me.

'Sten must die.'

BOOK FOUR

VORTEX

Chapter Thirty-Five

Venloe foresaw no major problems carrying out the Eternal Emperor's orders – at least as far as the murder of Iskra and any other Jochi politico who could be decoyed into the trap.

He wasn't especially in love with killing Sten to cover up the conspiracy. Not because he had any feeling for him – Sten and Mahoney had, after all, tracked Venloe to his hiding place and forced him to undergo the racking brutality of a brainscan – but he thought the Emperor was planning a flight when no one would pursue.

Venloe did not think that anyone in the Empire outside the Altaic Cluster would care if a slimeball dictator was assassinated. Many would even cheer a little, even if they suspected the Eternal Emperor had masterminded the killing.

But he had his orders.

So Sten would die.

It might, the more he considered it, be beneficial to Venloe himself. Sten was too slippery, too good at the double- and triple-think of intelligence ops. If he were in his meat locker, that might make Venloe's extraction less risky.

Venloe was still angry at the Emperor's orders that he, himself, had to be part of the murder plot. Stupid. And it showed a measure of distrust. But he eventually shrugged and forgot it. The Eternal Emperor wasn't the first to require the absurd – and he certainly was the biggest client Venloe had ever worked for and must be kept satisfied.

So the Emperor wanted Venloe to go back to the days of his youth and show his talents as an iceman once more. So be it. Venloe added an extra E-hour to his day's normal physical conditioning while he pondered where he would actually station himself on the day.

He was too wise to ignore the Emperor's orders. Most likely the Emperor's mention of 'other agents' in the Altaic Cluster was bluff – but why take the chance?

One – or a dozen – more corpses didn't matter to Venloe. After some thought he had figured out his back door. It was a simple and clean Break Contact and Exit, which meant it would work. Occam's razor also cut in wet work.

Once away from the butcher's floor, all Venloe had to do was get off Jochi and out of the cluster. Fine. He had had a private yacht secreted on an auxiliary field outside Rurik within two weeks of his arrival on-planet with Iskra.

Venloe, someone had once said, didn't even use a latrine without making sure there was a way out – even if it meant jumping directly into the drakh below. Venloe had chosen to take the statement as a compliment.

Having figured his egress, he also knew what weapon he would carry. He would have preferred an Imperial-made weapon for its quality, but since he planned to abandon the tool at the site, he thought it better to procure one of local manufacture. Since Venloe prided himself on his taste, he preferred even his murder weapon to not be an off-the-shelf item. He ended up with the perfect device: an obsolete sporting arm that had been custom-built a century before, to slaughter a wild animal that was now extinct. He had found a bullet mold and cast new bullets and then handloaded propellant into shell casings for the weapon.

Now, for his assassin.

Assassins, since the Emperor wanted the biggest bang for his buck.

That, too, was simple.

He started with Dr Iskra's Special Duty units. Every dictator, public or corporate, that Venloe had ever worked for or heard of had his own private thuggery, with its own label – from the Fida'is to the Einsatzgruppen to CREEP to Mantis to the Emperor's newly formed Internal Security to this unit of Iskra.

Venloe didn't think much of them. He referred to them publicly as 'beards,' or 'bearded ones,' and refused to explain why. Actually, Venloe was making a private reference to one of the least-competent murder organizations of all time, far back on ancient Earth.

The first and – so Iskra had thought it – preeminent cell of these Special Duty units, this one a deep-cover team, had been vanished from its supposedly secure safe house in a mansion outside Rurik. There had never been any rumors, nor had any of Jochi's other private hit teams claimed credit for the deed. Venloe had wondered idly, since that cell had been assigned to harassing the Imperial Guard battalion and had almost certainly been responsible for the barracks bombing, if Sten hadn't given himself a little private pleasure and obliterated them.

Regardless, the effect was immediate – and chilling. Several entire 'units' of Special Duty people requested reassignment to active duty status on other worlds, perhaps to fulfill duties against the Bogazi, Suzdal, or Torks. Still other cell members went inactive. That ended when beings still loyal to Iskra hunted them down and dealt with the traitors.

In any event, the Special Duty units were, to Venloe, a joke. But that didn't mean he could not use them. He had enquired of their 'Supreme Intelligence Leader' what beings, now serving in the Jochi armed forces, were considered potentially traitorous and capable of armed resistance that the Special Duty teams hadn't gotten around to dealing with yet.

That got him one list.

He got a second list from the army's own Counter Subversion Department. A list that was a little less hysterical.

Any name that was on both lists Venloe put on his own roster of possibly dangerous service types. He could not believe how big this short list was – hell, Iskra wasn't even all that good at purges.

Which gave him the direction for his final cut – anyone who had been friendly with or assigned to the same unit as any of the beings Iskra had purged when he arrived on Jochi, beings Iskra still swore were imprisoned in Gatchin Fortress. Venloe knew better, but had not bothered to find out where Iskra had disappeared the bodies to, so long as no trace could ever be found.

This final list he was quite pleased with. He was still more pleased when he found that some of these beings, all of whom had excellent reason to hate Iskra, had been carefully applying for assignment to certain units.

Venloe positively beamed, and permitted himself a single glass of Vegan vintage wine that night. The only thing more perfect than creating a false conspiracy was finding one already extant that could be used for his own purposes. Then he sent two of his most trusted freelance aides into the field, to find out who was running this conspiracy a-birthing.

The answer was four young officers. None of them appeared

to have any idea on what specific mission their conspiracy would take – but it would be used, and used soon, to destroy Iskra. They weren't particularly clever or Machiavellian. If Venloe hadn't found themselves, they would undoubtedly have been picked up by Counter Subversion or the Special Duty teams and body-bagged.

There were thirty of them he could use, he finally decided. Very good. The murder technique that would be used on the day, Venloe kept mentally filed as Crimson Ratpack. He collected, using Iskra's never-to-be-questioned authority, their dossiers from the counter-intelligence unit, and burned their files. They now owed him greatly. He had saved their lives. The least they could do now was sacrifice themselves, but this time to fulfill their dreams instead of ending as futile cinders at the Killing Wall.

His two aides approached the four officers, without saying that Iskra's behind-the-scenes adviser was planning to cut his boss's throat. Venloe had been right – they were more than happy to volunteer for the sacrifice.

Venloe had half of his players. Now all he needed was the other half – the victims.

And a theater.

That, too, was simple.

'I do not see,' Dr Iskra said, having scowled his way through Venloe's memorandum, 'what purpose this farce would have. What will I – which means the government of the Altaic Cluster – gain?'

'Solidarity,' Venloe said.

'In what way?'

'First, peasants love a dumb show, as you said in your essay, "The Revolution's Need to Understand the Soul of the People."'

'Correct.'

'Secondly, there have been some stories about certain offworld events involving both the military and the Special Duty Corps.'

'Idle talk should be punished.'

'It is,' Venloe said. 'Your Special Duty units are especially effective in that area. But we now have the opportunity to provide a positive image. How could anyone seeing the noble soldiery of Jochi parade past imagine them culpable in what these rumors hint.'

'Ah.'

'Plus such a parade is a magnificent opportunity for you to show that your government is solidly supported by everyone, including the Torks, when livie viewers see the Torks' leader near you on the reviewing stand.'

'Menynder will not attend.'

'Yes, he will,' Venloe disagreed. 'Because the alternatives that will be presented to him won't be to his liking.'

Iskra considered. 'Yes. Yes, Venloe, I see your thinking. And it has been too long since I showed myself to my people. As I pointed out, as part of my analysis of the Kha— that forgotten monster's tyranny, how he was planting the seeds to his downfall in many ways, not the least of which was hiding, invisible, in this palace. It was in the second volume.'

'I am sorry,' Venloe said. 'I have been too busy for any off-duty reading. One other thing,' he went on. 'The Imperial ambassador should be invited.'

'Sten? I have requested his relief,' Iskra said. 'Yet another necessity that's not been responded to by that *man* on Prime. Why should he be invited? And why would he attend, anyway?'

Venloe did not quite roll his eyes, but he wanted to. Iskra, for all of his millions of words and speeches about politics and ruling, knew less than nothing about it.

'He should be invited because that will show the populace you are supported by the highest. And that their worries about this new AM2 shortage must be pointless.

'And Sten will attend for one reason: He is a professional.'

Sten looked out the window at the weather, listening to Kilgour filter through the incoming messages behind him. The weather continued to fulfill Sten's expectations, alternating from humid, overcast, and oppressive, to humid, overcast, and raining, cloud-bursts passing so rapidly that no one knew how to dress when going out.

'Clottin' kilt maker. Ah dinnae ken th' clot'd hae th' brains t' track me doon. He'll whistle "Bonnie Bells" throo hi' fundament ere he gies credits frae Laird Kilgour.

'Gie'in me ae kilt thae's th' ancien' Campbell sheep-futterin' pattern, an' claimin't he c'd nae tell th' difference tween thae ae' th' tartan ae th' Kilgours.

'Hah.

'Noo, whae hae we here. Mmmph. Mmmph.' A chortle. 'Hah. Boss. Noo thae's int'restin'.'

Sten turned back around. 'Whatcher got, myte?'

'Y' rec'lect wee Petey Lake? Th' navy weatherman w' hae assigned, way back, i' Mantis?'

'Not really.'

'I' wae th' time we were t' be blowin't thae dams ae thae planet wi' the bein's thae lookit ae weasels an' smell th' same? We were suppos't t' bring thae boom jus' when th' rainy season broke, so's t' nae cause max damage, but jus' enow t' topple th' gov'mint an' send i' th' Imperial peacekeepers?'

'Oh yeah. Wait a minute. The weatherman? Human type? The guy we called Mr Lizard?'

'Aye. Thae's th' lad.'

'How the *hell* did he stay out of jail? Let alone beat the court-martial?'

'Ah hae noo idea. P'raps we w're wrong, an' th' lasses an' their ridin' hacks were enjoyin't whae he wae doin't, an' were just hollerin' frae their clothes. Ah dinnae ken. Anyway, Ah've hae letters frae him e'er noo an' then.

'He's doin't quite well. Runnin't a stables wi' real Earth horses f'r rich little girls noo. At any rate, Ah wrote an' asked why this clottin' weather's so clottin' clotted ae Rurik. He's tellin't me thae any big planet wi' fast rotation, braw seas, small landmass, tall bens, an' multiple moons'll most likely always be bloody.'

'Sure,' Sten said, not having thought about the weather much beyond just watching it – it was just another part of the general sewer that was Rurik.

'He hae a wee warnin't. Aboot thae cyclones Ah, at any rate, hae been takin't wi' a grain ae haggis. Here. P'ruse f'r y'self.'

Alex passed the long, handwritten letter across Sten's desk. Sten scanned it, until he hit the section Alex had referred to, then read hastily – he *did* remember Mr Lizard, and he wanted to get his hands off the document and into a sterile bath as quickly as possible.

. . . so it's going to be miserable on Jochi – miserable cold in the winter, miserable hot in the summer, and, oh yeah, capable of being either one out of season.

Serves you right, you clot, for sticking with the uniform drakh.

One thing you want to be careful of – and you can push that clot Sten in front of one for me – is tornadoes. Tornadoes are trick little circular winds that'll blast you straight out of your shorts if you aren't either underground or out of the way.

Take these suckers real serious – the whirlwinds'll get up to 4–800 kph rotational wind speed in the vortex, and will honk right along anywhere up to 112 klicks an hour. About here is where the measuring instruments break, so don't assume any of those numbers are maximum. You *can't* run, so you'd better hide.

I got a whole bunch of statistics in my files that I can ship along if you're morbidly curious as to what a tornado can do – kill a thousand people in forty minutes, punch a blade of straw through an anvil, throw five tacships weighing a few hundred kilotons each a quarter klick, without bothering the crews inside by the way, and so on.

The best example I've got is on Altair III, and the clots there who were dumb enough to build their capital city right in a tornado belt (sounds just like this Rurik place you're in) – and yeah, tornadoes have patterns. Anyway, summer afternoon, and the city, est. pop. of around five million, gets hit with seventy-two twisters in one afternoon. Killed one-fifth of the city's population – guess they didn't believe in storm cellars.

Just to show you what a good guy I am, I'll even give you a couple clues as to what to look out for, before the funnel lifts you into low orbit.

First, you get convection currents that overcome the usual inversion layers. The air will lift to up to 10,000 meters or so altitude, and will be affected by any jet stream you've got running overhead. This is gonna lift air from all over the region, and it'll destabilize the inversion layers.

The air from the jet stream is like a giant tube, rotating at altitude, and when the tops of cumulus clouds encounter that tube, it bends in the middle from the rising air, due to the rotational wind increasing with the height.

As the tube becomes more vertical, the winds increase with altitude, but more importantly veer from the southwest . . . right now you have a giant, rotating tube, embedded in one big mother thunderstorm . . .

. . . if you've got anything as primitive as a radar set, about now you can see this tube, which will look like an extended cat's-paw. Sometimes it's called a figure six or a hook echo.

This is the wall cloud . . . think of it as a horizontal tornado, usually black, but sometimes even green . . . wall cloud tilts . . .

Down on the ground you're gonna be sweating bullets, getting cranky if you believe in positive ions and getting wet, because there's almost certainly going to be a helluva thunderstorm going on.

You ought to be getting a little scared, too.

*

Sten scanned on.

. . . hail and storm . . . downdraft ahead of the updraft . . . an overhanging cloud . . . all of a sudden funnel clouds drop out of the wall cloud and rotate around the mesocyclone – the southernmost tube – don't remember right off the top how many tubes you get.

But only a crazy clot would stick around to count them, because right now, your basic vortex is about to ruin your entire week . . .

The letter went on and became a gibberish of equations – evidently Mr Lizard had gotten tired of ghosting it and looked the subject up.

Sten flipped the letter back. 'Thank you, Mr Kilgour, for giving me yet something else on this clottin' world that will try to kill us.'

'Nae prob, wee Sten.'

A screen dinged, and Alex scanned the scrolling letters. 'Noo, here's e'en better'n Lizard's wee whirlwind. Doc Isky's throwin't a review. Ae th' troops. An' he'd appreciate th' pleasure ae one Ambassador Sten, on th' stand. Th' intent i' plain. T' bore y' to death wi' his bootskies, bootskies, movin' up an' doonsky . . .'

Alex spun the screen around for Sten to look at. Nobody except a circus throws a parade just for drill. Why this one? He considered. To build the morale of the civilians, first. Second, to give Iskra a chance to pose nobly – all dictators liked that.

Not enough.

There was a tap at the door. A secretary entered and gave Kilgour an envelope. Alex opened it.

'Ah hae here th' confirmation ae th' review. Handwrote, i' Isky's braw scrawl, i' is. An' on real paper, Ah reck.

'Ah do wonder,' Alex mused, 'jus' whae villainy th' good quack's plannin' t' hatch?

'D' y' pass, lad?'

'No. I go.'

'Ah dinnae think thae's wise. Cannae y' d'velop a case ae clap, or aught?'

Sten just shook his head – both of them knew better. This was part of being an ambassador – even one that was not held in the highest regard by the current government he represented Imperial interests to. Sten would have to appear and lend authenticity to whatever Iskra's scheme was.

'I' y' go,' Alex announced with finality, 'y' dinnae do i' wearin't nae but y'r new spring frock, flowers i' y'r hair, an' ae doofus smile. An' noo Ah'm speakin't ae y'r security adviser. I' y' hae t' play that clot's games, y' dinnae hae t' play by his rules.'

Sten grinned. What Alex was evidently proposing was a fairly severe violation of protocol – for an honored diplomat to consider going armed, with backup, to a celebration of the host government.

But considering how events in the Altaic Cluster had been, and the honorable, upright beings Sten had encountered, he thought it very reasonable to consider double-armoring his own privy.

Kilgour's large, horned fist slammed down on the metal bench. Being intended for use as an engine stand for gravlighters' McLean generators, the bench's legs bulged but did not give way.

'If Ah c'n hae y' attention,' he bellowed, and the murmur of conversation died away. Kilgour stood in front of an assemblage of Gurkhas and Bhor, in one of the embassy's garages.

'Ah wan' y'r eyeballs hooked t' thae chart ae the wall, there.

'Ah'll keep this brief,' he went on. 'Y' c'n find y'r own duty assignments up ae they're listed. Thae garage's swept, no more'n an hour ago, by myself an' Cap'n Cind, and it's unbugged. So we dinnae hae t' use circumlocutions.

'Th' skinny is like so – th' boss is goin't twa thae review t'morrow. I' th' square ae th' late Khookoos. An' we dinnae think the deal's square-up.

'So we'll be i' position, aye?

'Ah wan' you Gurk's i' squad format. Two squads per grav-lighter. Otho, y're pr'moted sarg'nt, an' i' charge ae th' Bhor. Four per gravlighter, plus two heavy-weapons teams. Aye?'

'As you say,' Otho rumbled. 'But what of our captain?'

'Cap'n Cind hae th' countersniping detail. She's tucked e'er sniper-rated an' expert-qualified rifle shot under her wing. We'll be saltin' them, twa by twa, ae th' rooftops afore dawn.

'Now. Here's th' orders. I' there's aught attempt made ae Sten – Ah wan' thae hitter dead. Dead 'fore he can think ae violence, an' we'll nae consider gie'in th' lad th' chance t' touch th' trigger.

'We'll hae all coms open, so i' there's an attempt, Ah wan' all a' y' t' swarm th' reviewin't stand. Dinnae be worryin't aboot prisoners or such.'

'Question?'

'Aye, lad?'

'By my mother's beard,' the young Bhor growled, 'but you send in the lances just on the suspicion there will be danger.'

'Aye?'

'I am not arguing, sir. But what would you do if there was a confirmed threat to the ambassador?'

Alex's face went still, and his eyes glittered. After a pause, he said, 'In thae case, Ah'd hae Sten lock't i' th' cellar, an' th' reviewin' stand'd be a nuke ground zero afore th' ceremony'd begin.

'Noo. Thae's all. Y' ken y'r duties, y'r weapons, y'r gear. See to it. Stand-to is one hour before dawn.'

'Kilgour, this isn't my tailcoat.'

'Aye. Shut y'r lip an' be puttin' i' on. Th' piss i' review'll be nae more'n twa hours away.'

'Fits lousy,' Sten growled, frowning at his reflection. 'Who tailored this? Omar th' Tent Maker?'

'Th' coat's 'flatable, an' thae's inserts t' be put i' place.'

'For what? If somebody shoots at me with a cannon?'

'Ah.' Kilgour smiled. 'Ah always ken y'r noo ae stupid't ae Cind keep't sayin't. Cannon i' th' watchword.'

'Noo. Bolt y'self up.

'I' y' rec'lect, all a' thae silliness Ah been doin't since yesterday's i' y'r cause. C'mon, lad. Ah hae t' put on m' own wee drag. I' y're braw, Ah'll buy y' a pint a'terward.'

If, Kilgour thought, there is an afterward . . .

Sten evaluated the thick crowds on either side of the wide boulevard as his gravlighter approached the palace.

If this is supposed to be a holiday, Dr Iskra has miscalled it, he thought. The faces were angry, sullen as the darkling skies overhead. At first Sten thought the hostility was pointed at the two Imperial flags fluttering from the gravlighter's stanchions, then corrected himself. The rage was free-form and unprejudiced – Sten saw a man look up as one of the constantly patrolling military gravsleds slid overhead, then spit into the gutter.

Otho grounded the embassy's ceremonial stretch gravlighter just behind the huge reviewing stand that had been special-built to one side of the Square of the Khaqans. The gravlighter looked even worse now – the weapons mounts and most of the jury-rigged armor had been cut away, but there had been no time to refinish the body or repaint. The craft looked as if it had failed to qualify in a demolition derby.

Two Gurkhas in full ceremonial dress, which included kukris and willyguns, snapped out of the lighter and presented arms, first to the Jochi flag to one side of the stand, then to the main riser, where Dr Iskra's chosen symbol was mounted. Iskra had not yet materialized, but he was the only dignitary not in appearance.

Sten stepped out, Alex slightly to his rear. Kilgour had chosen to wear the full ceremonial rig of his home world: flat shoes, tartan stockings with a dagger tucked in the top, kilt with sporran – containing a pistol – another dagger at his hip, silver-buttoned black velvet and vest, lace jabot at his throat, and lace at his wrists. On his head was his clan's bonnet, and slung over one shoulder was a tartan cloak.

The outfit was not, however, exactly what he would wear on Edinburgh turned out as Laird Kilgour of Kilgour. The flat shoes were strapped on, so as not to come off if Kilgour had some running to do. The tartan pattern was very dark, which Alex blandly explained was the correct ancient hunting tartan of his clan. Sten had never been sure whether there really was a Clan Kilgour, or whether Alex, and the several thousand people on his estates, were making it up as they went along. The Scots were fully capable of doing something entirely that elaborate just to pull the chain of the sassenachs.

He was not carrying the usual ceremonial broadsword, again for efficiency. Swords got in the way. And the cloak thumped if banged against – Sten thought that the heavyworlder was likely carrying a full weapons shop in the drape.

Behind Sten came two more Gurkhas. Sten bowed to the Jochi flag and, mentally gritting his teeth, to Iskra's emblem. Otho lifted the gravlighter away – he would keep it ready in a park just behind the palace with the other backup units.

Two of Iskra's Special Duty goons were at the foot of the stairs, with detectors. Alex looked at them once. Even hooligans occasionally were guilty of sense, and the two stepped out of the way, awkwardly saluting.

The Gurkhas remained at the rear of the stand. Sten felt a bit more secure about his back. In front of the stand's base, standing shoulder to shoulder, were more of the Special Duty troops.

'A wee bit of info,' Alex whispered. 'All th' troopies thae'll pass i' review hae been told i' their weapons point anywhere close t' th' stand, Iskra's murthrers hae orders t' ice 'em wi' no questions. Whidney y' like a wee career i' th' Jochi gruntery?'

Sten was twice surprised at the top of the stand. First he saw

Menynder. Interesting. Someone or something had winkled him out of his period of mourning.

The second surprise – and it took him a moment before he recognized the being – was seeing Milhouz the rebel, now in the black uniform of this new 'student' movement that Iskra had created and Sten had vaguely noted.

There were two older beings beside Milhouz – his parents, Sten thought. Milhouz met Sten's gaze, started to flinch, then stared boldly.

Sten frowned, as if trying to remember the face, couldn't, but to be polite nodded slightly: Perhaps we were introduced at a social function some time?

Sten almost felt sorry for the clot. Turncoats were never trusted – and everyone knew that, especially those who doubled them. True in espionage, true in politics. Milhouz had only one future – to be used by Iskra as long as needed and then dispensed with.

Iskra being Iskra, Sten thought, that dispensing would almost certainly involve a shallow grave rather than an obscure retirement.

No more than Milhouz deserved.

Sten, Kilgour beside him, worked his way to his assigned seat. A polite greeting to Douw, who was wearing a full dress uniform hung with decorations old and new. Nods to other dignitaries and pols.

He stopped beside Menynder.

'I am glad,' he said, 'to see you have recovered from your family's tragedy.'

'Yes,' Menynder said, his head moving a bare millimeter sideways, toward Iskra's emblem. 'Nobody'll ever know how grateful I am to have some new friends who just cheered the drakh out of me, telling me how much the rest of my family means, and how my ancient estates should be worried about, and, in general, convinced me to dump the widow's weeds.'

As Sten had thought. Menynder had been blackjacked into attendance.

A military band blared what might be considered music, and Dr Iskra, aides at his heels, came down the steps from the palace's terrace and walked slowly across the vast open square to the reviewing stand.

'Any idea,' Sten whispered to Kilgour, 'why the doctor isn't reviewing his troops from the usual place?'

'Ah ask't,' Kilgour hissed. 'Ah wae told because th' terrace i' distant. An' the doctor wishes t' be closer t' his wee heroes.'

'That's a real cheap lie.'

'Aye. An' wha' worries me, is th' stand wae no built right.'

Kilgour was correct – it was no more than a meter and a half off the ground. A basic part of pre-riot crowd control was to build the bandstand high enough to make it difficult for the madding throng to rush the stage successfully.

The dignitaries came to the salute as Dr Iskra mounted the stand.

Cymbals crashed, and the military band crescendoed and broke off.

In the sudden silence, Sten heard, from a great distance, the twitter of a panpipe being played by some street minstrel working the crowd.

And then, as if cued, the clouds broke, a high wind rolling them up like they were dirty linen, and an impossibly blue sky shone above.

The band cacophonied into life again, and the review began.

The Square of the Khaqans was a crash of cleated bootheels, an eerily grating rumble of tracks, and the bash of marching music. Every now and then Sten could hear the cued cheers from the crowds watching.

He applauded with his forearm against his side, Altaic style, as yet another range of rankers bashed past the stand.

'Fifth Battalion, Sixth Regiment, the Iron Guards of Perm,' the unseen commentator told them over the square's PA system.

'Didn't we just see them?'

'Nae, skip. Thae wae th' *Sixth* Battalion, *Fifth* Regiment. Y' hae t' pay tighter heed.'

'How much longer can he keep running troops past us?'

'Damfino,' Alex whispered. 'Till our eyes bleed an' we start burblin' ae th' wonders ae ol' Isky. It's mass hypnosis, lad.'

'Time,' Cind said. Obediently, her spotter rolled away from the scope, behind his own rifle. Cind slid into position and began her own shift, sweeping endlessly across the palace rooftops and windows that she had taken for her sector.

Her other sniper teams were doing much the same – one being watches, the other waits behind the gun. A spotter could only work effectively for a few minutes before starting to see motion that was a curtain blowing in the wind, menace that was the shadow from a chimney, or just simply things not there.

The architectural style of the Palace of the Khaqans didn't

make their job any easier, having been built and then redecorated in a style that could be referred to as Early Unromantic Gargoyle.

Cind and her spotter had taken position on one of the palace's roofs, finding a fairly level area to keep their backup arms and ammunition in, then slithering very slowly to the roof's peak to observe. A dull scarlet hood, just the color of the metal roof they were lying on, hung over the scope, and both snipers had their faces camouflaged with a flat medium-brown wash.

Cind's eyes were watering from the strain in a few minutes. She swept the roofline, then swept it again, routinely. She stopped and moved the scope back.

'Earle,' she said, unconsciously and needlessly whispering. 'Three o'clock. That dormer window.'

'Got it,' the man behind the rifle said. 'The window's open. Can't see inside. Too dark.'

'Come left half a finger,' Cind ordered.

'Oh-ho.'

'I'll take the gun.'

Earle started to protest, then took the spotting position. Cind moved up, hands automatically readying her own rifle.

Across the square, to the side of that dormer window, a hatch onto the roof had been lifted clear – a hatch that had been closed earlier. And very close to that hatch was a low parapet that would make excellent cover for someone to use to move the thirty meters or so to where a wall zigged out, that provided a hidden crevice that would make an ideal escape route.

The window was about six hundred meters away from the reviewing stand below, and about . . .

'Range?'

'Twelve . . . twelve twenty-five.'

'I have the same . . .'

. . . twice that to Cind's post.

Cind slid her shooting jacket's fasteners shut, pulled the rifle sling tight around her upper arm until there was no circulation anymore, and was in the rigor mortis that was her firing position.

All that existed was that open window twelve hundred meters away.

She barely heard Earle reporting that they had a possible target and ordering another team to take over the routine scan.

Venloe was ready. He had his monstrous sporting rifle braced firmly on a tabletop, the table solidly sandbagged.

He was about three meters back of the open dormer window, in clever concealment. Neither the human eye nor a scope would be able to see him in the gloom, and if some extraordinarily paranoid security type was using an amplified-light scope the glare from the rooftops outside would blank that device.

He looked again through the rifle scope, then rubbed his eyes. He had forgotten how exhausting sniping was, and how short a time before the edge was lost.

Six hundred meters away was the reviewing stand.

Venloe had his targets chosen, and six cigar-sized solid projectiles resting in the rifle's box magazine.

If there was an error . . . first Iskra.

Then Sten.

Then . . .

The tiny com beside him, tuned to the review's public broadcast, spoke:

'Eighth Company, Guards Combat Support Wing. The Saviors of Gumrak.

'Afoot, Scout Company, Eighty-third Light Infantry Division.'

This was it.

Now for the Crimson Ratpack.

The combat support wing's gravlighters swept forward, three abreast, at low speed. Just ahead of them trotted the lightly armed scouts.

Each gravlighter carried a full complement of troops, sitting at rigid attention. The gravlighter's pilot concentrated on his formation, and the lighter's commander saluted.

Six ranks back, in the center row, was the first of Venloe's assassins. The gravlighter's pilot was one of the young officer/conspirators, as were all of the other soldiers.

'Sixteen . . . seventeen . . . eighteen . . .'

At a count of twenty, the gravlighter was, as calculated, about fifty meters out and twenty meters short of the reviewing stand.

The pilot punched full power to the McLean generators and pushed the control stick hard over to the right.

The gravlighter pirouetted, crashing into its fellow, which went out of control and dominoed into the parade formation.

The young officer fought his craft level, then slammed it to the ground, the lighter skidding forward toward the reviewing stand, skewing crazily.

It spilled out soldiers, soldiers who hit the ground running

– and firing, semiautomatic grenade launchers blasting the Special
Duty soldiers.

These guards took a bare moment to recover – but a third of
them were dead by then. Then they opened up, rounds sheeting
into the middle of the review.

The support wing's formation broke, gravlighters climbing for
the sky and getting shot down as other Special Duty units obeyed
orders to kill anyone or anything irregular.

A platoon of the scout unit broke from *its* formation and went
flat. Orders were bellowed, and rifles crashed.

Their target was the reviewing stand.

One burst and – 'Grenades!' came the shout, and the platoon
charged the stand.

A quarter second earlier, Sten's four Gurkhas had been at
attention, at the rear of the stand. Now, most suddenly, they
were on the stand, knocking fear-maddened pols aside, willyguns
braced on their hips, AM2 slugs slashing out and cutting down
the scouts.

Sten dug under his monkey suit for his pistol and was down
as Kilgour bodychecked him flat. Alex recovered, his cloak
pitched away and the willygun hidden under it up and chattering
rounds.

Douw was suddenly in an underwater trance, as he saw the
grenade thud down on the planking just in front of him – how
annoying – and he kicked it, grenade dropping off the stand and
then exploding, blasting him back into Menynder. Both men
sprawled, Douw half stunned.

Menynder started to shove the general's crushing weight off
his body, then reconsidered. What better shield could there be,
he realized, and then turned his thoughts toward camouflage,
concentrating on being the very model of a modern major
corpse.

Dr Iskra's eyes were wide open, his brows just beginning to
furrow like a professor about to chide a favorite pupil for being
unable to answer an easy question, when the blood-covered
woman levered herself up onto the stand in front of him.

Iskra's hands went out, trying to push this horror away.

The woman shot Iskra four times in the face before her body
was shattered by a burst from a guard's weapon.

Sten rolled sideways, pistol coming out of a rear holster, and
was coming to his knees, mind recording screams from the crowd,
gun blasts, crashes from the pandemonium that had been an army

in review seconds earlier, and the whine of gravlighters at full drive.

Out of a corner of his eye he saw the Bhor lighters rip out of their park toward the stand, then there were two men just below him, aiming, and he fired . . . tap, tap . . . tap, tap . . . they were down and dead . . . looking for another target . . .

The pleased smile was frozen on Venloe's face as he touched the sight stud, and it zoomed tight on the target, his field of vision narrowing.

Iskra was dead. Absolutely.

Menynder and Douw were hit – probably. It did not matter – they weren't major targets.

Now. Now for Sten.

There he is. The bastard's not killable. He's coming to his feet now . . .

Just coming up . . . hold the breath . . . exhale smoothly . . . touch the stud . . . brace for the recoil . . . firing pressure . . . now!

Shock-recoil-slam, gun butt against shoulder. Action crashing back, sending the smoking shell case spinning out, *clatter*, another round chambered, bolt locked in battery, dammit, the sights are off target . . .

'Sten is down,' an unemotional voice on the com said.

Shut up, Cind said. Don't look. Don't turn. Just hold on that dormer window and see the curtain flung out by the muzzle blast inside, bastard's trained, had enough sense to pick a stance back in the shadows, and she pumped three AM2 explosions through the window . . .

Sten's formal dress may have been bulletproofed by Kilgour. However, there is no way the human animal can withstand the impact of a solid bullet weighing just over one hundred grams being delivered at a velocity of around eight hundred meters per second, unless he or she is inside a tank, any more than a bullet-proof vest is worth drakh to a pedestrian hit by a bus.

But it had been too long for Venloe's old training, as his mind flinched away from that shoulder-cracking kick-to-come.

Six hundred meters is not significant with a modern weapon. But it is a factor. It is especially a factor if a projectile weapon uses conventional propellant to punt an enormously heavy round to its target. So the trajectory taken by the bullet from Venloe's dinosaur-killing rifle was a high, looping howitzer-arc, subject to crosswind and heat/cold waves.

The bullet should have hit Sten in the stomach. Instead, it first struck the heavy chair beside him, and shattered. Most of the bullet ricocheted away to who-knew-where. But its solid jacket impacted directly on Sten's monkey jacket, just on the base of one of those solid plates Kilgour had sheathed his boss with. Sten was knocked spinning off the stand. The self-inflating shock cushion realized that its finest hour had arrived, and suddenly the Imperial ambassador greatly resembled a floating bath toy; then, as he touched down on corpses, the shock cushion deflated, and there was somebody just in front of him with a bayoneted rifle.

Somehow the pistol was still in Sten's hands, and he shot the man dead, and was looking for a target, then realized he was still alive, and able to hear that wonderful wonderful *Ayo . . . Gurkhali* as his backup arrived.

Cind's AM2 rounds blew the attic room apart, sending Venloe stumbling back, dazed for a moment; then he recovered, staggering toward the open hatch, but no, there'll be someone out there, remember you planned for this, too, reach down, reach down.

Venloe's hands found the pull cord on the two smoke grenades he had taped on either side of the patch, and yanked.

Wait . . . wait . . . wait for the smoke . . . now. Through the hatch and away with you.

'Clottin' missed him,' Cind muttered, then her sights swung as the open hatchway gouted smoke.

'The ambassador is all right! I say again, the ambassador is all right,' the com bleated.

Did the explosion start a fire . . .

Hell. It's a smoke screen, she thought, seeing a flicker of movement that disappeared behind the parapet.

Oh, you cute thing, she thought.

'Earle. Three rounds rapid. Into the middle of that wall. Forward one meter from that rainspout. Now!'

Crash . . . crash . . . crash.

The ancient stone of the parapet shattered. Cind could see a tiny, jagged hole through her scope.

Now, you behind that wall, what are you thinking? Do you

think you're quick enough – or that I'm not a good enough shot – to wriggle past that little crack?

Cind sighted and fired. Her single round slammed through the crack and exploded somewhere on the parapet's far side.

Yes, you. I *am* that good a shot that I can slip a bullet through the hole if I see any movement.

Now, it would seem to me, were I stupid enough to be that man over there, thinking that twelve hundred meters and only one way out makes you bulletproof, I would now be considering modifying my avenues of egress.

'Earle, watch the smoke.'

'NG for him. It's thinning.'

Very good. So what do we have? We have you out there, lying prone behind that parapet. Your exit route is blocked by that hole Earle drilled and by the knowledge you have that I can see through it and shoot through it.

About twelve meters back of Earle's spy hole, the parapet ends against the dormer window. So you are lying somewhere within that twelve meters.

First we access the area . . .

She sent another round into the dormer window's sill, shattering away. Yes. Now, if I were lying there, would I be closer to the dormer, or to that little crack? I'd be closer to the crack, and waiting for some kind of miracle to cross that two-centimeter 'gap.'

Range to the dormer sill . . . *that*. She locked the range finder.

Cind moved her scope sideways, sweeping the cross hairs along the blank face of the parapet but keeping the barrel aimed exactly at the shattered window sill. About . . . there. The linear accelerator hummed. Ready.

Cind fired.

The AM2 round spat across the twelve hundred meters. Then, at the appropriate range, it turned a sharp right.

Venloe was lying flat, trying to figure what his next option might be, just where Cind had estimated.

The bullet hit him at the base of his pelvis and exploded.

Half of Venloe's body pinwheeled up into the air and over the parapet, and splattered down on the rooftop. Then it slid, greasily, hands splayed as if trying to hang on, over the edge of the roof and fell two hundred meters into the square.

The time elapsed since Venloe had set off his smoke screen was just under two minutes.

*

Milhouz stood alone on the reviewing stand. At length, he realized he was still alive.

He was the only one.

There . . . there were the bodies of his parents.

He would mourn them.

But the dynasty would continue.

Iskra was dead.

But Milhouz lived.

The beginnings of that look of saintly self-satisfaction crept across his face.

It was still there as the kukri slashed from behind, and his head rode a crimson fountain to bounce off the stand and paint a red semicircle on the square's paving.

Jemedar Lalbahadur Thapa stepped back as the headless corpse dropped. He sheathed his kukri and nodded once, in satisfaction.

The Gurkha had been at Pooshkan University.

The Square of the Khaqans was almost quiet, except for the moans and screams of the wounded and the roar of runaway engines from crashed gravlighters.

Sten heard wails and screams from the crowd as the equally stunned security forces began clearing the square. A few meters away was a sprawled body he identified as that of Dr Iskra.

Overhead, the bright cheerful day was gone, and storm clouds were rolling in. So much, Sten thought, for weather prophesying hurly-burly, witches, or anything else.

He walked over to the body and used a toe to turn it over.

'Th' lad's aboot ae dead as Ah've e'er seen.'

'He is.'

'Well,' Alex said as he walked up beside Sten. 'Th' king's croaked, an' long live th' king an a' thae. What the clot are we goin' t' do next?'

Sten thought about it.

'I will be double-damned if I have even the slightest,' he said honestly.

Chapter Thirty-Six

Thirty-seven E-hours later, thunder rolled across Rurik.

Sten was carefully composing his dispatch on Iskra's assassination that would give the full details – following up the initial flash sent to the Eternal Emperor and Prime within minutes of Sten's race back to the embassy.

Someone at the spaceport buzzed the embassy – an Imperial unit or units had just broadcast that they were inbound for landing.

Neither Sten nor Alex had time for more than a fast wonderment: Was this support? Some Imperials that had nothing to do with anything? An invasion?

The sky rumbled louder than one of Jochi's super thunderstorms, and ships swept overhead.

'Sufferin' Jesus,' Alex swore. 'Ah dinnae glim s' many putt-putts since th' war ended. Thae must be . . . twa, no, three squadrons. Wi' battlewagons. Somebody's through muckin' aboot – or else they've finally found us oot, lad.'

Sten didn't answer – he was also watching the sky. The second wave was coming in, behind the warships.

Troop transports, auxiliaries, and their screens.

Sten estimated that a full division of Imperial soldiers was arriving.

Now, just what in the hell . . .

'. . . are you doing here, Ian?'

'You want the answer as of the day before yesterday,' Ian Mahoney asked, 'or what it is after we intercepted your charming message to Prime?'

'Whichever one I can handle,' Sten said. They were on the flag bridge of the Imperial battleship *Repulse*, flying Mahoney's command flag. Outside, Rurik's once-deserted spaceport was studded with ships and looked like a central military field on Prime World.

Sten and Alex's estimates had been quite correct – Mahoney's force consisted of three battleship squadrons and Mahoney's 'home' unit, the First Guards Division.

Mahoney had greeted them, introduced them to the admiral in charge of the naval forces, a rather officious sort named Langsdorff, chased him off the bridge, and opened a bottle of the special liquor made for the Emperor called Scotch.

'I'll give you both sets of my orders, then. The Emperor ordered me to put together a peacekeeping force just after the barracks bombing. He told me he wanted me to arrive, with muscle, at the proper time. My job description was to be Imperial governor. I was supposed to back you up, and make sure Iskra stayed on his throne.'

Sten pursed his lips. 'So nothing changed his mind, then? About Iskra.'

'Was something supposed to?'

'Yeah. About twelve metric tons of the best stones I could polish and a solid silver bucket to keep them in. Never mind. I'll show you my rock collection later. The Iskra situation has taken care of itself.'

'So I got my orders changed,' Mahoney said. 'The Altaics are now to be put under direct rule from Prime.'

'Home rule,' Alex wondered. 'Thae's clottin' *ne'er* an answer. Sorry, sir.'

'Kilgour, the day you can't put in an oar is the day I'm ready to go back to wearing a uniform. I don't like it either. But that's the direct orders from the Man.'

'For how long?'

'I wasn't told.'

Sten rolled his yet untouched drink between his palms, looking for the right way to ask his question. 'Ian – what did your orders say about me?'

'Nothing. Should they have?'

'I don't know.'

Sten explained that he had asked to be relieved previously, and that the Emperor had refused. Now, with Iskra dead, and the Altaics even closer to the cliff edge of chaos, he assumed he would either be headed for home in disgrace or at the least offered another assignment.

'I guess,' Mahoney said, 'that you're to continue as ambassador. At least until the shock waves settle down. Then I guess one of us will be moved on. I can't picture the Emperor keeping both of his high-dollar troubleshooters in the same forty-holer for very long. There's too many barns burnin' out there.'

'Yeah.'

'I don't think we need to worry about any kind of pecking order, do we, Sten?'

'That wasn't why I was asking.'

'Okay. Everything's settled. Let's see if we can't jerk these clots into something resembling armed truce, starting tomorrow.

'Now, would you slug that back? You're getting touchy, being out here with all these murderous clots, touchy and paranoiac.'

'I guess I am,' Sten said, and followed Mahoney's orders, trying to relax.

Now, at least, he had something and somebody to lean on with some real clout. But the back of his mind told him that somehow, in some way, the Altaic Cluster would find a way to drag Mahoney, the navy, and the Imperial Guard down, into the bloody anarchy they seemed to love all too well.

Chapter Thirty-Seven

They sat on the banks of Menynder's desolate pond. The old Tork was silent as Sten painted the bleak future facing the Altaics.

'You're at one of those moments in history,' Sten said, 'when disaster and opportunity are equal options. What happens next is your choice.'

'Not mine,' Menynder said. 'Choices are made by people with hope. Right now, I have about as much hope for my people as I have of ever catching a clottin' fish in this pond.' He gestured at the dead waters.

'Someone *will* replace Iskra,' Sten said. 'Chances are, all you'll do is trade one despot for another. Why leave it to chance?'

'Because no single person can successfully lead the Altaics,' Menynder said. 'In case you haven't noticed, none of us are very clottin' easy to get along with.'

'I've noticed,' Sten said dryly.

'In fact, we're rotten at it. We'd as soon as kill each other as breathe. So the top man is top killer. By definition . . . It's the way our stupid system works. The biggest and baddest tribe kicks drakh out of everybody else as often as possible. Which is how it stays big and bad.'

'I was going to suggest something else,' Sten said. 'I was going to suggest putting together some kind of coalition government.'

Menynder snorted. 'Coalition? On the Altaics? Not clottin' likely.'

'You almost put one together before,' Sten said flatly.

Menynder's eyes narrowed. 'What do you mean?'

Sten didn't bother with being casual. 'The infamous dinner with the old Khaqan,' he said. 'I've never believed that story.'

'What *do* you believe?' Menynder's voice was cold.

'I think the Khaqan was never invited at all,' Sten said. 'He wouldn't sit down with a bunch of Suzdal, Bogazi, and Torks. Much less *eat* with them.

'I think you . . . General Douw . . . Youtang and Diatry . . . had no idea he was even going to show up. In fact, I think you were all sitting together in that room trying to figure out how to get rid of him. And *you* are the only being in this cluster capable of hammering together a plot involving all representative species.'

Sten gave a chilly smile. 'If that's true,' he said, 'it only follows that you are also the only being capable of putting together the kind of coalition government I have in mind.'

Menynder was silent. Sten's praise also included accusation.

'What I can't figure out,' Sten said, 'was how you killed the old bastard.'

'I didn't,' Menynder said. A beat. Then, '*We* didn't.'

Sten shrugged. 'It doesn't matter to me one way or the other.'

'You'd have a murderer as a ruler?'

Sten looked at him. 'Name one who isn't.'

Menynder thought awhile. Finally, he said, 'What if I don't go along with your idea? Will you just let it rest?'

Sten gave him a hard look. 'Not this time.'

'So I really don't have a choice,' Menynder said.

'Maybe not. But it'll work a whole lot better if you *believe* you have a choice.'

'Then I'd better say yes, real clottin' fast,' Menynder said.

'That's the way I see it,' Sten said.

'Menynder again,' the Eternal Emperor snapped. 'Why do you keep bringing up his name?'

'Because, sir, he's the best being for the job,' Sten said.

The Eternal Emperor fish-eyed him. 'Is that an "I told you so," Sten? Are you saying I screwed up by picking Professor Iskra?'

'It's not my place to judge your decisions, sir.'

'Why do I keep hearing reprimands in your voice?' the Emperor said.

'Professor Iskra was the best choice from a poor lot, sir,' Mahoney broke in. 'Anyone can see that. Which is why, sir, I think Sten's idea now has merit.'

'Committees make rotten law,' the Emperor said. 'They always have. They always will. Before you know it, every committee member has his own agenda, based on pure ego. Consensus becomes a joke. Paid for by power or money or lust or all of the above.'

The Emperor drained his drink. His holographic image gestured across millions of light-years for Mahoney and Sten to do the same. 'Clot a bunch of rule by committee,' he said. But his mood had changed.

Glasses were emptied and refilled. Sten started to speak, but Mahoney tipped him the wink, so he buttoned his lip and let Mahoney grab the ball and run.

'I couldn't agree with you more, sir,' Ian said. 'Government by committee tends to be bloody useless. But, in this case, sir, might it not be a temporary solution? In fact, might it not eventually lead to a permanent one?'

'Explain,' the Emperor ordered.

'The act of putting together a coalition,' Mahoney said, 'might also have the side benefit of calming things down. Putting a lid on the violence.'

'I can track that logic,' the Emperor said. 'Go ahead.'

'So, what if we give the coalition a time frame, sir? Such and such must be accomplished in such and such time. After that, the coalition ceases to exist. Automatically.'

'Some kind of sundown law,' the Emperor said.

'Exactly,' Mahoney said. 'The committee *must* be replaced by a more stable system by the date you mandate.'

The Emperor thought. Then he said, 'All right. You win. Put it into motion.'

'Thank you, sir,' Sten said, hiding the relief in his voice. 'One other thing . . .'

The Emperor waved this down. 'Yeah. I know. You need some kind of dramatic gesture that says I am going along with this coalition idea.'

'Yessir,' Sten said.

'How about a royal audience? Get Menynder and the others to Prime. I'll make a fuss over them in court. Bless their holy mission of peace, and all that rot. Send them back heroes. Will that do?'

'It'll do just fine, sir,' Sten said.

The Emperor reached for the button that chopped the connection. He paused. 'This had *better* work,' he snapped. Then his image was gone.

Sten turned to Mahoney. 'Ian . . . I owe you real clottin' big.'

Mahoney laughed. 'Put it on the tab, lad. Put it on the tab.'

'This is Connee George reporting live from Soward Spaceport. The delegation from the Altaic Cluster is due to land at any moment, gentlebeings. And look at that welcoming party waiting for them on the landing pad, Tohm!'

'A big Prime World welcome it is, Connee. My goodness. What an historic moment! I'm sure our viewers are glued to their livies, waiting to get an exclusive KRCAX Prime look at this distinguished delegation. I wonder what's going through our viewers' minds, now, Connee.'

'Probably the same as me, Tohm. Which is – wow! What a story!'

'Indeed it is, Connee. Indeed it is . . . uh . . . Give us some of your thoughts on this . . . uh . . . historic . . . uh . . . moment, Connee.'

'Well, the official release from the Emperor's press office tells us that on board are four beings bound for destiny. A destiny of peace. But, the release doesn't tell us the whole story, Tohm.'

'No, it doesn't . . . uh . . . does it?'

'Excuse me, Tohm, while I see if Captain P'wers can put us in a little closer. Can you get in over to the left of the landing pad, Gary?'

'I'll try, Connee. But the traffic is pretty fierce and the tower is giving us a hard way to go.'

'Just doing their jobs, I'm sure, Gary. And what a job that is!'

'Right, Connee . . . Okay . . . Hold on . . . Geesh, where'd that lighter come from?'

'Probably our competition, Gary. Ha-ha. Forgive my gloat, Tohm, but I'm sure the viewers at home will understand.'

'Absolutely, Connee. They know that's why we're the number one news team on Prime. KRCAX Prime, Connee.'

'It sure is, Tohm. Now, look at that view!'

'Sure is impressive. Good work, Captain P'wers!'

'Thanks, Tohm. Clot! Get outta my sky you bas—'

'Watch it, Gary. Kiddies at home. Ha-ha . . . Now that we've got an exclusive view for our exclusive live coverage, Connee, why don't you finish that rundown.'

'Right, Tohm. Well, in the wake of the tragic death of Professor Iskra, the Eternal Emperor has come up with what most authorities agree is a sheer masterstroke of a plan to solve the troubles of the vital Altaic Cluster.

'On board that ship are the beings who will lead their region into a new era of peace. Heading the distinguished delegation is one Sr Menynder. And his fellow Torks are one thousand percent behind this effort, Tohm.'

'As they should be, Connee. Now, tell us about the . . . uh . . . others. A pretty distinguished group, themselves, right, Connee?'

'Right, Tohm . . . The Suzdal are lead by Youtang, one of the most able diplomats in the Altaic Cluster. On the Bogazi side is a being of equal importance, Diatry. Last, but certainly not least, is Sr Gray – the leader of the all-important Jochi population.'

'Great rundown, Connee. Now, tell our viewers what festivities lie ahead for these . . . uh . . . distinguished . . . uh . . . delegates.'

'Well, you can be sure, Tohm, that Prime Worlders are not going to stint on our famous hospitality. First, there's the big welcoming at Soward.'

'Excuse me, Connee, but I want to remind the viewers that we'll be covering that live. As soon as the delegates land.'

'Go ahead, Tohm.'

'Uh . . . I just did, Connee. Ha-ha.'

'Ha-ha. Okay. After that, the Eternal Emperor has scheduled a big public celebration at the palace. Which we shall also be covering.'

'Exclusively, Connee. Live and exclusive.'

'Right, Tohm. Following the celebration, there's a big royal ball set for tonight. Then—'

'Sorry to interrupt, Connee, but the tower reports the ship is coming in.'

'Don't be sorry, Gary, you're just doing your job. Ha-ha. Now, let's see how close we can get. We'll give our viewers a real KRCAX Prime look at things.'

'Tower's gonna be mad.'

'Don't worry, Captain P'wers. They're all pretty good sports in the tower. Besides, they're just—'

'I know, Connee . . . doing their jobs.'

Menynder peered at the ship's vidscreen as the spaceport rushed up at them. He grudgingly admitted to himself that he was excited.

As excited as a kid, you dumb old Tork. But what harm is there? Let's be honest. You've never been anywhere in your life. And now you're actually going to get to see Prime World. Which has to be every being's dream since . . . since clottin' forever.

Menynder chuckled to himself and glanced over at the other members of his party. Damned if they weren't as excited as he was. He noted that Youtang's sharp grin had a silly pup tilt to it. And Diatry's beak was wide open, looking at all the marvels of Prime. He couldn't see the Jochi, Gray. But he heard him sniggering.

Knock it off, Menynder. There is serious business ahead. Yeah. Sure. But just for now, can't I be a kid again? I mean, I gonna meet the clottin' Eternal Emperor. At a big clottin' for-real castle. Maybe even shake the Emperor's hand. Damn. Damn. Damn. If Momma could see me now.

Menynder saw a gravlighter darting across the screen. The sign on the side read: KRCAX Prime. Some kind of livie news crew, he assumed. He idly wondered if the lighter captain might be cutting it a little too close. Nah. These were the best of the best, weren't they? A by-God news crew from by-God Prime World. Absolute pros. He was sure.

But – oh, my clot. It was still coming! Hey . . . What's going on?

'Look out!' Gray screamed. 'We're gonna—'

Menynder had an instant to feel the jolt and see the screen go from white to black to collapse. And then he felt the great heavy hand smashing into his back. Heard the crack of his seat giving away.

And then Menynder was ramming forward. The far cabin wall rushing at him.

He heard screamsscreamsscreams. And he thought . . . Aw, drakh!

'This is KBSNQ, reporting live from Soward Spaceport. For those viewers joining us late – there's been a terrible tragedy here at Prime World's main spaceport.

'A delegation of high-level beings from the Altaic Cluster – arriving here for crucial peace talks with the Eternal Emperor – has collided in midair with a lighter carrying a local news team.

'All beings aboard both craft are believed dead. Imperial investigators are at the site now. The Eternal Emperor has ordered all flags lowered to half-mast for a one-week period of mourning.

'We now return to our regular programming. Be assured we will interrupt if further developments warrant. This is Pyt'r Jynnings reporting live for KBNSQ. You give us twenty-two minutes . . . and we'll give you the Empire.'

Chapter Thirty-Eight

Sten sat brooding at the dark skyline of Rurik. The only light showing was the faint, far-off glow of the eternal flame burning in the Square of the Khaqans. All was silent . . . waiting.

He felt Cind's hand touch his arm. 'Menynder was our last hope,' he said.

'I know.'

'I talked him into going. All he wanted to do was sit by that damned dead pond. In peace.'

'I know that, too.'

'He was a crooked old dog. But – clot. I liked him.'

Her answer was a tighter grip.

'I haven't the faintest idea what to do next,' Sten said.

'Maybe . . . the Emperor will think of something.'

'Right.'

'Mahoney, then.'

'He's as lost as I am. Right now, he's battening down the hatches. Getting ready.'

'You think it's going to be that bad?'

'Yeah. Real bad.'

'But it wasn't anybody's fault. Except maybe that damned news crew. It was an accident, for clot's sake.'

'That's not what *they* think.' He pointed out at the silent city. 'They think it was a plot. That the Emperor lured Menynder and the others to their deaths.'

'That's ridiculous. Why would he?'

'They don't need a reason,' Sten said. 'They just need someone to blame. We screwed up last. So we're it.'

Cind shivered. Sten put an arm around her. 'Thanks,' he said.

'What for?'

'For being here . . . with me . . . That's all.'

She snuggled into the arm. 'You just try to chase me off,' she said. 'You just try.'

Even in his gloom, Sten was comforted. He leaned back and pulled Cind closer to him.

They sat there until dawn. The sun came up huge and red and angry.

A few minutes later, they heard the first gunfire.

'W' hae snipers 'n' rioters 'n' looters, oh my,' Kilgour said. 'Which is noo ver' good. But it's noo ver' bad, either.'

'What could be worse?' Sten asked.

'Ah'm feared w' hae thae comin' up, lad.'

'Which is?'

'A braw clottin' absence a' army.'

'Come to think of it, I haven't seen any Jochi troops about, either. But I thought that was good news. Go ahead. Tell me different. I'm getting used to this depression. I'll probably miss it when it's gone.'

'I's th' puir bein's here thae's turned matters topsy-turvy i' y'r wee nog,' Alex said. 'Bleak's happy. An' joy i' bleak. Afflicted by their clottin' weather, puir things. Eat hate 'n' ill will wi' break- fast haggis.'

'Thanks for reminding me about stuffed sheep's stomach, Kilgour. Yum yum. I feel much better, now.'

'Ah'm rejoicin't t' be lookin't oot frae y', lad.'

'Tell me about the army.'

'Absence of army, son.'

'Yeah, that.'

'Well, i' ain't clottin' there, aye? Nary a trooper or trooper's whore t' be glimt i' Rurik. Had m' Frick 'n' Fracks up f'r hours, snoopit an' poopit aboot. Zed th' barracks. Zed th' ossifers' and noncompoops' mess.'

'Where the clot did they get off to?'

'Braw question. So Ah query't an em'nent silvery-haired fox.'

'General Douw?'

'Aye. He's away, too.'

Sten sat up straight in his chair. 'Where'd he go?'

'Off wi' his troopies. Maneuvers, his ferret of a press officer said. Annual maneuvers in yon alps.' Alex pointed off in the general direction of the mountain range that half-ringed the wide Rurik valley.

'Maneuvers? Oh, bulldrakh. You don't believe it, do you?'

'Noooooo. 'Less th' Jochi troopies – brave lads an' lassies a' – go on maneuvers wi' ammunition all alive, alive-o.'

'Drakh,' Sten said.

'Hip high, old son. 'N risin' fast.'

Douw may have been a silvery-haired fool with a pennyweight brain. But perched on a camp stool in his mountain command center, he looked every inch a general. And acted like a very angry one.

'We don't need proof,' he snarled across the war table. 'Insisting on proof is the last refuge of cowards.'

'No Suzdal has ever been called a coward,' came a growl. It was Tress, warlord of the Suzdal worlds.

'Don't be so quick to take offense,' Snyder said. He was Menynder's cousin and, now, the de facto war chief of the Torks. 'That's our problem in the Altaics. Every time we consider unified action, someone gets his nose out of joint and the whole thing collapses.'

'Respect we must have,' Hoatzin said. His voice was harsh, weary. His wife, Diatry, had died with Menynder and the others. It was now Hoatzin's task to lead the Bogazi hutches into battle. If there was to be one.

'Divide and conquer. Divide and conquer. That's always been the Emperor's way,' Douw said. He was not being hypocritical. He had truly forgotten that Iskra had used those very words, though in a different – and Jochian – context.

'So, we fight,' Tress said. 'What chance do we have? Against the Eternal Emperor? His forces—'

'Who cares about the size of his forces?' Douw broke in. 'The terrain is ours. The people are ours. If we all stand together . . . we must prevail.'

'Emperor not so strong as he thinks,' Hoatzin said. 'Fight Tahn many years. He had victory, yes. But not so good a victory. Very long war. Soldiers, I think, are tired. Also, as general say, this not their land. What they fight for?'

'Still,' Tress said, 'the Emperor has never been defeated before.'

'It happen once,' the Bogazi said. 'Must have. Why else the Emperor disappear? I think he flee privy council.'

No one had ever put the Emperor's disappearance in that light before. It was wrong thinking. But it was the kind of wrong thinking that leads to treacherous conclusions.

'We must all join together,' Douw said. 'For the first time in our history, we must stand united in one cause. The cause is just. Our soldiers are brave. We only need the will.'

There was a long silence around the table. A nesting bird fussed overhead.

Tress rose to his haunches. 'I will speak to my pack mates,' he said.

'What will you tell them?' Douw asked.

'That we fight. Together.'

The sniper still made no sense to Cind.

'Dinnae fash, lass,' Alex advised. 'Th' shooter's peepers hae big crosses on 'em noo.'

'By my father's frozen buttocks, you're thick sometimes.'

'Now y're cussin' a' me in y'r heathen Bhor tongue. No respect f'r y'r puir gray mentor. Shame, shame on y' lass.'

'Come on, Alex. How did he get into the palace? Why was he able to pick the best window to shoot from? How come he had all the time in the world to set up shop, find out where Sten would be sitting, plus create a diversion for his escape?'

'We hae a team pokin' 'n' a probin' on th' dread plotters, wee Cind.'

'No hope, there,' Cind said. 'Too many suspects. Too many possible combinations. They've got a better chance at winning the Imperial lottery.'

''N' y're believin't y' c'n do better?'

Cind thought a moment, then nodded. 'Sure. Because they're looking in the wrong direction. The guy was a pro. From his choice of positions, to that old rifle he chose as a weapon, down to the hand-molded bullets.'

'Ho-kay. Yon dead shooter wae a pro. This is noo unusual i' a sniper. Wha' else is buggin't y'?' Despite himself, Kilgour was getting interested. Cind was maybe onto something.

'Two things. The first is personal. He was trying to kill Sten. Clot, he almost did!'

Kilgour knew this, tsked, and waved for the key point.

'What really gets me,' Cind said, 'was that he was the *only* sniper. Dammit, that makes no sense. Under the circumstances, there should have been a whole host of rooftop shooters. Or none. Not unless somebody wanted to be extra sure of exactly who died.

'Fine. We know he didn't have to go for Iskra. The coroner's report tells us the attack on the stands got him. But the same attack missed Sten. So . . . Wham! He tries to take him out. Thanks to you and your chain-mail tailor, it didn't work. But . . . still . . .'

Alex was thoughtful. 'Aye . . . Thae hae t' be more.'

'More of what?' came Mahoney's voice. 'What trouble are you two cooking up?'

They whirled to see that Ian had entered the room. Cind was used to big beings moving silently. Look at Alex. Look at her Bhor comrades. But Mahoney still astonished her. It wasn't that he was just, well, getting on in years . . . But his large Irish body and round friendly face didn't look as if they belonged to someone who could cat around corners and into rooms.

She started to snap to attention and acknowledge her superior officer. Mahoney waved her down. 'Just tell me what you two are plotting.'

Cind filled him in on the mysterious sniper. Mahoney listened closely, then shook his head. 'It's an interesting mystery, I agree,' he said. 'And the man was certainly a pro. Which means he was hired. Which also likely means whoever hired him would have had a cutout. Therefore, if you find out who the sniper is, *that's* all you'll learn. He even might be an interesting fellow, in an evil sort of way. But, I'm afraid in this case, x plus y can only equal: who cares?'

'I don't think so, sir,' Cind said. 'Not this time. And it's not a feeling, but an instinct. Professional instinct. See, when I was hunting him, I did my clotting best to try thinking like him.'

'Naturally,' Mahoney said. 'Go on.' The former Mantis chief found himself getting drawn in.

'Pretty soon I *was* thinking like him. Even named him "Cutie" in my mind.'

'So, what makes "Cutie" different?' Mahoney wanted to know.

Cind sighed. 'It boils down to his knowledge of the terrain *and* his target. Which means, I think Cutie had been around the palace for a while. I think he checked out every square inch of it.

'I also think he would have done his damnedest to get to know his target. Otherwise he wouldn't have been comfortable. No. Cutie would've wanted to know Sten. Real well. Have an idea about his private habits. Know which way he would duck when the attack started.'

'Aye . . . Quite logical, lass,' Alex said. ''N' maybe . . . Jus' mayhap . . .'

Mahoney smacked the table. 'Of course! He would have tried to visit the embassy. Or, at least attend some official functions that Sten would have been at.'

'Exactly,' Cind said. 'Which means either Sten, or Alex, might recognize him.'

She looked up at Mahoney. 'I want Sten to go to the morgue, sir,' she said. 'To see if he can ID the remains.'

'Tell him, not me,' Ian said, quite sensibly.

Cind lifted an eyebrow. 'He'll think it's a waste of time, sir,' she said. 'Maybe if you . . .' She let it dangle.

'I'll drag him along by the ear,' Mahoney said. 'Come on, Alex. Let's go chat with the ambassador.'

The basement morgue was white and cold, with antiseptically filtered air that didn't cover the occasional whiff of odor that put a rusty taste on the tongue.

'Hang on a sec,' the human attendant said. 'I ain't finished me lunch.' He waved a thick sandwich in their faces. Tomato sauce seeped through the bread.

Cind was about ready to rip his face off. Even with Mahoney and Kilgour prodding, Sten had stubbornly refused to go. He was too busy, he said. Up-to-his-ears-in-drakh busy.

Remarkably, however, she now watched him step in. Instead of barking orders, he slipped a sheaf of credits out of his pocket and waved it under the attendant's nose.

'You could always bring your lunch along,' he said.

The attendant snatched the bills, motioned with the sandwich-filled hand, and trotted off. They followed.

'It's the only way to get a bureaucrat's attention,' Sten muttered to her. 'Yelling just makes them stubborner – and stupider.'

The attendant was moving along the drawered crypts. 'Let's see . . . Where'd I put that Jon Doe?' He aimed a remote box, pressed the button, and a corpse drawer rolled out with a crash. Cold air blasted from the crypt.

The attendant peered into the drawer. A drip of red sauce fell onto the body. He wiped it up with a thumb, then licked his thumb clean.

'Nope. Wrong guy.' He jabbed the button and the drawer slammed shut. The attendant laughed. 'Sorry to stiff you with the stiff.'

Nobody laughed at his joke. He shrugged. 'We been pretty busy since the Khaqan died,' he said. 'Got more clients than we got time.'

He laughed again. 'My wife's happier'n pig in drakh. I been on golden overtime for months. One more big shootin' match and we can go buy that retirement cottage we been dreamin' about.'

'How fortunate for you,' Cind said.

The attendant caught her tone. 'Wasn't me that put 'em here, lady,' he said. 'That's *your* job. You frag 'em, I bag 'em. That's my motto.'

He aimed the remote at another crypt and pressed the button. The drawer slid out. He peered into it. 'Yep. That's the Doe you laid down your dough for. Still dead, too. Ha-ha. Belly up to the bones, boys. And see your future.' He snickered at Cind. 'You too, lady.'

But it was Mahoney who looked first. His reaction was quick. And it was massive.

'Mother of Mercy,' he intoned. 'It's Venloe!'

Sten was rocked back. 'It can't be.' He took his own look. 'Damn! It's Venloe all right.'

'Thae's noo possible,' Alex said as he was confirming their view. 'But i' bloody is!'

Cind didn't know what they were talking about at first. Then she remembered. Venloe was the man responsible for killing the Emperor!

'I thought he was—'

'In a maximum clottin' security prison,' Sten finished for her. 'Last I heard, he was so far under the ground they had to pipe in the sunlight.'

'He must have escaped,' Cind said.

'Another impossibility,' Sten said. He looked again. 'But . . . there he is.'

'Top part a' him, anyways,' Alex said.

Mahoney frowned at the waxen features staring up at him. He remembered the day he had brought Venloe to ground. And their subsequent conversation. Venloe was a being who could squirm out of just about any situation – even the Emperor's most secure prison.

'But – what was he doing here?' Cind asked. 'Who could have—'

The rest of her question was cut off by Mahoney's emergency beeper. He whipped it from his belt and keyed in. 'Mahoney, here.'

The officer's voice rasped through the speaker. 'You better get back here fast, sir. We just picked up a fleet heading for Jochi. They're confirmed unfriendlies, sir.'

Mahoney was already running as he keyed out. The others sprinted after him.

Venloe lay cold in his drawer behind them, his mystery forgotten in the impending attack.

The morgue attendant – who had overheard the news – hustled off to make his wife an even happier woman.

Chapter Thirty-Nine

Admiral Han Langsdorff had obviously either slept through or cut his class in Basic Military Mistakes some fifty years earlier.

He took the three Imperial battleship flotillas out to stop the Suzdal/Bogazi invasion fleets full of confidence and contempt. This would be a simple, if bloody, mission. First he expected these primitive beings – Langsdorff concealed it rather well, but he was a xenophobe – to freeze when confronted with the mailed fist of the Empire. After they recovered from their awe and terror, they might, at worst, form a battle line and attempt a frontal engagement.

Langsdorff dangled one cruiser squadron as bait and arranged his main battle force in a lopsided wing behind and to one side of the decoys.

The enemy would attempt to attack the Imperial force, and it would be simple for Langsdorff to turn their flank and have all of them enfilade.

It was not a complex plan. But simplicity was a virtue in battle. Besides, how could any consortium of oversize avians and canines stand against the Empire?

He certainly wasn't the first battle leader to hold his foe in utter contempt. History has made a very full list of occasions when the same thing happened:

The Hsiung-Nu long-term disaster in Turkestan. The Little Horn. Isandhlwana. Magersfontein. Suomussalmi. Dien Bien Phu. Saragossa. And on, and on, and on.

Even the name of his flagship might have helped. Langsdorff vaguely know that the *Repulse*, many incarnations before, had been a water-borne warship. He even vaguely remembered it was something called a battle cruiser. That was the sum of his knowledge.

He did not know that the *Repulse*'s namesake – and an accompanying battleship – had sailed calmly into harm's way, confident that the mere presence of battleships would create paralytic terror in the enemy; that no one would hazard land-based aircraft over the open sea; and that certainly no one from the never-sufficiently-despised Mongoloid subspecies of the human race would *dare* confront these magnificent examples of Empire.

It took the Japanese land-based atmospheric bombers just under one hour to sink both warships.

Langsdorff scanned the screen. The longer-ranging Imperial sensors had picked up the Suzdal/Bogazi fleets. He snorted. These beings could do nothing right. If he were invading a cluster's home world, he would certainly have come up with more warships than he was looking at – even if he had to bolt missile tubes to every lunar ferry he could requisition.

Two hostile cruiser squadrons smashed at the Imperial cruisers in a frontal assault. Bare minutes later, two more Suzdal/Bogazi formations – these formed around tacship carriers and heavy cruisers – came down on the Imperials from above and below, like the closing jaws of a nutcracker.

The Imperial cruisers fought back – but were outgunned.

The battle was joined. Admiral Langsdorff ordered his battle-wagons in, to envelop the Suzdal/Bogazi left flank, just as the human Turks had attempted in the sea battle called Lepanto. But unlike the Ottomans, he kept none of his forces in reserve.

The Suzdal/Bogazi fleet commanders believed, just as Langsdorff did, that in battle simplest is best. Their tactics were taken from the clichéd drawing of a minnow being swallowed by a slightly larger fish being swallowed by a shark being swallowed by a whale.

Because farther above and below the jaws that had closed on the Imperial cruisers were the real Suzdal/Bogazi heavies. Their admirals waited until Langsdorff's battleship formations were irretrievably committed.

And then they closed the bigger jaws on the far richer prize: the entire Imperial strike force.

Langsdorff was dead before he could bleat for help – help that just didn't exist.

The battle was a catastrophe – for the Empire.

The Suzdal/Bogazi lost five cruisers, fourteen destroyers, and a scattering of lighter craft.

The Imperial *survivors* were one battleship, three cruisers, one tacship carrier, and twenty troops.

The Suzdal/Bogazi fleets reformed triumphantly and drove on toward Jochi. Their victory would not, however, be studied at many military academies, even those of the victors.

Massacres, for some reason, aren't vastly interesting to soldiers.

Langsdorff's disaster left Jochi wide open for invasion – and the First Imperial Guards Division stranded on a hostile world.

Chapter Forty

The embassy shuddered under the heavy storm blasting down from the mountains. Even here – in the conference chamber buried far under the building – Sten could hear lightning crack and thunder roll.

He shivered. Not from the cold rain outside, but from the words being spoken by the strange being hovering a meter above the chamber floor.

'. . . I regret to say, my reasoning did not prove faulty. Perhaps that's why I went to such risk and trouble to visit Dr Rykor. False hope that I was in terrible error. And that our wise friend would gently guide me back to reality.'

Sr Ecu gave a flick of his tail and drifted to Sten's side. A sensitive tendril whiskered out and touched Sten's hand.

'But there was no error. The Eternal Emperor is quite mad – and only certain disaster can result.'

Sten said nothing. He felt orphaned for the second time in his life. He had worked and fought for the Emperor since adolescence – after his real family had been killed.

'I can barely bring myself to believe this,' Mahoney said. Although he had suspected as much for some time, he found the hard truth difficult to choke down.

'I am very sorry, my old friend,' Sr Ecu said. 'But you of all people know just how correct I am. However . . . there are two other things I should tell you both.'

He shifted position, dropping a little lower to the floor. A tendril whiskered through the open case. Mahoney found himself holding a fiche.

'That is an intelligence file my operatives have put together. You see, when I became convinced the Emperor was insane, I wondered who was advising him now. Who had his ear? Who was doing his bidding?'

Mahoney stared at the fiche. 'And you learned?'

'Poyndex,' Ecu said flatly.

Sten sucked in air as another blow fell.

'But the man's a turncoat,' Mahoney protested. 'He betrayed the Emperor to join the privy council. Then he betrayed them to save his own life.'

'This is true. And now he commands the Emperor's efforts to bring the Empire's provinces into dominion status. A job, my sources tell me, you rejected. On moral grounds.'

Mahoney slumped in his chair, a portrait of despair. 'How could things come to such a pass?' he said. 'After all these years?'

The Manabi's tendril drew forth more bad news. It was Sten's turn. He was presented with two paper-jacketed files. One was blue, the other red. He duly saw his name on both.

'Your personnel records,' Sr Ecu said. 'Forgive my intrusion into your privacy.'

Sten shrugged. What did it matter now?

'The first file – the blue one – is your official file. A record for public consumption of your many achievements in Imperial Service.

'A close analysis shows there are gaps in that record. Gaps that are artfully covered over.' Sten and Mahoney both knew that those so-called gaps were the secret missions Sten had undertaken in the service of the Emperor.

'Don't bother trying to explain those missing years to me,' Sr Ecu said. 'I'm sure I can easily guess the nature of missions you undertook in the Emperor's name.'

'Thanks,' Sten said wearily. 'I guess.'

'Please open the second file, Sten,' Sr Ecu said.

Sten thumbed back the red jacket, revealing a cover sheet, with the letter head of Internal Security. Sten looked up at Sr Ecu, bewildered.

'I'm being . . . investigated?'

'The investigation has already been accomplished,' Sr Ecu said. 'When you have time to look it over, you will see that the gentle-being at the Internal Security office had a different view of those gaps.

'A view that leads to the unalterable conclusion that you are a traitor, Sten. You, the most loyal of all the Emperor's subjects, have been the tool of his enemies.'

Sten quickly thumbed through and saw evidence piled upon evidence. He closed the red file. 'Ammunition, I assume?' he asked.

'Exactly. If you fail in any undertaking – or somehow anger the Emperor – that is the file which will come into play. And your achievements will go the way of the shredder.'

Sten felt the room swaying around him. It wasn't the storm. He steadied himself. 'I thank you for this warning, Sr Ecu. But – I assume you have more than just my reputation in mind.'

Sr Ecu was taking a terrible risk with this visit. Yes . . . he had used an absolutely secure transport provided by Ida of the Rom – Sten's old Mantis team friend. If anyone learned the nature of his mission, Sr Ecu was not endangering only himself, but his entire species.

The Manabi dropped all pretense of diplomatic fine wording. 'I was hoping you could help,' he said.

This shook Sten. 'Help? But – how? I don't control armies and fleets. I'm just—'

'Don't get alarmed, young Sten,' Sr Ecu said. 'I'm not sure what I'm asking you to do. Except . . . think . . . think hard. When this ugly business in the Altaics is over . . . come to me on my home world. You, too, Ian. We accomplished a miracle once before, did we not?'

'But that was just the privy council,' Sten said. 'Not the Eternal Emperor.'

'I think we should listen to him, Sten,' Mahoney said, his voice a rough whisper. 'I swore my allegiance to a symbol. Not a man.'

Sten was silent. How could he explain? There were no words for the loss he had just suffered. The king is dead, indeed. Long live the king. Suddenly, he thought: What's to hold me now? Whom do I owe? Besides Cind? Besides my friends? He thought about his retreat on Smallbridge. He ached for its forests and hills and his cabin by the frozen lakes.

'Find someone else,' he told Sr Ecu. 'I don't mean to sound

like an ingrate – but I'm going to do my best to take your warning and make very selfish use of it.'

'I'll still be waiting, young Sten,' the Manabi said. 'I have faith in you.'

'You'd better go,' Sten said brusquely. 'My people will get you back to your ship. Have a safe journey. And thanks for your trouble.'

Sten headed for the door. Mahoney came slowly after him.

'Rykor said you would refuse me at first,' Sr Ecu called after him. 'But in the end, she said you'd come around.'

Sten was unreasonably angry. He snarled back at the gentle being who had come so far. 'Clot Rykor!'

'Just think about it, Sten,' he heard the Manabi say as he went out the door. 'It will save us all a great deal of time.'

Sten stormed through the reception hall, his guts a knot of white-hot anger. He wanted to get away. Anyplace. Anywhere. Get drunk. Chew on a pistol barrel.

He barely noticed the pale, frightened face of the reception officer as he swept past the main desk and headed for the embassy doors.

Mahoney's big paw came down on his shoulder and swung him around. It was all Sten could do to keep himself from striking out at his friend.

'Sten! Listen to me, dammit! Remember what I said back on Prime? Before all this started? Now – I think I know where our answer might be.'

Sten shrugged off the hand. 'I've had enough with these games, Ian,' he said. 'Let somebody else look for answers for a change. Clot! I don't even care what the question is anymore.'

Four large individuals in the gray uniforms of Internal Security stepped into view. Sten's heart lurched as the meaning of their presence sunk in.

The IS beings strode up to them. The commander flashed his warrant card. Another whipped out plas manacles. Sten braced himself.

The IS commander pushed past him. Sten's head reeled as the man addressed Ian. 'Governor Mahoney, you will come with us, please.'

Sten gaped. What the clot was happening? Why weren't they after *him*?'

'By what authority?' he heard Mahoney's voice boom.

'By the authority of the Eternal Emperor,' the commander snapped. 'You have been charged with incompetence in the face of the enemy. You are hereby relieved of command. You will be escorted to Prime World where you will be indicted . . . and if an indictment is returned . . . you will be tried.'

Sten tried desperately to make sense of this. They must be talking about what happened in the Disputed Worlds. Admiral Langsdorff's foolish and humiliating defeat. He stepped in between the IS officers and Mahoney.

'But – he had nothing to do with that,' Sten protested.

'Out of the way, Ambassador,' the commander said.

Sten turned to call for help, wondering, even as he did, what fool would rush to his aid.

'That's all right, Sten,' Mahoney said. 'Let's not make things worse.'

He pushed Sten aside. 'I'm ready,' he told the commander.

Sten watched helplessly as they shoved Ian against the wall, kicked his feet apart, and put him through a thorough, spirit-grinding search. Mahoney's hands were bent behind his back. The manacles were snapped on – so tight that Sten could see Ian's hands engorge with blood.

A moment later, Mahoney was being marched out of the embassy.

'I'll call the Emperor,' Sten shouted after him. 'It's a mistake. I know it. A terrible mistake.'

'Just go home, lad,' Mahoney yelled as he was shoved through the door. 'Remember what I said – and go home!'

A hiss of doors . . . and he was gone.

Sten raced to the com room and pushed the night officer aside. He hammered out the code himself and punched the send button.

'I want to speak to the Emperor,' he shouted at the official who finally took his call. 'Right now, dammit!'

'I'm sorry, Ambassador Sten,' the official said. 'But I have been given explicit instructions. The Emperor does not wish to speak with you. Under any circumstances.'

'Hold on, you clot!' Sten snarled. 'This is Ambassador Sten, calling. Not some jerk-off clerk.'

The official pretended to scan a list before him. 'Sorry. No mistake. The Emperor specifically asked that your name be removed from the personal access list. My apologies if this inconveniences you . . . but I'm sure you can get what you need through official channels.'

The screen blanked.

Sten sagged back. The only thing he could do for Mahoney now was pray.

And this was impossible for a man who, quite suddenly, had no gods at all.

Chapter Forty-One

Mahoney's relief and arrest sent what little morale there was among the Imperial Forces into free-fall. To Sten, Mahoney was not just his mentor and friend, but the man who had saved his life back on Vulcan.

To Kilgour, a man who had little faith in officers, Mahoney was, among other things, a respected leader – he had been Alex's CO back in Mantis Section, years before he had met Sten.

To Cind, Otho, and the Bhor, Mahoney was an honored war leader and elder. If he had somehow offended the Emperor, they agreed, he should have been given a chance to cut off his own beard in council and await the verdict – rather than being escorted off by armed beings as if he were some kind of criminal.

To the First Guards Division, Mahoney was not just one of them, having begun his military service in their ranks, but their most venerated commander. During the Tahn war, he had been their commanding general.

Their current commanding general, Paidrac Sarsfield, had even been a company commander under Mahoney, back on a hellworld called Cavite.

None of them understood what mistake, let alone what name-less crime, Mahoney had committed.

Not that they talked about it.

The event, and the situation, were too objectionable for that. The soldiers didn't even bitch about what had happened.

Sten would have had to take some sort of action to build the esprit back up to a functional level – he was unsure what it could be – if there weren't a worse nightmare approaching:

The Suzdal/Bogazi invasion fleet, oncoming at full speed. There was no way Sten could see to stop the invasion.

Two elements kept their own counsel on the relief of Mahoney:

The Gurkhas.

And Fleet Admiral Mason.

Alex slammed into Sten's office, crashing the door behind him. The jamb splintered, but held.

'Ah hae,' he said, *sans* preamble, 'jus' decoded our marchin' orders. Except thae'll be none ae us marchin't. Eyes Only. Nae frae our clottin' respected Emperor, lang may he wave, but frae some clot i' th' Imperial office.'

He spun the printout across to Sten.

It was brief:

CONTINUE MISSION AS OUTLINED. IMPERIAL DIRECT RULE
WILL CONTINUE. MAINTAIN PUBLIC ORDER.

'Wi' no suggestion ae how,' Alex said. 'There's some clot oot there gone sarky – an' Ah know who. Thae braw flyin't ray was right.'

Sten wasn't paying any attention to Alex's ravings.

'So whae d' we do?'

Sten made up his mind. 'Can you mickey the code log?'

'Wi' m' left foot. Y' wan' a bogere message sayin't 'tis time t' haul, or what?'

'Negative. Too hard to back up. We just never received this.'

'Aye, sir.'

Kilgour turned to go. 'Y' know, lad. When we gie our arses off an' away, Ah'll no be servin't th' Emp. F'r better 'r worse, he dinnae deserve m' oath no more.'

'Let's worry about asses and away first. That's unlikely enough to happen anyway,' Sten advised in as neutral a tone as he could manage.

'Admiral Mason, I'm detaching you from command of the *Victory*.'

'Yes, sir.'

'I want you to take over what remains of that clot Langsdorff's fleet – and the escort ships that were left with the Guards' transports.'

'Yes, sir.'

'The *Victory* will be detached and placed under my direct command, as with the tacship carrier that made it back.'

'The *Bennington*, sir.'

'Thank you.'

'What are my instructions?' Mason asked, still in that chilling neutral voice.

'We're preparing to evacuate all Imperial elements from Jochi and the Altaic Cluster. How that'll be done, with the minimum casualties, I'm not sure.'

'What about the First Guards?'

'I'll be responsible for them, as well.'

'Yessir. May I comment?'

'You may,' Sten said.

'Do you really think you're qualified as a general?'

'Admiral, I don't think *anybody* is qualified to lead a retreat under fire, which is what we're going to undertake. But I'll remind you I've stumbled through one. During the war. On a planet called Cavite. Now, if you have any other insults?'

'No. But I have another question.'

Sten nodded.

'What changed things? I thought the Emperor wanted the Altaics held. I thought this armpit had some great diplomatic significance that I'm not aware of.'

'I filed an operations order this morning to Prime,' Sten lied. 'Saying the Altaics cannot be held. I've had no response. So I propose to proceed with the withdrawal. If the situation changes, you'll be among the first to be told.

'That's all.'

Picket ships announced that the Suzdal/Bogazi fleet was three E-days from Jochi's solar system.

'General Sarsfield, if you're alone?'

'I am, sir.'

'I want you to saddle up your division. Get all noncombat items wrapped and ready. Anything that's not absolutely vital to an on-planet combat mission can be stashed on the transports. What's the minimum time your division requires for a move?'

'The regs say ten E-hours when we're at full alert. We can do it in five.'

'Good.'

'Might I ask where we're going?'

'Home. I hope. But there might be a few detours on the way.'

'That's enough,' Sten ordered, rubbing eyes that were feeling, from the inside and out, like hard-poached eggs. He blanked all of the screens in the conference room, and as the yammer of impending doom stopped, the room fell silent.

He went to a table, where a previously unnoticed covered tray sat. He lifted one of the salver covers and picked up a sandwich. It was only a little stale. He tossed it to Alex and took one for himself.

Beside it was a decanter. He took the stopper out and sniffed. Stregg.

Was that advised?

Why not? Disaster would be the same sober as boiled.

He poured drinks, handed one to Alex, and they toasted.

Bless Cind. She must have had someone slip the refreshments in sometime after she had taken over as commander of the embassy guard.

'Y' hae any gran' strat'gy developed?' Alex wondered as he inhaled the sandwich and scooped for another.

'Not much more'n it better be better than Cavite,' Sten said. Mahoney had begun the withdrawal of the outmanned, outgunned Imperial Forces from that world, and Sten had finished the task. He had gotten the civilians out, and less than two thousand of the Imperial soldiers. Sten himself had ended up a prisoner of war.

He had been given the highest medals for this accomplishment, and he had been celebrated as a brilliant war leader. Sten had never considered that true – he thought Cavite a complete disaster and his efforts no more than damage control at best.

At least this time there weren't very many Imperial civilians, beyond the embassy staff.

'Aye,' Alex agreed, although he had never judged Cavite as harshly as Sten did.

'I have a couple of ideas,' Sten continued, 'but right now my brain seems to have spun out.'

''Tis nae wonder,' Kilgour said. 'It's lackin' but an hour 'til dawn. P'raps we'd best have a bit of a lie-down.'

Sten yawned, suddenly very sleepy. 'Good thought. Put a wakeup in for two hours.'

There was a tap on the door.

'I'll chase th'—'

'Enter,' Sten said.

The door opened. Three Gurkhas stood there. Sten felt quite grimy suddenly. In spite of the hour, all three of them were dressed as if for barracks inspection.

He held back a groan. The Gurkhas were Jemedar Lalbahadur Thapa, and newly promoted Havildars Chittahang Limbu and Mahkhajiri Gurung.

The last time the trio had confronted him was on Prime, when they had offered themselves and twenty-four other Gurkhas for Sten's service, breaking the long tradition that the Nepalese mercenaries served only the Eternal Emperor, an offer that had visibly put the Emperor's teeth on edge.

The Gurkhas saluted. Sten returned the salute and told them to stand at ease.

'We are sorry to bother you at this hour,' Lalbahadur said formally. 'But this was the only time we could find. We would like to speak in private, if it is possible.'

Sten nodded – and Alex swallowed the sandwich, washed it down with stregg, and vanished. He offered them seats. They preferred to stand.

'We have a question or two about the future that we are unable to answer,' Lalbahadur went on. 'This is utter foolishness of course, since without question those evil feathered capons who are flocking toward us will peck us into tiny bits and hurl those bits into the garbage pits, to be torn at by their jackal friends. Am I not correct?'

'You are without a doubt correct,' Sten agreed. All four of them smiled – or at least bared their teeth.

'But once we have withdrawn from this dung heap of a cluster, what will be our next duties?'

'I – I guess you will return to the service of the Eternal Emperor. At least until your enlistments are up.' Sten puzzled at this total irrelevancy, wondering why the Gurkhas were wasting his time now, but his backbrain told him that these soldiers often went obliquely to a vital interest that concerned the moment.

'I do not think so,' Lalbahadur said firmly. 'We must consult with our king, back on Earth, and with our superior officers in the bodyguard to be certain. But I do not think so.

'We Nepalese withdrew from Imperial Service when the

Emperor was killed, refused all offers from those yeti afterbirths who called themselves the privy council and other gangsters, and returned only with the Emperor.'

'Ancient history, Jemedar. And I am very sleepy.'

'I will make my point rapidly. It is our opinion that we were in error to come back. This Emperor we agreed to serve is not as the last one my people served. I think it is not he who was reborn, but a Rakasha, a demon who wears his face.'

'My grandfather's grandfather,' Mahkhajiri Gurung added, further confusing the issue, 'would have said his aspect is now that of Bhairava, the Frightful One, and can only be worshiped in drunkenness.'

'As much as I'd like to get sloshed with you gentlemen,' Sten said, feeling waves of exhaustion crash down on him, 'could we get to the point?'

'Very well,' Lalabhadur said. 'If we are not in violation of our contract, and even then I will consider breaking it, we would wish to enter your service on a permanent basis, sir. And once more I speak not just for the three of us, but for the other twenty-four as well.'

Wonderful, Sten thought. That would further endear him to the Eternal Emperor.

'Thank you. I am honored. And I shall keep your offer in mind. But – and I am not saying what I shall be doing when we get out of this dung pool – I doubt I shall need bodyguards.'

'You are wrong, sir. But you will see that, later. And thank you for honoring *us*.'

The Gurkhas saluted and withdrew, leaving Sten to wonder what the blazes *that* had been about.

The hell with it. He was too tired. And he still had to figure out a way to get out of the Altaics.

'Base . . . this is Little Ear Three Four Bravo,' the com drawled, in a voice that had been carefully built to *never* show strain, stress, or fear.

'I have many, many hostiles on-screen, headed yours. Estimated time of arrival, two AU off yours, twenty E-hours.

'Units' main course, main orbit—'

The signal from the picket boat stopped.

The officers in the com room of Mason's new flagship, the *Caligula*, knew Four Bravo would not make another one.

*

'Admiral Mason,' Sten said. 'Stand by for orders.'

'Yes, sir.'

'I want you to lift clear of Jochi with all fleet elements. I want you to take an *offensive* position – of your own choosing – about five AU off-planet.'

'Yes. Sir. I am not arguing, but I assume you are aware my ships are outnumbered at least eight to one.'

'More exactly about twelve to one by my calculations. But that does not matter. You are not, repeat not, to engage the enemy. You are only to engage any Suzdal or Bogazi ships attempting to attack you in your holding pattern. You are to maintain, as much as possible, the integrity of what we're going to keep a straight face and call our fleet. Is that clear?'

'It is. So you want to try a bluff?'

'Exactly. Feel free to make any kind of threatening feints or ugly faces, so long as they don't violate my orders.'

'What makes you think I'll be able to draw them off, or at least get their attention? I'm not sure they'll believe I've either got some kind of secret weapon, or else I'm about to make a suicide run.'

'If you were Suzdal or Bogazi, and you'd just seen the number that imbecile Langsdorff pulled, wouldn't you think that the Empire's capable of almost anything? Just as long as it's stupid?'

Mason considered. 'Worth a try.'

Without saying more, he palmed his screen switch and broke contact.

Sten really hoped Mason survived this. Clot the dark alley and the blackjack – Sten was going to turkey-gobble-stomp Mason into the pavement in broad daylight – in the middle of the parade ground at Arundel Castle.

'Okay, troops. Gather around.' Sten's shout echoed through the *Victory*'s vast tacship hangar. All of his tacship pilots, and the pilots from the other two squadrons from the *Bennington*, had been ordered to this briefing.

'We'll make this quick. You can brief your crews independently.

'Here's what's going on. The invasion fleet is coming in, hot and heavy. We can't stop them. What we're trying to do is make life difficult enough for the bastards so us cowardly civilians and the crunchies can haul ass.

'You guys are gonna do it for me, and justify those clottin' white scarves and the flight pay that comes out of my taxes.'

The pilots laughed and relaxed. All of them knew Sten's killer record as a tacship pilot/combat commander.

'Admiral Mason has what heavies we've got left offworld. He's going to do a tap dance and convince our friends he's about to attack. They'll *have* to at least form some kind of defensive line between the troopships and our BUCs. Then it'll be your turn.'

Sten was suddenly serious. 'Flight commanders . . . squadron leaders . . . attack in any formation you wish. Your targets are the transports. *Only* the transports. Kill them. If you hit them offworld, don't hang around for the finish. If they're in-atmosphere, make sure none of them will be able to make a forced landing. If they deploy troop capsules before you kill the mother ships, take out the capsules.

'If you're in-atmosphere, and close to the ground, and you see any enemy troops – hit them. This includes Suzdal, Bogazi, Jochians, or Torks. Draw double units of fire for the chain guns. If your ships are fitted for antipersonnel bombs, carry them and use them.

'That is a direct order.

'I want a big butcher's bill on this one. And any pilot who decides to play ace or dogfight star, I will personally ground and break.

'And remember – every soldier you let land on Jochi is a soldier who'll do his damnedest to kill an Imperial Guardsman.

'That's all. Dismissed.'

Sten was getting very tired of saying 'That is a direct order.' But he wanted to make sure none of his pilots or captains labored under any illusions this battle was anything other than a last-ditch fight for survival.

He had seen, years, centuries, geological epochs ago, what happened when one side attempted to fight a war in civilized fashion – and he not only had seen his first command wiped out, but had personally buried too many bodies of friends to feel anything other than murderous purpose toward the bloodthirsty beings of the Altaics.

The Suzdal and Bogazi admirals analyzed the situation as their fleets closed on Jochi. There appeared to be no Imperial units in-atmosphere or immediately offworld.

In fact, the only warships in the system were those of the small Imperial fleet far off Jochi, orbiting in a ready position between two of Jochi's moons. First question: Could this fleet be ignored? Negative. If the Imperial ships attacked they could wreak havoc among the troopships. Second question: Should the landings be postponed until the Imperials were destroyed? Also negative – the threat was not that significant.

Besides, as one politically perceptive Bogazi pointed out, 'Our confederation glue not sticky. Torks. Jochians. Suzdal. Sooner, later, they behave as normal and stab backs. Best sequence: Secure Jochi. Destroy Imperial soldiers. Destroy Imperial ships. With Jochi as base, any changes with allies easy for response.'

The Suzdal and Bogazi main battleships moved out from Jochi toward Mason's fleet and formed in a defensive perimeter. Waiting.

The thin-skinned transports gunned toward the ground, protected by only a thin screen of destroyers.

The first wave of Imperial tacships hit them in Jochi's exosphere.

Hannelore La Ciotat was a drakh-hot pilot – her phrase. Everyone agreed, including the other pilots in her squadron. Not as drakh-hot as she thought she was, and certainly not as drakh-hot as *they* were – but drakh-hot.

She had slaved a secondary weapons-launch helmet from her weapons officer's station to her own post at the controls. She claimed it helped to be able to see on-screen not only what her tacship was doing, but what the enemy was about to get bashed with.

The transport bulked large in the screen. Readouts blurring on either side, indicators moving across it, read, deciphered, understood yet ignored by La Ciotat.

'Closing . . . closing . . . range . . . range . . .' her weapons officer droned.

'Stand by . . .'

The transport grew larger.

'Downgrade launch from Kali,' La Ciotat snapped, and the weapons officer changed the weapons choice from the huge, longrange ship killer to the medium-range Goblins.

'Range . . . range . . . range . . .'

'Stand by . . .'

La Ciotat felt herself drakh-hot as a pilot – but more importantly, she had a secret: she was *not* a drakh-hot shot. So she never launched outside point-blank range, and preferred to get closer.

'Stand by . . . clot!'

The transport's sensors must have seen the incoming tacship and emergency-launched its troop capsules, spattering long tubes full of troops into Jochi's atmosphere.

'Transport . . .'

'Still acquired.'

'Launch One! Cancel backup!'

She flipped the weapons helmet to the back of her head, ignored the ghost image of the missile slamming into the transport as it futilely lifted for space, fingers and boots dancing on the controls, and brought the tacship back – a lethal hawk swooping as the waterfowl scattered.

'Range . . . range . . .'

'Goblins . . . Multiple launch, single target distinction . . . set!'

'Set! Range . . . range . . .'

'On automatic . . . fire!'

The tacship held eight Goblin missile launchers, each loaded with three missiles. The launchers chugged . . . the tacship shuddered as the 10 nuke-headed missiles blazed out.

Nineteen troop capsules shattered, spewing screaming, dying soldiers into the high atmosphere, soldiers clawing at emptiness as gravity spun them down and down toward the ground far below.

Suddenly for La Ciotat these targets stopped being inanimate simulations on a battlescreen and became beings – whose deaths had come swiftly in the blast, horribly as their lungs froze in the frigid atmosphere, or mercifully as they spun into unconsciousness.

And 'Bull's-eye' La Ciotat saw the deaths from very close range. Her stomach recoiled. She was violently sick, vomit splashing over the screen and controls.

She turned back for another pass, to kill the twentieth and last capsule.

Sten watched the slaughter from a battlescreen in the embassy's control room, refusing to let his mind translate those points of light appearing and vanishing into what they represented. He could have gone out of the sub-basement to an upstairs window and seen the great battle raging over the mountains ringing the valley that contained Rurik. But that would have been still worse.

Around him the last embassy staffers hurriedly packed what files and equipment they would take offworld.

Outside, in a courtyard, high fires raged, as the rest of the embassy's records were destroyed.

Sten had been somewhat surprised that there had been no panic or trouble. Kilgour had explained: he had borrowed a company of Guardsmen for embassy security, told the Bhor and Gurkhas to rack their weapons and help with the evacuation. With one experienced combat veteran to every four civilians, it was hard to start a proper panic.

'A'ready, boss, w' hae i' better'n Cavite.' On Cavite, Alex had been in charge of evacking the civilians – and had sworn his own oath of never again. 'Whae'll we do wi' th' embassy? Blow it? Or jus' leave some wee booby traps?'

'Negative on both. There might be another ambassador show up one of these years. Why make life hard for him?'

Kilgour's stare was glacierlike.

Who cared what happened with the next regime, or the next clot dumb enough to take the Imperial shilling?

But he did not say anything.

'Do you have a prog on the landings, General?' Sten asked.

'Tentative,' Sarsfield said. 'They appear to have come in with, oh, call it twenty divisions. Say five for the first wave, five for the second, the same for the third, and five for reserve. That's my guesstimate, and that's what I'd do. But none of the Intel progs disagree, so that's what I'm going with.'

'GA.'

'Right now, I'll say – and these are pretty firm – that they've managed to put no more than eight on the ground. The rest either were lost in the landings or are still in orbit after the invasion was aborted.'

Sten repressed a wince, even though the body count was enemy. The First Guards Division, at full strength, numbered about eighteen thousand beings.

Assume – and a screen nearby showing Imperial Intelligence's order of battle said the assumption would be fairly correct – the same book strength for the Suzdal/Bogazi landing force.

Three hundred and sixty thousand beings, and only eight made it – the invasion force had taken over fifty percent casualties before real battle had even been joined.

'Of course,' Sarsfield went on briskly, 'casualties were not total. Elements of all invading units are almost certainly on the ground. But as stragglers, casualties, and so forth – not to be taken seriously.'

Sarsfield was a true Guardsman, Sten thought. He didn't appear worried that at least 150,000 enemy were now on Jochi, reinforcing whatever Tork militia were deployed – probably around a hundred thousand beings, and then the half a million more serving in the Jochi army. Three-quarters of a million, versus eighteen thousand.

'I'm grateful they don't appear, at least so far,' Sarsfield added, 'to have landed any heavy armor or artillery.'

They wouldn't need it, Sten knew. Douw and the Jochians had more than enough to go around.

Now, he wondered, how long would it take for them to reform and attack the city?

He knew that answer, too. No more than three E-days.

Imperial losses were slight – only five tacships had been shot down. But those five were irreplaceable.

Sten, Sarsfield, and Mason were on a three-way sealed beam, trying to plan what next.

What should have happened was that the Imperial personnel should have been onboard their ships and scooting for deep space and home.

But there were two small problems: the Suzdal/Bogazi fleet off Jochi, and the oncoming allied army.

Almost a dozen Frick and Fracks had been infiltrated and blown out of the sky before Kilgour had a firm report that the Altaic Confederation was on the march.

Sten had two advantages: First, Mason's ships off Jochi – which were enough of a threat to worry the Suzdal and Bogazi fleet admirals. Second, he had in-atmosphere aerial superiority, or at least enough units to make the air overhead contested territory.

The Suzdal and Bogazi heavies would be unlikely to hang in space and lob heavy missiles down on the Imperial Forces inside Rurik. None of the allied forces, including the two ET races, would define noble victory as having destroyed the longtime capital of the Cluster. That was a shade too Pyrrhic even for these beings.

Nor would the fleet, except as a last resort, sacrifice maneuverability and come down to smash these sprats that were tacships – sprats that very likely could kill more than one-for-one as they died, and no one would trade a battleship or cruiser for a fifteen-being spitkit.

On the other hand, Douw's advancing army would slowly provide an AA umbrella that would deny the air to the Imperial ships, so this was only a temporary standoff.

He suddenly found two more shafts of sunlight in his mental sky. First was he had a trained, disciplined force – the First Guards – who were fresh and not brought to battle. Second was the realization that, if he *was* able to get his Imperial bodies off Rurik, there would be only limited pursuit.

Just bashing the Empire out of the Altaics would be defined as enough of a victory.

At least that's what the Altaics would think.

He listened in silence as Sarsfield and Mason ran various options through and shot them down, trying to figure a way to get out of this Altaic sandwich the Imperial Forces were trapped in.

Something glimmered. He rolled it back and forth. It seemed worth exploring. It probably wouldn't work. Even if it didn't, the situation couldn't worsen. Could it?

'Mr Kilgour,' he asked formally to Alex, who sat somewhat off-screen. It slightly jolted Mason and Sarsfield – they had been unaware of Kilgour's presence. 'Do we have a code that's sort of compromised? Not a complete joke, but something they'll be able to break, at least partially, without too much strain?'

Alex shrugged and called up the embassy code chief. Mason started to say something, but Sarsfield waved him to silence. Five minutes later, Kilgour presented a choice of three codes that the code chief was morally certain were splintered, if not completely busted.

'Very good. Why don't we . . .' and Sten outlined the first stage of his plan.

Sarsfield, since the first stage did not involve him or his command, didn't say anything. Sten could see Mason trying to be fair – but wanting to say that anything that clotting Sten could come up with was worthless.

'My biggest objection,' Mason said after a while, 'is that we already tried it.'

'Not quite, Admiral,' Sten said. 'We tried the simple version of the con. Did you ever play which hand's got the marble?'

'Of course. I *was* a child once.'

Sten doubted that, but continued. 'First time you tried it, you just lied. Then you told the truth. Then you lied again. Escalating dishonesty.

'That's what we're going to attempt, unless someone's got something better – or can point out where I'm completely full of it.'

And so the Bluff, Stage Two, was begun.

*

First a destroyer was detached from Mason's fleet and sent in the general direction of Imperial worlds and Prime itself.

Once beyond the range of any of the Suzdal/Bogazi units, it broadcast a coded message, both to Mason's fleet and to the besieged Imperial post on Rurik.

Sten waited for six hours, watching Alex's Frick and Fracks, as the Altaic army ground closer toward Rurik. Thank somebody, what the clot, give it to Otho's gods Sarla and Laraz, they were moving slowly. Sten attributed it both to caution, none of them ever having fought Imperial Forces before, and the inevitable incoherence of trying to coordinate an alliance, particularly one where everyone hated everyone else.

He had ordered his tacships up as aerial artillery, lobbing air-to-ground missiles at predetermined targets – crossroads, major roadways, and the like.

Then both his com officer, Freston, and Mason's equivalent officer reported: there had been a sudden flurry of intership trans-missions in the Suzdal/Bogazi fleets, transmissions that had been sent in a rarely used – which suggested high-level – code. Blurt transmissions were also beamed out in directions suggesting they were intended for the capital worlds of the Suzdal and Bogazi.

'Mr Mason?'

'Yes, sir. We're on the way.'

The fish were nibbling, it would appear.

Sten had, indeed, just come up with a second version of that bluff he and Mason had run, pretending to send messages back to an oncoming Imperial fleet.

The destroyer he had ordered sent out had transmitted a message, in that breakable code, that appeared to come from the vanguard of a heavy Imperial strike force. This mythical strike force ordered Mason to abandon his position off Jochi – the besieged forces on the planet would have to fend for themselves for a while – and serve as a forward screen for this strike force.

The transmission continued, saying that Mason would be fully briefed at a later date, but that this strike force had been specially detached to punish the dissident Suzdal and Bogazi – cleverly making no mention of any human dissidents – by attacking the ET capital worlds, returning tit for tat.

Sten was too elaborate in his deception – he forgot to allow for the fact that this was exactly what any of the races or cultures in the Altaics would have done if they were in the same situation as the Empire.

Three E-hours later, the Suzdal and Bogazi heavies broke orbit and struck, at full speed, for their own systems.

Sten, trying to keep the elaborate geometry of astrogation in his mind, thought they would probably set a course in *x* direction for their home worlds. A course that would be more direct than the one Mason was supposedly on, and certainly one that was predicted never to coincide with the *y* direction or directions the huge Imperial strike force would most logically track.

Uh-huh. All this exotica from someone who had needed coaching in basic one-ship astrogation back in Flight School. It would not work – at least not for very long. Sten hoped it worked long enough for the next step, and for Mason to duck around the Suzdal/Bogazi fleet and get back to where he would be needed.

Regardless, at least one layer of the sandwich had been stripped away.

Four hours later, scout elements of the Altaic Confederation's army entered the outskirts of Rurik.

Sten had told Sarsfield his hopes, not his orders. He did not want the First Guards to feel they were being commanded to pull some kind of impossible Bastogne or Thermopylae.

Stop them. Try to get them to dig in. Make them think we're counterattacking.

Sarsfield, like Sten, had counted noses. Neither of them thought this third ruse would work. It's very hard, after all, to bluff someone who's got three aces and the joker showing and both elbows keeping his hole card from being turned over, when you've got four different suits and one slice of bologna.

The enemy scouts proceeded unmolested.

However, their nerves were tested. Here they found an abandoned barricade. There vehicles were overturned. Up there, some kind of antenna spun. Cryptic codes had been sprayed on the pavement.

The scouts proceeded, more and more cautiously.

They saw no signs of Imperial soldiers.

It was unlikely they would – the Guards' forward recon elements were specialists in not being seen.

The Confederation's progress was reported.

Frick and Fracks were behind the lines, waiting for the first heavy armor and gravsleds to creep into the city. No one likes to risk his expensive track or even more expensive gravlighter in the rat trap of city fighting. But the Altaic soldiers had no choice.

They were in the trap.

Sarsfield ordered the artillery to open up. His own cannon and surface-to-surface launchers opened up on predetermined targets, targets that were now obscured by enemy vehicles.

The tacships were launched from the mother ships, which were grounded near the huge park back of the embassy, where Sten had ordered the transports grounded.

Drakh-hot pilot Hannelore La Ciotat popped her tacship up, saw the track platoon's cannon begin to swivel, blasted a volley of rockets from the rack jury-rigged on her ship's belly, ran two cases through her forward chain gun, and disappeared.

La Ciotat was swearing almost continuously. Clot. She might as well have joined the clotting *infantry*. She gunned her tacship down a street, well below the building roofs, looking for another target.

The platoon was destroyed – and the momentum of the attack temporarily broken.

But they kept coming.

The Jochi armor-infantry Combat Command moved swiftly and efficiently toward the city center. It was a highly trained force on familiar ground. The tracks would hit anything the infantry couldn't, and the grunts kept antitank gunners from killing their big friends.

'Battery A . . . fire!' and the four Imperial gravsleds appeared to explode. Each explosion was, in fact, forty-eight rockets salvoed from the racks mounted on the gravsleds' rear. The unarmored sleds lifted at full speed and headed for another location.

The rockets were just that – propellant, guidance vanes, and warhead. Their accuracy was plus-minus fifty meters at four hundred meters. Appallingly bad. But when 192 rockets, each with fifty kilos of explosive in its warhead, simultaneously impact on an area one hundred meters on a side, and that area is occupied by a crack armor-infantry unit, the results can be impressive.

The Jochi infantry died to a man.

A few of the tracks had been hit and crippled. But most of them were still combat-capable.

Then the two-man antitrack teams rose out of their hiding places in the rubble, fire-and-forget missiles streaking fire.

But the Confederation kept coming.

*

The skies were black, and there were high, building storm clouds in the distance.

Kilgour wiped sweat from his forehead. 'Th' weather'll break, noo, an' we'll lose th' wee tacships.'

Cind grimaced. The ships had all-weather capability. But no one had ever meant that to mean a spacecraft could fly in the heart of a city, fight an enemy on the ground, which meant with mostly visual target acquisitions, and not spend a lot of time revamping the local architecture.

Or, if the architecture was as solid as on Rurik, crashing.

Seconds later the storm broke, huge raindrops shattering down. Kilgour swore, ducking for shelter that wasn't there, and then his language went doubly purple as hailstones spattered him.

Clottin' wonderful, he thought. Tis nae enow we hae th' hands ae all men agin us here, nae t' mention a few ETs, but th' weather-gods hae us on the list ae well.

Warrant Officer La Ciotat stood beside her tacship, oblivious to the rain spattering in through the *Victory*'s open hangar doors. The ship was grounded just behind the embassy, and the other tacship carrier, the *Bennington*, nearby.

'Sir. I'm willing to try it,' she argued. 'We'll just use the Kali sensors out the front of the launch tube, and I'll go on instruments and get targets from the missile.'

'Negative,' her flight commander ordered. 'We're grounded. We'll be pulling drive offworld next.

'Or if not, we're *really* going to be making kamikaze runs, instead of just getting close like you want. That's an order.'

'I have reports,' Sarsfield said, tonelessly, 'that my artillerymen are firing sabot charges over open sights. They're getting close, Sten.'

'Tell them to blow their guns and move to the transports.'

'Yessir.'

'What's the loading status?'

Sarsfield consulted with an aide.

'I have all battalions loaded, except the one boarding now, and the First Battalion in its defensive position back of the square. Plus the arty batteries that are hauling for the ships right now.

'I guess,' Sarsfield said, 'the First will have to fight the rearguard action. Clot. At least,' he said sadly, 'they volunteered for it.' As had every other battalion of the First Guards, Sten knew.

'All embassy personnel are loaded,' Sten said. 'As ordered, you are to lift all Imperial ships when First Battalion has the attacking units engaged and counterattacks. The *Victory* will hold on the ground until the last possible moment for pickup for any Guards elements that can disengage after you lift. I'm shutting down this station now.'

'Roger, you're last. You're transferring now to the *Victory*?'

'Negative,' Sten said. 'I'll be with First Battalion. Sten. Out.'

Sarsfield had not even time to register his protest. Sten stood, stiff muscles stretching, and reached for his combat harness.

Alex, similarly outfitted for battle, held it ready. They went for the stairs. Kilgour turned and pulled a wire, then they went on up toward the ground floor.

Ten seconds later explosives shattered the coms and conference room.

'Y' hae a plan,' Kilgour wondered.

'Sure,' Sten said. 'Many, many plans. To pray for peace. To not get killed. To make it to the *Victory* before she hauls. To break contact at nightfall, and exfiltrate into the country and go to ground.'

'An' how long d' ye think,' Kilgour wondered, 'thae clottin' Emperor'll take t' send a rescue party f'r a man who disobeyed orders?'

'Have faith, Alex,' Sten said. 'Sooner or later, we'll just learn to levitate home.'

In the courtyard Sten saw Cind, the Gurkhas, and the Bhor drawn up. Waiting.

He wasn't surprised.

But he almost started crying.

Cind saluted him, rain dripping from her nose.

He returned the salute, and his pissant little formation doubled off – up the wide boulevard toward the Square of the Khaqans to join the last stand.

Fleet Admiral Mason glowered at the screen, which showed the Jochi system rushing toward him. This whole assignment has been clotted, he thought.

First I am chauffeur to that popinjay Sten on that clotting yacht he was given. Then I spend time dancing around playing peepbo and now you see it, now you don't with a bunch of geeks and ETs.

Hither, yon, hither yon, and it is all shadows, just like I told

Sten, back on Prime, a world where everything is gray and there is no truth.

He deserved better from the Eternal Emperor, he thought furiously. And wondered how, once this disaster wound to a close, he could remind his Emperor of that.

At least there will be no relief and court-martial, as happened to Mahoney for some reason, he thought. I have followed my orders exactly.

And a soldier cannot go wrong when he does that.

'Jochi planetfall . . . two E-hours,' his watch officer said.

The Altaic soldiers moved confidently into the Square of the Khaqans. Opposition had lightened, and then disappeared. Now they would take the palace, and move on to destroy unutterably the hated Imperials.

A cheer rose. This was the center, was the throne. From this place, all power came. Now – and each soldier's thoughts differed, depending on his race – the rulers of the Altaic Cluster would be different.

The counterattack struck.

The multiple rocket racks had been dismounted from the gravlighters and concealed behind balustrades, terraces, and even statues. Firing studs were touched, and the rockets crashed out, ripping horizontally across the square.

Explosions shattered and echoed, and then the First Battalion counterattacked, rolling up the Altaic soldiers and sending them reeling back.

Bare seconds later, more thunder crashed. But this was not from the storm or from the Guards' rocketry.

Fire blazoned into the darkness that was technically day as the Imperial transports lifted clear of the park and drove at full power for space.

Sten watched them disappear into the storm clouds. Very good. Very good, he thought. Better than Cavite.

Now let's see if there's any way to save my own young ass.

The rain was slamming in now, wind-driven, and thunder was crashing as the wind roared across the great square in front of Cind.

She was stretched prone, using a projectile-chipped staircase for cover, and paid no mind to the puddle she was lying in, the puddle that was scarlet from the blood draining from the Guardsman next to her.

Her own rifle lay beside her, disregarded.

A precision sniper weapon was no use here. Far across the square, which was littered with crashed gravlighters and destroyed tracks, fire flickering from their hatches in spite of the storm, the Confederation Forces were getting ready for another assault.

Time had passed. How much time, she didn't know.

The enemy had reformed and attacked.

They tried first with armor – but Guardsmen with AT weapons were stationed in the upper floors of the palace, firing down into the always-vulnerable top deck of the tracks.

Then fast gravlighters swept forward, trying to punch through the increasingly thin lines of the Guardsmen. They were stopped.

Next the Confederation began human wave attacks. Shoulder to shoulder infantry attacks, men and women shouting cheers and marching bravely, suicidally, into the near-solid gunfire.

They died – but so did Imperial Guardsmen.

She had seen Alex cursing and putting a field dressing on a bloody, if superficial, shrapnel wound on his upper leg before he had gone back to the slaughter. Otho, too, had been hit. But after his wounds had been dressed, he had returned to the line, spotting for a Guards' mortar crew.

Cind wondered if they could stand two, three, or just one more assault before that wave washed over them.

There had been no opportunity to break contact and try for the *Victory*, assuming the ship was still on the ground.

Sten splashed down beside her.

The two of them were grimy. Bloody – but at least the blood was not their own. Their eyes were glaring.

'Well?'

'Two tubes left, boss.'

'Here.' He passed her another magazine of AM2 rounds.

'Be melodramatic,' she suggested. 'Kiss me.'

Sten grimaced, started to obey, and then jerked back as he heard the grind of oncoming tracks once more. 'Well, I shall be clotted. Look.'

This time the attack was combined armor and infantry. And, standing in that lead track was . . .

Cind grabbed her exotic rifle and sighted. She saw the handsome face and silver hair. 'It's him! You want the privilege?'

'Go ahead. I've had all the fun lately.'

The man in the track was General Douw. Cind supposed he

thought this would be the final attack that would overrun the Imperial Forces, and had chosen to lead it himself.

Brave.

Brave, but dumb, Cind thought as she touched the trigger and the AM2 round blew Douw's chest apart.

'Thank you,' Sten said.

Cind scrabbled for the willygun. The death of their leader hadn't even been noticed by the oncoming soldiers.

Wave after wave of them poured into the square. Cind swept their ranks – then decided to wait until they were closer.

She lifted her head to see – and her eyes widened.

'Jamchyyd and Kholeric,' she whispered, her tone wholly reverent, actually calling on the Bhor gods as if she believed they might exist. 'Sarla and Laraz.'

Coming over the city's rooftops, swaying like a great dark snake, came the cyclone, cutting a solid swath as it came. And behind the first funnel cloud . . . another. One . . . two . . . Cind counted six of them, swinging back and forth like a dancer's hips as they came.

Sten remembered: '. . . *kill a thousand people in forty minutes . . . punch a blade of straw through an anvil . . . throw five tacships . . . a quarter klick . . .*'

The tornadoes picked up debris as they came. A roof. A shed. A gravsled. A personnel carrier. A crashed tacship. A man. Spun them, ruined them, broke them beyond recognition, and then used them as weapons.

Cind's ears cracked, and she swallowed.

The roar was louder now than the gunfire, and the Altaic troops stopped. They turned – and saw the cyclones.

Then the first vortex entered the Square of the Khaqans.

It swept through the soldiers and their weapons like a vacuum cleaner picking up dust balls. It picked them up and cast them aside.

Sten was on his feet.

Shouting. Screaming. Unheard.

He was waving – back. Back – away. For the *Victory*!

The second tornado entered the square. Both funnel clouds twisted and spun, hesitating, as if unsure if they should continue.

Imperial soldiers pelted away from this new demon that no one could be expected to stand against.

But they were not in panic. They ran – but slowly, helping the limping walking wounded. Bringing their weapons with them, or abandoning them to pick up the ends of stretchers.

Sten and Alex held, just where the broad boulevard opened, the boulevard Sten had sent the *Victory* roaring down toward the embassy, lifetimes earlier.

The square was a black swirl, as yet another tornado came onstage. Palace walls ripped away, spinning out into the near-vacuum low-pressure area, and were caught by the cyclone and lifted thousands of meters up, into the overhanging cloud.

Then the vortex stalked forward once more, wind roaring and speed building, toward and through the palace that had once been the pride of the Khaqans, then had briefly housed Dr Iskra.

The palace vanished in a swirl.

The tornado's fellows, spawn of that great brooding wall cloud, came on, inexorably planing the soldiers of the Altaics, the shaky Confederation they had fought for, and that meaningless vanity of a palace that meant power from the face of Rurik.

They left nothing – nothing but chaos.

The *Victory* was still on the ground, waiting.

One AU off Rurik, Sten sent the message *en clair*, punched through with max power, direct to the Emperor's private channel, second transmission to the Imperial office:

ALL IMPERIAL UNITS SUCCESSFULLY EVACUATED FROM RURIK IN GOOD ORDER. IMPERIAL UNITS NOW ON DIRECT COURSE FOR PRIME WORLD. ALTAIC CLUSTER NOW IN OPEN REVOLT AGAINST THE EMPIRE.

STEN

Now, court-martial me, he thought.
You insane bastard.

Chapter Forty-Two

Mahoney waited in a prisoner-for-transport cell beneath the large new building that was Internal Security's headquarters. It was a small room, with white plas walls, a fold-up sleeping bench, and a hole in the floor for body wastes.

In a few minutes they would take him to his hearing before the Imperial grand jury. He was dressed in the pure white coveralls required by law for indicted criminals. The color was symbolic. White indicated presumed innocence. It also indicated that the prisoner's statements had not been produced by torture.

Mahoney had to admit that in his case the latter was true. So far. He had been treated with rough but professional courtesy. Sure, he had been beaten. The first time when they loaded him on the transport to Prime. But that had only been to alert him to his new station in life – bruises and blood to show him who was boss. There had been no emotion in the beating. Nothing personal. The same all along the processing line, as he was transferred from one IS group to another.

When the beatings stopped, Ian knew his hearing date had been set. It was a routine precaution. To make sure everything had healed in time for his appearance.

Mahoney had weathered the experience well. Not that he was philosophical about his fate. He refused to think about it at all. To dwell on the betrayal would only serve to soften him up – for the probably inevitable brainscan.

Instead, he thought about old adventures. Friends. Lovers. He never thought about food. Mahoney was glad that prison fare was efficiently bland. Otherwise, those meals the Emperor had fixed for him with his own hands would have come back to haunt.

Ian's hackles rose, his old Mantis senses prickling. Someone was watching. He made himself relax. Then he heard rustling at the cell door.

Ah, they've finally come, Ian. Be still, heart. And you there, lungs. You're not needing so much air. Steady on, boyos. Be of good Irish cheer.

Poyndex looked through the two-way as the IS screws hustled Mahoney out of the PFT cell. He was surprised at how well the man looked and wondered if he could do the same in Mahoney's position. He pushed that thought away. It was a talent he would just as soon leave undiscovered.

He stepped out into the hallway to intercept Mahoney and the guards. Ian saw him. From the flicker in his eyes, Poyndex knew he was recognized. The flicker vanished and was replaced with a grin.

'Oh, ho. So the boss sent the first team in,' Mahoney said. 'I'd say I'm honored, but I'd be lying.'

Poyndex laughed. 'I don't want to be responsible for a lie,' he said. 'We wouldn't want to start the grand jury proceedings on the wrong foot.'

He told a guard to remove Mahoney's restraints, then waved the guards away. 'I'll be your escort,' he told Ian. 'I'm sure you won't try anything . . . foolish.'

Mahoney rubbed life back into his wrists. 'Why would I? I'm an innocent man. Joyfully waiting for justice to be done.' He laughed.

Poyndex grinned back and indicated the far corridor door. They both started walking, Poyndex just a half step behind Mahoney.

'Actually, I've come along to make sure that's exactly what you get,' Poyndex said. 'The Emperor wants complete fairness.'

'Oh, certain he does,' Mahoney chortled. 'And tell him his old friend, Ian, is humbly thankful for this courtesy.'

Poyndex forced a small chuckle of appreciation. He had decidedly mixed feeling about his mission. On the one hand, Ian Mahoney was his sole competition for the power he now wielded. Disgrace had ended that competition.

'Tell him not to worry,' Mahoney said. 'When questioned I'll stick to the facts. I have no intention of bringing his name into these proceedings.'

'An unnecessary promise,' Poyndex said smoothly. 'But, I'm sure he will be pleased you're still thinking of his best interests – that you remember your past relationship.'

On the other hand, Mahoney *had* once stood in Poyndex's

shoes. He had been the Eternal Emperor's faithful servant for decades. As he watched Mahoney walking tall toward his fate, Poyndex feared for his own. This is what will happen, he thought, if you should fall from grace.

A whisper in the back of his mind hissed: Not if . . . but *when*.

'Tell the boss I remember,' Mahoney said. 'I remember *very* well.'

'I'll do that,' Poyndex said. 'And that's a promise.'

His hand dipped into his pocket, then came out. As they reached the door, Poyndex pressed the silenced barrel against the soft spot at the back of Mahoney's neck.

There was a quick flinch of skin from sudden cold.

Poyndex fired.

Mahoney tumbled forward. Slammed into the door. Sagged down.

Poyndex stood over the body, amazed. Mahoney's face still carried that damned Irish grin.

He bent down, pressed the barrel against Mahoney's head, and fired again.

With a man like Ian Mahoney, you had to make double damned sure.

Chapter Forty-Three

'Fare thee well, you banks ae Sicily, fare thee well, thee brooks an' dells, frae thae's noo Scots soldier thae's mourn th' last of ye,' Alex hummed from memory, thinking fondly of a very tall brew as soon as the fleet was absolutely clear of anything, including vacuum, that resembled the Altaic Cluster.

He was idly punching through various public channels being cast from the Imperial worlds ahead. Nearby, Sten was collapsed in the *Victory*'s CO station – but no one asked him to move. Both of them still wore their torn, filthy combat uniforms.

The bridge was near-silent – probably because no one thought they would actually have gotten away with this one.

'Sports,' Kilgour muttered, finding another cast. 'Ah dinnae ken whae thae's bein's thae think thae's virtue in puntin' a wee sack ae leather frae one chalk't line t' another.

'Reminds me,' he said to Freston, who sat near the console, 'ae th' time thae tried t' make m' play a clottin' sport ae gentlebein'ts call't crickit. First Ah thinks thae's mad, goin't chirp—'

And his mouth snapped closed.

No one exactly remembered what the liviecaster on-screen was saying. But it was very clear:

Disgrace . . . once hero of the Tahn war . . . Governor General . . . supreme penalty . . . Ian Mahoney . . . name to be stricken from all records and monuments . . . traitorous . . .

Sten was standing beside him. His face was white.

'That's torn it,' he whispered.

Kilgour started to say something, then shook his head. He swallowed.

He heard the snarl from the watch officer behind him: 'Watch your screens, mister. What's that com that just ran?'

'Uh . . . sorry . . . it's coded.'

'I can tell it's coded,' the watch officer said. 'Who's it to? Who's it from?'

'Sir . . . I think . . . Prime. And . . . and it's intended for the *Caligula* . . . I think.'

'Don't think, mister. Know!'

'Sir . . . we don't have the code. It's not indexed.'

Sten forced shock and anger about Mahoney's murder away. 'What is the signal?'

'We don't know, sir. From Prime to *Caligula*, sir.'

'I heard *that*. Patch me to Mason.'

'Yessir.'

Caligula, this is Victory, over.

. . .

. . . This is Caligula, over.

This is Victory. What was the transmission you received? Wait one . . . signal being decoded . . .

'How th' clot,' Kilgour wondered, hair on the back of his neck starting to lift, 'd' thae hae' th' code an' we dinnae?'

'Sir! The *Caligula*'s broken contact.'

'Reestablish.'

Caligula, *this is* Victory, *over*. Caligula, *this is* Victory. *Do you receive this transmission?*

'Sir, the *Caligula*'s broadcasting.'

'GA.'

'Not to us, sir. To its DD screen. Burst transmission. I didn't get it.'

Sten was trying to figure out what the hell was going on. Then he noticed the main maneuver screen.

The *Caligula* had broken fleet formation, together with the four destroyers that normally screened the battleship. It set a new course . . .

'What's the *Caligula*'s new orbit?'

'Wait one, sir . . . it appears to be a near-reciprocal track from the fleet's. Straight – I'm estimating – back toward Jochi!'

There was a rumble of surprise.

'Quiet on the bridge.'

Sten forced his mind to function. What the clot was going on? He found he had spoken aloud.

'Sir?' It was Freston. 'I think I might know.'

'One ray of light. Talk to me!'

'Uh . . . sir, before I was assigned to you, I was com officer on the *Churchill*. And the captain had been given a private code when he took command. There was another copy in the ship's safe, to be given to the XO or whoever took over if the CO was a casualty.'

'GA. But why the clot would the *Caligula* – or Mason – have a code that we don't? We're the flagship.'

'Yessir. But – but we're not carrying a planet buster.'

Of course. The Empire did not like even to admit that it had weaponry heavy enough to shatter a planet. But it did. Planet busters were *never* used – even during the height of the Tahn war they had not been launched.

For the Emperor, it had little to do with morality. Genocide made lousy politics, he used to say. That *had* been the Emperor's view. Apparently, went Sten's grim thoughts, the Eternal Emperor had changed his mind. Perhaps it had never been a moral issue for the Emperor. But it certainly had been for Sten.

'Is the *Caligula* answering?' Sten asked.

'Negative, sir.'

'Commander, do you have a tacship flight on standby?'

'Of course.'

'I want one ship. The best pilot on the *Victory*. Kali-armed. Launch time as soon as I get to the hangar deck.'

Kilgour was on his feet, starting for the companionway.

'Alex! I want you here on the bridge. I'll be broadcasting from the tacship, but I want the com linked to the *Victory*.'

''Y' dinnae need me frae that, skip.'

'And I want a synth that'll match analysis.'

'Right. Ah hae it noo. Away wi' y' lad.'

And Sten was running for the *Victory*'s hangar.

The tacship flashed out from the *Victory*'s port and, barely clear of the mother ship, went to full AM2 drive.

'What's the IP?'

La Ciotat didn't need to look at a screen.

'Fifty-three . . . fifty-one minutes, sir.'

'Fine.' Sten sat at the weapons officer's station, adjusting the control helmet to his own head.

'Here's the drill. The *Caligula* is headed back for Jochi. It's going to launch a planet buster.'

La Ciotat, priding herself on her poker face, wasn't able to control her expression. 'But what – is Admiral Mason mutinying, or—'

'You do not need to know, Ms. I want you to hold a closing course on the *Caligula* and have your com person keep an open link to the *Victory*. I want you to notify me when we're within . . . five minutes of the *Caligula*. Do you have any trouble with those orders?'

'No, sir.'

'Keep us from getting tagged by the destroyers. I'm pretty sure they'll have orders to stop us.'

'*That's* not even a concern. Sir.'

Sten almost smiled – it sounded like La Ciotat *was* drakh-hot.

'*Caligula*, this is *Victory*. Admiral Mason, this is Sten, over.'

'Still no response.'

'*Caligula*, this is Sten, over. Patch me to your Six Actual. That is an order, over.'

'Seven minutes to intercept, sir.'

'God dammit . . .'

The screen on the tacship suddenly cleared, and Sten saw Mason's face.

Mason – or so Sten hoped, at least – would be seeing Sten, or a computer synthesis of Sten, back on the bridge of the *Victory* and never think that his response had been almost immediate and that he was, in fact, aboard a tacship bare minutes behind the *Caligula*.

'Admiral Mason, I think I understand your mission,' Sten began.

'I am under orders, sir, to not discuss my assignment with anyone.'

'I am not interested in discussing, Mason. This is not a debating society. And I know that you've been told to bust Jochi.

'You can't do it.'

'I have my orders, sir.'

'Did you verify them? Mason, do you want to be the first man in – who the hell knows how long? – to wipe out a planet? Not everybody down there's loony, Mason.'

The on-screen figure made no response.

'I see no point in continuing this transmission,' Mason said finally, mechanically.

'Mason . . . stand by for one moment . . .'

Sten closed his mike and pulled the weapons helmet down over his head. 'Ms. La Ciotat, I am launching the Kali.'

'Yessir. At full drive . . . IP will be one point three minutes . . . ship IP is now two minutes.'

Sten touched the red key on the weapons panel – the only physical act that he needed to do.

The monstrous missile was launched from a tube that was the tacship's spine. It was twenty meters long, and its warhead was a sixty-megaton deathstrike.

The missile spat out from the tacship, and Sten aimed it through the helmet at the rapidly closing tiny constellation that was the *Caligula* and her escorts, holding at three-quarter drive.

He opened his eyes, and Mason ghosted at him on-screen.

'This is my last attempt, Admiral Mason. You know you're working for a madman. We just heard – the Emperor had Mahoney shot.'

Mason's eyes flickered, then he became the automaton once again.

Sten tried once more – knowing it was futile. 'Look, man. Do you want your name to go down like this? Mason the planet-killer?'

Mason suddenly almost-smiled. 'Sten, that is the difference between us. You think that you have some sort of god-given privilege to judge what orders you should or should not obey. That's seditious behavior, and you know it. Maybe that's why Mahoney was executed. Did you ever consider that? I'm following direct Imperial orders, mister. No, Sten, I'll not be the traitor. Mason, clear.'

The screen was blank.

Sten closed his eyes and became only the Kali. He hit full emergency.

'Closing . . . closing . . .' he dimly heard La Ciotat's chant.

'You are spotted . . . you broke a DD's screen . . . I have a Fox-launch . . . closing . . . prog cannot intercept . . . Closing . . . Target impact . . . Mark!'

Sten's world fireballed.

He pulled the control helmet off and saw, on screen, the *Caligula* cease to exist. There had been a hint of an explosion, and then simply nothing. The screen might as well have been trying to look into a black hole. He wondered if the Kali had sympathetically detonated the planet buster.

He guessed the *Caligula*'s destroyers would still be trying to launch countermissiles, if any of them had survived – the screen stayed dark, overloaded.

He didn't care. Evading them was La Ciotat's job.

'That's it, Ms.,' he said, tiredly. 'Back to the *Victory*.'

Mason died as he lived – following orders.

Sten did not give much of a damn about that.

But more than three thousand beings had died with him – and Sten doubted there would ever be a monument to them, out here, in the darkness and silence of interstellar space.

Chapter Forty-Four

Sten was still on automatic. Back aboard the *Victory* he had gone to the bridge and numbly given the order to secure from general quarters.

'We're frae th' hangman now, son,' Kilgour said. His voice was low. But it dashed Sten back to reality.

He looked at his friend. The Scot's round face was as calm as if he were discussing dinner arrangements.

Sten glanced around the bridge of the *Victory*. It was suddenly crowded.

There was Otho with a knot of Bhor. The wiry forms of the Gurkhas, headed by Lalbahadur Thapa. And many others.

Faces he remembered – but names he shamefully didn't.

And there was Cind.

The expression on her face was the same as the others. Expectant. Waiting for his decision.

Sten wiped moisture from his eyes.

They were with him – all of them.

Sten badly wanted to haul Cind into his arms. He wanted to be comforted, soothed.

He wanted soft lies that everything would be well.

Then the full force of what he had just done hit him.

Sten was an outlaw, now.

And through his actions he had damned all these trusting souls.

Soon, the Eternal Emperor would learn of Sten's betrayal and loose his coursing hounds.

Sten had to run. They *all* had to run.

He started to speak. He knew dozens of places to hide. Sten only had to choose and issue the coordinates.

He stopped.

No place was safe. Eventually, the Emperor's forces would run them to ground.

Sten looked around at the loyal faces again. There might be others.

He thought of Sr Ecu. And his proposal.

What was the use?

He wished Mahoney were there. Ian would have known what to do. He would have said, Quit your whining, lad. You've got your health. You've your lady. You've got that ugly Scot, Alex Kilgour. And many other loyal friends. And you've got a bloody great battlewagon. The Emperor's own ship!

At that moment, Jemedar Lalbahadur whispered to his group. They all snapped to.

In the formal, kukris raised Gurkha salute. 'We are at your command. Sah!'

And Sten decided.

If he ran, the Emperor would get him.

So he had to get the Eternal Emperor first.

Sten issued the orders.

STEN 8:
EMPIRE'S END

To
Everyone Who Was There
When
'Death came quietly to The Row'

BOOK ONE

INDIAN OPENING

Chapter One

The ruins of the Imperial assault fleet fled through the 'dark' between star clusters. There was one tacship carrier, two heavy cruisers, one light, their destroyer flotilla screens, and, in the center of the formation, auxiliaries and the troop transports carrying the battle-shattered remnants of the First Imperial Guards Division.

Flanking and closing the formation was the huge battleship *Victory*.

On its bridge, Sten stared at a strategic battlescreen, not seeing either the glow 'ahead' that represented the Empire . . . nor the symbols to the 'rear' that were the anarchy-ripped Altaic Cluster.

Two E-days earlier:

Sten: Ambassador Plenipotentiary. Personal Emissary of the Eternal Emperor. Admiral. Medals and decorations beyond count, from the Galactic Cross down, including Grand Companion of the Emperor's Household. Hero.

Now:

Sten: Traitor. Renegade. And, he thought, don't forget Murderer.

Among the symbols representing what was 'behind' the *Victory* was one marking where the Imperial Battleship *Caligula*, its Admiral Mason, and over three thousand loyal Imperial sailors had been. They'd been slaughtered by Sten for following a direct order to planetbust the Altaic's capital world, an order issued in person by the Eternal Emperor.

'Boss, Ah hae a wee tip.'

Sten's eyes – and mind – refocused. Alex Kilgour. Sten's best friend, a rather roundish-looking heavy-worlder who probably knew even more about death and destruction than Sten.

'GA.' Part of Sten's mind, the part always removed from the

hue and cry, found it funny both of them still used slang from their now-long-gone days in Mantis Section, the Emperor's super-secret covert-operations unit. Go ahead.

'Giein' thae y' hae no 'sperience a' bein't an outlaw, y'r entire life bein't spent singin' hymns an' such, p'raps y' dinnae ken Robbie Roy types hae noo time t' be pausin't an' smellin't th' flowers i' thae dinnae wan' a halter an' a neck-stretch.'

'Thank you, Mister Kilgour. I'll get my thumb out.'

'Dinnae fash, lad. Any wee service, y' hae but t' snivel.'

Sten turned away from the screen. Around him, waiting, was the *Victory*'s bridgewatch. The top elements of his long-serving personal staff, who were in fact more Sten's own private intelligence agency than striped-suiters.

Twenty-three Gurkhas – Nepalese mercenaries famous for serving only in the Emperor's private bodyguard – but these had volunteered for special duties: guarding the life of their ex-CO, Sten.

Otho. Six other Bhor. Squat, shaggy monsters with long beards, yellow fangs, and ground-brushing knuckles. They seemed happiest either tearing an enemy in half the long way or else doing the same to his bank balance in a shrewd multiworld trade. They were also fond of eddaic-type poetry. There were another hundred of them elsewhere on the *Victory*.

And, most important, left to last, their commander:

Cind: Human. Expert sniper. Descended from a now-obliterated warrior cult. A highly respected combat leader.

Beautiful. Sten's friend and lover.

Enough bean counting, he thought. Kilgour had been right: a wolf could never chance lying in a sunny clearing listening to the bees buzz – not unless he'd suddenly decided on a new career as a fireside rug.

'Weapons?'

'Sir?' The young woman was waiting. The lieutenant's name, Sten recollected, was Renzi.

'Bring your people back to general quarters. Commander Freston' – this was his longtime personal com officer – 'I want – oh, clot. Cancel.'

Sten remembered. 'Both of you,' he said, raising his voice. 'And anyone else interested – listen up.

'Things have changed. I just declared war on the Emperor. Which makes me a traitor. Nobody's required to obey my orders. No one who remains loyal to his oath will be harmed. We'll—'

His words were interrupted by the ululation of the GQ siren as the weapons officer obeyed Sten's first command.

That was one answer.

Freston made another: 'Pardon, sir? There was some static there and I lost you. Your orders?'

Sten held up a palm for Freston to stand by.

'Weapons, I want all Kali and Goblin stations at full launch-readiness. Some of our Imperial friends might decide to bag a renegade. Plus there were four destroyers escorting the *Caligula*. If any ship begins an attack, put a Goblin in the vicinity and blow it off as a warning.'

'And if they keep coming?'

Sten hesitated. 'If they do – contact me. No Kali launches will be made without my orders, and any launch will be controlled by either myself or Mister Kilgour.'

The Kalis were operator-guided shipkillers.

'That's not—'

'*That* is an order. Follow it.'

'Yessir.'

'Commander Freston. Patch me a secure link to General Sarsfield on whichever transport he's riding.' Sarsfield was the Guards' CO, and the next-ranking officer to Sten. Freston touched keys.

'One other thing,' Sten said. 'You've been through C&S school?'

'Yessir.'

'You have any really terrible sins in your past? That'd keep you from being the very model of a shipcaptain? Ram the admiral's barge? Shine the ship's cannons with carbolic acid? Bootleg the beer? Badmouth the beef? Boast about buggery?'

'Nossir.'

'Fine. They tell me pirates get promoted a lot before they get hanged. The *Victory*'s your ship, Mister.'

'Yessir.'

'Don't thank me. That just means you'll probably be next after Kilgour for the high jump. Mister Kilgour?'

'Sir?'

'All offwatch personnel to the main hangar.'

'Yessir.'

And then Sten noticed Alex's hand move away from the small of his back. He might have been fingering an old war wound around the caudal vertebra. Kilgour was not – his hand had been touching the butt of a miniwillygun, hidden in his waistband.

Alex took no chances: loyalty to the Emperor in the abstract would be acceptable. But if anyone attempted to fulfill that promise to 'defend the Empire and its welfare onto death,' they would be prime candidates for martyrdom. And most likely Kilgour would loudly admire their fidelity at the wake.

A screen cleared. Sarsfield.

'General, you're aware of what's happened?'

'I am.'

'Very well. In view of events, you are now the ranking officer of the fleet. Until you receive differing orders from the Empire, I would suggest you continue the present course toward the nearest Imperial worlds.

'I will advise you that, regretfully, any attempt to interfere with the *Victory* or its movements will be opposed with maximum force. However, none of your ships are in danger if they obey these instructions.'

The old soldier grimaced. He took a deep breath, and started to say something. Then he changed his mind.

'Your message is understood.'

'Sten. Clear.'

The screen blanked. Sten wondered what Sarsfield had been about to say – that none of the Imperial ships had one-quarter the firepower of the *Victory* nor were they skippered by deathseekers? Or – and Sten cursed at himself for still having a bit of romance in him – Good luck? It didn't matter.

'Jemedar Lalbahadur?'

'Sah!'

'Turn out your people. I want them as flanking security.'

'Sah!'

'Captain Cind, I'd also like your people dancing attendance?'

'They're already drawing weapons,' Cind said.

'Commander – pardon, Captain Freston, have the captain's personal boat ready for launch. We'll steal you another one somewhere.' Interesting, Sten thought, how quickly one could lose that stifling straitjacket discipline the navy held so dear.

'Yessir.'

'Mister Kilgour? Shall we go draw the line with our saber and see if anybody's in an Alamo kind of mood?'

Alex hesitated.

'Sir, i' y' wish. But thae's another wee matter . . . a matter o' security . . . Ah think Ah'd best—'

'Oh Christ!'

Suddenly Sten remembered security. He had no idea what Alex was hesitating about – but Sten had recollected two trump cards of his own. If they still held value. He unsealed the front of his combat suit and lifted out the thin pouch that was hung on a tie around his neck. He removed two squares of plas.

'You people stand by,' he ordered.

Sten hurried across the bridge to the central computer station. He told the two operators to clear out of the cubicle, pulled a security screen around the station, and slid a keyboard out.

Touched keys.

The station was one of the three on the *Victory* that could access ALL/UN – the central Imperial computer net that reached every Imperial command on every world and ship of the Empire.

Should, Sten thought, rather than *could*.

Most likely the *Victory* had been cut out of any access to anything, just as the Eternal Emperor had cut Sten's usual direct line into his quarters.

Weeks passed. Months. Decades. Sten knew his body could have been carbon-dated before the screen suddenly cleared and ALL/UN blinked at him, then vanished.

Then: ACCORDANZA.

Sten input the *Victory*'s code.

Another long wait.

The next thing he would see would be the simulation of a stiffly extended human middle finger and STATION REJECTED.

Instead: ATELIER.

Sten input the program on the first plas chip. Again, a wait, then, BORRUMBADA. Damn, he thought. They accepted it. Once again: ATELIER. The second chip was fed in. And again Imperial All Units accepted the program. Now we pray a lot, and hope both those little bastards work their magic.

The chips were a gift from Ian Mahoney, Sten's former commander in Mantis, Fleet Admiral, and, for aeons, the closest thing the Eternal Emperor had for a friend. But Mahoney was dead now – accused of treason by the Emperor and executed.

It's a great pity, Ian, Sten thought, you couldn't come up with one of these for yourself – and deploy it before the Eternal Clot killed you. He caught himself. No time for that, either.

Sten pulled the security curtain aside and found Alex waiting. 'Ah'm thankin't you f'r warmin't th' chair frae me, boss. Noo, i' y'll get gone?'

'Yessir, Mister Kilgour, sir. Out of the way, sir, right away, sir. Can I have someone send in tea, sir?'

'Clottin' liquid fit only t' flow through th' veins ae sassenachs. Ah'll hae a dram in a wee.' And Kilgour pulled the curtain closed.

Sten started for one of the slideways connecting the bridge to the battleship's central transit tube and thence to the hangar near the stern. Without orders, the Gurkhas, willyguns at the port, were trotting behind him.

Cind and her Bhor were waiting at a junction. She motioned them, and the Gurkhas, to move on ahead.

For a moment, she and Sten were alone at the bend of a corridor.

'Thanks,' she said, and kissed him.

'For what?'

'For not asking.'

'Asking what?'

'You are a clot,' she said.

'You mean—'

'I mean.'

'But I never thought that you wouldn't, I mean—'

'You're right. I stay volunteered. Plus I never took any oath to any Emperor. Besides, I know how to pick a winner.'

Sten looked closely at her. She did not appear to be either making a joke or trying to build his morale.

'My ancestors were Jannissars,' she went on. 'They served tyrants who hid behind the lie that they were the voice of a god they'd made up.

'I swore if I could become a soldier, I wouldn't be like them. Matter of fact, the kind of soldiering I dreamed about was helping get rid of all those bastards like the Prophets. Or like Iskra. Or the Emperor.'

'Well,' Sten said, 'you told me that before. And now I guess you'll get your chance. Or at least a good shot at going down in noble flames.'

'Naah,' Cind disagreed. 'We're gonna kick his ass. Now come on. You've got a sermon to preach.'

Sten stood on the winglet of a tacship, looking down at the nearly two thousand beings – those sailors of the *Victory* not absolutely required at weapons stations or to keep the ship alive, plus the remainder of his embassy staff – spread out around him. He didn't think he was doing a very good job of preaching tyrannicide. He tried not to look up at the hangar's overhead catwalks where Bhor and Gurkha marksmen waited, in case someone planned any nonverbal objections.

'All right,' he finished. 'That's the situation. I shoved the Emperor's face in it. There's no way he can let me vanish and pretend nothing happened. Which I'm not going to do anyway.

'I won't say what comes next. Because I don't think any of you should volunteer to remain with me. If there's anybody down there who's good at running progs or who stayed awake in battle analysis, it's easy to come up with a prediction.

'I've got the *Victory*, and maybe some beings somewhere who believe the same as I do. Which is, that it's time to fight back. This, I plan to do.

'I've been serving the Emperor for most of my life. But things have gone nuts. Like the Altaics, for instance. All right, those poor beings were blood-crazed. And have been so for generations.

'But we're the ones who made it fall apart. We're the ones responsible for turning turmoil into bloody chaos.'

Sten caught himself. 'No,' he said, his voice dropping so that those in the back had to listen hard. 'I shouldn't say "we." You, me, all of us, did our best.

'But our best wasn't good enough. Because there was one being who was running his own program. The Emperor. We followed his orders – and look what it produced. And I was not going to let it be covered up with a planet buster.

'That's all I think I should say. We'll have the captain's own boat ready in a bit. It'll cross-connect to the rest of the fleet. You've got about one ship-hour to collect your gear and board.

'Do it, people. You'll live a lot longer if you stay with the Emperor, no matter what he is and no matter what he does. I have no other choices left. You do.

'One hour. Get yourselves out of the line of fire. Now. Anybody else, anybody who's had enough of serving a madman who's hellbent on turning the Empire into chaos, like the chaos we just left – move over against the hangar baffle.

'That's it. Thanks for helping. Thanks for your service. And good luck to all of you, no matter what you choose. Dismissed.'

Sten turned away. He pretended to be busy talking to Cind, but his ears were full of the low rumble of voices, and then the clatter of bootheels on the decking.

Cind's eyes weren't on him, but beyond, watching for a potential attacker.

Then the voices and movement stopped.

Sten made himself turn around. He blinked in astonishment. Before he could ask, Cind told him.

'The first people to move were your staffers. I'd say, maybe nine out of ten will stick. You've really corrupted them.'

'Hell,' was the best Sten could manage.

'No drakh,' Cind agreed. 'Plus you have what I'd estimate is two-thirds of the swabs. I thought nobody in the navy *ever* volunteered. But I think you got a whole bunch of prospective rebels.'

Before Sten could do anything – like fall on his knees and thank a couple of the Bhor gods that the *Victory* had been blessed/ cursed with over a thousand brain-damaged crewmen – a com blared:

'Sten to the bridge! Sten to the bridge!'

There was a slight note of emotion in the talker's voice – which meant that almost certain and immediate catastrophe loomed.

'These six screens are patch-ins from the *Bennington*'s internal com. They came right after the first contact.'

Sten glanced at them – they showed weapons stations and missile-control consoles, all deserted.

'I am not assuming they're realtime casts,' Freston continued.

Sten looked up at the main screen. On it was the *Bennington*, the tacship carrier that was the heaviest ship in Sarsfield's fleet. Flanking it were two specks that a readout ID'd as destroyers. Headed directly toward the *Victory* at full drive. Either Sarsfield had ordered a suicide run, since there was zero possibility the carrier could play hitsies with a battlewagon, or else things were getting weird out there.

'I have,' Freston said, 'six Kali stations manned, tracking and holding at four seconds short of launch.'

'Replay the first transmission from the *Bennington*.'

Freston brought the cast up on a secondary screen.

It showed the *Bennington*'s bridge, which looked as if it'd been the focal point for a bar brawl. The officer onscreen had a bandaged arm, and her uniform was torn.

'*Victory*, this is *Bennington*. Please respond, this freq, tightbeam. This is Commander Jeffries. I have assumed command of the *Bennington*. The officers and sailors of this ship have rejected Imperial authority, and are now under my orders. We wish to join you. Please respond.' The screen swirled, and the message repeated.

'We also,' Freston said, 'have a cast from one of the DDs – the *Aoife*. The other one's the *Aisling*. They're both Emer-class.' He indicated a projection from *Jane's* on another screen, which Sten ignored.

'Their cast is shorter, and key-transmitted *en clair*. As follows: "*Aoife* and *Aisling* to join. Accept Sten command. Both ships homeworld Honjo Systems." Does that explain anything, sir?'

It did – barely. The Honjo were known as supertraders throughout the Empire. And they were cordially hated. They were ethnocentric to a ridiculous extreme, dedicated to the maximum profit but absolutely loyal to whatever master they'd agreed to serve – as long as that loyalty was returned. They were also lethal, nearly to the point of race suicide, as the privy council had found out during the Interregnum when they tried to steal the Honjo's AM2.

Sten had heard rumors that since the Emperor's return the Honjo felt, with some degree of justification, they hadn't been rewarded properly (which meant monetarily) for their loyalty to the Empire.

'Divert the Kali watch from those two ships. Contact them as soon as I finish, tell them message received and stand by for instructions,' Sten ordered. 'We'll find out how far they're backing us in a bit. Get me through to this Jeffries on the *Bennington*.'

The connection was made quickly. And the conversation was short. The *Bennington* had, indeed, mutinied. The captain was dead; five officers and twenty men were in the sick bays. About thirty percent of the crew, now held under arms, had remained loyal to the Empire.

'Request orders, sir,' Jeffries finished.

'First,' Sten said, thinking fast, 'welcome to my nightmare, and I think you're all insane. Second, get all loyalists ready for transshipment. If you've got a supply lighter, use that. Otherwise, disarm enough tacships if that's the only alternative. Third, keep your weapons stations unmanned. Sorry, but we're not in a position to trust anyone.

'Fourth, stand by to receive visitors. Fifth, get your navcoms set up to slave to this ship's command. We're going to travel some, and you'll convoy on us. That's all.'

'Yessir. Will comply. Standing by for your personnel to board. And . . . thank *you*.'

Sten blanked the screen. He didn't have time to wonder why

another set of idiots were volunteering for the death chamber. He looked around for Alex and found him, sitting back from the main console, looking smug. Kilgour surreptitiously crooked a finger. Sten, wanting to growl, went over.

'Y'r pardon, boss, but afore we move on, Ah hae a report . . . We're still rich, lad.'

Sten repressed the suicidal urge to kick Alex. What the hell did that have to do with—

'Since we're in a hurry, Ah'll keep th' input short. While y' were doin't y'r usual job ae inspirin' th' idjiots, Ah hit our bank accounts.

'Another thing a wee outlaw needs is liquid'ty. So all our assets Ah could lay th' fast touch on, I dumped into an old laundry bank frae th' Mantis days.'

Sten started to say something, but then realized Kilgour wasn't being greedy – revolutions, like politics, are fueled by credits and fail for lack of same nearly as often as they do for not providing a proper alternative. Sten would need all the credits in the known universe if he was even to survive this war, let alone win.

And Kilgour had not exaggerated about their riches. Years earlier, when they were prisoners of war of the Tahn, their ex-Mantis companion Ida the Rom had pirated their accrued pay and pyramided it into vast riches. They were wealthy enough for Sten to have purchased his own planet, and for Kilgour to build half-a-dozen castles and surrounding estates on his home world of Edinburgh.

'Then, thinkin't thae'll prob'ly be someone followin' that trail, Ah then rescrubbed th' gelt t' Ida, wi' a wee message t' stan' by an' expect th' pleasure ae our company, fat cow thae she is. Ah think we'll be needin't th' Gypsies afore thae skreekin't an' scrawkin't is o'er.

'Plus Ah drop't a wee line t' our king ae th' smugglers ae well, although Ah dinnae ken i' Wild's dropbox is still good.

'Thae's all, boss. Noo, y' hae some work f'r me? Ah'm assumin't we're noo bein't sensible an' findin' a badger's den an' pullin' it in a'ter us.'

Alex was on his feet and at attention. Sten nodded appreciation.

'You've got that right. Besides, the Emperor would just send badger dogs after us. So we won't bother. Grab about half of the Bhor and get over to the *Bennington*. Make sure they're real sincere about things.'

'If not?'

'Do whatever seems right. But if it's a trap, make them bleed, not us. I'll keep two Kali stations launch-ready until you say otherwise, and I'll keep one flight of tacships out on CAP.'

'Ah'm gone.' And Kilgour was.

Sten wanted to take a deep breath and come up with a plan – but there was no time to do anything other than react. He went back to Commander – now Captain – Freston.

'Okay, Captain. You heard what we're doing. We'll have all three ships slaved to the *Victory*. I want an irrational evasion pattern on the nav computer.'

'Yessir.'

'I want one flight of tacships out around the *Bennington*. And I want another flight . . . gimme a hotrod – whatsername, La Ciotat – in charge . . . one light-second back of the formation, also slaved to the *Victory* as rearguard.

'Every time we hyperjump, we'll leave one of the *Bennington*'s Kalis behind, manned by one of Renzi's officers. I don't like being followed.'

'Yessir.'

'Now, get me double-ganged to those Honjo hardheads.'

'Aye, sir. Do we have a final destination?'

Sten didn't answer.

Not because he didn't have an answer, but because one secret of being a live conspirator was never telling anyone anything until just before it happened. In fact, he had two, now that true miracles had happened and he had not just a ship, but the beginnings of a fleet.

The first one he hadn't exactly decided on. But it would be close to center stage, since all good rebellions require some kind of Bastille-bashing to get started.

The second?

Mahoney had shouted 'Go home,' as he was dragged off to his death.

And Sten had finally figured out exactly where Mahoney meant. Even if he still had not the slightest idea why or what.

Or so he hoped.

Chapter Two

Ranett dug her elbow into a sleepy-eyed clerk's ribs, trod hard on a naval officer's toes, and, with practiced carelessness, dumped hot caff on a bureaucrat's swollen paunch.

As she punched through the crowd, she strewed apologies in her wake: 'Pardon . . . So sorry . . . How clumsy of me . . .'

If anyone had been awake enough to notice, they would have seen that Ranett moved with the oiled ease of a combat veteran. She slipped through the crowd at full tilt. Leaping across openings. Forcing gaps where none existed before. All the while she kept her eyes focused on her eventual goal – the enormous doors leading into the Arundel Castle pressroom.

At the door she was brought up short by a black-uniformed mountain. The golden insignia on the guard's sleeve was an ornate *I* with an *S* twisted around it like a snake. Wonderful, her mind snarled . . . Internal Clottin' Security.

She flashed her sweetest smile. Guaranteed to melt the hearts of most reasonably heterosexual males. 'Excuse me, please . . .' Ranett started to duck under his arm and slip into the pressroom. Inside, she heard a briefer's dry voice. The clots have already started, she thought. I'll skin somebody's hide for this.

Again, the IS man barred her way. 'Press only,' he snarled.

Ranett kept the sweet smile pasted on. 'Then, that means me.' She whipped out her credentials and held them steady for the big stupe's beady eyes. He looked closely at the credentials, then at her face. Taking his damned good time.

'Looks like you, all right,' he said. Then he gave her a malicious grin. Double wonderful, Ranett thought. A media hater.

'You still can't go in.'

'Why the clot not?'

The IS man jolted. The sweetness on Ranett's face was gone now. Her tone dripped icicles. But after the moment's hesitation, the guard failed to take warning.

'Orders, that's why,' he growled. 'The briefing's already in progress . . . No one may enter or leave until it's over.'

A heartbeat later his self-satisfied smile was replaced with a look of pure terror as Ranett unleashed her pent-up fury.

'Get out of my way, you pumped-up little scrote,' she snarled. 'You let me in there this instant, or I'll fry your pubes for breakfast.'

She let him have it for a full one and a half horrible minutes. Scorching him and the wall on either side with blasphemies and foul threats equal to anything the IS man had ever heard – up to and including introducing him to the Emperor's chief torturer.

As each second of the ninety dripped away like a full year, the name on the press ID started registering in his tiny brain. The woman flaying him alive was a legendary newsbeing. Ranett had covered the Tahn wars from the front. Survived the nightmare years when the privy council ruled. Produced prizewinning livie documentaries that even he had watched in awe. Mighty government and corporate chieftains had been known to flee like small boys caught in dirty little acts when she showed up with her recording crew.

When she paused for breath – or new inspiration – the IS man did his best to ooze out of her way. He was busy deserting his post – he'd rather face his hyena-voiced sergeant than this woman – when he heard the big doors hiss open, then closed. He looked behind him. Managed a breath . . . long and shuddering. Ranett was inside. He was safe until the press conference was over. And clot his orders.

Fleet Admiral Anders – Chief of His Majesty's Naval Operations – did a little mental swearing of his own when he saw Ranett duck into the crowded room and cozen some young fool out of an aisle seat.

Up until now, the thing had gone perfectly. When he had first gotten news of the drakh that had hit the fan in the Altaics, he had put his press crisis officers into motion before he had even gotten orders from the Emperor.

The admiral's critics – all silent now – believed him far too young for his post. Also too consciously handsome and smooth. A man who had climbed quickly to the top through political talent, rather than military. In fact, his combat medals had all been won by staged fly-ins to recently cleared enemy territory. He had fired many shots in anger, but all skillfully executed memos and press releases.

His first act as Chief of Naval Operations had been to create the emergency press-pool system the beings before him were operating under. The rules were simple: (1) Only newsbeings credentialed by his office could attend a Crisis Briefing. (2) Only questions pertaining to the 'facts' presented in the briefing would be entertained. (3) Only authorized spokesbeings were permitted to be questioned. (4) Any violations of the first three rules might be deemed a breach of Imperial security and all parties prosecuted for treason.

Still, there were certain realities to handling the media. Some of the beings before him were stars as popular as any livie heart-throb. And they commanded salaries of such size that they were powerful corporations in their own right.

Fortunately, most of them were tame. One part of Anders's genius was he recognized that even a gadfly must join the institution it torments to become a rich and famous gadfly.

Ranett didn't fit this mold. She was merely famous. She had no desire for wealth. Cared nothing for her fame . . . except as a powerful tool to be used to get her way.

Which was why when Admiral Anders drew up the list of reporters to be called, he was forced to include her name. But it went on the bottom. Careful instructions were given for the call to go out too late for Ranett to attend.

But here she was. In clotting person. Despite the hour – Anders had purposely set the crisis briefing for two E-hours before dawn – Ranett looked frighteningly awake. Unlike her punchdrunk colleagues who yawned and nodded all around her, halfheartedly bending an ear as Anders's pet briefing officer continued the jargon-laden drone.

'. . . So much for the history and physical makeup of the Altaic Cluster. You will find planetary thumbnails, relative-grav data, and time-conversion charts in the materials we've already handed out,' the officer said.

'Also included is a fact sheet on the four principal races: the Jochians and Torks. Both human. And the Suzdal and Bogazi. Both ET. It will be helpful to recall that the Jochians are the majority race. And each of the races harbored historical hatred of the other.'

There was a dry rustle of documents as the officer moved on. 'Next . . . the political backdrop. The details are well known to you all. However, to sum up. Anarchy threatened when the Emperor's trusted ally, the Khaqan, died. He was a member of the Jochian majority. It was unfortunate the heavy workload and detail-driven nature of his duties prevented the Khaqan from grooming a successor.

'The Emperor appointed Dr Iskra – a prominent Jochian scholar and devoted citizen of the Empire – as the new leader . . .'

Ranett was getting the range now. She could see by the glazed look on her colleagues' faces that nothing important had been said . . . yet. But they were over an hour into the briefing. The dry lecturer in front of her was only one of several who had come before. Obviously, all of them had outlined equally unimportant facts. It was certainly not news that things had gone into the slokhouse in the Altaics. A leakproof news blackout had been slammed down for some time now. Ranett herself had just returned from an attempt to visit the sector. Her ship had been ordered back to Prime by someone very powerful, just short of its destination.

She quick-checked through the sheaf of press materials she had snagged on the way to her seat. Found the Crisis Briefing Agenda. Sure enough, the first items listed on the agenda came under the heading of Background. That was followed by Crisis In Focus: Fleet Admiral Anders, Chief of His Majesty's Naval Operations. This was followed by a Q&A. Nowhere on the agenda – or in the other material in the folder – was there a hint of exactly what this crisis briefing was all about. Except for the fact it had something to do with the Altaics. And it was probably military, since the briefing was being conducted by the Chief of Naval Operations.

If Ranett was the type who whistled, she would have done so right then. There was some deep drakh about to come down. In her experience weaving through the maze of Imperial politics, good news was announced immediately. Bad news was shunted to the end.

She caught Admiral Anders dart a glance at her. He was clearly stewing over her presence. Gooood! She gave him her nastiest grin. Anders pretended to ignore her. Turned his solemn attention back to his briefing officer.

'. . . the greatest difficulty,' the man was saying, 'proved to be the numerous heavily armed forces at the command of the several highly volatile races. To begin with, a diplomatic effort was launched to meet with the commanders of the hostile forces arrayed against Dr Iskra. And, as quickly as possible, Imperial forces were sent in to assist Dr Iskra in keeping the peace. Those forces were commanded by one of the Emperor's most capable and loyal officers – Admiral Mason . . .'

Ranett's alarm bells started ringing. Why the lavish praise for Mason? She had also caught the past-tense phrase: '. . . forces *were* commanded.' Then the alarms grew louder still. The briefing officer had unaccountably left out the name of the man who had headed the diplomatic mission: Plenipotentiary Sten. She knew Sten was one of the most prominent beings on the Eternal Emperor's staff. The poor sod, Ranett thought. To her mind, Sten was either being set up as a scapegoat or was bound for execution. She wondered if maybe it had already happened.

'. . . Despite the many difficulties,' the briefing officer continued, 'we are happy to tell you today that the situation in the Altaics has stabilized. Order has been restored. Some time in the near future, we expect to be able to permit free travel and communication with the cluster.'

Riiight! Ranett thought. She knew when she was wading in drakh thigh-deep. 'Near future' most likely meant . . . never in her lifetime.

'That concludes the background portion of the agenda,' the briefing officer said. He made with an insincere smile. 'Thank you for your attention, gentlebeings. Admiral Anders will now bring us up to date on the latest developments. Please give him a warm welcome.'

There was a scattering of applause as Anders came forward. This frosted Ranett. She noted most of the applause came from the star anchors. Human or ET, they all looked alike to Ranett – gorgeous, rich, and self-satisfied.

'This is a solemn moment for me, gentlebeings,' Anders intoned. 'It is with heavy heart that I announce to you that one of our own has betrayed all that I . . . and the hundreds of thousands other members of the Imperial forces . . . stand for.'

Ranett leaned forward. Here it comes, she thought.

'Only hours ago, Admiral Mason stumbled upon a plot to overthrow His Majesty, the Eternal Emperor.'

A loud rumble erupted from the press corps. Anders held up a hand for silence. And got it.

'The coup attempt – using the disturbances in the Altaic

Cluster as a screen – was uncovered only moments after it was launched. Admiral Mason engaged the perpetrators. And shattered them . . .

'. . . Losing his own life in the process. As well as all hands aboard his ship.'

The rumble turned into a thunderclap. Newsbeings were on their feet shouting for attention. Ranett stayed in her seat. Intent on Anders. She noted that his left cheek was twitching. And his eyes were overly bright. Her conclusion: the Admiral was a lying sack.

Again Anders signaled for silence. Again he got it. 'The coup was masterminded,' he said, 'by a being we all believed to be loyal . . . a man who proved to be secretly nursing an insane desire to murder our Emperor, and once again bring disaster to the Empire.

'Plenipotentiary Sten! A man who once had the Emperor's love and trust.

'You will be pleased to know that although this intergalactic outlaw survived, his forces have been destroyed or scattered. As we speak, they are being hunted down one by one.'

Now, Anders skillfully allowed himself to be overwhelmed by questions.

'Any word on this villain's whereabouts, Admiral?' one of the overpaid anchors shouted.

'None that I am allowed to verify,' Anders said. 'But rest assured, Sten – and his underling, Alex Kilgour – can run. But they can't hide.'

'Were any of the rebel forces in the Altaics involved?' came another question.

'Again, I am hampered by concerns of Imperial security. I can say, however, that Sten was heavily involved with the rebels in the course of his duties.'

'Is there any danger of the conspiracy spreading?'

'I can't say no to that. But, I can say I believe we have it localized. Internal Security will be following up all leads.'

It's witch-hunt time, Ranett thought.

'What were Admiral Mason's total casualties?'

'I'm sorry . . . Again, security concerns prevent me from answering. Except to say all hands aboard his flagship died in the cowardly attack.'

'How many of Sten's forces have been killed or captured?'

Anders shrugged. 'I repeat my last . . . Imperial security, and all. I promise all of you these questions, and all others, will be answered . . . in the fullness of time.'

Ranett dipped into her bag of tricks and pulled out her favorite – the Donaldson. Her practiced bellow blasted over the other questioners. 'ADMIRAL ANDERS! ADMIRAL ANDERS!'

She could not be denied. Anders sighed. Motioned for her to GA.

'What evidence do you have against these alleged conspirators?' she asked.

Anders frowned. 'Evidence? I told you . . . There was a coup attempt.' He tried laughing at her. 'I know it's early, Ranett, but we do wish you'd pay attention when we speak.'

'I heard you, Admiral,' Ranett snarled. 'But, I assume . . . If this Sten is captured—'

'*When*, Ranett. When!'

'Your qualification, Admiral. Not mine. Regardless. If, or when, Sten – and this Alex Kilgour – are captured . . . what proof of a conspiracy exists? For the trial, I mean. For example, did you monitor any conversations? Discover correspondence between the alleged perpetrators? Witness them meeting with known enemies of the Empire? That sort of thing.'

Anders sputtered. 'Dammit. They attacked and destroyed Admiral Mason's ship! What other proof do you need?'

Ranett wasn't buying. 'An honest prosecutor might ask for more than your word, Admiral,' she said. 'Surely you can see that. Show us pictures of the attack, for example. Transcripts of bridge-to-bridge communications. Whatever proof you have.'

'I'll have to plead security concerns again,' Anders said. 'You'll have those things . . . eventually.'

'In the fullness of time?' Ranett said.

'I couldn't have put it better myself,' Anders said.

Ranett knew, at that moment, no one had any intention of capturing Sten. Not alive, at any rate.

The admiral buried a smile and started to turn away.

'One other question, Admiral . . . if you please.'

Anders buried a groan. 'Go ahead, Ranett. *One* more.'

'Does this incident with the plenipotentiary indicate a severe weakness in the diplomatic corps?'

Anders was honestly stumped. 'I don't understand. This is an isolated incident. One man acting in league with a small group of deranged individuals. Nothing more.'

'Then what about Ian Mahoney?'

Anders purpled. 'One has nothing to do with the other,' he snarled.

'Oh? Wasn't Ian Mahoney assigned to the Altaics as well? In fact, wasn't he Plenipotentiary Sten's superior at one time? And wasn't he just executed? Also accused – with great fanfare, I might add – as a traitor? And, like Sten, hadn't he too spent a lifetime in service to the Emperor?

'Come on, Admiral. Either one and one equals two or we have a coincidence that at the very least indicates dissatisfaction with Imperial policy. Loyal and able beings who have spent their entire careers fighting the Emperor's battles aren't suddenly transformed into traitors. Unless there is something seriously wrong.'

'Writing an editorial, Ranett?' Anders growled.

'No, Admiral. Just asking questions. That's my job. Answering them is yours.'

'I won't dignify your remarks by responding,' Anders said. He turned to the rest of the newsbeings. 'And . . . I warn you all . . . The area your colleague has just encroached upon is forbidden under the crisis-briefing rules. She – and the rest of you – *will* confine yourself to asking and communicating only those details authorized under those rules. Do I make myself clear?'

The press room was oddly silent. No one looked at Ranett. Angry enough to peel and parboil Anders, Ranett opened her mouth to bellow one more stinging question.

Then she saw the deadly look in Anders's eyes. Saw an Internal Security officer move forward, getting ready for a word from the admiral. Her jaw shut with a snap.

She smiled, shrugged, and buried her head in her notes.

Ranett was a survivor. She would get her questions answered – one way or the other.

As the press briefing broke up and everyone hurried out of the room, Ranett thought about Sten one more time.

Poor sap. He didn't stand a chance.

Chapter Three

'I am afflicted with fools,' the Eternal Emperor roared. 'Overpaid, overstuffed, smirking, self-satisfied fools.'

A variety of beings quaked in their footgear as the Emperor detailed his displeasure. There was Avri, the young woman with the very old eyes, who was his political chief of staff. Walsh, the handsome but exceedingly stupid boss of Dusable, who was the Emperor's toady in Parliament. Anders, the admiral who had run afoul of Ranett at the press conference. Bleick, the Emperor's chamberlain. And scores of other beings – uniformed and otherwise – were scurrying about the yawning Imperial chamber or hanging their heads in shame as the Emperor railed on.

The Emperor towered over Anders. Blue eyes shifting to the color of cold steel. 'What kind of a press conference was that, Admiral? You're supposed to be an expert on that sort of drakh. God knows, you can't pour piss out of a boot when it comes to *real* military business.'

'Yessir,' the Admiral said. He was drawn up, heels locked, like a raw recruit.

'And *you*, Avri . . . You were supposed to gameplan this thing with pube brain, here. I gave you the spin on a gilt-edged platter, for crying out loud.'

'Yessir,' Avri said. Licking lush lips with a nervous tongue.

'People, I do not have time to explain basic politics to you,' the Eternal Emperor gritted. 'Traitors – the privy council – put this Empire in its worst shape in two thousand years. And I barely pulled it out *that* time.

'Now I'm saddled with debt, harried by mewling allies, and

every time I turn over another rock, a new kind of traitorous slime crawls out.

'In my view – which, dammit, is the only view that counts – Sten is the worst of the lot. I nursed that snake at my bosom for his whole clotting life. Gave him honors. Riches. And how does he repay me? Conspires with my enemies. Plots my murder. And when discovered, he slaughters innocent sailors, and one of the best admirals in my service, in a cowardly sneak attack.'

The Emperor's voice lowered. He shook his head. Weary. 'Now, *that's* a spin, dammit. Guaranteed to turn a drakhhouse into a palace. Not so very hard, is it?'

'I'm very sorry, sir,' Anders said. 'I don't know how that reporter – Ranett – got in.'

'Oh, just shut the clot up, Admiral,' the Emperor said. 'If you can't make a plan that can stand the test of somebody with a little smarts, then get out of the clotting business.'

'Yessir.'

'Avri, it's damage-control time. I want *all* newscasts blanketed by our spin doctors. Hit the Op Ed programs extra hard. "Face The Empire." "Witness To History." "Countdown." That sort of thing.

'I especially want you to get into the pants of that Pyt'r Jynnings clown over at K-B-N-S-O. Half the Empire watches that piece of drakh he calls "Nightscan." I don't know why. Guess he makes everybody feel smart because he's so damned dumb.'

'Right away, Your Majesty,' Avri said.

'You! Walsh!'

The dimwit that was the ruler of Dusable blinked into semi-sentient awareness. 'How . . . uh . . . may I be of . . . uh . . . service, Your . . . uh . . . Highness?' he managed.

'I want those lazy sods in Parliament stoked up. Some kind of condemnation vote. Calling Sten and that Scots sidekick of his every filthy name in the book. And if that vote isn't unanimous, I'll nail your guts to a post, Walsh. And lash you around it.'

'Yessir,' Walsh gobbled.

'One other thing. Get ahold of Kenna. I have a little personal business I want him to transact.'

'Right away, Your Highness,' Walsh said. Kenna was possibly the sharpest old pol on Dusable. A world whose politics were so crooked infants gurgled the word 'mordida' before they learned to say 'momma.'

'Anders. I want all firstline forces on this. I don't care what fleets you have to strip. Sten *must* be found.'

'Yessir.'

'Bleick!' His chamberlain snapped to. 'I want—'

He stopped in midorder as the door hissed open and Poyndex, his chief of Internal Security, entered. His face was grim. Bloodless. A man bearing bad tidings. But the Emperor was too angry to immediately notice.

'Where the clot have you been, Poyndex? I told you I wanted that info on Sten and Kilgour immediately, dammit. Not tomorrow. Not the day after. But now, dammit. Now!'

Poyndex glanced quickly around the room. Then back at the Emperor. 'I think we need to talk in private, sir.'

'I don't have time for games, Poyndex. Spit it out.'

Poyndex hesitated. The Emperor's eyes got a sudden spooky glint in them. Clinical paranoia was Poyndex's diagnosis. 'If you insist, Your Majesty,' Poyndex said. 'But I would be remiss if I didn't warn you one more time. This should be discussed in private. I strongly urge you to reconsider.'

The Eternal Emperor turned to his people. 'Get out.'

They got. With feeling. In moments the room was empty. The Emperor looked back at Poyndex. 'Okay. Now report.'

Poyndex stiffened. 'I regret to say there is nothing *to* report, sir. All files on Sten and Alex Kilgour have been wiped clean.'

'Say clotting what?'

'It's as if they never existed, sir.' Poyndex's heart was hammering as he delivered the news.

'That's not possible,' the Emperor said.

'But I'm afraid it's true, Your Majesty,' Poyndex said. 'Even the Mantis computers have been penetrated. There is no record of Sten – or Alex Kilgour – in *any* record system in the Empire. I don't know how it was done. I've got every tech in IS working around the clock. The only thing we know for sure is it had to have been done by a very high placed insider.'

The Emperor stared at Poyndex for a long, uncomfortable time. He turned and palmed a switch. His personal computer terminal winked into life.

'Fortunately,' the Emperor said, 'I keep my own files for just this reason.' He laughed. Without humor. 'When all is lost,' he said, 'you have to depend on yourself.'

His fingers flashed across keys, beginning the search.

'I *used* to have a staff I could depend upon,' the Emperor said.

'Mahoney, for one. Sometimes I regret I had to have him killed. Ian was a strong right arm, that's for sure.' The Emperor, who normally appeared to be a man in his mid-thirties, suddenly seemed very old to the IS chief. His handsome features drawn. His voice high-pitched . . . and weak.

The Emperor looked up at Poyndex. '. . . The same with Sten. I tell you, Poyndex, the trouble with traitors is they tend to be your best people.' Another humorless laugh. 'Maybe that's what old Julius was trying to tell Brutus.'

'Pardon me, Your Majesty? I have no knowledge of these beings. Should I have IS put this Julius and Brutus on your Personal Enemies list?'

The Emperor grunted. 'Never mind.' He muttered to himself. Just loud enough for Poyndex to hear. 'That's the other thing . . . No one to talk—'

He suddenly broke off. 'What the clot?'

'Something wrong, sir?'

The Emperor hammered keys. 'No. I probably should have – Holy drakh!'

The Emperor bleared up at Poyndex. 'My files . . .' he gasped, 'they're . . .'

Poyndex glanced at the screen. Saw the display. 'STEN, NI. KILGOUR, ALEX. NO FILES ON RECORD. PRESS ONCE FOR ANOTHER REQUEST.'

The IS chief staggered back, as flabbergasted as his boss. The Eternal Emperor's personal files on Sten and Kilgour had been wiped absolutely clean.

The Emperor's heavy fist smashed on his desk. 'I want Sten, dammit! Get him, Poyndex. If you don't, I will. And I will personally put his head on a stake next to yours.'

Poyndex fled. And as he went out the door, he swore he could hear a growling, as if a great hound were snarling after him.

Chapter Four

'Good evening, gentlebeings. I'm Pyt'r Jynnings. Welcome to this week's edition of "Nightscan." The news program that examines the crucial issues of our time.

'Tonight we focus our full hour on an event that has stunned the Empire. At the heart of this broadcast is a disarmingly simple question . . .

'Sten: Traitor, or Misunderstood Genius?

'To my right, Professor Knovack. A renowned Imperial historian and expert on parliamentary power brokering. To my left, Sr Wiker. Former speechwriter for the Eternal Emperor. Current ambassador to the Tahn worlds.

'Professor. We'll start with you. What is your response to the question?'

'Oh, he's a traitor. No question about it.'

'What about you, Sr Wiker?'

'I couldn't have put it better myself, Pyt'r. Sten is definitely a traitor.'

'Ah! Agreement! And . . . uh . . . so soon. Goodness me. Well, let's explore the other side of the coin, then. Professor?'

'I went first before.'

'Ha ha. Too true. Well, Sr Wiker, what's fair is fair. Now, tell us . . . do you think Sten is a misunderstood genius?'

'That's an interesting question, Pyt'r. And I've come prepared to discuss it all night . . . if I have to.'

'Good. Good.'

'But, before we do, I think we have to talk about the nature of this man.'

'Oh? Did you know Sten? Personally?'

'Good God, no! Uh . . . I mean . . . I know *of* him. And I most certainly know *his* type.'

'Please share these insights with our viewers.'

'To begin with, he has enjoyed the favor of our Emperor his entire life. True, he performed some service. Valuable service, some might say.'

'But, would *you* say that?'

'I think that's . . . uh . . . open to interpretation. More importantly, he has been the recipient of a host of honors. So these services – however one might characterize them – have certainly been repaid. Besides these honors, he has also been blessed with great wealth. Thanks to his friendship with the Eternal Emperor.'

'How do you react to those statements, Professor Knovack?'

'I think this . . . this . . . traitor approached our Emperor in a rare moment of weakness. After that awful business with the privy council. And our beloved Emperor mistook his ambition for love and loyalty. And now it seems . . . the Emperor was . . . was . . . nurturing a snake at his bosom.'

'Very well put, Professor. Your reputation as a phrase-maker has once again been assured . . . Any comments thus far, Sr Wiker?'

'I think we're forgetting those poor Imperial Service beings who were the victims of Sten's traitorous and cowardly action. Especially Admiral Mason. Think of his family! Think of how much agony they must be in at this moment.'

'A most excellent point. I think we should all pause for just a moment. A moment of silence, if you please. Out of respect for Admiral Mason's family and the crew of the *Caligula* . . .'

As the vid recorders whirred for the billions of K-B-N-S-O viewers, the three men solemnly bowed their heads.

The director's voice whispered in Jynning's ear. 'For clot's sake, Pyt'r. Not the silence business again!'

The anchor whispered back into his throat mike: 'Shut the clot up, Badee. You're not the one who has to fill an hour with these two scrotes.'

'Well, think fast, bub. We've got fifty minutes to go.'

'Cut to a commercial, dammit.'

'You gotta be kidding,' Badee said. 'Who'd advertise on a piece of drakh like this?'

'How about a "Give Blood" spot, then?'

'Oh, maaann. Another house ad. Okay. If we gotta. On the count, then . . . One . . . Two . . .'

At that moment a porta-ram smashed through the studio doors.
'On the floor,' Sten shouted.

'Move't, or lose't, mates,' Alex thundered.

Jynnings, his guests, Badee, and the livie crew gaped for a full
two seconds. Sten and Alex strode over the ruined double doors,
willyguns at the ready. Behind them, Cind led a contingent of
Bhor and Gurkhas.

'It's Sten!' Jynnings uttered in absolute awe. 'And Kilgour.'

Sten motioned with his weapon. 'I said, Down!' He fired,
blowing a largish hole in the news anchor's desk.

Much diving for the floor commenced, Jynnings denting his
wavy head against the desk. Only the director had the presence
of mind to whisper into his mike: 'Holy mother . . . we've *got*
our hour! Keep rolling, fools. Keep rolling.'

Sten advanced, just out of pickup range. To his right, an emergency door creaked open. Sten saw a flash of many uniforms.
Guards. Then the air shattered as Cind put a burst through the
doorway. Howls of agony. The uniforms vanished.

A burly man stepped out of the shadows, swinging a heavy
light standard.

'Ooops, there, lad,' Alex said, catching the light housing with
one hand. Giving it a yank. 'Y've made a wee m'stake.' The grip
stumbled forward. Alex dropped the light and hoisted the man
off the floor. With one hand. ''Tis noo i' y'r job description, mon.
Y'r lucky Ah'm noo a taleteller. Ah'd put a bug in y'r shop stew-
ard's shell, otherwise.'

The man's eyes bugged out. Alex hurled him. A loud crash as
the goon hit, and monitors cascaded around him.

Alex turned back to Sten. 'Ah, think w' hae their attention
noo, wee Sten . . . I's showtime, folks.'

Sten stepped in front of the camera.

'Gentlebeings,' he said. 'Fellow-citizens of the Empire . . . My
name is Sten. The subject of this broadcast. I am addressing you
live from K-B-N-S-O . . .'

Anders gulped like a fish as he watched Sten address the Empire.
The man he sought was speaking from the station's main broadcasting center – in an orbit only a half-an-E hour from Prime
World. His propaganda-centered mind immediately caught the
full impact of the blow Sten had just struck. The man was standing
virtually in the center of the Emperor's stronghold. Waving a rude
finger at the mightiest military force in history.

'. . . The Emperor has branded me and my colleagues a traitor,' Sten was saying. 'History will judge if this is true. Just as history will judge the Emperor. And I promise you it will judge him harshly. My fate does not matter. It is your fate you should be thinking of at this moment. And your children's.

'I accuse the Emperor of betraying *you* . . . His people. You work in near poverty. While he enjoys lavish entertainment. As do his favored cronies. You labor in cold, in heat, in near darkness. While the Emperor's favored bask in the light of plentiful AM2.

'The Emperor has betrayed you. Only one of many crimes. I will detail those crimes over the coming days: Star-chamber justice. The imprisonment, torture, and execution of beings whose only sin was to trust their Emperor . . .'

Anders recovered and turned to his aide, Captain Lawrence. The woman's face was a mask of confusion.

'Scramble the fleet,' the admiral barked. 'I want to see a hole in the sky. And I want to see it quick.'

'But . . . all the civilians at the station—'

'Clot the civilians. I want that man dead. Now, move it!'

The captain rushed into action.

Anders turned back. Sten was still talking. Good. I'll see you in hell, you son of a bitch.

Alex signaled to Sten. A finger across his throat. Time to get the clot out.

'. . . The list of the Emperor's sins is far longer than I have time to detail. I suspect his fleets are on the way now. So, I haven't much time. Except to say this:

'I, Sten, declare war on the Eternal Emperor. And I urge you all to join me in this crusade. He's left you nothing to lose. And *all* your freedom to gain.

'Thank you. And good night.'

Sten lifted his weapon and turned the camera into molten metal and plas. The station jolted again and again, as Sten's forces blew their strategically placed explosives. No innocents would be hurt. But it would take many months and even more credits before K-B-N-S-O broadcast again.

Sten prodded Jynnings with his toe. The man whimpered and looked up at him with terror-stricken eyes. The anchor was sure he was staring a madman in the face.

'Thanks for the loan of your program,' Sten said.

'Sure,' Jynnings squeaked. 'Anytime.'

Cind shouted, 'We're three seconds behind schedule.'

Sten nodded, and sprinted through the blackened hole posing as a doorway, his team behind him. The last out was Cind. She paused and fired a long burst around the room to add to the terror and confusion. Molten metal and plas dripped from smoking walls.

Then she was gone.

Jynnings raised his head from the floor. 'Thank God,' he breathed. 'I'm safe.'

'Who cares,' the director said as he scrambled to his feet. 'You realize what we just broadcast? I tell you, the numbers we get on this baby are gonna blow our competition out of the water.'

Badee looked around at the ruins of the studio. Humming to himself. It was gonna be easy street all the way, now. He would have his pick of any job in the livie business.

He wondered if there was a com line undamaged. He had to call his agent. Real quick.

All the alarms were hooting warnings as Sten and the others dived aboard the *Victory*. Within minutes, Sten was on the bridge. Captain Freston's face relaxed slightly.

'Just in time,' Freston said. 'We've got a whole clottin' fleet after our tender young hides. Led by a big clottin' battleship . . . the *Nevsky*. Permission to run like hell, sir.'

'Negative,' Sten said, scanning the incoming blips. There was just enough time. 'I want to thin out a little of the competition, first, Captain.'

Sten swiveled to Lieutenant Denzi. 'Weapons?'

'All Kali and Goblin units at full launch-readiness,' she reported. The woman was ready to fight.

Sten hated to disappoint her. 'I'm afraid I'm going to have to do the honors, Lieutenant,' he said.

He raced for a Kali station. He called out to Captain Freston as he pulled on the helmet. 'When I say go . . . go, dammit!'

Freston nodded. He wouldn't need to be prodded. The monitors showed the *Nevsky* coming fast, accompanied by half-a-dozen cruisers and a forest of destroyers.

Sten's hand automatically armed the missile, then fired. His point of view was black space pricked with flares of color rushing by him as the missile hurtled out.

There was a cruiser bearing down on the *Victory*. Behind it he could see the battleship. There was just a chance he might slip his Kali past the cruiser. But Sten opted to play it safe. Especially when he saw the cruiser's missile bays' gunports yawn, ready to fire at the *Victory*.

Aboard the *Nevsky*, Captain Leech faced a similar problem. His battle monitors showed the *Victory* in a parking orbit to the side of the orbiting livie station. An alarm indicated an enemy Kali honing in on his lead cruiser. And that the cruiser blocked any possible shot at the *Victory*.

Then he saw the solution. The livie station.

Leech had become addicted to an ancient Earth game when he was a young officer on his first lonely outpost. It was called 'pool.' Why, he didn't know. One didn't puddle water on the green felt table. In a clutch, one of his favorite tactics was a 'power break,' which called for smashing the white cue ball into its brothers with all his strength. The results were messy, but sometimes miraculous.

The livie station before him presented a similar situation. A direct hit on the station would produce an explosion that would, at the very least, damage the nearby *Victory*. The bigger the blast, the greater chance he had to disable or even destroy Sten's ship.

It never entered Leech's mind it took a minimum of two thousand beings to run a livie station of K-B-N-S-O's size. His orders, after all, were to get Sten. At all costs.

A rush of orders to his weapons officer put his plan into action.

Moments later, three nuclear-tipped missiles spit from the *Nevsky*'s tubes.

Freston had never heard of pool. But he was blessed with a remarkably quick mind. When the enemy missiles winked into life onscreen, he at first thought the captain of the *Nevsky* must be incompetent. Their trajectory would take them nowhere near the *Victory*. His mind swiftly calculated their course . . . the livie station? What the clot? Then he got it.

There was no time to warn the station. Much less Sten, who was hunched at the Kali controls, his mind racing along with the missile he'd aimed at the enemy cruiser.

Freston's hand smashed down on the drive controls.

*

The cruiser jumped up at Sten, as the Kali closed. He thumbed controls, the image blurred, and his mind was falling away . . . back . . . back . . . back . . .

The Imperial missiles struck the station simultaneously. The nukes detonated. Two thousand beings ceased to exist.

Radioactive debris shrapneled outward. In moments the *Victory* would be riddled.

Sten plunged into awareness just as the *Victory* crashed into hyperspace. Kilgour's face bleared at him. Pale and worried. Behind him was an anxious Freston.

'Tell us y'r name, lad,' Alex said.

'Say clottin' what?'

'Y'r name. 'Tis a wee test.'

Sten snarled back. 'Kilgour, if you don't get your haggis breath out of my face, I'm going to stuff you into a ship's stomach along with the rest of the porridge.'

Kilgour turned back to Freston. A big smile wreathed his round face. 'Aye, he's fightin' fit. Altho' his slangin' c'd use a bit o' work.'

'What the clot's going on, Kilgour?' Sten demanded.

'W' hae to' leave, wi'oot waitin' on th' order ae our comin't, nor f'r you t' bash th' cruiser. Th' mad Emp hae stuck his foot in th' drakh i' whae's goin't on, young Sten.'

'I repeat my opening remarks, Kilgour. What the clot is going on?'

'Th' Emp's blow' it up his pet livie station.'

'What the clot for?' Sten was gaping.

Alex made a motion with his heavy-world shoulders. It was a shrug that came in a massive wave.

'P'raps he dinnæ like th' panto.'

Chapter Five

DOCUMENT ID: None (vice Originator)

TO: ALL IS STATION HEADS
   DESIGNATED/CLEARED EMBASSY SECURITY STATION CHIEFS
   OTHER PERS DESIGNATED BY P. OR HIGHEST

FROM: POYNDEX, HEAD, INTERNAL SECURITY

1. All stations have received orders for the immediate apprehension of STEN, (NO INITIAL). No task is to be given higher priority by IS personnel unless specifically notified otherwise by P. or designated subordinate.
2. This task is to include the apprehension or deactivation, by any means necessary, of all involved co-conspirators; both those identified to date in Imperial Bulletins and those who are clearly participants but not yet named.
3. To this end, you are authorized to commandeer or requisition any Imperial resources whatsoever, WITH HIGHEST AUTHORIZATION with no justification for actions of this nature required to normal-channel suppliers.

4. In addition, ANY intelligence of any nature pertaining to STEN, NI, and KILGOUR, ALEX, is to be forwarded to this station, PRIORITY ONE-ALPHA. Particularly sought is physical descriptions, habits, hobbies, specialty areas (civilian and otherwise), places where above are known to have frequented, in short, ALL data concerning above two individuals.

5. No, repeat no screening of raw data relevant to (para. 4) above is to be made.

6. (Para. 4) and (para. 5) are not to be discussed with local authorities nor any conventional division of Imperial Intelligence.

7. Any request for data in the area of (para. 4) cannot be answered at this time, and IS chiefs are advised to avoid mentioning reasons to anyone in (para. 6). This is due to some confusion and doubling of input, caused as an act of sabotage by STEN, NI, or some other conspirator yet to be discovered and indicted. As complete data becomes available on STEN, NI, and KILGOUR, ALEX, it will be immediately disseminated to all levels.

8. Under *no* circumstances is the information in (para. 4), (para. 5), (para. 6), and (para. 7) to be conveyed with any personnel formerly associated with the discredited Mercury Corps, nor, most particularly, with Mantis Section. In addition, any inquiries as to STEN, NI, by former operatives of this branch, especially Mantis Section, must be reported *immediately*, Priority One-Alpha, to P.

9. If possible, STEN, NI, is to be apprehended secretly and immediately prepared for transfer directly to Prime for trial. No information is to be released, particularly to media.

10. If, however, apprehension is made by operatives other than IS, and publicity is inevitable, STEN, NI, is to be charged with HIGH TREASON, MURDER, CONSPIRACY and ATTEMPTED REGICIDE. Other charges will be filed after STEN, NI, has been transferred to Prime World and is in high-security custody.

11. In the event of contact with STEN, NI, and apprehension is not possible, or in the event of attempted escape after apprehension, immediate termination *must* be made.

12. As a corollary task, all IS operatives are ordered to devote maximum attention to uncovering the degree of conspiracy attempted by STEN, NI. However, under no circumstances is this investigation to be regarded as a 'hunting license' to remove other enemies of the Empire. This task is too

important and too immediate to be allowed to broaden to such a degree, although operatives should maintain files on the above matter for eventual attention.

13. Successful accomplishment of this most vital mission will not only be deemed in the Highest Traditions of Internal Security, but a personal service to the Eternal Emperor himself, and so rewarded.

FOR THE ETERNAL EMPEROR

P.

Chapter Six

The school of fish broke the surface, scattering spray against the face of a wind-whitened wave, then skittered down across the trough.

Their flight was pointless. Death was close.

The sea exploded as the great creature arced out of the water in front of the school, mouth gaping as it inhaled the leader. A monstrous flipper crashed and two more of the half-meter-long fish writhed, then floated limply, momentarily stunned.

The com buzzed, and Rykor's focus on her alfresco midday meal was shattered. But she didn't answer immediately. Instead, she deliberately devoured both fish before they could recover, thoughtfully analyzing their taste.

Yes, she thought. These were not from our farm-spawnings. Yet another ground is breeding back to its proper level. True wild fish can always be distinguished. The taste is . . . more . . . more . . .

Pondering just what it was more of, the being that was the Empire's most gifted psychologist rolled on her back, oblivious to the raging hurricane and the below-zero-C temperatures. Rykor's flipper waved over the bone-induction com that fitted closely around her neck. Neck was an arbitrary designation – Alex Kilgour had once observed that 'it hae t' be th' lass's neck, since some'at keeps her head frae bangin' into her chest, aye?'

The caller was one of her assistants, in the luxurious quarters/ office she'd had lovingly built that some insensitive sorts compared to an arctic sea cave.

'I do not,' Rykor rumbled, 'particularly appreciate being interrupted in midmeal. Lunch, as the humans say, is important.'

'There is a priority message from Prime,' the assistant said, new enough to be somewhat awed by this communication from the Imperial capital. 'It requires that you stand by for special duties, at the command' – and his tone grew more hushed – 'of the Eternal Emperor himself.'

Rykor stiffened. 'What sort of duties?'

'The message was not specific. But it said the duties would almost certainly be protracted, so you are advised to bring a gravchair and pack accordingly.'

No mention of the late Ian Mahoney, Rykor thought. Nor of the recently outlawed Sten. Nor did the message suggest that perhaps the Emperor – or more likely his new head of secret police, Poyndex – might also be interested in why Rykor had conferred recently, in the greatest secrecy, with one Sr Ecu, Diplomat Extraordinaire.

Bad, bad, very bad.

'And how am I to get to Prime?'

'An Imperial ship has been dispatched. I have a confirm from the spaceport that its time of arrival is within two E-days.'

Worse and worse, Rykor thought.

'Shall I reply, or wait for your return?'

'Advise that . . . advise that you are still attempting to contact me.'

'Received. But . . .'

'For your own sake, if you are recording this conversation, I would suggest you blank the record immediately. By the way, that is an order.'

'Are you returning now?'

Rykor thought hard. She had two E-days before the ship that could only be carrying Poyndex's gestapo and an arrest warrant arrived. Time enough.

'I am. But only momentarily. For these new duties, I shall require some time to myself, out here at sea, preparing and focusing my energies.'

'Of course,' the still-bewildered assistant said. Like all aquatic races, Rykor's race needed the sea not only for physical health and nourishment, but for psychic replenishment as well. 'I shall have your usual travel pack ready.'

'Very good. I am returning. Close transmission.'

Rykor, without waiting for acknowledgement, shut the com off and bulleted back toward her home.

Two days.

Time enough for her to pack bare necessities and get to the in-atmosphere flier she had concealed underwater not far from the cave, the flier she had bought a few years earlier, when she sensed that somehow the Empire was going very wrong.

All of her expertise about intelligence was theoretical, but she had spent long years advising Mahoney when he was head of Mercury Corps and then Sten. She knew any conspirator worth his cloak always had a back door.

The rest of the back door was a small yacht she had hidden in a remote warehouse at a tiny spaceport on the other side of her world. She had two days until their arrival, then perhaps two more days while they fruitlessly searched the winter oceans for Rykor on her mythical wanderjahr – and then they would know she had fled.

Long enough, she hoped.

She even had a refuge – with the being that had first come to her with the horrid suspicion that the Eternal Emperor had gone insane.

Sr Ecu caught the updraft that rose close to the vertical, sunbaked cliff and allowed it to loft him out of the twisting canyon, high into the sky.

Before him, centered in the vast valley, was the towering spire of the Manabi's Guesting Center.

Sr Ecu had delayed his passage as long as he dared, following the course of the canyon as it wound its way toward the valley. He could dawdle no longer.

He'd taken his time in responding to the summons not out of rudeness – among the Manabi's qualifications as the Empire's diplomats and negotiators was an overwhelming sense of what could only be termed decency – but so he could make sure his carefully prepared lies would still stand up.

He also felt a relatively unfamiliar 'emotion,' to use the human term. Fear. If the slightest suspicion fell on Ecu, the Manabi's main protection, absolute neutrality, would not help him stay alive.

Ecu himself had broken that political and moral neutrality some time ago, when he had determined the Eternal Emperor was no longer qualified to rule, and that the Emperor was, in fact, destroying the Empire he had created. He'd then sought out Rykor, for confirmation of his theories and that he was not the first Manabi to go insane.

And then he had sought out Mahoney and Sten, advised them of the situation, and, still worse, announced he, and therefore the entire Manabi race, would be willing to assist in any attempt to prevent the seemingly inevitable collapse of the Empire.

Now Mahoney was dead and Sten was on the run.

Just ahead could be the instrument of Ecu's own dissolution into the nonmaterial racial presence. He wondered just who the Emperor's inquisitor would be.

Ecu's long black body, red-tinted at the wingtips, three-meter-long tail ruddering skillfully, floated toward the Center. Ecu found his senses at peak. Perhaps, he thought, because this could be the last time he experienced the quiet joy of his home world. At times he wondered why he'd ever chosen his career, a career that took him away, off Seilichi and its lake-dotted single supercontinent and occasional jagged mountain ranges.

Perhaps he should have stayed, and been no more than just another philosopher, drifting in his world's gentle winds, thinking, teaching. His early sketches at forming a personal dialectic were stored on a fiche somewhere underground, where the Manabi kept whatever machines and construction necessary.

The only artificial constructs to show above Seilichi's surface were the three Guesting Centers, and they existed only as a courtesy to whatever non-aerial beings chose to visit the planet. And they were intended to appear, as much as possible, like huge natural extinct volcanic necks, with the landing fields hidden in the 'crater.'

The Center sensed Ecu's approach, and a portal yawned. Ecu flew inside, tendrils flickering. He found traces of the signature scent he used, and followed those traces to the assigned confer-ence room.

Inside, sitting very much at ease, was the Emperor's emissary.

Solon Kenna was even fatter and more benevolent-appearing, if in a bibulous fashion, than Ecu remembered. Those who had taken Kenna as an obese caricature of a stupid, crooked pol over the years had generally not survived in the political arena long enough to correct their thinking.

Now Kenna was on Seilichi, as the Emperor's hatchet man.

'It has been long.'

'Too long,' Kenna said, coming quickly to his feet and smiling. 'I have been sitting here, lost in thinking of the marvels of Seilichi.' Of course Kenna pronounced the word correctly. He still showed the regrettable love for flowery speech the Emperor had noted years ago. 'I should have found occasion to journey here many times, especially now that the Empire has returned.

'But . . .' He shrugged. 'Time creeps up and past all of us. And I have had my own concerns. You know that I am preparing my memoirs?'

'Those will be most interesting.'

Ecu was being more than polite – he was constantly wondering why humans had such a love for the convolutions of dishonest politics when, from his race's point of view, a direct approach was far more likely to work. Not that the Manabi ever allowed this belief to hamper their appreciation for circumlocution, nor their abilities to practice it. So, indeed, if those memoirs were in fact produced, Ecu would be fascinated by how many ways Kenna could find to avoid the simple fact that he was, and had been since he was a baby ballot-box-stuffer, Crooked to the Gunwales.

'But now I am here on business,' Kenna said, mock-mournfully. 'The business of the Eternal Emperor.' He slid a card from his pocket, and the Imperial emblem glowed to life, keyed to Kenna's pore patterns.

'Regarding Sten, I would imagine.'

'You imagine correctly.'

'Of course,' Sr Ecu said, 'I will render what service I can. I see no problem in cooperating, since my race's neutrality has never extended to a confessional seal about criminals – which Sten is, correct?'

'Of the worst order,' Kenna agreed. 'He betrayed the Empire – and for no reason that anyone can ascertain except personal ambition.'

Kenna tried to look pious, a laughable attempt. It was supposed, the Manabi knew, to look stupid, and the witness then encouraged to think Kenna the same, never noticing the razor gleam from his piggish eyes.

'Ambition . . . something that makes mockery of us all, as the poet said.'

'Sten,' Ecu mused, as if assembling his thoughts. 'I frankly know very little, since the time I spent in his company was rather . . . frantic, might be the correct word.

'The Tribunal and the privy council was far more on my mind than anything else. But, as I said, what help I may render, I shall. But I'm puzzled, frankly. Considering all the time Sten passed in Imperial Service, I would think your . . . I mean Imperial . . . records would be far more thorough, even considering that the greater percentage of his career was spent in . . . irregular pursuits.'

Kenna frowned – and it seemed this expression was honest. 'I thought so, too. But evidently not. Or else the Emperor needs to cross-correlate what records he has. Or, and this is the most likely, he's dredging for any scrap that can bring this traitor to the bar.'

'Where would you like to begin, then?'

'Would you consent to a brainscan? A machine and the finest technicians of Internal Security are aboard my ship.'

Ecu jolted, wingtips involuntarily twitching. A brainscan was not only the ultimate mental rape, but likely to produce longterm psychic damage or death, even when performed by the most highly skilled operator.

'I will not,' Ecu said firmly, after he recovered. 'While I have served the Emperor, I must officially remind you that I was never in his service, nor were any others in my race. And we have our own secrets, of course, which are not of the Emperor's concern.'

Kenna nodded acceptance and reached to a side table. On it were the refreshments the Manabi had provided – Kenna's favorite brandy from Dusable, a glass, and a tray of snacks, supposedly intended to sop up the affects of alcohol, actually chemically synthesized to compound them.

'The Emperor said you would decline, and told me I was not to press the point. He did, however, add – and this is off the record, so if you are recording this meeting you are requested to so cease – the following, and I am quoting directly:

'"When Sten is apprehended, tried, and brainscanned prior to execution, any being involved with him or his conspiracy, no matter if they're neutral, will be considered a personal enemy, and dealt with accordingly."'

'That,' Ecu said, feeling proud that his wing tendrils did not even flicker slightly at the threat, 'is not the most diplomatic statement I have ever heard the Eternal Emperor make.'

'These are not diplomatic times,' Kenna said. 'And he takes the threat of Sten and the others far too seriously to waste time with niceties. However, my personal apologies for the bluntness, even though I was merely the messenger. And I also wish to apologize for the amount of your time I am now going to consume, since the Emperor wants *everything*.

'I must now advise you that this conversation is being recorded. You have a right to counsel, legal advice, and medico-watch to ensure you are not under any influence, physical or pharmacological.'

'I understand, and thank you for the dual apologies,' Ecu said. 'But for me, at present, there is nothing but time. Shall we begin?'

He carefully began his story. He would tell it very slowly, with great exactness, and the tale would take several days.

And at the end of each day he would carefully check his story, Kenna's reactions, and what should come next with his own mentor, hidden far below the conference room in one of the Manabi's laboratories.

Rykor.

Chief (Investigative Division) Lisa Haines came suddenly awake – but made no move whatsoever.

First . . . ears.

Nothing.

Smell. Nothing.

What, then?

Motion. Her entire 'houseboat' moved slightly.

She opened her eyes a pinhole.

Moonlight filled the large single room of her home – a McLean-powered barge moored several hundred meters above one of Prime World's forest refuges.

The room was empty.

Her husband, Sam'l, snored gently beside her.

Haines's hand slid to the side of the bed. Down the side of the watertube mattress. Touched the butt of the miniwillygun. The always-loaded gun was in her hand and the safety slid off.

Again, the houseboat swayed.

Someone trying to climb up one of the mooring cables? Yes.

Haines was in bed/Haines was suddenly crouched, naked, combat stance, in the middle of the floor, gun ready. Confirmed. She was alone.

She snaked to an armoire, took out and pulled on a one-piece phototrophic coverall. The coverall, like the pistol, was strictly Imperial-issue, and not even a police chief like Haines was entitled to own either one. But, as always, cops don't follow the laws they enforce.

Haines had been expecting this.

Now to confirm.

She slid to the door leading out to the houseboat's deck, and opened it a notch. Then she took a pair of light-amplifying goggles from a hook beside the door and pulled them on.

Daylight. A little green, but daylight.

Out, onto the deck.

The houseboat swayed again.

Not yet. First worry about . . . she scanned the darkness of the hillside across from her. Nothing. She switched modes, into thermal imaging, and looked again. Ah. A tidy little glow over there. Several beings.

The command post, she speculated. That's what it would be, if what she had been anticipating was in fact happening.

Or else the kingpins, allowing for the other possibility – that some of the gangsters she had harassed and crucified regularly over the years were coming to wreak revenge. Unlikely. Crooks only looked for nonprofitable vengeance in the livies.

Haines switched the goggles back to light amplification, went flat, and slid forward, peering over the edge.

Quite correct.

Someone . . . three someones . . . were coming up the mooring cable. Skilled climbers – but as they climbed, the cable unavoidably swayed, and the houseboat jerked minutely. All three someones wore identical phototropic coveralls, combat vests, and holstered pistols. Some kind of special-ops team.

All right, Haines thought. What you were hoping wouldn't happen is happening. You've worried about it from the time you heard Sten was named traitor – she came close to goddamning her ex-lover – and there is no way you are going to stand still for a brainscan or any of the other lovely devices you have heard Internal Security is using for 'deep interrogation.' Not you. And *by God*, not Sam'l.

A whole clotting lifetime being on the right side of the law, and just because of a minor love affair – all right, a major love affair – way back when and you're now a crook.

A completely unknown fragment drifted through her mind, translated from some long-forgotten tongue: '. . . where every cop is a criminal/and all the sinners saints . . .'

She shot the first climber in the face.

The crash of the detonating round echoed into the stillness, and the man dropped soundlessly, straight down, cleaning off the second infiltrator as he fell.

A scream, and Haines was rolling back to the doorway, flipping open the cover of what appeared to be an outdoor power socket but was a switch, switch closed, and . . . thank the Lord for the blessing of paranoia – the three saddle charges blew her mooring cables in half.

The third climber shouted in surprise, then fell silently to his death as the houseboat, unanchored, lifted like a balloon under the power of its antigrav generator.

Now, Haines thought, let us hope these 'nappers didn't want to disturb my neighbors' sleep with nasty old overhead aircraft, because we're screwed if there's top cover.

Inside, she heard grunts as Sam'l woke, crashed to his feet, and evidently walked straight into a side table.

'What the hell . . .?'

He was no Sten, no cop, no soldier, took half an hour to grunt awake enough to be able to hit the ground with his hat, and Haines loved him for all of those reasons . . . and a lot of others.

The nightwind caught the houseboat and sent it spinning over the forest. Haines heard crashes from inside as paintings came off the wall and plates shattered. She went inside, one hand steadying against a wall as the boat started drunken sashays through the air.

'A kidnap team,' she announced, even though in his present stupor it would probably take Sam'l several minutes to define kidnap. 'All of them in uniform. Imperial thugs.'

Sam'l, astonishingly, was suddenly quite alert.

'Oh,' he said. Then nodded.

'Well, I suppose it had to happen,' he said. 'Although I wish we could think of something more . . . active to do than just running.'

'First we run,' Haines reminded him. 'Then we hide. We'll have all the time in the world to figure out paybacks.'

She crossed to a chest, opened it, and took out two personal 'chutes' – steady-drain McLean packs with harness that would drop an average-weight human safely from any distance up to two kilometers before the batteries went dry.

When the houseboat hit about four klicks altitude, they'd go out the door and free-fall half the distance to the ground, targets too tiny – she hoped – to be picked up by Imperial sensors. Sam'l was the one who'd taught her that sport.

Time enough for paybacks. Yes. With luck there would be, she thought, but didn't say it aloud as she helped Sam'l into his rig.

Even now, even in the darkest part of the night, the tower still was a muted rainbow at the end of the gorge.

Inside, Marr and Senn slept uneasily, curled around each other. They looked almost the same age as they had been years earlier, when they were *the* Imperial caterers and Sten a young captain, in charge of the Emperor's Gurkha bodyguard. Perhaps their fur had darkened slightly, to a deeper gold. But nothing else had changed. The two Milchen, financially stable in their retirement, still loved beauty and love itself. The lovers were not only Sten's friends, although it had been years since they had seen him, but they had thrown the Grand Party after which Haines and Sten had become lovers.

Marr suddenly woke. Sat up. Senn whistled questioningly, huge eyes blinking.

'It was but a dream.'

'No. A gravcar. Coming up the valley.'

'I see nothing. You were just dreaming.'

'No. There. Look. It's coming without lights.'

'Oh dear. I feel those fingers touching my soul. Cold. Cold. At night, without lights. If it stops, we do not answer.'

Marr didn't respond.

'I said, we do not answer. In these times, with the Emperor not as he was, only a fool goes to the door after midnight. Those who move by night are not friends.'

Silence. The gravcar had stopped outside.

'The cold is stronger. Don't you feel it?'

'I do.'

'The bell. Who is it?'

'I don't know.'

'Don't turn on the lights. Maybe they will go away.'

Marr's slender hand moved through the air, and, outside, four single beams marked the parking area.

'You fool,' Senn snapped. 'Now they know. Who are they?'

Marr peered out. 'Two. They are human. One is a man. The other a woman. I don't know the man . . . the woman looks familiar.'

'Yes. She does. Marr. She is carrying a gun. Turn out the light.'

'I know her,' Marr announced. 'She is that policeperson. She called me on some vague pretense just days ago. I wondered.'

'Which police . . . oh. Haines.'

'Yes. The one who loved Sten.'

'Then she is a fugitive. The Emperor must want to question anyone who knew him. And she must know something, or else she would not flee.'

'Senn. Think. Would you not run from that horrid Poyndex? The one who personally murdered Mahoney?'

'Turn out the lights. Come back to bed. We do not play human politics.

'See? Now they are turning away. Someone else will take them in.'

Marr did not answer. He thought he could hear the crunch of footsteps outside and below, in the parking area.

'I once was told,' he said slowly, 'by a human, that if he was ever given the choice of betraying a friend or betraying his country, he hoped to be courageous enough to be a traitor.'

The two leaned close to each other, their antennae twining. Senn pulled back.

'All right,' he said. 'But don't try to talk to me about loyalty and all those other complicated human emotions. You just want to have houseguests to cook for again.'

His hand moved in a semicircle.

And suddenly the tower of light glowed in full life, welcoming Haines and Sam'l.

Chapter Seven

Once again the Eternal Emperor's chambers were jammed, the air freshers working overtime as he barked orders to the flowing stream of staff members.

'Avri.'

'Yes, Your Highness?'

'What's the status on the K-B-N-S-O operation?'

'Not good, sir. I've got our best spin doctors working on it. But nobody's buying our angle.'

'Which is?'

'That it was a quote tragic accident end quote triggered by Sten's attack on the station. That we were merely trying to quote protect the innocent civilians end quote.'

'Change "innocent civilians" to attempting to "limit collateral damage."'

'Thank you, sir.'

'Then I want you to set a backfire.'

'Like what, sir?'

'Easy. The airwaves belong to the Empire. Which means me. Inform them I'll yank their licenses to lie if they don't start telling more of mine.'

'Yessir . . .'

'You sound doubtful. What else is bothering them?'

'They're scared. Afraid Sten will raid them next.'

'No problem. Anders.'

'Yes, Your Majesty.'

'Hustle up some spare ships and troopies. I want all the major Imperial broadcasters ringed. I want a net a flea couldn't get through, okay?'

'Yessir. But we don't have that many to spare. What with the budget cutbacks. And the heavy commitments to help stabilize our weaker allies. Then there's the garrison forces. We've got them spread all over—'

'*Find* them, Anders. Just find them.'

'Yessir.'

'One other thing.'

'Sir?'

'I'm not forgetting your fine Italian hand in this station foul-up.'

'No sir. I take full responsibility, sir.'

'Shut up, Anders. And while you're doing my bidding, I want you to think about a nice post I can send you to after this whole thing is over. An island, someplace. A cold island. And make it small, while you're at it. No more than a kilometer in any direction. Now, get busy.'

'Uh . . . Yes, Your Majesty!'

'Walsh.'

'Yes, Your Highness.'

'What's the status on the AM2 tax bill?'

'I'm not sure we have enough votes to carry Parliament, sir.'

'What's the hangup?'

'The Back Benchers are arguing that the tax increase goes against your promise.'

'Big deal. They break promises all the time. Why can't I? It goes with the territory. Which is politics. Which is nothing more than lies and damned lies.'

'Yessir. But they don't feel the same now they've given up their independence. We offered AM2 at bargain-basement prices if they became Dominions of the Empire.'

'Sure, I remember. I also remember that I'm the boy with the hand on the AM2 nozzle. I'm the sole supplier. Ergo, I get to set the price.'

'Yessir. I know that, sir. It's the other members of Parliament. They say they've all got deficits that are choking them.'

'Well, tell them they're going to have to join the club. Because that's why I've got to have my tax increase. My treasury is tapped out. Nary a bone in the cupboard. I can't believe those people. Clot, I'm the one with the whole burden. Without me, they've got zip. I figured six years of being under the thumb of the privy council would have proven that.'

'True, Your Highness. But I've heard some whispers in the halls that maybe things weren't so bad, uh, when you, uh, were gone, and the privy council was running things.'

'Don't worry about whispers in the hall . . . Kenna?'

'Yes, Your Majesty.'

'I want you to help Walsh on this.'

'Delighted, sir. As always.'

'I want Dusable behind me when it comes to a vote. I want a big push. And I want a bigger vote margin. Unanimous would be nice, but I'll settle for 99 percent.'

'I'm not sure that's possible, sir.'

'Dusable is one fat and sassy system right now, is it not?'

'Yes, Your Majesty.'

'I've made you guys a principal AM2 depot. Which means you get to skim all you like.'

'I protest, Your Majesty. The good citizens of Dusable—'

'Knock it off, Kenna. If you weren't stealing I'd be suspicious. Point is, I've been giving you all the goodies. Made you one of the top jewels in my crown. Now it's time to pay the piper. And get out the vote.'

'I'll do my best, sir.'

'That's not good enough. Theft is required. And arm breaking. I want this Parliament brought into line. At least until it recesses. I can always pack it with more of our own people afterward.'

'Consider it done, Your Highness.'

'Bleick.'

'Yessir.'

'You're working with Poyndex on that high priestess character, aren't you? What was her name?'

'Zoran, sir. High priestess of the Cult of the Emperor.'

'That's the fruitcake I mean.'

'Yessir. I have that assignment.'

'What's going on? I was expecting a few godheads in my pocket by now. I badly need to boost my image with the ignorant masses. Damn, but the poor can be hard on a ruler. We've got riots all over the place. Bad for business.

'A few temples built in my honor could restore faith in the economy, and seriously trim this depression.'

'To be frank, sir . . . I haven't had much luck with the woman. She's either not available, or, when she is, she talks in circles and giggles a lot. I think she's crazy.'

'Like a fox, Bleick. She's a nut, for sure. But she's smarter than most people in this room. Tell her I'm getting tired of pouring credits into her organization. With no return.'

'I spelled that out for her, sir. In absolute no-nonsense terms.'

'Hmmm. I smell a skunk. Fine. Forget her. Exile her or something. Tell her it's time for her to reflect on the Spheres. Tell Poyndex to have her sent to her proper reward. Something quick, and not painful. Then suborn her second-in-command.

'If that doesn't work, keep going down the list until you find somebody with big eyes and a small brain. Talk to Poyndex. He'll know what I mean.'

The door hissed open. Poyndex entered – with the pinched bad-news look on his face again.

The Eternal Emperor made immediate motions for his staff to make themselves scarce. They did.

'Sit.'

Poyndex obeyed, sitting stiff in his seat, almost at attention. The Emperor pulled a bottle of Scotch from his desk. The ancient Earth whisky had taken him years to reinvent. He poured a glass and braced himself with a long swallow. The Emperor pointedly didn't offer Poyndex any.

'Okay. What's happening this time?'

'It's Sten, sir.'

'I figured that. What about him?'

Poyndex leaned forward across the desk. The man was honestly bewildered. 'Sir. My people have been over every connection you gave us a hundred times. And we've come up with many more. But it's no dice, sir. No one, but no one, knows him, sir. Except in passing. We've brainscanned people. Had them worked over by experts. But as near as I can tell . . . Sten doesn't have a friend in the Empire.'

The Emperor *woosh*ed, then took another heavy slug of his drink. Poyndex noted that his once-clear features were getting puffy and there was a small red web of a blemish beside his nose.

'That doesn't scan,' the Emperor said. 'Even the lowest being in the Empire has at least *one* friend. Even the misguided attract their own. Or, I should say, *especially* the misguided.'

Poyndex turned his hands palms up. 'It's true, just the same, sir. The real trouble is, with all the records on Sten and Kilgour wiped . . . we don't have much to go on.'

'Except my memory.'

'Which is excellent, sir. The few breaks we've had have all come from you.'

The Emperor stared at Poyndex, reading his face. No. The man wasn't catering to his ego. He meant it. The Emperor wondered for a moment if maybe he was beginning to lean on Poyndex more than was healthy.

Beings could get very dangerous ideas . . . if one depended on them too much. Only Poyndex, for example, knew of the bomb that had once been planted in his gut. A bomb wired to that . . . that *thing*.

That great ship, out there beyond the Alva Sector, through the discontinuity.

The great ship that controlled him.

The Emperor's mind shuddered at the thought of the ship with the white room and the disembodied voice that spoke to him.

He shivered. Took another drink. Then he remembered. Correction: former controller. It was Poyndex who'd set up the special surgical team that had removed the bomb from his body and cut his link with the controller.

Another drink. Yesss. Much better now. He was the last Eternal Emperor. Until the Empire's end . . . Which would be?

Never.

He pulled himself together. 'There's only one thing to be done,

then,' he said. 'Somehow, I have to make more time. Get an interrogation team on standby. Every spare second I have, I'll devote
to my memories of Sten. Any detail the team digs up from me,
you can get cracking on immediately.'

Poyndex hesitated. 'Are you sure that's wise, sir?'

The Emperor frowned. 'I *know* it's not wise. I've already fallen
into the jimmycarter, for crying out loud. Micromanaging every
detail in my empire. Next thing you know, I'll be going over the
damned new year's greeting list with Bleick. But . . . dammit . . .
what choice do I have?'

'Sten is just one being, Your Majesty,' Poyndex said. 'Let us
deal with him.'

'I can't take that chance. Sten is the symbol of everything that's
gone wrong. Citizens have no faith. They won't follow orders.
They question my every pronouncement. When I'm the only one
who really cares about them.

'Who else can take the long view? I mean the *really* long view.
I see things not in years, but generations.'

The Emperor fell silent a moment. 'No. This is something I
have to do,' he finally said. 'Damn his eyes!' And the Eternal
Emperor drained the glass.

Chapter Eight

Home.

It was strewn across a thousand thousand kilometers of space,
a slowly whirling sargasso of industrial junk.

Vulcan.

Sten stared at the ruins through his suit's faceplate. The sound
of his breathing seemed loud.

This was the hellworld where Sten had been born, an artificial
factory planet built and run as a violent, dangerous industrial

plant by The Company. His parents, Migrant/Unskilled laborers, and his brothers and sisters had died here, killed by an executive's callous decision about secrecy.

The boy that was Sten exploded into futile rebellion. He was caught, and sentenced to Exotic Section, an experimental area where the workers were assured of a slow, painful death. But Sten survived. Survived, learned to fight, and – his fingers touched the deathneedle sheathed in his arm – 'built' his knife from alien crystal.

He had escaped Exotic Section, and become a Delinq, living in the secret ducts and deserted storehouses of the planet, trying to stay one theft ahead of The Company's Sociopatrolmen and brainburn. He had met Bet here, his first real love. And here he had been saved from death by Ian Mahoney, coldcocked after a blown raid and drafted into the Imperial Guard.

Mahoney had again 'volunteered' him – this time from infantry assault training into Mahoney's own covert force: Mantis – where he learned the dark alleys of intelligence and the darker skills of secret violence. How to kill any being without leaving a mark. Or, more importantly, how to seduce or corrupt them into your service, without them ever realizing they'd been used.

And then Mahoney had sent him back to Vulcan with Kilgour and the rest of his Mantis Team. Mission: destroy the man who killed Sten's family.

His first great success. In the course of that destruction, Sten, three ETs and three humans, including Ida the Gypsy, had created and led a planetwide revolution.

That mini-rising brought in the Imperial Guard, and Sten's team came out, Sten himself on a life-support system.

He had never found out what happened afterward to Vulcan. And he had never wanted to know. He assumed that new management had come in Vulcan as an only slightly less lethal factory.

Evidently not, he thought, looking at the shambles in front of him. Or, anyway, not for very long. Even if it was needed for defense during the Tahn war, the privy-council era would have made Vulcan unprofitable – AM2 had simply become too rare and expensive to waste running a heavy-industry vacuum-based plant.

Vulcan had been abandoned, looted, and gutted. At its height it resembled a junkyard anyway – factories, quarters, and warehouses had been built, used, and discarded without being wrecked out.

But now it looked as if the gods of Chaos had looked on man's work, found it amateurish, and decided to improve matters.

Somewhere in this scatter would be – or so Sten hoped – whatever secret Mahoney had guided him toward.

At first, when Sten considered Mahoney's cryptic shout, he had thought of Smallbridge – the world Sten had bought some years earlier that was the only home he had ever known, besides Imperial Service.

Improbable. If Mahoney meant 'home' to be something useful to Sten – best theory: a weapon against the Emperor – he would not have stashed it in a place known to Sten's friends and enemies. Plus, to the best of Sten's knowledge, Mahoney had been on Smallbridge exactly once, and that was to warn him the privy council's goon squad was on its way. Not exactly time enough to build a hidey-hole.

No – not Smallbridge. It was far too obvious – even considering a purloined-letter device – for an Irisher as subtle as Mahoney.

And so Sten had forced himself to look up the interstellar coordinates to Vulcan and issue the orders. Even if nothing is here, he thought, this is an adequate temporary hideout. Destroying Thoresen had been a nonrecord Highest Authority mission, which meant Vulcan's importance and its relation to the Grand Traitor wouldn't show up, even on Sten's fairly accurate, highly classified Mantis file. Sten, experienced soldier that he was, was operating on the assumption that Mahoney's trick program hadn't worked and the Empire knew everything.

Of course, there's yet another possibility, his mind went on, spinning further into the double- triple- quadruple-think that eventually drives all counterintelligence types into the gaga ward. If the Emperor's got a real fine memory, and has put together his own private termination file, then he's just liable to remember the orders to destroy that mysterious Bravo Project on Sten's home world.

'Lad?'

Sten came back to the present thankfully, before he took this feedback nonthinking any further and attempted to disappear down his own throat.

'Ah dinnae want to seem like Ah'm noodgin', but i's gettin' on, 'n' Ah'm noo lookin't forward t' bein't a Resurrection Man. Shall we be gettin' at it?'

The Mantis soldiers who had died on Vulcan – Jorgensen, Frick, Frack – had been friends of Kilgour's as well. Alex himself had almost died, defusing a nuke.

Sten nodded, then realized there was no way Alex could see the gesture through the thick alloy helmet.

'Let's move.'

He touched controls and sent his suit jetting forward, on its tiny Yukawa drive, toward the main clump of wreckage – Vulcan's central core.

He was probably being foolish, but rather than use one of the deep-space worksuits – which were really small spaceships with a tiny bicycle-type seat and room enough to scratch when and where it inevitably itched – he and Kilgour had corseted themselves into fighting armor.

Vulcan, he had rationalized, might still have a McLean generator on, and some gravity. Or maybe its whirling bulk would give some weight, and it would be better walking rather than trying to fly the canister-shaped deep-space suits through the corridors.

Behind him the *Victory* hung, with the destroyer *Aoife* as screen. He had ordered the *Bennington* and *Aisling* to proceed directly to Sten's eventual final destination, after his minifleet had spent several ship-days after the raid pursuing nonrational trajectories, eluding pursuit.

Beyond the *Victory* he also had a full flotilla of tacships on CAP around Vulcan.

A trap was unlikely.

But Sten had not lived to his present age without being careful, native caution his training had amplified. One commandment, going back into prehistory and old Earth, was from an odd unit called Rogers' Rangers – 'Don't never take no chances unless you have to.'

The question now was, Where in this scrapheap was he to look?

'Sten.' It was Freston, back aboard *Victory*. He had demoted himself from captain to man the com board and was sitting on an open-miked tightbeam caster to the suited men.

'I've got a transmission.'

'Where?'

'From Vulcan. A very weak broadband signal's coming from the core. Weak, and erratic. Like an SAR beacon that's running dry. I've gotten a triangulation from the *Aoife*. On your orientation, it's at twelve o'clock, near the tip.'

'That was called the Eye,' Sten advised. 'Stand by.'

He braked the suit, killing velocity and steering toward Alex, aiming himself so his suit's own directional com pointed directly toward Kilgour.

'Ah heard,' Alex said, without preamble. 'An' thae raises more sarky questions thae i' answers. If Mahoney left somethin' aboot, p'raps he'd bolt a wee transponder to it. T' make life simpler f'r us.

'But Mahoney whidny hae left i' runnin', i' i's a truly deepy darky secret, aye? He would'a keyed it t' go off frae somethin' or someone when thae got close. Playin' Cold an' Warm wi' the bairns, as it were. Nae t' mention battery life an' such, which i' Freston's watchin' his gauges, seems to be runnin't doon.'

'Possibly,' Sten agreed. 'Which means that somebody else set it off.'

'Wi'out knowin' it or wi'out bein' able to retrieve th' goodies. Or th' whole thing's booby-trapped an' th' mad bomber had nae th' patience t' let us find his handiwork blind an' then blowin't ourselves oop.'

'Right. Which gives us something to really worry about – once we're onboard.'

'Aye. Noo. Home's been narrowed, assumin't we're thinkin't correct, an' yon beepitybeepity's noo a wild signal frae some bit ae forsook electronics.'

'Agreed. Home's somewhere in the Eye. Something that we knew about. Or I did, anyway. Our hideout – that old liner – was around there. Nope. DNC. Mahoney wouldn't know about that. Maybe his old office, when he was spying out the land, pretending to be a recruiter? Maybe – but that does not compute easily, either. Mahoney wouldn't chance us remembering where it was, which I don't . . . Oh clot,' Sten said.

'Aye. Th' main man. Duke, or Dynast, or wha'e'er he'd dubbed himself.'

'Baron. Thoresen.' That name he'd never forget. In a final duel, Sten had taken on the murderer of his family barehanded – and killed him.

His quarters had been just at the top of the Eye, in a palatial dome that covered Thoresen's office, garden, and quarters.

'That's it. But we'll not go in direct. Nor hang up here being big fat targets anymore.'

Sten put full drive on his suit and, Kilgour in his wake, eye-calculated a trajectory that would intersect Vulcan just above the old ship-porting area. He would not chance that dockyard – that was too easy to booby-trap.

To one side, as they flew 'over' Vulcan, was the great rip in the planet's skin where the laboratory that was Bravo Project had been until Kilgour's bombs went off.

That also meant that somewhere below Sten was the cramped apartment he had grown up in. For all he knew, the muraliv that haunted him might still be mounted on the wall, the snowy landscape on a frontier world that his mother had sold six months of his life for, a muraliv that had broken in less than a year. Sten had unconsciously duplicated that scene in reality on Smallbridge – a cluster of domes sitting in his planet's arctic regions.

No. He would not – could not – go there. It would be too much.

He shut that part of his mind off. They were closing on Vulcan.

Sten landed on a bare stretch of hull. Finger-point. Make me a door, Alex.

Kilgour took a prepared charge from a carrying case, extended its small legs, and clipped the charge to Vulcan's skin. He started a timer, then motioned Sten away. Alex, demolitions expert that he was, pushed off into space unhurriedly and hovered a safe few meters away.

The timer went to zero, and the charge blew, blasting a stream of molten metal through the hull in a widening cone. It was a violent but relatively silent way to B&E. No air *whoosh*ed out. Vulcan – or at least this part of it – had lost its atmosphere.

Kilgour the perfectionist then trimmed a few ragged edges, ripping them off with his hands. Massively strong heavy-worlder that he was, he almost certainly could have done it without the suit's pseudomusculature cutting in. But he felt lazy.

They winkled through the hole.

Blackness. Both of them turned on their helmet spotlights. They were in some kind of machine shop.

Sten pointed himself back through the hole.

'Inside,' he broadcast back to the *Victory*. 'No prob. Tag on. Moving.'

He set his suit's inertial navigation system as a guide toward the Eye, in the probable event of Vulcan's twisting corridors getting them lost, and they started out. His 'tag' – a transmitter broadcasting on an unlikely freq – would tell the *Victory* where, in this metal maze, they were.

Zero air, zero gravity.

It was quicker to use the suit's drive and 'fly' toward the Eye. Sten wondered what the seventeen-year-old Delinq that had been

Sten would have thought, given a bit of clairvoyance, seeing somebody actually fly inside Vulcan.

He would probably think it wonderful and then promptly figure out how to use the newly accessed dimension in a raid.

It was tempting to increase their speed, particularly when their course led through some of the huge open assembly lines. Tempting – but that could be quickly fatal if there *was* a trap. Or if something jagged lurked at the end of an insufficiently braked swoop.

They moved on, 'up' into the docking area. Huge ship-size airlocks yawned into vacuum, and fittings had been roughly cut or blasted off. The scavengers hadn't bothered to close the doors behind them.

A slideway – or where a slideway had been. Someone had ripped the alloy top away, exposing the aircushion plates below. The slideway led due 'north' – toward the Eye.

Suddenly there was a great gap, a rip of metal extending through several decks directly out into space. Here was where one of the Imperial assault ships had deliberately smashed into Vulcan's skin, making a breach for the Imperial Guardsmen to pour through.

'You should be within range of that broadcast,' Freston's voice whispered. 'Tune Six-Three-Kilo-Four.' Sten obeyed on a secondary com. He heard it. A whine that broke off now and again, and whose note rose and fell. It did, indeed, sound like a search-and-rescue transmitter whose power was about dry.

Now they were close to the 'top' of the Eye, close to Thoresen's dome.

Even though he wanted to go faster, Sten forced himself to slow. Ahead was a great door. One of the periodic emergency barriers – airlocks – intended to keep an accidental rupture from dumping Vulcan's entire atmosphere into space.

Alex started to push on it, then caught himself before Sten could warn him.

Resistance. How interesting. That probably meant there was atmosphere on the other side.

And then Six-Three-Kilo-Four fell silent.

The link to the *Victory* opened, and Freston began a transmission, probably to tell Sten what had just ceased happening.

'Received,' Sten said in a whisper. 'Break 'cast. Monitor. Do not transmit. Click code.'

He'd always known it couldn't be this easy.

Kilgour curled his hand, and his willygun slid down on its harness. A lifted eyebrow. Shall I blow the door, boss?

Headshake no. Motion – back.

Sten hit the cycle button.

Grindingly, the lock emptied its air back into the main chamber. He started forward, and Kilgour waved him back. Cover . . . and Sten did. Alex moved forward and ripped the door open, spinning back flat against the corridor's wall.

Nothing. Inside. They forced the outer door closed again.

Now they were well and truly trapped. Both of them shut off their helmet lights. Being an obvious target was one thing – there was no necessity to put a spotlight on the bull's-eye.

Cycle.

The grinding stopped, but the light that would signal ATMOS-PHERE EQUALIZED did not go on. Burnt out. Possibly.

Nor did the inner door open automatically.

Sten pushed at it, and it reluctantly slid aside.

They were in Thoresen's dome.

Both men were crouched on either side of the lock, weapons ready. Sten could feel his suit press against him from atmospheric pressure outside before it adjusted. So where had the atmosphere come from? Was Thoresen's dome built so well that it held air after being abandoned all these years? Not clottin' likely.

He looked at a gauge. Neutral gas, 75 percent; oxygen, 18 percent; garblegarble trace gases. Oh really. Half a percentage of carbon dioxide. Exhalations from an oxygen-breathing creature? Possibly.

Breathable – no gases analyzed.

Pressure half E-normal.

There was enough light from the stars and a far-distant sun through the dome's skylights for Sten to see without needing his helmet light.

Kilgour pointed and Sten saw the piled racks of empty oxygen containers. That was where the atmosphere had come from – a hand-carried flask at a time.

Thoresen's dome was huge. Envision a jungle, now petrified when it lost atmosphere sometime ago. A garden. Up ahead would be Thoresen's office/living chambers. Sten and Alex would have to fine-comb the dome, their task complicated because they had no idea what they were looking for – nor if it was even there.

Sten turned on an outside microphone and listened. Nothing. He of course did not chance opening his faceplate and breathing the dome's atmosphere, no matter what his suit's analysis told him.

He went into the chamber.

In front of him was the twisted, desiccated drought nightmare that had been Thoresen's lush forest.

Very strange, trying to move silently, as if he were walking point for an infantry patrol, deep in a planetary jungle. In a spacesuit. Toe first . . . touch, test the ground under you, heel down, full weight down, other foot lifted straight up, brought forward slowly, close to Sten's center of gravity . . . toe touching . . .

The dead boughs twisted up around him, agonized arms stretching for, never to reach, the far-distant stars.

A crunch. Sten tensed and looked down.

Gleaming bones.

He remembered. One of Thoresen's 'pet' tigers. The one he'd killed with a desperation thrust-kick with both legs, crushing its throat. Sten shivered. He was the one who should have died.

Kilgour followed Sten. He, too, looked down at the tiger's skeleton, then, without realizing it, at Sten's back. Clot, he thought. Ah heard th' story, but really didna believe it. Ah ne'er, ne'er woulda gone f'r it.

Somewhere across the dome, Sten heard a noise. Or thought he did.

He froze, waiting. Nothing. He chanced a look back at Alex. He could see Kilgour shake his head from side to side through the faceplate. He'd heard nothing.

Sten continued on.

He half expected to find Thoresen's skeleton next, rib cage shattered where his heart had been torn out, still beating. But the body would have been removed and given some kind of burial, or at least dumped into space.

Wouldn't it?

Here was the wall where Thoresen had hung his weapons collection, everything from an archaic flamethrower to a broadax. The racks were empty, weapons most likely souvenired by the victorious Guardsmen as they poured through the dome.

Over there. Thoresen's office. The huge slab that had floated, held invisibly up by McLean generators, was canted against one wall.

And then Baron Thoresen walked out of the gloom.

Sten's willygun was up, finger pulling through to full auto, mind screaming, *Goddammit, you aren't there, you aren't there you're dead goddammit or by Christ you're going to be because there aren't any ghosts full magazine right in the middle of that clotting robe, right between where those skinny arms are stretching out for my neck* . . .

He heard the baron's voice through the open mike:

'Don't kill me. Please don't kill me.'

A scratchy, wavery old being's androgynous voice.

One thousand out of one thousand normal people would have already opened fire. Nine hundred and ninety-plus Guard-trained combat-experienced soldiers would have, too.

Sten's finger came off the trigger.

'Don't kill me,' the old voice said again.

Sten's helmet light slashed on.

In front of him was an emaciated man, ancient skeletal claw arms and hands outstretched, trying to ward off the death he saw from the suited killer in front of him. The few strands of hair left sprayed wildly out above his head.

'I won't hurt you,' Sten managed.

The old man *was* wearing a set of Thoresen's formal robes, the same sort Sten had seen him wear once, when delivering the mock-pious funeral oration for his parents. Stolen from Thoresen's unlooted wardrobe?

Sten lowered his weapon.

Kilgour did not.

He crabbed sideways, around Sten.

'Who're you?'

His voice, amplified, boomed through the chamber. The old man winced.

'Please. Please. Not so loud.'

Kilgour brought himself back out from *Controlled Panic – Lethal Mode*, and his outside speaker control down as well.

'ID yourself.'

'I'm not anyone. I'm Dan Forte.'

'Where's your ship?'

'I don't have a ship. The others have the ship. They left me here. They said I had no right to live. They said I was . . . it doesn't matter what they said I was, does it.'

'Somebody stranded him,' Sten wondered. Alex nodded – he guessed so.

'Ah wonder whae th' lad did t' get marooned?'

'Maybe we don't *want* to know.'

'Aye. Dinnae y' turn y'r back on th' rascal.'

Kilgour went to Forte – the man flinched – and swiftly, expertly, checked him for weapons. 'He's clean, metaphoric'ly speakin't . . . but Ah'd noo be openin' m' faceplate t' hae a sniff.'

'How long have you been here, Dan?' Sten asked.

'Not long. Not long.' The old man started laughing, and then singsonging: 'A bottle here/A bottle there/A ratpack here/A ratpack there/Breathe it out/Breathe it in.' His singsong stopped.

'You know, the sun is going to die. They are going to kill it. The Tahn know things like that. What they know/They always know/What they do/They always do.'

'Laird hae' mercy,' Kilgour said. 'Th' puir clot's been here since durin't th' war!'

'And I watch,' Forte went on.

'I always watch.

'Take me with you. Please. Don't leave me. There was another man. He wore a suit. Like yours. He had a gun. Like yours. I was afraid to ask him. He had a gun. But I was young, then. And afraid of more.

'Now I'm not afraid. There's nothing to be afraid of. Is there?'

Kilgour let his sling snap his rifle back against his chest to carrying port arms.

'No, old 'un,' he said heavily. 'Thae's nae t' fright y'self. W're nae but friends.'

'That man,' Sten said carefully. 'Did he leave something here?'

Forte quivered.

'And Moses smote the rock twice . . . and the congregation drank . . . and the Lord spoke . . . because you believe me not, to sanctify me in the eyes of the children . . . ye shall not bring this congregation into the land.'

'Uh . . . we believe you, Dan.'

'Then strike ye against the wall!' Forte shouted, waving.

Alex and Sten looked at each other. Sten nodded. Alex shrugged, aimed his willygun against the wall Thoresen had hung his weapons on, and snap-fired four times. Once against each corner of the wall.

And it crumbled and fell, as one piece.

Behind the wall, high-piled in a hidden chamber that could have been built by Thoresen or Mahoney, was the Secret. Stack after stack after stack of identical file-storage cases.

Sten rushed forward. Knelt in front of one case. It was neatly labeled, in Mahoney's militarily perfect handwriting:

ASSASSINATIONS, SUCCESSFUL
Official Denials
Suppressed Evidence
Rumors Circulating Following
Personal Theories

Another case:

THE SECRET YEARS
System Politics
Murders Ordered
First AM2 Supplies Provided by
Philanthropic Foundation Institutes

Yet another:

THE 'CIBOLA' EXPEDITION
Scientific Journals – Expedition Suggested As Possibility
No Other Info Available
No Hard Data Could Be Found
Personal Theories Only

Sten realized what he was looking at.

He didn't know – and suspected Mahoney didn't either – if these cases held The Secret that would destroy the Eternal Emperor – or even A Secret that might help. But he *did* know these cases contained enough dangerous data for the Emperor to be willing to sacrifice most of the Imperial Guard to recover. These were the notes for the never-written biography.

After the Eternal Emperor had been assassinated by the privy council, Mahoney had found it expedient to retire, and begin plotting the destruction of the council. As a cover he announced that, in deep mourning for his old leader and friend, he would write the Eternal Emperor's complete biography. At first, just a cover. But as he had told Sten, Mahoney would have been quite happy being an archivist instead of a general, and so his files got larger and larger, more and more thorough.

The thought floated up: perhaps if Mahoney *had* become a researcher he would have lived longer. But he shut that idea out.

The cover had become a fascination, as Mahoney discovered that *all* biographies of the Eternal Emperor were fraudulent, either authorized or unauthorized. Deliberately false data had been given; incompetent writers, researchers, and foundations had been encouraged while capable ones were shunted aside.

Mahoney found many, many versions of given events, versions that had been deliberately created by the Empire and used as red herrings.

Sten had wondered what the Emperor had been trying to hide, and Mahoney had retorted, 'Damned near everything, from where he came from to how he got where he is . . . I'll just mention two of the murkiest areas, besides where the clot the AM2 is. First is that the son of a bitch is – or was, anyway – immortal.

'And the second thing is . . . he's been killed before.'

Sten had scoffed – and Mahoney had offered to show him the files sometime. But events moved too fast and too bloodily, and the one time Sten had thought about those files, he had decided they were certainly explosive, and that anyone interested in staying on the Emperor's fair-weather side would probably be wisest not even considering their existence.

Or, as the Z-grade livies put it, just after the scenarist had failed to come up with an even vaguely believable explanation for all the drakh he had come up with earlier, 'There are some things in this universe, boy, man was not meant to know.'

All right, Sten thought. But this time man's gonna find out.

Because Mahoney, in a way, died for these files.

Sten got to his feet. He started to key his com, to order the *Victory* to send down a cargo lighter and some strong deck apes. He – or somebody, anyway – would begin analysis when they reached their intended destination, Sten's intended base of operations.

'You're my friend, aren't you?'

Sten remembered Forte – and, when he called the *Victory*, he told them to send down a bubblepak stretcher, with the interior controls sealed.

Dan Forte, completely insane, would either be cured, if that was possible – and Sten would dedicate all resources he had to help – or else given a long, happy life in whatever luxurious asylum Sten could put him.

Because he had very possibly given Sten the keys to the Empire.

Chapter Nine

'Your success thus far has bordered on the miraculous,' Sr Ecu said.

'Correction,' Sten said. 'It's been nothing but a series of *real* miracles. But, I can't keep on counting on smiles from the gods. I need a goal. And a plan. All I've been doing is shooting and scooting in the dark.'

'I can see how operating without a plan would be especially disturbing to you, Sten,' Rykor said. 'You always were a being in search of structure.'

Sten laughed, unfazed by this instant bit of analysis from the Empire's most eminent psychologist. 'Another delusion destroyed. Here I always thought I was a real seat-of-the-pants kind of a guy.'

'Oh, but you are,' Rykor said. 'I remember the first profile I drew up on you. Your inventive skills were among the best I've ever seen. But you tend to be displeased if your actions must take place in a vacuum. It's a typical trait of most special-operations experts. You like the illusion of complete freedom. But there must be structure just the same.'

Water splashed as she eased her bulk in the tank. 'In the past, it was service to the Emperor that provided that structure.'

Sten shuddered. All too true.

'Guilt is not necessary in this situation,' Rykor said, reading him like a crèche-level fiche. 'It is my own misfortune to share some of these same traits. I too found comfort in the bosom of the Emperor.'

As Sten mulled this over, one of Sr Ecu's tendrils whiskered out to touch a hidden switch. A small 'bot bearing a tray churned out of an alcove. In a moment, Sten was gratefully slugging down stregg.

'I hate to sound like an old-fashioned dipsomaniac,' Sten said. 'But boy did I need that. Thanks.'

Sr Ecu's tendrils wriggled with humor. 'The circumstances cry out for inducements. Besides, Rykor and I are ahead of you. Appropriate stress relievers have been added to the atmosphere. As well as to that liquid our largish companion is lolling about in so casually.'

Rykor barked and ducked her head under the spiked water. She emerged again, lips parted between her big tusks in what Sten was sure was a grin.

'That's why I'm being so pedantic,' Rykor confessed. 'I tend to be pompous when I imbibe.'

'I see I have some catching up to do,' Sten said. He raised the stregg. 'Confusion to our enemies,' he toasted. He drained the glass and refilled it.

Although Sten's situation hadn't improved, he was feeling much better. It had little to do with the stregg.

He'd left his minifleet tucked away offsystem while he made this visit to Seilichi to seek Sr Ecu's counsel. Sten had immediately been whisked to the hidden chamber beneath one of the planet's Guesting Centers.

Finding his old friend Rykor waiting there was not only a surprise, but a bonus. Having two beings like Sr Ecu and Rykor on his side made him feel that the odds had shifted slightly in his favor. Now he figured he only had a ninety-nine percent chance of winding up quickly and horribly dead.

He gulped more stregg. As he did, a sudden thought jolted him. 'Sr Ecu, do you *usually* keep stregg on hand? Somehow I can't imagine that many diplomatic types with a lust for this evil Bhor brew.'

More tendril wriggling. 'No. It's for you. And you alone.'

Sten puzzled. 'I can't imagine why you'd keep it in stock. The last time we met, I rejected your invitation. I was pretty damned firm about what I intended to do next. Which was to get the clot out of the Emperor's way and bury myself somewhere. And mind my own business.'

He was referring to Sr Ecu's secret visit to the Altaics, bearing proof from Rykor that the Emperor had gone mad. The Manabi had urged his help. Sten had given him a definite no.

'I said I had faith in you. I laid in the supply of stregg as soon as I returned.'

'I am in a room full of beings,' Sten said, 'who know more about what I am going to do next than I do myself.'

Rykor woofed through her whiskers. 'Illogical. But understandable in the circumstances . . . Oh, brother. There I go being pedantic again . . . Still, I hope the thought gives you no distress.'

'No. I just hope the Eternal Emperor isn't as good at calling my shots as you are.'

There was no answer to this. Silence for a moment, as each being contemplated various sins and partook of his or her own favorite brand of poison.

'Back to that visit, Sr Ecu,' Sten finally said. 'I assumed at the time that when you asked for my help, you had something in the works.'

'Ah . . . The illusive plan,' Rykor burbled. Before Sten could react, she added, 'Which is a very natural assumption for two fugitives such as ourselves.'

She hoisted herself higher in the tank. Waved a flipper at Sr Ecu. 'You do have a plan, don't you, my dear friend? I would hate to think I was facing a life on the run. It's difficult to dodge about for someone of my needs . . . and size.'

Sten buried a sudden hilarious image of Rykor ducking in and out of dark alleys, hauling her tank behind her.

'Actually, I don't,' Sr Ecu said. 'I'm a diplomat. Not a soldier. And I fear this situation requires military action first. Negotiating, later.'

'The Emperor won't negotiate,' Sten said. Flat. 'Even before . . . when he was—' The word stuck in his throat.

'Normal?' Rykor completed it. 'How can a being with apparent immortality ever be normal? No. He was mad all along. I understand that now. Something only made his condition worse . . . A judgmental word, I realize. But I think it applies.'

'Here is the situation as I see it,' Sr Ecu said. 'I speak for the Manabi, now. All our progs come to the same conclusion. The Empire is finished. The future will be nothing more than a slow, miserable descent into chaos.

'We predict the bloodiest wars in the universe's history. Starvation and plagues on an unimaginable scale. A complete collapse of all societies and cultures. In the end, we will all end up where we began. As barbarians.

'All the progs call for only one solution. The Emperor must relinquish power. Quickly. Because all progs also indicate delay will produce the same disastrous results. To use diplomatic jargon,

"The window of opportunity is very small." We act now. Or it will soon close.'

Sten had been too battered by recent events to be shocked by this doomsday prognosis. It all made very tired sense. 'Fine. The window's open. How do we get through?'

'I have nothing I can dignify with the word *plan*,' Sr Ecu said. 'But I do have a proposal . . .'

'Thank God. Let's hear it.'

'All over the Empire, many beings feel exactly as we do. Perhaps all they need is encouragement. Now . . . You have forces at your command. What if you waged a guerrilla campaign? A series of blows that would arouse the citizens everywhere. Many of them might join us.

'When the pressure builds until the Emperor can no longer bear it, we make an offer. We demand he abdicate . . . or agree to a constitutional monarchy. There have been successful governments of that type in the past. He would be Emperor still. Have all the glory. But not total power.'

Sten's hopes sagged. 'We don't have a prayer for that,' he said. 'You're right. Sr Ecu. You're no soldier.

'Here's the reality. The Emperor holds *all* the cards. The only reason I've kept my head on my shoulders so far is because he's still in a reactive position.

'He may be mad, but he's certainly the smartest being I've ever met. The Empire's enormous. So it takes a very long time to come up to speed. If the Emperor wants to throw a punch, thousands and thousands of details have to be dealt with first.

'But, believe me, when that punch lands – which it will, and I guarantee he won't miss – we'll all be bloody smears on the pavement.'

Rykor rolled in her tank, spilling water over the side. 'He's right, Sr Ecu. I've lost count of the number of operations the Emperor has consulted me on. And that was how it always came out in the end.'

'Another flaw,' Sten said, 'is even if we could bring that much pressure to bear, he'd never agree to step down now. Much less share power. Why should he? He's the Eternal Emperor. Practically a god to some beings.'

'No wonder,' Sr Ecu said, very grim. 'He appears immortal. A key definition of godhood as I understand it.'

'I really doubt that,' Sten said. 'No one can be immortal. Claudius proved that.'

'But we all saw what happened when the privy council struck,' Sr Ecu protested. 'All over the Empire, billions witnessed him die. Then . . . six years later . . . we were there to greet him, you and I, when he stepped off that ship. As if he had risen from the dead.'

'Mahoney said it's happened before,' Sten said. 'Several times. And each time he was assassinated, according to Ian, there was a very large explosion. Just like this last time. As if he had a bomb implanted in his body.

'Also, each time he was quote killed endquote, he returned approximately three E-years later. This time it was six. The longest it has ever been.'

'But you don't believe our late friend?' Sr Ecu said.

'I have to admit Ian knew more about the Emperor than any other being alive. I have whole cases of research he compiled aboard my ship. When there's time, we plan to go through it. See if there are any weaknesses we can uncover.

'But as far as immortality goes . . . No. I don't believe it. He's as human as I am.'

'Then how do you explain what happened?' Sr Ecu asked.

'I don't,' Sten said. 'The historical facts say it occurred. Natural facts say it can't. I'll stick with nature over history every time. History has been known to lie.'

'Now I know what the Christians were envisioning when they invented Hell,' Rykor said. 'We are living it. And are doomed to stay here until the end of time. And after listening to Sten, I see no possible solution.'

Sten sipped absently at his drink. Scattered thoughts were beginning to coalesce. He slammed the glass down. 'We're going to try, dammit!'

'But how?' Sr Ecu wanted to know. 'I'm afraid your argument has convinced me. I'm with Rykor. There is no hope.'

'Maybe just a sliver,' Sten said. 'But forget about trying to make His Highness see reason. Emperors, he's told me time after time, don't need to *see* reason. They *are* the reason.

'Therefore, we either have to capture him . . . or kill him.'

'This is the part I always like,' Rykor burbled. 'Goal setting. It makes one feel so satisfied.'

Sr Ecu said, 'But you just explained – quite logically, I should add – that the Emperor is too powerful for us to defeat.'

'We have to keep making his size work for us,' Sten said. 'Keep him in a reactive position as long as possible.' He drummed his fingers on the table. 'If we can draw his forces out . . . stretch them to the limits . . . then . . . in theory . . . size won't matter. We look for a hole – or make one, dammit – and punch through. We don't have to take all the pieces. We only need to kill the king.'

'Assuming all these impossible things become possible,' Sr Ecu said, 'we are still left with the same dilemma as the privy council.

'Without AM2, the Empire will collapse. You know as well as I that all modern industry and transport is based on that substance. And only the Emperor knows its source.'

'The privy council spent six years trying to find it,' Rykor agreed. 'And they didn't come close.'

'I've thought about that before,' Sten said, remembering a late-night talk with Cind after they had first suspected the Emperor had gone mad. 'I'm not so sure it's that bad a fate. To live without AM2, I mean. When we were running out – during the privy council's reign – things were bad, true. But at least a whole lot of beings were learning to fend for themselves.'

'It will be the end of interstellar travel,' Sr Ecu said. 'Which means we will all quickly become strangers again.'

Sten shrugged. 'Maybe it'll be good for us. Starting all over again. Besides, maybe someday somebody'll figure a way to synthesize AM2.'

He filled his glass with stregg. 'Of course, it'd be easier if I can get him alive. Toast his toes, or something. To get the secret of AM2 out of him.'

Rykor shifted her bulk. 'One large problem . . . just to add to the others. What if you're wrong about the immortality aspect? What if there's another big blast – I'm assuming you'll take this in consideration and stay at a safe distance – and he disappears. Only to return. A few years later.'

'I still think it's a trick,' Sten said. 'Sleight of hand. Or maybe he does it with mirrors. Whatever. If I can pull this chess match off – and pin his royal behind – I promise you that whatever cosmic misdirection he's been pulling won't make me look the other way.'

'I see no other choice,' Sr Ecu said. 'Speaking for the Manabi – and I do have that authority – I pledge our complete support.'

'I'll need it,' Sten said. 'I'd appreciate it if you can lay the diplomatic groundwork. Obviously with total secrecy.'

'As a matter of fact,' Sr Ecu said, 'I put out a quiet word or two already.

'There are many natural allies . . . the kind that come with some successes. Your attack on the broadcast station was a good start. Actually, the fact that you are still eluding the Emperor's minions is an even better one.'

'I'll try to keep it up,' Sten said dryly.

'What about me?' Rykor asked. 'How can I assist in this grand crusade?'

She burped daintily. 'My, but that's an interesting potion, Sr Ecu. I must acquire your recipe.'

Sten rose to his feet. 'Rykor, my gentle sot, you're coming with me. We're going to put that tricky brain of yours to work skewering the Eternal Emperor.'

'Ah ha. I fight at last. To arms! To arms!'

When they rolled her tank aboard the *Victory*, Sten's newest gallant warrior was snoring blissfully.

Chapter Ten

'We appear,' Sten observed, 'to be trapped.'

Cind grunted at him, still recovering her breath.

'Was *this* on the aerial?'

'Negative. Or if it was, I didn't pick it up on the viewer.'

'Doesn't matter, really. Other than we're going to have to do some serious backtracking.'

He slid out of his heavy pack, nearly falling on the steep icy slope. Backtracking? He glanced behind him.

Way, way, *way* down below, he could see the double herringbone tracks of their skis, leading up the slopes toward this clotting excuse for a mountain they were stuck on. About two kilometers before, the gradient had become too steep, and they had strapped their skis to their packs and put on crampons. A klick after that, the two of them had roped up as the grade grew steeper still.

Two klicks . . . one kilometer . . . that was the distance in a direct, near-vertical line. In actual travel, they had been off their skis since just after dawn, and the day was getting late. And they had better reach a decision on what to do next quickly – Sten would rather not spend the night in a sleeping bag that he would have to anchor to keep from sliding off the mountain.

If for no other reason than that he had designs on Cind's virtue . . .

Sten had arrived at his planned base of operations – the Bhor home worlds in the Lupus Cluster – without encountering any Imperial warships. Next, he would prepare his specific campaign and go to war.

He still had to get approval for using their worlds from the Bhor Council. But at least he had been greeted with cheers, invitations to drunken feasts, and volunteers who wanted to join him killing someone, anyone.

However, it took time for the Bhor elders to assemble, and even longer for them to reach a decision, given the Bhor tendency to endlessly explore any aspect of anything – all spokesBhor welcome. Which was probably a legacy from the severe lack of entertainment in their primitive days during long arctic nights.

Rykor herself had wanted some time and privacy to consider what could be done, from her perspective, against the Empire.

Neither set of Sten's potential allies had materialized. Not that there was any guarantee they would – both the Rom and Wild's smugglers might have realized an alliance with Sten was more likely to produce death than freedom.

And Sten's troopies – from his embassy assistants to his Bhor and Gurkha heavies to the Imperial sailors – had suffered through a very long tour. Essentially no one had had any time off since they had arrived in the Altaics. Even the Gurkhas were tired and weary of blood.

Tired beings make mistakes, and Sten could afford none.

He spread his four ships out among the Wolf Worlds, hid them well on rural airports, and gave his troops some R&R. Sten worried his presence among the Bhor would be discovered by the inevitable Imperial agents, but Kilgour had told him not to fash. He already had a Plot, and would take care of that little matter before his own vacation. Which involved Otho, vast amounts of stregg, and whatever trouble he could get into.

Cind had the op order for Operation Vacation already drafted. A conventional lover might have looked for tropical oceans and romantic islands with ten-star resorts and twenty bow-'n'-scrapers for each guest. But Cind was a descendant of the Jann, 'had grown up among the Bhor, and was a hard, experienced field soldier. To her, vacations meant the wilderness – and Sten's own ideas weren't that different.

The Bhor home planet was still glacial, even though the Bhor had reluctantly removed some of the glaciers as civilization and the birthrate increased. Scattered across the world were volcanic 'islands' – oases in the midst of freeze. Most of them had been settled aeons ago by the Bhor, but there were still a few that were unpopulated.

Cind had planned on kidnapping Sten and taking him to one of those, and had been trying to figure out which of the possible areas could provide the best skiing and even some winter climbing. Sten had taught Cind rock scrambling, and she was determined to become at least his equal and, she hoped, his master.

She had found something better on a recent aerial photomosaic. Not on any map. Completely unknown. All that was necessary to get there was to grab a pilot and a gravsled and they could be there in an hour.

Cind sneered. That, too, was no vacation. Getting there was half the fun.

And so, carrying packs heavy enough to give them the trail staggers, they had Kilgour drop them off where the dirt path ended, with a promise to return in five days to pick them up – or start the search parties in motion.

Among the reasons their packs were so heavy was that neither Sten nor Cind fancied carrying dried rations – they could stay in the barracks and on duty and get ratpacks. They were willing to break their backs carrying some other, minor creature comforts.

Their route on skis through the foothills to the base of the mountain. Where the mountain steepened, they would follow the course of a generally frozen river upward, through a gorge, to Cind's secret spot. Since the maps of the wilderness were rotten, they would navigate from the aerial.

And so it had been – until they reached this place not too far below the mountain's summit, where the river went vertical, and became thirty meters of frozen-solid waterfall. They were trapped.

This was a helluva fix she had gotten him into, he thought. And so observed.

'Shut up,' Cind said helpfully. 'I'm trying to figure out if we can slither back down this slope to that ravine we passed an hour or so ago. And maybe go up that to the summit. Then we could drop back down to where we want to go.'

'That sounds like work.'

'Stop whining.'

'I am not whining. I am sniveling. How much rope do we have?'

'Seventy-five meters.'

'Dammit,' Sten swore. 'See if I ever play climbing purist again. Right now a couple of cans of climbing thread, jumars, and a grapnel would be welcome. Or a stairway. But oooo-kay, we'll do it the hard way.'

He unclipped from the rope, set his pack down where it hope-fully wouldn't start sliding all the way back down to the foothills, reroped his harness, took a deep breath, and started climbing.

Up the ice of the waterfall.

'I don't like this,' he muttered. And he didn't – the only reason Sten knew that ice cubes could be climbed was because he had seen it done once in a livie and also because he had once spent a weekend with one of his instructors in Mantis – and whatever happened to her, he wondered – who had been a nut on climbing waterfalls when the temp went below zed Centigrade.

He had come off twice and had to be near-hoisted to the top, he remembered. No. His memory was wrong. None of the four of them had made it that long and bruised weekend.

Follow Cind's advice. Shut up.

It wasn't that bad, he thought. No worse than, say, dangling by your hands and having to do a pull-up every two minutes.

At least the ice is good and frozen. Don't have to worry about any kind of a spring thaw.

And you've got a good place to stand every now and then. As he was doing at the moment.

'What's that called?' Cind wondered from five meters below him.

'Suicide,' Sten panted. 'Front-pointing.'

His good place to stand consisted of two front metal spikes of his crampons – alloy plates clamped to his boots that had vertical two-centimeter-sided spikes around their edges and hori-zontal ones sticking straight out from the toe.

One foot suddenly *skriiich*ed out of the ice, and Sten went back to dangling. He twisted back and forth for a while, getting the hang of things, did another pull-up, reached out for a hand-hold, found a handjam, kicked in his free boot. Half a meter farther up.

Two wheezes, and try it again.

And again. And again.

Eventually, there was no ice above his hand to grab, and he flailed a little. Hand moved to one side. A rock projection. Rock? Such as no more waterfall?

No more waterfall.

Sten pulled himself to blessedly level ground, and rested. Then he tied off, and shouted down to Cind.

First came the packs, tied to the rope and hand-over-handed up. More wheezing. Not only getting old, but old and weak, Sten thought.

Now for Cind. He waited – in spite of an impatient shout – until he'd gotten *all* his wind back. He wouldn't mind losing a pack, but . . .

Cind tied on.

'I've never done this before,' she shouted.

'All the girls say that.'

Cind started climbing. Naturally, Sten thought in some disgust, she's a natural. She swarmed up the waterfall as if it were liquid and she an Earth salmon in spawning season. Nor was she breathing very hard at the top.

'I didn't know you could even *do* that.'

'All the girls say that, too.'

Sten shouldered his pack. Helped Cind on with hers. They were next to a frozen pool, rocks sticking through the ice. Sten noticed the ice looked hazy the further back it got.

Just ahead of them – not more than fifty vertical feet – a cloud drifted toward them from a draw. Wonderful. Now they'd be climbing in a fog.

Sten was wrong: the rest of the climb – a gentle walk on level ground – took only four minutes.

They moved through the draw, into a winter paradise. The draw opened into a tiny valley. Shrubs. Grass. Wildflowers.

'Well, I'll be go to hell,' Sten marveled. To one side of the valley a hot spring bubbled, its water flowing across the minimeadow and joining the larger river, still hot enough to melt the ice. Pools dotted the course of the spring's flow, and they were anywhere from boiling to frigid, the farther away they were from the spring.

Sten thought it was almost worth the climb.

The steaming springs drew them – but both of them knew the unchangeable ritual: first shelter, then fire, then food, then fun.

Shelter was easy – snap three sets of shock-corded wands
together, slide them through slots, and their tiny dome tent was
up. They staked it down for security. Fire was also not a problem
– their stove was a Mantis-issue item no larger than Sten's
palm. But it was AM2-fueled and could run at full blast for at
least a year without a recharge. Sten took it from his pack and
set it near the tent, between a circle of small rocks that his
small fold-up grill would sit on. Food? They skated on that
one for the moment – their muscles were sorer than their bellies
empty.

Or at least that was the pretext.

'Damn, but these rocks are cold.'

'Of course they're cold. Get in here where it's warm.'

Sten, naked, slid into the pool near Cind.

'What,' she asked, 'is in that bottle?'

'You will observe what appears to be a standard alloy camp-
flask, which disgusting people who espouse clean living and good
thoughts probably fill with some sort of healthy soyagunk. But
some subversive clot happened to dump the organic glop, and
fill it up with stregg.'

Sten uncapped it, *whooo*ed, put the cap back on, and tossed
the flask to Cind.

'There are three more like it in my pack.'

'Oh, boy. I brought two myself,' Cind said. 'So much for the
clean life.' She drank.

Sten eyed her lasciviously.

'They float!'

'Brilliant observation. You're only just noticing, and we've been
together how long? Is that why they made you an admiral?'

'Yup.'

'What a guy to go Empire-toppling with,' Cind said. She rolled
over and kicked against the rocky wall of the pool, sealing out
into its center.

'Hey, you can almost swim out here in the middle.'

'Uh-huh.'

Sten had no interest in swimming. He lay on his back in
shallow water, parbroilingly close to where a stream of water
bubbled into the pool. Years of trouble and blood seemed to
wash out of his body and mind.

'I think,' he managed, 'every muscle in my body just turned
to rubber.'

'Oh dear.'

'Not quite. Come here, wiseass.'

'Observant, romantic, and complimentary to boot. Well, here I am. Now what?'

'There . . . like that. Now. Down a little.'

Cind gasped as Sten arched his body. He moved his hands up, across her breasts and moved her up, into a sitting position across his body.

And then neither of them had any words.

Dinner, somehow, never was prepared.

The only light in the world was the tiny candle hanging from the tent's ceiling, glowing through the tent's thin red-synth walls.

'I . . . think,' Cind managed, 'that I am dishrag city for the rest of the night.'

'I didn't suggest anything.'

'Then what are you doing?'

'Just . . . sort of stretching.'

'Yeah. Right.'

'I read someplace once that you didn't need to do any moving. That you could focus your attention, concentrate, and *whambo*.'

'I don't believe it.'

'I never lie. It was called Tantric or Tentric or something,' Sten argued.

'At least you're trying it in the right place. Hey. You're moving.'

'No, I'm not. You are.'

'I . . . am not. Would you . . . at least slow down? Hey! If you try to put my leg up there, I'm . . . liable to get burnt!'

Sten blew the candle out.

Neither Cind nor Sten woke the next day until very late in the afternoon.

'How long do we wait, Mister Kilgour?'

'A min. An hour. A lifetime,' Alex said with complete indifference. 'Intel's noo frae th' impatient.'

The com tech, Marl, shifted. Perhaps she was impatient, perhaps she felt a bit strange, stuffed into the gravsled's shell rear between the beefy Scotsman and an equally looming Bhor police constable.

The amount of room available was further decreased with the jam of electronics.

But she didn't say anything – Alex had handpicked her as being the most likely candidate for intelligence training of all the *Bennington*'s com crew.

Kilgour already had an extensive spookery section as part of Sten's embassy team, plus some likelies he had spotted among the *Victory*'s crew and trained on the Altaics. But he needed more. Marl was a good candidate, he thought. Enough time in life and the service so she wasn't still a mewling infant. And built proper, not like the wisps Sten seemed to favor. Not that Kilgour would consider doing anything – romancing a subordinate under your command was about as unethical to him as, say, inviting a Campbell up to your castle for a drink. But he could look.

A box clicked. A needle swung. A screen lit. A sweep swept. The gravsled was a disguised mobile locator.

'Ah-hoo,' Kilgour said in satisfaction. 'See whae Ah said aboot patience? Oh whistle an' I'll come t' y', m' lad. Right on schedule.'

'First lesson. I' y're t' be a spy, Technician, dinna be stickin't t' any schedule. Nae y'rs, an' 'specially nae y'r control's. He/she's more worried't aboot makin' dinner than whether you're blown. One a' y'r few real weapons i' bein' unpredict'ble. You lad's signalin' away like a clockwork mouse.'

Quite suddenly all the gadgetry went to respective zeros.

'Nae quick enough,' Kilgour mourned. 'Ah'll say third floor, back. Whae's your call, Paen?'

The policeman keyed his com, linked to a second locator. 'Right.'

'Ah,' Kilgour said. 'Jus' th' lad we thought. Human, t' boot. Another lesson. I' y're runnin' field agents, ne'er use your own people i' y' can recruit locals. They're nae as easy to spot.'

'And,' the technician-in-training said, 'if they get blown, you don't lie awake as if it were one of your own.'

'Y're learnin'. Y're learnin'. Noo. Let's go visiting.'

The agent, who was using the cover name of Hohne, was carefully combing gel into his hair when the door came down. He spun away from the mirror.

'Help! Police!'

'Button it!' the Bhor snarled. 'I *am* the police!' He held out his ID shield.

'Who are you? Who's he? What do you want?'

Kilgour wasn't listening.

'Const'ble Paen,' he said casually. 'I' y'll pick up yon door, an' prop it up, wi' you on th' other side, Ah'll be wantin' a wee word wi' this fine, upstandin' young man.'

The policeman followed orders.

'You don't have any right—' the man said.

'Tsk,' Alex said. 'First mistake. Lass,' he said to the technician, 'he had his game right th' first time. Full a' prop'it outrage thae his privacy's been invaded. Which he should'a kept oop, an' shoutin' aboot how some clottin' human dinnae hae jurisdiction here i' th' cap'tal ae th' Bhor.'

'I want to see some kind of warrant,' the man said firmly.

'Thae's no warrant,' Alex told him. 'Y're nae under arrest. Thae's noo record ae police activ'ty i' this district t'night.'

Hohne paled, then recovered.

'Aye,' Alex said. 'Thae 'tis th' price ae spyin't. But thae's a price y' ken already, Sr Hohne. Y're noo a baby spy, y're the senior Imperial agent i' th' cluster. 'Sperienced, an' thae. Although Ah mus' admit thae Ah noo c'nsider you lads frae Internal Security fit t' wipe th' arses ae th' lowliest Mantis bairn. But thae's m' prejudice. Noo. Let me ap'rise y' ae where y' stand. In th' middle of a deep, deep bog, my friend.

'Dinnae be talkin' an' sit y'self doon while I 'splain. Oh. One wee thing thae'll pertain. Ah hae *all* y'r net rounded up an' in a holdin't pattern.'

Hohne followed orders and sat down while Kilgour went on. The Empire had quite naturally always spied on its friends and allies as well as its enemies. As every sane power had done throughout history. With Internal Security having replaced Mercury/Mantis, and the Emperor's new fears, the spying grew more intense.

Sr Hohne was, indeed, a senior operative for IS, which really wasn't that impressive, given that Internal Security was a newcomer to espionage, crippled by the Emperor's and Poyndex's decision that no one from Mercury Corps was capable, loyal, or honest.

Hohne had been in the Lupus Cluster for some time now, working under the cover of a native crafts buyer/exporter. The cover wasn't exactly original.

Bhor Counterintelligence knew, of course, that they were being spied on. Just as their own External Bureau spied on anyone it could. Most of the subagents Hohne had been running were Bhor or, if they were human, at least natives of the cluster. Only their Control was from outside – a wretched mistake in Kilgour's estimation. Field Control should also have been a Bhor, and whoever was running the net should stay safe in the Imperial embassy.

But the Emperor trusted no one, and neither did Poyndex. In the Lupus Cluster the Imperial embassy was staffed by numbwits and timeservers.

The field agents reported – regularly – to Hohne. Their broadcasts or drops had been monitored or picked up, copied, and then replaced for pickup for some time by Bhor CI. All the Bhor lacked was Hohne. Not that they had tried for him particularly hard – the Empire and the Bhor were still technically allies, although the cluster was under Imperial suspicion, just as anyone or anything who'd had the slightest contact with Sten was a potential pariah.

Kilgour had taken only a few hours at CI headquarters to work out a pattern for the Imperial field agents, and found they worked on a schedule. Reports were to be filed by X time/date, whether the spy had gotten any hard data or not. A response would also be provided – another no-no – at Y time/date at Z location, different from the drop box, so the still-unknown Imperial wasn't a *total* yutz.

Now to find Control. Kilgour worked on the assumption of like slave, like master. A broadband sweep found unknown transmissions being tightbeamed toward a known Imperial base 'near' the Wolf Worlds, transmissions that were 'trapped,' logged, and then located.

Which was what led Kilgour to Hohne's apartment.

'So,' Kilgour finished, 'since zed a' y'r reports aboot ex-Imp sailors rootin' around th' Wolfie Worlds hae got throo, y'r master'll be gettin' concern't. He'll be wantin' a report, mos' rickety scratch, aye?'

'You want me to double.'

'No. Ah *wan*' very little. A pint, a dram, a lass, a side ae smoked salmon no bigger'n y'r ego. You are *goin't* t' double, lad. Y' hae no choice. It dinnae matter whae reason y' hae f'r spyin't, f'r gold, f'r th' flag, or f'r y'r own reasons. Y're noo workin't f'r Alex Kilgour.'

'There's no way,' Hohne said, 'that I'll help you cover Sten and your treason. I imagine you want me to sit here and file reports that this clottin' cluster is 152 percent Loyalist, that nobody's ever seen Sten out here, nobody's ever heard of him, and they'd spit on his grave if he did show up.'

'Twa points, mate:

'First, Ah dinnae wan' y' t' lie aboot th' cluster. Nae like that, at any rate. Nae. 'Tis dangerous oot here. Y'll be wantin' more agents. Agents by th' squad, by th' pl'toon, by th' bleedin' clan i' y' can score 'em.

'Second, y'll be helpin' me. Ah hae nae a doubtin' shadow a' thae, an y' should no either. An' Ah'm sure it'll noo take but hours til y' ken th' wisdom ae my words, an' reck wha' a *fine* laird Ah am.

'Aye? Ah. Y' still dinnae believe me.

'Mister Paen, i' y'd step in? Y' c'n take th' lad wi' you. Ah'll be wantin' further words wi' him a' another time.'

Not gently, Sr Hohne, Internal Security, was removed.

'Will he come around,' Marl asked.

'Oh aye,' Alex said, as their civilian gravsled took them back to where Kilgour and his team were quartered. 'He'll sit i' th' wee dungeon, contemplatin' his sins, which are many, an' his future, which i' bleak, an' he'll come aroun'. Spies bein't th' failed bein's they are, they always do. T' make sure, th' Bhor'll play some awful tapes ae pris'ners under inter'gation, screamin' ae they're flayed alive an' forced t' listen t' political speeches.

'Ah'm quite th' screamer, gie'en good recordin' techniques an' a wee throat spray. Y' see, y're learnin', Marl. F'r openers, y' hae learned th' virtues ae patience. T' elaborate, Ah'll noo hae a parable. Are y' religious, lass?'

'Nossir. But my crèche was.'

'Then th' fable be e'en closer t' y'r heart. Seems thae was a man. Nae a puir man, nae a laird. But he's livin't i' a wee house, an' he dinnae like it, but he canna fin' th' money frae a bigger one.

'So he hears aboot a wise man. Ver', ver' wise, he is. An he determines t' consult thae wise man.

'Bein't wise, a' course it's a t'rble journey t' find him. But eventually our hero climbs t' th' top ae th' mountain where th' magi hangi't his beanie, an' he pleads, "Great One, what c'n Ah do? M' house i' wee an' Ah canna stand it."

'Th' wise man thinks, an' asks, "Hae y' a coo?"

'"A coo?"

'"Aye, a coo."

'"Aye, Ah hae a braw Hereford."

'"Move it i' y'r house."

'An' th' wise man refus't t' say more, i' spite ae th' man's pleadin't an' cryin't. So th' man goes back home, an' aye, it's e'en more a t'rble trek.

'An' he's thinkit, an wonderin't, but he knows th' wise man's truly wise, an' so he moves his coo in t' sleep wi' him. An' his wee house is e'en wee-er.

'An' he canna stand it. So he goes back, t'rble journey thae it is, all th' way t' th' wise man, an' again asks th' question.

'Th' wise man thinks, an' then he says, "Hae y' a goat?"

'"A goat?"

'"Aye, a goat."

'"Ah hae a goat."

'"Move it i' th' house, too."

'An' once again, th' wise man refuse't say more.

'So th' man, noo puzzled sorely, wander't back t' his wee home, an' thinkit. But 'cause th' sage i' truly wise, he move th' goat i' wi' him an' th' coo.

'An' noo he *truly* canna stand it, f'r his house is e'en smaller.

'So again, he goes back t' th' wise man, an' asks f'r help, sayin't "Ah hae a wee house, noo wi' a coo an' a goat i' it, an' i's bleedin' crowded, an' Ah canna stand it."

'An' th' wise man think't, an' then he says, "Hae y' chickens?"

'"Chickens?"

'"Aye, chickens."

'"Aye, Ah hae chickens."

'"Move 'em i' th' house. Come t' ponder, i' y' hae ducks, an' swans, an' pigs, hae them i' the house ae well."

'An' despite th' man's pleadin', th' wise man sayit noo more.

'But th' man goes back home, an' puts th' chickens in th' house. An' noo i's worse, i's so bad i's intolerable. Thae's no room left i' th' house f'r th' man, i's so crowded.

'An' he journeys back yet again t' th' wise man, an' says, "Ah canna stand it! M' wee house hae naught but animals i' it, an' there's noo room ae all f'r me! Noo, Ah'm pleadin't, help me!"

'An' th' wise man sayit, "Go home, an' take all th' animals oot ae th' house."

'An' thae's all he'll say.

'An' th' man rush't home, an' clear oot all th' animals, an' y' ken whae he discovered?

'He still hae a wee house.

'But noo it's *entire* full ae animal shit!'

Marl stared at Kilgour for long moments. She had been warned. She should have known. But . . .

'What does that have to do with patience?'

'Y' listened all th' way through, di'nt y'?'

Cind was the first to spot Kilgour's gravsled as it sped up the dirt track toward them.

'It's over, isn't it,' Sten said, just a bit sadly.

'It is. It was time to come back anyway, since we were out of stregg. But we've still got three containers of the herbed anchovy pâté, right here in my pack with the dead soldiers. We could've stayed out another week on that wonderful tastebudtingling delight you had to go and discover.'

'So I made a mistake. The label made it look trick. Cut me some slack – I'm the one who brought the adobo.'

'True, and forgotten if not forgiven,' Cind said. 'Now, all we have to do is explain why we're sunburned in places nobody gets sunburned climbing rocks.'

'The cover story is that we were learning how to ski nekkid. Not that anybody better ask.'

Sten turned serious. 'Thanks, Cind. Five days – I wish we would have had five fives. This'll be something to remember in a few weeks.

'When things . . . heat up again. A good reminder that it doesn't have to be crazy all the time.'

Her answer was a kiss.

Sten pulled her tight. And the gravsled grounded, so neither of them had to continue the thought that something like this might never happen again for them.

They had expected just Alex. Instead, Ida ploomped out of the front passenger seat beside him. She was even fatter than the last time Sten had seen her, and her brightly colored gown was even more expensive. Obviously her vitsa – family/band – hadn't completely lost its senses, and she remained as chieftain – Voivode.

She may have been fat, but she unloaded from the gravsled as smoothly as she had moved years ago as a Mantis operative with far fewer years and kilos.

Of course, she did not greet Sten with any sort of compliment, any more than she would have met Kilgour without an insult.

'You are still disgustingly outdoorsy,' was all she said. Then she looked Cind up and down.

'So you are the one.'

'I don't know,' Cind said. 'What is the one?'

Sten intervened. 'Ida, since when are you vetting my life?'

'I always did, imbecile. You just weren't smart enough to realize it.'

'Oh.'

'She appears all right,' Ida judged. 'A good companion. A man should not sleep alone. Nor a woman.'

'Th' coo's snapp't, gettin' all sentimental an' a',' Kilgour said. 'Pinch'd m' thigh on th' way out.'

Ida merely sneered at Kilgour's cheap lie.

'Greetings out of the way,' she said, 'can we get out of this clottin' snow and somewhere close to a fire and some alk?'

The four loaded, and Kilgour lifted the gravsled back for Otho's castle, where Sten was quartered. Ida – who hadn't, of course, offered to get in the back and let Sten ride up front – swiveled around to eye him.

'So. It is finally time to end all this nonsense with the Emperor, eh?'

'You go right to it, don't you?' Sten said.

'Enough is enough. It was barely tolerable back then for the Rom, with all these laws and beings with their borders and boundaries who start wars for this clot who dubbed himself Emperor. And back then all of them were considered sane, at least by the thinking of the gadje. We Rom always knew better. Freedom cannot be served by making laws and fences.

'The Empire had become too much for us, even before that bastard on Prime went mad. There had been discussions at tribal gatherings of this. Perhaps it is time for the Rom to move on.'

'To where?'

'Beyond.' She gestured upward, forgetting about the gravsled's roof and putting a minor dent in it. 'Beyond the Empire, beyond where it stretches now, beyond where it will ever reach. It is time to search out treasures and beings we can't even imagine. This little Empire has suddenly become hard to breathe in.'

Sten suddenly had a dizzying, entrancing vision of swirling, unknown galaxies, stars, and systems whispering the invitation to adventure, instead of this seemingly endless series of wars and slaughter. Beyond. It drew his soul like a magnet.

'Load the ships with our most precious and compact trading

goods, fuel them and slave some barges as tankers, and set a one-way course,' Ida continued. 'I have heard stories some Voivodes have already convinced their tribes to move on, and it is true that some vitsa are not seen at council anymore. After all, it is said we Rom did not originally come from the worlds of men.'

She turned back to the subject at hand. 'But that is a matter for later, after we have killed this gadje who's called himself Emperor too long. Here is the situation for us Rom, Sten. We have come to serve the star of freedom. Which, at least for the moment, means you and your allies. If that changes – or if *you* change – then we shall reevaluate the situation.'

'Thank you,' Sten said. 'I accept.'

'We hae also,' Alex said, without taking his eyes from his piloting, 'heard frae Wild. He offer'd t' set doon, but Ah advised him to hang offworld. P'raps th' fewer who ken we hae a bargain wi' th' king of the smugglers, th' better it might be.'

'Good,' Sten approved. 'We'll send one of the Bhor ships up to pick him up and any lieutenant he wants for a strategy session when it's set.'

He settled back in his seat.

The forces of rebellion were gathering . . .

'I have,' Sten began, 'what, for want of a weaker term, might be a plan. Or at least the beginnings of one.'

The seven beings listening to him were dwarfed in Otho's great banquet hall, which could easily hold two thousand Bhor in cheerful riot.

The hall would have satisfied the most critical Viking as an acceptable place for *Valholl*, even though the roof wasn't made of war shields, and there wasn't a goat with aquavit-flowing teats handy. Far overhead were monstrous wood-beamed ceilings, with skylights in the roof, now snow-covered from the driving storm outside. Four huge fireplaces that it seemed a tacship could park in roared at each corner of the building, and the AM2-powered radiators that provided the real warmth were hidden behind false stonework.

Thick carpets covered the flagstone floors, and the walls were hung with war and hunting trophies. The furniture – long tables and benches – were as solid as anything else in the hall. Necessary, when an acceptable way for a Bhor to deliver a categorical syllogism's conclusion was with a knobkerrie.

This was a high-strategy preliminary planning session. Listening intently, and sipping only non-alk drinks (although Otho kept looking thoughtfully at his great stregghorn and a barrel of the deadly stuff on a nearby table) were Freston, who represented Sten's minuscule conventional military force; Ida; Wild, who would carry as much or as little of Sten's plans as he chose to the loose group of smugglers and confidence men who considered Wild's advice worth taking; Otho, who, even though he had formally retired as Head of the Bhor Council to serve as a mercenary soldier under Sten, was still regarded by the Bhor as an elder statesman; Kilgour and Cind, Sten's closest aides; and Rykor. No one except Cind and Alex knew about Sr Ecu, and that the Manabi were now part of the conspiracy to overthrow the Emperor. Rykor would report whatever was necessary to Ecu, back on Seilichi, who hopefully would *never* be publicly seen as one of Sten's chesspieces.

'Here's what we want to do, and forgive me if I get a little obvious. So far, we have the Empire in a reactive position. We want to keep things that way as long as possible, because the minute we slow down, we'll get squashed like bugs.

'We'll hit the Emperor every chance we get – but we don't ever want to hit him in the predictable places. The bastard is smart, and he's got people almost as smart working for him.

'So we'll bash him in unexpected places . . .'

'Like K-B-N-S-O,' Otho rumbled approvingly.

'Right. Any of you who come up with wide-open targets like that, feel free to add them to the pot. We'll also want to be hitting the Empire in embarrassing places as well. For instance, if anybody knows where the Empire's main supplier of toilet paper is, that could be a viable target.

'We won't be able to hit him with a knockout, but maybe we can dazzle his ass with some fancy footwork and jabs and get him to stumble over his own feet, in which case we'll kick hell out of him while he's down.

'We want the damage to be as public as we can make it. We want to make him look like a mess. I'll stick with the stupid hand-combat comparison – I want him to be wandering around leaking blood from some good solid eyebrow slashes. Fat lips. A shiner on each eye. An ear chewed off. Like that.

'If we can get him mad, that's all to the good. I don't think he's that stupid, but we can try. When we're thinking of these raids, also consider how they'll play to anybody who might be an ally. For instance, we've already got two Honjo ships. Believe me, their actions will be quietly praised on their home worlds. With any luck, we can get the Honjo to declare openly for us, if we can convince them the Emperor's a loser. Rykor's handling that, and the rest of the propaganda, which we'll get back to in a minute.'

Sten broke off for a minute, and drained his mug of tea.

'The second priority will be AM2. We want to steal it, destroy it, divert it. I'm operating on the premise that the Emp is the only one who knows where it comes from, or how to make it if it's synthetic. Fine. We're gonna mess with that capability. And we want to take as much of Anti-Matter Two as he's trying to give his toadies, and pass it along to our allies. We'll get specific about that later.

'Kilgour will be running the intelligence end. So anything you pick up on AM2, even if it's a weird rumor that it's really the Emperor's crap and smells like attar of roses, put it in for analysis and possible addition to the databank.

'Same deal for anything on the Emperor himself. Any stories about where he came from, what he's done, girlfriends, boyfriends, sheep, goat, or octopi he used to get romantic with back in the dark ages . . . anything, anything, anything. This is a critical part of the whole campaign, and we'd like to keep it fairly quiet that we're putting together a personality fiche on the Emperor. So don't be putting anything in writing to your intelligence staffers. It'd be too easy for our Eternal Opponent to start a disinformation campaign as an ambush.

'Don't ever forget – the Emperor himself is our target. We're going to capture him if we can, and convince him to see the light if we can. But more likely, we're going to have to kill him. That's also *sub rosa*, of course.'

'Sten?' It was Freston.

'GA.'

'Right now the Emperor is staying on Prime. The few times he's been offworld have been unannounced and on the run. Is that right, sir?'

'Aye,' Alex agreed. 'Th' lad's holed up in his wee castle. Which i' a stronghold Ah dinnae think w' can take on an' reduce.'

'Agreed. We've got to smoke him into the open.'

'Good luck,' Wild said cynically. 'He did not get to where he was by doing what *anyone* wanted him to do.'

'We're still going to try. More in a shake on that.

'We want him out, in the field, where we can nail him. And once he's in the open, we'll smash him.'

'Admirable,' Ida said. 'But my vitsa'll want some nice specifics before we start wadin' through the gore. Such as how we're gonna winkle the clottin' Emperor out of his nice, safe shell.'

'Rykor?'

'We're going to embarrass him out,' Rykor said. 'First you gentlebeings will set the stage. Make his forces appear foolish. Make his generals and admirals appear incompetent. Every time you can win an engagement, that victory will be publicized. Publicized on two levels.

'The first is the open one. We must tell the truth, no matter how painful it is. With luck, the Emperor will play into our hands with his own propaganda. One of the many faults the Emperor has evinced of late is a large and growing ego. If anyone questions this, look at his Imperial stupidities in the Altaic Cluster.

'Egomaniacs, just like power-seekers, can never be satisfied. So we hope that the Emperor's people will take any victory or accomplishment, and go big with it. The technique is called the Big Lie, and the theory behind it is that if you tell a great enough falsehood, the listeners will, at most, argue over its size, not over its truth.

'This is correct in some instances, but not when its practitioners are completely watchdogged. And every time they blow trumpets for their latest untruth, someone points that out immediately – using nothing else but the truth. The eventual result will be that *all* information from that Big Lie's parents will be questioned and disregarded, which is just what we plan to do with the Emperor.

'But our side *must* always tell the truth.'

'A frightenin' concept,' Alex said.

'Don't worry, Mister Kilgour. That's only with white propaganda – stories that clearly emanate from our side. Gray and black . . . you'll still have the ability to try to outlie even the Emperor himself.'

'Ah dinnae ken i' Ah'm *that* bonnie . . . but Ah'll gie i' a wee shot.'

'As for black propaganda,' Rykor continued, 'this is what Sten was referring to earlier. We shall spread some awesome rumors. Stories that the Emperor in fact never returned. If we can get him out of Arundel, and present at a battle, rumors will spread that he was killed in that battle. There will be stories that he is mentally, morally, or even physically crippled. We shall play to the worst of human male fears in *that* particular area.'

'Small things,' Otho rumbled. 'The Emperor is a warrior. He cares not if there are back-alley rumors he is a eunuch.'

'Small things,' Rykor agreed. 'I shall tell you a joke, Otho. Do you know the difference between the old Emperor, the new Emperor, and the privy council?'

'I do not.'

'If somehow all three entities were aboard a ground vehicle, and were informed the vehicle is stalled, their responses would be as follows: the privy council would have ordered the controllers be shot, the crew sent into exile, and someone new brought in. The old Emperor would have ordered the problem investigated and then the most competent crew members given promotions and the vehicle be put under way once more. The new Emperor would pull down the shades and pretend the vehicle was still moving.'

Otho considered, then politely chuffed a minilaugh. 'As you said, Rykor, a small thing.'

Cind got it. 'Uh-uh,' she said. 'Isn't the point of the story to get beings thinking in terms of *old* and *new*? Which ices the whole Majesty of Ages, Eternal Emperor belief?'

'Just so. Once we have accomplished that mental division, then the stories, the back-alley rumors, will start to be believed.

'Another area – I think it is profitable for us to look at this Cult of the Emperor that has been tacitly encouraged. Once you have two beings convinced that the immaterial exists, and can affect the material, you can then make one proclaim the other a heretic. Possibly you can even convince the first being that the new deity is, in fact, the antigod.

'Beings, particularly humans, will harbor the most imbecilic thoughts and commit the most appalling acts in the name of whichever god they've created and decided to worship . . . But I am sorry. I run on.'

'Not at all,' Sten said. 'You, at least, have a specific campaign. At this point all I have is some generalities and a possible first target. Gentlebeings, the floor is open for ideas, suggestions, and stupid ramblings.'

'All a which,' Kilgour said, 'is vasty improved wi' a whiff ae th' grape. Or stregg. Boss, whae are y' drinkin't?'

Sten shook his head. 'No thanks. Somebody's got to drive.' He was starting to realize that among the many things wrong with being the one for whom the buck stops, a fairly high degree of sobriety was one.

As it happened, the only drinkers were Otho, Kilgour, and

Freston, and Freston stopped after one heavily watered glass of alk.

Otho looked them up and down, then growled. 'Wonderful. Simply wonderful. By my mother's beard, I appear to have cast my lot with a group of bluestockings.'

And he promptly drained the great horn and refilled it, determined to compensate for this shame single-handedly.

The session did not break up until nearly dawn. It had been productive – and that possible first target was a definite.

As everyone yawned toward their quarters, and a few hours of unconsciousness before the Dream would be broken down, bit by bit, ship by ship, duty by duty, weapon by weapon, ratpack by ratpack, into an operations order.

Cind lingered on and caught Otho's eye. He nodded, knowing what she would ask.

He filled his horn and grunted a question. Cind nodded, and Otho filled one for her.

'When will we gather?' Cind asked.

'I have already heard from the elders. They wait on our convenience.'

'Soon,' Cind suggested. 'Do you know what you will say?'

Otho's brows furrowed. His great fangs bared. He snarled. To anyone not familiar with the Bhor, it would have been taken as at least a threat, at worst the beginnings of a possibly cannibalistic attack. Cind knew it to be a smile.

'By Sarla and Laraz, I do. But it is not what I had planned. By my father's thawing buttocks but I am surprisingly thick at times. But now I have the words, and shall cut my beard if necessary to make the elders listen.'

Beard-cutting was the way the Bhor had of bringing a matter to an immediate 'vote' in front of the assemblage – and something that, if the 'vote' did not go in the favor of the beard-cutter, would almost certainly result in his dismemberment.

'Yes, I now have the words,' Otho repeated.

'I shall inform the elders, and we shall meet at nightfall of this day. Advise Sten and the others to remain in their quarters after dusk. I do not mean to embarrass great warriors such as them – but this business must be done with only our people present. Time has run out for the Bhor to continue as they have been.'

And that was all that Otho would tell Cind.

*

Near dusk of the next day, the Bhor arrived, singly and in groups. 'Trickled in' might be a correct phrase, but tsunamis never runnel. Cind was one of a handful of humans – all natives of the Lupus Cluster, and all high-rankers in the Bhor military – permitted at this enclave. She, like the others, wore full battle harness.

Otho had the great tables laid out for a banquet, and sideboards held cold roasts and dishes for late arrivals. Everything had been presliced, since a Bhor political discussion did not need further encouragement by allowing edged weapons.

Great barrels of stregg were set out at strategic intervals. Which meant arm's length.

At full dark, the subject was formally announced by the Bhor elders: Should the Bhor declare against the Empire? If so, should they declare independence and war openly – or merely back Sten to the hilt, protesting innocence all the while and declaring anyone whose name/profile showed up on a WANTED poster a renegade?

That ancillary topic was taken care of rapidly. In spite of the brawling style of the Bhor, they were not imbeciles – and the mere mention of the size of the Imperial fleets, the existence of planet busters, and the probable willingness of the Emperor to deploy those weapons sent a cold chill across the great hall.

Even the greatest warrior may have a mate and offspring, and somehow hope to still have a home he/she/Va might return victoriously to.

Then the major issue was mounted.

By midnight, several topics had been discussed:

Whether it was wise for the Bhor to involve themselves with *any* cause with a human at its helm.

Whether Sten was in fact human or a Bhor reincarnated under a curse in that puny body.

Whether Alex Kilgour was actually a Bhor (passed by acclamation).

The most successful way of thawing frozen buttocks.

Whether, if the motion to go to war against the Empire failed, the Bhor ought to declare war on *someone*, since the new warriors were little other than mewling milksops.

Whether the W'lew Peninsula still contained any wild stregg.

Whether the W'lew Peninsula offered better fishing than C'lone Bay, assuming you could not find any stregg.

Whether the problem with the Eternal Emperor could be settled by a chosen Bhor warrior challenging him to a winner-take-all duel to the death.

Six tables had been broken, two over Bhor heads. Twelve warriors were on their way to hospital. Cind was nursing a black eye and bruised heel of palm from a badly conceived but extemporaneous rebuttal. Five very promising duel challenges had been issued. Seven warriors had been tossed through a window into a snowbank to sober up.

The Bhor were merely getting started – this was the first big issue to come up in several years, and it might be a week before it was settled, assuming the stregg held out and there were Bhor still left unhospitalized to argue.

Otho had enough.

The elders had already attempted to manipulate the 'dialogue' toward Otho, with small success. Otho waited until Iv'r was in midperoration, surprisingly close enough to the subject at hand, being a diatribe that even the best of the Imperial Guard would not be a worthy adversary to the Bhor, no matter how greatly they outnumbered the race.

Iv'r, a longtime friend of Otho – Otho'd once bested him in a trial of endurance over the stewardship of a disputed arctic oasis – saw him fondle his beard, knew what Otho would do as a last resort, and yielded the floor to a 'point of order.'

This meant he knocked another Bhor unconscious, who'd been shouting claims about the shortness of Iv'r's mother's beard, and sat down.

Abrupt silence.

Otho began. These were parlous times, he said. The Empire had turned murderous, and its leader no more than a beardless dacoit. The Bhor must respond to this threat in a new fashion, or face obliteration. Otho reminded them of how they had been following their ancient enemies, the stregg, to extinction, courtesy of the prophets of Talamein and their swordsmen the Jann, before Sten came to the Wolf Worlds.

Now it was time to choose – and there could be but one choice.

'The choice is yours,' Otho bellowed, roar booming back from the ceiling high above, 'and it is clear. Or have we become a race who flees across the ice from a stregg?'

That put the matter in quite a clear light. The Bhor would declare for Sten.

Iv'r's shout rose above the clamor: 'Then let us choose a leader. The greatest warrior of all, to lead us in this battle.'

Pandemonium. There were those who agreed, those who

disagreed, fearing tyranny – although choosing a single warchief in an emergency was a respected Bhor tradition – and most loudly those who knew they were the only possible candidate for the post.

Iv'r began chanting: 'Otho! Otho! Otho!'

Eventually others started chanting as well.

Otho's bellow went to sonic boom – and he got the silence he wanted, or at least the noise reduced to mere agony level. 'No!'

That got *real* silence.

'I am old,' he began.

Shouts agreeing or disagreeing. Otho paid no mind. 'I will assist, I will aid. But I am in the nightwinter of my life, and this struggle might go on for years. I wish to serve in the coming conflict as but a simple soldier. Or, perhaps, battleforce leader.

'I said we must respond to this threat of the evil Emperor in a new fashion, and that I meant. Which means someone who can look beyond our cluster, and see what is best, and convey that vision to our elders.'

Otho should have built his 'nominating' speech to some kind of 'Happy Warrior' peak. Instead, he stepped off the table, filled his stregghorn, poured it down, stregg spilling across his chest, gasped for breath, and jerked his thumb across the table.

'Her.'

Her, of course, was Cind.

A very long silence, followed by an even greater bedlam.

Cind, after she recovered, attempted to argue. She was but a human. She was still young, and not fitted for this honor. She was—

Whatever else she had tried to stammer went unheard. And the bleat went on.

Near dawn, the controversy was settled. Those still conscious who knew and respected Cind's battle and leadership abilities, plus those who were intrigued by the novelty of a human speaking for the Bhor, 'won,' although the field looked less like a political debating chamber than Hattin from an infidel's perspective.

Cind would speak for the Bhor.

She went to wake Sten, wondering how he would take the news.

Sten, of course, was delighted. First that the Bhor had declared, and second that they had picked such a talented and capable leader. He also found it funnier than hell that he and a Bhor were bedpartners. Although he did suggest she must immediately concentrate on beard-growing.

*

Alex Kilgour had not slept that night either. Near dawn, he found himself outside, on one of the fortresses' high battlements. A sentry saw him, started to challenge, then recognized him and left him to his thoughts.

The storm had broken, and the stars gleamed cold overhead.

Kilgour stared up, his eyes going past the strange constellations of the Wolf Worlds, far into interstellar space, toward the unseen galaxy that held his home star and system.

Edinburgh, where he was Laird Kilgour of Kilgour, with castles, estates, and factories. A hard three-g world, that bred hard men and women.

A world that Alex suddenly felt he would never see again.

An' whae ae thae, he reminded himself. When y' took th' Emp's shilling, wae it noo wi' th' knowledge th' service would likely put y' in y'r grave, as it did y'r brother Kenneth? Or, ae best, leave y' crippl't, like Malcolm?

Aye. Aye. But th' gutcrawl thae y'll noo live t' bear th' corpse ae th' Emperor t' his final rest i' a hard one.

But would y' rather die abed, years hence, wi' y'r mind a snarl ae th' past, y'r body withered an a', snivelin't graybeard?

Alex shivered, as his mind laid out all the paths before him, and all of them led only to his death.

He shivered, and it was not the cold.

Then he turned and went inside, to his chambers.

I' death comit, was his final thought, ae th' wee Jann put it, S' be't. W' hae a war t' fight i' the meantime.

Chapter Eleven

Dusable was one E-year away from its quadrennial elections. At stake: the office of Tyrenne and two-thirds of the seats on the Council of Solons.

All across the big, densely populated port planet – the industrial and political linchpin of the Cairene System – the upcoming elections were heatedly debated. Even the big news of the Imperial hunt for that traitor, Sten, was buried in an avalanche of pontificating and speculation on the livie newscasts.

Everyone from sewer worker to industrial baron was testing the political winds. Parents discussed the chances of Tyrenne Walsh and Solon Kenna at the dinner table. Joygirls and joyboys spread the mordida thicker among the local cops. Ward bosses counted and recounted the promised votes. Dirty tricksters pored over graveyard registries. Even children were recruited from the crèche play yards to snoop about the wards for scandal.

Politics, the Eternal Emperor was fond of saying, is big business. On Dusable, it was the *only* business.

Patronage was the axis upon which the world spun. It was unlikely there was a being on Dusable whose existence didn't depend upon it. Cops were tithed by their precinct captains for prized mordida-collecting beats. Business owners bribed inspectors for their licenses. Unions traded influence for feather-bedding jobs. Even dishwashers sold their votes to become pot wallopers. And pot washers paid mordida just to keep on scrubbing.

In short, Dusable was the most corrupt planet in the Empire. But in its fashion, the system worked. A citizen careful to always back the right horse was assured a chance of a happy life. Only the losers plotted and schemed to 'throw the rascals out.'

When the Eternal Emperor had made his long and twisted return from the grave, it was a Dusable election that had given him his first large step up to the throne. Since then, he'd repaid that debt many times over.

To begin with, Walsh and Kenna owed their current exalted status to the Emperor's not-inconsiderable political savvy. He'd stolen the election from Tyrenne Yelad – a boss with three decades of experience in ballot-box larceny.

But the Emperor was a fervent believer in that ancient law of politics, 'He who was with me before Chicago . . .' and had ladled favor with a heavy hand.

Against this backdrop Solon Kenna hit the stump. Electioneering as if the big date were a week away, instead of a year, even though all his advisers said the election was in the bag. They pointed out that Dusable had never been so prosperous. The landing orbits of its big shipping ports were jammed. Factories were working twenty-four-hour shifts. The GNBI (Gross National Bribery Index) at record levels.

AM2 was not only plentiful and cheap, but the Eternal Emperor had gifted the system with a brand-new AM2 depot – servicing two vast sectors in this area of the Empire.

Kenna refused to be soothed. As the president of the Council of Solons and the power behind Tyrenne Walsh, he had a great deal to lose if there were any miscalculations. Which was everything. Kenna had no intention of repeating Tyrenne Yelad's most crucial error: overconfidence.

He approached his first major speech of the campaign season with special care.

To begin with, he chose a friendly audience – the Cairenes division of the giant shipping union, the SDT. The union had been one of Kenna's power bases since his days as a rookie member of the Council of Solons. The brawny shipyard workers could always be counted on to deliver, whether it was votes, hefty campaign-chest contributions, on-demand wildcat strikes, or strong-arm goon squads to raid rival wards.

Next, he dipped deep into his private war chest to provide the entertainment. There would be three hundred refreshment tables, creaking under the weight of tons of food. A hundred more would serve as open bars. A central stage was erected, and scores of musicians, comedians, and scantily clad dancers were pressed into service for dawn-to-dusk entertainment. Fifty tents were thrown up at the edges of the big main shipyard and staffed with teams of patriotic joygirls and joyboys, who were called on routinely during the quadrennials to give their all for Dusable.

Finally, he put gentle pressure on the Emperor to provide him with suitable ammunition for his speech. And the Eternal Emperor, Kenna was pleased to tell his aides as he mounted the platform to address the assembled SDT members, had come through with more than he could have hoped for.

The roars of greetings that met Kenna were loud enough to drown the sounds of an inbound liner. He stood for long minutes under the rolling thunder of applause and huzzahs. He affected an attempt at interruption – a weakly raised hand for silence. Then the hand fell . . . Helpless before the enthusiasm of his admirers. As a newscaster's camera pushed in for a close-up, Kenna flashed that humble grin he had perfected over decades of working the hustings.

Three times, Kenna attempted to halt the applause. And three times, he had to bow to the will of the masses and accept their praise. On the fourth attempt, Kenna made a small hand signal, which was instantly picked up by the shill captains, who passed the word to their minions peppered heavily in the crowd to cool down. This time, the applause and glad shouts slowly diminished to a hush.

'I have one question before we get started,' Kenna intoned, his voice blasting over the portaboomers. 'Are you all better off today than you were four years ago?'

The crowd noise was even louder than before. A news tech watched the needle of his popularity meter bang against the max peg and hold for a full minute. He nudged his anchor, whose eyes saucered. It was a near record.

Then the claque brought the crowd to a hush again, and Kenna continued.

'It is with great pleasure and humility that I stand before you once again to ask for your support,' he said. 'Now, my worthy opponents think I'm a fool for rubbing elbows with good, honest, working beings such as yourselves . . .'

He allowed a space here for a growl of anger at his snobby 'worthy opponents.' The growl came on schedule.

'But I say to them, without the working class, where would Dusable be?'

A shill shouted a carefully crafted impromptu from mid-crowd: 'In the drakhouse, that's where!' The crowd hooted laughter.

Kenna made with the swamp-beast-eating grin again. 'Thank you, sister!' More laughter from the crowd.

The smile was replaced with Kenna's patented frown, in which his two gloriously thick eyebrows met in a dramatic, inverted V. 'There's change in the wind, my friends, and no one, but no one, knows it better than the working being. And of all the hard-laboring folks of Dusable, it is the SDT Union which has led the vanguard in promoting these changes.'

It took no prompting by shills to get a deafening shout of approval here. Kenna waited until it died of its own accord.

'Now you all know I'm not one for false humility,' Kenna said. There was laughter. 'But, I'm going to have to be honest with you good people here.

'These winds of change I'm speaking of have graced Dusable with the greatest prosperity in its history. Full employment. Record wages. Prices at near-record lows.

'All these things we've enjoyed partly because of the enlightened leadership of Tyrenne Walsh . . . and my humble self . . . but, there is really one being all of us have to thank for our good fortune. And that is . . . the Eternal Emperor himself.'

The crowd went wild at this. Shouting. Pounding on one another. On and on it went, the shills working the lines with fervor. This time the news tech's needle pegged out for one and a half minutes.

Kenna stepped in again. 'My opponents say all the benefits we have received since that historic day when the Emperor revealed himself among us, are charity, pure and simple.'

There were loud boos at this. Kenna smiled in acknowledgment, but pushed on. 'They say Dusable is at the beck and call of its master, the Eternal Emperor. That since we've become a dominion of the Emperor, we've abandoned our traditional independence.'

The crowd hooted.

'You've heard all these lies, and more,' Kenna continued. 'But, the truth is, Dusable is being listened to for the first time in its history. And I mean *really* listened to. We can hold up our heads in all the great capitals of the Empire now. And who does the Emperor turn to for advice in these trying times? Why, our own Tyrenne Walsh, who labors as we speak in the great hall of Parliament on Prime World.'

Kenna sipped at a special throat-soothing drink as the crowd applauded.

'Yes . . . Dusable owes a great deal to the Eternal Emperor. There's no doubt about it. But, the Emperor owes us as well. And in these trying times, he needs us more than ever. I spoke to him personally, just the other day, and he told me to thank the people of Dusable for their undying efforts for freedom.

'And he said he especially wanted to thank the workers of SDT. He said he wanted you all to know that without the great shipping unions of our Empire, all his struggles would be for naught.'

The crowd took forty-five seconds to thank the Emperor back.

'But as you all know,' Kenna said when the applause waned, 'the Eternal Emperor is not just a being of words. And I'm here to tell you this day, that once again he's putting his thanks into action.'

Kenna lofted a large, old-fashioned piece of parchment. The news cameras pushed in to show the Imperial seal at the bottom. Then panned up to Kenna.

'First off, our brand-spanking-new AM2 depot – orbiting now high above our blessed world – has just been raised to a Triple A rating!'

The crowd really took off on this. A triple A rating would bring even more business and work to the port.

'But, that's not all,' Kenna said. 'Along with our new rating, comes an even greater responsibility.

'My friends, I'm pleased to announce the Emperor has diverted an enormous AM2 shipment from a less deserving system. The amount is enough to supply all the needs of this entire sector for two E-years.

'As we speak, this AM2 shipment is approaching Dusable. And when this shipment is safely stowed away in our state-of-the-art depot – constructed, I might add, by our own talented people – Dusable will be able to rightly boast of the Emperor's respect and faith in us.

'For, from this glorious day forward, Dusable will be the only supplier for AM2 in this sector. And that, my friends, is anyone's definition of loyalty repaid.'

The applause, cheers, and general pandemonium greeting this statement rolled across Dusable's capitol. Beings in distant wards looked up and wondered at thunder on such a cloudless day.

Aboard the *Pai Kow* – sixty-seven million miles away – the cheers became a sudden blast that nearly cracked the com unit's speaker cells.

Captain Hotsco chopped the volume, chortling to herself over Solon Kenna's lavish promises of AM2 aplenty. She hit a monitor touchpad and Kenna's face – silently mouthing the words of his speech – became a small window in the right-hand corner of the screen. Space filled the remainder.

Hotsco scanned the monitor, singing, 'Mushi, mushi ano nay, ano nay . . . mushi, mushi ano nay . . .'

Then she saw it. Lights winked at three o'clock.

'Ah so desca.' Hotsco laughed. 'Come to Momma, bright eyes.' She glanced at Kenna's round face, still flapping its jaws to the union masses. The captain gave Kenna a mock salute. 'Solidarity, brother!'

Fingers brushed touchpads and Kenna's face vanished. The winking lights shifted to dead center. And the monitor snapzoomed in.

Hotsco sucked in her breath as the robo 'train' came into view.

The lead element looked like an Imperial battleship chopped in half. In a way, it was. The ship had been turned out decades ago in one of the late, not so great, Tanz Sullamora's yards. The command and weapons part of the ship had been buzzsawed, a new nosecone installed, and now it consisted almost entirely of engine. Tractor beams ringed the center. Starboard was a hump that was the brains of the ship.

The sole job of this giant engine was to tow the eighty-kilometer formation of barges trailing behind.

Hotsco started an automatic count of the container ships, then quit in awe as the sum reached into the scores.

And each and every one of them was filled with the most precious substance in the Empire – AM2.

Captain Hotsco, part-time pirate, full-time smuggler, was gazing upon a dream prize. The value of the AM2 train bound for Dusable's depot was unimaginable. Even allowing for a Kenna lie involving the quantity – clot, cut it in half – Hotsco knew she was looking at not one fortune, but as many as the number of ships in the convoy.

And it was just sitting there for the taking. Okay, she couldn't get it all. But she could certainly cut out enough to buy two or three systems the size of the Cairenes.

Wild would be livid enough to cut her pretty throat.

Clot Wild.

But, what about that cute Kilgour? It was his intelligence that had turned up word of the AM2 shipment. She had fallen in lust with the tubby Scotsman as he had laid out the plan to Wild and a group of his captains – which had included Hotsco.

The drill was for the smugglers to use their normal runs to the Cairenes – usually carrying expensive illegals for the pols and their cronies – as a cover to sniff out the AM2 train.

It was a damned good plan, too. Proof was looking out at her from the monitor.

And there was no one, but no one, around to know.

But if she followed her instincts, she might never learn the answer to that age-old question of what lies under a Scotsman's kilt.

Clot the kilt.

Look at all that AM2.

After all, she hadn't promised anything. Not really. She had only said she would take a look. And she was looking, wasn't she?

Then a terrible, dream-souring thought trickled through. What would she do with it? Who could fence that amount? And if she tried dribbling it out, someone would eventually fink. And the Imperials would soon be hot on her trail.

Clot the Imperials. Hotsco had practically been born on the run.

Yeah . . . But . . . She had never had to run from entire fleets. Which is what would happen. All that AM2 double-damned-guaranteed it.

Oh, well.

Hotsco decided to do the honest thing – no matter how much it hurt.

To cheer herself, she thought of Alex's broad, smiling face. And that short kilt.

She quickly coded the message, including the coordinates of the AM2 supply train. Then she sent it in one short, powerful blast.

Hotsco waited for two, or three breaths.

Her com unit bleeped.

It was the *Victory*.

Message received.

Hotsco quickly shut down and scooted out of the area, thinking, I hope you're worth it, Alex Kilgour.

Dusable's new AM2 depot was the size of a small moon. In looks, it resembled a quartered sphere. Each 'slice' was placed in the corner of an imaginary square, then linked with its sisters by enormous tubes. All traffic and freight flowed through these tubes. Laid over this configuration was an elaborate spiderweb of com lines, repair walks, and pipes carrying everything from industrial liquids to recycled air and sewage from the life-form units.

The depot normally required six hundred beings to operate. But there was nothing normal about Dusable. Even here, parked in high orbit, the rules of featherbedding applied. There were twice that number lazing away when the AM2 shipment arrived.

Most of them were asleep. Or partying in the rec center. Kenna's announcement hadn't been a surprise to the depot people. They had been alerted days before to get ready for the shipment. Not that there was much to do. The depot was almost entirely automated.

A sleepy operator noted the approach in his log. He half checked that all automatic units were functioning, and then returned to his bunk and spooned up to his joyboy's smooth back.

For a moment, he thought about waking the lad for a little fun. His loins stirred mildly. Then sleep overtook him, and he was snoring away.

On the monitor, the image of the giant AM2 train closed in. Then it stopped as the convoy reached a synchronous orbit with the station. Signals went out. The com board lit up with computer-exchanged messages.

The first container units separated from the train. They moved in a slow arc toward the depot where 'bot units waited to snag them and guide them aboard.

If the operator had been looking, he would have seen one of those AM2 container units detach itself from the convoy and scoot away from its fellows.

The depot's shadow fell across the scene. And all became darkness.

'I'll never be able to hold up my head in the stregg halls again,' Otho mourned.

'It'll do you good,' Cind said, as she jockeyed the phony barge away from the pack of container ships closing on the yawning main depot bay.

'You could stand to lose about eighty kilos. Get your girlish figure back.'

'By my mother's beard, you have no heart, woman,' Otho said – keeping an eye out for the patrol boat it was his job to track.

He figured they had about fifty-five minutes before it completed its routine circuit.

'I, Otho, have been ordered to do a thing that is less than glorious.'

'Poor baby,' Cind mock-sympathized.

She was getting used to the controls now. It had been awkward at first. After all, she was basically piloting a hulk – except it had been gutted, and a standard ship's lifeboat hidden inside. The only clue that the container wasn't standard was the slight cutout in the stern for the boat's drive-tube. It was so battered from millions of light-years of travel that only a close inspection would reveal the exit bay the *Victory*'s sailors had cut out with torches under Kilgour's direction. The lifeboat contained herself, Otho, and half-a-dozen Bhor warriors.

'When my good friend Sten informed me that our first target

was the quisling politicians of Dusable, I thought my old heart would break with joy,' Otho said.

'By my father's frozen buttocks, I thought, but this is a true brother of the stregghorn. For there is nothing a true Bhor loves to hate so much as a politician. And here I was offered a whole planet of these vipers to slay.

'I tell you, Cind, I dreamed of a long-old age, spinning the tale of all the thick political skulls I cracked. Their blood would flow like stregg at a blessing. The only sorrow I foresaw was that there would be so many souls to drink to hell, I would not live to honor them all.'

'Quit trying to soften me up, Otho,' Cind said. 'First off, you're not that old. Secondly, you've done more than enough killing to boast for six lifetimes. So, forget it. I'm not going to suddenly feel sorry for you, and say, "Well . . . if you feel so strongly about it, dear . . . let the slaughter begin."'

'A slaughter wouldn't be necessary,' Otho said. 'If only I could crush a throat or two, I would be satisfied. A happy Bhor.'

'No,' Cind said. 'And that's my last word on the subject.' Just then, the container coasted against one of the depot slices. It bumped once. Twice. Then she had it steady against the steel walls.

She applied small bursts of power, edging the container along the station's hull. Finally, it came to rest against a repair port. Cind locked on.

'Now, let's get inside,' Cind said. 'And remember, Otho . . . No killing. We're freedom fighters, remember? And a bloody trail of innocent civilian victims makes for a lousy image.'

'If you insist.' Otho sniffed. 'I suppose I'll become accustomed to these modern ways in time.'

A few blurred minutes, and they'd peeled the sealed port door with a small charge and were inside.

Cind clicked her com unit twice. A moment later, there was a return click from the *Victory*.

Step one complete.

Cind had never seen an AM2 depot in person, much less been inside one. Onscreen, the mission had looked easy. The schematic Kilgour had ferreted out of a reference library showed a very dull, functional structure. Only its purpose was dramatic. A storehouse and distribution center for the most efficient power source ever discovered.

The schematic showed that almost the entire depot was devoted

to this purpose. There was only AM2 in the Imperium X-shielded
bays. Living and work quarters. And a big-son-of-a-clot computer
to keep things humming along.

Onscreen, it looked easy . . .

Cind glanced around the corridor she and her squad were
slipping silently along. Nothing but gray walls, gray ceiling and
floor, bathed in a faint glow of indirect lighting. From the repair
port, the corridor ran straight for half a klick. Then it elbowed
to the left. A quarter of a klick more, and they had reached the
central computer.

For a change, Cind thought, the practice looked as easy as the
theory.

Then they reached the elbow. Turned. And it quit being easy.

'By the curly hair on my dear mother's chin,' Otho groaned,
'it looks like the inside of a streggan's lair.'

His comparison was quite accurate. The streggan – a mortal
enemy of the ancient Bhor, now hunted to extinction – had lived
in deep caverns reached through elaborate mazes scraped out of
rock. To this day, the Bhor played a complicated game based on
those legendary mazes.

Cind was looking at something very similar. Dusable's engineers
had only partly followed the schematics. Instead of one corridor
leading in a single direction, the main tunnel split a dozen times.

There was not a clue which entrance she should take.

'How much time do we have?' Cind asked, a little desperate.

'It doesn't matter,' Otho said.

'Dammit, it does. If that patrol boat—'

'You have surpassed your old mentor in many things,' Otho
said. 'But I see there is still some things you can learn. By my
father's scrawny backside, I tell you . . . that gives me hope.'

His brows beetled fondly at Cind. 'A maze,' he said, 'is a thing
of purpose. The purpose can be to amuse, or to hide.'

He glanced at the tunnels snaking out before him. Shadows
deep inside each one indicated other corridors celing off to who
knew where. 'The beings of Dusable,' he said, 'most likely are
concerned with the second. From what I have heard, the politicians have almost everything to hide.'

'Why would they want to hide their central computer?' Cind
asked. 'I would think quick access would be important.'

Otho nodded. He strode down the center tunnel a short distance,
thumping on walls. Solid. Then a hollow sound. He lifted a belt
torch from his harness and quickly cut a small opening.

Otho peered inside. Then he chortled. 'I knew it.' He waved for the others to join him.

Cind peered into the hole. There was a large compartment beyond, stacked with crates and barrels of contraband.

'The depot serves a double purpose,' Otho said. 'To store AM2 for the Empire. And to enrich the black marketeers of Dusable. You see. I was correct. As usual.'

'Well, good for you,' Cind said. 'But that still doesn't tell us which corridor to take.'

'Oh . . . *That*. No difficulty at all,' Otho said. 'I was merely curious as to the purpose of this puzzle.'

'You mean you know the way?'

'Certainly. These dimwits of Dusable would have chosen the most basic maze design. We take the tunnel on the far left. From then on, no matter what opportunity presents itself, you always choose the left. Eventually, we will arrive.'

'If you're wrong,' Cind said, 'then we could be lost for hours. The entire mission blown. Not to mention our own buttocks being held against the fire.'

'You doubt me? I, Otho. The master of the maze game?' Otho's red-rimmed eyes were wide at her lack of confidence.

Cind hesitated, then shrugged. 'Lead on,' she said.

Otho did. They moved quickly down the left-hand corridor, which twisted and turned and then spread out into many other possible routes. But Otho always chose the left. Sometimes this route would dead-end. And they would have to retrace their steps. Then plunge on.

Suddenly, the corridor made a left elbow like the first that had confounded them. Ahead was a door. Behind the door came a gentle hum of electronics.

With high drama, Otho waved a hand at the door. 'Our destination,' he intoned. He beamed at Cind, expecting a gush of admiration.

Cind simply nodded and raced for the door. She unsnapped a listening device from her harness. Put it to the door and bent an ear. A moment later, she signaled the all-clear, palmed a switch, and the door hissed open.

Light flooded across the elaborate computer that controlled all functions of the AM2 depot.

Cind plunged inside, went directly to the computer. She stared at the various options, touched some keys, grinned, and then took a programmed fiche from a beltpouch and fed it into the machine.

Otho and the other Bhor took their preplanned security positions. 'The young are so rude, these days,' Otho complained. 'They do not see value in the experience of their elders. Why, when I was a stripling – too young to drink stregg unless it was in my milk – my mother would have skinned me for showing so little respect.

'Oh . . . well . . . No sense complaining. At least I had the joy of playing the maze game.'

He thumped his corporal's back. 'Was that not a most splendiferous achievement?'

Before the corporal could respond, there came an incredible shrieking wail, followed by a loud hooting of alarms.

Cind sprinted out of the control center as the computer voice blared down the corridor and sounded all over the depot.

The depot has just been impacted by a meteorite. Point of impact, the main AM2 storage center. An AM2 explosion is imminent. All personnel are ordered to abandon the depot immediately. Use emergency procedures 1422A. Do not panic. Repeat do not panic. Impact.

'Let's get the clot out of here before they do,' Cind shouted. And they raced away – this time bearing to the right as they wound their way back through the maze.

All over the depot, beings scrambled for the lifeboats. As the alarms hooted and the computer advised them not to panic, they scratched and fought for positions aboard the boats. In a few minutes the depot had emptied. And a small area of space was filled with lifeboats hurtling for the safety of the planet's surface.

Cind's container craft quietly kicked off.

She clicked her com three times.

Mission accomplished.

Aboard the *Victory*, Freston keyed acknowledgment. Then he gave swift orders for the *Aoife* to scoop the team up and head for home.

Freston turned to Sten. 'Ready, sir.'

'Proceed.'

As the AM2 train and abandoned depot swung in their orbits, the *Victory* suddenly appeared out of hyperspace. Missile ports swung open, baring the *Victory*'s teeth. Six Kalis spat out.

Before they struck, the *Victory* was gone.

*

On Dusable, there was no sound as the Kalis hit home and set off the massive AM2 explosion. Kenna and the thousands of SDT workers still gathered at the shipyard election party were suddenly aware that something was different. It was an odd, swimming sensation as all objects suddenly lost dimension. As if they had all been transported to a world of dots on paper.

They looked up at the sky. And it was gone.

All they could see was blinding white light.

There were loud screams. The crowd wavered as a gut-gripping hysteria swept over it.

Kenna fought for self-control. He raised a hand – to plead for calm.

Then all was abruptly normal. The white light gone. Dimension returned.

Kenna sucked in breath. Then his heart jammed against his ribs as he saw the enormous vid screen at the edge of the crowd wiped clean of his transmitted image.

Another man's face looked down on them. Vague familiarity clawed at his memory. There were loud, frightened mutters from the crowd. Then Kenna knew.

It was Sten.

'Citizens of Dusable,' Sten's voice boomed. 'I bring you grim news. Your leaders have callously chosen to gamble with your lives. And they have sold your right to be a free and independent people to the Eternal Emperor. And now you are his slavish allies.'

Kenna shouted frantically for his tech to wipe Sten's face from the monitor. But it was no use. And it wasn't only at the shipyards that people were hearing and watching Sten speak. The broadcast was overpowering all transmissions, all freqs on the planet.

'Considering Dusable's importance to the Empire of Evil, I have no choice but to remove it as a threat to me and all freedom-loving beings.

'The first attack has already been launched. We have destroyed the AM2 depot the traitor Solon Kenna was boasting about. We have also destroyed the AM2 shipment that was the price your Judas leaders set for your betrayal.'

The crowd was transfixed, hanging on every word that fell from those gigantic lips on the vid screen. Kenna was looking for a bolt hole.

'My forces are launching a series of attacks on your world,' Sten said.

People in the crowd looked wildly about, as if missiles were going to fall at any moment.

'However,' Sten said, 'it is not our wish to harm innocent civilians. Therefore, I now give you warning on which military targets we shall strike. I urge you all to abandon those areas immediately.'

Sten held up his doomsday list. And began to read out: 'In Ward Three, the arms facility . . . In Ward Fifty-six, the tooling facility . . . In Ward Eighty-nine, the shipyard . . .'

Kenna and the union minions didn't wait to hear the rest of the list. Sten had just named the shipyard where they all stood and gaped.

Screaming, weeping, calling to forgotten gods for mercy, the crowd poured out of the yard and raced away for safety.

Kenna was too scared to be ashamed to be among them.

The missile swooped lazily out of the sky, dropped to twenty feet above the broad boulevard, and slowly made its way along the avenue, on a hastily installed McLean drive. Broadcasting as it went:

'Warning. I am a Kali missile. I carry a low-yield nuclear device. Please do not interfere with my progress. I have no wish to harm innocent civilians.'

All over the street, beings scurried for cover. Windows slammed as the missile cruised by at second-story height.

In one apartment, a child reached out with a stick to touch the missile. His mother grabbed him just in time and pulled him back.

In Ward Three, the workers at the targeted arms factory dashed out of the sprawling complex. Fleeing on foot, gravcar, and occasionally on one another's back.

A Kali slowly approached, skimming over their heads.

'Danger. Danger. I am a Kali missile. My target is this arms factory. Please clear the area immediately. Do not panic at my impact. I am set to explode in fifteen minutes.'

Still broadcasting, the Kali sailed through an open door of plant headquarters.

A plant supervisor watched in awe as the missile entered the main work area. Then settled to the floor.

'You now have fifteen minutes to evacuate. Please leave at once. I have no wish to harm innocent civilians . . . You now have fourteen minutes and fifty seconds to evacuate. Please leave at . . .'

The supervisor and his team needed no further prodding. They ran.

At a bearing factory in Ward Forty-five, a missile was buried up to its nose in a crater.

'. . . *please abandon this area. I am armed with twenty-four explosive devices. The first will detonate in one hour. Please do not return to the area after the first explosion. The other explosives have been programmed to explode every hour on the hour. Warning. I am a Kali missile. Please—*'

A burly ward boss, frustrated at being cheated out of contracted overtime, rushed forward. Swinging a two-meter-long hunk of steel.

He connected. Then disappeared from the face of Dusable as the Kali exploded.

Two factory buildings collapsed as the force of the blast hammered out. But only the ward boss and four of his crew were dead. Good sense saved the thirteen thousand other workers. They had fled long ago.

Dusable's biggest shipyard was now empty of politicians, hangers-on, and sentient life. Scattered all over were hundreds of abandoned freighters, transports, liners, and private flitters.

Kalis rained down. These fell with no warning.

In two awful minutes the yard was a smoking hole. Surrounded by twisted frames and molten metal.

And every launch pad had been turned into craters. The port would be useless for decades.

Sten studied the damage on the monitor. Image after image of destruction leaped up at him.

Factories gone.

Smoke and fire bursting upward from other points as delayed explosions went off.

Not just one, but thirty shipyards in total ruin.

It would be a long time before Dusable would be a threat – or a support to anyone again.

As the mind-clouding scenes of destruction swept by, he had a sudden, giddy moment. He felt lightheaded. Powerful.

Almost . . . godlike?

For just a heartbeat he knew what it must be like to be the Eternal Emperor.

Sten shuddered and turned away, disgusted at himself.

Captain Freston stopped him just as he was about to exit the bridge. He had a puzzled frown on his face. 'A strange thing has happened, sir,' he said.

'Go ahead.'

'That AM2 shipment? Well, according to the com officer, just before the missiles hit, there was an odd transmission.'

'You're sure it was from the ship?'

'Yessir. I double-checked it myself. The message was coded. Naturally.'

'Where was the signal being sent?' Sten asked.

'That's even stranger, sir,' Freston said. 'I've run the coordinates over again myself. And I keep on coming up with the same answer.'

'Which is?'

'To nowhere, sir. It was being beamed to nowhere.'

BOOK TWO

POISON PAWN

Chapter Twelve

Sten's hammer blow to Dusable caught the Eternal Emperor completely unprepared. As Sten had hoped, he was still in a reactive mode, concentrating his energies on the massive hunt he had launched for the ragtag band of rebels.

When word of the attack was flashed to Arundel, the Emperor went into instant overdrive. Military and political aides were scrambled. Whole fleets were diverted to guard other AM2 depots. Diplomats were yanked from their posts and flung across the Empire to shore up weak alliances.

The hunt for Sten was doubled and then redoubled again in intensity.

Before he ordered any of these things, however, the Emperor cracked down with the heaviest news blackout in the history of his reign. All over the Empire, news organization CEOs got the word: there was to be no mention of Dusable or the Cairenes until further notice.

The Emperor's emissaries didn't bother mentioning what the penalty might be if the edict was violated.

They left it to the corporate chieftains' vivid imaginations.

But between the orders and their implementation, there fell one brief moment.

A journalistic no-man's-land . . .

'This is Ranett reporting live from Dusable.

'A terrible blow was struck against the Eternal Emperor today, when the fugitive rebel leader, Sten, launched a surprise attack against the Emperor's most important ally.

'In one swift action, Sten's forces destroyed a crucial AM2

depot, along with what local sources claim is two E-years' worth of AM2 supplies. The attack was followed up with a devastating series of surgical strikes against key military and transportation facilities.

'High officials on Dusable say it will be a decade or more before these facilities can be rebuilt . . . if ever.

'Eyewitnesses to the attacks say Sten's forces appeared to purposely avoid civilian population centers. Casualties to civilians were described as extremely minimal.

'The precision strikes apparently lasted only a few hours. But during that time, sources in Dusable say, this once-thriving port planet was effectively eliminated as a key transport and energy-storage facility.

'The devastation wrought here – which experts say will easily mount into several trillion credits – may have an even broader impact on the Empire at large.

'High-placed sources say Sten's raid did even greater damage to the Eternal Emperor's prestige. Many allies, they say, will question the Emperor's ability to guard his friends against similar action.

'One source said the humiliation the Emperor suffered, and the David versus Goliath image the rebel Sten—'

Ranett reeled back as her image on the monitor shattered into a blizzard of interference. The shriek of a powerful jammer howled from the speaker cells.

She wasted no time deciphering what had happened. Actually, Ranett was mildly surprised her broadcast had been allowed to run so long. At best, she had hoped to deliver the first two graphs of her report before the Emperor's censors pulled the plug.

Ranett punched in the commands that would blast her small ship from its hiding place in a grove near Dusable's now-ruined main port. The craft was a luxury yacht she'd muscled out of a businessman who owed her big-time for keeping his name out of a series on slave labor.

In reality, her inaction had been no favor at all. Crucial evidence had been lacking to really nail the scrote to the wall. It was a missed opportunity she had always regretted. But the injustice would now be corrected when Imperial agents hunting Ranett knocked on his door with the registry numbers of his yacht.

Ranett laughed at the thought of the little pube's well-deserved misery. Then she got busy getting the clot away from Dusable.

She would go to ground. Just as she'd done before, during the privy council's reign of terror.

There she would remain until the heat was off. She had no illusions. It was likely she would have to remain in hiding for the rest of her life.

As the ship broke free from Dusable's gravity and headed for the first stop on Ranett's elaborate escape itinerary, she reflected on the report she had just filed.

Unfortunately she would never be able to follow up on it. In her view this was almost certainly the opening shot in the greatest news story in the Empire's long, tortured history.

Bigger than the Emperor's assassination. Bigger than his return. Bigger than any war.

The Eternal Emperor, she thought, might have just met his match. The impossible had now become a slight probability.

The romantic side of Ranett's weatherbeaten soul wondered what would happen if somehow Sten won the fight.

Would he then rule in the Emperor's stead? Quite probably. If so, would Sten be that mythical beast fuzzy-headed scholars called 'an enlightened ruler'?

Give it a rest, Ranett, she snarled to herself. There's no such thing as good guys and bad guys. Just those who are in. And those who wanna get in.

No way was this Sten character any different from the others.

First chance he gets, he'll screw us all.

Avri believed she had seen anger many times in her life. But nothing in her wide experience among the powerful had prepared her for the Eternal Emperor's face.

His skin was a ghastly white, his brow ridged with pent-up fury. His eyes shifted back and forth in their sockets like great hunting birds tracking their prey.

The most frightening thing of all was the rictus grin upon that face.

The second most frightening was his complete calmness.

'This is the time for cool heads,' the Emperor told his assembled staff. 'Hysteria never improves a crisis. We have to approach our problems as if they were routine irritations.

'Now, to business . . . Avri? What's the mood in Parliament?'

Avri jolted, nerves jangling from being called upon first. She recovered quickly. 'Not good, Your Highness. Tyrenne Walsh had to return home fast, of course.'

'Of course,' the Emperor said, maintaining that odd overly mild tone.

'No one is saying anything openly . . . but I spotted a lot of shuffling positions among your allies. And lots of quiet conversations with the Back Benchers.'

'I'll rein them in,' the Emperor said. 'After all, who do they have to run to? But I get your drift, Avri. I'll work up some programs to stiffen their spines.

'Meanwhile, hit the floor expressing my sorrow and concern. Deplore anything you think needs deploring. Promise them plenty of forces. Lots of hands-on support. Oh, yeah. Make some noises about Sten being brought to justice any minute now.'

'Yes, Your Majesty,' Avri said. 'But . . . next to Sten . . . what they're most worried about is the AM2 supply. They're saying things were bad before Sten struck. But, now . . . I don't know . . . They're pretty edgy about the future.'

The Eternal Emperor curled a lip into that rictus grin again. 'I'll take care of the AM2. And *that's* a promise they can count on.

'As a matter of fact' – the Emperor indicated his personal com center – 'I put new shipments into motion not fifteen minutes ago. The first convoys ought to be arriving fairly soon.'

'Yes, Your Highness. They'll be delighted to hear that, sir.'

'Poyndex?'

'Sir!'

'That broadcast from Ranett . . . Any prog yet on how many of my subjects it actually reached?'

Poyndex tried very hard not to show his relief. He had expected much screaming over that slip-up. Still, like Avri, the man's calm demeanor worried him.

'Yessir,' he answered. 'And the news is equally bleak in that direction, Your Highness. Although the damage from the initial broadcast was not as bad as we feared.

'Only about 6 percent of the available audience were tuned in at the time. The big problem, sir, is that copies of her report are the hottest thing anyone has ever seen in the underground market.'

The Emperor waved, seemingly unconcerned. 'Okay. So some pirated copies got out. Couldn't pick up more than another three or four percent viewership from that.'

'I wish it were true, sir,' Poyndex said. 'The figures are more like 20 percent . . . the first day. Then – in their jargon – it almost instantly hit breakthrough.'

Poyndex paused and swallowed hard for what he had to say next.

'Go on,' the Emperor said.

'Yessir . . . Uh . . . They're figuring that within two E-weeks more than 80 percent of the Empire will have seen Ranett's report.'

Absolute silence from the Emperor. Poyndex and the other beings quaked as they waited for the expected explosion from the absolute ruler of the known universe. He remained perfectly still for a long, agonizing moment. As if, Poyndex thought, he were consulting some demon deep within.

The Emperor stirred in his seat. He forced a slight chuckle.

'Not the most wonderful news, I'll admit,' he said. 'However, as I said at the beginning of this audience, this is no time to focus on the negative. If we act in a calm, deliberate manner, this crisis will soon pass. I've been through this sort of thing before. And it always ends the same. My enemies dead or in disorder. My subjects praising my name.'

The Emperor's eyes swept over the small crowd in the room. 'Of course, there will be a great deal of blood spilled meantime. There always is.'

He stopped. As if he had forgotten their presence. Absently, he reached into the desk drawer. Pulled out a bottle of Scotch and poured himself a drink. He sipped. Musing.

Then he began to speak again. Very quickly. Conversationally. But it wasn't the people in the room he seemed to be addressing. It was more like he was having a late-night talk with a few old friends.

It scared the hell out of Avri. Like the others, she stood quite still. Instinctively they knew this was no time to draw attention to themselves.

'I blame myself for Sten. What could I have been thinking? From the moment Mahoney brought him to my attention, I believed I saw a young man with vast potential. Potential to serve me. I should have seen how badly flawed he was. And that flaw was ambition.

'Amazing how you can miss something like that. Because we're talking about an ambition that goes far beyond any kind of norm. Yes. I can see it now. He wanted my throne all along.'

The Eternal Emperor sipped at his Scotch. 'Yes. That explains it. Sten is quite mad. And he's been mad all along.'

For a moment he fixed his gaze on Poyndex. 'I believe that explains it, don't you?'

Poyndex did not make the deadly mistake of hesitating. 'Absolutely, Your Highness,' he said. Fervent. 'Sten is quite mad. It's the only possible explanation.'

The Emperor nodded. Absently. 'I suppose he rationalizes his actions, however,' he said. 'Very few beings like to think of themselves as having evil intent . . . He probably thinks I'm mad as well.'

His eyes darted to Avri. Like Poyndex, she did not falter. 'If he thinks that, sir,' she said, 'he *must* be insane.'

Again, the absent nod. 'Of course, his view will have some public appeal,' the Emperor said. 'Albeit limited.'

'*Very* limited . . . if at all,' Poyndex said quickly.

'Ah, well,' the Emperor said. 'Bleak economic times seem to always draw out the worst in a monarch's subjects.'

Cold laughter.

'There seems to be this persistent point of view in any age that times of plenty are normal. Hard times an aberration. Usually caused by the rulers of the offending state.'

The Emperor topped up his drink. 'Actually, the opposite is true. In most times . . . for most beings . . . life is sheer hell.

'And they give us – their rulers – even greater hell for somehow failing them.'

The Emperor lifted his rictus grin at Avri. 'But it would be bad politics to point those facts out to them, of course.'

'I agree, sir,' she said. 'Promises are always better than getting into pocketbook negatives.'

He motioned for her to come to his side. She did. An arm snaked out and drew her closer. He began stroking her slowly. Avri flushed. But no one dared notice. They kept their eyes on the Emperor as he continued.

'Still . . . the pressure is tremendous on a ruler to deliver the impossible.' Avri shuddered. Fear, not desire, as the caresses grew more intimate.

A bitter laugh from the Emperor. 'And . . . if we should falter . . . it is the monarch who gets the blame . . . Our subjects desert us.'

The Emperor shook his head mournfully. 'But it isn't good for a monarch to dwell on these things. Otherwise . . . his subjects will drive him—'

He stopped, staring into nothingness. Then his eyes blazed to life again. He shouted, 'God, I wish my subjects had a single throat. I'd slit it, without a thought.'

All around the room, hearts jumped. Poyndex found himself staring into the Emperor's eyes, pinned there, frightened to keep looking, yet frightened to look away.

Then he realized the Emperor wasn't seeing him. His face was blank, his thoughts inward. A creak of swivel chair as the Emperor turned away, his eyes lifting to take in Avri.

Suddenly, he pulled her into his lap. Fingers fumbling at the fastenings of her clothing. Avri instinctively twisted to help.

Poyndex made frantic motions to the staff. Very quietly, they slipped out of the room. He was the last to exit.

But just before he was safely gone—

'Poyndex?'

He spun. Avri was sprawled naked in the Emperor's lap.

'Yessir.'

'That wish was not original with me,' the Emperor said. Absently, he traced a finger along Avri's flesh.

'Nossir?'

'It was from one of my colleagues . . . a long time ago.' The finger stopped its trek. Thumb joined against finger on tender flesh.

'His name was Caligula.'

'Yessir.'

'A much-maligned ruler, in my opinion. He had no head for money, of course. But in many ways he was very talented. Unfortunately, the historians tend to focus on his personal habits.'

His pinch bit deeply into Avri's flesh. A small moan of pain escaped from her lips.

'Very unfair,' the Eternal Emperor said.

'Yessir.'

The Emperor's eyes dropped back to Avri, Poyndex forgotten.

'Lovely,' the Emperor said.

Poyndex stepped quickly away, letting the door hiss shut. Just before it closed, he heard Avri scream.

Chapter Thirteen

The Cal'gata, Sr Tangeri, whistled shrilly, breaking the long silence that had hung across the chamber while he'd considered Sr Ecu's words. The whistle signified mild amusement and interest.

'I see,' the being went on, 'why you chose your words with such care. It would be entirely too easy to misunderstand what you just said, and interpret your words as a very subtle inquiry as to whether the Cal'gata have any particular dissatisfaction with the Empire as it has been reconstituted since the Emperor's return.'

'Fortunately,' Ecu said, 'I knew I was not speaking to a being of lesser intellect, so I have no fears whatsoever about being misunderstood.'

Tangeri whistled again, Ecu allowed his tendrils to flicker, also showing appreciation for this fencing match that had gone on for nearly two E-hours. It was a pity, Ecu sometimes thought, that all of the recreations Ecu found intellectually stimulating, such as historical analysis or the human game of go, made Tangeri's black/white fur bristle in boredom; and Tangeri's own pastimes, such as fourth-level equations in topology, mapping a posited universe containing an additional, fictional, eighth or ninth dimension, Ecu thought intellectual masturbation.

The only common ground they had was the subtleties of diplomacy. Each of them knew, however, that he was actually only humoring a friend: in a 'real' contest, there would be no contest at all.

The reason the Manabi were preferred to Tangeri's race as the Empire's diplomats was their innate pacifism and neutrality. The Cal'gata had no problem, if they saw an advantage to their species, in getting involved, even if it meant wading through blood up to their incisors.

'If I understand a passing reference of a while ago,' Tangeri continued, 'you brought up the name of this human, Sten. I further understood you to imply that his quixotic and kitlike gesture of waving his private parts at the Empire was seriously meant.'

'Your understanding is not too distant from what I said,' Ecu said. 'Pray continue.'

'Most romantic. One being against the Empire. Or so it would appear. Do you know, I have run some analyses of late, based on the data you were kind enough to send me under sensitive cover. The data I'm referring to is the amusing situation you created that the Empire is destroying itself. You have a rare ability to synthesize fiction.'

Both of them knew the Empire's kamikaze rush toward doom was no fiction whatsoever.

'From your data, as I said, I made some extensions. Sheerly in the spirit of the mental exercise you created. I will give you an abstract if you wish.

'But briefly, given the proper conditions, which I posited, it is indeed possible for one being – such as this outlaw Sten – to shake the Empire. If the Empire failed to respond correctly to this minor stimulus, it is not inconceivable this would produce a multiple-loop feedback situation, and that the ensuing oscillation, if continued for a not-particularly-extended period, might bring the entire system to a halt or – accepting ultimately favorable conditions and no successful damping – its destruction.

'Most interesting.'

Tangeri fell silent and stroked his long face-sensors with a tentacled paw, then sat motionless braced on his tail, a fat, furry black-and-white tripod. He could maintain this immobility for hours and days if necessary or desirable.

'That *is* interesting,' Ecu agreed. 'And I would like to see your equations. Strictly for their amusement value, of course. But you mentioned something I perhaps did not understand.'

'My most sincere apologies. I find the older I get the more likely I have become to use circumlocutions or even inaccuracies.'

'No,' Ecu said. 'You were most clear. I would merely be interested in what you generally mentioned as "favorable conditions." If you could be more specific?'

'I posited many such,' Tangeri said smoothly. 'Perhaps the most fascinating was if this Sten made a secret alliance with another race, one that normally maintained, or tried to maintain, neutrality when it came to Empire-wide politics.'

'Ah?' Ecu wondered if Tangeri's point would be to expose the Manabi as being on Sten's side. No. He would hardly take pride in doing something which was that obvious to the Cal'gata – Ecu had done everything except put up a flagpole and run Sten's battle emblem up it.

'Yes. I further envisioned a large race. Somewhat warlike.'

Sr Ecu floated, completely motionless.

'A race that had also been loyal to the Emperor during the Tahn war, and one which maintained hostile neutrality during the Interregnum.'

This was it! This was why Ecu had made the long journey to this world in secrecy.

'Mmm,' Ecu said. 'Could you possibly have added to this hypothetical race that after the Emperor's return they were hardly rewarded for their loyalty, perhaps because the star clusters they controlled, no matter how numerous, were far from the Empire's heart?'

'More than two hundred and fifty such clusters.' Sr Tangeri whistled sharply, and the fencing match was over. 'Some of our most respected beings were murdered by the privy council. We lost two million during the Tahn war.

'And now we are forgotten. Our AM2 supply is tightly rationed. If it were possible to burn wood in stardrive chambers, we would be exploring that as an option.

'Yes,' Tangeri went on, his whistled speech losing its sharpness. 'The Emperor has set and locked his controls for the heart of some great sun. The Cal'gata will not make that journey with him.

'Contact your Sten. Tell him what I said. All we lack is enough AM2 to fight the war. Ask him what he needs. Ships. Fighting men. Factories. Whatever.

'The Cal'gata are declared. And even if we are wrong, and this rebel Sten is destroyed, bringing some or all of the Empire down with him into near-barbarism, that will still be better than the absolute chaos which is the only thing at the end of the Emperor's path. Tell him that, as well.'

Two hundred and fifty clusters sounded like a massive host, Ecu thought, after he had returned to his ship to rest and prepare for the next day's formal banqueting. But to the enormity of the Empire, which swept across many galaxies, it was little more than a company-size formation.

Still, it was a beginning.

He floated next to a wallshelf – what the free-floating Manabi called a desk – and sorted through papers a courier ship had delivered while he was negotiating with Tangeri.

Being a disciplined creature, he first went through official fiches, but his vision kept straying to the small pile that was personal – fiches from colleagues, friends, and one female exbreeding partner. And something else. Something that shimmered.

He could stand it no more. A tendril slipped it from the stack, and held it up. The small fiche swirled a kaleidoscope of light at him, colors washing across the surface of the fiche in waves.

A commercial solicitation. He should have expected something like it. The question was, how had whichever business sought his custom found Ecu's private shipping code? He looked more closely.

The return code was hand-scribed. Marr and Senn? Ecu thought, then remembered. The former caterers for the Imperial Household. Ecu remembered them with pleasure. He, like almost everyone who had encountered the lifetime-bonded same-sex lovers, had been enchanted by the two Milchen. He had first encountered them at a formal banquet and been impressed that they had not only gone to the trouble of finding and synthesizing examples of the Manabi's native diet, but also to the trouble of somehow finding out some of Ecu's favorite 'dishes.' He had also been invited to a couple of parties at their famed 'tower of light' home that was in an isolated sector of Prime.

But why would they contact him? They were, if memory served, in retirement.

He touched one of the sensitized areas.

Two small holographs hung before him. Marr and Senn. Their antennae waved.

'We send you our fondest greetings, Sr Ecu,' they chimed, then vanished. A personalized advertisement, then.

Aromas floated up to him, aromas of a great kitchen. A tiny holograph of a steaming platter appeared next. It vanished. Another hologram, this of a formal banquet table.

Ah. They had evidently begun some sort of catering operation, and no doubt thought Sr Ecu was somewhere near Prime and might wish to take advantage of their services.

How odd, he thought. They could not need the credits. But

possibly the boredom of a long retirement had driven them back into the business world.

The table disappeared, and again Marr and Senn appeared. They confirmed that they were now available for custom catering. And they offered—

There was a chime. Ecu glanced at a wallchron and realized he was late.

He looked at the play time on the fiche and was surprised. There was almost thirty E-minutes' play time left. What had Marr and Senn done, list their complete menu and how all the dishes were prepared?

Very strange. He set the fiche down. He did not have time to go through the rest of Marr and Senn's message. He was already encroaching on time that could be best spent readying himself for Tangeri's gathering.

But he hesitated, his attention still drawn by the fiche. No. This *still* did not make sense, as his mind occamrazored away.

Very, very odd indeed.

But he was now *very* late for the banquet . . .

Perhaps later.

The convoy slid through hyperspace, eighteen troopships, with only two picketcraft as forward escorts.

They were unaware of the two sharks lying in ambush, only light-minutes away.

'Like a school of cod,' Berhal Flue, commanding officer of the rebel destroyer *Aisling*, said to his brother berhal, Waldman, aboard the DD *Aoife*. 'Blinded by the sun and swimming happily into the shallows toward the net.

'Or,' he corrected his analogy, 'toward the spearman.'

'Tactics, sir,' Waldman asked. He was one class-year junior to Flue, despite their common rank as berhals.

'As we agreed,' Flue said. 'Hit them and split the formation.'

'One pass and gone?'

Flue hesitated.

'Most likely. But stand by for emendation.'

'Sir? I think it most unlikely that this convoy is almost completely unescorted. Perhaps we might lay doggo until it passes, make a full globesearch to make sure there are no surprises, and then hit them from the rear?'

'My orders stand, Berhal,' Flue said shortly. 'If they sense us, they could scatter. We have an opportunity here to strike the first great victory for the rebellion. And for our names to ring across our home worlds forever.'

Waldman, like most Honjo, had less interest in glory than in honorable survival and profit, but he made no further protest.

'At your timetick,' he said, and turned away from the screen.

The crew of the *Aoife* was already at general quarters waiting for the command.

Ship-seconds ticked away . . . and zero flashed.

Both destroyers went to full drive and 'dove' on the convoy.

Aboard the Imperial ships, alarms yammered, and the two picket-craft shot between the attackers in a useless if brave attempt to at least slow the convoy's attackers. They were instantly obliterated.

And then the wolves were among the sheep, and the 'flock' split, fleeing in all directions as rebel ship-to-ship missiles sought them out. As the destroyers swept through the disintegrating convoy, both skilled captains brought their warships close enough to the Imperial spaceships for chainguns to be employed, even if for only a few nanoseconds.

The *Aoife* and *Aisling* cleared the far side of the convoy.

Four troopships no longer existed; three others had taken crippling hits.

'One more sweepthrough,' Flue ordered. 'Then take individual targets and we'll destroy them in detail.'

Waldman again thought of protest. This was not only against common sense, but against Sten's direct orders. When he had sent them out on their roving commission, with instructions to create as much havoc as possible, it was with the direct command to never take a chance. 'You have fast ships,' Sten had said. 'But that gives you no license to sail in harm's way. We are only four – the Bhor units are still forming and unready for combat. Fight hard – but come back!'

Before Waldman could decide whether to say something, the rear-lagging escort appeared onscreen.

Four Imperial light cruisers, and eleven heavy destroyers.

Honjo screens flashed a warning.

There was neither time nor need for Flue to shout orders. Both rebel destroyers went to emergency power, set irrational zigzags into their computers, and set final orbit for the prearranged RP.

Weapons officers launched Kalis as a rearguard action.

And the Honjo sailors prayed.

One destroyer flameballed as it took a solid Kali hit, and the bow of one light cruiser vaporized.

But prayer wasn't valid – or whatever gods controlled this sector of hyperspace were more interested in slaughter.

The Imperial ships counterlaunched.

Both destroyers sent out a barrage of Fox countermissiles. But there were too many launches.

Waldman flashsaw: Screen A: Imperial Kali closing on the *Aisling* . . . Flue's onscreen face, eyes widening . . . prox detectors howling.

And the screen to the *Aisling* went blank as the tightbeam severed.

'The *Aisling* is hit, sir,' Waldman's OD said, completely tone-lessly as he'd been trained. 'Wait . . . wait . . .'

Waldman ignored him.

'Nav! Orbit! I want a collision course with the *Aisling*'s last position.'

'Sir!'

'Wait . . . wait . . .' the officer of the deck monotoned. 'Clear screen. No sign of *Aisling*, sir.'

'Thank you, Mister. Powerdeck, I would appreciate it immensely if you happen to have a few extra PPS hiding back there.'

'Missile closing,' Countermeasures reported. 'Impact . . . seven seconds . . . countermissiles failed to engage . . . four seconds . . .'

And the *Aoife* swept through the near-empty vacuum where the *Aisling* had been. Near-empty, but full enough to confuse the Kali's controller, as she lost contact with her missle and manually detonated the bird.

A miss. An Imperial officer at Central Tracking tonelessly reported the *Aoife* was still intact. Still under drive. A second launch went out.

But it was too late. The *Aoife*, tail between her legs, outran first the missiles and then the pursuing destroyers. The Imperial cruisers were far 'behind' in her 'wake.'

Seven ship-minutes' battletime.

Imperial casualties: Two light escorts destroyed. One heavy destroyer destroyed. Four troopships destroyed. One light cruiser crippled beyond repair. One troopship abandoned and blown up after survivors were evacuated. One slave-towed to a shipworld and then scrapped as hopeless. The other two would require long months of repair before returning to service.

Almost fifteen hundred Imperial sailors as casualties.

Seven thousand trained Imperial soldiers were corpses.

Against:

One rebel DD destroyed.

Two hundred and ninety-three Honjo rebels dead.

A smashing victory for the Empire.

Sten gloomed back from the memorial for the *Aisling*'s dead. Christ. He was very glad that Berhal Flue was an exploded corpse on an endless orbit to nowhere. Because, if he had survived, Sten would have had him shot.

He had been tempted to relieve Waldman as well, and would have if he wasn't concerned about losing whatever support he had on the Honjo worlds.

Instead, he declared the dead Honjo martyrs to the revolution, announced that a new warship would be named the *Flue*, and ordered medals and bonuses in all directions for the sailors of both ships.

Privately, he told the officers of the *Aoife*, the *Victory*, and the *Bennington*, and his Bhor officers-in-training that if anyone else fancied himself a General Kuribayashi they should so announce it now, and he would save them the bother of having to cut their own bellies after an appropriate amount of suicidally brave resistance. Sten would be delighted to perform that duty right now and avoid the summer rush.

He made particular emphasis to the Bhor. They had a strong interest in self-preservation, as did any trading culture. But there was that species fondness for berserker rages, and Sten wanted no more memorials for a while.

He put that aside.

Ran his strategies once more. Was there anything more he could do at the moment, beyond what plans were already in motion? He thought not. Recruits from the Cal'gata clusters would be slipping secretly into the Wolf Worlds shortly, and Sten was braced for the howl of outrage when he began stripping veterans from the Bhor escort ships and his own vessels for training and command cadre.

He still needed somebody to analyze Mahoney's files. At first he'd considered Alex, but he needed the Scotsman mobile and heading up his intelligence branch.

The worst thing about beginning a revolution, he thought, was being so light in the ass when it came to Available Personnel.

What little he could think of, and what he could logically carry out, given his limitations, was being done. An image crossed his mind: a huge massed ball of collapsed material from the heart of a pulsar. Hung from a cable. And Sten was a midget, swatting at that ball with a feather.

Very good, he told himself. Any other mental images occur to you that'll cheer you up?

There was one. Hunt up Kilgour and Cind and chew on a bit of stregg. Two, actually. Chasing Kilgour out after a while and nibbling on Cind's toes for a month or so.

Cheered, he sought out his compatriots in revolution.

He found them packing.

Cind explained. She might speak for the Bhor, but they were an engine – actually a juggernaut – that mostly ran of itself. Her other ostensible duty, bodyguarding Sten, was already well covered by the Gurkhas.

Besides, she had suddenly felt her horizons open, even before Otho had used his ploy – and was starting to see the limitations in just being a headbanger and tactical leader of headbangers.

She had become interested in AM2, and found a possibly unique avenue of exploration, Cind went on. The privy council had looked very hard for the material, and found nothing. She was investigating – as best she could from this distance and without being able to get near Prime – any trail they had gone down.

'A' firs',' Alex interrupted, 'when th' lass told me aboot th' notion, Ah crook't a wee brow an' wonder't why, since th' council went up blind alleys, 'stablished, what's th' int'rest?

'An' a course Cind remind't me thae's no better way t' save time thae t' know whae y'r pred'cessor did wrong, an' y' noo hae t' waste time duplicatin' th' effort.'

Cind continued.

The initial investigation hadn't produced much of interest, and she was wondering if maybe the time *was* wasted. Then she ran across, in a declassified overview of the council's final months, that they'd appointed a special energy czar – with the title of AM2 secretary. A Sr Lagguth, who had suddenly vanished not too long after the first full-member meeting of the council in some time, a meeting, rumor had it, that was an emergency called to deal with the AM2 crisis.

'So,' Sten wondered. 'He probably stood up, announced "I ain't got none," and they geeked him.'

'Maybe,' Cind said. 'But he was taken under Kyes's wing first.'

Kyes. The ET artificial-intelligence specialist, who'd also

disappeared, shortly after the council lifted Poyndex from his post as head of Mercury to a seat on the council itself. No explanation for that disappearance, either.

Sten had, in fact, investigated as part of his general work investigating the council. He'd discovered that Kyes's race was symbiotic, its real intelligence provided by a parasite. In time, the parasite claimed its due, and a Grb'chev went into drooling senility. Kyes, well past that well-known age, had most likely been discovered one fine morning watching sunlight crawl across a windowsill, murmuring 'It's shiny,' and been quietly medevacked to the Grb'chev Home for the Terminally Bewildered.

'Possibly,' Cind allowed. 'The Cult of the Eternal Emperor believes he was taken directly to commune with the Holy Spheres, whatever the hell they are.

'However, consider what we have here. Kyes, a computer genius, and his cohort, another specialist in the field. Both interested in AM2. Oh yes. One further thing. When Kyes became Lagguth's rabbi, all data that the council had stored on AM2 was removed. It vanished, too.'

'Uh-uh,' Sten said, alarm signals going off. 'I think your report's a mickey. The Emperor had somebody wipe those files – *after* his return. And then put out the fiche you're using as disinformation.'

'Could be,' she said. 'However, I'm off to Lagguth's home world. Just to ask some dumb questions. Unless you have something better in mind?'

Sten did – but it wouldn't further any cause beyond his own morale.

'And you're going with her,' he inquired of Alex.

'Thae's a big clottin' naaaaaay, ae i' Ah was a foalin't mare. Ah'm off t' see th' weasand. Or whae Ah hope i' th' Emp's windpipe, at any rate.

'Th' lass's thinkin't makit a wee bit ae sense, Sten. An' Ah took th' same tactic. 'Cept Ah went peepin't aboot th' Emp. Y' rec'lect whae we were i' th' Altaics, oop t' our pits i' ter'rists, y' were skreekin't frae th' Emp and c'dnae get a response? A'ter Iskra massacreed th' students?'

Sten did. Very well. He had made call after call on the secure hotline between the embassy and the Imperial palace on Prime. The Emperor, he had been told, was indisposed.

'I always thought,' Sten said, 'that he was just ducking me. For some reason I never figured out, and haven't really considered since.'

'Aye. Mayhap th' Emp dinnae want t' chat wi' y', lad. But Ah took th' trouble ae checkin't. Thae's still secure lines onto Prime, i' y' hae old friends who retired frae Mantis t' a sin'cure wi' Imperial Communications, aye? An' more mates who've gone int' private security.

'Int'restin' thing Ah hae discovered. Aboot th' same time, though no one's runnin't ae timetable, th' Emp wen' t' Earth. Wi' no notice, wi' no fanfare.'

'Why?'

'Ah c'd nae find e'en a theory. But i' dinnae wash thae he'd gie himself a fishin't vacation whae th' drakh's hittin' th' fan e'erywhere. Th' lad's nae prone t' kenn'dy oot ae th' wee'est prov'cation.

'An' one other wee thing Ah hae heard, fraw m' sources wi'in th' Emp's soldiery. At aboot th' same time ae th' Emp wae goin't fishin, some laddies frae th' service wae detached, on spec'l duties, t' th' Imperial Househol' itself. EOD laddies.'

EOD – explosive ordnance disposal. Bomb-defusing and countermeasure experts. Why would the Emperor want them on Earth? Sten thought for a moment, then nodded. It was time to filter somebody onto Earth and find out what the hell had happened.

'Ah'm away,' Alex said, seeing the nod. 'Altho' Ah dinnae hae pleasure i' this. Thae's bad thoughts oop thae, i' th' mist an' th' fog.'

There were. Sten had led an assassination team against the privy council onto Earth, where they'd held a summit meeting at a palatial retreat up Oregon Province's Umpqua River from the Emperor's old fishing grounds.

Of the ten beings in the contact team, Sten had been the only survivor. And all of them had been longtime Mantis operatives, friends as well as fellow operatives, of Sten and Alex.

Another place, like Vulcan, with blood-drenched memories.

'Are you looking for anything in particular?'

'Ah hae no leads. Just wanderin' aroun' keepin't m' nose up i' th' air an' m' arse doon. Ah ask't Sr Wild i' Ah c'd borrow a wee ship an' a pilot.

'He's loan't me ae zoomie, an' a pilot he's claim't be one ae his slinkiest. Human lass, nam'd Hotsco. Wild's sayin't she volunteer'd. So we ken she's brain-damag't.

'Ah hae spokit t' her. Pretty, i' y're fond ae th' slender lassies wi' wee hips an' boobies an' a waist y' can span wi' one paw. M'self, Ah always fear't Ah'd gie romantic an' snappit such a one i' half. But, since she's noo hard on most human eyeballs, Ah'll us't th' old deep-i'-love duo ae m' cover. I' anybody'd believe this Hotsco, wi' her hair hangin't doon t' below her waist an' flashin't eyes, hae an' int'rest i' a tub like m'self, aye?'

Bhor Intelligence would monitor Alex's work while he was gone, and he had appointed Marl, his agent-in-training and the Bhor Police Intelligence Specialist, Constable Paen, as acting case officers on his personal project, the counter-agent program he was running through the successfully doubled Hohne. The Imperial spy had seen the light, just as Alex had predicted to Marl, after only a few cycles at the bottom of one of the Bhor's more colorful prisons.

'So. Everything's goin't tickety-tickety, like a wee sewin't machine. Worries me, 'cause we're noo i' a sewin't machine.

'An' noo Ah'm off? D' either ae y' wish t' kiss me 'bye? Ah brusht m' fangs nae more'nt two epochs gone.'

Instead, Sten bought him a farewell drink. Or two. Cind found time for one herself.

He loudly mourned, over the stregg, that he had now discovered the problems of being a figurehead. He never got to have any fun.

Cind patted his cheek.

'It's like the old song goes,' she said. '"You just stand there looking cute/And when something moves you shoot."'

Just stand there, Sten thought.

Like hell I will.

Ida, too, was disobeying Proper High Level Leadership Rule Three, SubParagraph D: Keep a Lotta Grunts Between You And Where The Bullet Goes Bang. Sten had determined to keep the Rom in the background as long as possible, and use them as deep-cover recon and for surreptitious transport of small attack forces. Eventually they would be blown – but Sten hoped to get the maximum utilization from the traders before they were exposed as the Emperor's enemies.

That, of course, meant that Ida herself shouldn't even consider going operational.

Ida had come up with a Grand Scheme, one that Sten had heartily approved of. She hadn't bored him with details such as who was the field agent who would plant this 'bomb.'

Ida planned to plant the Fiendish Thingie herself. Romantics, or those who had never spent any time around Kaldersash, might have thought she was providing a noble example by leading from the front or, possibly, indulging in some homesickness over the old glory days of Mantis.

Of course, the reality was that Ida had seen vast opportunities for the initiating agent to make Noble Profit, a reality Jon Wild also sensed instantly.

And so a grossly overweight and overbearing woman, accompanied by her mousy husband, arrived on the trading world of Giro. It appeard that he had the money, but she had the clout. But since they arrived with several millions in hard credits, E-transmitted one day after their arrival, no one cared about their personal arrangements.

Civilizations, human or otherwise, tend to accept certain fictions. One of the most convenient is that securities – stocks, bonds, and the like – actually have some relationship to the actual prosperity of the government/corporation they're issued by. The Bourse, Wall Street, Al-Manamah, the Drks'l System, all have worked about the same over the centuries.

Ida had figured out a long time before that the two best rules of security trading are: (1) Avoid the perceived wisdom, and (2) The stock is not the company. Her non-Aristotelian approach to the market as pari-mutuel system had made her several squillion credits.

One of the many odd facts she had collected in her periodic economic looting/maiming expeditions was that Giro was one of the worlds specializing in securities/finance where the entire system's main computers were housed.

Ostensibly, however, Ida's – and oh, yes, her husband's – reason for being on Giro, instead of using one of the brokerage houses on her – unnamed – home world to trade was that she liked to be in the center of things. That also wasn't particularly interesting to anyone.

She and Wild made their grand entrance one morning, when the trading firm of Chinmil, Bosky, Trout & Grossfreund opened. Ida had chosen the firm carefully, not for its massive size and far-scattered branch offices, but because CBT&G were known for their 'liberal' interpretations of the Empire's security laws. Ida knew that a white-collar crook is one of the easiest to hoodwink. He's not only convinced he's the first to come up with whatever scam he's running, but is convinced that everyone else, from the coppers to the marks, are utter fools.

Ida and Wild announced their intent of increasing and

broadening their holdings beyond their home system, and mentioned the huge amount they were prepared to play with, and were rapidly passed through the hands of a receptionist to a junior trader to a senior trader to a partner, Sr Bosky himself.

Ida pretended to listen to his advice, accessed a central terminal, and began buying. And selling.

Talking in a steady stream as she did:

'Sr Bosky, now, if I do as you advise, and go long on TransMig, keep what I have in Cibinium, consider this new issue of Trelawny . . . Jonathan, stop fidgeting, we know what we're doing . . . ah, getting out of Soward five percent municipals . . . see *that* quote . . . I could have told them . . . good advice, Sr Bosky, as I was saying that I consider Trelawny, although the prospectus hardly seemed to be complete—'

She had completely lost Bosky in one-half an E-day.

Ida sneered inwardly – she figured anyone as crooked as Chinmil et al were, most especially a partner, would have to be able to see which walnut Ida's pea was under for a day or so. But she continued her prattle as money went here, there, and everywhere.

Bosky was tempted to tell this annoying woman to go away – but he noticed that within two trading days, Ida had doubled her investment.

He started listening. Hard. And spending his own, and the firm's, money, chasing Ida's investments.

Of course, what Ida was really doing with her capital was very different than what Bosky thought, but it would take at least one cycle for the confusion to subside and Bosky to figure out just how many megacredits he had lost.

He also failed to notice that Wild, in the chatter, had been unobtrusively feeding a program into the firm's main computer. Stage One. It took one E-week to get the program exactly positioned.

That night, Stage Two was mounted. Ida and Wild, well after midnight, slid out of their hotel suite to a completely clean and anonymous gravsled Wild had procured and lifted into the night.

The next day, Ida got the obligatory terrible message from home. A cheap, hack, dumb device that'd get her busted out of Basic Extraction Tactics 101 at any spy academy. But business-people, in spite of loud boasting that they study history/espionage/military strategy, in fact do nothing more than memorize enough catchphrases to convince their fellow drinkers they're Tigers.

Ida promised Bosky they would return shortly.

And they departed on a great luxury liner, a liner they immediately left at the first planetfall, where they picked up one of Wild's ships that had been prepositioned for them. Then they disappeared completely. Even the ship they had used for their escape was completely wiped and given new registry, from engines to nav equipment to hull numbers. That was but one of the cultural specialties of the Rom.

Even before they had gotten off the liner, Stage Three, a completely automatic program previously fed into one of CBT&G's smallest branch offices half a galaxy away, activated.

All of Ida's investments were liquidated immediately into hard currency, and the credits E-moved. Later investigators managed to follow the money through three laundries before the trail vanished.

Both Ida and Wild, already rich enough to consider hiring Croesus as a flunky, had trebled their personal fortunes. They had made so much, in fact, that Ida had felt almost guilty, and made Sten and Kilgour an additional bundle, just for recreational purposes. 'How clottin' nice it is,' Ida observed, 'to be able to do well by doing good, or whichever way the grammarians say I should put it.'

Stage Two went off, predawn, just as the market opened for the next trading 'day.'

Literally.

Twenty-six small but exceptionally dirty nuclear demolition charges blew Giro's automated computer center – which meant the Empire's main securities computer – off the face of the planet. The charges had been designed and built by Kilgour, the supermad-bomber, before he had wandered off on his own mission.

Total casualties: one custodian who had passed out in a mess area instead of clocking out in a mess area, and a handful of security goons.

Nanoseconds later, the disaster rippled out, across livie channels and business 'wires.' Panic. Who . . . why . . . what could anyone . . . how could anyone . . . anarchy . . . atrocity . . . against the rules of something or other . . .

The market free-fell hundreds of thousands of points. And then instantly recovered, as sanity returned.

The horror was not that horrible. There were backup computers, of course. And certainly the monster who could even think of destroying a staple of civilization wouldn't know that.

The main backup computer went online.

Wild's program began running.

A junior trader saw it first, as he activated his workstation. The screen, instead of giving him a market display, showed a portrait of the Eternal Emperor. Scowling. In full uniform. Finger pointing directly at the clerk. The voicesynth boomed, 'YOUR EMPIRE NEEDS YOU.' And the image hung there, hung there, and the trader swore something about clotting politicians and clotting – stopped, broke off, looked guiltily around, since Internal Security had begun investigating the business community, and rebooted.

The rebooting activated Ida's virus, and quite suddenly the Empire wanted *everybody*, and everybody swore to themselves just as they swore when the omnipresent antipiracy warning came on their screen when they fired up their stations and then *they* rebooted. . . .

. . . and the virus spread some more. Spread and grew and spread and grew . . .

. . . and the backup computer system blew, and, as it blew, sent the virus on to yet another backup system.

The Empire's securities trading network went to La-La Land.

It was almost a full cycle before any trading floor approached normalcy. The first panic reaction of a good capitalist is to go for the gold. Liquidate everything into something secure.

Orders went out – but could not be implemented. Several exchanges were closed for trading. Banks declared holidays. Some very healthy corporations were forced into bankruptcy as shareholders dumped their holdings. And, conversely, some truly hemorrhaging entities were not only given a prolonged lease on life, but able to establish themselves firmly as successes. Traders sometimes had to actually keep notes – in *hand* writing. Buy/sell orders were handled verbally and manually!

Sten was quite pleased. Especially since Ida's grand scheme produced the desired end result: as investors liquidated, and bought into safety, which of course was the AM2-secured Imperial credit, those credits became more expensive as they became scarcer. And for a while, no matter how many credits the Empire's main bankers dumped out, the crash seemed unstoppable. Eventually the Empire's emergency financial dumping worked and the pendulum stopped swinging.

But the midget had swung his feather – and the ball had moved. It was yet another beginning on another front of Sten's total war.

*

Sten was rather morosely preparing himself a solitary meal, trying to remind himself that the best revenge is living well. Yet another pastime he had sort of picked up from the Eternal Emperor.

His meal was, by description, a simple Earth sandwich. Its filling would be a rib-eye steak from a steer.

But it may have been the Ultimate Steak Sandwich.

Earlier that day, before the paperwork and Go Higher And Hither orders had a chance to consume him as usual, he'd cut diagonal slices in the three-centimeter piece of meat. The steak went into a marinade – one-third extra-virgin olive oil, two-thirds Guinness – the remarkable dark beer he had been introduced to just before his last face-to-face meeting with the Eternal Emperor – salt, pepper, and a bit of garlic.

Now it was ready for the charbroiler.

He took softened butter, and beat a teaspoon of dried parsley, a teaspoon of tarragon, a teaspoon of thyme, and a teaspoon of oregano into it. He spread the butter on a freshly baked soft roll, foil-wrapped the roll, and put the roll in to warm.

Next he sliced onions. A lot of onions. He sautéed them in butter and paprika. As they started to sizzle, he warmed, in a double broiler, a half liter of sour cream mixed with three tablespoons of horseradish.

Next he'd charbroil the steak just until it stopped moving, thin-slice it on the diagonal, put the meat on the roll, onions on the meat, sour cream on the onions, and commit cholesterolcide.

For a side dish he had thin-sliced garden tomatoes with a vinegar/olive oil/basil/thin-chopped chive dressing and beer.

The com signaled. It was Freston.

He asked if Sten's com was shielded and scrambled. It was, of course. Freston said he had just finished an interesting analysis on that strange signal that had been beamed into nowhere from the lead ship in the AM2 convoy as it arrived in the Dusable system and robotically realized it was under attack.

Sten decided to wait until Freston was finished before eating his ass out and reminding the officer he was no longer a techno-wonk communications specialist but a combat leader with his own ship, and to leave his clottin' com techs alone.

The signal, Freston went on, didn't go to nowhere. It went to a dead system, somewhere between forgotten and lost. Freston had chanced borrowing one of the Bhor ELINT ships, bread-boarding their sensors into some measure of the sophistication he was used to in his access to the Empire's best gear, and then sneaking the ship into the dead system.

On one world the ship had found a small relay station. He didn't chance ordering a landing or trying any electronic probings, since he surmised the station would be booby-trapped.

He started to explain what he thought he had accomplished. Sten didn't need one. Freston had traced the mysterious robot AM2 supply convoys back one stage.

Sten surmised that the robot convoy would appear in this particular system from its origin in a still-unguessed place and receive either a GO, NO GO or DIVERT COURSE from the relay station, and, depending on the signal, either continue to Dusable or whatever other AM2 depot it had been intended for, or divert to a secondary destination, or . . .

Or any number of interesting possibilities.

'Is the ELINT ship still in-system?'

'That's affirm,' Freston said. 'I ordered it to lie doggo, all passive receptors on full, and not to attempt any active sensing without a direct order from me.'

'Were there any transmissions when the Bhor ship first arrived?'

'None reported.'

'Have there been any since?'

'Technically, none,' Freston said. 'However, the electronics ship has recently reported increased power output from the station on all lengths. As if it's coming up from standby.'

Freston's reaming – and Sten's dinner – was forgotten.

'Is the gear on the ELINT ship good enough to pick up another transmission like the one you flagged off Dusable?'

'Easily.'

'What's the distance?'

'You could be there in three E-days.'

Sten grinned: Freston knew his boss. 'Okay. Is the *Aoife* ready to lift?'

'Affirm.'

'I'm on the way. Tell its skipper—'

'Waldman, sir.'

'This is his or her big chance to step off his sex organ for that convoy disaster. I want couplings ready to hook a tacship up to the *Aoife*. And I want you to set up a tightbeam com, set up to link between the tacship and destroyer. Yesterday.'

'Yessir. I assume you'll be commanding the tacship?'

Sten started to nod: *Of course.* Then he caught himself. Come on, son. You're busting common sense in the chops enough, already. Don't be a complete grandstander.

'Negative,' he said, to Freston's surprise. 'I want a drakh-hot pilot – And I've got just the candidate. Out.'

Sten went out the door of his quarters before the com blanked. The Gurkha sentry outside was one count into his present arms and Sten was gone, a flicker that might have been a waved return of the salute in his wake.

Sten had a helmet bag in one hand, weapons harness – pistol, ammo, cleaning kit, kukri – over one shoulder, and a daypack carrying three days' rations and toiletries in the other, three things that were never more than an arm's length from him.

Ida, unintended, *had* set an example.

Now was the time to scrape off some of the rust.

The three greatest talents a diplomat must have, Sr Ecu had realized a century or so earlier, were to never take things personally, to always look pleased when served what was generically dubbed rubberchicken on the banquet circuit, and most importantly to endure boredom.

Not just the boredom of long, droning conferences while amateur pols tried to score points as if governing were Beginning Debate, but also the boredom of endless hours traveling.

Ecu had wondered how spaceship crews, particularly on the torchships in the early days, kept from going berserk, and researched the matter. Reading of the murders, mutinies, and worse aberrancies, particularly on the pre-stardrive longliners, told him they didn't.

Now, on this long flight back from the Cal'gata worlds, especially as his ship was under enforced com blackout, he had started to feel like perhaps mutinying a little himself, even though he tried to remind himself that boredom was not an emotion the Manabi felt, and that the way he was feeling could be no more than a conditioned response from all the decades he had spent around humans.

Still, he was getting what he had heard described as the Jeabie Heabies.

He had viewed every livie aboard the small yacht, read every book available, written reports and progs beyond count, and they were still four ship-days out from Seilichi.

Finally his ennui led him back to Marr and Senn's flier.

He had wanted to look at it before, but had refrained. Thinking of the succulences that the two Milchen might concoct might be the last straw, especially considering the less-than-inspired rations the yacht's bellyrobber served up.

Ecu now thought he could tough out the four days before real nourishment would become available.

Again he touched the sensitized area, and again Marr and Senn appeared and greeted him by name. Again the wonderful scents floated toward Ecur's tendrils.

And again the two beings announced their catering service and began presenting a menu.

Ecu's senses flickered. Trouble. The menu was being presented in a perfunctory drone, as if Marr and Senn had been forced into this new business through economic desperation. But that could not be. Perhaps—

Both holographs stopped. Marr and Senn looked at each other.

'That's time enough for anyone busybodying through your mail to get bored,' Marr said.

'I can only hope,' Senn said. 'Sr Ecu, we need your help. I trust it is you who is viewing this, and that some others –'

He shuddered and crouched, as if an icy windblast had caught him. Marr moved closer, protecting.

'– some others,' he went on, after collecting himself, 'are not.

'We are in trouble. We need to contact Sten. We are not aware if you know where he is, and the only reason we are sending this is because the two of you worked on that Tribunal, back in the awful days of those five beings whose names I will not pronounce.

'This is our only hope. We need Sten to help us. And someone else. I cannot mention the being's name. But tell Sten that the being is someone he will remember. Tell Sten to remember the party and what came later. In the garden. The black ball against the moon that happens but three times a year. The being does.

'If Sten remembers, tell him that this being is in trouble. The being is being hunted by the Emperor. We—'

Marr interrupted.

'We have *heard* where this being is,' he said. 'And if the Emperor learns of our knowledge, we too will be hunted. We do not know this being's exact location. We feel that even now a net is being cast, somewhere out there, by beings who intend us harm. Sooner or later, if that fisherman keeps casting, we shall be netted.'

The beings moved together, finding what little love and security was left in their universe, and fell silent.

'We should say no more,' Senn said finally. 'Tell Sten of our problem. Ask him if he can help. He will know where we are. We do not have any suggestions.

'But . . . but tell him this. Tell him he must not chance all. We say this, and his friend says it as well. If help might risk his crusade, he must not try to help.

'Sten *must* not be defeated.'

Drakh-hot pilot Hannelore La Ciotat had wondered – as much as anyone might wonder in a profession where two of the pre-requisites were an inability to talk without moving one's hands and a mild curiosity about what the O-club's got for its dinner special – just why she had joined the rebellion.

No one but her fellow rebels knew she had been Sten's pilot when he had ambushed Admiral Mason and the *Caligula*. And even if accused, she probably could have skated on that, and claimed to be in fear of her life if she disobeyed his commands. Instead, she had been one of the first of the *Victory*'s tacship pilots to throw in on Sten's side.

She settled on three reasons: First, that the Empire to her was represented by lard-assed senior officers who never could under-stand the tactical importance basic to underflying every single bridge that ran through the middle of her planet's capital world at mach speed, officers who would one day insist that she park the ship and start flying a desk. Second was that Sten was a pilot too, and spoke her language. Third was that she surely would have more combat time and flight hours with the rebellion than sticking with the monolithic Imperial forces.

She shied away from the fourth reason, which was Why The Clot Not, because that might imply that pilots are frequently lacking in any sense, let alone that of the common type. Especially tacship drivers.

She listened to Sten's briefing aboard the *Aoife* with some degree of skepticism, which Sten noted with amusement.

'You have a question, Lieutenant? Sorry, Captain. Congrats on the promo, by the way.'

La Ciotat shrugged. More stars on the shoulder meant only more credits on the O-club bar payday night since sergeant-pilots and admiral-pilots still flew the same ships – and bore in.

'Last time you had this great plan,' she began as tactfully as she knew how, which meant not very, 'it was, "Hey there, Hannelore, let's you and me ambush a battlewagon."

'Dumb, dumb, truly dumb, but we blindsided the clot, and got away with it. Now you want to try again, except even bigger. As I understand it, my tácship, supported by one lousy non-Imperial tincan—'

Sten interrupted. 'The *Aoife*'s only there to pull our tails out of the crack. She won't be there for the binga-banga-bonga.'

'Even more wonderful. One spitkit, *not* supported by one lousy non-Imperial DD, to jump an entire convoy, a convoy carrying what's only the most important resource the Empire's got, and you think we're gonna accomplish the mission?

'Hell, I don't think we'll limp away, let alone do what you've got in mind. Who's gonna take care of the escorts?'

'There won't be any.'

'Hoo. You weren't listening . . . By the way, what the clot do I call you? Besides "sir"? I mean, what's your post-rebellion rank? Leader? Hero? I assume you've given yourself more tabs than just clottin' Admiral.'

'Try Sten. No rank. No "sir."'

'Right. Anyway, you're saying the Empire lets its goodies travel unescorted?'

'I am.'

'Sten, I gotta question how good your skinny is.'

'You can question the intelligence and you can ask, La Ciotat. But you aren't going to get an answer. Need-to-know and all that.'

La Ciotat stared at Sten for a long moment. 'I'm not hot for your carcass,' she finally said. 'Nor needing any kind of an adrenaline rush. But I'm thinking I'm gonna be party to this silly-ass operation. So it's gotta be that I was born twins, and Momma said drown the dumb one and Daddy blew it. Okay, skipper. I'll brief my crew.

'They're gonna love this. Fearless Volunteers Into the Valley of Slok and all that. One of these years I gotta ask them before I toss them into the crapper, I guess.'

Just beyond the dead system, Sten, La Ciotat, and her crew boarded the tacship, the *Sterns*. The com link was opened between the *Aoife*, the *Sterns*, and the Bhor ELINT ship, the *Heorot*, still monitoring from its silent parking orbit not too far off the relay-station world.

And then they waited.

La Ciotat, as was her custom before battle, retired to the tiny cubbyhole that was the captain's cabin, which meant on a tacship a closet-size room with a pulldown desk. But a cabin for all of that – there was a drawcurtain that everyone on a tacship called a door. She depilled from head to foot and bathed in water she had brought over from the *Aoife*'s supply, water that had been augmented with aromatic oils from her home world. She painted her face in the ancestral battlepattern of her house, and then cleared her mind of evil, of lust, of desires.

She was ready for battle.

She wondered what Sten – who occupied the only other cabin on the tacship – formerly belonging to the XO and engineer, given up at their request – was doing. What customs did *his* world practice? If any?

She considered the possibility of imminent nonexistence. And the ramifications if she were to pull on a wrap, slip through the curtain, walk two meters to the next compartment, tap politely, and . . .

She caught herself. She went through the exercises again, forcibly clearing lust or ambition from her mind.

Besides, what was she worrying about, knowing that the void only beckoned her enemies, not her? She put on a fresh flightsuit and tried to sleep.

Sten, in the next compartment, slept deeply. Woke. Ate. Thinking of nothing except the taste of what he had put in his mouth, the hum of the air freshers in the background, the drone of the ship's internal power, the small jokes and large laughter at the mess table, as all thirteen beings on the *Sterns* waited for battle, trying not to snarl at or massacre the being beside them.

He slept once more. Perhaps he dreamed.

If he did, his mind chose not to record them when he woke to the yammer of the GQ siren.

He glanced at the overhead telltale. It was less than four shipdays since he had arrived insystem. Freston might have crystal balls and talent beyond that of being a mere battleship commander.

Heorot: 'All stations! I have incoming—'

Aoife: 'At battle stations!'

Sterns: 'We have them.'

Sten, from *Sterns*: 'All stations! Maintain silence!'

The three ships watched the huge convoy bulk out of hyperspace toward them.

AM2. Twice the size of the convoy the rebels had ambushed off Dusable.

A com officer on the *Heorot* picked up a convoy relay-station blurt – a response to the convoy's initial inquiry from the planet. He resisted a temptation to run an analysis. Instead, he reported the transmission.

'All stations,' Sten said calmly. 'All recorders, all sensors on full. Stand by . . . stand by . . . stand by . . . *Now!* Captain! Full drive!'

La Ciotat obeyed. The *Sterns* flashed toward the monster convoy.

The com officer on the *Heorot* 'saw' the convoy panic. Nothing physical happened, but the convoy began broadcasting on many frequencies.

'Ms La Ciotat,' Sten went on, 'I would like a Kali launch . . . individual control . . . area target . . . convoy on main screen . . . on my command . . .'

'Ms Castaglione,' Hannelore said in turn to her weapons officer. 'Acquired. . . .'

'Target acquired, sir.'

'Launch,' Sten ordered.

'Fire.'

The huge shipkilling missile lurched out of the center firing tube of the *Sterns*.

Screens flashed on the *Heorot*.

'We have a convoy-station 'cast,' the Bhor com officer reported. 'We have a response from the relay station . . . direction unknown, power strength massive . . . we have a signal transmitted on EM subspectrum . . . unclassifiable single spectrum . . . computers suggest between Omicron Sub Two and Xeta Three . . . no known previous use of spectrum by any known – *by the clottin' beard of my clottin' mother*!'

The fairly irregular interjection from the com officer occurred as his screens told him that the entire convoy had committed seppuku, a monstrous blast as if a star had gone nova! The explosion was beyond even the cataclysm that had resulted when the smaller AM2 convoy off Dusable had been hit by the *Victory*'s Kalis.

A second later, another screen showed him the robot relay station on the dead planet had also self-destructed.

Aboard the *Sterns* all screens overloaded and blew out.

Finally, one emergency screen cleared. It was a tertiary screen, 'casting from the Kali missile. It showed a great deal of nothing. Castaglione ran the pickup through all available bands.

Nothing but parsecs and parsecs of parsecs and parsecs.

La Ciotat forced herself to appear quite calm, as if a thousand-ship convoy suddenly blew itself up in her sights every E-day or so.

'All right,' she grudged. 'Your intelligence is One-A. But what a piddle-poor excuse for a battle this was.'

Sten didn't answer immediately. Instead, he picked up the open mike on the three-way circuit.

'*Heorot*. *Sterns*. Six Actual. Trap? Angle?'

'*Heorot*. Affirm both.'

'Do you have a receiving station?'

'Negative. None known. Analysis will continue.'

'*Sterns* clear.'

And now Sten smiled. 'It was clottin' wonderful,' he said.

'So what did we get?'

'We've got,' Sten said accurately, 'an Emperor with a major case of the hips, which is almost a case of the ass. We've just cut off a big chunk of the AM2 he'd be doling out to his cronies and allies. A *big* chunk.'

His smile grew larger. La Ciotat looked at him skeptically – she wasn't sure she was hearing all of it.

She wasn't, although the fact that merely jumping out of the bushes and shouting boo had been enough to make the Big Bad Wolf drop dead of heart failure was significant – and certainly a tactic that could be repeated indefinitely, if they could continue finding the courses of the AM2 convoys.

Sten was realizing that one of the Eternal Emperor's primary weapons – that *no one* but the Emperor was permitted to get close to wherever AM2 came from – was a double-edged sword. Just as the shutdown of AM2 subsequent to the Emperor's disappearance would destroy any coup, so, too, Sten's boo-shouting could wreak economic havoc on the Emperor himself.

Possibly. Or at least until the Eternal Emperor figured out a response.

More importantly, the *Heorot* had recorded a second, equally mysterious signal to nowhere, this time from the relay station.

If they could home on its target . . . Sten would be one step closer to finding the AM2.

And one step closer to destroying the Emperor.

Chapter Fourteen

41413 . . . 31146 . . . 00983 . . . 01507 . . .

Far beyond the stretch of the most sensitive sensor, far beyond the Bhor picketlines, an Imperial destroyer, modified into a special-missions delivery craft, dumped a tacship into space and fled.

The tacship, completely unarmed, its weapons systems replaced with massive electronic suites, slid toward Vi, the Bhor home world and capital of the Lupus Cluster. There were just five crewmen aboard, plus one Internal Security agent, fresh from her training and initial intern assignment.

09856 . . . 37731 . . . 20691 . . .

It found a parking orbit offworld, hiding behind one of the planet's moons until the ordered time came around.

Then, under partial and muffled drive, it set a landing trajectory. A somewhat unusual one. From the ground, it would appear that the tacship was coming 'straight down,' toward one point on the planet – a wilderness near the capital city. Speed was kept low to reduce skinheating and subsequent infrared printing by Bhor scanners.

It was still waiting for the correct moment, which came when one of the great Bhor intercontinental suborbital transports lifted from a field and bellowed for nearspace.

The tacship went for ground, using the cover of the transport's electronic, infrared, and physical turbulence.

On board, the dispatcher waited next to the spy. The compartment was lit with eye-saving red nightlights.

The spy was heavy-laden, McLean pack on her chest and a backpack containing a weapon and a travel case that would pass unnoticed as a civilian's valise. Inside the case were clothes, normal espionage gadgetry, plus a great sheaf of Imperial credits and Bhor currency.

Strapped to her leg was the heavy dropbag containing that most necessary and dangerous tool of a spy, a transmitter/receiver. The com buzzed.

'Coming in on Delta Zulu,' the tacship pilot announced.

'Aye, sir,' the dispatcher said.

'We're at dropspeed. On approach.'

The dispatcher felt the tacship chop power and level out of its dive.

'Aye, sir. Hatch opening.'

The dispatcher touched a button, and a circular hatch yawned. There was moonlit night and, far below, gleaming snow. Two corrugated steel plates slid out, into the middle of the open hatch. To one side, the dispatcher could see the flickering from the Bhor transport's stern as it drove on and upward, unseeing.

The spy shivered. But the compartment was heated.

'Looks cold down there.'

'Your friends'll be waiting,' the dispatcher soothed. 'Now. Position.'

The spy stepped onto the plates. She swayed in the air-blast from the hatch, then recovered. As trained, she locked her hands tightly on the two handles of the McLean pack. One of them held the drive activation switch.

'Count thirty before you drop your bag,' the dispatcher reminded. The spy nodded, not really hearing.

The com buzzed.

'Ten count . . . nine . . . eight . . . seven . . . six . . . five . . . four . . . three . . . *GO!*'

The steel plates snapped back into their housing, and the spy plummeted down toward Vi. The dispatcher keyed the mike, as the hatch slid shut.

'One away, sir.'

'Affirm. Return to your post.'

The tacship lifted toward space. The temptation was to hit full drive and hare away. But the tacship pilot was a professional – the drive signature at full power would very likely be picked up, wasting all the trouble they'd gone to for the insertion. The dispatcher looked down at the now-closed hatch.

'May all your eggs,' he said, 'be double-yolked.'

A spy needed all the luck that could be wished for.

*

43491 . . . 29875 . . . 01507 . . .

Marl, now promoted out of tech ranks and commissioned as
ensign, and the Bhor constable, Paen, watched one of the night-
screens in their gravlighter.

The image blurred, and Marl touched a button, and the picture
was razor-sharp.

'You would not ever get me leaving a perfectly good tacship
in flight,' Paen observed.

'Nor me,' Marl agreed.

The message had been coded and blurted out from Vi toward
an Imperial Intelligence receiving station, located as close as safety
would permit to the Lupus worlds:

41413	urgently
31146	require
00983	additional
01507	agent(s)
. . .	
30924	reports
32149	s
37762	t
11709	e
23249	n
03975	begins (beginning?)
26840	plans
41446	to use
37731	system(s)
03844	the basalt has come in again
. . .	
09856	delivery
37731	system
20691	m
. . .	
43491	will
29875	recover
01507	agent(s)

Marl was particularly proud of 03844, since she'd observed
that Hohne was not exactly the most skilled of coders. Kilgour
had been right in thinking Hohne a bit of an amateur since he
was using an extant code. It wasn't significant to Alex that at
least Hohne had chosen a prehistoric system, dating back to the

dark ages when idiocies like obsidian daggers and onetime pads had been used.

She figured the Imperial who decoded the message would swear a lot, scratch his/her/its head(s), reconsult the code fiche, substitute 03843, meaning *for a base*, and the message would make sense. The mad Scotsman would be proud of her sneakiness.

Damn, but she was starting to miss Alex. When he got back, now that she was commissioned and all, and he was technically not in her chain of command, she planned to cozen him into drinks, dinner, and . . . who knows?

If nothing else, she wanted to find out the truth about that title, Laird Kilgour of Kilgour. If he was really some kind of baron, what was he doing in this revolt, instead of sucking up to the Emperor?

'The human looks cold,' the Bhor said, not a shred of sympathy to his rumble.

'She does.'

Marl felt momentarily empathetic for the doomed spy drifting toward them, still about a kilometer above the ground. She pushed it away. The woman has a choice.

'More stregg?' Constable Paen asked.

'I say again my last – humans can't be swilling stregg like you folks, and still function.'

'Kilgour can.'

'Kilgour isn't human, either.'

'That is true.'

Paen drained his cup – a duplicate in miniature of a drinking horn – folded it, and put it away.

'Shall we collect our new friend?'

Both beings slid out of the gravlighter, careful to not shut the doors behind them – the sound of a slamming door carries forever on a silent night. Around them, hidden in the blackness of this thicket, were twenty heavily armed Bhor policemen.

Above them the spy touched buttons, and her rate of descent slowed as much as the McLean generator could overcome gravity. The age of the fantasized strap-on-your-back personal flier still hadn't arrived, even with the antigrav capabilities of the McLean system. But at least it had replaced all varieties of the incredibly dangerous parachute.

The spy directed her descent toward one end of the huge open meadow that was the dropzone, the final end of delivery system M. Below her was tranquil forest. Far, far away – at least five klicks, she estimated – she saw the lights of a tiny farmhouse.

Just as planned. No ambush waiting.

Perhaps, she thought with a chill, her friends – the Imperial spymaster whose cover name was Hohne, or his chosen representatives – weren't at the rendezvous, either. But, that was not a problem. She would go to ground for one planet-day as instructed. There were rations and heat tabs in her case, and her jumpsuit would keep her very warm.

Even if they didn't materialize then, she would still be all right. Bury the jumpsuit and McLean pack, and make her way to the capital city. She had memorized three alternate pickup points.

Groundrush – under twenty-five meters – as she swung toward the snow.

She forced her eyes off the earth below, earth she knew had needle-sharp stones just under that innocent-looking snowy blanket, and onto the horizon. She suddenly remembered the dispatcher's warning, and her hand slammed the knob on her harness, letting the dropbag unspool on its five-meter cord so it wouldn't still be attached to her leg on the landing slam.

The bag with the transmitter dropped less than half a meter when the ground came up and smote the spy.

She did a classic three-point PLF: toes, knees, nose . . . and the pain crashed. She blurted, then buried an outcry and lay motionless in the snow.

'Clot,' Marl swore, as the police spread out toward the spy. She and Paen hurried toward the sprawled agent. 'If she ruined the com, I'll use the thumbscrews. We're two back now as it is.'

Building a replica of one of the Empire's secret, compact superpower transmitters took a great deal of time – time when a spy would be out of circuit and would have to come up with some explanations when she reopened contact.

And there was no question in Marl's mind that this agent would eventually be tamed. Or else she would be brainscanned for her code phrases, contacts, electronic 'fist,' and then executed.

Only three Internal Security agents had chosen Patriotism and the Road to Tyburn so far – three of the twenty-nine whom Poyndex had ordered into the Wolf Worlds in response to Hohne's bleating about Sten's imminent arrival.

The other twenty-six were quite comfortable in quarters on various worlds that weren't quite prisons but were certainly not freedom, broadcasting exactly what they were fed.

Marl, and through her, Kilgour, and through him, Sten, were

running the Eternal Emperor's entire espionage net in the Wolf Worlds.

Just as Alex had planned.

Some time before, a colleague of Rykor's had been given an unusual assignment. A specialist in military recruiting, she had been ordered to prepare a campaign intended for the defeated Tahn worlds. At first Rykor had thought the idea somewhat unsavory, but she was pragmatic enough to realize that the military always recruits from its defeated and most generally downtrodden enemies.

But her colleague had gone on to explain that her orders had specifically stated that the campaign was to focus around a resurrection of the old Tahn samurai culture, a deathway the Emperor had sworn to extirpate after he had defeated the Tahn.

Interesting – and Rykor found it aberrational that the Emperor could believe that poverty could be cured by putting the poor in uniforms. But there was more to the concept than just that – and a full analysis revealed another indication of the Emperor's growing psychopathy. He was evidently building an army that he planned to use. Since there was no known external foe requiring a huge army to stand off, this newly restructured military would have as its purpose to destroy the enemy within. In other words, the citizens of the Empire.

Since the Tahn Way encouraged xenophobia, a racial superiority, the belief that mercy was a weakness, and the firm conviction that the strong had rights over the weak, this new model army of the Emperor's would be barbaric.

Rykor had subtly investigated – and found that other worlds with their own feral cultures were suddenly the focus of Imperial recruiters.

Very interesting.

Fortunately the campaign was very easy – at least easy for a being with Rykor's skills in mass psychology – to destroy.

Rykor had swept up every psychologist or psychological student she could find who was able to fulfill some fairly basic requirements: Do you like to travel? Do you mind being alone? Can you tell a necessary lie without feeling guilty? Can you take on a job that you will not be able to see the results of? Can you accomplish a task and accept that you will not be rewarded immediately? And so on and so forth.

It was unfortunate she wasn't able to field battalions of

counterpropaganda specialists, as she would have had she still been serving the Eternal Emperor.

But the antitoxin to this murderous psychological virus spread rapidly enough by itself. It worked because it addressed the Emperor's campaign at the root – and contained just enough truth to be unpleasant.

For instance, one of Rykor's volunteers was named Stengers. He was given a clean background and inserted on an Imperial world where he traveled openly as a student of sociology to Heath – the former capital of the Tahn. It was purest chance his wanderings were just behind an undercover Imperial Recruiting advance man, and just ahead of the recruiting team itself.

All Stengers did was ask some puzzled questions, especially to those young Tahn who were considering taking the Imperial shilling.

Questions such as: 'Well, if the Emperor wants you to rise up and redeem the honor of the Tahn, why does he want you to serve so far from your home? It is hard to gain honor in the darkness, as one of your own proverbs states.'

Sometimes, he was a bit more direct: 'Interesting. You say that eighteen Tahn from this farm district alone have gone off to serve? And none of them have returned from Imperial duties? Two of them have died? How sad to die, so far from home, serving someone who seems to never notice such a sacrifice.'

Or closer to the bone: 'If the Emperor suddenly thinks so highly of the Tahn, and their elders, why is this district pig-drakh poor? With all of the Empire's riches, why are we shivering in front of this peat-bog fire? Why, the world I come from, which is no richer than this, and I live far in the hills, has AM2 heating in every home. I don't understand.'

Or brutal: 'Seems to me a pretty good way for the Tahn to never amount to anything if the Emperor's taking your best and sending them out to the fringe worlds to die.'

Stengers and his fellows planted livie items, a revival of carefully chosen Tahn war ballads that centered around the belief that the Emperor and all his minions were worms beneath a Tahn's feet . . .

The next overall recruiting report to Prime contained some disappointing statistics about the sudden drop in volunteers to the Eternal Emperor's armed services . . .

*

Sten had cautioned Kilgour to be most careful on Earth. Even though the blown mission on the Umpqua River was against the privy council, security beings are security beings. There was a very good likelihood that the goons who would be wandering around the near-abandoned hamlet of Coos Bay, which Sten and Alex had used for their base, might still be carrying the same occupational specialty but serving another master. Gestapo is gestapo, as the seemingly meaningless archaism put it.

No problem, Kilgour swore. He planned to stay well away from the province of Oregon. Alex hoped that the secret he was looking for – the purpose of the Eternal Emperor's mysterious trip to Earth – was far, far away. In this case, far away meant the nearest full-range spaceport.

San Francisco, California's biggest city, boasted a population of almost 100,000. The young lovers – Hotsco, at least, qualified – claimed to have arrived in California Province on a shuttlehop into one of the desert retirement communities to the south, around the tiny province capital of Santa Ana. From there they had boarded one of the luxury gravcraft that swept over the San Joaquin Marshlands at the hamlet of Bakersfield, and leisurely found their way north.

Actually, Hotsco's smuggling ship was parked fifty meters underwater in the city's great bay near the Isle of Pelicans. One beep from Hotsco's transponder, and robot rescue would be inbound.

Playing tourist, they took lodgings in one of the new pseudo-Victorian guest houses that were being built in the wilds atop the Twin Peaks. They marveled that there had once been a bridge across the headlands, and listened as visionaries told them one day the straits would be bridged again. They declined an invitation to hunt a man-eater in the overgrown jungles of what had once been a park. They listened to arguments as to whether the foothills of the Mission District should be cleared – some swore the low mounds were rubble from high-rise buildings that had fallen in some great quake. They danced in the restoration of a huge clifftop mansion patterned after one that had been destroyed pre-Emperor and three monster earthquakes ago.

They politely refused an invitation from two rather lovely human females to join them in sexual ecstasy, in the Lovedance of the Ancient Merkins. Free. Alex thought Hotsco looked interested and then somewhat disappointed when he reminded her that, generally, new lovers are in love for a while before kinks occur. He did make a mental note to himself that the woman appeared to have interesting recreational ideas.

And they ate. Crab they caught themselves with a rented pot near another ruined bridge which led directly across the bay. Long loaves of wonderfully sour bread. Broiled fish. Raw fish artfully arranged on pats of rice. Rack of lamb. Chicken roasted under a brick. Alex, never a sybarite, let alone a gourmand, thought of changing his ways.

And they talked. Talked to anyone and everyone. Especially in the bars and hangouts around the small spaceport just south of the city. Alex claimed to be a freelance import/exporter in the luxury trade, and Hotsco his new business/life partner. What, they wondered, did people think could be exported from Earth, considering that it was Manhome, that would interest customers throughout the Empire? More specifically, what *could* be exported – legally and morally?

Six E-days – and Alex smiled to himself: these really *were* Earth-days – later, without anyone seeming to realize that they had been grilled, Kilgour found his being. A customs official, someone with a sense of mission – which meant a built-in nose for a grievance, especially when it meant that someone had used higher authority to avoid proper procedure. Tsk, Kilgour assured her. Neither of them would ever . . . kind of thing that's despicable . . . business must be run in a proper manner . . . matter of fact, Ms Tjanting . . . one of the more terrible things about my own profession . . . some traders . . . even heard stories of very high officials bending the laws . . .

The pump didn't need much priming.

Very high officials, indeed. Straight from Prime, in fact. And during the time frame Alex was interested in.

Customs, through Earth Spaceship Control, had been notified that the province of Oregon was closed to all nonstandard in-atmosphere and nearspace traffic. Which mattered not at all to Tjanting. She knew that the Emperor had his estates up there, and what he, or his people, chose to do was none of her concern. She might have been curious, being a good citizen, if the Emperor had been present. But of course, he had not been there.

How did she know that, Alex wondered?

Well, there would have been something on the livies, wouldn't there? But that wasn't why she was red-arsed, though. If the Eternal Emperor knew what liberties had been taken in his name, Tjanting knew, he would not be pleased.

About two weeks before the announcement, Tjanting went on, a commercial transport had grounded at San Fran, intending to clear customs at this entry port and then proceed immediately to its final destination – the Imperial Grounds some hundreds of kilometers away. She boarded the ship and immediately found things unusual. The ship was immaculate, and the crewmen followed orders as if they were in the Imperial Navy. But that was sheer conjecture. What had upset her was the cargo.

The skipper of the transport had, at first, refused to allow her access to the hold, claiming that what it contained was a classified cargo – property of the Imperial Household. But there was no paperwork to verify his claim. He could be carrying any sort of basic supplies to the river complex, supplies that the Emperor, like any other citizen, would have to pay duties on to the Earth government.

Tjanting insisted he open the hold – or else she would call for security and impound the ship and cargo and arrest the crew. The captain yielded gracelessly.

The cargo was medical – sophisticated equipment and supplies, as if someone were establishing a very small, but very superb, surgical ward. Or so, Tjanting said, a colleague specializing in med supplies had told her when she called back and read him the bill-of-lading fiche.

The problem wasn't that the cargo was dutiable – it probably wasn't, under humanitarian grounds. The question Tjanting had, and the one that wasn't answered, was why was this equipment necessary? Customs was also responsible for quarantine and health. Was someone in the Imperial Household ill? Or needing some kind of surgical help? For all she knew, there was a plague breeding.

She reported the matter to her superiors and was told to wait. They would contact the Emperor's staff in Oregon. That took minutes – no one in Oregon knew of such an incoming shipment. Tjanting was sure she had uncovered a strange sort of smuggling ring whose members had the maximum amount of gall.

Then another call came from the north, and before her shift ended, she was hauled in and reprimanded severely for what her supervisor called 'unwarranted snooping into the business of the Eternal Emperor.' Tjanting was also told she had a nasty reputation for being a busybody, and had best correct this character flaw lest it cause a downgrade on her next efficiency hearing.

By now the woman was seething, and Alex soothed her, and

bought her another drink – a truly awful concoction of a sweet liqueur called Campari, charged water, and a brandy float on top. It was a monstrous waste of cognac, Alex thought, but said nothing.

So, while Hotsco covered for him with chattered sympathy, Alex mused: Jus' afore th' Emp dances on, some laddie wants t' set up an OR. An' it's gowky to conceive th' Emp's retreat nae has a wee medical kit an' such. So, somethin' special mayhap wae intended, aye? An op'ration?

On th' 'Ternal Emp'rer himself?

A wee bit ae surgery thae's carefully kept under th' rose . . .?

Aye. 'Tis odd. 'Tis ver' ver' odd, Kilgour thought.

Actually, 'tis ver' simple, he realized, considering the presence of the bomb-disposal experts at the Emperor's compound. Surgically implanting a bomb in somebody wasn't unknown to Kilgour – the ruse had been used successfully by fanatics before. Kilgour had also heard of brave beings having a bomb installed inside them before they went on a suicide mission, to prevent any possibility of capture, torture, and exposing their fellows.

However, taking a bomb *out* was a new twist. And this is what he now thought had happened.

Mmm, Alex mused. So. Noo we ken where th' boomie thae goes off whae th' Emp dies com't frae, aye? I's installed i' th' loonie's gut, p'raps where th' 'pendix was. I' dinnae matter. Th' *real* puzzler i' who put th' clottin' thing in, i' the first place!

Th' further an' further Ah dig an' delve, Kilgour mused, th' less an' less Ah knoo thae's f'r certain.

Ah well. I' y' want'd a life where thae was naught but th' abs'lute, y' coulda been a WeeFreesie. Or stay'd a common so'jer.

Alex refused to continue. Reasoning from insufficient data almost invariably produces suspect conclusions. He would think more on this later.

They fed Tjanting a couple of drinks, then announced that they had to get back to their hotel.

Tjanting watched them leave. After a moment, she frowned, and a queer expression crossed her face.

Halfway across the Empire, two men were drinking raw alk and knocking the shots back with homebrew in a portabar not far from a construction site. One man was a contact welder, the other a bank vice president, slumming.

'You heard,' the welder began, 'about what happened when

the Eternal Emperor picked up a joygirl? First time he says I'm gonna ravish you and make you moan. He does and she does.

'Then he says I'm gonna ravish you and make you scream. He does and she does.

'Then he says I'm gonna make you *sweat*. And the joygirl pulls back and says Huh? And he says because the next time's gonna be midsummer . . .'

The banker chortled politely. 'Way I heard it, the Emp just thinks that there's some things a man's gotta take care of himself. And in his case, it's th' little stuff.'

The welder returned the compliment of laughter, turned serious. 'You never notice, Els, that the Emperor never shows up on a livie cast when he's somewhere doin' something ceremonial with a woman?'

'Why should he?'

'No reason,' the welder said. 'But if you was top dog, I'd assume there'd be a ton of honey trying to lurk on you, right? Like if you got promoted Chief Suit tomorrow?'

'Maybe. But my wife'd have words about that.'

'Something else the Emperor's lacking.'

'Maybe that's why he lives forever,' the banker suggested. 'He's just saving his precious natural resources.'

'Assumin' he's got any.'

Both men snickered, and attention was drawn to the livie screen and the gravball match's third quarter just beginning.

Both 'jokes' were the work of Rykor's staff. Funny or not, they were intended to accomplish just what they were doing: to reduce the Eternal Emperor's image of omnipotence. In this particular instance, quite literally.

These jokes, and a hundred hundred others, coupled with some really nasty whispered rumors and legends, were moving through the Empire at a speed slightly above stardrive.

The nighttime ritual was for Alex to check their room to see if they had been blackbagged or bugged. Then he would wash up in the fresher. Afterward, Hotsco would get showered and powdered and join him in the great, old-fashioned feather bed. But only to sleep. Alex, the professional and the moralist, would never dream of taking advantage of a cover. Nor was he attracted to the slender young woman. Not at all his type.

Or so he lied at increasingly frequent intervals.

He lathered and scrubbed, luxuriating in the soft water that needled against his body, remembering times and missions when there was no water for anything but drinking, and barely enough for that. He turned to adjust the shower from NEEDLE to BLAST, and a giggle sounded in his ear, a giggle whose Alex's expert ear sonared at two centimeters' distance.

'Move over,' Hotsco said. 'And give me the soap. Your back needs washing.'

'Uh, lass . . .'

'I said, move over.'

Alex did as he was told. Hotsco began scrubbing his back, soap moving in slow, sensual circles.

'I'm not looking,' she said. 'But I have a wager on what a Scotsman has under his kilt.'

'Aye?' Alex said, a smile beginning to grow across his face. 'An' y'd like t' feel someat thae's twenty-five centimeters? Reach under m' sporran twenty times.'

Hotsco laughed. Her fingers moved on. Traced a red, ragged trough on Kilgour's biceps.

'What's that?' she wondered.

'Thae's where Ah zigged like a clot when Ah should'a zagged. Wounds are a good way t' keep y'r ego frae gettin' overweenin't.'

'Lass, thae's noo m' chest y're scrubbin't.'

'That's all right,' Hotsco said dreamily. 'That's not the soap, either.'

'If Ah turn aroun',' Kilgour said, his voice a little husky, 'Ah'll be startin' t' take th' wee game a bit seriously.'

'Mmm.'

Alex turned, reached down, and lifted Hotsco in his arms. Their lips met, and her legs closed around his thighs.

A bit later, they got out of the shower. They had to use Kilgour's robe as a towel, since the fresher looked like the site of a water-main explosion.

Outside was the moon shining on the bay and the dying lights of San Francisco.

'An' noo,' Alex said, 'we'll hie ourselves t' th' feathers, an' Ah'll noo hae t' worry aboot whether m' McLean powers are runnin't dry.'

'Is *that* what you call it,' Hotsco wondered. She crossed to her dresser, picked up a tube of aromatic oil, and slowly began rubbing it into her skin, smiling over her shoulder as she did.

'If y're th' lass wi' th' soap,' Alex volunteered, 'dinnae it be justice if Ah'm th' lad whae goes slip-slidin' away?'

He took the tube from her, squeezed some oil on his fingers, and then, suddenly, his instincts cut through the lust. He flipped Hotsco sideways, across the bed. She thudded into the feathers, too startled to shout – and the dressing-table mirror exploded.

Kilgour backrolled to the door, came up, pistol magically in hand, kneeling, braced . . . three rounds crashed as one . . . and out on the balcony the assassin's chest exploded.

Someone or something crashed against the door, and Kilgour sent three more AM2 rounds through it, the wood wisping and charring. There was a scream outside.

Alex grabbed the tiny transponder that was their only back door, shoved it in his mouth, and scooped up Hotsco in one arm. He took two gigantic steps across the room, shattering what remained of the balcony door's framework, high-stepped onto the balcony, and jumped. Hotsco yelped.

It was seven meters to the grassy turf below, and as Alex fell, he twisted his body, feet together, and used the uniformed cop who was gaping up at him as a trampoline.

The cop's ribs snapped, and he screamed a bloody gargle. Kilgour collapsed to his knees, absorbing the shock of the landing. Then he sprang back up, and, without pausing or dropping either Hotsco in one hand or his pistol in the other, hurtled toward the brushy cover around the inn.

An AM2 round exploded turf next to him – so, i's th' Emp's boyos, Kilgour recognized – and he spun and, without bothering to aim, pumped four rounds back up into the room they had just vacated.

Then he was juggernauting again.

By the time the pickup/hit squad of San Francisco cops and Internal Security operatives recovered, the white blur that was the naked heavy-worlder had vanished into the scrub.

Sirens ululated then, and lights flashed and coms crackled.

But Kilgour was gone.

Two kilometers away, Alex stopped running. He estimated that he was somewhere in that great jungle close to the end of the peninsula, where tigers who had been freed from the zoo aeons earlier stalked the night.

The tiggers, he decided, would hae t' take their risks.

'Ah'm in no mood t' be trifled wi',' he announced softly. 'Ah had plans f'r th' remaind'r ae th' evening.'

Even though Hotsco had grown up on the far side of what

most beings called the law, she was not used to this sort of thing – especially when it came at a blur of lightspeed. But she was clotting damned if she would lose face in front of Alex.

'I assume,' she said, 'the Empire just caught up with us.'

'Aye,' Alex said. 'Thae hae willyguns. Th' customs lass narked on us. Ah dinnae catch her last name, Hotsco. Dinnae y' ken i' it wae Campbell?'

He seemed completely oblivious to the fact they were both stark naked – and that their sole assets, against a city and a world that would be raising a hue and cry against them, were a pistol and a transponder.

'What next?' Hotsco asked.

'W' hae twa choices,' Alex said. 'First, an' most palatable, i' w' hunt doon th' two lassies ae th' Lovedance ae th' Merkins. Thae'll noo blanch ae th' sight ae a couple ae young lovers comin't t' them ae th' Laird made them. An' we c'n continue whae we barely – sorry, lass – begun't till th' heat dies doon. I' y' hae their card?'

'I left it back there,' Hotsco said. Her shock had died away, and quite suddenly she found this whole situation funny. 'In the hotel. You want me to go back for it?'

Alex considered.

'Nae,' he said, straight-facedly. ''Twas nae but a passin' fancy. Option two. We'll work our way t' th' docks, an' either steal a curragh, or else swim oot t' thae island ae th' big-jawed birds. Alcatruss?'

'Swim. I can't swim.'

'Nae problem, lass. Ah'll need but one arm t' be bashin't th' sharks away. Ah'll hae y' wi' th' other, an' th' bangstick between m' fangs. A braw measure ae a Scotsman.

'Kickin't wi' m' feet an' steerin' wi' th' rudder th' Laird provided. It canna be more'n a klick 'r twa awa'. Brisk, refreshin' dawn swim. Ah hae a strong desire t' gie back t' th' wee game y' w're teachin' me wi' a minimum ae time loss. Shall we?'

He bowed formally, took her arm, and they started south, toward the fishing village.

Fleet Admiral Anders, the Imperial Chief of Naval Operations, looked at the progs on the five wallscreens, then at the sixteen fiches projected across his desk. His face was impassive, just as he had learned a proper war leader should look in his moment of decision.

He was not sure what he thought, since he was, or so his Intel chief had assured him, the first to see, let alone have the chance to analyze, this data. After all, there was just the possibility, his mind thought vaguely, that the Eternal Emperor had not been jesting when he said some time ago that when the Sten problem was over, Anders would find himself in command of two rowboats and a tidal bank on some forgotten planet. He really didn't want to make another mistake.

He decided to start with skepticism. Because he was a man of lists, that was the way he worded his doubts.

'Give me,' he said, 'three reasons why I should believe that this system – Ystrn – will be the jumping-off point for the traitor Sten's next raid? And why, in fact, does your intelligence suggest that Al-Sufi is, in fact, the target?'

Anders's Two, Sheffries, wondered whether she was supposed to come up with three reasons or six, considering that he had asked two separate questions. In either case, she was disappointed in her clot of a boss. She had three threes ready.

'One: Al-Sufi is one of the three largest AM2 distribution centers in the Empire. Two: Sten has already hit one such depot. Three: Revolutionaries with limited means, such as Sten—'

'That should be the *traitor* Sten,' Anders interjected.

'Beg pardon. Traitors like Sten, who have little in the way of combat ships and troops, normally become enamored of spectacular targets. Particularly if those targets appear to provide the maximum damage to the enemy, sorry, the home worlds, they're rebelling against. The term is "panacea targets." In other words—'

'In other words,' Anders went on, 'he somehow had a small measure of success against Dusable, which is why he'll hit Al-Sufi next.'

'Thank you, sir. You summarized my thinking admirably. Four: The Al-Sufi/Durer battle, commonly called Durer by the masses, was one of the Emperor's biggest victories during the Tahn war. Therefore it makes perfect sense that the traitor Sten would want to ruin this image.

'Five. Since Sten was evidently, although we still have incomplete data, not serving with the Imperial forces during the Al-Sufi/Durer battle—'

Anders waved Sheffries to silence. 'Very well,' he said. 'You have convinced me.

'Three fleets will be required for this operation. Alert my staff. I shall brief them on what the oplan shall consist of.'

'Three fleets, sir?'

'Exactly. I propose to obliterate, at one stroke, this rebellion. So I shall wish all of my sailors to be aware of their participation in this moment of destiny.'

'Sir. My plus/minus of accuracy on the prog is only eighty percent. And I haven't run *any* progs as to whether Sten – I mean, the traitor Sten – would be personally in charge of the raid.'

'Of course he would,' Anders said impatiently. 'I would. You would.' He smiled. 'The Eternal Emperor will be very glad of this news. When the traitor Sten is finished, Sheffries, I shall personally see that you are rewarded with flag rank.'

Sheffries managed to express delight, saluted, and was gone. Wonderful, she thought glumly. And if anything goes wrong, it'll be, Commander Sheffries, would you mind crossing your legs? We only have three nails . . .

Sten was plotting the 'raid of Al-Sufi,' and just how the rendezvous point in the Ystrn system should appear, when the EYES ONLY message from Sr Ecu, on Seilichi, was hand-carried up from the message center.

He swore, found a decoding machine, and keyed in pore pattern, retina flash, personal code, and all the rest.

Then he scanned the covering message and that appeal from Marr and Senn.

Clot. He knew who the other being was. Haines, of course. Yes, he remembered only too well, his body stirring, the party and the garden and the black ball against the moon.

It made sense that the madman who called himself the Eternal Emperor would be rounding up anyone who knew Sten for brainscan.

He was glad that somehow Haines had escaped the net. Then he wondered if the Emperor and his satrap Poyndex had cast again, and gotten her. Or if they had widened their quest and gone after Marr and Senn, after they had sent the 'flier.' Yet a third and even more likely possibility was that Poyndex's IS elements had discovered Marr and Senn's amateur attempt at cryptography and had laid an ambush.

First response. Saddle up and go for a rescue.

Stopped cold in its adrenaline rush.

Like hell. You are beyond that, now. You have had the gall to stand up and declare yourself outlaw and rebel against the Empire. Which is fine. Any being is entitled to find his own suicide.

But there are others who've joined you. You're responsible for them, aren't you? So you sure as hell can't head out on some forlorn hope, can you? You've got to worry about the bigger things.

Besides, this wouldn't be the first time that you've had to abandon a friend or even a lover to accomplish the mission, right?

Of course.

The com buzzed. Sten slugged the contact switch.

'GA.'

'Mister Kilgour,' the com officer reported. 'Inbound. ETA one E-hour. Mission accomplished. I have him onbeam now.'

Sten started to say that he would talk to Alex when he grounded, then stopped.

'Sealed?'

'Of course, sir.'

'Patch it through.'

The screen cleared. Onscreen was Alex; to one side of him was a demurely smiling woman. Oh yes, Sten thought. That must be the smuggler captain who volunteered to insert Kilgour onto Earth. Sten looked at his friend.

'Welcome home,' he said.

'Thanks, boss.'

'No offense. But you look like slok.'

'Lad, i' wae a noisesome task Ah set myself.'

'You were blown?'

'Aye. But noo by th' Emp, thoo Ah hae an int'restin' run in wi' India Sierra as we w're runnin't th' mission. An' noo on Earth. An Ah'll noo 'splain. But Ah hae traces ae whae Ah wen' lookin't for, which Ah'll noo 'splain till we face-t'-face.'

'Whae's been th' haps i' m' absence?'

And Sten found himself briefing Alex. Further, telling him about the com from Ecu/Marr/Senn. He stopped short, without mentioning his decision.

'Ah.' Alex nodded. 'Ah ken. Y' noo hae a choice, do y'?'

Sten didn't answer.

'Ah'll hae th' *Victory* packed an' liftin' wi'in an E-day after Ah return, lad.'

Sten blinked.

Alex smiled. 'Y' noo thought thae was whae Ah meant, did y'? Y' were thinkin't about duty an' respons'bility, aye?'

'Something like that.'

'Well . . . consider all thae lads an' lassies thae went rebel wi' y'. Some went oot frae selfish reasons, some went oot frae reasons ae' aidin' th' gran' cause ae civil'zation. But more went oot 'cause they're servin't y'r wee smilin't face, lad.

'I' some ways, 'tis noo a good part ae life, wee Sten. We all should mak't decisions wi' logic an' frae th' good ae all livin't things.

'But thae's noo how it works.

'An' i' the foolish ones who're servin't you because y're one wee mon, shouldnae you be thinkin't th' same? Willin' t' spend y'rself f'r th' life ae one wee fellow rebel? 'Cause if you're noo willin't t' go doon i' flames like thae, then we're noo dif'frent thae the Emp, and p'raps should cast i' our lot immed'jately.

'Y' sh'd noo be sendi't frae which fool th' bell tolls frae, an' thae, aye?

'Ah reck y' hae noo choice othern't to gie y'self a'ter Haines an' th' two furballs.'

It was completely wrong, and one of the more stupid things that Sten could do. And why he decided to go for it. What the clot, the rebellion was doomed anyway. He had zip-burp chance of toppling the Empire. So why not go down in flames on a noble gesture?

'GA,' he started. Then he caught himself, and an evil smile spread across his face. He remembered a scam he had worked once before on a prison break, and thought he could ring yet another change on it.

'Negative, Mister Kilgour. I won't need the *Victory*. All I need is one Bhor robohulk and the *Aoife*. There's no reason I have to be a complete Don Quickshot. Oh yeah. And one livie crew and some actors. I want three pilot sorts, two goons, and one idiot with steel teeth. Unbathed and whacko-looking. All human. Oh yeah. I need about fifteen or so terrified cute children.

'Now, get your butt down here. I have need of your talents. And somebody to hold the fort while I'm off playing Sir Gawaine. Clear.'

Sten's plan took less than half a day to accomplish.

He was still going out to his death, but at least in a sneaky, dirty, underhanded sort of way instead of the imbecilic 'charge in full dress uniform waving an ivory-hilted can opener' that he had always despised.

'Soward Control, this is the transport *Juliette*. Now in normal space, coordinates transmitted . . . now. Using commercial orbit Quebec Niner Seven. Request landing instructions. Over.'

And so terror came to Prime World.

'*Juliette*, this is Soward Control. Have your coordinates.

Transmitting landing data . . . now. Please enter data and activate
ALS at termination of your orbit Quebec Niner Seven, over.'

'Soward, this is *Juliette*. Wait one . . . uh, I've got a slight
problem with your data, Control. That'll park us on the far
southeast corner of the field, correct?'

'That's an affirm.'

'Got a favor to ask, Soward. Any possibility of getting closer?
I've got a shipload of scholarship kids aboard, and they'd get a
boot out of seeing things a little closer. Plus that's a long walk
to the terminal. Can we get a shuttle?'

'This is Soward. No problem. We'll tuck you right over here,
near the tower. Transmitting new data . . . now. And for a shuttle
. . . all we've got is commercial. Shall I notify a carrier?'

'This is *Juliette*. Thanks for the shift. And, uh, negative on that
commercial carrier. My kids don't have a lot of money. This is
one of those starving-students hops.'

'Roger. Maybe we can—'

And the *Juliette*'s signal cut.

'*Juliette*, this is Soward Control. *Juliette*, please respond to this
transmission.'

Static. No response. The controller automatically hit EMERGENCY
and STANDBY buttons.

'This is the tower,' he said. 'I've got an inbound, closing on
final, and they went off the air. Info from pilot said they've got
children aboard. Stand by.'

Rescue crews rolled into their vehicles.

The controller fingered a touchpad, and went to both the
standard landing and the Imperial Standard emergency freqs.

'*Juliette*, this is—'

'Who is this?' It was a new voice, from the *Juliette*.

'This is Soward Landing Control. Identify yourself. Is this the
Juliette?'

A laugh.

'Yeah. Yeah. Is this the visual-transmit switch . . . yeah. Here
we go.'

A screen cleared, and showed an appalling scene. It was the
control room of the *Juliette*. The four beings in the flight crew
sprawled in bloody pools. In front of the pickup was a wild-eyed
man, wearing a filthy, stained shipsuit. He held a gun.

Behind him were two equally repellent assistants. Each of them
held a wriggling child in one arm – and held a knife pressed to
that child's throat.

'See what you got,' the man said. 'Now. I want a straight patch to an Imperial livie station. Now!'

'I can't—'

The man gestured, and one of his assistants slashed a throat. Blood gouted, the other child screamed, and a body flopped on the deck.

'Get another one,' the man said, and his pet goon vanished, and came back dragging another preteenager. 'You see? We ain't drakhin' around. Get a—'

And the dispatcher was hitting keys.

'You better sound convincing,' the hijacker said. 'Because I got me another fourteen crumbsnatchers I don't mind thinslicin'. Or doin' . . . some other things to them. Stuff that's worse.'

So began the drama of the *Juliette*. The feed went live on K-B-N-S-O, back on the air, but broadcasting from a temporary, planetary headquarters.

Prime World came to a stop as the battered transport orbited over Soward Spaceport. The man announced what he wanted.

'I want a link to the Eternal Emperor. Not on a clottin' com like this. But face to face. He's gotta settle something. He's gotta stop doing to my family what he done. It ain't right for nobody that big to be feuding like he was some kind of backcountry pencilneck, it ain't. And it's gonna come to an end, it is. My family's near wiped out.

'Hell, if there ain't no clottin' change, I'm subject to send this clottin' transport at full drive straight into that clottin' palace of his. You tell the Emperor that.'

Hostage-rescue teams were assembled, and waited to see if they'd be called on for the last resort of boarding the *Juliette*. The Imperial fleet patrolling offworld closed on Prime. Arundel's already alert security elements were ready with AA missiles held one count from launch, and would fire if the *Juliette* headed toward the Emperor's palace.

Of course there would be, there could be, no meeting between the Eternal Emperor and the men aboard the *Juliette*. Terror must not be surrendered to.

Negotiators began the long slow drone, trying to bore the hijackers into surrender. But the hijackers didn't respond – the only response they made was either to repeat their preposterous demand, to stare blankly at the pickup, or occasionally to shut down without a warning.

The livies ate it with a spoon. The story had everything. Crazed terrorists. The cutest on-camera kids since they caught child star Shirlee Rich in bed with her orangutan. Understanding shrinks analyzing everything endlessly. Experts trying to figure out just what world the still-unknown hijackers could have come from. Warships blasting back and forth across the sky. Unknown movement of forces that not even the biggest sleaze livie show host would speculate on, to avoid possibly exposing a secret rescue plan. Lloyds insurance executives explaining what might have happened to the transport *Juliette* since it had disappeared into Imperial Special Service all the way back during the Tahn war. Noble-looking special-weapons teams ready to sacrifice their all.

Best of all, it was *real*.

The only challenge the *Aoife* got as it closed on Prime was mechanical, perfunctory, and at least three cycles out of date. Berhal Waldman didn't even have to analyze the challenge, but found it in a standard code-fiche. Everybody was preoccupied.

The *Aoife* went straight in for a landing.

No one noticed, even in the tiny village at the far end of the narrow valley. That abominable monster aboard the *Juliette* had just butchered another child.

The destroyer may have been a tiny ship – in space, and compared to a battlewagon/carrier like the *Victory*, or on the wide, bare tarmac of a landing field where the eye couldn't provide any scale. But it made the tower it landed beside into a toy. Waldman's fingers ran across the keys, keeping the *Aoife* hanging just clear of the ground on its McLean generators. It would not do to leave a five-meter-deep impression in the middle of the beautifully-laid-out garden. Not only for aesthetic reasons, but that might suggest to the curious what had happened.

There was no movement from the tower.

The *Aoife*'s chainguns swept the pinnacle, Honjo fingers hovering above firing keys.

The ship's ramp slid down, and Sten came out. He was wearing combat armor, and carried a willygun. But his helmet face was open.

Waldman thought that was truly insane – Internal Security could be waiting just inside. But Sten couldn't figure out any other way to let beings know they were being rescued, not attacked.

He was nearly at the door before it opened.

Marr and Senn stood there.

'I must say,' Marr said. 'You certainly arrive in a baroque manner, my young captain.'

'Yeah. Baroque. Let's get the clot out of here before somebody baroques us in half. Later for the aphorisms, troops.'

And Haines was there, in the doorway.

'Took you long enough.'

'Sorry. Hadda stop and tie my bootlaces.'

Behind Haines, a human male. Slender. Balding. Early middle age. Dressed about ten years out of style. Sten flashguessed that was Haines's husband. Not at all the sort of man he would have expected her to end up with.

Don't be considering that, idiot. Like you just told everybody else. Book.

Senn, Haines, and Sam'l ran for the ship. Marr hesitated for a moment, then bent and picked up a small, multihued pebble.

'There might be nothing left to come back to.'

And then he, too, boarded the *Aoife*, Sten close behind him.

'Lift, sir?' Waldman asked as Sten boiled into the control room.

'Wait one.'

He looked at a screen, which showed the bridge of the *Juliette*. No one was in front of the pickup, either hostage or terrorist.

'Send it.'

'Yessir.' The com operator next to the screen hit a button, and the *Aoife* broadcast a single letter in code to the *Juliette*.

Onscreen chaos.

Shouts. Screams. The hijackers, bellowing incomprehensibly. A young girl broke away and tried to run. She was shot down. The hijacker was shrieking in some never-to-be-translated tongue. His pistol swayed, then blasted. Straight into the pickup! Dead air.

'Oh my dear, oh my dear,' Marr moaned, arms around Senn. 'Those poor baby humans!'

'Yep,' Sten said. 'Terrible, terrible. And it's going to get worse. Berhal Waldman, take us up. About five hundred meters, please.'

The *Aoife* shot skyward.

Sten was quite a prophet, as a second screen went to life, this time on a commercial station.

Blur . . . snap-focus . . . a battered spaceship . . . McLean units off . . . haze from the ship's stern as the Yukawa drive went to full . . .

Screaming incoherence from some liviecaster: 'Horror . . . Horror . . . oh the horror of it all . . .'

'Full drive, if you please. Home, James.'

The *Aoife* slammed into hyperspace, sonic boom as air rushed to fill the vacuum left by the destroyer.

That explosion went unheard, buried by a greater one as the *Juliette* crashed straight into the center of Soward's main landing field. There was no fire, no rubble. Just a smoking crater.

Sten turned sadly as the *Aoife*'s pickup lost the commercial 'cast.

'What an awful thing,' he said. 'All those beautiful little children, spread over the landscape like so much strawberry preserves. Strawberry? Tomato. Saltier-tasting.

'And *so* coincidental, too. Unfortunate for them, although they'd probably all grow up to be ax-murderers or lawyers or something, but certainly providential for us.

'As Mister Kilgour says, God never takes away with one hand but he gives with the other.'

Marr and Senn uncurled from their woe and their great eyes focused on Sten. Haines verbalized it.

'You know, you're an utter bastard, Sten.'

'That's what my mother always said,' Sten agreed happily.

'Thanks,' she said, quite seriously.

'Hey. It wasn't that much. You know me. Saint Sten. Slayer of Virtuous Maidens. Rescuer of Dragons.'

Amid the banter Sten felt very, very good about himself. And very surprised they'd gotten away with it.

Officially, the *Juliette* incident remained a tragic event, another example of the growing collective psychopathology of an over-complex civilization. Privately, though, investigators were fairly sure they had been snookered. Not that any trace of the tape Sten's actors had carefully prepared during the flight out from Vi remained. *Nothing* remained of the Bhor robohulk except a hole in the tarmac and a wisp or six of greasy smoke. But investigators knew they would have found some carbon traces of the eighteen or more beings who died before or in the crash, no matter how thorough the splatter.

When Sten heard that, as a passed-along rumor, he swore mightily. If he had given the situation one more thought, he could have scored ten or so beef carcasses from a butcher shop, and no one would *ever* have known.

Three mighty Imperial battlefleets flashed out of hyperspace in the Ystrn system, all weapons stations manned and ready to obliterate the rebellion.

Six worlds and their moons and moonlets orbited a dead star. Nothingness.

No Sten.

No rebel fleet.

No nothing.

And as far as the most sophisticated analysis could determine, no known ship had *ever* entered this system. It had been named on a star chart and never explored. Not that there was anything worth exploring.

Sten's big con had worked. Or, rather, was working. He had never considered raiding Al-Sufi, of course, nor going anywhere that close to Prime World with his tiny battlefleet.

The deception that had been leaked through Hohne's doubled net and other agents around the Empire was just the first step.

Sten was playing liar's poker with the Emperor.

This time, there was nothing there.

Next time, in another system, there might be traces that Sten or some of his ships had recently passed through.

Not only was this game something that could be played over and over again – the Emperor could not and would not ignore any reports of Sten's presence – and burn AM2, Imperial ships and supplies, whatever faith the Imperial Navy had in its intelligence, and the Eternal Emperor's arse, but it would have a payoff.

One that would shake the Imperial forces to their souls.

Chapter Fifteen

Subadar-Major Chethabahadur snapped a crisp salute. 'Sah! Reporting as ordered, sah.'

'Sit down, Subadar-Major,' Poyndex said. 'No need for formality.'

Chethabahadur sat, his small, slender body stiff in the seat.

'I'm afraid I have some very bad news,' Poyndex said. 'I'm sorry to be the one bearing it. But there's no sense beating about the brambles and making things worse. So here it is. As you know, the Eternal Emperor holds *you* people in high esteem for your years of dedicated service.'

Chethabahadur blinked. Very quickly. All other reactions were caught in time. The phrase 'you people' was clearly an insult worthy of a cut throat. The 'years of dedicated service' numbered in the hundreds, which meant that Poyndex should have had his throat cut a second time. As for 'high esteem' – well, it was almost too much.

The subadar-major kept his expression mild, wondering at the several miracles allowing this toady to remain alive after mewling such nonsense.

'Very high esteem, indeed,' Poyndex continued. 'Unfortunately, he has found himself in a terrible position. Money is very tight now, you understand. Cutbacks and belt tightening has been ordered all through the services.'

'Yes, sah,' Chethabahadur said. 'The Gurkhas have done their part, sah. But if further reductions are required, sah . . . be assured we are ready.'

Poyndex smiled condescendingly. 'How generous. But that won't be necessary. Under the circumstances. You see, I have been ordered to disband your unit. As I said, I'm very sorry. But we all have to make sacrifices in times like these.'

Without hesitation, Chethabahadur said, 'No need to apologize, sah. Tell the Emperor the Gurkha stand ready for any command. If he needs us to disband, sah . . . and return to Nepal . . . well, it shall be done. And without complaint, sah. Assure him of that.'

Another Poyndex smile. 'Oh, I will. I certainly will.'

The subadar-major came to his feet and snapped another salute. 'Then if that is all, sah, I will depart to inform my men.'

Poyndex made with a weak reply to the salute. 'Yes . . . That is all . . . And thank you very much.'

'It is you who are to be thanked, sah,' Chethabahadur said. He spun and marched from the room.

Poyndex eased back in his chair, pleased with himself for a difficult task well done . . . although he was surprised at how easy the Gurkha major had taken the news.

Such loyalty.

Blind, ignorant loyalty.

Poyndex laughed. He keyed his com and ordered his Internal Security troops to the posts of the departing Gurkhas.

Outside, in the corridor leading away from Poyndex's office, one floor below the Emperor's private quarters, Chethabahadur had to force down the sudden desire to leap high in the air and click his heels.

For a long time now he and his men had worried over the Emperor's deteriorating personality. His actions turned their stomachs. They could not understand how a soldier they admired – Ian Mahoney – could become a traitor. And there was absolutely no way they would believe Sten, once their commander, and still, as far as anyone knew, having one platoon of Gurkhas serving under him, would turn his coat, even against the rabid beast the Emperor had become.

All of the Gurkhas had wanted to quit. The only thing that had stopped them was their sworn oath – and the certain knowledge the Emperor would consider the action a grave insult.

He would kill them all.

Worse, they feared for their people in far-off Nepal. None of the Gurkhas doubted that the Emperor would remove Nepal from the face of the planet for such a betrayal.

But now – joy, oh joy, the heavens smiled and the Gurkhas were fired. What a bessing to come from such a barbarian as that Poyndex.

Not that Chethabahadur forgave him his rude behavior Someday he would kill the man.

If this was not possible, Chethabahadur's son would kill Poyndex's son.

For the Gurkhas had very long memories.

Poyndex watched with amazement as the woman, Baseeker, abased herself before the Eternal Emperor.

'Oh Lord, I am blinded by your exalted presence. My limbs tremble. My brain is a fever. My tongue a thick stump unable to form words befitting your full glory.'

Poyndex buried a smile. He thought her tongue was working just fine. The new high priestess of the Cult of the Eternal Emperor was prostrate on her god's office floor.

'You may rise,' the Emperor said solemnly. Poyndex was only mildly surprised at how seriously the Emperor seemed to be taking this interview.

Baseeker came to her knees, beat her head several times against the ground in further obeisance, then came the rest of the way to her feet. Poyndex saw the glitter of pleasure in the Emperor's eyes and congratulated himself in his choice to replace Zoran as the new high priestess. Baseeker had absorbed his coaching and then bettered it by several hundred percent.

'Please. Do sit down,' the Emperor said, fussing over the woman. 'May I offer you any refreshment?'

Baseeker slid into the indicated chair, poised at the edge as if relaxation would be a blasphemy. 'Thank you, Lord. But allow this humble seeker of truth to reject your kindness. I could not possibly take mortal nourishment at this time. Permit me, instead, to continue to feed my spirit upon the ethers of your holy presence.'

Poyndex doubted whether Baseeker ever fed on much of anything – except personal ambition. She was all bone and gristle, wrapped tight with skin so pale it was nearly translucent. She was of indeterminate age, with a severely pinched face, sharp incisors peeking through thin lips, and eyes like small bright beads. Like a rat's, Poyndex thought.

'Whatever pleases you,' the Emperor said, waving grandly.

Baseeker nodded, tucking her white robe around bony knees.

The Emperor indicated a sheaf of paper on his desk. 'I've studied your proposals for reorganization quite thoroughly,' he said. 'An impressive job.'

'Thank you, Lord,' Baseeker said. 'But it could not have been done without your inspiration. Frankly, the cult was left in complete disarray by my late predecessor – Zoran. Our purpose is to glorify you . . . and educate your subjects on your divine mission. But these things were left shamefully undone.'

'I see you have added a new program,' the Emperor said. 'A proposal to build worship centers in all the major capitals of the Empire.'

Baseeker bowed her head. 'I'd hoped it would meet your favor.'

Poyndex lifted his eyes to keep from laughing. They fell on the painting above the Emperor. It was an ultraromantic, ultra-muscular portrait of the Emperor, posing heroically. The painting was in commemoration of the Battle of the Gates, which the portrait indicated he had won single-handedly. Poyndex happened to know the Emperor never was even vaguely near the fighting in question.

The painting was one of a whole gallery glorifying the Emperor. They were from the awful collection of the late Tanz Sullamora. Ordered to track them down, Poyndex's IS agents had found them rightfully discarded in a museum trash heap. Now they hung frame edge to frame edge along the office walls. The effect was unsettling, to say the least. All those saintly Imperial eyes staring down at him. It was like hallucinating on spoiled narcobeer.

He forced his attention back to the interview. He saw Baseeker's small eyes fire brighter. 'This proposal is nothing, Lord, compared to my true vision,' she said, full of holy fervor. 'I see temples to your exalted self in every town and city of the Empire. Where your subjects can gather together and bask in your glory.'

'Really?' the Emperor said. 'I had no idea there were so many potential converts.'

'How can it be otherwise, Lord?' Baseeker said. 'For is it not written in our holy scriptures that soon your worshippers will outnumber the stars in the heavens? And that they will praise your name as the one true God of us all?'

Even the Emperor was embarrassed by this. He coughed into a closed fist. 'Uh . . . Yes. The way you put it . . . I suppose it does make sense.'

'We only lack funds, Lord,' Baseeker said, 'to put this program fully into motion.'

The Emperor frowned. 'I've already supplied a sufficiency of funds. Have I not?'

'Oh, but you have, Lord,' Baseeker backpedaled. 'And in my opinion, this has been an unfair – bordering on blasphemous – burden. In my view, those who benefit most should bear the cost. Your humble subjects, Lord, should be the ones to pay.

'I do not think it seemly for a living god to pay for his own temples. But, we – your faithful subjects – have been denied this small pleasure, Lord. And it is the fault of our political leaders, I fear. They're too busy lining their own pockets instead.'

'Very well put,' the Emperor said. 'And refreshingly so.'

He turned to Poyndex. 'I'm getting tired of those penny-pinchers in the Parliament. It's time for them to put their credits where their mouths are. Get together with Avri and work up some kind of funding bill. A subject so loyal as this woman shouldn't have to go begging for funds for such a worthy proposal.'

'Yes, Your Highness. I'll do it immediately.'

The Emperor shifted back to Baseeker. 'I have one request.'

'Anything, Lord.'

'I'd like you to sift through the membership. Ferret out the most ardent believers.'

'We would all lay our lives down for you, Lord.'

'Yes . . . But some are always going to be more willing than others. You know the type I mean.'

Baseeker nodded. The word 'fanatic' was the unspoken answer.

'I want them organized into a core group. I have some of special training in mind for them. Training, Poyndex's people can supply.'

'Yes, Lord.'

'They are to hold themselves ready. Until they hear from me. Then they are to act instantly, and without question.'

'Yes, Lord. These . . . missions . . . you have in mind? I assume they will be dangerous?'

'Yes. Possibly even suicidal.'

Baseeker smiled. 'I know just the type of individual we'll need,' she said, rat teeth snipping off each word.

Poyndex shuddered. There was nothing new about using religious fanatics as assassins. But the image of a wild-eyed cultist waving a bloody knife was decidedly unsettling. He wiped the image away. As frightening as the idea was, he could not deny its merit.

'Fine. We have an understanding, then,' the Emperor said, winding things up. 'Now . . . if you'll forgive me . . .'

Baseeker leaped to her feet. 'Certainly, Lord. And thank you so much for gracing me with these precious moments of your time.'

She dropped to her knees again and bounced her head on the floor three times. 'Praise thy name, Lord. Praise thy name . . .'

And she was gone.

The Emperor turned to Poyndex with a huge smile. 'Amazing. They really *do* believe I'm a god.'

'No doubt about it, Your Majesty,' Poyndex said. His survival instinct, however, kept him from smiling back. 'Their beliefs may be childlike . . . but they certainly are sincere.'

The Eternal Emperor looked at the door Baseeker had just exited. 'Out of the mouths of babes,' he murmured.

The mood broke and the Emperor slid a bottle of Scotch from his desk. He briskly poured a drink. And as briskly downed it.

'Now. From the sublime to pure damned foolishness,' the Emperor said. 'I have a complaint from my chamberlain involving you.'

Poyndex lifted a brow. 'Yes, Your Highness?'

'Apparently those honors I asked you to process have yet to reach his desk. And he has an awards ceremony to prepare for. A ceremony, I might add, scheduled for less than two weeks from now.'

'I am so very sorry, sir,' Poyndex said at his most humble. 'It's my fault. And I have no excuses for it.'

'Damned straight,' the Eternal Emperor snorted. 'For crying out loud, Poyndex, I know and you know these things are meaningless. But medals and honors are good public relations. Especially in these times.'

'Yes, Your Highness. I'm sorry, Your Highness. I'll get on it right away.'

'Never mind,' the Emperor said. 'Send the list to me. I'll deal with it.' He shook his head. 'Might as well. It seems like I have to do everything *else* myself.'

'Yes, sir.'

The Emperor drank more Scotch, his irritation waning. 'I suppose you do have your hands full at the moment,' he said.

'It's still no excuse, sir. But thank you.'

'Don't thank me yet,' the Emperor said. 'Because I have another rather large item for your plate.'

'Yes, sir?'

'I've been thinking about our problem with Sten. He's been doing us a great deal of damage. But only because he's the one with the momentum. And while we're still coming up to speed, he can continue to hit us at will. Build up his image as a bold hero of the masses and all that rot.'

'He's bound to falter soon, sir,' Poyndex said.

'I don't like depending on luck or another being's mistakes,' the Emperor said. 'We need to grab the march now. Put so much pressure on him he won't know which way is up.'

'I don't mean to be negative, sir,' Poyndex said, 'but we've already stretched our forces to the limit. And then some. At this point, even our reserve units are strapped.'

'Strap them some more,' the Emperor said.

'But . . . if there should be some emergency, sir . . .'

The Emperor's eyes blazed. 'Clot that! Sten's been surprising us at every turn. Hitting us from every angle. My pet news stations, to AM2 depots, to the financial market.'

Poyndex puzzled. 'The financial market? I assumed the economy was merely suffering because of the crisis. What could Sten have—'

The Emperor gave him a scornful look. 'Don't be a fool. That had all the marks of a guerrilla action. Nothing natural about it. No. It was Sten's doing. Or one of his people.'

'I see . . . Your Majesty,' Poyndex said haltingly, not really seeing.

The Emperor snorted, frustrated. 'Now get this through that thick skull of yours, Poyndex. This *is* the emergency. And if we don't put this fire out soon, we're going to be in even deeper drakh. Do I make myself clear?'

'Yes, sir.'

'Good. Now, take a look at this.' The Emperor moved aside the bottle of Scotch and spread out a map of his empire. Poyndex bent over it, noting the many circles, crosses, and arrows the Emperor had scrawled.

'These are the areas I think are the most vulnerable,' the Emperor said, jabbing here and here and here. 'The most likely places for him to hit next. We can cover if we move the Fifth Guard from Solfi . . . then shift the fleet at Bordbuch . . .'

Poyndex watched in amazement as the Eternal Emperor jabbed at the map, rejiggering his forces.

And every time his finger touched paper, hundreds of ships and thousands of soldiers were hurled across the stars.

In pursuit of a single man.

Much later, secure in his own small kingdom in Arundel Castle, Poyndex reflected on the state of the Empire.

He touched a sensor at his desk and the mural on the far wall of the command center shattered, and was replaced by an electronic version of the map the Emperor had shown him: the situation board. Crisis lights winking.

Poyndex scanned the bad news. Food riots. Rolling blackouts. Wildcat strikes. His eyes moved on. Money markets in disarray. Commodities seesawing. Panicked corporate reports. Appeal after appeal for more AM2.

The bad news wasn't limited to the civilian sector. Sten's attacks against the Empire were indicated all over the board. As were the declarations of war or independence from many of the Emperor's former allies.

Dead agents, blown missions, and other intelligence failures were also added to the Empire's burden.

A normal being might have despaired. Poyndex was far from normal. In each failure he saw opportunity. In each disaster, a hidden treasure trove.

Poyndex had learned much from the Eternal Emperor in a very short time. Success required perspective . . . and patience.

In this case the long view was Poyndex's – not the Emperor's.

As his black-uniformed aides hustled about the enormous room,

Poyndex once again weighed the odds. And once again he came to the conclusion that the Emperor was wrong. He was taking the threat of Sten far too seriously.

In fact, it was Poyndex's view that Sten was actually being propped up by the Emperor's attention. His antics would be seen as just that if he was officially ignored. But the more the Emperor ranted and raved and flung about ships and troops, the more attractive a figure Sten became to the Emperor's enemies.

All data suggested that the dice were loaded against Sten. His forces were puny and his resources slim, when compared to the juggernaut that was the Empire.

Sten could not afford one mistake. The Emperor could afford many.

For some reason the Emperor couldn't see this. He was completely obsessed with Sten. Very little else was getting his attention.

A large blind spot.

A small smile began to grow on Poyndex's lips. He couldn't help feeling clever for encouraging the Emperor's obsession. And slipping around that blind spot.

He'd warned the Emperor of this and that. But only to protect himself – if things went wrong. Meanwhile, he'd successfully isolated the Emperor from the outside world, moving in his own people.

The Gurkhas were the last of the old guard to go.

Now, the Emperor was totally dependent on him. It was Poyndex who had chosen Zoran's successor. Poyndex who controlled all people permitted in the Emperor's presence. And it was Poyndex who encouraged the Emperor in his madness whenever possible.

As a matter of fact, he had become so indispensable to the Emperor that he'd deliberately started making a few mistakes. Such as the mishandling of the honors-banquet nonsense.

The Emperor might be mad. But he was certainly no fool. He knew as well as Poyndex that there was nothing so dangerous as an indispensable man.

So Poyndex had to foul up once in a while. Just enough so the Emperor wouldn't resent him.

He looked up at the situation board. Not at the bad news. But at the sheer expanse of the Empire.

An Empire that in some ways bent to *his* will.

Not the Emperor's.

And as each day passed – and the Emperor deteriorated – Poyndex's influence grew.

He did not make the mistake of ever seeing himself as Emperor. At least not very often.

During the time of the privy council, Poyndex had viewed first-hand what happened to the Empire when there was no figurehead to give it form.

No. The Emperor was a necessity. At least his presence was. His legend.

There was only one large flaw. Poyndex would eventually grow old.

Weaken.

And die.

But the Emperor was immortal.

What if Poyndex could some how learn that secret?

What if he could live . . . forever?

Poyndex brushed the sensor and the situation board became a mural again.

There were more possibilities here than even Poyndex could ever dream of.

And Poyndex was a practiced dreamer.

Chapter Sixteen

'I don't know how they discovered your whereabouts,' Sr Ecu said. His holo image was shadowed on the edges from the strength of the scrambler.

'The point is, they're on their way to the Lupus Cluster right now. A 260-being delegation. Headed by the three top leaders of the Zaginows.'

'Speaking as one trained diplomat to another,' Sten said, 'this is not what I call clottin' wonderful. I'm going to have to move our base of operations. Fast.'

'I think it would be a mistake not to meet with them,' Sr Ecu said, his tail agitating the Seilichi atmosphere. The flick sent him drifting across the chamber.

'I know it's dangerous to assume innocent intent.' Another flick, and Sr Ecu's body steadied. 'However . . . if the Zaginows do join with us . . . it will be a major blow against the Emperor. Think of it. An *entire* region – representing hundreds of clusters – defecting to our side. The propaganda value would easily equal any military venture you might be considering.'

Sten tapped a nervous foot against the cold, stone floor of the Bhor com room. 'I know. I know. But I still can't get past the frightening little detail that somehow the Zaginows not only connected us, but also figured out where I'm holed up.'

'I was as startled as you,' Sr Ecu said, 'when they arrived at my front door, demanding to meet with you. My first assumption was there had been a leak. The second was the Manabi were doomed. I had visions of an Imperial planet buster in our immediate future.

'But after speaking with them, running all the progs through my techs, combined with my personal knowledge of the Zaginows – I see very little possibility of a trap.'

'It's the *little* possibility that scares me,' Sten said. 'Also a largish "how come" . . . In other words, if they want to sign on with the revolution . . . how come they didn't do so with you? Why is it so important they have a face-to-face with me?'

'Because the Zaginows are not entirely convinced,' Sr Ecu said. 'They're only sure we share the same enemy. They're *not* sure we have the means to do something about said enemy.'

Sr Ecu drifted closer to the camera lens. 'It's up to you, Sten. They're already leaning heavily in our direction. Otherwise they wouldn't be taking such a risk.'

'So, what you are advising,' Sten said, 'is a little diplomatic razzle-dazzle so we can reel them the rest of the way in.'

'Razzle-dazzle? I don't understand this term.'

'A big show.'

'Oh. Very descriptive. Yes. That's precisely what I advise. A very big show.'

Sten hesitated. 'Did you ask how they figured it out?'

'Yes. They said they added one plus one to a great deal of

wishful thinking. They used the same nonlogic to pinpoint you in the Bhor worlds. Although, I certainly didn't confirm their belief. Actually, the Zaginows didn't even ask. When they left, they just kindly asked me to notify you they were on the way.'

Sten sighed. 'Okay. I'll do it. What the clot? If we're wrong, I'll be too damned dead to count how many ways I was played the fool.'

'You won't be alone, Sten,' Sr Ecu said. Dry. 'The afterlife, it is rumored, is mostly composed of fools like us.'

'I feel a lot better already,' Sten said with a grimace. 'Thanks.'

'You're quite welcome.'

Sr Ecu's image was gone.

Sten began pacing to work out his thoughts. But his mind was already crammed with so many odd details of the complex war he was waging against the Emperor that he soon found himself spinning about his own fundament.

He needed advice. Badly.

'So, Sr Ecu claims it was mostly luck that led them to us?' Rykor said.

'That pretty well sums it up,' Sten said.

'Ah dinnae believe i' luck,' Alex said. ''Cept when i's m' own wee hide thae's beggin' f'r it.'

'Of course there's luck,' Otho insisted. 'The Bhor know it well. It comes in three varieties. Blind, dumb, and bad.'

'We've been in kitchens,' Marr said, 'where we've encountered all three.'

'And in one dinner rush as well,' Senn said.

'I have to accept Sr Ecu's word for it,' Sten said. 'But I still think it was a helluva gamble for the Zaginows to take. What if they were wrong? They might as well have flung themselves into the Emperor's arms and shouted, "Take me, I'm a traitor."'

'Very kinky,' Marr said. 'I like it.'

'Shush. We're being serious, here,' Senn said.

'So was I, dear.' He patted Senn's knee. 'I'll explain it to you some night.'

'When you really think about it,' Rykor said, easing her bulk in the tank, 'their actions make an odd sort of sense.'

'Good,' Sten said. 'I've been short that lately. Spell it out for me. And don't use any big words. Like "the" or "and."'

'I believe it's the nature of the Zaginows, Sten,' Rykor said. 'They are all economic refugees. Refugees have always been willing to take great risks for tenuous gain. When you have very little, the act of gambling sometimes makes you feel empowered. As if you have finally taken control of your own fate.'

Sten nodded. Good sense, indeed. He had dealt with the Zaginow region before. Almost all of the many billions of beings inhabiting the area were descendants of poor working stock – human and ET alike – who had followed scarce work opportunities across the Empire. The slightest tilt in the economy impoverished them.

Like Sten's own family, they had little but dreams and strong backs to sustain them. Some ended up in slave factories like Vulcan. The lucky ones – that word, again! – drifted into the jumble of star clusters that made up the Zaginows. There the wandering ended. The refugees took root.

A strange sort of unity and common view persisted in the Zaginows. Although there was no dominant species, or race, folks were considered folks. Whether they were black, white, or green. Solid-formed, or jellied. Skin or scales.

Sten remembered the enormous gamble his father had taken in a get-rich-quick scheme involving Xypaca fights. The fact that he'd promptly lost – adding years to his work contract – had not dissuaded him from further risk. If anything, it only made his father more willing to gamble everything – anything – to escape the grind of Vulcan.

Yeah. He understood.

'P'raps i's a gamble, wee Sten,' Alex said, 'but thae dinnae hae much t' lose, y' ken.'

This was also true. Shortly before the debacle in the Altaics, the Emperor had sent Sten to the Zaginows to do some basic diplomatic stroking. The mission had been a success, he supposed. At least he'd been able to patch some kind of agreement together without *too* much lying.

'When I saw them last,' Sten said, 'they were in a helluva mess. Not of their making. The Zaginows had a fairly self-sufficient and prosperous region before the Tahn war.

'They had a healthy agricultural base. Some heavy industry. Mining. Big population to do the work. And mostly well-educated.'

Otho's heavy brow beetled forward. 'I was unaware of that background,' he said. 'I thought the Zaginows were known for their weapons industry.'

'Like I said . . . that was before the Tahn war. Then old Tanz Sullamora showed up with the Emperor's money and the

Emperor's clout. Before you knew it, he'd transformed the entire region into an immense defense industry.'

'Then . . . when the war was over . . .'

'Ah ha,' Alex said. 'Th' bad luck Ah was mentionin'.'

'You can't eat guns,' Marr said.

'Exactly. The factories were idled and their economy collapsed.'

'But . . . my mother's beard . . . Why didn't they change back?'

'It wasn't possible,' Sten said. 'Not without a major investment for retooling and so forth. When the money dried up, the privy council couldn't dump them off the sleigh fast enough.

'Now I can see it was even worse for them when the Emperor came back. Sure, he strung them along. Sending me, for instance. But it was easier – and cheaper – to cut them loose. And let them die quietly.'

'Thae're no goin't quiet int' th' night noo,' Alex said.

'Remember,' Rykor warned, 'Sr Ecu said this was far from a sure thing. We still have some convincing to do.'

Sten nodded. 'He said put on a show. A big show. Trouble is, when you look around, there isn't much to boast about. We don't have legions of troops to inspect or fleets to do flybys. Anyone with half a brain can see the Emperor only has to breathe a gentle puff and we'd be blown away.'

Senn scrambled off his chair and thumped to the floor. 'No difficulty at all,' he said. 'First off, they're here to see *you*. Not troops and fleets.'

Marr dropped to the floor beside his lover. 'The Emperor has all the troops and fleets that exist,' he said, 'Our friends *know* what that got them. A great big screwing.'

'Without even a kiss first,' Senn said.

Rykor heaved in her tank, water sloshing against the side. 'The furry ones are making several major points,' she said to Sten. 'I would listen if I were you.'

'I'm listening, dammit,' Sten said. He looked down at the odd little pair. 'What do you have in mind?'

'If we want them to climb into bed with us,' Marr said, 'we're going to have to set the mood.'

'In other words, a little foreplay.' Senn giggled. 'Which has been sadly lacking in their love lives.'

'And you, Sten dear, are going to help us,' Marr said.

'Me? How?'

'It's time, O Great Leader of the Revolution, to give your gray cells a rest,' Senn said.

'You need to climb down from those lofty heights of leadership,' Marr said in mock high drama, 'and mingle with common folk.'

Sten eyed them suspiciously. 'Doing what?'

'Oh. Fetching and carrying,' Marr said.

Senn giggled. 'And scrubbing pots.'

'Now, why would I volunteer to do something like that?' Sten said.

'Because in this case, Sten, dear,' Marr said, 'diplomacy begins in the kitchen.'

'We're going to throw a little dinner party,' Senn elaborated. 'For two hundred and sixty plus lovelorn beings.'

'By the time we're through with the Zaginows,' Marr said, 'they'll be down on their knees begging for your hand in matrimony.'

'Or, at least in lust,' Senn said.

Sten wanted to object. Not to the idea of a dinner party. That was wonderful – especially with the Empire's greatest caterers staging it. But much as he'd like to learn some of their secrets, he just wasn't into scrubbing pots to earn a look.

Then he saw the grin on Kilgour's face. Otho practically had a paw stuffed into his mouth to keep from laughing. Rykor was studiously avoiding looking at him, but the violent trembling of her girth gave her away.

Sten sighed. 'Well, what are we waiting for? Let's get started.'

Off he marched. Sten. The Most Wanted Being in the Empire. AKA Hero of the Revolution.

Now promoted to Chief Pot Scrubber of the Cause.

Sten wiped chicken gore on his apron and took the message from the runner. He scanned it.

'It's official,' he said. 'The Zaginows will be here tomorrow night.'

Senn fretted. 'Not much time.'

'It'll do, Senn, dear,' Marr soothed. 'Otho's pantry is far better stocked than I imagined. We shouldn't have to cheat *too* much.'

Sten hoisted a cleaver and resumed whacking chicken into parts. 'Not that I doubt your abilities,' he said, 'but I don't see how you plan a menu for something like this.'

'Well . . . We want them to be *impressed*,' Marr said. 'So the dinner should reflect on your success. However, we want to do business with these people . . .'

A claw taloned out of the exquisite softness of Marr's fur. It speared a tomato and plunged it into boiling water. 'We want them to *like* us. We don't want them to think we believe we're better than they are, for heaven's sakes.'

Marr lifted the tomato from its hot bath – spun it toward the opposite paw. Where another claw whisked away the skin. Snip. Slide. Just like that. Sten's jaw dropped.

On automatic, Marr speared another tomato and repeated the process. And another tomato was peeled. Snip. Slide. Just like that. 'Haute cuisine is definitely out, out, out,' he said.

'It wouldn't do,' Senn agreed. 'Not at all.' His wickedly sharp claws were blazing through a stack of yellow onions. Skinning and chopping so deftly, Sten didn't feel the slightest sting in his eyes.

'We've decided on native dishes,' Marr said. 'Food one might imagine came from an ordinary being's kitchen. But still a little exotic and daring because it *is* from someplace else.'

'Also, it gives us a theme,' Senn said, disposing of another onion. 'A Flag of All Nations sort of theme. It fits with the jumble of beings that make up the Zaginows.'

'We *like* themes,' Marr said.

Sten was only half-listening. He was busy gaping at the Milchens' skills. They were living kitchen machines. Full of all kinds of little tricks.

'Great. Great. Themes and all,' Sten said. 'But, before you go any further, I have to ask you a question.'

'Question away, dear,' Marr said, thunking down the last peeled tomato.

'I can't do onions like Senn . . .' he said, pointing at the furry little whirlwind, chopping up big mounds of the stuff. 'I'm not built for it. But that trick with the tomatoes . . . Every time I have to peel tomatoes, I mutilate the suckers. One pound of peel for every ounce of tomato.'

'Poor thing,' Marr said.

'You *only* have to dip them in boiling water,' Senn said in a small – I really, really, don't think you're stupid – voice.

'And he's the leader of us all,' Marr said.

'I did read about it, *once*,' Sten said, weak. 'But I never got around to testing it out.'

'There, there, dear,' Senn said. 'Of course you didn't.'

The kitchen was filled with the delicious odor of tomatoes, garlic, and onions sizzling in olive oil. Marr tasted, adjusted the paprika, stirred some more, then nodded to Senn, who poured in fresh chicken stock.

Marr clamped a lid on the pot and set it to simmer. 'When dinner is served,' he told Sten, 'you might want to go easy on the soup.'

Sten eyed the big pot. 'Sure looks like enough to go around to me.'

Senn laughed. 'Oh, there's plenty, all right. But this is a special recipe. A guaranteed first-course tension-breaker. For the guests, that is. Not the host. Hosts should beware of this dish.'

'You see,' Marr elaborated, 'after we strain it through a sieve, we're going to stir in some flour and sour cream. Just enough to make it smooth.

'Then . . . a moment before we serve it . . . we add vodka. Lots of vodka! And . . . voilà,' Senn said. 'We give you . . . Hungarian tomato vodka soup! It's quite potent, too.'

'A tongue loosener, huh?' Sten said, dry. 'Did you guys ever consider a career as Mantis interrogators?'

'Amateurs,' Senn sniffed.

'No challenge at all,' Marr said.

'After we get the Zaginow delegation nice and soothed,' Senn said, 'we need to work on their courage.' He was dusting chunks of meat with flour, spiked with lots of salt and pepper.

Marr was assembling chopped-up onions, bell peppers, and crushed garlic. 'Build them up for a firm commitment,' he said.

Senn giggled. 'So to speak.'

'Don't be dirty,' Marr said, putting on a pan doused with olive oil to heat.

'I can't help it,' Senn said, the giggles building. 'My mind just *works* that way. Especially when we're cooking mountain oysters.'

Sten frowned. He picked up a chunk of the floured meat. Sniffed it. 'Don't smell like oysters to me.'

'They're calf testicles, dear,' Marr explained. 'Cut from the little dickens before they're old enough to know what's missing.'

'We're going to do them Basque style,' Senn said. 'The image is *so* sexy. Muscular brutes with large libidos.'

'Makes you want to fry balls all day,' Marr said.

Sten looked at the meat he held in his hand. 'Sorry, boys,' he said. 'I hope you know they went for a good cause.'

'Now, we need to engage their minds,' Marr said.

Sten looked doubtfully at the large heap of bird parts he'd

carved up with his cleaver. 'Brain power through a clottin' chicken? You've gotta be kidding.'

'Stupid animals, yes,' Senn said. 'But they're so *willing*. Especially plucked and dressed out. See how patiently they await their marinade?'

'Like the Zaginows?' Sten guessed.

'Excellent, Sten, dear. You're beginning to get the idea,' Marr said. 'At this point we should have our new friends primed and ready for fresh approaches . . . Alert them through their taste buds there are endless possibilities once an alliance has been achieved.'

'Don't be so stuffy,' Senn said. He waved a spice-dusted paw at Sten. 'Ignore him. The dish *is* called jerk chicken, after all,' he said.

'I like it . . . mon,' Sten said.

Marr set down the bunch of scallions he was dicing up. 'You've heard of it?' He seemed disappointed.

'From Jamaica, right?' Sten said. 'One of the old Earth islands. A place where they smoke rope fibers and drink silly fruit drinks with little parasols on top.'

Marr sighed. 'Aren't we running out of clean pots yet?'

'Not a chance,' Sten said. 'I've only heard of jerk chicken. I'm not moving until I see how this is done.'

'In a kitchen,' Marr said, 'only the chef is permitted to be clever. Pot washers laugh at Chef's cunning jokes. Pot washers peel potatoes. Pot washers are in a constant state of awe at Chef's genius. Pot washers scrape slime from floors. Pot washers duck a lot when sharp objects are thrown at them when they make poor Chef mad. These are only some of the things pot washers do.'

Marr sniffed. 'What they don't do, is be clever. Pot washers are *never, ever* clever.'

'I promise it'll never happen again,' Sten said.

'He really wasn't *that* clever,' Senn said.

'Very well,' Marr said. '*It* can stay. But only if *It* promises to button *Its* lip.'

'Mmmmph,' Sten grunted, pointed at his zipped lip.

'Actually, this is a dish even a pot washer could master the first time,' Marr said. 'It only tastes complex.'

He touched a switch under the chopping board and a metal processor revolved up. Pawfuls of chopped hot pepper and scallions went into the processor, along with a few bay leaves, some grated ginger, and diced garlic.

'Now the allspice,' Marr said. 'That's the anchor. You use about five tablespoons for every kilo of meat. Along with one teaspoon each of nutmeg, cinnamon, salt, and pepper.'

He dumped the spices into the processor and hit the button. As it whirred, he slowly poured in oil.

'Peanut oil,' Marr said. 'Just enough for it all to stick together.'

In two beats it was done. Sten peered at the goo.

'Another thing pot washers get to do,' Marr said, 'is smear goo over chicken.'

'This is true. Chefs never smear goo,' Senn said. 'Especially when they're furry.'

Sten, the comparatively hairless pot washer, began spreading the marinade over the chicken. Actually, he didn't really mind. It smelled wonderful. His mouth watered imagining what it was all going to taste like when Marr and Senn tonged the chicken off the barbecue.

In the corner, he could hear Marr and Senn arguing over the relative merits of pine nuts in Lebanese pilaf. All about him were the warm smells of a dozen dishes bubbling and simmering.

He felt relaxed . . . clear-minded.

On the whole, he thought, he'd much rather be a pot washer than a Hero of the Revolution.

Marr and Senn observed Sten's beaming face as he slathered marinade over chicken.

'Do you think he's ready?' Marr whispered.

'Absolutely,' Senn said. 'I don't like to pat myself on the back, but I think this is one of the best jobs we've ever done.'

'Beings don't realize,' Marr said, 'that the first – and only – real secret of a dinner party is getting the host prepared first.'

'A little kitchen magic,' Senn said. 'It works every time.'

The Zaginow leader forked one more bite from the creamy pastry dish in front of her. She looked at it . . . as if not believing her body was capable of handling still more. The fork continued its journey and the pastry disappeared into her mouth.

She closed her eyes. Ebony features a portrait of bliss. Tasting. Mmmmm.

Her eyes snapped open to find Sten grinning at her.

'Oh, burp,' she said. 'Oh, heaven. But, I *just* couldn't eat anymore.'

'I think the chefs will forgive you, Ms Sowazi, if you resign the field of battle,' Sten said. 'You've certainly given it your best.'

He glanced around the banquet room. Marr and Senn had turned the drafty Bhor hall into a wonder of festooned flowers and subtle lights.

The other guests were as dazzled and replete as Sowazi.

For two hours, Marr and Senn had commanded convoy after convoy of deliciousness through the room. Whether the dish was meant for a human or an ET, each was greeted and devoured with great enthusiasm.

Beings had their elbows – or equivalent parts – on the tables now. Chatting warmly away with Sten's colleagues as if they were all long-lost friends.

As a capper, Marr and Senn had printed up souvenir menus for each member of the Zaginow delegation.

'We always do it,' Marr said. 'Beings like to show the folks at home what a good time they had. It's wonderful advertising for us, as well.'

'Not "advertising," dear,' Senn said. 'Not in this case, at any rate. Remember, we're revolutionaries now. The military term is "propaganda."'

'Same thing,' Marr sniffed.

'True. But "propaganda" is much more romantic.'

Sten had to admit that the souvenir menus fit the bill perfectly as propaganda.

On the back was a picture of himself, flanked by the master caterers, Marr and Senn. On the front, Senn got his theme: 'A FEAST FOR ALL BEINGS.'

This was the menu for the humans:

SOUP
Hungarian Tomato Vodka
Miso Saki Shrimp

SALAD
Cambodian Raw Fish
Tomato Cucumber Raita

APPETIZERS
Basque Mountain Oysters
Russian Blinis and Caviar
Armenian Stuffed Mushrooms

ENTREES
Jamaican Jerk Chicken
Moroccan Roast Lamb
Broiled Salmon Steaks
Mesquite Broiled Vegetable Kabob

SIDE DISHES
Lebanese Rice Pilaf
Rosemary Potatoes
Cuban Black Beans & Rice

DESSERT
New York Style Cheesecake
Swedish Pancakes With Lingonberries

The items listed on the menus for the ETs were equally impressive.

Sten saw Marr peering from a doorway. He spotted Sten and waved. It was time.

Sten turned to Sowazi. 'I think we're being called for coffee and brandy,' he said.

She laughed, deep and pleasurable. 'Cigars, too?'

'Cigars, too,' Sten promised.

'Lead on, Sr Sten.'

As he rose to do her bidding, Sten made a furtive thumbs-up motion to Marr. Everything was going according to plan.

'Here's our position,' Moshi-Kamal said. He was the second member of the troika that ruled the Zaginows. 'We're willing to come on board. But we need some assurances.'

'I can't give you any,' Sten said. 'Remember, I started the conversation by saying the odds are decidedly against us. If you join us . . . it may be an act of suicide.'

'But your own behavior does not bear that statement out, Sr Sten.' This was from Truiz, the ET member of the troika. 'You fight well. Logically. Certainly not like a suicidal being. You also have had many successes.'

'They look good,' Sten said, 'but they're not near enough. The Emperor has had a lot of bad days. He can afford to. If I have *one* . . . it's over.'

'Why are you being so candid?' Sowazi wondered. 'I would think you'd be pointing up the positive. The fleets you command. The victories. The growing number of allies.'

She waved at the cozy paneled den Marr and Senn had converted an old weapons room into for this conversation. 'You sit here at ease, dining luxuriously, thumbing your nose at the Emperor and his hellhounds. Why aren't you boasting of these things to win us to your side?'

'I could,' Sten agreed. 'But the trouble is . . . Once I'd won you over, I wouldn't be able to count on you. When something terrible happened – and I promise you it will – you'd see that I'd lied. And desert me.

'There can be no mistake about this,' Sten said. 'This is a fight to the finish. The Emperor will never give us quarter. We lose – we die.'

'I can understand this,' Truiz said. The little tendrils wriggling beneath her eyes were red with frustration. 'But the picture you paint is so bleak. Give us some hope.'

Sten leaned forward. 'Right now, I have the Emperor's forces strung across the map. What I don't have pinned down . . . I have chasing its own tail. But I can only keep this going for a little longer.

'I need two things right now. Reserves. And an opening. Without the first, it will be difficult to support the other.'

'Do you think you will get this opening?' Moshi-Kamal asked.

Sten paused, as if giving serious thought. Then he nodded. 'Without a doubt,' he lied. 'No matter how we read the progs, they keep on coming up with the same thing. The thrust of the fight is with us. Sooner or later, we're going to have a break-through.'

'Then we want to be there,' Sowazi said. 'This . . . this . . . *being* has become unbearable.'

'He is forcing us to become one of his dominions,' Moshi-Kamal said. 'Putting us under his heel. The beings of the Zaginows have long memories. We all come from working people. The class the bosses put in dark holes full of sharp machinery.'

'This is true,' Truiz said. 'All of our ancestors fled from some despot or other. We can't condemn ourselves to the lives they escaped.'

'Did you know,' Sowazi hissed, 'that he is even putting himself up as a god? He has these . . . these . . . *beings* bounding about proclaiming him a holy thing. They want to put temples up to him in our cities. It's . . . filthy!'

It wasn't necessary for Sten to comment. Instead, he looked from one to the other.

'Then you'll join us . . . even without assurances?'

'Even without assurances,' Moshi-Kamal said. 'We will join you.'

'And we might also be able to solve your first problem,' Sowazi said.

'How, so?'

'Why, the reserve forces,' Truiz said. 'We assume you have more beings at your disposal than ships and weapons?'

'You assumed right,' Sten said.

'I'm sure you are aware that we have thousands of factories – forced on us by the Eternal Emperor – designed and tooled to build those things.'

'I knew that,' Sten said. 'But I also know they've been shut down for some time. I figured most of the machinery had either rusted or been sold for scrap.'

'Only a few,' Moshi-Kamal said. 'Mostly, they are in excellent condition. It's one of the benefits and curses of the Zaginows. We can't stand to see good machinery go to ruin.'

'People didn't have any work to go to,' Sowazi explained. 'But they kept the factories up just the same.'

'Are you trying to say that you've got a turnkey operation?' Sten asked. 'That all you have to do is give the word and you can start building ships and weapons again?'

The little tendrils below Truiz's eyes wriggled with pleasure. 'We can be up and running in one E-week,' she said. 'Then bring on your troops.'

Now all Sten needed was the opening.

The pale, slender Grb'chev towered over Cind. The splash of red across the smooth skull throbbed with curiosity. 'Your request is most unusual,' he said. 'Few humans have ever come to this place.'

Cind looked about the small building whose mirrored walls reflected the sprawling gardens surrounding it. 'I can't imagine why,' she said, 'it's such a lovely place.'

The Grb'chev touched a switch and the door slid open. He escorted her inside. 'Sr Kyes had a love for beauty,' he said. 'Especially understated beauty.'

Cind's smile was humble. 'I've learned about that side of Sr Kyes in my studies,' she said. 'He was quite a complex being. Even for a Grb'chev.'

'Even for a Grb'chev,' her escort agreed. 'But this leads me back to my first remark. In our culture, Sr Kyes is a hero. His intelligence, inventiveness, and business acumen have already taken on mythlike characteristics.

'We've converted his old headquarters into a museum. A shrine, for some.' Cind and her escort were pacing through the museum's cheery foyer. 'But I would think only someone of our culture would appreciate Sr Kyes.'

'Then I apologize for my species,' Cind said. 'After all, no one would argue that the Grb'chev are easily among the most intelligent beings in the Empire.'

'This is true,' her escort said. There was no modesty necessary.

'And Sr Kyes was arguably the most intelligent Grb'chev in this age,' Cind said.

'Some say, of all time,' the escort said.

'Then, how could any reasonable being – especially a student such as myself – not want to see firsthand how Sr Kyes lived and worked?'

'You are a very bright young woman,' her escort said. Another switch brought another door open. They stepped into the library. Across the way, a figure worked at a monitor. A human.

'This is a most fortunate day for you and your research,' her escort said as he spied the figure. 'As I said before, only a few humans share your interest in Sr Kyes. One of them has a position on the museum's staff. And to my surprise, your visit happily coincides with his shift day.' Her escort tapped the figure on a shoulder.

The man turned. An expectant smile on his face.

'Ms Cind, allow me to introduce you to one of our senior researchers . . . Sr Lagguth.'

Lagguth rose, and put out a hand. They shook. 'Pleased to meet you,' he said. 'It is a pleasure I almost missed. This is my normal rest day. But one of my colleagues called in ill.'

'A happy coincidence,' the escort said.

'Yes. A happy coincidence,' Cind echoed, looking her quarry up and down.

It was no coincidence at all. And for Lagguth, it certainly wasn't going to be happy.

Lagguth had suffered through countless nights of torment, envisioning the hard-faced beings who would come to get him. They were always large. Always dressed in black. Sometimes they came with drawn guns. Sometimes with bloody fangs. But they always said the same thing: 'You know too much, Lagguth. And for this, you must die.'

The woman confronting him now was that nightmare, but in a disarmingly soft package. She had no visible weapon. And small, bright teeth instead of fangs.

'You know too much, Lagguth,' Cind said. 'And if you don't help me . . . they'll kill you for it.'

'I was just a functionary,' Lagguth groaned.

'I wouldn't call being the head of the privy council's AM2 bureau a mere functionary,' Cind scoffed.

'I had no power. No authority. I followed orders. That's all. I did nothing to harm anyone!'

'Your very presence meant you conspired with the Emperor's assassins,' Cind said. 'As for authority . . . Thousands of beings whose loved ones died of cold or starvation from lack of fuel might want to have a word with you for the authority you *did* exercise.'

There was nothing Lagguth could say. He bowed his head.

'So. Speak to me, Lagguth. Or I'll drop the word. And either the Emperor's goons will get you, or the mob. I almost feel sorry for you, you poor excuse for a life-form.'

'You'll speak up for me?' Lagguth begged. 'You'll tell Sr Sten I cooperated?'

Cind let her voice soften. 'Yes. I'll speak up for you.' Then – cracking the whip: 'Now. *Tell* me, Lagguth! Tell me everything!'

Lagguth talked. He told her about the strange program he'd set up for Sr Kyes. Its ostensible purpose was to search for where the Emperor hid his AM2. This was what Kyes told his fellow members of the privy council, at least.

'But I got the idea he really wasn't all that interested in AM2. His search was much deeper than that. Highly personal.'

'In what way?' Cind asked.

'Well, we did gather together everything that was known about AM2. From composition, to the few known courses AM2 shipments followed before they so mysteriously stopped. We fed it into this marvel of a computer he'd developed.'

He pointed to a small terminal in one corner of the library. 'That's linked to it,' he said. 'It's still functional. But, sadly, it can only be one of a kind. I doubt any being in several lifetimes would ever be able to decipher the program he created to run it.'

Cind prodded him away from reveries of Kyes's genius. 'Go on. I don't have much time.'

'Yes. As I said, we fed in all that data on AM2. But we also fed in everything that was known about the Emperor. We had help on this from Sr Poyndex.'

Cind's eyes widened. 'Poyndex. He was in on this?'

'Absolutely,' Lagguth said. 'He got something on Kyes. I don't know what. But, Kyes turned that knowledge back on him. Pulled him into our circle. It was he who made Poyndex a member of the privy council. So, obviously some kind of a bargain was made.'

'Obviously,' Cind said. The detail of the deal was interesting, but she doubted it was of any use. 'Okay. So you fed all kinds of raw data into the computer. Then what? What did Kyes learn?'

'I'm not sure,' Lagguth said. 'But I do know he learned something. He suddenly became very excited. He was a being, you realize, who rarely showed any kind of emotion. Anyway, he became excited. Ordered the program shut down. And then he left. In a great hurry.'

'Where did he go?' Cind wanted to know.

'Again, I'm ignorant. Except that I know he left Prime. For some far place. And when he returned . . . his brain . . . had died.'

Cind knew what this meant. The Grb'chev were the only known example of a higher species created by symbiosis. Their bodies – large, handsome things – originated in an exceedingly dimwitted race. Their 'brains' were actually the result of a sort of virus that settled into the brute's plentiful sinus passages. And prospered into tremendous intellect.

The curse of the Grb'chev is that the 'brain' had a near-absolute lifespan of 126 years. Kyes was one of the few examples on record of a Grb'chev brain that had lived a few years longer. The tragedy was the body lived happily and moronically on for at least another one hundred years.

Cind had seen many examples of this living death shambling through the streets of the Grb'chev's home world. Constant and horrifying reminders of what each member of this species faced.

Cind pointed to the terminal. 'Have you tried to learn what Kyes was doing, during those final days?'

Lagguth hesitated. Then he sadly shook his head. 'I'm not a very brave person,' he said. He croaked laughter. 'In case you haven't guessed. I've been frightened every day of my life someone – like you . . . or worse – would find me. And I'd be killed, or brain burned for the little I know.

'And so . . . although I desperately wanted to learn what Kyes was up to . . . I never could bring myself to actually do something about it.'

A sound came from behind a door, just to the side of the computer terminal. Cind's hand snaked down to the place where she had hidden her weapon.

'Don't be alarmed,' Lagguth said. 'He just wants to be fed.'

Cind's brow furrowed. '*Who* wants to be fed?'

'Sr Kyes, of course,' Lagguth said. 'Would you like to meet him?'

'He's here?' Cind was astounded.

'Why not? It's a good enough home for what's left of him as any. Actually, it's a damn fine home. They've put him out to pasture, so to speak. Like one would a fine racing beast. He gets everything he could possibly want. Although, to be frank, he's too stupid to really know what he wants. Sometimes . . . we have to help him with his treats.'

Lagguth rose. 'I really should go feed him. It's cruel to make him wait.'

Cind followed him into the room.

It was a bright and cheery place, filled with toys and decorated in the bright primary colors of childhood. Kyes was perched in a vastly oversized chair, giggling at the large vid monitor. It was showing a kid livie: small things scurrying about, smacking one another.

Kyes saw Lagguth. 'Hungry,' he said.

'Don't worry. I've got your yummies for you,' Lagguth said.

Cind shuddered as she watched Lagguth spoon-feed a being who had once ruled an empire.

Food dribbled from Kyes's mouth. He pointed at Cind. 'Who, pretty?'

'A friend come to see you, Sr Kyes,' Lagguth said.

Cind came out of her shock and moved to Kyes's side. She took the food from Lagguth. Kyes looked up at her. Eyes wide. Not a clue of intelligence in them. He opened his mouth. Cind fed him. He smacked his lips loudly as he ate. Belched. Then giggled.

'Make funny,' he said.

'Very funny,' Cind said. 'Good boy.'

Kyes patted her. 'Happy,' he said. 'Like happy.'

'Aren't you always happy?' Cind asked.

Kyes's head bobbed up and down. 'Happy . . . Always.'

Cind braced herself. Only cruelty could follow. 'What if the Emperor comes?' she said. 'What if he comes to take you away?'

The innocent thing that had once been Kyes reeled back in horror. 'No. Not him. Not take away. Please. Not go other place!'

Cind leaped on it: 'What other place?'

'Other place,' Kyes moaned. 'Bad place. Emperor there. Not happy me.'

'Let him be,' Lagguth pleaded. 'He can't tell you more. Can't you see how frightened he is?'

Kyes had curled into a ball. Sobbing. The huge chair made him seem small and helpless.

Cind did not relent. 'What did you find?' she gritted. 'What did you find in this bad place?'

'Emperor. I say.'

'What else?'

Kyes shrieked at some dim memory. A genetic haunting. 'Forever,' he cried. 'Find forever.'

'You see what I mean?' Lagguth said. 'It's only nonsense you'll get. He says that all the time when he's frightened. "Forever." Over and over again, "forever."'

Kyes nodded. 'Not happy, forever. Not happy.'

Cind patted him. Soothing. Then turned to Lagguth. 'Now, I want to see the computer,' she said.

As they left the room, Kyes was beginning to recover. He squirmed upright in his seat, dried his eyes, and started tentatively giggling at the little things on the livie screen.

The moonlet was a silent wilderness of destruction. Cind moved through bomb-blasted craters and twisted, melted hulks whose designed functions were barely recognizable.

The sensors on the small device in her hand were winking frantically, as they took in data. Cind scrambled over the surface of the moonlet, pausing here and there to scan wreckage with the device. The facts were fed to the mainframe aboard her orbiting ship. The conclusions were quickly beamed back. Chirping in her helmet com.

So far, they confirmed everything she had found in the data banks of the computer in the Kyes museum.

The moonlet had been an elaborately constructed communications center. A byway on the road to the mystery that led to the Emperor's ultimate hiding place for the AM2.

But, Kyes hadn't come to this desolation with this goal. Cind was sure of that. Instead, he had come to find the Emperor. A being, most others in those days, believed dead. And he'd found him. Here on this planetoid.

She imagined Kyes, driven nearly mad by fear of his impending 'death,' pleading with the Emperor. Offering anything. Desperately begging him to rescue Kyes.

The gibbering hulk back at the Grb'chev museum was sufficient evidence his pleas had been rejected.

Cind worked the area for some hours. Finally she was done. It was time to tell Sten what she had learned.

The outpost was a place where the paths of two secrets had once intersected.

The first was the secret of AM2.

The second, the Emperor's apparent immortality.

Cind was weary when she messaged for pickup. Not from the work. But from the depressing thought that although she had learned a great deal in this hunt . . . the knowledge didn't necessarily add up.

And she prayed to all the beards of all the mothers of the Bhor, that she wasn't exiting the same door she'd only recently come in.

Haines rattled the papers in her hand, coldly professional. 'Once we put his files in order,' she said, 'it became quite clear what Mahoney believed he had learned about the Eternal Emperor.'

'Which was?' Sten waved impatiently at the ex-homicide detective's holo image. It was being beamed from the small Bhor resort he'd stashed her in – along with her husband and Mahoney's treasure trove.

'Don't be in such a hurry,' Haines said. 'Facts should be given their due.'

Sten grimaced. 'Sorry.'

'First, I'm sending you a psychological profile of the Emperor. Mahoney drew it up as a model. My husband and I confirmed it by our own work. And double-checked with Rykor. It's absolutely dead on. Look it over when you have time.'

'I'll take your word,' Sten said.

'Next, I'm sending you the matches Mahoney made against that profile. He set the guide against the other times the Emperor allegedly died . . . and then returned, big as life. Each time, it was definitely the same being. There was no possibility of a surgical double. Again . . . we confirmed all Mahoney's data.'

Sten groaned. 'That resurrection business again. That clottin' Mahoney reached out from his grave and converted you.'

'I'm no convert to anything,' Haines said. 'But if these facts were clues pointing to a murder suspect . . . I'd bust the son of a scrote and lead him with confidence to my prosecuting attorney. Face up to it, Sten. It's a clear possibility.'

'I'll face that ghost when I see it and touch it myself,' Sten said. 'Meanwhile . . . where does this get us?'

Haines paused, considering how she was going to put this. 'What it gets us, is a far more frightening puzzle. You see, my husband and I took Mahoney's work and punted it one step forward.'

'What did you do?'

'We took that profile of the Eternal Emperor – the one we all agree is a perfect match. Updated it and ran it against the man we're all ducking and dodging right now.'

'And?' Sten almost didn't want to ask. 'It's still the same guy, right?'

'Yeah. It's the same guy. But it isn't. The Emperor's the same overall. But when you put a closer microscope on him, he's *very* different in his behavior.'

'Clottin' wonderful,' Sten groaned.

'Sorry to dump it into your lap, Sten,' Haines said, her voice warming in sympathy. 'But, as they say in the livies, "It's just the facts, ma'am."'

Sten thanked her, and broke the connection.

He leaned back, letting the information churn around. They settled into this uncomfortable equation: Same but different still equalled different.

The com buzzed. The watch officer said she had Cind on the line. It was important.

As Sten leaned forward to answer, a question tingled at his back brain: If it wasn't the Eternal Emperor . . . who the clot *was* he fighting?

Chapter Seventeen

Solon Kenna stood upon the broad speaker's platform, a block of pure white marble tabernacling out from the far wall of the Hall of Parliament. Posed beside him at his handsome best was Tyrenne Walsh. Behind them was a three-story-high portrait of the Eternal Emperor.

Kenna's powerful, polished voice rolled out across the hundreds of assembled politicians: 'Distinguished Representatives . . . Loyal Imperial citizens . . . Gentlebeings.

'It is with deep humility that my colleague and I stand before you on this most historic day.'

Kenna's voice dipped into an oiled, humble tone. A twitch of a finger signaled the dimwitted Walsh to bow his head.

'The people of Dusable have already enjoyed vast honors from our beloved Emperor,' he said.

Kenna's old-pol brain made note there was not one titter from the group – which represented every nook and cranny of the Empire. Nor was there one whisper he could detect of the recent humiliation his people had suffered at the hands of the Emperor's enemy – Sten.

Kenna gestured to the enormous portrait of the Emperor staring out at all of them. 'For reasons only our wise leader can determine, the people of Dusable have been honored once again.'

Kenna's trained eyes scanned the crowd, as he spoke. Sussing out his strengths and weaknesses. Supporter and enemy. He may have been humiliated by Sten, but humiliation did not diminish his skills as a manipulator.

He and Avri had prepared well for this moment. When he was done, the Emperor's bill would be presented. A highly controversial bill, whose passage at one time had been difficult to assure.

Many favors and heaps of coin had exchanged hands in the dark corridors of the Hall of Parliament. The old mordida moved a plenitude of votes into the Emperor's column. Poyndex – for reasons Kenna chose not to ponder – had also volunteered assistance. Old files on the opposition representatives had been sifted for pressure points and blackmail. More votes were added.

Still, the matter would be close.

But, in politics, close is enough to win a kingdom.

'Gentlebeings, I am here to put before you this remarkable proposal. We are being asked to lift the veil from our eyes. To see what we have been too blind to realize for so many tragic years.

'And that is, we live in so fortunate a time that a living god walks among us. And that god is our good and holy Eternal Emperor. Whose immortality stands as an unyielding shield against the hard blows of history.

'In his sanctified embodiment, our glory goes on and on before us. Our glory. Which is his glory. And his glory, ours.

'Gentlebeings . . . I put the question to you. Let us now declare, once and forever, that the Eternal Emperor is our rightful god.'

There was a stir. The gauntlet was down.

The Emperor was demanding godhood by parliamentary decree.

Kenna turned to the Speaker, an old, distinguished puppet of the Emperor. 'Sr Speaker,' Kenna intoned, 'call the question.'

The Speaker's grizzled snout pushed forward, virile tusk implants an odd vanity in an ancient, wrinkled face. 'In the matter of PB 600323 – titled, Declaration of the Eternal Emperor's Godhood; subtitled, Be It Resolved to Amend the Emperor's Title to Read, "Holy," and Any Other Word Forms Recognized As Terms of Worshipful Respect – how do you say, gentlebeings?

'All for approval . . . say Yea.'

A choreographed chorus of 'yeas' began to rise in the hall. Broken by loud shouts of protest. The shouts became a roar, drowning out the proceedings. One voice soared over that roar.

'Sr Speaker! Sr Speaker! Point of order, please! Point of order!'

The Speaker tried to ignore the voice. His gavel hammered down. He was particularly humiliated because the voice came from one of his own species. It was Nikolayevich, a young firebrand of a tusker.

The gavel rat-tat-tatted. Lectern pickups magnified the blows and the sound thundered through the hall. But an unruly crowd took up Nikolayevich's cry: *'Point of order! Point of Order!'* More voices were added, drowning out the thunder. *'Let him speak! Let him speak!'*

The Speaker turned helpless old eyes on Kenna. There was nothing that could be done. At least not in public. Kenna motioned: *Let him speak*. Then he slipped a hand in his pocket to trigger an alarm to Arundel.

'The chair recognizes Sr Nikolayevich, representative from the great and loyal Sverdlovsk Cluster.'

The Speaker keyed the pickup that would amplify Nikolayevich's remarks.

'Sr Speaker,' the young tusker shouted, 'we protest these procedures in the strongest possible terms. The issue before us is an obscenity. We will not be manipulated into seeing this become law over the will of the majority.'

'From where I was sitting, young man,' the Speaker said with dramatic sarcasm, 'the majority was quite clear. The "yeas" were overwhelming. Now, if you will permit me, I will call for the "nays." And you will see how weak is your support.'

'It is our right to refuse a voice vote. To demand a roll call,' Nikolayevich insisted. 'Let us stand up and let our peoples see how each of us votes on this matter. If the Emperor is to be a god . . . let his citizens see us declare it so. And on our heads be it.'

The Speaker shot a look at Kenna for help. Kenna made stretching motions: *Delay this*.

'Very well,' the Speaker said. 'I will call the roll.'

Nikolayevich grunted in pleasure. Sniffing victory.

The Speaker snorted. 'However, since you believe this matter so sensitive – although how any of you could doubt the sanctity of our Emperor is beyond me – I will put another question to the floor first.'

'Objection!' Nikolayevich shouted. 'The chair may not pose another question while a previous one is still in action.'

The rebel from Sverdlovsk knew his legal ground. So did the canny old Speaker. A puppet he may have been, but he was a skillful puppet.

'But the assembly *does* have the right – duty, as you are insisting – to decide the means of its voting. You say it should be by the numbers. I say it should be by vigorous acclaim.'

Nikolayevich looked about him. His cronies were doing a quick count, polling their strength. The answer came back. Waverers had been heartened by Nikolayevich's boldness. For this brief moment, he had the edge.

'Call the question, Mr Speaker,' he said. Flat. 'And I think you'll hear the loud shouts of "nay" put pay to this blasphemy.'

He slammed back into his bench, nodding all around, pleased with himself.

The Speaker raised mild eyes. 'Under the circumstances of your protest,' he said, 'I believe it would be unseemly to settle the matter with such dispatch. There will be no yeas, or nays, sir. No. Tit for tat, sir. I'll call the roll.'

Flabbergasted, Nikolayevich popped up again. 'Sr Speaker, this is incredible. You're going to call the roll to see if it is permissible to call the roll?' He turned to his fellow rebels, shoulders humped in amazement. Barking laughter. But the laughter was forced.

'Yes. That's exactly what I mean,' the Speaker said. 'I'm elated that my thoughts to you were so clearly expressed. Sometimes, I must confess, young representatives have me wondering if somehow senility has crept up on me.'

Laughter roared out from the Emperor's allies. Nikolayevich refused to be intimidated.

'But this foolishness will take hours, Sr Speaker,' he protested. 'Polling us one by one on a thing so easily settled is the height of folly.'

'Nevertheless,' the Speaker said, 'this is how we shall progress.'

He turned to the master of arms. 'Master of Arms, call the roll!'

The master of arms bristled forward. He opened the thick official logbook.

He began to drone them out: 'Ms Dexter . . . From the great region of Cogli, how do you say?'

'I vote yea, Sr Speaker.'

And so it went. One by one the representatives rose. Each vote was carefully entered in the logbook.

Kenna's forces fanned out through the great hall. With the Speaker's help, he had redrawn the battle line. If he won this vote, the second victory would be assured.

Nikolayevich's cronies worked desperately to shore up their support. But time . . . slow, dragging time . . . began to wear against it.

Still, Kenna was fuming. Yes. He would win. But now the old

rule of close being good enough would be turned on its head. After Nikolayevich's outburst – loudly supported by many others – anything but total victory would appear manipulated.

This was not how the Emperor wanted to start his first day of being God.

The vote ended. Kenna had won. But the margin was slender. He could see Nikolayevich and his people out twisting append-ages and shouting into hearing orifices.

And he could see that the young tusker was making progress. One of his agents on Nikolayevich's staff flashed a message to Kenna's lectern com. When the voice vote came, the message said, Nikolayevich and his cronies were planning to disrupt it with a boisterous demonstration.

Kenna racked his brain for some other means of stalling. No matter how hard he wrung it, however, nothing came. When this was over, the Emperor would have his hide.

Where the clot was he? Some god. Not even around when you need him.

The Speaker signaled. Frantic. What should he do? Kenna had no choice. He motioned. Call the question.

'Gentlebeings,' the Speaker intoned, 'for the second time this day, I call the question . . . In the matter of PB 600323 – titled, Declaration of the Eternal Emperor's Godhood—'

Doors boomed open. Boots hammered down.

The master of arms gave the cry: 'Gentlebeings, I present to you . . . the Eternal Emperor!'

Startled faces churned around.

A white-robed contingent of cultists danced through the enor-mous doors leading into the great main hall. Their faces beamed in ecstasy. Some swung clanging incense pots on long chains. Others strewed rose petals down the long avenue. All wore small knives in the ropes belted around their waists. The knives were sharp and festooned with streaming red ribbons.

At their head was the skeletal figure of their high priestess – Baseeker.

Behind them, boots crushing the rose petals, came a troop of black-uniformed IS officers. Their eyes sweeping the assembly of representatives for danger. Weapons at ready.

In the center was the Eternal Emperor.

When Kenna and the others saw him, they didn't notice the other little details of the entrance. The second IS troop that followed just behind the Emperor, led by Poyndex. Or the camoclad sniper teams that sprinted off to take up position. Or Avri directing nondescript figures to mingle among the representatives. When they'd been dispatched, she sighted Nikolayevich, and slipped toward him.

But these things blurred past the assembly's side vision. The Emperor commanded their full attention.

He was garbed like they had never seen him before. Long golden robes flowed over his muscular figure. The material phosphored, giving off a ghostly glow. Encircling his dark locks was a thin band of more glowing gold. In his hand, he carried a staff of yellow metal that flared at the top into a round standard. On the standard burned the symbol of AM2.

The Imperial formation swept along the avenue and wheeled onto the marble speaker's platform. The Eternal Emperor strode directly to the edge and faced Parliament. Weapons thunked and boots crashed down as the troops took position on either flank.

Baseeker and the cultists flowed around them to the Emperor. Then they lay on the platform at his feet. A nest of white-robed angels with knives.

Kenna stared. The others stared. For a moment he – and they – could almost believe. All the old myths stealthed into the room, spreading like fog among them. An ancient fog. Swept up from the cold depths of several thousand years. This was the being who had ruled them for all that time.

Perhaps he *was* a god.

'It has come to my attention,' the Eternal Emperor said, 'that there has been some mewling in this assembly.' His voice was low. But they didn't have to strain to hear. Menace buzzed all around them.

'I don't usually pay attention to your whines,' the Emperor said. 'I gave you that right when I empowered this Parliament in the Imperial Constitution. It's a nuisance, I admit. But that is the nature of democracy and I have had a long time to get used to it.'

In the audience, Nikolayevich barely noticed as a figure moved close to him. It was Avri.

'It is the nature of this current mewling, however, that brings me before you. I understand some honors were about to be conferred upon your Emperor. These honors, I should add, I did not seek. They were pressed on me by my subjects.' The Emperor's hand flowed out to indicate the white-robed cultists.

'They say I'm a god. They have built temples to me. Temples

where millions of other like-minded subjects worship. In those temples, they preach wisdom and patience and gentleness. These attributes, they believe, are at the heart of my godhood.'

Nikolayevich felt a motion at his beltpak; a small lump dropped in. He brushed at it impatiently. A message from an ally, he assumed. He ignored the figure slipping away.

'I have always encouraged freedom of worship among my subjects. So, it was with some shock that I learned that these gentle folk who worship me were being brutally persecuted for their beliefs.

'In fact, I now have incontrovertible proof that this persecution was at the heart of the conspiracy launched against me by the traitor Sten. Unspeakable acts were committed by Sten against these believers because he feared their deeply felt truths stood in his way to my throne.

'For, if I am a god, who would possibly join him against me? So, you see, even my greatest enemy is a believer. A Satan set against his perfect master.'

This odd dance in logic momentarily broke the spell gripping Nikolayevich. He slipped the message from his beltpak. A lump wrapped in paper. He unrolled it. The lump was a tusk, slender and finely curved – then a horror of gore at the stump. On the tusk was an ornate ring.

The ring Nikolayevich had given his lover on their first pairing day.

'This is the background to the bill your Speaker has presented on this day. A background which I kept to myself until this moment, for reasons of state security involving the traitor Sten.

'The decree will end the persecution of these innocent beings. A decree that will strike a moral blow against my greatest enemy.

'A decree that will recognize what has been so painfully obvious these many millennia. I have watched over you and your ancestors for long years. I have fed you. Clothed you. Given you the means to prosper in peace.'

The Emperor's head dropped. 'Ah,' he said, 'sometimes I am so weary . . .'

'Hail the Holy Emperor!' Baseeker shrieked. 'Hail, O Great Good Lord.'

The other cultists took up the cry: 'Hail the Holy Emperor! Praise Him. Praise Him!'

Kenna gave Walsh an elbow poke. Then another. Walsh's eyes unglazed. 'Praise Him!' shouted Kenna. Another nudge into Walsh. 'Praise Him!' he shouted again.

Walsh gave him a dumb grin. 'Praise Him!' he shouted. 'Praise Him.'

Out in the crowd of representatives, Nikolayevich and the others were suddenly very much aware that beings very close to them were watching.

Nikolayevich almost choked, knowing that his lover's tusk was not the only bloody message delivered this day.

'Hail the Holy Emperor,' Nikolayevich chanted. A moment later hundreds of other voices joined in. '*Praise Him! Praise Him!*'

The Emperor smiled and spread his hands. Then he wheeled around and swept off the platform with his contingent.

He rushed down the aisle, nodding here and there as he went. Even in his speed, Poyndex could see that he was savoring the shouts of '*Hail the Holy Emperor!*'

Poyndex was the last out. He could hear the Speaker's hammer coming down. Then his cry: 'In the matter of PB 600323 – titled, Declaration of the Eternal Emperor's Godhood . . . how do you say, gentlebeings?

'All for approval say Yea.'

And the thunder came back: '*Yea!*'

Poyndex didn't bother sticking around for the 'nays.'

Chapter Eighteen

'Nothing?' Fleet Admiral Madoera glowered to the com watch officer. He refrained from adding, 'Again?'

'Nossir. The *Neosho* reports no transmissions on any freq from any planet in the system. All unnatural EM bands are clean. And no sign of any ships, either, hostile or friendly.

'I had it make a double-sweep. We're picking up a lot of crap from that radio star, so I wanted to make sure before reporting.'

'Right. File a preliminary report to Prime that Intel blew it again. No Sten, no nothing. We'll take the task force through on a high pass just to confirm.'

'Sir . . . we won't be able to transmit until we're clear of the star ourselves. All long-range com links are blanketed.'

'It doesn't matter. We'll report fully after we clear the system. Not that this'll be a surprise . . .'

He stopped before adding '. . . to those clots who think they're Intelligence.'

Madoera's task force had spent too many ship-days and months chasing will-o'-the-wisp sea stories about the elusive traitor around their assigned galactic AOR to be surprised. In Madoera's estimation, this new Internal Security that'd replaced Mercury Corps wasn't capable of pouring pee out of a boot if the instructions had been printed on its heel.

None of the Alpha One-rated stories had turned out to be true. Either Sten had never been there, Sten had passed through rapidly a long time ago, or some unknown ships had been reported in a particular cluster and assumptions made they were rebel.

Why, he wondered, didn't IS realize *all* of the stories were almost certainly a crock, since every system his fleet had been punted toward was dead, abandoned, or a backwater. Just like this one. It didn't even have a name – and its only coordinates were from a charter radio pulsar, NP0406Y32.

Maybe *he* should name the damned thing. Poyndex, perhaps.

Right. And face a loyalty board when he got back to Prime. Although at the moment he didn't think he was ever going to see civilization again. He and his sailors and marine infantry would waste their substance and years pooping around the hinterlands until one day somebody discovered this Sten had died of old age and they could all go home. Or maybe they'd just lose the task force's fiches in toto, and the fleet would wander on, until the Last Donald, like some sort of *Flying Duchess*, or however the legend went.

Hell.

Madoera slammed out of the daycabin onto his flagship's bridge. He glanced at one wallscreen that showed the system, a scatter of burned worlds too close to the radio pulsar, whose image – virtual, of course, as was everything else on the screen – flashed near the screen's top. He reached over a watch officer's shoulder, and tapped three pads.

Another screen opened, this one showing just Madoera's task force. A heavy combat fleet – a tacship carrier/flagship, the *Geomys*

Royal; a modern battleship, the *Parma*; two cruiser divisions, one with two heavies, the second with three light cruisers; and seven destroyers for a screen. A second crudiv was in support, with three light cruisers and four destroyers in its screen. His logistics tail was small – two supply ships and one tender, escorted by two destroyers.

A force to contend with. If he ever – and he privately thought never – could bring the rebels to battle, the action would be brief. But bloody, he was certain. Sten was misguided, but not stupid, and he and all of his fellows must know that if they surrendered they'd be merely prolonging their lifespan until a tribunal could be set up to try and execute them.

Knowing this, Madoera had issued as part of his standing orders instructions that if any rebel ships were encountered, extreme caution should be taken – they would certainly try any subterfuge or trick and fight to the last being. Certainly Madoera would do the same, if he ever slipped his shackles as badly as Sten.

Staring at the screen, Madoera wondered if there were any drills he hadn't run lately, or some highly obscure false emergency he could produce, just to keep his sailors from slacking off.

Clot it, he decided. It was bad enough they were hither-and-yonning so much. At least this time his swabs didn't need to think the old man was messing with them, as well as everyone else.

'In-system,' the watch officer reported.

'Thank you, Sr One pass. Double-diamond formation.'

That, at least, would be a test of how well his navigators could handle a complex formation. Especially with the real external problem of trying to keep their coms open while that pulsar sent out its tsunamis of white noise in the background. Now, just hope there's no collision while they're doing it, which probably would get me a nice reassignment to some water world with real ships. With oars.

Madoera listened with half an ear to the chatter as his flag navigator issued orders for the fleet's exercise in synchronized 'flying.' He yawned.

The rebels attacked.

There was no warning – the two DD's on flank security simply ceased existing. Someone shouted an alarm, and ships blinked onto the *Geomys Royal*'s screens. From 'behind' the Imperial task force.

They must have known, Madoera realized, exactly what orbit

the task force would set to approach this NP0406Y32, and followed them in.

The Imperial ships were at general quarters – but weapons stations were still at standby, and some missiles hadn't even been loaded in launch tubes. It had not made sense to chance damaging an expensive missile – or a more valuable crew-being – in another empty run.

A moment of panic, shouted down by Madoera and other officers throughout the task force. Steadiness returned – Madoera had turned his recruits into hardened professionals in long months of drill.

Numbers swirled across the screen showing the incoming attackers.

'Sir,' a watch officer reported. 'Six cruisers, estimated heavy, ten destroyers attacking.'

'Thank you, Mister. I can prog that myself. What class? What origin?'

'Sir . . . the *Jane's* has no data,' the woman said. 'Unknown. Except – they're state-of-the-art design. *Jane's* offered the theory they're new construction.'

Another wave of attackers appeared – this one from 'below' the task force.

'Three battleships, seven cruisers, twenty destroyers incoming, sir. I have an ID, sir. On the battlewagons. *Jane's* has a make. All three of them were designed and built by the Cal'gata. Pre-Tahn war. *Jane's* has them as mothballed and for sale. Five of the destroyers are Honjo origin, and we have a positive ID on one. The *Aoife*.'

Sten. For certain.

Now where the hell was the *Victory*? The bastard would be masterminding his ambush from its bridge. If Madoera could ID Sten's flagship, perhaps a suicide run by a couple of DD's might take out the puppetmaster. It wasn't on any screen. In some ways, that was worse. It meant the rebellion and the rebel forces had grown to the point that its leader no longer needed to accompany his beings to battle.

'All stations,' an antimissile tech monotoned. 'We have a multiple Kali-class launch from hostiles . . . attempting to divert . . .'

'Fox stations. Shift to local control. Acquire and launch at will.'

Madoera gnawed at his lip, calculating.

'Put CruDiv One on a direct attack against the BBs,' he ordered. 'And punch a line through to the *Neosho*. Order it to avoid battle and break for open space and report. Captain, get your tacships out there.'

'Yessir.'

'Sir . . . the *Neosho* is not answering. And we have no sign of *Neosho* onscreen.'

He hadn't even seen the destroyer get killed.

Madoera thought hard. 'All right, then. Put CruDiv Support out, wide on a flank. Get the supply elements in with the main fleet. And tell the *Parma*—'

'Signal from *Parma*, sir. Four hits. CIC wiped out. All weapons stations under local command. Drive regulation lost. Ship being conned from engine room.'

Another screen showed a third swarm coming in at the task force.

Someone shrilled, 'Where'd they get—'

Snapped retort: 'Silence at your station, Mister! Report as you've been trained!'

Madoera kept his calm. Closed his eyes, and let his mind battlechamber.

'Do you have contact with CruDiv Two?'

'Affirm. Staticky. A lot of interference from the pulsar.'

'Order them to avoid battle. Withdraw past *Parma*, past *Geomys Royal*, and set an erratic orbit clear of action. Do not engage the rebels. Do not attempt to stay in contact with the task force.'

'Message sent, sir. Will comply.'

'All right. Captain. We're going to circle the wagons . . .'

Madoera ordered the remnants of his task force – a crippled battleship, his flagship, and the rest – to take a globe formation, with erratic orbiting to keep them from being targets. He issued no change in orders to the two heavy cruisers he'd sent on a flanking attack.

He'd lose them, but perhaps they might serve to confuse the rebels, at least long enough for Madoera to begin some sort of breakout.

'Sir,' a talker said. 'Contact from the *Aleksyev*. It reports—'

The *Geomys Royal* shuddered as a missile impacted. Metal and men screamed. Flashdark/light as primary lighting went down, and a secondary circuit cut in. Nausea swept through Madoera's guts as the McLean generators went off and he free-fell, then they came back on – but 'down' was what had been to the side seconds ago.

'All stations, report damage. . . .'

The *Aoife*, at full drive, closed on the 'center' of the battlefield. Berhal Waldman stood behind his deck officer, not feeling his fingers trying to dig into the steel back of the chair.

His destroyer was at the front of the vee. The other four ships were also Honjo – officers and men who had mutinied to take their ships to join the rebels. They were actually regular volunteers. And all of them had sworn to avenge the *Aisling*.

'All units, all units,' Waldman ordered. 'Weapons systems slaved to my ship . . . on command . . . now.'

The ships obeyed. Then, 'All stations, ready to launch.'

'Very good. Target . . . enemy battleship. Goblin . . . half drive. Launch!'

Medium-range antiship missiles exploded from their tubes toward the *Parma*.

'Target . . . enemy battleship,' Berhal Waldman said. He ignored his weapons officer – she hadn't been on the *Aoife* when its sister ship was obliterated. This was his party. 'Kali launch. One tube per ship. Kali officers . . . maintain contact with your missiles . . . launch!'

The Imperial battleship seethed flame as its antimissile batteries and lasers went after the incoming missiles from the Honjo destroyers. In the dazzle, TA systems confused the monstrous shipkilling Kalis with the smaller Goblins, and did not correctly assign priorities.

One Goblin got through and knocked out two weapons stations – and forty men – on the *Parma*. And then both Kalis struck. The *Parma* blew in half, half again, and then into fragments.

The Honjo turned for the *Geomys Royal*.

On Madoera's main screen, Imperial units were blanking – or else transmitting DAMAGE/OUT OF BATTLE signals to the *Geomys Royal*.

That was enough. Fleet Admiral Madoera lifted a mike, and broadcast *en clair*.

'All Imperial units . . . all Imperial units. This is Admiral Madoera. All units break contact. Repeat, break contact. Set individual orbits, emergency power, for base. That is an order.'

He dropped the microphone.

'Captain, contact your tac squadrons. I want them to hold the rebels to the last. This is an all-units rearguard action. We must—'

'Missile closing . . . closing . . . negative diversion . . . negative acquisition . . . impact!'

The Goblin struck about two hundred meters behind the *Geomys Royal*'s bridge. Just behind the missile was a Kali. The Kali operator saw opportunity, and sent her bird directly into the fireball, counted once, and manually detonated.

Novablink . . . and there was empty space where the *Geomys Royal* – and Fleet Admiral Madoera – had been.

The survivors of the Imperial task force – one heavy cruiser, one light cruiser, three destroyers, and the fleet tender – fled at emergency drive. Their orbit would sweep them very close to the radio pulsar, then out, deep into the emptiness between the stars.

This was one sector from which the rebels had not attacked.

It was where Sten, and the *Victory*, waited.

'All tacships,' Captain Freston broadcast, 'we have six Imperial ships in-sector. All units, acquire data from central computer. Under squadron command: Attack. Repeat, attack.'

Hannelore La Ciotat and her fellow assassins with silk scarves went in for the kill.

Sten watched from the bridge of the *Victory* until the last Imperial indicator had vanished. His face was a mask. Just as had happened with the *Caligula*, beings who wore the same uniform Sten had worn, beings he might have served with or under or drank with in gin joints, were dead.

Kilgour's face was equally blank.

'All—' Freston hesitated, then continued, '—enemy elements destroyed.'

'Very well. Phase Two.'

And Sten's forces would not be permitted to ride clear of the battlefield, eyes averted from the slaughter.

Forty transports, provided by the Zaginows and the Cal'gata, swept the system. Ten Bhor armed merchant ships went with them. They hunted down any fragment of any Imperial ship they could pick up onscreen. The fragments were either further destroyed by demolition teams crossing to the wreckage and setting charges, or, if they were larger, the armed auxiliaries blasted them with Goblins or lasers.

It wasn't necessary, at least, to kill any survivors they found.

Not that there were many. Space war is no more merciful than naval battles far from land.

Any Imperials picked up would be given medical treatment and then transported, with uninjured survivors, to a planet at the fringes of the Lupus Cluster. Food, shelter, and continuing medical supplies and treatment would be provided on this forgotten, rather Eden-like world.

But that was all, until the war ended and either Sten or the Emperor was victorious. No mail, no notification to the survivors' families or friends.

Because the purpose of this long roundelay, back to the spoof in the dead system of Ystrn, was for an entire Imperial fleet to vanish.

Sten had deliberately chosen the area near NP0406Y32 for his plan's payoff. Any initial reports of his attack would be blocked by the pulsar. His strategy had worked perfectly.

Twenty-six warships, their admiral, and crew had disappeared.

Without a trace.

That would send a shiver through even the bravest warrior's soul.

And just as Ystrn had created the stage for this battle, NP0406Y32 would create a larger arena.

The essay purported to be a speech made by the Eternal Emperor at the graduating ceremony for one of the Empire's most prestigious naval academies, and was reprinted in *Fleet Proceedings*. In the speech the Emperor announced that these were parlous times the newly commissioned officers would face, but that they were also times of greatness. And as always, those who led from the front would be noted and rewarded.

The second item was buried near the end of the *Imperial Times*, a fiche no one in his right mind ever consulted for pleasure, but to check on the promotions, awards, and transfers of all Imperial officers.

Seven admirals had decided to take early retirement. All seven, analysts discovered, were respected – but all seven believed in the principle of leadership through battle analysis and ratiocination rather than noble posturing from the missile-torn bridge of a battleship.

The next item was the commissioning of a new super-battleship, the *Durer*. It had been especially honored by being picked by the

Eternal Emperor himself as a command ship. Command ship, the analyst noted. Not yacht or personal transport.

All these smallish items were published in specialized fiches.

A larger item was the lead story in the *Imperial Times*. A mass assemblage of the Imperial battle fleets was ordered, on a most tight schedule. There would be barely six E-months for combat elements to ready themselves.

The last was big and public, however. With full fanfare, it was announced the Eternal Emperor had been requested by Fleet Admiral Anders and the rest of the Imperial General Staff to provide them with his centuries of wisdom and experience to extirpate the last, lingering traces of the bandit Sten.

The rebels had winkled the Emperor out of his bunker.

Now he was vulnerable.

Next, Sten would strike for the heart of the Empire and the Emperor himself.

Chapter Nineteen

The great fleets of the rebellion rendezvoused in intersteller emptiness near a monstrous whirlpool galaxy. Emptiness – but emptiness very close to Prime World and the heart of the Empire.

There were thousands of ships. Zaginows. Cal'gata. Honjo. Bhor. Other ships from beings, cultures, worlds, even star clusters, Sten had never heard of. Systems' entire navies had joined the rebel forces. Squadrons had 'deserted' *en masse*. Other ships, and even in some cases individual beings, had found their solitary way to the rising.

Sten sometimes wondered at their motives. Gold? Gods? Glory? Perhaps sometimes a burning, inchoate sense of injustice, a desire to end the Empire's tyranny. It had taken generations and centuries, but at last the hammer had lost its velvet padding.

The indicator lights in the battle chamber of the *Victory* now represented fleets instead of ships.

But less than one-tenth of the Empire was now in open revolt.

Sten thought that might be enough.

The orders went out. The rebellion would move into the Empire's heart, ostensibly making an attack on Prime itself. Before they could attack the Empire's capital, Imperial fleets would certainly come out to stop them.

That would be, Sten prayed, the final battle.

The real objective was not Prime at all, but the fleets themselves. Once the Empire's ability to wage war was crippled, Prime and any other world could be easily attacked, seized, isolated, or ignored.

It would be, his own sense as well as his staff's analyses, a near-run victory. Estimates were, given the present level of forces and that the rebellion had thus far maintained a tactical edge, 61 percent to 39 percent, favoring a victory for Sten. Expected casualties would be a staggering 35 percent of the rebellion's forces.

But blood was the argument, and there appeared to be no peaceful alternatives.

So be it.

'So the traitor is moving,' the Eternal Emperor said. What might have been a smile moved his lips, then disappeared.

'Yessir,' Admiral de Court said. 'Just as your estimate and our progs said.' De Court was one of the seven computer-brained admirals that the *Imperial Times* said had taken early retirement. In fact, they had been detached for special duties and were serving as a shadow general staff directly under the Eternal Emperor himself.

Their role would never be known, of course. None of the seven would be disloyal enough to mention that the final obliteration of Sten came from the brilliance of anyone besides the Emperor.

They were not disloyal . . . or suicidal.

Admiral de Court did not appear pleased that the anticipated events were, in fact, occurring.

'What are the numbers,' the Eternal Emperor asked.

'Fifty-one percent chance of Imperial victory.'

'That is all?' The Emperor was startled.

'Yessir. Too many Imperial elements lack real battle experience. Or else they're relatively new formations.'

'I ordered the secret mobilization months ago.'

De Court was silent. Not even the Eternal Emperor could create Weddigens or *Golden Hind*s simply by the laying on of hands.

'Anticipated casualties?'

'Well over 70 percent.'

A long silence. Then, 'Acceptable.'

De Court licked dry lips. He'd been chosen, as the most diplomatically gifted of the technocrat-admirals, to handle this presentation.

'One other thing, sir. We have two single progs, not entirely quantifiable, but a probability estimation of approximately 82 percent, that the traitor Sten will be killed in this battle. And – and yourself, as well.'

The Emperor was very quiet.

'Sir.'

Still nothing. Then, finally, 'Thank you,' the Eternal Emperor said. 'You're dismissed.'

Scoutboats, then destroyers, then light cruisers met between the galaxies in a sudden snarl of blood. Ships swirled, launched missiles, took hits, died.

The engagement was all the bloodier because it was unexpected.

'So the bastard mousetrapped us,' Sten hissed.

'I wouldn't put it that baldly,' Freston said. 'But the Emperor hasn't just been sitting there waiting for us.'

Kilgour was in a glower of rage.

'Skip,' he said. 'Ah dinnae ken whae's th' matter wi' our intel. But Ah'll hae some gonads frae breakfast kippers. Later. A' th' mo, Ah dinnae hae time frae 'crim'nations. Th' sit's as follows:

'Th' Emp's got its fleets already mob'lized, aye? I's nae a total disast'r, unlike th' Emp mos' likely thinks it t' be. But it'll noo be a bonnie prog.'

'GA,' Sten said.

'We'll trash th' clots. Est 80 percent a' th' Imps'll nae see home again. But wi' a price. We'll take 75 percent hits ourselves. I's a Kilkenny cat's war, lad.

'But we'll mos' likely kill th' Emp i' the bloodbath. An', same prob'ility, die i' th' doin't.'

Sten nodded.

He stared at, but did not see, the screens as he ran his own set of numbers.

He would probably die in this battle in the galactic dark. Very well. Sten was surprised he could accept that with a certain equanimity – or at least he had fooled his mind into thinking that.

At least the Eternal Emperor would die, as well.

And the Imperial forces would be shattered.

But a navy could be rebuilt.

Especially if – and he'd completely accepted Haines's verification of Mahoney's improbable theory – the Emperor would return. Return, and be handed the throne in exchange for the resumption of AM2.

The Emperor would be gone for at least three, possibly six, E-years. During which time the 'civilized' universe would sink further into chaos. And then a madman would return, slashing out to regain his kingdom. A fifth horseman of the apocalypse.

How long would it take for another rebellion? A rebellion that wasn't aimed at the New Boss replacing the Old Boss? A rebellion unlike the Tahn war or the Mueller Rising before that?

No.

Sten issued orders, then retreated to the solitude of the *Victory*'s admiral's walk. The rebels were to take a defensive posture. He could not – would not – allow the projected orgy of mutual destruction to occur. Not when it would be unlikely to completely excise this tumor that called himself the Eternal Emperor.

No. If necessary, they could retreat. Regroup. Rethink. Or, in a worst-case scenario, follow the example of countless liberation forces through the centuries – dump arms, go to ground, and try again.

Hell, Sten thought. If this is where it ends, I can disappear into the woodwork. Change my face, change my name, and try again.

The next time, by myself.

The next time, with a bomb or a longarm.

No surrender, Sten promised himself. But now it's time to keep the beings who followed you from dying.

Inaction, his mind told him. Retreat. Passivity.

No other options occurred.

He thought of alk, or stregg. Neither was acceptable. He slumped into a chair. Stared out at the kaleidoscope that was hyperspace.

Seconds . . . minutes . . . hours . . . centuries later, the com blatted at him.

Sten slapped the switch and started to growl. Stopped himself. It was Alex onscreen, his face and voice carefully bland.

'Com 'cast frae th' Imperial forces,' he said, without preamble. 'Tightbeam. On a freq thae Freston says is exclusive t' th' Emperor. An' th' *Victory*'s one ae th' few ships wi' th' capability t' receive it. Y' recollect the Emp built this ship frae his own use?'

'Do you have a point of origin?'

'Ah dinnae, Sten. Noo frae any listed world. Frae a ship, Ah reck. Wi' th' Imperial forces, Ah'd guess.

'An . . . i's *en clair*. Vid an' voice. Wi' a card sayin't it's f'r y'r eyes only.'

Sten started to order it to be transmitted to his com, then caught himself. No. Even at this time, at this moment before the storm, it would not be unlikely for the Eternal Emperor to transmit something meaningless – and then leak the story that the message contained private instructions from the Emperor to one of his double agents.

'Hang on,' Sten ordered. 'I'm on my way down. Set it up for projection on the bridge.'

'Boss? Are y' sure?'

'Hell, yes. I'm getting too old to play games. Stand by.'

The screen showed the Eternal Emperor. He was standing alone on the awe-inspiring bridge of a warship. The *Durer*? He wore a midnight-black uniform with his symbol in gold on his breast – the letters AM2 superimposed over the null-element's atomic structure.

'This message is intended for Sten, and only for him.

'Greetings.

'Once you were my most faithful servant. Now you have declared yourself my most deadly enemy. I do not know why. I thought you served me well, and so I made you ruler over many things, and thought that would bring you joy. Evidently it did not.

'And I have seen, to my great sorrow, that some of my subjects believe themselves to be ignored, believe they have been somehow slighted, in spite of my efforts to help them as best I can in these troubled times.

'I could reason, I could argue, I could attempt to present a larger view of the chaos that looms before all of us in the Empire.

'But I shall not. Perhaps some of my satraps *have* enforced their own immoralities under the cover of my rule, which has always been intended to provide the maximum benefit to all beings, human and otherwise, a rule of peace and justice that began before time was recorded and, with the goodwill of my fellow citizens, will continue until time itself must have a stop.

'Beings – many of them my good and faithful servants – have died. Died in this murderous squabble that history will not even dignify with a footnote. It shall not be remembered because I propose a solution, a solution that no one could argue with.

'You, Sten, say that my rule is autocratic. Dictatorial, even. Very well.

'I invite you to share that rule.

'Not as a co-ruler, because you, or those who rose in rebellion with you, could well define that as a cheap attempt at bribery. At co-option.

'No. I propose a full and complete sharing of power between myself, my Parliament, and you and your chosen representatives, in whatever form we agree to be the most representative and just.

'I further propose an immediate truce, to avoid further bloodshed. This truce will be of short duration, so that neither side can argue it is being used as a device to seek an advantageous position to destroy the other. I would accept two E-weeks as an outside figure.

'At the end of that time, you and I should meet. We should meet with our best advisers and allies, to prepare the grounds for this new and promising time for the Empire.

'I further suggest that our meeting ground be on Seilichi, the home planet of the most respected, most neutral, and most peaceful beings this universe has ever known, the Manabi. I would also ask that their most honored savant, Sr Ecu, mediate our negotiations.

'I ask you, Sten, as an honorable being, to accept my most generous offer.

'Now, only you can keep innocent blood from showering the stars.'

And the screen went blank.

A blast of babble on the *Victory*'s bridge. Then silence, as everyone turned to look at Sten.

Son of a bitch, he thought.

He has us.

And there's no way out.

No way whatsoever.

Chapter Twenty

Sten rubbed tired eyes and tried to think. He hadn't gotten a lot of sleep in the past two weeks. What little he'd had time for had been constantly interrupted by messengers, coms, and delegations arriving from his allies. Even his thoughts, when he was alone with Cind, yammered at him.

Cind had run everyone out twenty hours ago, and forced Sten to take a sopor. He had slept hard, but not well.

Now, he was in his final briefing. His allies had presented what they wanted and expected in this Brave New World of Powersharing, a certain percentage of which was either wishful thinking or else shouldn't be mentioned until the transition was complete. And that last assumption was well up there with progging the belled cat . . .

The briefing, like everything else about Sten and the rebellion, was irregular, consisting less of those with the clout than the old guard. Himself. Kilgour. Cind. Rykor. Even Otho, who at least could be counted on to provide the nonsubtle touch.

Sten wished Sr Ecu could have been present, or could at least have monitored this session. But no one could chance even the vague possibility the Emperor would discover the Manabi and Sten were in collusion.

The *Victory*, escorted by five cruisers and eleven destroyers, was orbiting an unpopulated world less than twenty light-years from Seilichi.

Not that there was much to say in this meeting – it'd all been gone over time and again. Sten wondered about Alex, who'd been unnaturally quiet for the past few days, keeping his own counsel.

Sten poured a glass of herbal/protein drink, and sipped. He shuddered at its taste. Why were things that were supposedly good for you so frequently abominable?

'I wonder,' he said, 'just how long it will be before the Emperor double-crosses us?'

'It will depend,' Rykor said, 'on how we handle the first crisis after the Emperor grudgingly moves over on his throne to allow your presence, whatever it might be. If our solution coincides with the Emperor's, and in no way detracts from the perception that he alone really holds the reins of power . . . two E-years from that date.

'If there is a divergence of views, and ours becomes the plan operated on . . . three cycles.

'In any event, there will be an attempted counterrevolution within five E-years, either planned by the Eternal Emperor himself or, possibly, honestly mounted by his loyalists.

'But we should be, given foresight and proper planning, as well as an ocean and a half of pure luck, able to survive the first attempt to destroy the new government.'

'All those estimates,' Sten said dryly, 'give the coalition more time than we would have if we'd accepted battle. Time enough to figure how we're going to RF the Emperor before he does it to us.'

Kilgour shook his head. 'Ah'll noo be rain't on th' march-past, but Ah'm sittin' here rec'lectin' a place called Glencoe, a clan called Campbell, an' a pol named Dalrymple.'

'Which means?' Otho rumbled.

'Naethin' 'cept m' own buddin't fears, lad. Whae dealin't wi' a madman, y' cannae use logic.'

'We've gone through this before,' Sten said. 'The Emperor is hardly going to try a double cross now. He proposed the meet in the first place, so it'd be his flag of truce that'd be dishonored. Of course he's mad, and of course he wants my skin for his drumhead – but he certainly would not try anything while we're all under the protection of the Manabi.'

A com whispered, and Alex crossed to it and read the message onscreen. He keyed an answer and blanked it.

'Ver' well,' he said. 'Y'r ride t' th' conference's inbound.'

'And why will we not descend from the *Victory*?' Otho asked. 'Should Sten arrive like a beardless one? Perhaps on a trading ship?'

'Close,' Alex agreed. 'He'll be usin't a transport. Ah' borrow'd a liner frae th' Zaginows. An' dinnae be sayin't "we," less y' think

Sten hae a mousie i' his pocket. Sten'll be descendin' ae a man of peace, which i' whae we want ae th' perception frae all. Aye, Rykor?'

Rykor wallowed in her vat, considering.

'How dimwitted of me,' she said. 'And I am the being who prides herself on not automatically making assumptions. Yet I've always taken for granted Sten would land from the *Victory*, properly escorted by his allies.

'However . . . what exactly do you propose, Sr Kilgour?'

'Sten arrives on Seilichi wi' but one aide. M'self. We'll hae a tightbeam frae th' liner t' the *Vick*, which we'll hae offworld, an' well awa' frae th' Emp's fleets.

'We'll nae look like bloody-handed rebels, but ae wee an' Ah do mean wee, peacelovers, i' y' ken. Dav'd agin' th' Phar'sees, or howe'er thae tale goes.

'It'll make a braw point, frae th' livie crews, Ah wager.'

Rykor closed her eyes and ran the visuals. Yes. It would look impressive. Sten, one small man standing victoriously against the Emperor.

'Rykor, we'll hae y'rself oop here, listenin't t' all thae haps, an' keepin't ae clear mind.'

Cind was on her feet. 'Sten isn't going down there without any escort.'

'Well spok't,' Alex said. 'But he will. Y'r Bhor an' th' Gurks cannae stand up t' a laserblast frae a battlewagon. An' thae's noo point i' a martial show, solely t' be showin't th' size ae our claymores, noo is there, lass?'

Cind was about to go on – but Alex moved his head slightly to the side. She stopped cold.

Sten, too, was looking at Kilgour. Alex just stared back, expressionless. Ah, Sten, thought. And is there any harm if he's right?

'We'll do it Alex's way,' Sten said, before Otho could come in with a bellowed rejoinder.

'The Emperor wears plain dress whites when everybody else is in full dress uniform. We'll play another version of the same card.

'Somebody grab one of my dogsbodies, and make sure I've got a Boy Virgin Outfit. Now, I'm going to run everyone out. I want something disgustingly dull to eat and some more sleep. We're ready.'

Sr Ecu hovered in the center of the huge landing field within the 'crater' of the Guesting Center. His senses were at their finest tune. This meeting, and the subsequent series of conferences, could be not just the culmination of his own life, but that of the Manabi as well.

His race had always viewed the Emperor, and Empire, with skepticism and a measure of dislike. His authoritarianism brought continuity, a degree of peace, and a degree of plentitude, to worlds beyond worlds. But at a price. The price of tyranny. Sometimes it had been somewhat benevolent, sometimes it had been otherwise, such as the terrible conflicts like the Mueller Rising and the Tahn war, which, when all the rhetoric died, had been only fought to guarantee the rule of the Emperor. Ecu had long wondered whether it could be possible to correct the Eternal Emperor's excesses and still maintain the benefits.

Could this be the chance?

How romantic, his brain said. This, from a being whose life has been spent in the labyrinth of diplomacy, trying to ferret out true meaning from babble.

You expect Eternal Peace to come from a meeting between a being you believe to be quite mad and a young rebel who not many years ago was that madman's assassin? Who – knowing the nature of humanity and its lust for power – will take only a short time before he sees himself as the Emperor?

But still.

The livie cameras scattered along the 'rim' of the Guesting Center had gotten tired of the nearly dead air – motionless footage of the Manabi's red-and-black bulk hovering over bare tarmac – and had returned to a pursuit they seemingly never tire of – interviewing themselves as to what anything and everything meant.

A sonic lash broke into their circle game, and, overhead, the Eternal Emperor's ship lowered toward a landing, with a small scoutboat as its landing guide. Ecu recognized the *Normandie* – the Emperor's old, heavily armed secret transport. How odd. Ecu would have expected him to make as impressive an appearance as possible, and arrive aboard his new super-battleship, the *Durer*. He knew that overhead, just offplanet in a geosynchronous orbit, hung a full Imperial battlefleet as cover.

Ecu felt a flicker of hope. Perhaps the Emperor didn't want to present a warlike image.

But that was not the case, he realized seconds later, as a landing ramp sliced out and heavily armed Internal Security humans in their black uniforms doubled out in squad formation and took up position around the ship.

No one else came down the ramp.

Overhead, a whine, and Sten's ship – the civilian liner Ecu had been told to expect – lowered down toward the field. It shifted from Yukawa drive to its McLean generators, and grounded on its sponsons.

A wide portal yawned in one of them, and two beings stepped out. Sten and Alex Kilgour.

Kilgour wore the full regalia of an Earth Scots laird, from bonnet to cloak to kilt to sporran. But there was no *skean dhu* in his stocking, no daggersheath at his belt, and the scabbard for his great broadsword was empty. Kilgour did not even have a pistol concealed in the sporran worn over his crotch.

Sten wore a pale blue tunic that buttoned to his neck, and trousers of the same color. He was bareheaded and wore no decorations.

No security beings followed them. The two walked out into the soft sunlight and waited.

Across the field, bootheels clashed and weapons crashed as the IS troops came to attention.

The Eternal Emperor and his entourage came down the ramp. As expected, he wore a plain black uniform with the Imperial Emblem on its breast. Around his neck was one decoration – one of the liviecasters correctly identified it, in a hushed voice, as the Giver of Peace decoration that he'd received at the conclusion of the Mueller Rising.

The 'caster went on to identify the Imperial dignitaries: Avri, his political chief of staff. Tyrenne Walsh, figurehead ruler of Dusable and the Eternal Emperor's usual stalking-horse in Parliament. And so on down, from Count This to Secretary of Protocol That. The liviecaster misidentified one being, but Ecu knew him well: Solon Kenna. The Eternal Emperor was bringing his sharpest political minds to this meeting. Ecu felt that horrible stir called hope move in his soul once more.

Best of all, Poyndex was not part of the throng. Once more, a favorable sign that perhaps this conference was intended to bring a measure of peace to the Empire.

Sten and Alex moved to greet the Imperial troupe. The entourage stopped, and the Eternal Emperor walked forward alone.

'Sten.' It was a completely neutral acknowledgment.

Sten, foolishly, had to stop himself from saluting. The habit of years died very hard.

'Your Highness.'

'Shall we begin?'

Sten forced a smile to his lips and nodded.

Sten and the Eternal Emperor were alone on a balcony near the crest of the Guesting Center. The balcony appeared to be just a ledge on the outer near-vertical slope of the volcano-styled Center.

After the conferees had been shown to their quarters, the Emperor had asked Ecu if he might have the pleasure of talking to Sten alone for a few moments. The meeting was not to be recorded.

Ecu asked Sten, who hesitated, then agreed.

It was just twilight, and purple drifted across the sky above them, coloring the wide valley around the Center. The young Manabi who escorted them to the balcony told them it was screened against anyone, especially a liviecaster, who might be indiscreet enough to focus a parabolic microphone on the two of them. Sten and the Emperor looked at each other, and Sten half smiled. No one would be *that* indiscreet, he knew.

There were two chairs and a large cart equipped with a McLean generator at the rear of the balcony. The Emperor walked to it and opened the doors.

'Scotch. Stregg. Alk. Pure quill. Beer. Teas. Even water. The Manabi certainly worry over dry throats.'

He turned to Sten. 'Would you like a drink?'

'No,' Sten said. 'But thank you.'

The Emperor picked up the flask of stregg. Turned it back and forth. 'I used to drink this,' he mused. 'But I found I've lost my taste for it. Isn't that unusual?'

He looked directly at Sten, then his eyes shifted back and forth. Sten found the gaze uncomfortable, but did not allow himself to look away. After a few seconds, the Emperor looked elsewhere.

He walked to the edge of the balcony and sat on the low railing, looking out at the valley.

'Unusual beings, the Manabi,' he mused. 'The only real trace of their civilization is underground. I would feel unsettled, bothered, that if I vanished in the night, there would be no sign whatsoever that I had ever existed . . . no mark of my own on the face of the planet.'

Sten had no answer. Again, the Emperor looked at him, his eyes doing that mad dance.

'Do you recall our first meeting?'

'Formally, sir?'

'No. I meant the night of Empire Day. When you were head of my bodyguards. I assume you have heard that I dismissed the Gurkhas. Romantic as they are, I found their capabilities limited. Anyway, that night was when I asked to see your knife. Do you still have it, by the way?'

'I do.'

'May I see it again?'

Now Sten smiled. 'I hope there are no security types out there who might misunderstand,' he said. He curled his fingers and let the weapon slip down into his fingers. He passed it across to the Eternal Emperor, who looked at it curiously and handed it back.

'Just as I remembered it. You know, I have dreamed about this knife from time to time. But I don't remember the circumstances of the dream. Yes. I should have realized its symbolism to you back then.'

It took a moment for Sten to understand what the Emperor meant. Before he could protest, the Emperor went on: 'That was an interesting night. You introduced me to stregg, as I recall. And I cooked. I don't remember—'

'It was something you called Angelo stew.'

'Oh yes.' The Emperor was silent for a moment. 'That's something else I find I don't have much time for any more. Cooking. But now that this . . . disagreement . . . will be cleared up, I'll be able to return to my old ways. Who knows? Maybe even think about trying to build a guitar again.' His expression hardened. 'It's good to have a hobby in your twilight years, isn't it?'

Sten thought it best to remain silent.

'Empire Day. That, I suppose, is where the dry rot set in. Hakone. The Tahn. Mahoney. The Altaics . . . Christ!'

The Emperor peered intently at Sten. 'You don't know what you have asked for, Sten. How all this goes on, and on, and it never slows and no one ever is grateful.'

'Sir. I did not ask for anything. This powersharing is—'

'Of course you didn't ask,' the Emperor said, a note of pettishness in his voice. 'But after all these centuries, don't you think I know? Give me credit, at least, for not being a fool.'

'That is something I have *never* thought, Your Majesty.'

'No?' The flickering gaze turned away, back to the darkening landscape far below. 'How bare,' the Emperor mused. 'How barren.'

He rose. 'I plan on eating in my quarters,' he said, and smiled.

'I would think that any banquets or public feastings might well wait until we have reached an arrangement. Don't you?'

'It doesn't matter to me,' Sten said. 'But I'm not particularly inclined to ten courses and having to come up with polite toasts.'

The Emperor's smile became larger. 'That was one of the reasons I respected you at one time. Even, perhaps, liked you. You had no truckle for pretense. I sometimes wonder how you found yourself capable of *this*.'

He nodded, and, still smiling, went inside.

Alex Kilgour saw Sten to his chambers, and, yawning mightily, went to his own rooms.

Once inside, he doffed the outfit he mentally referred to as th' Laird Kilgour drag and shrugged off the pretense of exhaustion. He took from the lining of his valise a phototropic camouflage suit and zipped it on. The valise's straps became a swiss seat, and he took a small can of climbing thread from his sporran.

An' noo, he thought, we'll ken i' th' luck ae th' spidgers appliet t' all Scots, or solely t' Bobbie th' Brucie.

The problem was that he was not sure exactly what luck would be defined as.

The IS technician ran and reran his tapes. He was trying to figure out just where an annoying buzz on a low freq was coming from. Not from the *Normandie*, nor from any of the Imperial staff. Nor from any of the liviecasters' equipment.

He had tracked the static to the Guesting Center itself, but it wasn't from any of the Manabi's electronics.

The tech had finally nailed it. The buzz was coming from the portable com that the rebel's aide was carrying. Typical, he thought. Can't even use a handitalki without mucking it up.

But it was annoying. Sometime, during this conference, he would ask one of his superiors to talk to the clot and tell him to get a new chatterbox.

He went back to his main task, ensuring that the link between the picketboat and the newly installed apparatus aboard the *Normandie* was functioning perfectly.

The Eternal Emperor took Avri twice, in the manner that pleased him most. The woman bit hard into the pillow. A scream at midnight would be ignored by sensible beings if it came from the

Imperial quarters in Arundel, but here on Seilichi an unnecessary and foolish alarm might be raised.

The Emperor went to the fresher, then stopped by a case and took a tiny object from it. He returned to the bed, ran his hand down Avri's close-cropped hair in what might have been a caress, and, as the injector's tip touched the woman's medulla oblongata, he pressed the bulb.

Avri slumped into deep unconsciousness.

It would be her last sleep.

The Emperor rose and put on a black coverall from his baggage, a coverall that had built-in climbing harness bonded into it, and thin, rigid-sole rock-climbing shoes. He pulled a mesh vest over it and closed its fastenings. He wished again for a pistol, but he knew that there had been little chance of getting a firearm through the Manabi's automatic security devices. This would be enough.

He flexed his knees. He pushed the double windows onto the balcony open. Far below him, in the crater's center, was Sten's ship, his own *Normandie*, and the picketboat. It was very dark, and very quiet. He thought he saw the single sentry posted at the *Normandie*'s ramp walk out into the open, about-face, and pace back. He didn't matter. The day the Emperor could not slip past a gate guard was the day he was ready to admit to being the fool that Sten, and it seemed the rest of the Empire, considered him.

To either side of this apartment his aides and supposed confidants slept. Dream on, my servants, he thought. For now you are performing the finest duty to the Empire you could dream of. And your sacrifice will not have been in vain.

He looked at the naked sleekness of Avri. A slight feeling of pity crossed his mind. But not for long. The only way for a sacrifice to be convincing is when something important is really given away.

Besides, she had started to bore him.

He had already begun to consider other, more skilled women who had drawn his eye.

He unclipped a can of climbing thread from the vest, touched its nozzle, and the end of the single-molecule chain bonded to the edge of the balcony. The Emperor slipped his hands into special jumars – trying to climb down the thread barehanded would be exactly like trying to climb down a flexible razorblade.

The Eternal Emperor slid over the edge of the balcony and,

nerves thrilling and blood singing as had not happened in years, went down into the night.

Kilgour was quite comfortable. He had one toe on a firm stance almost three centimeters wide, a safety loop around an outcropping, and one arm around it as well.

He could have danced.

He kept watch, a great spider, invisible, as his phototropic uniform was now on exactly the color and pattern of the false rock the Manabi had built the Guesting Center from.

A bit below him, halfway across the crater, he saw movement. He focused the night glasses more exactly and zoomed in.

Th' Emp's apartment, aye. And one lad comin' oot.

Luck, eh? P'raps th' worst. Good luck – an impossibility – would have been Alex spending a cramped night out here with nothing happening, and the conference beginning as expected.

Noo. Who's th' wee lad danglin' frae th' rope o'er there? Th' Emp his own self?

Alex frowned, reanalyzing his various progs of possible Imperial blackguarding.

He had anticipated some kind of double-dealing here on Seilichi, but none of his plans matched what seemed to be occurring.

Back aboard the *Victory*, following the final briefing with Sten, Alex had led Cind and Otho to his own quarters. That was the only place on the *Victory* that he knew was unbugged by anyone, not Freston, not Sten. Especially not Sten. Although, from the look the boss had given him, Kilgour was pretty sure Sten knew what was going on.

'Whae we're on th' ground,' he'd started, 'Ah'll wan' you t' be standin't by. On command frae me, or frae Sten, or i' th' event com is lost wi' us, y're t' take th' bridge, an' read an' follow th' orders Ah'll hae gie'en y' afore we depart. E'en i' thae means relievin' Cap' Freston i' he gets arg'ment'ive.

'Ah knoo 'tis a hard thing t' ask, but Ah'll hae t' request y' to oath me thae y'll follow th' 'structions wi'oot fail. Trustin' me thae Ah hae noo but th' best ae intentions frae Sten, an' frae this clottin' rebellion thae's likely t' cause th' death ae us all.

'I' y' trust me, i' y' trust Sten . . . y'll do as Ah'm desirin't.'

Cind and Otho had considered. Cind had been the first to nod. Besides, she had suspected that Alex was planning for what had become Cind's worst nightmare – a nightmare she saw herself not being able to end, save in a suicidal battle royal. Then Otho had grunted. He, too, would obey.

Kilgour expressed pleasure in their confidence. Sent them out.

He had reflected . . . Glencoe . . . An eerie, narrow, rain-dripping desolate valley on old Earth, whose laird had delayed taking an oath of allegiance to the usurper king until the last minute, and then had been further prevented from an unpleasant if necessary duty by winter storms.

The laird had not considered that the usurper would have a pol named Dalrymple who wanted to make an example of someone who'd failed to sign, nor that there was a treacherous clan named the Campbells, all too willing to garner favor from the sassenach William.

Campbell soldiers appeared in the glen, and were given traditional Highland hospitality. Treachery was in their heart, treachery they did not wait to implement. That night, fire and the ax came to Glencoe, and women and children went howling into the snow and ice and frozen death.

Glencoe, Alex had thought. Aye. Sometimes, contrary to whae all th' finest planners think, treachery dinnae wait till th' perfect mo, i' th' dark ae th' moon whae th' raven rattles its deathcry.

And so he came to Seilichi prepared for the Emperor to double-cross them, from the moment the liner he'd cozened from the Zaginaws landed, till now, when he saw that man in black, who appeared to be the Eternal Emperor himself, abseil out the window.

He already had the corridor outside the Imperial apartments covered with a mechanical sensor, and Alex knew any movement from any of the Emperor's retinue would be met with alarms from the Manabi who, though no warriors, kept a cautious watch through the night.

Alex puzzled one more moment, wishing desperately he had somehow been able to wangle a sniper rifle onto Seilichi – an' then we'd ken whae a *real* expert ae duplic'ty's capable of, aye?

Then he thought he had figured the Emperor's scheme and touched a switch at his wrist. Then Alex went back up his own climbing thread like a spider fleeing the flame, a flame Kilgour knew would be real in moments.

The Internal Security technician was sound asleep, far from his instruments. He never knew that the annoying static, that buzz, stopped the instant Alex touched his handitalki. The static was a deliberate broadcast.

There are at least two ways to broadcast a warning. The first and most common, is to start a commotion when trouble threatens. The second, and sneakier, is to have a commotion *stop* at the sign of danger.

Like Sherlock Holmes's famous dog, which did nothing in the nighttime, the end of the deliberately generated static from Kilgour's com was a tightbeam alarm linked to two spaceships.

The GQ alarms yammered aboard the *Victory*. The ship, already at standby, went to full combat readiness.

Cind, Otho, Freston, and Lalbahadur had not been asleep, nor had they intended to go offshift until Sten returned, even if they'd had to progress to stimulants and cold showers.

'All stations ready, sir,' the officer of the watch reported. 'No external signs of GQ readiness apparent.'

'Very good,' Freston said. He turned to Cind. 'My orders from Mister Kilgour in the event of alarm were to place myself under your command, and obey your instructions absolutely. Take over.'

'Thank you.' Cind took a deep breath, and keyed her pore pattern into the small fiche holder Alex had given her when they left the *Victory*.

The instructions were simple:

WAIT IN PRESENT ORBIT UNTIL THREATENED. DO NOT, REPEAT DO NOT, ATTEMPT OFFENSIVE MOVES AGAINST EMPIRE. DO NOT, REPEAT, DO NOT ATTEMPT TO CLOSE PLANET OR MAKE PLANETFALL. MAINTAIN WATCH ON FREQ QUEBEC THIRTY-FOUR ALPHA. IN THE EVENT IMPERIAL COMBAT ELEMENTS ATTEMPT TO ENGAGE, BREAK CONTACT, MOVE COVERTLY TO [A SET OF COORDINATES]. THIS WILL BE RENDEZVOUS POINT. IF NO CONTACT MADE AT SECONDARY RV, VICTORY IS TO REVERT TO INDEPENDENT COMMAND AND TAKE WHATEVER ACTION OR ACTIONS IS DEEMED CORRECT AT THE TIME. GOOD LUCK.

. . . and the squiggle that was Kilgour's signature.

'We just wait,' Otho interpreted.

Cind growled – a noise that dignified her Bhor training – and then gritted, 'We wait.'

*

The Emperor's feet touched down, and he slid down to his knees. He broke the climbing thread off and discarded the jumars.

A few guardspots glared around the three ships on the landing field. Once again, there was no movement except for the single sentry at the *Normandie*'s ramp.

Crouching, he made for the picketboat.

The broken static-buzz signaled to yet another ship.

Hannelore La Ciotat was awake, feet out of her bunk and on the tacship's deck. Her tacship's GQ alarm was a civilized *bong*ing, the synthesized sound of a bell. It was more than loud enough to cover the cramped crew area.

La Ciotat sealed the front of her shipsuit and damned near physically threw her onwatch weapons officer/XO out of the command seat.

'I relieve you, Mister.' Her fingers were like fluid across the panel. POWER . . . UP . . . SYSTEMS STANDBY . . . CREW READY . . . WEAPONS READY . . .

She touched keys, and the tacship lifted clear of the ground on McLean drive, ripping away from the camouflage net that La Ciotat and her crew had staked over the tiny ship a day earlier.

The tacship was hidden just inside the first twist of one of the canyons leading to the great valley the Guesting Center was in the middle of.

La Ciotat ghosted the ship around the bend.

'I have the center on visual,' she told her XO.

'Roger. All screens show same.'

'Drive status?'

'Drakh-hot, Hannelore.'

And she, too, waited.

'Up, lad! Th' Emp's movin'!'

Sten's mind groped out of a disremembered, terrible dream, and Kilgour was pulling him up.

'What's the—'

'Shut up!'

Alex tossed him a phototropic suit, and Sten pulled it on. He looked around for some boots.

'No time, Sten! Move!'

Kilgour shoved him toward the door that yawned into a deserted open corridor, light glaring, and Sten was in a stumbling, nightmare run, not sure if he was still asleep and dreaming, but the rough carpet hurt his feet, and Alex slung him around a corner and up a ramp, toward the top of the crater.

'Which way—'

'I' y' speaki't again, Ah'll coldcock y', Ah swear! We're i' th' eye ae th' storm!'

A great door, barred, that led out onto a balcony on the outer wall of the crater. Alex, without slowing, crashed into the door and sent it pinwheeling away. Some sort of alarm – fire, intrusion, it didn't matter – began sounding.

The Eternal Emperor came in the picketboat's port. The duty officer jerked in surprise, even though he'd been briefed.

'Lift ship,' the Emperor snapped, as he turned and slapped the PORT CLOSE switch.

'Broadcast as ordered!'

'Yessir.'

The officer lifted a security cover, and slid the port of the recently installed control across, and the machine across the field, in the *Normandie*, began ticking seconds.

Overhead, in space, the signal yammered the *Durer* and its escorts and sailors into combat alert.

The McLean drive brought the tiny picketboat clear of the ground.

Across the landing field, the sentry at the *Normandie*'s portal came fully awake, his willygun coming up in his hands. What the clot was going on? Nobody told him anything? Clottin' corp of the guard hadn't said anything—

A predawn wind whistled across the balcony, a wind Sten never felt. Alex had his com up.

'Pickup! On this station!'

'Got you,' came a calm, unhurried woman's voice that Sten thought he recognized. 'On the way.'

'So you were right,' Sten recovered.

'Aye. The bastard's ducking out the back door. Solo.'

'Oh, Christ. We've got to alert the Manabi,' Sten said, knowing futility.

'What can they—' Kilgour winced as the com screamed at him, as a transmitter aboard the *Normandie* obediently began jamming cast on all freqs.

Across the valley, they saw a tiny miniature sun. La Ciotat's tacship, blazing toward them.

The Imperial picketboat's commander lifted his ship onto its tail, and kicked in full Yukawa drive, shooting the craft straight toward the stars. Barely clear of the crater, he went to stardrive, and the picketboat vanished into space.

A relay closed aboard the *Normandie*.

The whine/roar of the picketboat shattered Ecu's sleep. His sensors came instantly aware, forcing him from that other universe he inhabited in times of differing consciousness, a universe of soft-chiming crystal in mild winds where thought itself was sentient, beautiful and visible, a universe of non-flesh and forever widening horizons.

He had drifted toward one clear panel in his alternate state, a panel looking out on the center of the Guesting Center. His sensors picked up the flash as the Imperial picketboat went into space.

Ecu felt the wings of his mind spread, spread like his own great lifting sails, and that other universe open to him, welcoming him, like a silken bridge.

La Ciotat bashed the com into silence when the jamming started its screech.

'Ma'am, I lost—'

'Shut it!' She had the balcony on visual. La Ciotat brought the tacship screaming toward the Guesting Center, flipped it end for end, McLean antigrav lagging far behind trying to define down, braked on Yukawa drive, and skidded down on the balcony, backward, fins grinding at the synthetic stone.

Her bosun had the port open, just as Sten came through it – in the air. Alex had picked him up and hurled him five meters as the port opened. A second later, the bosun was ground zero as Kilgour impacted on her. The woman wheezed, sure that ribs were broken. Kilgour rolled off, not noticing, hit the port-closing switch, shouting, 'Get out of it!'

La Ciotat hit the Yukawa switch, spitting the tacship off, into the air. Her thumb was stretching for the STARDRIVE panel when

The final switch closed.

The Emperor had chosen the *Normandie* not only because he

was reluctant to sacrifice the *Durer*, but because the yacht/liner had great galleries and banqueting rooms.

Great rooms that had been stripped and filled with AM2. And now, on command, they detonated.

An unanswerable question: Was Sr Ecu 'dead' – by conventional beings' definition of the word – before the blast, or when the kilotons of Anti-Matter Two, the single mightiest power known, were detonated?

When the Emperor's bomb went off, it would have looked from deep space, for nanoseconds, as if the Guesting Center were a real volcano that had erupted.

Then the valley itself vanished in a sympathetic explosion, a blast moving faster than the eye could see, catching and obliterating its own debris.

Perhaps half of the Manabi died in that instant holocaust, as a quarter of their planet ripped and tore in a quake beyond all measurement.

And then, from the *Durer*, a planet buster was launched, a nearly destroyer-sized missile, or rather two-stage missile, given a stardrive generator, Imperium X armor, and more tons of AM2 as a warhead. The first stage impacted directly where the Guesting Center had been, and the second stage was set off, driving at full power, toward the planet's core.

It did not need to break through the mantle before the main charge detonated to function, but, given the head start of the Anti-Matter Two blast from the *Normandie*, nearly did.

For a moment the Manabi home world looked like a holiday lantern, as if its landmass were clear and a viewer could see directly to the planet's molten core. It bulged . . . grew . . . and exploded.

Seilichi rocked and shattered, pitching its land, its oceans, and its atmosphere up, out into space, and then the planet itself broke, magma spilling like the liquid center of a child's candy.

In space, battlescreens blanked, then secondary power went on.

The Eternal Emperor looked at the boil that had been Seilichi without expression. 'Do you have contact with the *Durer*?'

'Affirm.'

The Emperor took the proffered microphone.

'This is the Emperor,' he said without preamble. 'Were any transmissions or ships picked up from Seilichi after we lifted?'

'One moment, sir . . . No sir. One minor transmission, intended receiver unknown, no response found, from the Center itself. Nothing else.'

The Emperor gave the microphone back to the picketboat officer.

Very well, he thought. It is over. There will be a certain amount of housecleaning and damage control necessary. But the problem has been solved.

It was almost a pity Sten hadn't had a chance to know he'd never been a serious threat to the Empire or the Eternal Emperor. No one had, really. Not ever.

Not from the beginning.

And when, his mind rambled, *was* the beginning?

Perhaps . . .

Perhaps on the island of Maui.

Thousands of years ago. When time's measurement dated from the birth of a dead god.

Maui . . .

And a shatter of broken glass . . .

BOOK THREE

DRAGON VARIATION

Chapter Twenty-One

Maui, A.D. 2174

The boy hurtled across the sagging plank onto the next hulk, arrowing across its foredeck. He saw the tarred cable anchoring the scow to its brother just in time, and jumped – foot skittering on the gunwale – then he was in the air, the muck and slime of Moaloea Bay below him, sullen tide splashing the polluted water against the black hulls. He landed, almost falling, and darted around the high-piled scrap on the bow's deck and flattened.

Behind him yelps turned to shouts. There were six of them. All of them older, all of them bigger.

All they had wanted, they said, was to see what the boy had in his ragged military-surplus knapsack. What they said, what they wanted, did not matter. Their intent was clear. The boy had taken a new way across the bay, moving through the maze of grounded ships, half-sunk hovercraft, trawlers of the fisher families, and oared houseboats that might have belonged to the rich two generations ago. He slipped past the tiny junks of the Chinese boat families, unchanged for thousands of years, working steadily toward the ship channel. Across the channel was the far shore and Kahanamoku City.

The boy knew that when the six found him, they would not kill him. Probably not, at any rate. But he would certainly be beaten. That was not a problem. He'd taken beatings before, and would take them again. And those who would thrash him would have bruises of their own for mementos. It was what was in the knapsack that had made him run, and would make him fight.

Because they would take the pack from him, and open it. The

treasures inside would be mocked, ripped, and tossed into the murky waters. Three books. Real books. Books the old man who owned the pierside junkshop had not wanted. One fat book. Two slender. The fat one was very old, had small type, and was called *The Thousand Nights and a Night*. He knew nothing of what it was about, but a glance inside promised adventures with strange beings in strange places, with creatures called rocs and djinn. The second book looked equally impenetrable, but was equally promising: *Freedom From Gravity, The Equations and Early Experiments of Lord Archibald McLean*. Perhaps he could understand just how those great landbarges could fill themselves with cargo, and then effortlessly lift into the sky and float over the watery slum of the bay, out past the barriers to where the great torchships berthed. The last volume was medium-sized: *Starchild. Growing Up in Deep Space*. The holo of the author inside the front cover made her look a proper dwonk, but what did that matter? She'd at least gotten off this planet, and she looked to be not much older than the boy.

Thumps. Now they were on this barge. Gleam of violet, gleam of yellow. No. Leong Suk would be shamed. A thought crossed his mind – a thought far older than the boy's years. There's nothing wrong with being ashamed of yourself – if you're alive to feel that way later.

A howl. He'd been seen! A hand clawed down at him, to drag him up to meet a balled fist or a stick. The boy grabbed the long-abandoned glass vase and slapped it across the stanchion next to him. The glass shattered, and the boy bounded up, whipping the vase like a saber across the face of the older boy.

Blood. A scream. Another scream, from the boy himself, as the older one fell away, and the boy leapt toward the second of his pursuers. Again he slashed, and blood spurted from the second one's arm. Then there were shouts, clattering, and five teenagers ran like a demon of the sea was behind them. One lay writhing on the barge, hands covering the ruins of what had been a face.

The boy came back to himself. He twisted sideways and pelted down the deck of a dredger, ignoring the shouts of the crewmen cleaning the chains and buckets, jumped over its stern, onto a small boat, then another leap . . . and he disappeared. He did not stop his flight until he'd scrambled onto the stern of a just-departing crosschannel towboat. He slumped against its wire railing, panting. He still held the broken vase in one hand. Now it was violet, yellow . . . and scarlet. The boy dropped it into the water.

He thought about what had happened. He did not feel as if

he'd won a victory or something. He didn't feel proud. But the three books were still safe in his knapsack. He decided he knew something he hadn't known before. You had to know what you might encounter. And you always should give yourself an edge. More than anyone knew you had. Maybe a weapon . . . maybe . . . maybe just knowing something. He shook his head. He was not sure where this thought was taking him, but he would return to it later. He had learned something valuable this day.

The boy's name was Kea Richards. He was eight years old.

By the twenty-first century, Hawaii was a rotting slum. Its few natives were living on reservations, supported by government guilt checks. Its native flora and fauna were nearly extinct outside of a few botanical gardens and zoos. And its population was close to twenty million humans. As always, world events had not been kind to the islands, from the Chinese descent into barbarism before they once more closed the bamboo curtain at the end of the twentieth century, to the anarchy that disrupted Japan, the religious wars that turned Indonesia into an illiterate theocracy, and the earthquakes and exclusionary (anti-Asian) laws passed by the government of North America in the opening decades of the century, before its collapse and takeover when Earth finally achieved a single government.

Of the islands, Kaui and Oahu were the least spoiled, since they had the greatest wealth. Least spoiled from original paradise in the same sense that Manhattan Island of the twentieth century was identical with the rock Peter Minuit purchased in the seventeenth century. The Big Island of Hawaii was not rural, not urban, but dirt-poor, serving as a labor pool for cheap manual workers.

The center of Hawaii was now Maui/Molokai/Lanai/Kahoolawe/Molokini. In the dim past, they had been a single island, and Man was now in the process of making them one again, with floating barricades and causeways. The reason was Space. Hawaii was the perfect midpoint launch station for torchships headed offplanet to the terraformed worlds of Mars and some of the Jovian/Saturnian moons. Or else, less frequently, to where the great sail-ships waited to build their crews for the generations-long journey to the stars. And Hawaii had been the launch point for two of the five true starships Earth had been able to build and send out on their government-bankrupting explorations.

Businesses blanketed Maui, from bars to machine shops to import/export to who-really-knew. The sea itself was covered with ships, anchored or tied one to another, from skiffs to huge restaurant boats. The islands were encircled with huge floating Hamilton barriers, patterned after the Thames tidal palisades that required only a few minutes to automatically lift into floating breakwaters, in the event of hurricanes or tsunamis. There were even larger breakwaters circling the deeps – what had been Kealaikahiki Channel – where the torchships ported.

When Kea Richards was born, his family ran a small diner on Big Island, in the city of Hilo. Kea vaguely remembered his father and grandmother talking about the old days back on the mainland. The diner served anything and everything, and Kea remembered his father boasting they could make anything anybody wanted, given a recipe and the ingredients. He even thought they'd been challenged a few times, and, he dimly remembered, had been victorious making some strangely named and even-more-strange-tasting dishes. He himself was thrilled when his father would pile a box on a chair near the grill and put his infant son atop it, and pretend to consult him as he cooked. To this day, he still remembered recipes or parts of recipes.

He had trouble remembering his mother, except that she was very pretty. Or maybe he remembered her beauty because Leong Suk would talk about it. But not in a complimentary way. She was half-Thai, half-Irish, which is where Kea got his eyes, as blue as the skies above in the winter, when the trade winds blew away the pollution. Kea was her only child and that was just as she wanted. The boy never knew why his father would sometimes sing a song, which Kea couldn't remember any of the words to except 'Oblahdee/Oblahdah/Life goes on . . .' but it would instantly spark a blazing row.

When Kea was only five, his mother disappeared. His father searched, fearing the worst, not sure what the worst meant. And he found his wife – or, rather, found what had happened to her. She had volunteered for a longliner. The elder Richards shuddered, a reaction Kea did not understand for years, until he was able to find some of the declassified accounts of the misery, murder, and insanity that happened on the monstrous sailing ships, even before they were beyond contact in their reach for the stars.

Kea Richards cried a little. Then they told the boy that it did not matter. His mother would be happier, somewhere out there. And they could be happier here. Just the three of them. Two years later, the tsunami struck.

*

Kea was climbing a tree when the ocean left. A girl had said that the tree had a coconut, and Kea wanted to see what the fruit looked like. Pollution had killed the native coconut palms decades earlier. He had looped rope between his feet, put a single safety line around the tree trunk, and was shinnying up the palm when he chanced a look out to sea. He gaped. It was as if the tide was going out, except going out in a roar, receding far into Hilo Bay. He had never seen such a sight. There were fish, stranded and flopping in the exposed bottom mire. A wreck of a boat was being turned over and over as the Pacific was sucked away, just as if someone had pulled the plug from a washtub.

Two thousand kilometers at sea, there had been a suboceanic earthquake. The quake set three waves in motion toward the Hawaiian Islands. Each of them was only half a meter in height – but there were a hundred kilometers between wave crests. Instruments sensed the quake. They should have sparked alarms. But there were none shrilling across the city of Hilo when the tsunami struck. The great barriers protecting the Maui Complex and the torchship port slid smoothly into position. There were none around Hilo.

Kea heard screams. Saw people running. Some were running for the waterfront in curiosity, others were running away. Down the street he saw his father. He was shouting for Kea. Kea whistled, and saw his father gesture frantically. Kea obediently started to slide down the tree.

He heard the roar. And the sea returned to Hilo as it had four times in a little more than a century. The ocean floor had slowed the base of the seismic waves and now, as the water shallowed before land, the waves crested. The first wave was not the biggest Kea had seen – his father had taken him to Oahu and shown him the North Shore during a winter storm, and he'd shuddered as the great breakers, as high as ten meters, thundered against the land. This wave was only five meters tall, they said later. But it traveled at a speed of almost eight hundred kilometers per hour.

The first wave shattered the great breakwater as if it had never existed and rolled on, breaking, foaming, destroying. It ripped apart buildings, ships, houses, groundcars, hovercraft, men and women. Ripped them apart and used them as battering rams. The front of the wave was a solid wall of debris. Kea thought he remembered seeing his father try to run, and the wave catch him and their tiny home and diner. But perhaps not.

He woke, a day and a half later, in a charity hospital ward.

He had been found by a fishing boat, still lashed to that tree, floating nearly a kilometer out to sea.

No one ever found the bodies of his father and grandmother.

Kea did not end up in an orphanage. An elderly woman appeared at the hospital. Leong Suk. She told the officials that she had once worked for the Richards family, and they had treated her well. Kea did not remember her. Kea went home with Leong Suk that day. She had a small shop on a back street in Kahanamoku City, selling nonperishable groceries and sundries. She and Kea lived upstairs. That first day, she informed Kea what the rules were. He was to be a good boy. That meant he was to keep certain hours and help in the store when she needed him. He was not to give her trouble. She said she was too old to be able to raise a hellion. She did not know what she would do if he was bad. And one more thing. Kea was to learn. That would be the only path out of the slum. She did not care what he became, but he was not going to spend his life in Kahanamoku City. Kea nodded solemnly. He knew she was right. This place had already cost him his entire family. He felt it was trying to kill him, as well.

Kea, already a well-behaved child, gave Leong Suk little trouble – except when it came to school. He came home after two weeks at the local grammar. He was not learning anything. Leong Suk was skeptical. The boy proved it by reciting, chapter by chapter, what his class was supposed to learn during the next quarter. She wondered whom they could find for a tutor. Kea soon ferreted out a likely candidate.

Three streets away was the Lane of the Godmen. Tiny storefronts, each one with a different shaman or priest, each one looking for converts and acolytes. Kea came dashing home, shouting about one. The Temple of Universal Knowledge. A bit bigger than the other hovels – and filled with fiches, microfiches, and piles and piles of books. It even had a battered computer link to the university library.

Leong Suk told the boy they would go to this temple. Inside, it smelled a little musty, a little bad, as did the 'priest,' a balding, obsequious man who called himself Tompkins. Yes, he meant what he said. No one could know too much. Only when a being knew All Things could he achieve perfection, and he must study all his life and, if blessed, other lives to come. Then would come translation. He listened to Kea read aloud. Asked him some questions – questions that might have puzzled a secondary-school graduate. Tompkins beamed. Yes, he would happily take Kea as a student. His fee would be . . . it was astonishingly cheap. Leong Suk saw the way Tompkins was looking at the boy, and told Kea to go outside. She told the man that he was not to preach his religion to the boy. If Kea decided to become a believer . . . that was as it would be. That was not a problem, the little man smoothed.

One more thing, the old woman said . . . and Tompkins shrieked slightly, as mother-of-pearl blurred around Leong Suk's wrinkled hand, and the point of a double-edged butterfly knife touched his chest. 'You will never touch the boy,' she said, nearly in a whisper. 'You will never *think* about touching the boy. Because if you do . . . you will wonder why your friend, death, took so long to find you.' Tompkins shuddered . . . and the knife vanished.

Whether Leong Suk was correct or not, the man was never anything other than a perfectly correct teacher to Kea. In fact, whatever Tompkins's private desires might have been vanished in his awe, as the boy seemed to effortlessly inhale anything that was put in front of him. He particularly throve on mathematics. Engineering. Physics. All practical, though. He seemed to have little interest in pursuing theories. When he was twelve, Tompkins asked Kea why he seemed less interested – even though he read voluminously – in the social sciences. Kea looked at Tompkins seriously, as if not sure whether to trust the man.

'Hard science is what will get me out of here, mister. Out of here . . . and up there.' He gestured upward – and it took Tompkins a moment to realize that the gesture swept out, out to the stars themselves.

Richards learned other things. How to make change quickly and efficiently. How to spot snide, and refuse it without making a bother. To speak four, and get along in three others, of the more than twelve languages spoken in his neighborhood. He grew tall, strong, and handsome. His smile, and his blue eyes, brought him other teachers, in other subjects. Some were the giggling girls his own age. Some were young and teenaged. And some had husbands. He learned to look behind all curtains in a bedroom before he took off his pants. He learned how to jump from a second-story balcony and roll-land on the mucky street below without breaking something.

He learned where to hit someone and hurt them worse than you hurt yourself. And, more importantly, he learned when to hit and when not to. Sometimes he needed more than a fist. Sometimes he needed an edge. He learned how to use those things, too. He did not lack teachers. The riot police found it necessary to patrol Kahanamoku City in squads, with gravsleds overhead for backup.

When he was fourteen, Tompkins gave him a series of examinations. He passed them, handily. Tompkins did not tell Kea what they were – but he did inform Leong Suk that the boy had just passed the standard entrance examinations for the Academy of Space on the mainland.

'Should he go there?' Leong Suk wondered. Tompkins shook his head. Even though Kea wanted to go into space, that was not the way. The Academy would fit Richards for the military – and that would be not enough for what he thought Kea was capable of. But he refused to tell her more.

The spaceship was tiny – at least compared to pictures Kea had seen of the longliners that hung off Earth, or the torchships that sat like so many oranges, torches underwater, out beyond the barrier. There was no sign on the ship, nor a special marking on the berth. But Kea knew the *Discovery* was a starship. It was one of the five true starships, and the only one still on Earth. Two others had been scrapped: the others were in mothball orbits off Mars.

The ship's stardrive was simple. Idiot-proof. A blink – Alpha Centauri. A word – Luyten 726-B. A full sentence – Epsilon Indi. Half a cup of caff – Arcturus. The problem was fuel for that engine. It had made two voyages and was unlikely to make a third. The fuel for each voyage, an exotic synthetic, had taken five full years, a Manhattan project commitment, and the resources of an entire government to synthesize. Even so, the synthetic only let the engine develop half-power. The ship was a freak, like Leonardo's tank, Lilienthal's airplane, the *Great Eastern*, or the *Savannah*.

Kea stared, hypnotized at its sleekness, dreaming of where it had gone and where it might go again. He left the port at dusk. But he came back again. And again.

Kea was sixteen when Tompkins died. After the morgue crew had left, he and Leong Suk looked at each other. 'We must find,' she said firmly, 'if he had a family, and communicate with them.' They searched through the ruins and baled papers of a failed man's life. They found no sign that Tompkins had any friend or loved one anywhere on Earth or the planets. But they found a small antique safe. Leong Suk agonized, but eventually told Kea that perhaps they should open it. Perhaps he knew someone with that skill?

Kea did: himself. An older boy had once shown him. Kea twisted the dial, ear pressed against the door, listening. And he could hear the tumblers fall, just as the other boy had told him he would. Inside, there were two envelopes. One of them contained almost two thousand dollars in new credits, and a will. The money was for Kea. The other contained forms, and exact instructions on how they were to be filled out and who they were to be sent to. The old woman and the boy stared, in that reeking, moldy store. But the instructions were clear.

Kea filled out the forms and sent them off to the named person on the mainland. Within a week, a thick letter came back to him. He was to contact a certain person in Oahu. That person would have him take some tests. Kea followed those orders, too. They waited.

Six weeks after they had decided the whole matter was either a joke or complete madness, another letter came to him. This one was from the Director of Admissions, California Institute of Technology, Pasadena City, Province of California. He was welcomed to the Entering Freshman Class, Fall, A.D. 2182. Kea Richards had won. He would not live, or die, in Kahanamoku City. Now he would be free.

Chapter Twenty-Two

Pasadena, A.D. 2183

Kea sat on the edge of Millikan's Pot, waiting to meet the smart guys. So far, there hadn't been any. Cal Tech was a rather large disappointment, which he was just now realizing at the beginning of his sophomore year. His freshman year had been a blur of auditorium-sized classes, expensive fiches, loneliness, and work. He'd had little chance to evaluate the world he was now in. The blur had probably been increased by Leong Suk's death, just before Christmas of 2182. Kea hadn't been notified of her death until after the funeral.

Cal Tech was just as much a fraud as any of the faiths on Godmen Lane. And like all good swindles, it looked great from the outside. It had more Nobel laureates than even Houston or Luanda – but most of them taught one or two survey courses and perhaps a doctoral-level program with a handful of specially chosen disciples. The school, with more than 25,000 students, was approaching its three hundredth anniversary, and was a soar of the most modern architecture and imagination. About the only buildings left from the 'olden days' – before the institute had begun its cancerous expansion, devouring not just a nearby city college but the city's main center as well – was the fountain he was sitting on, and the nearby Spanish-style Kerkhoff Hall, now used for freshman orientations.

The work, while hard, largely consisted of swotting: rote memorization and regurgitation at periodic examinations. Both of the Theory courses he had qualified for this semester seemed to preach enhancement/modification of the past's breakthroughs rather than instilling any truly original thought in the students.

He wasn't so cork-topped that he had expected Cal Tech to be perfect, that it would give him the Secrets of the Ancients. But he had thought the school would have *some* original thinkers, scientists who were looking beyond this system/time's moil of rote repetition of the past's errors. Maybe there were sages, he thought, and he was just too damned young and dumb to know who, or where, they were. Yeah. Or maybe the original thinkers had gotten fed up and were teaching offplanet on Ganymede or Mars. If so, why were there so many offworlders going to Cal Tech?

Not that any of Kea's doubts had shown up in his work – he was holding a flat 4.0 average and had been on the Founder's List both semesters of the previous year. He was set. All he had to do was keep his grades, smile, morale, and genitalia up, and he would be a Twenty-second Century Surefire Success. Which meant, he thought wryly, he would be sucked into one of the super design-plants like Wozniak City and, eventually, if he behaved properly, allowed to put his name on a 'particularly elegant' computer path. Or, even more dizzyingly, to have a tertiary process in some synthetic industrial plant named after him. Perhaps they would reward him with a two-week, all-expense-paid trip to Nix Olympica. On one of the lesser peaks, of course.

Kea suddenly grinned. You're right, my lad, he thought. There's no option but suicide. Lie down in front of the next railbus as it passes, baby blue. Speaking of which . . . He looked at his watch – this year the fashion was to wear a timepiece on the wrist – and realized he'd best bust buns, or he was going to be late for work. He'd have just time to drop off his fichecase at his far off-campus rooming house, where he paid far too much for a tiny attic room, and change clothes.

Now forget all that crap you were thinking. You will not end up a cog in somebody else's machine. Hell, you can go back to Maui and start all over again as a gangster before you allow them to do that to you. Or you could volunteer for a longliner . . .

He shivered, and ran a thumb up the fastener of his jacket. He felt suddenly cold. The fall sun, no doubt, wasn't as warming as it appeared.

The hashhouse/ginjoint Kea worked in was in the middle of a bad district. About a million or so years ago, Kea had discovered after he peeled through geological layers of wall-board, paint, and flocked wallpaper, the place had been named the Gay Cantina. Now it had no name as far as anyone knew – it was just the dive over there. All the licenses were in the name of the owner, a glowering goon named Buno, and everything was paid in cash.

Buno hadn't believed anybody as good-looking – i.e., without any of the district's *de rigueur* face scars – as Richards, let alone anybody who was attending Cal Tech, would want a job in his dive. But Kea, who had spent a lot of time remembering his father's cooking and over the past several years had done the meals for Leong Suk and himself, persisted. Besides, he thought, it'd be a hoot seein' what happened the first time a yayhoo decided to hurrah the kid. Buno tried him out.

Now there was a smallish vee-notch in the countertop – and a wide dark stain around it. After that the district left Richards alone, especially when they noted that after he'd taken the chef's knife out of the counter – and the thug's hand – he hadn't called the police.

Kea worked from sixteen hundred hours until some vague time

called closing, which meant when the last drunk had stumbled out and no more were reeling in. Mostly the dive was pretty quiet and Kea could get his studying done. But not this night. The house was very busy, with a steady stream of hungry and even partially sober customers. About 2100, ten very unhappy drunks fell in. It was just another night. And then Austin Bargeta showed up. Kea, putting together a fried-egg-and-ham-and-cheese sandwich for one of the boozers, didn't see him when he entered. But he did recognize Bargeta's rather remarkable voice when he asked for a menu. Kea had heard it several times before – he and Bargeta were both suffering through Particle Theory and its Immediate Application in Common Yukawa Drive Situations.

The Bargetas were richrich. The family had been founded four generations before when a brilliant designer had made his trillions, building among other things one of the first portable triple-lobe astrographic instruments. Then he had married the daughter of one of Japan's most respected *yakuza*/bankers and the dynasty had begun. The family was very old-money now, with most of the wealth in holding companies. The rest was in interplanetary building/ transport. Each Bargeta generation was presented with a choice – a child could become either family head or else a trust baby. The family head would prove himself by running the high-risk building/ transport division, and the behind-the-scenes bankers would take care of the rest of the nearly automatic money machine. Being the Chosen One meant wealth and power beyond comprehension.

Austin Bargeta was making a run at being the heir apparent, or so Kea had heard. The problem and the gossiped wonderment was how long the family name would carry him before he was punted into the outer darkness, a failed heir apparent.

'Austin.'

It took three blinks for Bargeta to sort of recognize Richards. He wasn't being a snob, Kea realized. He was not much more sober than the ten drunks behind him.

'Oh, it's Richards,' he said. 'You're in one of my classes. *What* are you doing *here*?'

'Some of us,' Kea said, 'have to work. You've heard of work, haven't you? What most people do? For money?'

'Oh. Oh, yes. I'm sorry. Didn't mean, and all . . . don't mean to sound like . . . been gazing on the wine while it was red, you know.'

'Yeah. Austin, I've got to tab you to something. This isn't exactly your kind of place.'

'Why not?' Bargeta turned and looked around, and nothing, from the graffiti on the wall to the stained ceiling to the clientele, seemed to register. 'Seems quite . . . you know, authentic.'

'It's that. Okay.' Kea shrugged. Feed the kid – which Richards thought of Bargeta, even though Bargeta was a year and a class senior to him – and slick him out of here. 'Can I get you something to eat?'

Bargeta focused on the menu. He was studying it when one of the drunks shouted, 'Hey, cookie, if you're through blowin' in y'r bitch's ear, I'd like to order m' eats.' Kea ignored the shout. Bargeta did not. He swiveled off the counter stool, face turning red, as if he were in a vid. Wonderful, Kea thought.

'I understand,' Austin said with great clarity, 'that you call your mother Piles, because she is such a bleeding ass. Or am I mistaken?'

The drunk came up in several waves. Kea noticed, as he slid unobtrusively to the cashbox, that the man was a Samoan. There weren't that many humans wandering around Pasadena measuring two meters in any direction. Kea also knew that the Samoan culture is maternal, and that, very shortly, Bargeta was going to be steamrolled. Bargeta took on some kind of half-assed martial arts stance as the Samoan juggernauted toward him.

Kea took a wrapped roll of quarter-credit coins from the cashbox. Bargeta hit the Samoan with a snap-punch. The man grunted, but did not otherwise move or react. Then he swung. His punch took Austin in the shoulder and sent him spinning back, to sprawl across the counter. Kea slid the roll of coins into Bargeta's hand. Austin's fingers kinesthesiaed over the roll, told his brain what he was holding, and he came back up, whatever too-doo-woo self-defense system he'd been practicing forgotten. He swung a roundhouse punch, quite wildly.

The Samoan didn't bother moving aside. Austin's punch caught the man on the side of the jaw, and Richards could hear bone break and cartilage crunch. The Samoan shouted pain as blood spattered, and he slumped to a sitting position. His jaw hung slack and to the side. His friends were on their feet – and Kea had his cleaver out and had fingered the memory code for the cops before they could close on Bargeta. It was perfectly all right to call for heat in this instance – none of the drunks were local lads.

By the time the riot squad materialized, Kea had unobtrusively gotten the roll of coins from Austin's fist and busted it into the appropriate change drawer. They tucked the brokenfaced Samoan into a meatwagon and told his friends to haul butt out of there. Then they turned to deal with Austin. Kea, again impulsively, said he would take care of him. Kea called a cab, made sure Bargeta had enough credits to pay for the ride to wherever he lived, and started shutting down the kitchen. A thought crossed his mind that he would *never* make a good Machiavellian.

Three days later, when Particle Boredom Etc. met, Kea checked the results of a particularly bastardly verbal they'd had at the last class. What the course lacked in interest, the instructor made up for in severity. Second from the top. Not bad, Kea thought. He would've maxed it, but he had gone home the night before with one of the waitresses, who wanted to show him her new flat and other things of possible interest, and had been more than a little hungover. Austin's voice gloomed over his shoulder. 'Oh crap. And I actually *studied* for the brute.' Kea spotted Bargeta's name. In the subbasement. As usual.

Kea turned. Bargeta looked about him. No one else was near the bulletin board. 'You know,' Bargeta said, slightly lowering his voice, 'I was not *that* drunk. And I never forget anything. You would appear to have prevented me from being mashed across one of your restaurant's walls.'

Kea grinned – Bargeta, if one disregarded that voice and his born-to-the-manor manner, wasn't unlikable. 'You weren't in any trouble. Clean-living sort of aluno like yourself . . . you would've beanoed him, easy. Or, anyway, a bolt of lightning would've come through the roof and saved your butt when Vishnu decided to jump in.'

'He was *that* big?'

'Bigger.'

Austin laughed. 'As I said, I owe you. When – or rather if – this class comes to an end, lemme buy you a sudser. Not that I'm what I think that railbus was accusing me of being. Unless,' he said with mock alarm that became real as his mind considered that once again he might have inadvertently offended, 'you're a pledger? And not that I have anything against, uh, well, if you're the kind of man who, well, you know, doesn't really, well; like women all that much.'

Kea shook his head. 'Nope. I'm a normal red-blooded lusher.'

'Good. Good. And now the thought occurs that perhaps we could talk about some other things. About some other difficulties I seem to have stumbled into that you could advise me on.'

Over several beers, Austin made his proposal. He wasn't exactly the shining star of Cal Tech, he freely admitted. And a GPA of 1.5 was *not* gentlemanly enough to keep him at the institute, which would seriously displease some people. Some people, Kea was sure, were the decision-makers in the Bargeta family. Austin wanted to hire Kea as a tutor. Richards started to take a pass, and then, in one frozen instant, caught himself. Go ahead. Somebody's trying to give you the edge, just like that broken vase. Just like that roll of coins you passed this kid. Don't turn it down. He accepted.

Tutoring wasn't hard – Austin was a quick study. Admittedly, whatever Kea'd crammed in one ear slipped out the other within a week, but what of it? There didn't seem to be any professors interested in anything more than a proper regurgitation of their own magnificence. And it wasn't as if Austin would ever have to *use* any of the knowledge he supposedly had. At that point, Kea became fascinated as to just how smart he could make Bargeta. Assuming he was willing to play any angle – just as he'd been willing to play any angle to get away from Kahanamoku City. The answer was, very smart indeed, as Richards discovered the university had its own underworld, just as crooked as anything on Maui. Exams could be purchased. TAs could be bribed to write papers. Or to mark someone in attendance. In some cases, where the instructor was a complete mountebank, even change grades. By the end of the semester, Austin was scoring honorable 2.5's–3.0's in all his courses, and in one massive six-credit lab course that was in reality a gut run, an amazing 3.5. 'And,' Austin marveled, 'it's all because you showed me how to focus on what's important.'

Austin asked Kea if he wanted to move in with him before the next semester started. Richards jumped at the invite. It wasn't as if they would get in each other's way – Bargeta actually had a *house*, sitting on an open lot by itself. Six bedrooms. A maid, a cook, and a yeeves to take care of the details. Austin took his new friend around to meet *his* friends. Kea, tall, rugged, with a strange and colorful background, was at first the latest wonder in Bargeta's circle. It was assumed that sooner or later he'd pass on, as did all of Austin's new best friends, male or female. But Kea did not. And he became an accepted part of their gatherings.

Kea studied these rich young people and their mannerisms carefully. He learned, in fact, all that the upper crust could teach. It was fascinating. The rules were as exact as any of the triads back on Maui would require from a member. And the penalties for error, even if they weren't as physically fatal, appeared to be almost as damaging. At times he felt he saw Austin Bargeta for what he was – a shallow, superficially charming user, who in fact was playing Kea like a marionette. And he saw the Bargeta family, even though he had only met one member, as part of a great conspiracy of the status quo, a status quo that was keeping mankind from its real destiny.

Of course, that immediately produced a question from within: What destiny, Kea? He did not have an answer to that, only the feeling that mankind was holding itself back from some great goal, a goal out among the stars, a goal that would be shared by other beings as intelligent or more so than mankind.

Space travel was more than two centuries old now, and what had been accomplished? The Solar System was explored and a few worlds terraformed. Fifty or so longliners had set sail into the unknown, and those who had managed to message back reported emptiness beyond, and horror and degeneracy within. A few stars had been touched by the astronomically expensive starships. One extraterrestrial race had been contacted. What an accomplishment, he jeered.

Austin's senior and Kea's junior term passed smoothly as well. Bargeta graduated. Not with honors – no amount of cheating and bribery could have managed that – but comfortably in the upper third of his class. Kea was First Junior. Next year he knew he would be the Prime graduate of the institute. With that degree, Kea would have little trouble finding a suitable position. Perhaps with Bargeta Shipping. Perhaps elsewhere. Soon – perhaps in only three or four years – Kea would go into space. The future looked quite bright. It became dazzling on that long, celebratory weekend after Bargeta had received his diploma and sprang the great surprise. He felt he owed Kea, and he wanted everyone to know it, especially his family. He wanted Kea to be his guest for the summer – or at least part of it, since this summer would last twice as long as any Kea had known. Kea would also have to make minor alterations in his own plans – he wouldn't be able to start his final year at Cal Tech until the first semester of '85.

Austin's smile grew as he saw Kea frown at the proposed changes to his life. Then he paid off the buildup. The reason Kea would have to start school late was passage time. Come September, he'd still be at the Bargeta family's vacation compound, the one they called Yarmouth. Near Ophir Chasm, now a freshwater ocean.

On Mars.

Kea felt, as Austin beamed, as if he'd suddenly entered freefall aboard one of the early spaceships. School could wait, his career could wait. Space. It was the beginning of the end.

Mars, A.D. 2184

Her name was Tamara. She was seventeen. Tall. Dark-haired. A lean curving body. Pert breasts. Eyes that dared, and told Kea no dare was forbidden – if he had the courage to follow through. She was also Austin's sister.

She did not look more than passingly like him. She was perfect. Perhaps Kea realized that what the gods had failed to give Tamara, the finest plas surgeons had. But he probably would not have cared. It was a measure of Kea's intoxication with other things that it took some time before he became aware of her.

His brain-drunk had begun as soon as the ship had lifted. A Mars trip was still a rich man's pleasure, costing, in real credits, about what a first cabin on an Earth ocean liner would have cost during the days of the Cunards. The suite he shared with Austin, and one of the family factotums burdened with reports, was one of the largest on the transport. It measured four meters wide by seven meters long. Austin told Kea that this was always the worst part of the passage – he felt trapped.

Kea never noticed. For one thing, the suite was not much larger than the cramped apartment he and Leong Suk had shared. And for another, the suite had a 'port' – actually a vid screen linked to through-hull pickups mounted at various places around the transport. Mars grew in the forward pickup. As the transport closed on the wargod's world, Kea could pick out details. Valles Marineris. Tharsis. Olympus Mons. All spectacular – but what most riveted Kea's attention were the works of man. Not just the haze of Mars's new atmosphere, or the oceans and lakes, or the twinkled lights of the new cities, but the offplanet marvels, some of which had been allowed to remain, as reminders and memorials. A space station. The First Base on Deimos. One of the great mirrors, in a geosynchronous orbit over the north pole, that had helped melt Mars's ice caps.

That, he realized, wasn't a deliberate monument. It was the centerpiece of a junk heap. He cozened his way to the bridge, learned how to use the pickup's controls, and scanned the orbiting scrap, for reasons he was never sure of. There were dead deep-space ships he recognized from books, museums, or models he'd never been able to afford as a boy. A longliner that had never been completed or launched. A space station, peeled and shattered – Kea remembered reading about that disaster of a hundred years earlier.

And, to one side, by itself, a tiny ship. Another one of the starships. The second one he'd seen. He wondered why he seemed to be the only one who saw them as a mingle of triumph and defeat. Promise and tragedy. For want of a nail. Hell, for want of a goddamned energy source . . .

Kea went back to the 'suite' and prepared for landing. Bargeta senior, Austin's father, was waiting for them. He was frightening. Kea wondered if he would have felt the same about the older man if he didn't know how much power he wielded. He decided yes, he would. It was Bargeta's face. Hard, measuring eyes. The thin lips of a martinet. And yet the jowls of a sybarite and the body of someone kept in shape only by highly paid trainers, not from physical labor. It was, Kea realized, the same face Austin would wear, if he was chosen to replace Bargeta, in forty years or so.

Mr Bargeta was very friendly to Kea. He was grateful to the man who'd helped his boy out of that imbecilic school slump he'd fallen into. In his letters, Austin had mentioned Richards frequently, he said. Kea knew this to be a lie – Austin never communicated with his family except to plea, directly and briefly, for an advance on next period's allowance. The older man said that before Kea returned to Earth, they would have to talk. About the future. Kea's future.

Kea felt as if he were in the middle of a twentieth-century mafia vid and about to be made a member of a crime family. Perhaps, he thought, that wasn't just a piece of romantic foolishness. He put the thought aside.

There were ten or fifteen Bargetas – including cousins and relatives-by-marriage – resident in the compound. And the family retainers. He asked – and was told that thirty men or women were required for each 'guest.' More, for 'special occasions.' Kea was reminded that, truly, the very rich were not as common folk.

The Bargeta compound was only a hundred meters from the near-vertical cliff that led down to the sea that had been the Ophir Chasm. The compound had originally been one of the earliest bubbles; it had been acquired by the Bargetas and truly turned into a pleasure dome, even after the no-longer-needed plas was stripped away. There were main buildings and outcabins. Halls for drinking or playing tennis – even Kea became fascinated with what a ball could do in a low-g world. Lawns. Heated pools. A cabana had been recently built on the cliff-edge. From it, a round clear elevator shaft, with McLean plates, dropped down to a floating dock and the effervescent ocean.

That was where Tamara swam into his consciousness. Literally. He was perplexing over the sails and rigging of a trimaran tied up to the dock. Kea had done some sailing on Earth, but only on a monohull. He was trying to figure out, if he tacked sharply, whether the boat would spin out, a wing would shatter and he'd be trying to navigate a catamaran, or if the craft would just go into irons, when Tamara sealed out of the ocean onto the deck.

At first he thought she wasn't wearing anything – and then realized the color of the small one-piece suit was exactly matched to her deeply tanned skin. He wondered – after he'd begun recovering from the basic arrival, why she wasn't shivering. He himself was wearing a one-piece shorty wetsuit against the chilly breeze and cold water. Then he noticed the tiny heatpak in the suit, tucked at the base of her spine. Tamara padded forward, without saying anything. She eyed Kea intently. Kea turned slightly to the side. His suit was tight, and he would rather not embarrass himself.

'You are Austin's Saint George.' Her voice was a purr.

'I am. I left my card in my other armor. Dragons rescued, virgins slain, my specialty.'

Tamara laughed. 'Well, there certainly aren't any dragons on Mars, either. So you can relax.' She introduced herself, curled down beside him, shoulder touching his. 'I guess the family owes you for helping my brother,' she said.

Kea shrugged. 'Not by my calcs. The scale's zeroed.'

'Perhaps. You'll be staying with us all summer?'

'Right. My return ticket's an open booking. But Austin said we'd best take the . . . what is it, *Copernicus*. It's set to lift on . . . hell, I still haven't figured out the months here . . . Earthdate in the first week of September.' Kea dimly realized he was babbling.

'A long time,' she said. 'We'll have to make sure you aren't bored. Won't we?'

'I, uh, don't think that – I mean, how can you be bored on *Mars*?'

'That is not,' Tamara announced conclusively, 'the sort of boredom I was talking about.' She ran her fingernail down Kea's arm, and it seared like a branding iron. Then she was standing.

'You know,' she said, 'moonrise is special on Mars. The best place to see it is from the cabana. It's away from the compound so there's no lightspill.'

She walked to the edge of the trimaran. 'Far enough,' she went on, 'for as much privacy . . . as anyone could ever need.' She smiled as if at a secret memory or thought, and then flatdove into the bubbling, CO2-charged water. Kea's mouth was dry.

The cabana had four bedrooms, each of them made up. It was staffed by four blank-faced men. They asked if Kea wished anything, or any service. Showed him where drinks were iced and snacks were kept. Told him he had but to touch the com and someone would be there within minutes. Then they disappeared. The cabana's main room was circular, with glass walls that would opaque at the touch of a switch. In its center, a huge sunken sofa was around a hooded fireplace, with wooden logs arranged to roar into flames at the touch of a match. A fireplace? On Mars? Not likely, between pollution laws and the incredible permits required to do anything to a tree. It was, of course, false, as Kea discovered. After a few moments, he found the correct setting, so that the logs were guttering down, flames flickering shadows against the walls. Now, for the drinks.

And Tamara was there. She wore a teal-green pair of flaring pants, and a matching sleeveless top. The pants were scooped far below her navel, and the top ended approximately at Tamara's rib cage. Approximately. Tamara picked up two already-filled glasses she must have poured from the cloth-wrapped bottle that sat in a bucket beside her.

'To . . . to the night,' she said. They drank. And they refilled their glasses, and went back to the couch. They talked. Kea could never remember the exact conversation. But he had told her his life story – and Tamara listened, completely fascinated, sitting very close to him. He ran out of words.

Tamara put her glass down. Somehow they'd emptied that bottle of sparkling wine. She reached out, and touched his lips.

'Soft,' she murmured. She leaned closer, and her tongue flicked across Kea's lips. He started to kiss her – and she pulled back. She unfolded, and walked away from him – hips swaying. There must have been some sort of hidden fastener on the halter top, because it was suddenly gone. Tamara flipped it over her shoulder. Turned back and looked at him. Her face serious.

She touched her midriff, and the pants fell into a silk pool about her ankles. Tamara stepped clear of them. She stretched, long and lingeringly. Kea stared, unable to speak or move. She walked slowly into a darkened room. She looked back at him and smiled. Then she disappeared into the bedroom. Light flared, as a mock candle was lit.

Kea was free. Free to follow her.

'No,' Tamara said. 'This time . . . this time you'll just watch.' She unwound the scarf, and began knotting it at intervals. 'Next time . . . *that's* yours.'

Mars became a shadow, a blur. The center of the world was Tamara's body. Nights were a swirl of movement, ecstasy, a sudden flash of sweet torture. Days were exploration and daring, making love anywhere and everywhere. Tamara's passion seemed to increase the greater the risk of discovery or embarrassment. Particularly if the discovery might be made by a member of the family. Not that Kea came to Tamara's bed as an innocent. She learned from him, as well. She wanted something new. And so, reluctantly, he showed her some of the techniques he'd heard of or even, once or twice, had demonstrated in the cribs of Maui.

She learned well and then eagerly practiced those dexterities. She combined them with other skills she was already familiar with. The style of lovemaking she preferred was prolonged, exotic, and would have a lightning-shock of pain/pleasure at the climax. Kea felt as if he were a bit of wood, floating at the edge of a maelstrom, and then being drawn down, deep into its center.

He was in love with Tamara. That could mean disaster. Ruin. But it was a fact. What made it worse – or, perhaps, better – was that Tamara seemed to be as besotted, as passionate and over-whelmed, as Kea. Kea allowed himself to dream of a future – a very different future than he had conceived of before. One which would be for two people.

Kea was amazed. Anything he wanted to do, Tamara seemed delighted to oblige him in. It was as if he were the ruler, instead of . . . His mind shied away from the rest. Once, they went to the dockyards at Capen City. He was fascinated by the array of ships of varying types. Here, torchships were landed in great aboveground cradles rather than ported in water, and Kea could even walk under their bulging enormity and fully realize just how huge they were. Tamara, not terribly interested in the ships them-selves – 'Darling, we *own* half of them' – was fascinated by the color, squalor, and lurking danger. Several times she told him how safe she felt with him.

Something was bothering Kea. Why were the spacecrews dressed in such a slovenly manner – very different from the heroic posturing of the vid that still occasionally dealt with space travel? Why were there so many notices tagged outside the local hiring hall? And why were the notices so weathered, as if they'd been posted for a long time, with no one desperate enough to answer them?

Tamara and Richards found seats in a crowded dive that called itself a cafe, drinking some terribly sweet concoction Tamara'd ordered from the barkeep, and he tried to think it out. Ignoring the groundpounders, almost everyone they had seen was a spaceman(woman). High vacuum and all that. So, why were all of the conversations he overheard about drink or drugs and how iced they had been the previous night. Or else how terrible the conditions were aboard ship, and which was the least ghastly hellship to sign aboard on. Their language wasn't that of science or engineering, but the lazy-palated monotones or drunken sudden rage of the poor and desperate. It sounded like Wino Row. Why were the eyes of these brave space pioneers so dull? So dead?

He heard, for the first time, of Barrier Thirty-three, the term used as if it were some sort of gateway to Hades. He asked – and found it was the standard bulkhead division between the crew/engine spaces and the cargo/passengers. Something was very wrong. But he didn't know what. He drained his glass and took Tamara's hand. She was staring, entranced, at a woman down the bar whose tattoos covered every inch of skin that could be seen outside the stained cut-down shipsuit. The woman seemed as interested in Bargeta.

Tamara frowned when Kea said he wanted to hat up – but didn't say anything. She gave the tattooed spacewoman a long smile – and Kea remembered that smile from other, private times – as they left the bar. That night, he slept alone, not wanting to disturb Tamara with his dark mood, still disturbed by what he had seen and still wondering what it meant. She laughed away his apologies the next day. She had gone back into Capen City. And looked up some 'old friends.'

The end came in bright sunlight, on the deck of the trimaran where it had begun, about an Earth-week later. Kea had spent the morning preparing himself. Making sure he had the correct words. Then he was ready – as prepared, he hoped, in this matter

of the heart as if it were the most important examination he
would ever take. Which it was.

Tamara listened quietly to his stammer that grew into fluency.
Then he was finished. Kea waited for her response. It came as a
giggle. Then a full laugh. 'Kea,' she said, when the laugh died
away. 'Let me understand. You're saying that you think the two
of us should . . . be together? When this summer is over? Back
on Earth, even?' Kea, feeling his guts writhe, as if he'd just stepped
into a gravshaft and the McLean power was off, nodded.

'*Live* together? Or – do you mean like a covenant? Kea, darl',
you sound like an oldie, talking about *marriage*! Oh dear. This
is delicious. *You*? With me? Oh, my, my.' And she dissolved into
laughter. Kea got up, and walked numbly across the dock, and
found the elevator up to the clifftop.

Sometime later, he found himself in the main house. It was dark.
Kea had not eaten, nor gone back to his room. He had tried to be
invisible, especially to any of the Bargetas. A couple of the retainers
asked if he needed anything. Kea shook his head. He saw one
woman's eyes soften. She started to say something, but just put her
hand on his arm. Then she looked frightened and hurried away.

He didn't know what he would do next. How could he stay
out of Tamara's way for the rest of the summer, a summer that
had gone from paradise to purgatory? He couldn't just leave.
Austin was his friend. All he wanted was a secret, hidden place,
to crawl into and lick the gaping tear Tamara had ripped.

He heard laughter. Austin. 'Oh dear, oh dear,' he said. 'Was he
serious?'

'If not, he's the best japer on Mars.' Tamara.

'I guess it shouldn't be unexpected,' another voice said thoughtfully. Bargeta senior.

'I'm sorry, Father,' Tamara said. 'But I thought—'

'You needn't bother with an apology,' her father interrupted.
'I'm hardly concerned that you found the rustic to be handsome.
Nor how you chose to scratch an itch. It would be most hypo-
critical for me to suggest my daughter behave as if she were a
Renunciant, when we know the family has always had a taste
for the . . . rawer side of life, eh?'

There was laughter. Shared laughter. Family laughter at the
casual mention of a minor secret.

'So it's my fault.' Austin.

'Not really,' his father explained. 'You've just been reminded of a lesson you perhaps let slip from your mind, when you rewarded this young man's assistance by letting him into your life. But it's not a new lesson. Remember how hard it was when you realized your nannies weren't Bargetas and had to be treated a certain way? Or the children we allowed the servants to have, so you'd have playmates, and how you cried when it was time for them to be sent away? So don't chastise yourself, Austin. It's a lesson we have to learn and relearn.'

'So what do we do?' Tamara. 'I mean, I can see that letting Kea sulk around for the rest of the summer like some moonstruck swain out of a poem will be really dullity.'

'Don't worry,' Bargeta senior said. 'Perhaps he'll simply vanish. Or jump off a cliff. Or sail off into the sunset. Moonstruck yokels do things like that.'

The clink of glasses as someone poured a drink. Then, Austin's voice: 'Actually, Father, when you stop to think about it, this whole thing is *very* funny. Isn't it?'

Tamara's titter. A chuckle from Bargeta. And then all three of them were laughing very hard. Harsh, unrelenting laughter. Kea heard no more. Their mirth vanished. As did the Bargetas and Yarmouth itself. The only thing in the entire universe was a tattered, yellowing PLACES AVAILABLE notice, on a spacecrew hiring hall.

Chapter Twenty-Three

Alva Sector, A.D. 2193

The pinlight was a frantic red pulse on the monitor. 'There it is again, Murph!' Vasoovan twittered. 'At one o'clock.'

Captain Murphy 'Murph' Selfridge squeezed into the navigation cubicle. He was a big, formerly athletic man, gone to seed. He bent over his first officer. The light pulsed back at him. Kea

Richards watched his commander's broad features take on an oxlike look of puzzlement as he studied the winking light. 'I don't get it,' the captain finally said. 'Same damn coordinates?'

'Same damn coordinates, Murph,' Vasoovan said.

'Sure you didn't make some kinda screwup?' Murph asked. 'Maybe you better run it through again.'

The Osiran sighed the martyred sigh of the constantly incompetent. 'If *you* say so, Captain,' she twittered. Slender pink tendrils moved swiftly over the com unit. Touching sensor pads. Spinning dials.

Richards and the two scientists kept silent. Their card hands forgotten on the tiny rec table of the cramped instant-bucket-of-bolts some corporate sales veep had misnamed *Destiny I*. There was no *Destiny II*. The first model was so poorly designed and built that only the ten ships had been completed. And those had been sold for kiloweight. Richards's skinflint company had bought two and put them into service. For the past five E-months, it had taken all of Richards's skills as chief engineer to keep the *Destiny I* in one piece and headed for the mysterious signals emanating from Alva Sector.

Vasoovan rebooted. The monitor blanked, then came back on. The light was still blinking. But this time at six o'clock. 'What the hell's goin' on, Vasoovan?' Murph demanded. 'How come the sucker keeps movin' around on us?'

'Don't blame me,' Vasoovan protested, anger building. 'I just do my job. Same as anybody else.' She turned her large oval face full on the captain. Vasoovan had the permanent grin of a carnivore. Even after five months in close proximity with the ET, Richards found the face unsettling. He watched two of Vasoovan's eyestalks check out Murph for signs of argument. The other two craned over Murph's head to study Richards and the scientists.

One scientist pretended not to notice. She stroked a straying dark curl from her eyes. The other – the man – turned his handsome profile away. But Kea stared back. He knew better than to give the Osiran an edge. 'What're you looking at, Richards?' Vasoovan's twittering was shrill.

'Apparently not very much,' Kea said. 'In my book, watching my captain and his first officer doing tight twirls around their backsides hardly qualifies as entertainment.'

'You've got no cause to gripe,' Murph said. 'You're getting triple time for this trip, with some pretty hefty bonuses all around if we come up with something.'

Richards pointed at the wandering light on the nav board. 'If that's our bonus, Captain,' he said, 'I wouldn't be making plans for any big spending when we get back. From where I sit, the company's money is pretty damn safe.'

'Come on, Kea,' the captain urged. 'Let's not be negative. We got a good team here. And, by God, we're gonna take this thing all the way over the top.'

Kea shrugged. 'Sure, Murph. Whatever you say.'

'It's *their* fault,' Vasoovan said, indicating the scientists. 'This whole thing was their idea. Know what I think? I'll tell you what I think—'

Dr Castro Fazlur – chief scientist of the expedition – broke in: 'It actually believes it has a thought process, Ruth. Amusing, isn't it?' He crooked his lips into a smile of non-amusement.

Dr Ruth Yuen, Fazlur's assistant and lover, ducked her pretty head. Trying to stay out of the line of fire. 'Oh, come now, Ruth. Be honest,' Fazlur pressed. Handsome gray-fox features pushed forward. 'Don't you find it tragic that the only sign of allegedly intelligent life mankind has found is this tentacled thing?'

'Watch it, Fazlur,' Vasoovan hissed.

The scientist ignored the warning. 'I'd say it was the eyestalks,' Fazlur said. 'What IQ exists in an Osiran is mostly consumed controlling that primitive biological function. This would explain its limited language capabilities. You will note, Ruth, dear, that it speaks the argot of a common ship rat. Obviously, its mental powers are too taxed to achieve a civilized person's vocabulary.'

Vasoovan's features turned from pink to parboiled. A powerfully muscled tentacle reeled out, searching for a heavy object to hurl. Then snatched back as the captain slapped at it. 'Come on, guys. Lighten up. I got enough problems without you piling on more,' Murph pleaded.

It was at this point that Kea felt a warm, shapely foot press against his calf. It rose up his leg, caressing higher . . . higher. Ruth's dark eyes flashed. A red tongue tip licked an upper lip. It was that Tamara kind of look. Suddenly, the already-cramped world of *Destiny I* slammed around him. He tossed in his cards. 'I'm going to catch up on some sleep,' he said. 'When you figure out where we're going . . . be sure to wake me.' He rose, avoiding Ruth's hurt look, and stalked out. The too-familiar sound of quarreling voices faded as he made his way down the corridor.

Surprisingly, he found the fresher room unoccupied. The rest of the crew, fifteen in all, was either at work or bunked down.

This was a rare opportunity to scrape off some of the grime the overtaxed atmosphere system aboard the *Destiny I* kept spewing out. He peeled coveralls from his greasy body, then groaned as hot spray needled his flesh. No one ever got really clean aboard *Destiny I*. For months, they had all been walking around in the thickening miasma of their own smells. Eating stale packets of heavily manufactured chow, since scarce water also meant a crimped supply of fresh vegetables from hydroponics.

The needle spray cut off as his hot water allotment was used up. Kea suffered zed guilt as he punched the button and the shower resumed. Crap on those company pinchcredits. A delicious fog filled the room. He spread the soap on thick and lathered up.

The expedition to the Alva Sector had been a bust from the get-go. Kea had signed on against his own good sense. Being chief engineer of a bucket of bolts had never been his idea of a life's work. He'd had big dreams, once. Dreams that seemed to be worth achieving. Then he had thrown it all away over that inbred, high-society woman. If it had happened to somebody else, the situation would be laughable. But the memory of the other, harsh laughter on Mars would be with him for years. He was so young and dumb he didn't ask why the first deep-space company he had hit up leaped on him as if he were solid gold. Sure, he had aced their aptitude test. And gone through the exams in a third the allotted time. Kea had half expected to be rejected, despite his high test scores. After all, he had no experience. He had also assumed the competition would be fierce for something so exotic as a career in deep space. Especially now that private companies – sniffing fat profits and guaranteed monopolies – were venturing out on the few bridges to the stars that had been built with government money.

He started getting an idea how wrong he was in his first job as a wiper aboard a cargo hauler making the jump out to Epsilon Indi. His fellow crew members were as stupid as his chief engineer. And *his* brain cells numbered fewer than the fingers on his mangled left hand. What the crew members lacked in intelligence, they made up for in greed and sloth. Any time the ship ported, it was all the captain could do to rouse them from the drinking and narco dens to make the next flight.

His next job – a long jump out of Arcturus – proved the first ship was no exception to the rule. If anything, the feebles making up that crew and officer staff were *less* competent. That journey had ended in near disaster when the captain ignored the clearly charted meteor belt and wound up hulling his ship. Four crew members had died before Kea had jockeyed a patch into position and sealed the hole. His knowledge of Yukawa drive had been tested when it was discovered the engine was damaged. And no one aboard had the skills to repair it. There had been a lot of praying for the next seventy-two E-hours as Kea jury-rigged the stardrive into some kind of working order. The jump home went without incident.

It was then he had been recruited by his present company – Galiot Inc., a division of the megagiant SpaceWays. 'Galiot's a brand spankin' new division, son,' the recruiter had boasted. 'You'll be seein' places and doin' things folks are just startin' to dream about. Our mission's to come up with new ways and ideas for SpaceWays to make money. They're puttin' big credits behind us. If you join, son, you'll be joinin' quality. Nothin' but the best for Galiot Inc. Cuttin' edge all the way.' Kea had hired on at a two-grade jump in position. And it wasn't long before he'd worked his way up to chief engineer.

Yeah, he thought, as the needle spray soothed tension-knotted muscles, the road might not have been long, but it sure was torturous. It wasn't the risk that made it so. Hell, risk was spice. Here he was getting his chance to act out his boyhood dreams. Starships bound for adventure in the beyond. But the company did its best to spoil all sense of wonder. They hired and bought cheap, making intellectual companionship minimal and turning the most routine labor into knuckle-busting frustration for lack of quality machines and tools. The company had a knack for turning any assignment into boredom – interspersed with fear of a pointless death as shoddy equipment failed at a touch.

What the bejesus are you doing here, Richards? Stuck on a one-E-year-minimum expedition. Surrounded by the sorriest, most cantankerous, ill-mannered employees of Galiot Inc. You could have stayed at Base Ten. Waited for another contract. Okay, you were bored out of your skull. So, what's new about that when you work for Galiot Inc.? You could have guessed. Hell, you *knew*, Richards. Knew at the time you had best tell them to put that contract where the sun doesn't shine.

He heard the fresher door open. Through the clouds of steam he saw a lush, female form slip out of tight-fitting coveralls. The warning bells hammered. Dr Ruth Yuen smiled through the mist, then slowly lay down on the fresher's small changing bench. 'Mmmm,' she said. 'I *like* my men nice and clean.'

The last time she had left his bunk, Richards had sworn to himself that was it. The end. The woman was more dangerous than anything aboard the ship or outside in cold, cold space. A guaranteed knife in the back. So, tell her no, Richards. Tell her no. Send her back to her full-time lover and boss, Dr Castro Fazlur.

Go ahead, Richards.

But his feet were moving forward, taking him out of the shower. Ruth's smile grew broader. She looked up at him, eyes half-closed. Her hand reached up. Caressed Kea's stomach. Slid downward. Her left leg lifted off the deck, knee bending, and she put her foot on the bench. She let her leg fall open, then reached down and touched herself, stroking.

'What're you waiting for, Richards? Do you need a written invitation?' As he knelt over her, her legs came up, locking around his waist.

Sure, Richards. Tell her no.

Just like you told the company no.

He had heard the rumors about Operation Alva even before he had been approached by Captain Selfridge to join the crew. Word was that a routine scan of the remote Alva Sector had come up with a strong but intermittent disturbance in the normal background radiation. The pulse came from an area no known body existed. It was not a black hole. Or any of the theoretical formations posed by twenty-second-century physicists to explain the newly unexplainable. Also, as far as anyone could tell, the blips or buzzes showing up against the radiation background charts came from a 'natural' source.

Kea was oddly stirred by rumors of the unexplained phenomenon. The small-boy/adventurer in him wanted badly to see for himself. To be the first to know a thing before anyone else. To rediscover his sense of wonder. Then his hard-won cynicism reasserted itself. Unless there was proven money in it, the company would ignore the whole thing. The required government report would eventually be drawn up, filed, and forgotten in a bureaucratic black hole. So, he'd returned to the room the company provided 'tween-contract workers and buried himself in his steadily growing collection of historical works. Then he had gotten the news of Dr Fazlur's arrival. The scientist was reportedly an expert on alternate-universe theory.

Kea had nearly dismissed this news outright. He had met too many of the company's pet experts. They always proved to be nothing more than Ph.D.s for hire, with no qualms about bending fact to meet an employer's expectations. He had figured Fazlur was there merely to draw up the report, to maintain the company's license requirements with the government. This guess had been reinforced when he heard about Fazlur's gorgeous 'assistant' – Dr Ruth Yuen – and how he liked to nuzzle and paw at her in public. The man was obviously more playboy than scientist. Then he'd heard about the many metric tons of equipment being unloaded from the ship that had borne Fazlur and Yuen to Base Ten.

'Company's turned on the money machine,' an old space jock had said at one of Kea's favorite dives. 'Somethin's gotta be up!'

A small forest of special antennas had been erected on Base Ten's exterior skin by around-the-clock crews. Kea had seen it for himself upon his return from a quick, one-week hop. As his ship had floated toward Base Ten's docking bay, he had noted the odd configuration Fazlur had ordered constructed: wires knitted together and strung from towers until they formed an immense gill-net receiver. The old space jock had not exaggerated when he talked about the money machine going full bore. Something was up, indeed.

Kea had paced his room. Picked up Gibbon. Tossed it. Flipped through the *Anabasis*. Tossed it, too. Ditto *Plutarch's Lives*. And Churchill. Too many hours dragged by. When he had gotten the message from Captain Selfridge that he was putting together a crew for an expedition to the Alva Sector, he had bounded to the meeting as fast as a strong young man can bound in three-quarters gravity.

'Company thinks real well of you, Richards,' Selfridge had said.

'Thanks, Captain.'

'Hey, none of that captain business,' the man had protested. 'I like my ship loosey-goosey. Informal. Makes for a better team. That way we all pull together when you-know-what hits the fan . . . Call me Murph.'

'Sure . . . Murph,' Kea had said, thinking then and there he ought to blow out. Only a fool would sign on a ship run by a captain who said, 'Call me Murph.'

'That's right, Richards. Loosey-goosey. And we'll get on fine. Anyway. Company put you top of my list for the chief engineer's slot. Now that I metcha, and we talked . . . I can see why.'

Kea hadn't responded. He would have blown the deal. He had spoken maybe fifteen words since he had arrived at the captain's temporary HQ. If old Murph spent an equivalent time checking out the others, they'd wind up with a crew that would give Long John Silver the heebie-jeebies. 'One thing I oughta mention,' Murph had continued. 'I gotta Osiran for my new first officer. Name's Vasoovan. Any problem with that?'

Murph had instantly misunderstood Kea's raised eyebrow. 'Now, I won't blame you if you're sorta prejudiced against Osirans. Taken a good man's job, and all. But this Vasoovan comes highly recommended. Even if she is a bug.'

'No. I've got no problems with Osirans . . . Murph,' Kea had finally said. This was no lie. He was too much a mongrel himself to be prejudiced. He had heard fine things about Osirans in general. But not as company employees. Osirans were a pretty proud group. Hated the idea of being beholden to humans because they'd been the ones to make first contact. The only ones who would work for humans, Kea knew very well, were malcontents and incompetents. Which meant Murph's first officer was a likely loser with an attitude. Another bad sign. So, if his own name was on the recommended list, what did that make him?

'Now, this is a real ticklish mission we got here,' Murph said. 'So you get hazardous-duty pay. And that's triple time, friend. One year guaranteed.'

Kea had smiled, acting pleased. So that explains it, he had thought. As one of the company's youngest chief engineers in grade, triple time would be pretty cheap. Which explained the Osiran. Rock-bottom wages there. And good old Murph looked like the sort of guy who had to work cheap. 'Plus bonuses if we bring home the bacon,' Murph had said.

'What exactly are we after?'

'You probably heard the scuttlebutt in the bars about the weird readings they're gettin' out of Alva Sector, right?'

'Yeah. *Everybody* heard.'

Laughter. 'Figured that. No secrets on Base Ten. Anyway, they got the readings. Clerk drew up a filing, like we're supposed to. Law says the company's gotta report unexplained stuff like that. Part of the license with the Powers That Be. Public duty, and all that BS.'

Public duty, meaning pure research and intellectual development, was a sop the big companies threw the opposition when they won the right to commercialize space. Little money was actually spent. SpaceWays and its fellow franchisees met only the vaguest spirit of the law.

'The report got punted forward,' Murph continued, 'and everybody figured that was that. It'd get buried along with all the other jerkoff stuff. Which is where Fazlur comes into the story. The doc's an expert on alternate-universe theory. Don't ask me to explain it, I'm a space jockey, not a domehead.'

'I promise I won't,' Kea had said.

'So Fazlur sees the report. Gets all excited. Runs it through the computers, and bingo, it comes up three cherries. Proof there's an alternate universe, he says. A leak in space.'

'Why is the company listening?' Kea had kept his features bland. Inside, his heart was hammering. 'What do they care? Unless there's money it in for them.'

'No money,' Murph had said. 'Not a chance. This expedition is, and I quote, "purely in the interest of the advancement of science," end BS quote.'

Kea had just stared at him – a working stiff's Don't Con Me stare. Murph had laughed. 'Yeah. Right. Actually, what's goin' on is that our fearless parent company – SpaceWays – has got its tit in a political wringer. Some government types say they're skinnin' the research credits too fine.'

'So they're looking for a nice bone to throw to the dogs, right?' Kea had guessed.

'You got it. And so did Fazlur. He may be a domehead, but he's got a good business nose. He pulls some strings. A junior veep sees a chance to make senior. And son of a gun, all of a sudden, we got us a scientific mission.'

So, that's all it was, Kea had thought. A little cheapie non-effort to spread oil on troubled political waters. This thing was bound to be screwed from the get-go.

'So, Richards. I did my dance. Give you my best dog-and-pony show. What do you say? You with me?'

Kea had rolled it over. And over again. It still didn't look good. However . . . An alternate universe? The other side of God's coin? And there was a measurable leak . . . A door. Into . . .

What?

Richards had to know. 'Yeah,' he'd said. 'I'm with you.'

Kea watched Ruth ankle down the corridor. She paused at the door, turned, flashed that wicked grin, then the door hissed open.

She disappeared inside. He waited a few moments. It wouldn't do for them to arrive together.

Murph's call for a meeting had caught them in the middle of another wild session of lovemaking. The voice on Kea's room speaker had barely died away before they were pulling on their clothes. Now he was cooling his heels to allay any suspicions Fazlur might have. Kea cursed himself for getting into the predicament. The woman had come on from the start. She had a body and look that dared you to find out what she knew. Which was a helluva lot. She had told him Fazlur was a pig. She put up with his demands because it was the only way she could keep her job. Otherwise she would be just another scientist with a sheepskin for hire.

'I have to use what nature gave me,' she'd said, tracing a shapely finger along even more shapely naked flesh. But Kea had noted that for her the danger of getting caught – and the ensuing trouble it would cause – lent heavy spice to sex. Again, like Tamara. Don't point fingers, Richards, he thought. It gets to you, too. Every time she comes knocking . . . you open the door.

The most maddening thing about it, Kea realized, was that the situation was right out of a basic frosh psych text. An obsession directly related to his failure with Tamara. It helped that the sex was absolutely fabulous. Feeling far younger than twenty-eight and ashamed of his addiction, Kea decided enough time had passed. He paced down the corridor and entered the bridge. They were all waiting. Murph and Vasoovan and Fazlur. Behind them, Ruth threw him a kiss.

'What kept you, Richards?' came Vasoovan's irritating twitter.

Fazlur looked at him. Did he suspect?

'A little trouble in the engine room,' Kea said.

'Leak in the seals again?' Murph misguessed.

'Yeah, Murph. Trouble in the seals again.' Kea watched Fazlur turn away . . . satisfied? 'What's going on?' Kea asked.

Murph thumbed at Fazlur. 'Doc's got some kinda answer.' He turned to Fazlur. 'Why don't you run it down?'

'Yeah, Fazlur,' Vasoovan prodded. 'Tell us why you've had us chasing a big fat zero for five months.'

'It is not a phantom, my dimwitted companion. Of this I assure you. When we started out, the signal we were picking up from the apparent discontinuity in the Alva Sector was certainly steady and strong enough. Our dilemma came only when we grew close. The steady pulse we were receiving appeared to shatter.'

'I think your equipment is all screwed up, is what I think,' Vasoovan said. 'You were seein' something that wasn't there.'

'Then what, you fool, do you think those blinking lights were on the monitor? That's not *my* equipment.' Vasoovan was silent. Eyestalks astir. Wandering or not, the blips on the screen did indicate *some* kind of presence. Fazlur smirked at Vasoovan, then turned serious. 'What I did was gather up all the recordings of Vasoovan's sightings. Then I crunched the data. To see if there was some sort of pattern.'

'Which there was,' Kea guessed. Otherwise they wouldn't be here talking about it.

'Which there was,' Fazlur confirmed with relish. 'Viewed in isolation, it appeared the signal was wandering all over the clock. One o'clock to six o'clock. To nine . . . When one steps back for perspective, however, one would observe that it repeats the nine, then six, and on to one, again.' He sketched as he talked. The result looked a bit like a tilted *U*.

'What's causing it?' Richards asked.

'Some of it is due to the presence of black matter,' Fazlur said. 'No doubt about it. A very strong gravitational force is at work here, and I'll be the first to admit I hadn't considered it. But that's not the whole answer. I think what's really happening is that we're viewing an alternate universe bleeding through the discontinuity. It's well known that early in the life of our own universe, positive ions were so compressed that no light could escape. As the ions separated – we now imagine – light began to burst out of that dense ionic fog. I believe something similar is going on in our not-so-theoretical alternate universe. Dense ionic fog – or its equivalent in that universe. Light pushing to get through. And finding the path of least resistance through the discontinuity and into our own universe.'

'Good work, Doc,' Murph said. 'I guess. But I'll leave that to our bosses. Tell the truth, though, what you're tellin' me may be *the* answer. But that answer don't have the ring of Bonus City. Hope you can punch it up better'n that when we get back to Base Ten.'

'Oh, I can do *far* better,' Fazlur said, preening. 'I can take us there . . . and prove it!'

'Hey, come on, Fazlur!' Vasoovan protested, predator's grin stretched wide on her long face. 'Let's not get stupid about this. I'll buy your theory. I'll even back your act with the company to earn my share of the bonus. But, we gotta face facts, here. Which is – ion fog or no ion fog – we don't know how to get from *here* to *there*.'

'Yes we do,' Fazlur said. He drew a line straight through the tilted *U*. Made a circle at eleven o'clock. 'This is our course for the next jump.' Silence all around. Kea saw Ruth puzzling. Judging. Then he saw her nod. She believed he was right.

Murph finally broke the silence. 'Gee, Doc. That's good crap, and all. But I think we got enough. The politicos will be happy we really *did* something. Which means the company'll be happy. End story.'

'Don't be a fool,' Fazlur said. 'If I'm right, we're talking about the greatest discovery since Galileo. Redefining reality itself. Forget the fame. Although every member of the crew will go down in history. Think of the fortune, man. The fortune.'

Murph turned to Kea. 'What's our status?'

'Engine's in okay shape. Everything else is so-so. Including fuel.' Kea had no choice but to be honest.

'I don't know,' Murph said. 'I just don't feel right making this kind of decision myself.'

'Can't buzz the Powers That Be,' Vasoovan said. 'We're way out of range.'

'If you turn back now,' Fazlur warned, 'I swear I'll see you fired and blackballed for life.'

'Come on, Doc,' Murph said. 'Don't be like that. I'm just sayin' I feel real uncomfortable decidin' this whole thing solo.'

'I'll take responsibility,' Fazlur said.

'That wouldn't be right,' Murph said. All he meant was it wouldn't be enough to protect his big-hammed behind. 'How about we vote on it? Just the officers and you two. We don't need to ask the crew anything.'

Kea almost laughed aloud. A ship's captain calling for a vote. Instead, he said, 'Why not?' He raised a hand. 'Start with me. I say we go.'

'Crap on you!' Vasoovan said. 'I vote for home.'

Fazlur and Ruth joined Kea. Murph could see which way the land lay now. 'Okay. I'll go along with the majority. Sorry, Vasoovan, but I gotta keep the peace. It's my job.'

And so the last stage of Operation Alva was launched as cynically and halfheartedly as the first. Kea didn't care. He was determined to see the other side of God's big coin. An old line crawled into his brain: 'This is the stuff dreams are made of.'

A fine rain of fire curtained across space. And that curtain seemed to swirl and billow against a gentle cosmic wind. It was a place where two universes touched . . . and bled through.

Kea peered at the image on the ship's main screen and watched birth and death enacted instantly as small particles from one universe touched one from another and exploded in pinprick bursts of light. Pinbursts that played up and down the shuddering curtain that Fazlur called a 'discontinuity.' Kea thought, Discontinuity? No. More like the Gate to Paradise. Or Hell.

Fazlur's voice came from behind him: 'Now, Richards . . . if you could take the sweep in a bit farther . . .'

Kea worked the joystick. Onscreen, the sweep he'd helped Fazlur and Ruth deploy swooped into view. It consisted of a small cylindrical unit designed for use as a 'tween-ship short-range courier, now pushing a net made of specially treated plas wires. On a bar across the bottom of the screen, numbers jumped and played.

'Just a little more . . .' Fazlur's voice coaxed. 'A little more . . .'

Suddenly the sweep's net was alive with pinbursts. Antiparticles colliding against particles. A small drama being played out against the plas wires of the net. Kea kept the sweep steady on its dip-in-and-out course. It wasn't hard. The joystick's sensors showed no interference. Then the pinbursts stopped abruptly as the sweep completed its journey and returned to normal space.

Fazlur's voice gloated behind him. 'I've done it! Done it!' Kea knew Fazlur was seeing his name in history books. The first scientist to explore another universe – albeit by remote. He punched in a command putting the sweep on autoreturn and swiveled in his chair.

'Done what?' came Vasoovan's annoying twitter. 'We're in on this same as you, buster. It's a team. Right, Murph? We all get equal shares.'

'Uh . . . Gotta get back to you on that,' Murph hemmed. 'See what the book says.'

Kea could tell that good old team player Murph would like the bonus cut in the rank-share system. He could see those crafty old eyes in that disarming hail-fellow face buzz in calculation. Let's see, now, he'd be thinking . . . That way me and Fazlur split fifty percent . . . That'd be . . . Uh see . . . what's the biggest bonus the company ever put out?

'I don't gotta read the book, Murph,' Vasoovan shrilled. 'This is expedition rules, fella. Fazlur as team leader gets twenty. We all split the rest. Equals.'

'Will you all just stop it,' Fazlur stormed. 'Who cares about the company bonus? Put it in a glass, swallow, and urinate.'

'Say . . .' Murph said. 'If you don't want any part of your bonus, we'll be glad to split up your share. Won't we, Vasoovan?'

'You got it, Murph.'

Kea broke in. 'Why don't you explain it to them, Fazlur?' This was the third time he'd taken the sweep through. And he'd watched over Fazlur's and Ruth's shoulders as they figured and refigured. He had a faint idea what Fazlur had discovered. But it was very faint.

Fazlur nodded. He turned his craggy, handsome face to its best profile. 'It's as simple as this,' he said. 'We have just reached into another universe – and brought back evidence of its most basic material. This material – in our own universe – would become the source of unlimited power. A small flask of it, my friends, might supply all the wants and needs of a city and its inhabitants for a hundred years.' Fazlur giggled. The giggle turned to laughter. The cabin was silent until he stopped. 'So much for your damn bonus,' he said.

The faint idea bloomed to understanding in Kea's head. Power . . . Fuel. Wars had been fought over it. Hundreds of thousands had died on oil fields. Power . . . Weapons. Hundreds of thousands more had died in the nuclear fires of the past. Power. Wealth. The greatest fortunes – and families – had been founded on its gold. He looked around the room at the others. Each in his or her own way understood. Even the lowliest grease monkey would have understood. You did not come to space . . . and stay . . . and not understand these things. Kea looked at Murph: Jock's face. Clown face. But somehow oddly solemn. Vasoovan: Pink features paler than he'd ever seen. Big predator's grin. Tentacle curling and uncurling. Ruth: Eyes alight. Red tongue-tip flicking out. And himself.

He wished he could see himself.

'Uh . . . Doc . . .' came Murph's voice. Throaty. 'What do you call this . . . uh . . . stuff?'

'A good question, Murph,' Fazlur said. Kea didn't blame him for sounding so pedantic. 'It's the opposite of matter in our universe. But we can't call it anti-matter. Because we already have anti-matter in this universe. Perhaps we should express it in its simplest terms.' He turned to Ruth. 'Something commercial. Recognizable even to the ignorant. I find it always helps when I make my presentations to funding boards.'

'Easy.' She shrugged. 'If it isn't anti-matter, exactly . . . then it's new anti-matter. Stress the newness, somehow.'

'How about Anti-Matter Two?' Kea suggested.

'I like it,' Ruth said. 'Simple.'

'Anti-Matter Two . . . Yes. That'll do. Very very well. The heading will get their attention.' Fazlur was satisfied.

'What I like,' Murph said, 'is it fits real nice on the side of a building. AM2.' He drew the symbols in the air: AM2.

'How sure are you about this, Doc?' Vasoovan twittered. 'You got proof?'

Fazlur rose, turned from them, and looked up on the screen at the curtain of fire. 'I'm sure. Very sure. And I have the proof. But it is not absolute. And in this, my friends, we must be absolute. Otherwise . . .' He turned back, the fire raining on the screen behind him. 'There are those who would kill to control this. You *must* realize this.'

Fazlur stared at them hard. One by one. He came to Kea. Richards thought of the Bargetas. The other great families – and fortunes. And the opportunity *and* threat they would see in AM2. The issue was control. The Haves against the Have Nots. The man was right. The Haves would attack with lawyers, writs – and assassins. Kea nodded. He knew. As did the others.

'If we want any rights – bound-in-steel guarantee rights – to our discovery,' Fazlur said, 'we must make that proof patentable. A patent so strong that no one can question our rights.'

'How do we get proof, Doc?' Murph asked.

Fazlur pointed at the screen. 'We have to go in there to get it,' he said. 'And come back again.'

Kea had never heard silence to thick. There was no argument. No heated questions: Can it be done? . . . Are you sure? . . . What if? . . . The struggle was within each of them. They all knew Fazlur would answer, Yes. I am. I don't know . . . I've never been there before. Kea swallowed. He looked at the screen. He saw the gentle fire rain, the billow and curl of space, as alluring as any woman he'd ever known.

He . . . Just . . . Had . . . To . . . See.

That line again: 'The stuff dreams are made of.'

Kea cleared his throat, startling the others to life.

'I think we should go,' he said.

it was a place like the other.
but not familiar.
it was . . .

not.
I don't like it.
why?
i don't know.
is it colder?
no. but i'm . . . cold.
is it darker?
no. but i can't . . . see.
what's wrong, then?
i'm . . .
lost.

A juddering into normalcy. They all looked at each other, dazed. Ruth's hand crept toward Kea's. Fazlur saw it. An odd light came to his eye. Then the screen caught his attention. 'We're on the other side,' he said quietly.

Kea looked up. The remotes were panning along the rear of the ship. The curtain of fire was behind them.

Destiny I was through.

'Reckoning by the discontinuity,' Murph said. Voice crisp and professional. 'On time-tick . . .'

Vasoovan's twitter was modulated: 'Check. Coordinates . . . x350 . . . Proceeding . . .'

'Half power . . .' Kea broke in. 'Drive steady. All functions normal.'

'Readings . . . positive on the port sensors, Doctor,' Ruth said. Calm.

'Course starboard nine now . . . Thank you, Ruth. A little less on the data stream, please . . . There you go.'

Fazlur's fingers flew across his key unit, monitoring the incoming data. He nodded. Yes. Yes. And yes. Then he keyed out. 'I think we can go home now, Captain,' he said. Formal.

Murph nodded to him. Stiff. 'Thank you, Doctor.' Then, 'Vasoovan. Set the course for XO . . . We're going home.'

It came as a spot on the screen that blazed the colors/no colors of this strange universe.

An infinitesminal spot.

'Murph! Eleven o'clock!'

'What the crap is it?'

'Dunno. Pint-sized moon, maybe.'

'Don't look too close.'

'Naw. Not real close. But maybe we oughta—'

Two bodies approached in space. Composed of mass. Potential of that mass. And gravitational displacement.

But one was the stuff of one reality.

One another.

Opposites attract.

What do double opposites do?

The explosion took *Destiny I* midships, cutting it like a shark ripping into fat-bellied tuna.

Fifteen died.

Five survived.

The gods of this place were kind to the fifteen.

Kea came awake. It was dark and bloody. Acrid.

There was no pain.

Numbness.

He heard voices.

'All dead.' A wail.

'There's us, Murph! There's us. We're alive.'

Me too, Kea wanted to say. I'm alive, too.

Not even a groan escaped.

'What'll we do? Oh God, what'll we do.'

'I'd kill you, Murph. I'd kill you if it wouldn't leave me all alone.'

'Gotta think. Gotta think.'

'It's your fault, Murph. We never shoulda come, damn you!'

Check the damage, Kea wanted to say. The urge was desperate . . . Check the damage.

He felt his lips tighten to speak.

A wave washed in and took him away.

He was thirsty.

God he was thirsty.

A voice. Ruth's.

'Hell, I don't know. He's broken up, or something. Inside. I'm no physician.'

'What about Fazlur?' Murph's voice.

'Who cares?' came the twitter – Vasoovan. 'He got us into this.'

'Castro's worse,' he heard Ruth say. 'I followed the directions in the medkit best I could. The stump stopped bleeding, if that's any consolation.' Her voice was cold.

'Still out?'

'Still out. Thank God. Those screams were awful.'

Water, Kea thought. I'm so thirsty.

'We've got practically no rations,' Vasoovan shrilled. 'And very little water.

'I say we put them both out of their misery. And we can live a little longer.'

'That wouldn't be right,' Ruth said. Perfunctory.

'Naw,' Murph said. 'Guess it wouldn't . . . Besides, long as they're out, they ain't costin' us anything. Except air. And we've plenty of that.'

The tide lifted Kea up again and carried him off.

Pain. Waves and jabs of it.

But it was bearable pain. And there was no numbness.

There was still no light. Eyes . . . felt . . . crusted shut. Dried . . . What? . . . Blood? Yes, blood.

'Jeez, this suit stinks,' he heard Murph say.

There were sounds of fastenings being opened. The clank of equipment falling.

'Did you get back as far as the drive unit this time?' Ruth asked.

'Yeah. Wasn't hit too hard, either. And the input to the controls checks out.'

'Can we run it?' Came the twitter.

Kea heard Murph sigh. 'I *said* it wasn't hit too hard. Meaning . . . it's fixable. But not by me. And not by anyone else here.'

Kea struggled the word out. 'Water.'

'Hey, it's Richards,' Murph said.

'What's he want?' Vasoovan asked.

'Water. He said water,' Ruth said. 'I'll get it for him.'

'Hey, Murph,' Vasoovan said. 'We didn't talk about *this*, Murph. Last we talked, you said they ain't costin' us anything. Remember?'

'I remember.'

Kea was suddenly frightened that a decision was being reached. And even more frightened how it would come out. Where was Ruth? Why wasn't she speaking up for him?

Don't wait for Ruth!

'I can fix it,' Kea croaked.

'He *really* is awake,' Ruth said. Meaning: he heard us talking.

'What's that you say, partner?' It was Murph. Jovial. Kea felt him move close. Imagined him peering down. 'You say you can fix it? Fix the drive?'

Kea wanted to say more. A lot more. But he hadn't the strength. So there was only one response. 'Water,' he croaked. Then he fell back. It was his first and final offer.

A rustling. Then cool water touched his lips. He lapped it until he'd had enough. Perfume floated down to him, along with a voice. 'Oh, darling,' Ruth said. 'I'm so very happy you're alive.' A kiss brushed his cheek.

He slept.

Kea hoisted himself on his good arm to get a better view. The other was strapped tight to his body. 'That's a good seal,' he said. 'That's a keeper. Now . . . lift it up and you'll see a Y-shaped impression.'

On the screen he saw Murph's suited hands do his bidding. He was crammed into a space between the drive unit and a bulkhead. 'Got it,' Murph said.

'Good. You'll find a tool that matches in your beltpack. But before you open the cover . . . make sure you set up the shield.'

'Damn straight,' Murph said as he went to work.

'No sense worrying about cancer,' Vasoovan twittered. 'None of us are going to live that long.'

'Humorous,' Ruth said. '*How* jolly you keep us all.'

Kea ignored the start-up of another bickering match. He fell back into the cot. 'Get me some soup,' he said. Ruth turned a deadly look on him.

'You had your ration,' Vasoovan said.

'Soup,' Kea said. He was sick. He needed more. End discussion. Kea looked up at Murph working in the drive room. When the cover was off, the next step should go pretty easy. Hunger knotted under his ribs again. As sharp as if they were broken clean. Instead of cracked.

He lifted himself up to look for Ruth, his back barely supporting him. She was still sitting in the chair. Vasoovan was watching, enjoying herself. 'Who are you to give people orders?' Ruth snarled. 'Who are you to break rules and eat and drink more than the rest of us?'

'Doesn't matter,' Kea said. 'Do it – or they'll make you.' Hysterical twitter. 'No eat. No work. Guy drives a hard bargain.'

All four of Vasoovan's eyestalks turned on Ruth. 'Get him what he wants,' she said. 'Or we'll put you in the soup with Fazlur.' Ruth did as she was told.

Kea settled in to wait. Murph should be ready for the next

little step in about four hours. Then Kea would trade yet another bit of knowledge for nourishment. And another. Until it was done. Two more weeks, he thought. And then we shall see what we shall see.

Fazlur had died three days earlier. He'd tossed and groaned for an eternity, never quite conscious, nor quite out enough to not feel pain. No one had moved to help him, much less feed him or bring him drink. Kea hadn't spoken up for Fazlur. Why bother? They would have refused him help. Kea's bargain would not be stretched to include Fazlur. Murph, Vasoovan, and Ruth were the strong here. Kea was helpless until his injuries healed.

Besides, in Vasoovan's predator logic of survival, Fazlur was the most expendable. 'We get lucky and make it,' Vasoovan had said, 'we don't need him. Not alive. We got his proof. His absolute proof. All in his data file.'

'I just wish he would get it over with,' Ruth had said. 'I can't stand his infernal groaning. He used to sound like that sometimes when we made love. A pig.' Kea had turned away from them. To his own thoughts. And sleep.

Sometime later, Kea had come to semiconsciousness. Fazlur was groaning. The others made the noises of sleep. Then he heard movement. A softer patter of feet. The smell of sweet perfume. The groaning stopped. Abrupt. Then the soft pad of feet.

They found Fazlur dead the next day.

'Run him through the reclaimer,' Vasoovan had twittered. 'Add him to the soup.' He was referring to the sort of nutrition stew produced by their own waste and the dwindling supply of plant protein being produced in the damaged hydroponic room.

'Why not?' Ruth had said. 'Make some use out of him. It seems so fitting, somehow.'

Kea had watched them lug the corpse out of the room. Hunger gnawed at him again. He heard light footsteps. Ruth's perfume. He took the mug from her without looking up. He drank. There was no taste at all.

Poor Fazlur.

The curtain between universes hung before them, beckoning. If things had worked out differently, Kea supposed it would have been called Fazlur's Discontinuity. He looked about the room. Vasoovan. Murph. Ruth. No one here would give Fazlur a drop of the credit. As for himself . . . well, he had ideas of his own. Just formulating.

'We're ready,' Vasoovan said.

Kea struggled up. Some life was returning to his bound-up arm. He was getting stronger. Barely. 'One thing more,' Kea announced, 'before we go through.'

They turned to him, alarmed.

'Don't worry. The drive unit's fine,' he said. 'But what I want you all to remember when we get to the other side is that it's five months home.'

'Yeah? So?' From Murph.

'So now that everything's working okay, some of you might get the idea you don't need me anymore. That the chief engineer is expendable – like the chief scientist.' No protests. No offended denials. Only silence. 'I took out insurance to keep us friends,' Kea continued. 'I fixed the drive unit, okay. But I slipped Murph a little extra task to do. An extra step.'

'Like what?' Murph demanded angrily.

'Like I rigged the unit to go down in a couple of months. And when it goes busto, my dear companions in adversity . . . you're going to need me again. I guarantee it.'

Kea fell back into the cot. 'Now, go, dammit!'

They went.

They found the air leak a week later.

'It's not my fault, Murph!'

'You were supposed to check, dammit!'

'I checked. Not my fault, if I missed something. I'm no engineer.' Two of her eyestalks turned to peer at Kea's figure, prone on the cot. His duties had been shared out among them. Kea stayed silent.

'Let's not get into this bickering again,' Ruth said. 'The leak's plugged. Fine. Now, the question is, Do we have enough?'

'Not a chance,' Murph said. 'Not with most of the five months to go. And—' He broke off. A long silence.

Then Vasoovan finished it: 'And four of us breathing.'

There it was. Kea had been waiting.

'Yeah,' Murph said.

'Yes . . . I can see that,' Ruth said.

They all turned to look at Kea. Eight eyes upon three living forms peering at his own, air-consuming self.

'It'd be close,' Murph said. 'Still be maybe a month short.'

'By then,' Ruth said, 'we might find other means . . .'

'What about the drive unit?' Murph said. 'The little trick he played on me?'

'I think he lied,' Ruth said.

Kea smiled at them. A big, broad smile. A smile right up from the warrens of Maui.

'Yeah, and maybe he didn't,' Vasoovan said. The eight eyes turned away. But Kea remained watchful.

'What'll we do?' Murph asked.

'Simple,' Vasoovan said. 'We gotta have Kea. We gotta have you. And we gotta have me. I'm the nav—'

Kea didn't know where the hatchet came from. It was painted the slick red of emergency tool gear. The handle was short. The blade blunt. Ruth brought it down between the four eyestalks. She was a small woman, barely coming to Kea's chin. But she swung with the force of survival. The hatchet buried itself in the Osiran's brain globe. The haft protruded back – giving Vasoovan a protuberance that looked like a long human nose. Pink goo blobbed out and dripped to the floor. The tentacles shuddered, then were still.

Ruth stepped back. She looked Murph full-on. 'Well?' she said.

'She kinda got on my nerves, anyway,' Murph said. 'All that twittering.'

'The rations are getting low,' Ruth said.

'I noticed. Let's make some soup.'

He dreamed of kings. Of empires.

Menes was the first. A crafty old devil who welded upper and lower Egypt into the first empire. He ruled for sixty years. And was killed by a hippopotamus.

The Persians bowed before Alexander's sword. He died in a swamp. Kublai Khan got it right. He quelled the mighty Chinese. And died of old age.

The Romans pushed the bounds of the known world and beyond. They fell to thieves on horseback.

Elizabeth was fine. The best of them all. She was the dazzling acrobat of the monarchs. Kea sometimes wondered why she hadn't killed her sister sooner. Instead she bore the threat of deadly plot after deadly plot. The romantics said it was deep, sisterly feeling. Kea believed it was simply because Elizabeth hadn't thought it was time.

He had learned much from these people during those long hours of offwatch reading. His interest was not casual. The nature of the powerful had confounded him. He had been smacked on his ignorant blind side. Kea was determined to understand. So he had gone at it like an engineer. Taking each monarch and his kingdom apart. Putting it back together again. Piece by piece. Sometimes rearranging those pieces to see how it might have turned out. An empire, he had discovered, could take several forms. It could be crown and throne. Altar and blood sacrifice. An army standard with its accompanying secret police. A presidential seal resting on stolen votes. A company logo above a penthouse suite. But they all had one thing in common: an idea. An idea of a perfect life. Real, or promised. And for the idea to work, it had to satisfy from top to bottom. Starving masses do not praise their monarch's name on Feast Day.

In one of the folktales he had read, one of the ancient kings went among his subjects in disguise so he could learn first hand how to sweeten their disposition. The king's name was Raschid. In the real world, the ward bosses, commissars, and priests fetched food and comfort up tenement stairs to sell for votes. The Robin Hoods – Huey Long, Jess Unruh, Boris Yeltsin – stole from weakened kings to create their own power bases.

Dictators preferred triage. Kea thought of it as rule by the three G's: genocide, gulags, and gendarmes.

Still . . . No matter the form of the empire, or the means to maintain its rule, all of it circled back to the idea that was in the heart of the king who founded the empire.

And Kea had AM2.

His arm hurt. This was good. Like the pain before. He would be able to use it soon – though he had kept this from Murph and Ruth. He had a fever. An infection. A boil on his belly the size of a saucer. He'd have to hide that, too.

Kea heard whispers in the darkened room:

'C'mon, honey. I'm hurtin'.'

'Get away from me.'

'We done it before. What's another hunk?'

'You reneged on your bargain. You lied.'

'I couldn't help it, honey. I was hungry. Real bad hungry. I'll give you halvsies in the morning. Swear it.'

'Get it now,' Ruth said. 'Give it to me, now.'

Silence.

Ruth laughed. 'What's the matter . . . Daddy doesn't want to play slap-belly anymore. What's this. *Tsk tsk. It's* hungry. But Daddy's going to be selfish, isn't he?'

Murph made no response.

Then Kea heard Ruth gasp. And for one . . . two . . . three heartbeats, a violent, muffled struggle. Then a distinctive crack.

Kea felt a knot in his gut untighten. A sudden release of pressure. A terrible odor rose up from the burst boil. Then sudden chills. And sweat. Good.

The fever had broken . . .

He awoke with Murph standing over him. 'You're lookin' better,' he said.

Kea didn't answer. And he didn't look around the room for Ruth.

Murph stretched. 'I'm hungry,' he said. 'Want some soup?'

'Yeah,' Kea said. 'I'm hungry, too.'

'It's gonna take longer than we thought,' Murph said.

'I can see that,' Kea answered. He was looking at the latest computations on the screen.

'Damned Vasoovan,' Murph said. 'Lousy nav officer. Good thing you spotted her screwup and set us right.'

'Real lucky,' Kea said. He hobbled back to his cot and eased himself down.

'Maybe it won't be so bad,' Murph said. 'Maybe we'll get picked up when we first get inta range and they hear our SOS.'

'That could happen,' Kea said.

'Only one bug in that chowpak,' Murph said. 'And that's if we lose a buncha time puttin' that little trick of yours straight. When it blows.' He grinned. 'How long did you say it would take to fix again?'

'I didn't,' Kea said.

Murph looked at him. 'Naw. You didn't . . . did you?'

Kea clamped his bound arm tighter and felt the edge of the filed-down plas spoon. An old, familiar boyhood friend. Murph came closer to him peering down with bloodshot eyes. Flesh hung loosely from his big jock's frame. His cheeks were hollow, face pale as death. 'You don't look too worried,' he said. 'About the delay and all. 'Specially with your delay on top.'

'We'll make it,' Kea said.

'I'm not what you call clever,' Murph said. 'I know that about myself. And it don't bother me. I leave clever to guys like you. More power to ya, I say.'

He moved to the edge of the cot. Kea could see roped muscles play through the sagging flesh of his neck. He scratched his bound arm. Slipped the knots free.

"Course I woulda thought of lyin'," Murph said. 'I'm clever enough for that. Don't make captain in this man's company if you ain't quick on your feet.'

'I guess you don't,' Kea said. He scratched again. The spoon slipped upward.

'Naw. You don't,' Murph repeated. Kea saw Murph make the decision. Saw the click in those cunning eyes.

Kea came off the cot, right hand striking up to the chin, left hand – the bound arm – free, the spoon thrusting. It took Murph in the windpipe. Kea saw the eyes widen. Felt the flesh give. The sharp rush of air. He collapsed back as Murph flopped to the floor. A hand beat against his leg. He heard the whistling horror of Murph expelling his life.

Stillness.

Kea moved his foot. It thumped against Murph's body. There was no reaction. Kea let the weakness take him. All tension drained away. He would rest now. Later, he could get up and recheck the course. Let his eyes run over the readings of happy machinery at work.

Then he would make some soup.

There was plenty to eat and drink, now. Plenty of air to breathe. It would have been a lot closer, though, if Murph hadn't figured out that he had lied.

Chapter Twenty-Four

New York City, A.D. 2194

Mankind was a little low on heroes when Kea Richards, sole survivor of the *Destiny I*, returned from Base Ten to Earth. Kea was not sure how the hero card would help him with this ultimate edge he had happened on, but he was canny enough to not let it go unplayed. He had worked out the tale he would spin on the long journey home. He told the truth about the cause of the disaster. A collision with a meteroite. He merely left out it had occurred in another universe. And he certainly didn't tell them about the AM2.

Richards came on humble. He played up the image of an ordinary, hardworking space engineer who had been able to snatch victory from the jaws. He also made much of the 'fact' that when those fearless scientists and self-sacrificing space crew members around him died, generally with Expressed Noble Sentiments As Their Last, it was his great good fortune that his formal education at Cal Tech, even though it had been interrupted by financial problems, was remembered and applied directly to the various emergencies.

He took an enormous advance and cooperated cheerfully with the ghost preparing his autobiographical fiche. He went to the banquets and lectures, charging whatever his newly hired agent could cozen. And he was delighted to attend the parties and presentations afterward. He smiled, listened intently to the men and women he met, the ones with power, who glorified in their ability to attract the latest hero. He lied, and lied again.

Sometimes he wondered what the old Kea Richards would have thought, the Richards of Kahanamoku and the first two years in California. The Richards before the Bargetas or long hard years in space, on the far side of Barrier Thirty-three. Shaft him, he decided. A man had to grow up sometime and get over the idea that life was a pretty pink wonderland full of bunnies and lambiekins.

Besides, now there was Anti-Matter Two. The key to personal power, he was honest enough to admit to himself. But it was also the ultimate gift for man, and any other species he would encounter in his explosion out into the universe. Richards could not afford the luxury of an Ethics 101 debate, even within himself.

He was undecided as to what to do next. Anti-Matter Two. Whole galaxies of cheap, raw energy. As Fazlur had said, it would change everything, creating a civilization – or barbarism – unlike whatever had gone before. Richards was determined the vast changes would be for the better. *He* would make damned sure it was properly directed to the benefit of all. Neither fuhrers nor premiers, doges nor Rockefellers, would fatten from what he already thought of as his discovery. Nor the Bargetas. And this energy wouldn't be diverted to evil, as most everything from gunpowder to petroleum to the atom had been.

Consider the immediate problems you have. The first and most important, he thought, is to stay alive, and always guard your back. This secret has already cost lives – and is worth the death of entire worlds. Richards knew any hint of the secret of Anti-Matter Two and the Alva Sector would also be enough to put kidnappers with mind-draining tools and assassins on his trail, hired by those who stood to gain/lose the most from AM2. At the very least, charges might be trumped up against him by planetary governments.

Very well, then. So he would need to treat the Alva Sector as if it were some kind of hidden mine, deep in a jungle, that only he knew the directions to. He must not return to the Alva Sector, and that discontinuity in N-space, unless he knew he was not being tracked. Nor was it worthwhile returning to in the immediate future, his mind ran on. Before Anti-Matter Two could be developed, someone must create a handle. A shield. Some substance, synthetic or natural, that was a solid, that was malleable, and that was absolutely neutral to both matter and anti-matter.

Richards gnawed his lip. That was a real problem. He grinned – as if the thought of assassins and brainburners was gathering nuts in May. He continued analyzing and thinking, and came to the wonderful catch-22 – except this was a triple whammy: To utilize Power (AM2), he would have to achieve Power (wealth/clout). Which could most easily and safely be accomplished by cultivating Power. Catch-222.

That third Power was the men and women whose egos he was stroking as he toured his saga. And they were the beings he was determined to transform or destroy as he helped the human race achieve its destiny. He remembered the ancient saying, If you are not part of the solution, you are part of the problem. But this suggested his next move.

A job. He had no intention of renewing his contract with Space Ways/Galiot. Not with all these other offers that were coming in. Corporations wanted him solely for the Hero Factor, just as they hired gravball stars for the same reasons. Richards would be expected to continue pressing the flesh, except this time for the benefit of whoever was paying him. That would give him a chance to travel the halls of power. He carefully examined the various letters, verbals, and messages he'd gotten – glork that he'd more or less ignored.

One was from Austin Bargeta. Call him, anytime, day or night, on a private line. The message slip was balled up and hurled into the trash can in a reflex. Kea caught himself. Bargeta? A known entity. Someone he'd had unlikely dreams of encountering – on Richards's terms and turf – someyear. This could be someyear. He'd heard, in spite of his mind's promise to never concern himself with the Bargetas unless he found them in some sort of gunsights, Austin had fulfilled his early promise and become The Man – replacing his father at the head of the Bargeta octopus.

Bargeta senior had suicided three years after Kea's life had been shattered – or at least changed inalterably – on Mars. Suicided under conditions the tabs could only hint at being unthinkably disgusting.

He smoothed the slip out and stared at it, thinking. Possibly. He made his way to a library and did some research. Very possibly.

Bargeta Ltd. still was one of the colossi of the twenty-second century. But it was tottering. Bad investments had been made. Bargeta Transport, the tree all the lovely money-bearing branches grew from, was blighted. The old man had ordered new plants built, plants that never came up to full production. He'd commissioned new-model spacecraft, models that were offered on an already-saturated market, and craft that seemed to offer no more than a new crew/compartment/drive configuration rather than any real engineering improvements. And then he'd 'passed on,' and Austin had been given the scepter.

Austin had done no better than the previous generation, the business rags told Kea. He had been reluctant to newbroom the greedheads out of the holding corporations until almost too late. Then he had decided there was a far brighter future transporting people instead of commerce from world to world, and had a quarter of the Bargeta fleet converted to liners, just as a medium-size recession had cycled through the Solar System. Austin had proudly and personally bid on new transport routes, routes that thus far had failed to be profitable. Kea laughed quietly then, a sort of laugh Bargeta senior would have found familiar.

Now, as to Austin himself. Covenanted, naturally. To an ex-poser, Ms Smiling Breasts of a few years back. Two children. Mansions. Travel. Philanthropy. Ratchetaratcheta, Kea thought. Where's the dirt. Ah. Austin travels alone a lot. With his staff. Richards squinted at the holo showing Bargeta and staff boarding a spaceship. Even with the retouch, it appeared that Austin considered eye appeal a definite factor in his choice of advisers. There was more explicit gossip, and even some holos, in the sleazier and less controllable tabs.

That was enough. Kea placed the call. Austin was thrilled. Delighted his old friend, his roommate, the man who had taught him everything, would take the time. They must get together. What's the matter with tomorrow? Kea wondered, deliberately pushing it. Oh, well, there was this meeting. Stuffy, dull, but you know, I must wave the banner and look concerned, make a couple of real Decisions. Take all day. Ah, Kea said. I understand. Let me check the old logbook here (Kea had found that the execs he socialized with loved it when he used nautical terms, terms that no self-respecting swab back of Barrier Thirty-three would have recognized unless he heard them in dialogue on a vid). Oh. Hell, you can't believe how tied up I am, Richards said. He was sched-uled, pretty close to fourblocked himself. Let's see here. McLean Institute next week . . . that thing in New Delhi . . . plus you know I've been talking to some people about some interesting things I've considered, things that directly came out of what happened Out There. There were some interesting commercial possibilities I'd discussed with the late Dr Fazlur that seem to be worth developing. But we'll get together. Sometime. Maybe after I put together some venture capital.

Suddenly Austin's meeting was unimportant. Tomorrow it was! Smiling, Kea clicked off, and the smile vanished as quickly as Bargeta's image. All right, you bastard. On my terms this time. And we'll talk about me becoming your Pet Adventurer.

In fact, they talked about a lot of things, over three days, several meals, and many bottles. Everything except Mars. Austin tentatively mentioned Tamara once. She was now married – how old-fashioned – to some transoceanic hovercraft racer five years younger than she was. They were living in the new offshore resort near the Seychelles.

Kea nodded. Hoped that she was quite happy. Be sure and say hello, if you happen to talk to her. And remember the time you got blasted, and we sprayed CALTECH with acid across the Rose Bowl's synthturf just before that stupid groundball match they used to play every Newyear's? Ah yes. Those were the days.

By the end of the marathon session, which Kea's always-sober backbrain labeled as mental coitus interruptus, Richards had a job. The amount, terms, and exact definition of which were undefined. 'You know,' Austin went on, still in that nasal tone and collegiate slang that Kea had almost forgotten, 'we'll let the suits finagle everything after the decimal.'

That wasn't exactly how it worked. Two mornings later, Kea showed up at Bargeta Corporate, ready to work. The press, mysteriously tipped the wink, arrived about an hour later for the announcement and a press conference. The negotiations began. They were handled by the same legals who had gotten Kea the sizable advance on his memoirs. Kea had told them to shoot for the stars, and they did. One of the Bargeta Ltd. negotiators had gone, in outrage, to Austin's office. Bargeta wasn't interested in tiddly little numbers and clauses. Make the damned deal. This man is my friend. Besides, he said, after a pause, the media's been talking about how we stole a march on everyone getting him to work for us. Do you want to be the one to say that Bargeta could not afford the universe's biggest hero? Do you? I certainly won't. He stared at the negotiator. The negotiator returned to his office, contacted Richards's attorneys, closed the deal, and sent out his résumé.

At first, Austin and Kea traveled together a lot. Austin never got tired of saying that it was just like the old days, and Kea never missed a chance to agree with him. It was going very well, Kea thought after half a year. He was meeting the real movers and shakers.

Plus, he had been able to offer a few real suggestions to Bargeta. Suggestions that were obvious to anyone who didn't live with a solid gold suppository up his bum. Suggestions that'd made Bargeta Ltd. a few million credits. Bargeta was starting to think that he'd made a real bargain adding Kea to his staff – and boasted to his mate that he had always been able to fit the right person for the right peg, and he had seen the worth in Richards years and years ago, back as far as Cal Tech. Now it was time for the next stage. A good swindler always salts the mine with a little real gold. Gold, or whatever valuable the mark will easily recognize. Cal Tech was the salt this time.

Kea hunted down the most respected, most recondite professor on the campus. A double Nobelist. Kea had conned his way into one of the woman's seminars when he was a freshman, and suffered mightily. Dr Feehely remembered Richards. What had he been doing since he'd taken her class? Well, she hoped. She remembered him as not being gifted in theory, but showing great practical promise. Was he well? Was he happy? Had he perhaps achieved some post at a university somewhere? Kea, trying to keep from laughing, came up with some plausible story about labwork and study. The reason he had wanted to consult with this woman, whose mark had been made in microanalysis, was that someone had presented Kea with a particle concept. He did not understand anything on the fiche, and, remembering Dr Feehely, had sought her out. Could she take a few minutes? And would she mind if Richards recorded her?

She normally did not take consulting jobs . . . but for an old student . . . Feehely scanned the fiche. Raised eyebrows. Snorted. Raised eyebrows. Snorted. Raised eyebrows, and shut off the reader. 'If this particle existed,' she said, 'it would be quite interesting. Your friend did not present an adequate synth, and the only way I could see this model existing mathematically is if one posited it were some sort of nonconventional matter. I would hate to use a popular term such as "anti-matter," because that would be a misnomer.'

'How would this particle . . . if it could exist, work as a tappable source of energy?'

Eyebrows. Snort. The doctor chose her words. 'Again, this is an incorrectness. But I will take an analogy from ancient history. Assuming – and this is also an impossibility – this particle could be handled safely, the effect would be that of using nitroglycerine . . . you know what nitroglycerine was?'

'No. But I'll learn.'

'As I said, using nitroglycerine as fuel in an internal-combustion engine. An enormous amount of energy, but one that the engine could never handle. Of course, all this is mere amusement. Fairly puerile, I might add. Such a particle could not exist in any sane universe.'

'Thank you, Doctor. I have won my bet. Would you mind giving me the mathematics on that?'

'Well . . . all right. But I am afraid I will have to charge you for that, so I hope your bet is of a consequential nature. Perhaps . . . a lunch?'

The description, of course, was an abstract of the AM2 particle. Kea had laboriously taught himself how to write the description over the last six months. And Kea knew of an engine that could handle that power. Stardrive. Again, all he lacked was a 'handle.' And the bet *was* of a consequential nature: The Universe.

Richards would have liked to have bought Dr Feehely more than a meal. Hell, he would have purchased a restaurant, dedicated to making only Feehely's favorite meals and delivering them to her study for the rest of her life. But he didn't – he bought her lunch at the faculty dining room. And he could reward her no further. When business progressed further, any link with Richards or AM2 could well be lethal to her. And beyond that, she could be in even greater danger – from Kea himself. Kea Richards knew once he came close to achieving power for himself, some beings would have to die. Another saying he took as gospel: Three beings can keep a secret, if two of them are dead . . .

With the doctor's mathematics in hand and a copy of his original abstract, he sought out Austin. He told him he had something of the greatest importance to show him. But privately. This was far, far too big. He began with a story. The story of how, just before catastrophe struck on the *Destiny I*, Dr Fazlur had been analyzing some observed phenomena taken off a darkstar they'd made close passage by. And he had been coming up with some remarkable equations. Equations that suggested a certain substance could be synthesized. A substance a bit like something he had observed off that pulsar. If his suggestions were correct, the substance could be synthesized, and modified into . . .

At that point, he gave Austin Dr Feehely's equations. He scanned the first page on the screen, frowning. 'Kea, old sock,' he protested. 'You, better than anyone, know how easily I parse numbers. Can't you give it to me straight?'

'I just wanted to make sure you'd believe me. Because otherwise you'd think I was completely gonkers.' Kea had found it useful to sometimes use the old Cal Tech slang that Austin was so fond of. Then he played the abstract. Austin sat in silence, thinking. Then he managed an 'Oh.'

Kea watched closely – did he really track?

After a moment, Bargeta said, in a small voice, 'If this particle, this substance, you know, could be synthesized . . . Oh. Kea, I see why you sought me out. I see why you were so mysterioso about some things that you planned to develop. You know, Kea, I feel like . . . who was that person? Speechless on a peak in Darien? Although what could be so impressive about Connecticut, I've never known. This is very big, Kea. Very, very big.

'I . . . I could be Rutherford. Better. I could be a Dr McLean. Bigger than him, even, because this is more than just dinky little antigravity. This is everything. Stardrive first, then I am sure there will be some way to modify the substance to power anything. Everything. I feel like the first man who pumped gasoline out of the ground, whatever his name was. Oh my. Kea, this is not some kind of wicked joke, is it?'

It took almost a week of vacillating – this was too big, too important, it couldn't happen, there would have to be some government notification, perhaps a consortium of transport corporations, we could at least mount a feasibility study, actually, this would make us all richer than whoever that old Greek was, are you sure, Kea, that we should be doing something, I mean, you know, there are things that man simply wasn't meant to know, although I don't have much truck with tract-thumpers, and Christ, you know they say that genius deteriorates generation by generation, and this would certainly prove that a canard, you know, I'd be thought bigger than Father, bigger even than the first Austin, the one I'm named after, you know, the one who started this company . . .

Finally, 'We'll do it.'

A special team of lawyers and accountants were set up. They were to be firmly under Kea's direction. As was the lab he would build under supersecrecy. This might be expensive, Kea warned. Austin was willing to commit up to 10 percent of Bargeta Ltd.'s pretax resources per annum. The lab was built and top-line scientists hired for the project. Deep-space test and research ships were planned. Everyone in the corporate world knew Bargeta Ltd. was R&Ding something spectacular. Fortunately – for Kea's purposes – Austin had such a reputation as a lightweight the project was an instant joke, thought of in scientific slang as an edsel, whatever that might've been. Kea told no one why he had dubbed the operation Project Suk.

All of the hardware, and all of the personnel, were real. But it was a complete tissue. Kea knew AM2 could never be synthesized – or if it could, it would be even more gawdawfully expensive than the present fuel for stardrive. He caught himself. Never say never, he thought. Anti-Matter Two couldn't be synthesized at this moment in history, nor, most likely, at any other. Leave it at that. Besides, who would bother – once we find a way to shield the particles, which will also mean that we'll have a way to shield mining/processing ships, AM2 would be dirtcheap. For me, at least, he thought.

There were three reasons for this elaborate charade. First, it would provide an acceptable screen for where the substance really came from one of these years. Not that important. Second, it would provide exploration ships, who were sent out with explicit instructions. The instructions were known but to those crews. They would search for an element that could be used, modified to create this shielding, which Kea had dubbed X. The exploration reports were also carefully studied, in the event they could produce a line of thought that would justify research that might lead to the synthesis of this shielding.

Yet another benefit Project Suk provided was a very quiet recruiting station. Richards sought out the best researchers on the project, which meant some of the best workers mankind could produce. The best – with two additional requirements. The first was that each person was either unattached, their family could travel with them, or they were estranged from any relatives. And the second was that each of them had some secret. An unpunished crime. Their sexual habits. Unpopular political or social theories in their home provinces/planets. Alk. Drugs. Or, best of all, that they were simply misanthropic. These people, if Richards's efforts produced anything, would be used to finish the development of AM2. Richards bought First Base on Deimos for a lab. He told Austin this was where the core research for the X particle would be conducted. There would be no possibility of leaks to business rivals – because no one except cleared Bargeta personnel would be allowed on Deimos, and all of the ancillary laboratories would be limited to a segment of the overall problem.

Finally, and most importantly, Operation Suk was Kea's cash cow. Of course there were comptrollers and such. But the day an experienced spaceship engineer couldn't steal the company's shirt, while it yet thought it was wearing a formal, was the day the sun would die. Especially when Operation Suk was run in such extreme secrecy.

Six years passed. Kea was, as one of his better-liked, less-reputable, and richer mining-ship friends put it, busier'n a onelegged man at a butt-kicking contest. Colorful, but accurate.

First, there was Operation Suk to run. Since he was the only one who really knew what the project was supposed to produce, he was required to go through all lab and operational summaries each reporting period and, frequently, call for the raw data. It gave him the reputation of being a very hands-on manager, as well as someone who was grudgingly respected because you couldn't slip one past *him*. But respect did not replace enough sleep, or personal relaxation.

Second, he was busy 'helping' Austin run Bargeta Ltd. In fact – and Kea made sure that all of the people he was meeting found this out, subtly – he was running the dynasty. Austin was now regarded as even more of a numbnuts, to one level of the work force, and a dilettante, to their superiors. And Kea encouraged Austin to get out more. Travel. Get away from the job. Stay fresh. Stay active. If you bury yourself with all this little crud like I'm doing, who's going to make sure we don't stumble into a manhole?

He was careful to let Austin make the decisions, and let him make some that were very poor without protest. Kea could have done a more exact job of stage-managing, but he knew just how sensitive and paranoiac the incompetent were. The last thing he needed was to be fired. Except, at his level, being canned would be phrased as 'resigned to pursue exciting interests of a personal nature.'

He also traveled extensively incognito. There were people he needed to meet and industries to research that had nothing to do with Bargeta Ltd. Sometimes he traveled under a false name, with false papers. One of his favorites was H. E. Raschid, in tribute to Burton and Scheherazade. Now and again people grinned – and Richards made a mental note of the person as worth cultivation.

His new contacts and friends extended far beyond the business world. Politicians. Some people who had interesting trades, some of them quite beyond the law. He spent money lavishly, but cannily. He was always willing to contribute to a pol's coffers, without regard to the man or woman's party. Eventually he controlled a significant number of Ganymede's traditionally available estates general. He also owned about a quarter of the moon itself. The estate he had constructed was more a small, ultra-secure industrial park than the sprawling demesne of a rich man.

Which is just what Kea was now. Not only was he lavishly paid by Bargeta, with his own keys to the vault with Project Suk, but his new friends offered tips and suggestions. Kea played the market in every legal and illegal manner possible, so long as it was fairly subtle. Eventually there might be an investigation and an accounting – but when or if that day came, he would either be dead, have disappeared, or have made himself beyond the law.

Then came the breakthrough, a few months into the new century. An expedition returned. Not from the stars – Kea had chanced gross amounts of Bargeta's capital to fund two stardrive expeditions – but from the Solar System's backyard. Just beyond Pluto, just beyond the shatter that had once been thought to be an eleventh planet of the system. A meteorite, almost a quarter kilometer in diameter, had been found, tested, and brought back. The ships' captain reported more drifting bodies out there that spectroed as being the same matter.

It was the X material. Nonreactive to anything that the Bargeta labs could come up with. Hard to work, but not impossible. It would not retain radiation or anything else it was bombarded with. It even failed to react to a small bit of laboratory-produced 'conventional' anti-matter.

It had a melting point high enough on the Kelvin scale to be suitable for ship armor, but low enough to be workable in a high-tech foundry.

Sensing victory, and allowing himself a flash of arrogance, Richards named the X substance. Imperium X. And he ordered a certain, very unusual ship to be moved from its parking orbit around Mars to the secret lab on Deimos. There it was given a plating from bow to stern, just a few molecules thick, of the new element. The ship was that old starship he'd seen drifting in a junkyard above Mars's polar regions years ago, which he'd purchased earlier and had modified in several ways, among them so one man and several computers could run it. It was already fueled – a good segment of Project Suk's resources had gone just to power the ship. Now for the Alva Sector, the discontinuity, and the final test.

The company announced Richards was finally going to take some time off. Kea told Austin that he would be absent for a minimum of three Earth-months. He was going somewhere, somewhere he wouldn't even tell his best friend about. Just as Austin had told him to do, a year or so ago.

'I did?'

'You did. We were fairly gassed at the time. Remember? Hey, you're the one who forgets nothing, right?'

Austin didn't laugh. Lately he had been wondering about Kea. He seemed . . . sometimes . . . as if he were setting his own course. Or, at least, behaving as if Bargeta's knowledge of the dynasty weren't that important. Perhaps, he thought, he'd have to talk to Kea. He *was* his friend, of course. But Austin remembered Mars, and remembered his father's reminder that the lesson of proper place must be learned and relearned, taught and retaught. There was no such thing as an irreplaceable man at Bargeta Ltd. That applied even to family members – Austin had sacked a couple of cousins just this year. No one was that vital – except, of course, Austin himself.

Two days before his planned disappearance, Richards was working out – on his private, single-station, no-links computer – the erratic series of orbits he would take to the Alva Sector. He was buzzed. His receptionist – Kea quite deliberately hired men or women for their competency and, preferably, homeliness, in deliberate contrast to Austin's office harem – said he had a visitor. She refused to announce herself. What should the receptionist do?

As she spoke, appearing to be puzzled, she kicked a pickup under her desk in the outer chamber, and a screen lit up, as instructed. This would not be the first person who preferred not to give a name to arrive at the boss's sanctum. Kea stared at the image. He was quite proud that he took less than two seconds, by his count, before he said, in a clear, normal voice, 'Ah yes. Show her in.'

Tamara. Still lovely. She wore a business suit that appeared to be styled for a man – once again, androgyny was the in cycle – but with a silken-looking blouse underneath, a blouse whose colors shifted and changed as sunlight and shadow crossed it. Under the suit, she would have nothing on, Kea knew. She still had that look. You may take me, any way you wish. If you can. He swam weightless for an instant. But he did not show it. He would be damned if he did.

He was delighted to see her. Embraced Tamara like a long-fondly-thought-of friend. He refused to let his mind tell him he felt her erecting nipples under the coat against his chest. Hold all calls. A drink. He seated her on his office couch, and sat close to her. But not that close. He had dreamed of seeing her again, all these years, he said. What was she doing in town? Recovering, Tamara said, her voice still sending chills, chills to match the time she'd showed him what could be done with nothing more than a few ice cubes and a leather strap. Recovering from what?

'My husband and I . . . are no more.' She shrugged. 'He's obsessed with his racing, although he certainly hasn't won anything of late. Boys and their toys, and that. I guess he never grew, and I did.'

Well. Sorry, and that.

'I've been thinking about you a lot. For a lot of years. And I thought . . .' She stopped, waiting for Kea to pick up on the signal.

Richards waited, his expression patient, interested. Perhaps this old, respected friend was about to present an entirely new idea? Tamara tried again.

'You know, there are a *lot* of things I remember very, very well. Fireplaces. Silk. Laughing a lot. A hard-to-explain windburn.'

She forced a giggle, and Kea frowned for a moment, then visibly 'remembered' the circumstances. Tamara's brows furrowed for an instant. This was not going as she'd planned . . .

'But mostly, I remember mistakes. Especially one.'

'Yes. I do, too.'

'I think,' Tamara said, her eyes now humbly down, on her hands clasped in her lap, 'that all I can say is that I was a little shit in those days. And it took me a while to grow up. And that you'll never know how sorry I am, and how much I want to make it up to you.'

She managed a tear. Kea found her a handkerchief. He shrugged. 'Neither one of us,' he said, 'was exactly an adult in those days. One mistake balances another.'

Tamara started to say something, then stopped. She puzzled, unsure of what Kea had meant by his last. Then she went on. 'At least,' she said, 'Austin wasn't as stupid as I was. So it's not like you vanished, and it's not like life only gives you . . . I mean, we're in the real world. And people get a second chance, don't they?'

He took her in his arms. Kissed her. Not in a brotherly manner – but not with any marked passion. 'Of course they do. And . . . you know, I've never forgotten you.'

Kea stood and gently lifted her with a genteel hand under the elbow. 'Now we have the time to get to know each other properly. Look. As soon as I'm back from this . . . business trip, I'll give you a call. Maybe have dinner or something. We have a *lot* to talk about.'

He walked back to his desk. Tamara stared at him. She painted a smile across her face. He responded. She slowly went to the outer door, and opened it. She looked back at him. He was still smiling. Tamara stepped outside, and the door hissed closed. Just before it shut, and just before the insulation cut sound, Kea laughed.

Loudly. A harsh, unrelenting laugh. A Martian laugh. Then he forgot her.

Kea Richards vanished from man's haunts. He and the starship he had never bothered to name. He zigged his way across the galaxy toward the Alva Cluster. He tracked toward the discontinuity. Against interstellar blackness, he saw once again the sparklers flashing, an independence fireworks against the moonless night as tiny bits of normal matter collided with AM2 particles.

He set his course. Through the discontinuity, and into that other universe, the universe of black and all colors. He navigated, at quarter-drive, by the blind-flying system he had developed after years of hard thought, a sophisticated evolution of the navigational system Murph and Doctor Fazlur had improvised.

He had a prox detector mounted in the ship's nose. It signaled. He was closing on some interstellar debris. Perhaps no more than half a meter in size. But it would be Anti-Matter Two, more than enough to shatter this tiny ship he was aboard. He killed stardrive, went to secondary Yukawa drive, then cut all power, braked, and let inertia close him on the chunk of Anti-Matter Two.

He looked at another instrument and felt hope. This registered any object impacting on the ship's skin and was sensitive enough to go off if an Earth raindrop landed on it, when the ship was parked. Or less, actually. The readout showed his starship had been hit by particles after entering this mad universe. AM2 particles. With no adverse effect to the ship.

The prox detector's signaling was a continuous *bong*ing. Richards moved to another workstation. He fitted his hands into waldos and concentrated on instruments. From a bay just below the ship's nose, a probe extended. A claw. Another modification of Kea's. A scoop. Plated with Imperium X. He worked for long minutes with the unfamiliar controls. Sweat spattered on the controls in front of him. If he had been wrong, not only would all these years have been wasted, but he would be very dead as well, if Imperium X was not the perfect shield he had thought it to be, and the AM2 detonated in its beyond-nuclear hell.

The probe's instruments said the chunk was inside the claw. Eyes involuntarily closed, brain expecting mindshatter explosion, he closed the waldos. And again, nothing happened.

He was the proud possessor of a chunk of Anti-Matter Two. He moved the long arm back inside the ship and the bay hatches closed. The inside of the bay was also plated with Imperium X. He touched controls, and the ship went to lightspeed, on an orbit out of the discontinuity. This was the moment of real victory. Right now, even before the research, development, mining, and rest, Kea Richards had just made himself lord of the universe.

The world ended less than a year later, in two cataclysms. The catastrophes occurred a month apart. The first bannered every liviecast throughout the Solar System and to the scatter of settled worlds beyond. Deimos had blown up. The moon was now a blasted irregular asteroid like Phobos. An impossibility. Moons do not self-destruct. Deimos was uninhabited, except for three or four caretakers at the old First Base. More facts surfaced. In fact, Deimos had been well-populated. Several hundred men and women had been working in a secret complex of laboratories around the old First Base. The development belonged to Bargeta Industries. The screamers grew larger. Five – no, six – no, four hundred and fifty beings had vanished. Someone must pay.

The livie and newscasters stalked Bargeta Ltd. headquarters. Its CEO, a white and shaken man, stumbled through a prepared statement. Yes, the laboratory was a project center for his corporation. No, he would not say what it had been developing, except that it pertained to spaceship development. No, Austin did not know what happened. Bargeta scientific investigators were already trying to determine the cause of the disaster. No . . . no further comment. The 'casters found Kea Richards. He had no statement. No ideas. And absolutely no comment.

'What the blazes happened?' Bargeta screamed.

'I don't know,' Richards said. 'I had a com two E-days before, from Dr Masterson, the director. He said that one of the exploratory teams had a new and fascinating lead, but it was so out of the ordinary he declined to be specific, for fear of embarrassment until further tests were made. Maybe something went wrong with those tests.'

'Christ,' Austin moaned. 'All those people. The best scientists we could find. It wasn't like they were worker bees or anything. My God, my God. Do you realize what they're going to say at the annual meeting? How am I going to explain this to the stockholders?' Kea didn't know.

The second disaster was internal. Auditors had prepared a final report on Operation Suk. It was like some kind of financial black hole, Austin thought as he scanned the fiche. Thirty-eight percent of all convertible assets of Bargeta Ltd. – not just the transport company, but some of the holding company's assets as well – had vanished into the project. Worse was the classified scientific report attached – it appeared that the attempts to synthesize Kea's X substance had not only failed, and in the failing destroyed Deimos, but the entire idea had been proven absolutely fallacious. The Philosopher's Stone. A pollution-free oxygen-combinant combustion engine. Cold fusion. Bargeta was . . . if not bankrupt, lurching toward it. The huge conglomerate was broken now. It would be lucky to survive two more fiscal years, unless some kind of miracle happened, a miracle no one could see on any horizon.

Austin scrolled through the last page, and went looking for Kea. He found him in his office. The chamber was stripped bare. Travel boxes were stacked in one corner.

'What—'

Kea indicated an envelope, hand-addressed to Austin, on his desk. Bargeta read it. It was Richards's resignation. 'All this,' Kea said, in what appeared to be a shell-shocked monotone, 'was my fault. I . . . I was wrong. No gold, no rainbow.'

Bargeta looked for words and didn't find any. Kea started to say something, but merely put his hand on Austin's shoulder. Then he left.

Bargeta walked to the window and stared out and down the two hundred stories to Madison Avenue. The world had just ended for him, for his family, and for Bargeta Ltd. What next? What now?

Next was Bargeta and allied stocks plummeting even before the emergency stockholders meeting was called. Somebody had leaked the report to the Street – and Wall Street had divisions on every continent and planet. Investigators later found someone had also dumped Bargeta stock a day or so before the report had been released internally by the audit department. They could never determine just who'd been the original holder of the stock, since the certificates had traveled through a dizzying number of hands before being sold.

Kea Richards was gone, abandoning his Earth estates, his friends, his women, and his possessions. It was odd, and showed a previously unknown Spartan side, that in fact he didn't own that much. His mansions were only half-furnished, the half that someone on the outside might happen on. Or else they were leased furnished. The same with his yacht and his gravcars.

Austin Bargeta stammered through the emergency meeting. The corporate shareholders were as shocked after they had read the report as Austin had been. They adjourned, to meet again on the morrow. Austin was not there for the meeting. Immediately after the adjournment, he had taken a pistol from his private wallsafe. It was an antique 13mm caseless automatic, firing gunpowder-charged rounds, that had been in the family since the beginning. He had recently had shells custom-made. Now he pulled the slide back, and let it go forward, chambering a round. Turned the large pistol awkwardly, held it against his temple, thought at least the Bargetas had some honor, and pressed the trigger. The bullet blew most of the frontal half of his brain away. Unfortunately, it did not turn him into a corpse. Austin Bargeta, blind, mute, brain capable of only providing motor responses, lived on.

Kea Richards, from his self-exile on Ganymede, sent a shocked com. Could he help? He had some personal credits, and if they could be used to keep Austin from becoming a public ward, the family had but to ask. The family declined. Bankrupt they might have been ·– but they were not reduced to charity. Kea felt a flicker of regret – the bastard should have been a better shot.

Kea was revenged. As, he felt, were many, many others. His unknown mother, driven to the horrors of a longliner. His father and grandmother and the other citizens of Hilo, drowned because most likely whichever fat-cat company had been supposed to maintain the tidal barriers had cut corners on maintenance to fatten their coffers. Leong Suk, who had never had a chance to know anything but poverty, from her native Korea to Maui. Hell, even that poor sad bastard Tompkins, who surely deserved better than to spend his life as a crackpot down a filthy alley. All the bluecollars he had grown and lived with, who sweated, worked, and died, so that people named Bargeta could have trimarans on Mars. The spacemen who killed themselves with alk or died in industrial 'accidents' because shipline owners had little interest in safety standards beyond the letter of the law. The Bargetas and their gutted conglomerate were on the first. There would be more. Many more.

Kea was ready to build his 'weapons' for the takeover. Only one man had died when Deimos blew up. He was one of the blasters Richards had hired from Mars's underworld, a demo expert who evidently hadn't been as expert as he had bragged. All the others, scientists, machinists, support people, and their mates, had been evacked days earlier to Ganymede, where the real task would begin. Kea Richards was ready for his 'wilderness years.'

Chapter Twenty-Five

Ganymede, A.D. 2202

Kea had given himself twenty years to reach a throne – a throne that he would have to create. But it didn't take him that long – everything went to lightspeed. Some of the acceleration was deliberate. Richards knew he had only so much time to establish a completely secure physical, moral, and economic stronghold before They would try to take it away from him. The 'They' would include not just business tycoons and supercorporations, but planetary governments as well. So he moved very fast. What little personal life and recreational time he'd had as Bargeta's troubleshooter appeared like a lifetime of idle luxury now.

At first, it seemed to everyone Kea Richards really had retired to piddle about on his vast Ganymede estates with scientific toys. What actually happened was that his starship was modified to accept AM2 for fuel. The 'fuel tank' was no bigger than Richards's torso and was made of Imperium X, as were the feed lines and chambers in the engine itself. There had been a seemingly insur-mountable problem keeping the engine lubricant from ever contacting Anti-Matter Two, but eventually the problem had been solved.

When all ground tests were completed satisfactorily, Richards and Dr Masterson quietly boarded ship. Overhead, filling the sky, was the reddish bulk of Jupiter. Kea lifted the ship on McLean power, then went to Yukawa drive. Offworld, he checked the ship's ultrasensitive receptors. The ship was not being monitored. And then the ship went to stardrive. AM2 stardrive.

Nothing spectacular happened. Stardrive was stardrive was

hyperspace was boring. Nothing was exciting about this test flight – except that the drive-activation control was closed, and drive automatically cut before Richards could take his hand from it. Arcturus's red-yellow bulk and its twelve worlds hung onscreen. Three other star systems were reached that E-night. And on return to Ganymede the fuel 'tank' appeared to be as 'full' as on departure.

Cost? Not calculable. The fuel was a bit of the small chunk 'mined' by Kea beyond the Alva Sector. There was still three quarters of the debris left, held in an Imperium X vault on Ganymede. Now the dream was a reality. The ship was further modified, its hold gutted and lined with Imperium X.

Again, Kea vanished. Three E-months later he returned with a full cargo of AM2. That was enough Anti-Matter Two to provide energy, he calculated, for the entire career of every spaceship ever built, with enough left over – but this was on fairly shaky mathematics – to run all of Mars's power plants for three E-years. Sooner or later Kea knew he would have to build roboticized mining ships, everything in them either made of or plated with Imperium X, move them through the discontinuity into the other universe, and set them to work. He would also have to come up with some kind of long-distance on/off switch, a com whose signals would have to be at least as eccentrically targeted as Richards's chosen orbits to the Alva Sector.

Kea had studied, with some amusement, the attempts of the so-called oil sheikhs to use their control of the petroleum resource to reshape the culture of Earth. Perhaps admirable in its appalling egocentricity, the plan had of course failed in unreality, greed, and hypocrisy. If Kea had to play that card, however, he was determined it would be the highest of trumps. But the on/off power switch could wait. Now it was time to start rattling some cages.

Kea stepped out of retirement and announced plans to build luxury ships – spaceyachts, really – and run them from Earth to Mars as a first-class service. At a rumored price three times that of conventional passage. There was some quiet scoffing in the resorts, bars, and clubs catering to the gigawealthy. Nice thought, but there weren't that many superrich fools. Not enough to support Kea's scheme. Oh well. He would go bankrupt, and come looking to them for a position, which any of them would be happy to provide.

The ships were built. They looked to be more medium-size

freighters than luxury carriers. And back of Barrier Thirty-three, some compartments were left empty. Modifications would be made on Ganymede. Kea had some odd ideas of his own, which would be made at the small port on his estates. On Ganymede, the ships were fitted with stardrive engines. Fueled. And crewed.

Since no one gave a diddly damn about spacemen, no one had noticed that recruiters had been filtering through spaceports. Looking for the best, those who hadn't lost their illusions and those who looked to the stars as a challenge, not a swamper's scut job. Those who passed the amazingly stringent tests were brought to Ganymede and trained. Surprisingly, about 15 percent were paid off and regretfully returned to their home worlds – psychologists discovered that even a spaceman might be afraid of the stars beyond the 'known' worlds. Eventually the men and women were shown the new ships. Taught to navigate, pilot, and service them. And sent out. To the stars. Looking. For valuables. And for extraterrestrials.

Two years after Kea had launched the first starship, *seven* intelligent – human or near-human equivalent as a minimum – extraterrestrial races had been found. Three of them were evolved enough to have interplanetary travel. None had stardrive. They would. On Kea Richards's terms.

Kea's espionage reported, a little worriedly, that there were some amazing rumors about what Richards was doing out on Ganymede. Kea sighed – the secret couldn't have been kept forever. Too many people on Ganymede, in spite of precautions, had seen starships lift from Richards's port and simply vanish. And spacemen/women tell bar tales. It was time for the next stage.

A new corporation was chartered in the no-questions-asked, flag/ bank-of-convenience Province of Livonia. Clive, Anon. The charter was carefully written to be so vague that the new company could do anything from painting itself blue and dancing widdershins to terraforming the sun. Livonia's laws being what they were, the only person whose name appeared on the charter was a local, one Yaakob Courland, as Livonian law required. He was paid, in cash, for the use of his name when the papers were filed, and promptly forgot about the event, since it was the fifth set of papers he had signed that day. But that was the last time the company was anonymous.

Earth vid/livie crews were asked if they would be interested in attending a press conference, in which Kea Richards would make a major announcement. It was to be held at New York's near-abandoned Long Island spaceport, at a certain time. Another conference was announced. On Mars, at Capen City's port. Kea Richards would appear, to make a major announcement. Both conferences were on the same day, two E-hours apart. No one noticed the apparent error. Both conferences were moderately well attended – although not one-tenth as many journalists actually showed up as later claimed to have been present.

Because Kea *did* attend both events. In fact, having gotten lucky with takeoff clearance, he had to waste almost a full E-hour on the ground at Capen City, waiting for the press. His announcement was simple. His research company had made certain major improvements in the stardrive engine, improvements which, attorneys said, in fact, qualified the engine as an entirely new invention. Some thousand patents were being filed in The Hague, on Mars, and on Earth. Any infringement on these patents, once they were granted, would be met with the most severe legal penalties. Kea figured the crockola of Superengine would satisfactorily murk up the cesspool for a while, anyway.

On Mars, after he had made his announcement, some fifteen starships that had been waiting offworld landed. Each of them carried a cargo like man had never seen before. Unknown minerals. Gemstones. Sealed 'plants' from beyond the stars. In two cases, extraterrestrials landed with the humans, ETs previously unknown.

Kea offered man the stars. But at a price. The new, improved engines would *not* be offered for sale, nor would they be licensed. All transport with the new engines would be the sole province of the Clive, Anon., starships. The little corner of creation man thought of as his universe went insane. And everyone went after Kea Richards.

He retired to Ganymede and went deep into his bunker. Quite literally – he'd had many levels excavated below his mansion. He could take anything up to and including a nuke with zero damage – at least to himself and his immediate staffers. And he watched the fun. Everyone wanted to ship aboard his craft. There was a monstrous waiting list, a waiting list that almost made it practical to ship or travel conventionally. Almost, but not quite. And Richards had set his rates to be exactly what they should be – he allowed a 30 percent markup for profit and, for the moment, another 20 percent for risk.

His fellow capitalists were frothing, lawyers charging back and forth from court to suite to corporate headquarters. The situation was quite simple – Richards had just announced the steamship to his friends, who were sitting, paddles in hand, on their floating logs. This sounded like Kea Richards had a monopoly. Incredibly illegal. Civil and criminal charges were made.

Richards, through his lawyers, had but one standard announcement. He was innocent. But he firmly believed in justice, and had full faith in the wisdom of the courts. Unfortunately, though, he had been advised that he would have to cease shipping to any city, province, country, or world where such charges pended.

That immediately brought battalions of new heavyweights onscene, filing *amicus curiae* briefs on behalf of Clive, Anon. Their companies were as varied as mankind's choice of trades, but all of them had one thing in common – they wanted/needed to be able to ship/receive something from Point A to Point B in less than a lifetime. The shipping companies, and their hastily if massive filings, vanished.

Still heavier guns rolled up. Governments themselves. Kea Richards was seen as a Threat. He should share this miracle engine with everyone, for the Good of Mankind. Richards declined. Mankind would benefit quite well, thank you, through Clive, Anon. Orders were issued for his arrest. One came from the tiny province of Rus, the other from Sinaloa, both traditional places where influence and credit could purchase anything. Kea's lawyers informed the courts that under no circumstances, being in fear of his life, would Kea surrender to these warrants.

Very well, he would be arrested on Ganymede and extradited. Armed forces would be provided by the as-yet-unnamed men who'd charged Kea with crimes. The furies after Kea next discovered that all the credits invested in Ganymede's politicians had been well spent. The pols were honest – that is, they stayed bought – and Richards remained free and unextraditable. 'Trapped,' at least for the moment, on Ganymede. But what of it – he had access to any ship he wanted and any destination that could be navigated. With galaxies opening in front of him, Kea imagined he could live without caviar or cabrito for a spell.

Eminent domain was suggested next. His ships would be seized. It was pointed out it might be a little difficult to 'stop' a spacecraft that would outperform, at quarter-drive, any conventional starship. And how, exactly, did any government propose to do this, in deep space? Eventually even the bureaucrats were convinced that Halt in the Name of the Law was a little ludicrous between planets, let alone between stars. It was rumored someone had laboriously defined inertia to them.

Government ships could be armed, came the bumble. That brought a stinging release from Richards's headquarters. First, all basic interplanetary treaties had banned military development in space. Second, and more to the point, Kea's ships were armed. This was a fact – Kea had purchased some tiny lunar lighters, given them AM2 stardrive, put in a prox detonator in the nose next to a warhead – also AM2, of course – and adapted a standard commercial robot piloting system to the lighters. Each starship had been given a missile. Now each looked like a chubby shark with a remora. The ships themselves were also equipped with remote-controlled chainguns mounted inside each ship's cargo port.

Very well, the pols floundered. His ships would be arrested – seized for an Admiralty court – when they made planetfall. Kea's main lawyer announced quite coolly that, first, if Clive, Anon., became aware of any warrant being issued, the firm's craft would blacklist the city, province, etc., as before. If force was used, that would be regrettable. Any such country attempting this deviousness would be considered as beyond the law. No better than a corsair nation. And not only would charges be filed in the still-extant if ludicrous World Court, but force would be met with force. The uneasy peace continued. It was prolonged by the rumor – never verified – that all of the new starships were booby-trapped, so that any intrusion beyond Barrier Thirty-three would be a disaster.

Evidently there were disbelievers. Because, quite suddenly, as one of Richards's ships was clearing for lift from Ixion Port – Alpha Centauri's most developed world – the ship, most of the port, and some of the city's industrial section vanished in hellflame. Richards's enemies seized on this – the new engines were unsafe, and should be banned, and Richards himself prosecuted. Kea was worried – and then an amateur shipfreak surfaced with an amazing audio track. He had been recording ship–tower chatter, and, quite clearly, any listener could hear the takeoff drone being interrupted by shouts, the clanging of a hatchway out of crewspace, gunfire, and then silence. The critics were not only answered, but somewhat discredited. But that was too close for Kea.

He had been carefully winnowing through the personnel roster of his retained spookshop, and hiring away the absolutely loyal, and those who were qualified in certain irregular areas. The truehearts he used for personal and estate security. The others made up a very specialized hunter-killer team. They went looking for whoever had hired the hijackers. And they found them – the woman and her son who headed SpaceWays/Galiot. Somehow a commercial gravlighter went out of control and crashed into a mansion on a tiny, private Aegean island. Without any surviving heirs, SpaceWays went into receivership until the situation could be sorted out. Just to make sure that the robber barons and their thugs got the message, Kea hired more security people. These had a new task – to baby-sit, unobtrusively, his spacemen. Anyone interfering with one of his crew members, whether it was pumping for info in a barroom or trying a backalley snatch for interrogation, was intercepted and 'handled roughly.'

Kea bought more shipyards and commissioned more ships, and they went out to the stars. For deployment around the worlds of man, he had a different class of ship built. These were AM2 warships, missile/rocket/laser/chaingun – armed patrol craft, which escorted the liners and freighters safely away from the dangerous – i.e. inhabited – worlds. Governments may have been banned from building warships, but no one had mentioned private enterprise, for the simple reason that before AM2 drive, a spaceship/starship built for combat was absurdly wasteful. Kea was spending a fair amount of his time thinking about weaponry. One of his technicians, a Robert Willy, had pointed out that there was no particular reason a tiny particle of AM2 could not be given a shroud of Imperium X and made into an explosive bullet, if the shielding was cast with a deliberate, high-impact-sensitive fault. He also believed that, if this 'bullet' was made small enough, and the latest generation of hyper-powerful portable lasers was used, that the AM2 bullet could not be 'fired' by laser. Kea Richards, thinking grimly of Alfred Nobel, his invention that was intended for the benefit of all mankind, and the effective if terribly dangerous 'dynamite guns' that were produced, gave Willy his own research team and access to Anti-Matter Two.

The vids and the livies, reflecting public perceptions and feelings as the media have always done instead of creating it as too many fools believe, were beginning to banner Kea as a liberator. Greater than Edison, greater than Ford, greater than McLean, even. Kea knew they weren't even close, although the thought sounded like it came from a megalomaniac. They still didn't understand, any more than someone in the middle of massive change ever does, the total revolution that was going on. But they would.

Everything was running at full drive. Kea was worried, because he knew what would come next and wasn't sure that he would be able to block the next attempt to deny man the stars.

Perhaps the assault team had forgotten about Jupiter light and thought they would have complete night for their cover. Or perhaps they didn't care. But it was no more than three-quarters dark when they attacked, Jove hanging overhead like the largest color-streaked party light ever built. They were well-trained commandos and must have practiced on full-scale models or at the least livie-simulations of Richards's estate.

Alarms screamed, and Kea rolled out of the bed he had slumped into, exhausted, less than an hour before. Not awake, he stumbled to a closet and pulled on a dark coverall. Hanging nearby was an LBE harness with a pistol and ammo belt. A machine carbine dangled next to it. Wishing that he'd had more time, and Willy'd been able to perfect his AM2 weapon, he jacked a round into the carbine's chamber, tugged on zip-closure boots, and headed down the hall. The ground roiled beneath him, and Kea tumbled down. He didn't find out until later that was a small picketboat, under robot control, that had been sent smashing into one of his compound's perimeter labs as a diversion to attract emergency crews. Kea came up, ran on. Into one of the mansion's lobbies.

'Mr Richards! The bunker!' Security's watch commander was waving at him. Then a crash, and supposedly impact-proof plas and reinforcing alloy fell into the chamber. The officer spun, shouted, died, as two black-dressed men dropped into the room, weapons firing. One of them saw Richards, gun came up, recognized their target, the gun was knocked away, and they dove toward him. Kea held the trigger full back and three rounds on full auto/control shattered the pair. So they were under explicit orders, he thought. I'm not to be killed. That'll slow 'em down a little.

Richards's security men swarmed into the lobby. One of them flipped a blast grenade up, through where the skylight had been blown away. Another explosion, and screams. The hell with the bunker, Richards thought. If the bastards know enough about this mansion to hit close to my bedroom, they've probably got that targeted as well. Gunfire chattered from outside the main entrance and lasers flashed seen/never-seen red eye-memory. Shouts.

'Let's go,' he yelled, and ran toward the main door. Absurd, absurd, he thought. Are you leading from the front, or are you playing Roland? You are an engineer and maybe a back-alley brawler. You've never been a combat soldier, nor been much interested in being one, or even watching the livies that glorify their slaughter.

The mansion's main anteroom was a haze of smoke and gunfire. Kea watched his 'soldiers' – and most of them had been trained in one or another of the various armed forces of the Solar System – fire, cover, and maneuver forward. Amazing, he thought. Just like the vids. Just like the livies. Another thought came: Did the livies reflect reality, or are all of us aping what we've seen done by actors? Come on, man! You don't have time for this slok! There were four attackers left, crouched behind the solid planters, containing now-bullet-shattered ferns. More grenades rained – never liked the ferns anyway, and there'll sure be a redecorating bill after this, amazing how the mind can spin all these stupid things out – and the first wave was obliterated.

Kea's security may have been surprised by the first assault – but now their training and constant practice took over. Great doors that appeared to be part of the three-story walls slid open, and wheeled autocannons were rolled out. They were set up – as intended – behind those planters that had been designed to double as a firing point, and ammo drums slammed home.

Outside, on the vast reaches of the grounds, Kea counted three, no four, small ships. This was not a small-time operation, he realized. The second wave rose from cover and charged. The front of Kea's near-palace had been laid out with graceful, flowing, low, close-barred railings that swept the viewer's eye toward the splendor of the house itself. It was considered part of the magnificence that had made the house a prizewinner in architectural circles. In fact, the flowing walls had been drawn up by Kea himself, working with his head security man, and were intended to channel not the viewer's eye, but an attacker's charge.

The railings were just high enough to be hard to hurdle, and the bars were far enough apart so they offered neither cover nor concealment. Now, they worked as intended, channeling the attackers directly toward the main entrance. Directly into the killing zone of the autocannon.

Guns yammered again, and blasts fragmented the night, and men and women shouted and died. A wounded, bloodied man stumbled through the smoke, gun hanging down, and was shot down. He was the last. Without a pause, the autocannon were pushed out into the open, and opened up on the four spacecraft. Two of the ships blew apart, the other smoked menacingly, and the last gouted flames.

Kea's security split into three elements. One group took up a defensive perimeter around Kea, a second charged the ships, their task to make sure all the attackers were down. The third element quickly, skillfully, began searching the bodies and, after making sure the wounded were disarmed, dragging them toward a common collecting point. Kea watched, his mind suddenly dulled. After some time, his Head of Security approached. 'Sir, I have a report.'

'Go ahead.'

'There were at least seventy-three invaders, possibly more. We don't know how many were aboard the ship. Twelve are still alive.'

'Who are they?'

'No IDs on any of the bodies. The two that're talking claim they're indies, hired out of Pretoria by freelancers they'd worked with before. Neither of them know who's the original hire. Assuming that this *was* a for-hire hit, which I don't.'

'Keep looking. Will your two injured stand up to interrogation?'

'Negative, sir. Not now, maybe not ever. Those thirty-mill rounds tear hell out of everything.'

'Do you have a prog?'

'Not really,' the security commander said slowly. 'Maybe mercs, working for one of your enemies. Maybe coverts that got sheep-dipped and this is a deniable black.' Kea nodded. It could have been the Federation, Earthgov, Mars Council, or any of the supercorporations.

'What about the wounded, sir? I mean, after we've gotten whatever we can?' Kea hesitated, as an aide approached.

'Sir, we have a com from NewsTeam Eleven. Leda. They say they've gotten six calls reporting gunshots and explosions, and want to know what happened. They'd like to talk to you . . . and they want to dispatch a team.'

Kea thought quickly. At first his reaction was to welcome the newsies. He'd have time to change into a bathrobe and bewildered expression, and throw a conference on the basis of Who Would Dare, Why Would Anyone Attack an Innocent? and so on and so forth. He reconsidered. 'You can tell them that my security was conducting an extremely realistic exercise. They're welcome to send a newsteam – Ganymede is a free world – but they are not welcome to land on my property. As for me – I'm offplanet. Testing a new ship. You have no contact with me at the moment. You can tell them that when I return, you imagine, I would be willing to talk to them, although about what, you have no idea.'

The aide blinked – a thickie, Richards thought – frowned, then scurried away. Kea turned back to his security commander. 'Does that answer your question?'

'Yessir.' The officer took his pistol from its holder, chambered a round, and walked toward the enemy-casualty collection point.

Kea walked out of the shambles and looked up, beyond the sky-filling bulk of Jupiter, his eyes going beyond, toward the settled worlds. *Now we'll wait. Until someone whines. And then we'll know who my biggest enemy is.*

But he never found out. There were not even rumors in the grayworld of the mercenaries.

Kea grew even more concerned. *This attempt could have worked. And it wouldn't be the only one or the biggest. It had been handicapped because 'They' wanted Richards alive. But sooner or later someone would determine that at least the status quo must be maintained – and surely one of Kea's people knew the secret of stardrive.*

No one did, of course. But that would not bring Kea Richards back from the grave. He needed a miracle.

Chapter Twenty-Six

Clarke Central, Luna, A.D. 2211

The miracle arrived in late spring. It was first observed and tracked by a Callisto–Mars Yukawa drive ship. It was an irregular chunk of rock not much more than a kilometer in diameter. It might have been considered a small asteroid, but its characteristics showed no semblance to the rocks tumbling beyond Mars. The navigator noted the orbit and roughly calculated the meteor's speed. He reported and forgot it. The report was logged, and the navigator's figures checked, rechecked, and extrapolated. The tech at MarsNavCentral blinked, swore, and ran the problem again.

The figures indicated that this chunk of interplanetary/stellar debris was on a collision track with Earth's moon, plus-minus 15 percent probability. The tech told his supervisor. His supervisor, realizing the navigation center's annual budget was up for review, commed the existence of this hurtling rock to a local vid science-news reporter. And the reporter's editor knew what built ratings and sold ads: FLASH: Scientists Report a New Interstellar Meteor on a Collision Course with Luna! Superspeed Asteroid to Crash into Moon in 158 E-Days! Mars Entire Population in Jeopardy! Earth Itself Endangered!

Chaos and craziness, from scientists to the media to the public. Early on, a literate antiquarian named the rock Wanderer. The name was seized on as the only thing everyone agreed about as the Solar System's sanity level dropped like the long-ago ocean in Hilo Bay. Kea, from Ganymede, watched and read in growing amazement and concern.

Theories were offered. Studied. The Solar Federation set up an emergency headquarters on Mars, in the central Clarke complex. It took a week or so, but eventually enough pols had been reassured there'd be more than enough time and ships to evac them before Wanderer impacted. And then the speeches and the 'viewing with concern' went on. A state of emergency was declared. But nothing was *done*. Worse, as the probable impact time grew closer, nothing was even suggested.

Should the Moon be evacuated? How? There were almost two million people living under its cratered desolation. And what about Earth's population? Should everyone move to high ground, in the assumption Earth would experience the most erratic and deadly tides in humankind's history? Words, words. No actions.

Kea had thought his cynicism to be unshakable in his belief that society, as presently constituted, could muck up a rock fight. He should have been unsurprised as the media hollered, the pols debated, the scientists chased ever-receding decimal points, and the people clamored. The clamor included new prophets preaching that the sins of the past were about to be paid for. Mobs who knew that the world was coming to an end, and therefore utter license should be the order of the day. Cops and soldiery who seemed more worried about the possibility of riots than what response they would have to the catastrophe.

Words, and more words, as Doomsday grew nearer and nearer. There were even some utter stiffs who suggested *nothing* should be done. This was part of nature, was it not? Man had evolved through catastrophe. This was Intended to Happen. This would usher in the Next Level of Being. Intended by Whom varied from fruitbar to fruitbar.

Seventy-three days.

Kea sent for Dr Masterson, his head scientist. He respected the man, as much for his pragmatism as for his ability to keep secrets and administer equally individualistic and iconoclastic scientists and technicians. Masterson ran his own prognoses: Prog: that Wanderer would collide with the Moon. 85 percent. Prog: that Wanderer would bankshot and crash Earth. 11 percent. Prog: that the Moon will shift its orbit closer to Earth. 67 percent. Prog: that the impact would be great enough to shatter Luna completely. 13 percent. Prog: that Wanderer would knock some fairly impressive chunks off the Moon. 54 percent. Prog: that one or more of those moonlets could impact Earth. 81 percent.

The effects . . .

Kea did not need to listen. He was enough of a scientist to envision the radioactivity that would be produced if a decent-sized chunk of Luna, say about the size of Wanderer hit land. And to consider the likelihood of great earthquakes and even the slight possibility of tectonic plateshift? Wanderer promised the cataclysm – but still no one proposed any action as a rushed onward. Pols were besieged with solutions, it was true, from using all the Solar System's rockets to push the Moon out of the way to building a great cannon that would blast Wanderer out of its lethal orbit. But none of them, even those that might be possible, were implemented. Studies were authorized. Military and police forces were put on alert.

Forty-one days.

Kea thought there were only two alternatives. First was that he was living in a completely mad universe. The second was that he was mad himself. Because a solution seemed quite obvious. But no one had taken it. At least yet.

Kea moved. First was to punch a com through to Earth. He snarled at the time it took to get through, and then at the fuzziness of the hyperspace link. Someday, he thought, he would have to find himself an R&D dwonk, give him assistants, a few million credits, some AM2, and tell him to come up with some kind of system that'd enable one being to talk to another across a distance without both of them sounding like they're sitting in barrels and looking like so many triple-imaged blurs. Someday.

He eventually got through to his target – Jon Nance, the highest-rated liviecaster going. Nance was busy. The world was coming to an end, or so everyone said, and he was occupied being Chicken Little. Kea said very well. He would go to the competition. What did Kea have? He would not say. But it was big. And it involved Wanderer. Nance was very interested – there had to be something new to the story besides reporting the latest hysteria or drone of inaction. Richards told Nance to pack. Stand by with a full crew. A complete recording setup, plus two remotes. And a link to go live to Terra. A ship was on its way to pick them up.

'Oh Joy,' Nance said sourly. 'I'm going to have to unfasten an entire crew. Walk away from the desk, and put in my summerman to anchor. And just a smile for the cheeses and the producers. You've got to give me more than that.'

'Never mind,' Kea said. 'This link isn't secure, and I don't always trust you, anyway. I'll still have the ship at Kennedyport in . . . two E-hours.'

'Christ, it'll take me longer'n that to get a gravcar out to the port!'

'Sounds like a personal problem. Two E-hours. Or else I'll rent a doculivie crew and your net can bargain for their reels. Along with everybody else.' He shut off. Then he let himself grin. Masterson may have been the prog specialist in some areas, but Kea wasn't that bad himself. Prog: that Nance would be there with bells and recorders? 79 percent. Minimum.

He ordered the ship that was on standby at his own field to lift for New York. That was one ship. He needed two more. One of his newer transports would serve. He ordered Masterson and the best sober pilot he could winkle up to get ready. He sent for his own ship, the starship he had seen so many aeons before in its junk orbit off Mars. The ship that had been the first fitted for AM2. So what? – he had avoided sentimentality when it came to objects. He had never even given the ship a name beyond its registry numbers. It was time to get rid of the starship – increasingly he'd wondered, if the ship ever fell into the wrong hands, if it might somehow provide a clue to the Alva Sector. This would be a fitting way – if Kea was correct – for its end.

He had a pilot lift it to a clear area outside one of his experimental workshops. One minor modification was made to the controls. Starships are not normally fitted with timers. Then he himself lifted the ship, and hovered it into the super-secure AM2 storage areas. A remotely controlled, Imperium-sheathed cargoloader took a chunk of Anti-Matter Two from a vault. Kea, as he delicately took it in his own ship's grabclaw, thought the less-than-500-kilogram-in-weight block might even be what was left of that first chunk of AM2 he'd grabbed on this ship's maiden voyage into the alternate universe. He was ready to roll.

The two ships cleared Ganymede and set an orbit to intersect Wanderer. Waiting for them was the third ship. And, as Richards had known, a grumpy, evil-tempered Nance was aboard. Evil-tempered, until Richards told him what he proposed. And then he melted.

Kea had one remote set up in the control room of his own ship, the second in the port of the ship Masterson was aboard. The three ships were powered into Wanderer's path. Richards fancied he could feel the whirling chunk of rock moving toward him, like a railbound train in a tunnel. Enough. He told Nance he had better patch down to New York, to his net. There wasn't much time left.

Nance's ship hung about fifty kilometers from the other two. Richards thought it was far too close, but Nance said uh-uh. He had to get his 'picture,' and little dots of dark against a greater dark wouldn't cut it. Kea shuddered again, thinking about the nature of livies. How could anyone allow – let alone spend a career lifetime ensuring – other beings to gather in his mind, smelling what the liviecaster smelled, seeing what he saw, and even experiencing the 'caster's conscious, controlled thoughts? Masterson's ship was less than fifty meters from Richards's. Kea donned a spacesuit and dumped ship atmosphere, leaving both lock doors open. A line linked the two ships.

Nance was 'casting. Inside Mars's orbit, he said, in his calm-but-excited patented manner. About to witness what might well be the most spectacular feat in man's history. Kea Richards was about to attempt to destroy Wanderer, using a new and unspec-ified method, but one that involved his secret engine. And as coached by Kea, Nance wondered why the Federation hadn't even *tried* anything, but were still sitting on the Moon, jacking their jaws . . . (though he worded it far more politely than that).

Kea was ready. The remote – a vid, of course – showed a spacesuited man moving around a control room. What was not shown was the outside bay port opening and the ship's grabclaw extending that huge chunk of Anti-Matter Two in front of it, exactly like a fearful peasant trying to ward off the evil eye.

For melodramatic effect, Richards had told Nance to begin a countdown when signaled. It started. There wasn't much to do – the trajectory was set, and the controls were linked to the downcounting timer. At three minutes thirty seconds, Kea headed out. He swarmed across the rope, severed its connection to his doomed starship, and closed the lock door, his every action recorded by that second remote. He shut the vid off – Masterson had been emphatic that he never wanted to be seen on vid or livie – and went into the other ship's control room.

One minute, he heard Nance cadence. Twenty-seven seconds. And ten . . .

And zero . . . the timer closed, and the ship across the way vanished. Vanished into full-power stardrive. Not even a second later, it impacted into Wanderer.

The livie-recorder that Nance wore like some great helmet, and the accompanying vid camera aboard his ship, overloaded into the ultra and burnt out. Kea had warned him. But the audio pickup was still active, and Nance's voice continued, live, straight to the net headquarters in New York, and from there to man's worlds.

Kea barely noticed the 'caster's excitement. He was busy. He'd taken the ship controls and sent the transport, under half Yukawa drive, toward the meteor. What meteor? A collection of gravel in loose formation. Of Kea's ship, there was nothing whatever remaining.

Kea listened to the broadcast, still live, coming from Nance's ship. He had not known there were so many synonyms for 'hero.' Richards smiled. Actually, this time, he *was* a bit of a hero. He was surprised he felt a shade embarrassed. Hero, eh? Kea the Galactic Hero, he thought in amusement. Now Kea had the name. The tools. Wanderer had given him the stage and the floodlights for his grand entrance. All he needed was the fanfare. And he was fairly certain what it would be, even if he didn't know who'd show up to blow in his ear.

Chapter Twenty-Seven

Ganymede – A.D. 2212

One was the prime minister of a commonwealth. He represented the big families. One was a businesswoman, a member of the board on two thousand blue-chip firms. Another represented Big Money. He controlled the skim on two-thirds of all electronically transmitted cash. The last was labor chieftain of three continents.

'Most of the military is behind us,' Labor said. 'The rest will follow if we do a deal.'

'Amazing how timid generals can be,' Kea said.

'They would have come,' the prime minister said, 'but they were worried – despite our assurances to the contrary – that they might be spotted . . . They send, however, their humblest apologies and warmest greetings.'

Kea snorted. 'Like I said . . . timid.'

Big Money cut to the bottom line. 'But still with us,' he said. 'You know we wouldn't be here, Mr Richards, if we didn't have all our i's dotted and t's crossed.'

'The point is,' the businesswoman said, 'the Federation's presidential election is upon us. Time is short. We need to know *now* if you'll be our nominee.'

'I'll have to be honest with you,' Kea said. 'The other side has come to see me as well.'

Labor laughed. 'if you didn't figure we already knew that, Mr Richards,' he said, 'you wouldn't have let our shadows fall upon your doorstep.'

'We're not amateurs,' Big Money said. 'We came prepared to substantially increase the offer.'

'I think we had better stop right here,' Kea said, 'while I explain my position.'

'Explain away,' Labor said.

'I'll tell you the same thing I told them. I don't need this. I'm richer than anyone has a right to be. I'm forty-seven years old. I was thinking of taking it easy for a while. Resting on my laurels, as it were.'

The businesswoman clapped. 'Lovely speech. We'll see the spin doctors use it.'

'The think-piece writers will devour it with relish,' the prime minister said. 'I can see the Op Ed headline now: "Hero who saved civilization spurns all offers from grateful public."'

'We let that kinda thing bounce around for a week or so,' Labor cut in. 'Then play up the mess the fat cats and back-room boys have got the Federation into. Before you know it, folks will be beggin' you to save 'em again.'

'Then you reluctantly . . . and humbly . . . agree to a draft,' the prime minister said.

The businesswoman graced him with her most charming smile. 'Is that what you had in mind, Mr Richards? More or less?'

Kea laughed. 'The others believed me just a little longer than you people,' he said.

'That's why we're number one,' Big Money responded.

'Number one . . . but without a candidate,' Kea said. 'Which is the same boat your competition is in. At this rate, both parties will wind up in a tie out of sheer electoral boredom. And even if you win . . . The Federation is in a mess. You guys have put it in the crap house. What are you going to do about it? What are your big ideas?'

Dead silence greeted this. But Kea believed it necessary to drive his point home. 'The current state of the Federation is no fantasy, my friends,' he said. 'The economy is in shambles. You've got twenty wars of various sizes. Famine. Drought. Industry is stalled. Inflation running amok. Interest rates sky-high . . . if there was anyone with money to borrow. Besides that, lady . . . and gentlemen, you look in fine shape to me.'

'You must be interested,' Labor said, 'or you wouldn't have bothered to fill up your stone bucket before we got here. If you get my point.'

'I got it,' Kea said.

'Which brings us back to the price,' Big Money said.

'What *could* I want?' Kea asked. 'I've got AM2. Which means I already control everything – from the stars on down.'

'You tell us, Mr Richards,' Labor said. 'What *do* you want?'

Kea told them. Unlike the first group, there was no quibbling. No negotiation.

The deal was cut right there.

Port Richards, Tau Ceti – A.D. 2222

It was a gentle sloping hill, carpeted with a thick lichenlike plant – purple with green pinhead buds – that released a heady perfume every day at dusk. Kea breathed in the scent as he strolled up the hill – alone, except for the ever-present security screen spread out around him. He stopped to rest just before he reached the summit, puffing with effort.

Kea turned back to view his vacation campsite. The cynical street kid in him laughed. The encampment consisted of his personal tent – a two-story-high gold fabric pavilion, really – and more than sixty smaller tents to house staff, security, and other bits of his entourage. Kea snorted. Publicity had billed the trip as a simple camping vacation. A well-deserved rest from the awesome burdens of his office as President of the Federation. The fact that he had chosen to take his vacation upon a newly opened world – named in his honor – in the Tau Ceti system, was given much significance by his pet livie commentators.

'Is it not fitting,' one commentator had said, 'that this simple man . . . this ordinary man of the people . . . President Kea Richards . . . should seek to refresh his spirits in the stars?'

'Most analysts see this journey as symbolic,' another said. 'Through Kea Richards, civilization has pushed its boundaries into the great beyond. Now, President Richards is reminding us that there are many more worlds to conquer. That our future is a never-ending frontier.'

This trip to the frontier was just another stone mortared into the legend Kea had been building for ten years. The legend of the common man. A self-made man. A man who remembered well the plight of the poor from whose ranks he had emerged. A genius in the rough, continually seeking new ways to better life for all.

Some of that was even true.

In ten years he had created a commercial empire greater than anything before. New ideas and renewed vigor had birthed industries that churned out goods – priced within easy reach of all. Food flooded out of giant agricultural combines in unprecedented volumes. Science and invention had exploded. Star probes were bridging vast distances. Terraforming engineers were at work on scores of worlds like Port Richards – adding territory to the Federation. Even the arts flourished in an atmosphere of free-flowing money and ideas. There was no denying Kea Richards was the engine that had made all those things possible. And AM2 was the fuel powering that engine. The robot delivery system had been tested and perfected. AM2 was being shipped regularly, and in large quantities – with zero chance of anyone learning the source.

Naturally, he had enemies. Many enemies. Kea watched one of his guards aim a sniffer at the path ahead, checking for booby traps. He divided his enemies into three groups: the idealists, the covetous, and the insane. The idealists he nurtured. Especially the weak. Free expression and open debate gave such a wonderful patina of democracy. The covetous he co-opted, or crushed. As for the insane . . . Kea saw two other guards swing to the top of the hill, weapons ready . . . well, there was not much you could do about them. Except take care.

Kea's intellectual side insisted he'd accomplished a miracle in ten years – two terms in office. Fazlur had been a pessimist when he had predicted AM2 would turn the known world upside down. With Richards controlling it, Anti-Matter Two had also turned it inside out. But his gut twisted in revolt. Beware, it said. If you stop now, all will be lost. All will be reversed. The Bargetas and their ilk will be running things again. And all will return to inbred stagnation. Some of the old families were still holding out on Earth. These were a few of the covetous ones Kea had allowed their head. Let them have their outmoded factories. Let them continue spewing their pollutants across the planet. Let them break the back of the Earthbound poor. Each day hundreds were joining the migration off Earth. Climbing aboard ships powered by AM2 supplied by Kea Richards. Fleeing the chaos and misery Kea's enemies had created to new worlds their president was opening up.

It's going so fast, Kea thought. So fast and so well. In ten years, what I've built will easily double again. In fifty more . . . who knows? Pity I won't live to see it. A great yearning pit opened in Kea's stomach. A yearning as deep as the one that had clutched at him when Fazlur first proposed that they enter another universe. God, he wished he could see how it would all play out.

He heard a thundering from the far side of the hill. Kea hurried to the hilltop. He saw an official Federation ship settle into its berth. Around it was the enormous raw wound of the new spaceport being hurled up on Port Richards. It was the official delegation from the Federation's electoral college. Come to tell him that the people had begged him to stay on as president. Not just for a third term. Not for another five years.

Kea Richards had been elected President For Life.

Surprise.

The boys in the back room had come through.

But that had been the deal.

On Ganymede – ten years before – the guy from labor had gawped. 'Whaddya mean, for life?'

The businesswoman had hissed at him. 'Until he's dead, stupid. Or wants to retire.' She had turned to Kea. 'Right?'

'That's the deal,' Kea had said. 'If I'm going to run it . . . I want to run it like my own company. Elections every five years will tie my hands. I'll always be forced to take the short view.'

'What'd the other side say?' Big Money had asked.

'They weren't happy,' Kea had answered.

'Because they couldn't swing it?' Labor'd guessed.

'Yeah,' Kea had said. 'They said they couldn't swing it.'

'I don't see the problem,' the businesswoman had said. 'Not for us, anyway.'

'We couldn't do it all at once,' the prime minister had said. 'We would have to smooth the way. Prepare the groundwork.'

'We could do it by the end of his second term for sure,' Labor had said. 'He's pretty damned popular. If you get my drift.'

'If we agreed to this . . .' Big Money had ventured. 'As your loyal supporters . . . and dearest friends . . .'

Kea had bowed . . . almost kingly . . . 'and soon to be trusted advisers . . .' he had added.

Big Money had smiled . . . acknowledging . . . 'Yes. We would. And as your advisers, could we presume you would listen if we had a word or two about your policies on AM2?'

'Absolutely,' Kea had said. 'As a matter of fact, I have been discussing my long-range strategy with my managers. It has become time for what people have termed a monopoly to end. We're presently arranging a plan to license sales of AM2, Imperium

X, and the modified drive engines to . . . the proper concerns.'
He'd given them a meaningful look. 'I'd be happy to listen to
your suggestions . . . for individual cases.'

The room had brightened immensely. Aglow in the vision of
new private fortunes to be won.

'Let me be the first to call you Mr President,' Labor had said.
He stuck out a hand. Kea shook it.

That had been it. A presidency conferred with a handshake.
Details to be filled in later by constitutional lawyers. It was the
first time Kea had really tugged on the AM2 line and reeled in
the fish. And as time had gone by, he had gotten better and better
at it.

Kea watched the delegation descend from the ship. A gravlighter
was waiting to take them to his encampment with formal word
of his new title. Tonight they would all celebrate. Tomorrow he
would pay off a few more IOUs.

Then it would all be his.

It was like an old-fashioned marriage, really. The monarchs of
old had understood. A kingdom was the source of your greatest
grief and happiness. You were wedded to it. For life. Kea was
Emperor, now, in all but name. He didn't have even a niggling
of guilt for having bought and paid for it by keeping one of the
greatest discoveries in history to himself. The Chinese emperors
had kept the secret of the workings of time for centuries. What
would the people do with it? they asked their court scholars.
They do not have the skills or fortitude to take responsibility for
its appointment. This should be left for us to decide. This should
be our burden, and our burden alone.

Kea remembered a line from his early childhood. 'What's time
to a damned hog?'

He thought of the piggish greed aboard *Destiny I*. Ruth
murdering Fazlur and the Osiran. Her murder at Murph's hands.
Murph's intentions on his own life. Kea had vastly refigured his
concept of evil since that time. He had drawn up his own scale,
and found civilization wanting. But shouldn't these things be left
to a Higher Authority? To God? Maybe. But Kea had been to
another universe . . . and returned. And found no god in either
place. Perhaps there was Something. A god on his throne far
beyond the stars. But until that god was found, this world would
have to make do with Kea Richards.

He started back down the hill. If he hurried, he would have
time to change before he greeted the delegation. Kea picked up

the pace. The guard beside him looked surprised. And began to lope. Kea ran faster. Feeling young . . . and lightheaded.

Suddenly, there was a sound in his ear of a thunderclap. Distant, but somehow very close. A red haze fell before his eyes.

His mind shouted, 'Not yet! I'm not . . . done.'

Kea was unconscious before he hit the ground.

A panicked guard knelt beside him. Tumbled him over. Clumsily felt for signs of life. Found the faint hammer of the pulse. Frantically she keyed her com unit. In moments, the hillside was thick with frantically rushing vehicles and people – fighting to save the life of their new President For Life.

Ganymede – A.D. 2222

'Your doctors made no mistake,' the great physician said. 'It was a stroke.' Her name was Imbrociano. In the field of anatomical damage and regeneration, she had no peers.

Kea unconsciously gripped the numbness that was his left arm. Remembered his helplessness on *Destiny I* when it had been bound to him. This time, however, it was his whole left side that was useless. Imbrociano nodded at his arm. 'We can get that going again,' she said. 'Nerve implants will do the trick. Some rather complicated rewiring should take care of the rest. Although I should warn . . . you will be definitely weakened.'

Kea steadied himself. He needed courage now. 'That was not my greatest concern,' he said. 'What about the remainder of their diagnosis?'

The physician sighed. 'Unfortunately for you, I have no quarrel with that either,' she said. 'There is a good chance it will happen again. There's no telling when. A week? A year? More? I can't say. But I *can* say . . . it is unlikely you will survive a second attack.'

Kea laughed. Harsh. 'You're not much on bedside manner,' he said.

Imbrociano shrugged. 'Lies are time-consuming,' she said. 'And time is something you are definitely lacking.'

Kea laughed again. This time, it was a full-bodied chortle. The joke was on him. Hadn't one of his last thoughts been about the emperors who held dominance over time? But not all time, he thought. Not biological time.

Imbrociano peered at him, then nodded, satisfied. 'You're taking it well,' she said. 'No hysteria.'

'I'm not the type,' Kea answered.

'No. I guess you wouldn't be . . . Mr President.' She rose to go. Kea raised a hand to stop her. 'My staff spoke to you about the need for secrecy?'

Imbrociano shuddered. 'They stressed it . . . quite intensely. Really, sir. There was no need for threats. President or not, you are my patient. I have my oath.'

'Forgive their enthusiasm,' Kea said. Dry. Thinking that if his enemies got wind of Kea's illness, they could soon change her mind. 'I'd be in your debt,' he said, 'if you stayed on . . . until I decide what to do next.'

'You're still considering surgery,' she asked, 'even though the ordeal is most likely to be pointless?'

'I'll let you know,' Kea said.

She left, a puzzled woman. But no more puzzled than Kea. What *was* he thinking? What could he do? The best physician in the Federation had just told him he was doomed. His advisers were urging him to choose a successor. Meaning one of them. Unspoken – but implicit – in their constant hammering was that it was also time to reveal the source of Anti-Matter Two.

If I die now, he thought, the system – that perfect system – he had designed would automatically shut down. All traces wiped. And the secret of AM2 would die with him. The system had been the only *real* protection against his enemies. A shield of knowledge against their assassins. But what was the point of it now? Without AM2, the Federation would collapse. All his work for nothing.

So? Giving them the secret would be worse, wouldn't it? There would be terrible wars over control of AM2. He'd run the progs countless times. Each time the death toll burst through the top of the scale.

It was too late to produce an heir. Besides, he had dismissed that prospect from the beginning. He knew too much about kings and their children. They lived miserable lives waiting to succeed. Sometimes plotting against their parent. Almost always overseeing the death of the kingdom that parent had built. You had to look no further than the Bargetas to see the deterioration from generation to generation.

Enough wandering. He had to make up his mind. Who should succeed him? Who could he trust with the secret of AM2?

The answer came back: No one.

I *must* decide, he argued. I have no other choice.

There must be another option, came the insistent voice. There must be.

But . . . everyone has to die . . . Eventually.

But we're different, the voice said. Special. We know a thing no one else knows. A great pure thing that sets us apart from anyone who lives now . . . or has ever lived before.

Kea wrestled with this insanity – for he thought he must have gone insane – for a long time. Finally, he slept. Floating. Dreamless. Aides and nurses monitored him. Noted the peacefulness of the bio charts.

He awakened. Refreshed. Alert. Ravenous.

He sent for his breakfast.

And he sent for Imbrociano.

She answered all his questions, then listened closely as he outlined his proposal. Calmly. Dispassionately. 'Yes. I could do it,' she finally said. 'I could build a living body . . . a human form . . . exactly like yours. There are theoretical obstacles, to be certain. But with the right team and sufficient funds . . . it could be done.'

'Then you'll do it?' Kea asked.

'No. I won't.'

'Why not, for godsakes?'

'You can't deny death, Mr President,' she said. 'And that's what you're doing. You must see this whole thing is highly irrational. I can make a copy of you. Duplicate you. But . . . I can't make that new organism be *you*!'

'What would be the difference?' Kea pressed. 'If it had all my thoughts . . . my knowledge . . . my motivations . . . identical cells . . . all the stuff that makes me . . . then it would be me. Wouldn't it?'

Imbrociano sighed. 'I'm a doctor. Not a philosopher. A philosopher could better explain the difference.'

'I can make you very rich,' Kea said. 'Bestow many honors.'

'I know,' Imbrociano said. 'Enough to overcome even my ethics. But if I participated in such an endeavor – and succeeded – I can't help but think I would more likely be signing my own death warrant. It would be dangerous knowledge, you must admit.'

'I thought of that,' Kea said. 'However, for you to accomplish what I have in mind will most likely take the rest of your professional life. It will be a very secure, very lavish life. This I guarantee.'

Imbrociano thought for a long time. Then she said, 'If I don't do this, you'll find someone else. Albeit not as skilled.'

'Yes, I will,' Kea said.

'Which would once again leave me in jeopardy. For knowing too much.'

'This is true,' Kea said. Flat.

'We'd better get to work, then,' Imbrociano said. 'We might not have much time.'

Ganymede – A.D. 2224

His luck returned. Along with health, bestowed by Imbrociano's talents. The nerve rewiring was simple. The rehabilitation exercises torture. But it was worth it.

Richards rose from his chair and walked to the far end of his office. He was alone. He watched his progress in a mirror. Approved. Now, only a slight limp betrayed the lingering traces of his paralysis from the stroke. It had been easy to hide this from the public. Politics has long experience keeping those kinds of things hushed up. In FDR's time, Kea recalled, few people were even aware he was bound to a wheelchair for life. He walked back to his desk. Eased his fifty-nine-year-old bones into the soft chair. And poured himself a drink from a decanter on his desk.

It was Scotch.

He savored it. Just as he savored a few moments' peace from the breakneck pace of his duties. Then he tensed as a headache twinged. His heart fluttered – was this it? But the pain fled along with fear. Thank God, he thought, that worry will be over soon. One way or the other.

Imbrociano was almost ready. Everything was in place. He only had to say the word and great, shadowy forces would be put in motion. Kea had worked feverishly to reach this point. Shifting staff. Pulling strings. Creating and collapsing whole bureaucracies. Covering his tracks in a hailstorm of governmental actions and decrees. Vast industries were at his disposal, with no one manager aware of what the other was doing. Starships had been flung here and there at his bidding. He had spun an elaborate, supersecret network, with cutouts and switchbacks and complex electronic mazes created by canny old spies. During that time Imbrociano and her team had worked at equally as furious a pace. With the entire Federation's treasury at their disposal as a budget.

Kea sipped his Scotch, letting the warmth tease the kinks in his side.

The first part of his plan to cheat death had been relatively simple. Imbrociano would build a walking, talking, thinking duplicate of Kea Richards. The second part – yet to be put into motion – was simpler still. Horrifically so.

He steered his mind away from yowling terror. He'd have to deal with it when the moment came.

The third part of his plan was vastly complex. To begin with, he'd had new improvements of the old model in mind. Tinkering with several genes to make his alter ego invulnerable to disease and aging. When the organism was in place, the aging process would be gradually reversed. He had picked thirty-five as the place to stop. Kea thought that had been the best time for him. His peak in many ways. With the process spread out over many years, his people would barely notice their President For Life shedding middle age like a snake its skin. In theory, the new Kea Richards would be able to go on and on throughout the centuries without wearing out. Virtual immortality.

'In practice,' Imbrociano had said, 'I doubt very much this is possible. An organism – especially a thinking organism – is too complex. Vulnerable to many things we are ignorant of. Not just physically vulnerable, either. There is the psychological to consider.'

'I could go mad,' Kea had said. With no emotion. Imbrociano had only nodded.

'I could also be assassinated,' Kea had said. 'Or, held against my will. Forced to do and reveal things.'

'There is that, too,' Imbrociano had said.

These problems had led to the key part of the grand scheme. An engineer at heart, Kea had started with a machine. A judgment machine. Fitted with powerful reasoning programs. Remote sensors to monitor the alter ego. Judging mental and physical conditions, as well as outward threats. The organism itself would have a bomb implanted in its gut. Threatened by torture, brain-scan, or fatal attack, the bomb would blow with an enormous force. Killing all within its range. The same would happen if the judgment machine decided he was no longer mentally fit to rule the Federation. Kea called it the Caligula Factor. He had no wish to become a tyrant who ruled over an endless hell.

He had been proud of himself for thinking of that. Proud of it still, he thought, touching up his glass with Scotch. It was his own secret gift to his forever kingdom. If he was absolutely honest with himself, however, he would have to admit he was a little broad in his definitions of mental disturbance. But during these fits of honesty, he had rationalized that his future self might require some leeway to survive. It was impossible to imagine all the circumstances he might face over the centuries. What seemed insane today might be expeditious in the far tomorrow.

The machine orchestrating all of this was contained in a completely automated hospital ship; a ship not only built with redundancy on redundancy, constructed with bus bars a meter thick when a centimeter would give a lifespan of decades, but given complete self-analyzing and repair capabilities.

He had hidden it where no enemy could ever find it – the alternate universe. The source of his AM2 operation.

He thought of it as N-space.

And just in case his enemies ever tracked the ship down, it was defended by the best weapons of this age. It was unlikely anyone who attacked would survive. The hospital ship would sit in readiness, waiting for the signal to call it into full life. At that signal, the ship's robotic staff would build yet another Kea Richards – to replace the one that had just been . . . removed. The flesh would be grown from the genes Imbrociano was even now stockpiling from frequent biopsies. The mind – the id of Kea Richards – would be perfectly reconstructed as well. Right up to the final thoughts before . . . death.

'This will take time,' Imbrociano had warned him. 'A little more than three years before the duplicate is constructed. You'll have to be aware of these gaps.'

He had overcome the problem by having an elaborate library computer installed. It would constantly monitor every newsfeed and knowledge resource in the Federation. All this data would be fed to the new organism after the awakening – during tutorials. But he must be wary. The organism would be new. Untried. Imbrociano's psych techs told him too much pure knowledge without practical experience could doom it before it started.

The return to power would be gradual. A ladder of experience. With awareness fed in along with each step upward. And at any point, the judgment machine could decide the new organism was lacking in some way and destroy it . . . to start again.

Oddly enough, the easiest of all his tasks in preparing for immortality had involved the political.

Because his hole card was AM2.

When he died, the AM2 shipments would automatically halt. There would be no more for a usurper until Kea's rebirth and

return. Economic chaos would result. A three-year power drought.
The throne stealer would be so weakened, he would topple at a
touch when Kea Richards rose from the dead.

A hero reborn.

It was a powerful legend to build on.

Kea looked up at the antique clock on the mantel. It was time
to start.

Imbrociano was waiting.

He finished his drink. Replaced the glass on the tray and pushed
the whole thing away. And he buzzed for Kemper – his chief of
staff. They went over the things to be done in his absence. Last-
minute legislative details. Appointments to higher office. That sort
of thing. His staff was grudgingly getting used to his mysterious
absences. He had slipped away regularly to add to that tolerance.
Sometimes in his guise as the common engineer – Raschid.
Sometimes with a few chosen people for a little stealth diplomacy.

'What if there is an emergency, Mr President?' Kemper said
dutifully. He knew the answer, but thought he'd be remiss if he
didn't ask. 'How can we reach you?'

Richards gave him the usual response: 'Don't worry. I won't
be gone long.'

After Kemper departed, Richards pulled a bulky travel kit from
a drawer. Then he pressed a stud beneath his desk. A panel swung
away in the wall. Kea plunged into the dark passage. The panel
closed behind him. A short time later he was aboard a small space-
yacht, listening to the captain chatter with the first officer – waiting
for tower clearance. He turned in his seat to see if Imbrociano and
her people were comfortable. Imbrociano waved to him. Smiled.
A sad smile. Kea waved back. Settled in for takeoff.

There was the shock of the thrust . . . a roaring in his ears
. . . then weightlessness. Kea savored every sensation of the flight.
As if it were to be his last.

Imbrociano's voice came in his ear: 'Would you like a sedative?'

He turned to her. Motioned for her to sit next to him. She
did. Her eyes were hollowed from lack of sleep. 'I'd rather not,'
Kea said. 'Somehow . . . I don't know . . . I want to be aware.'

'I understand,' Imbrociano said. 'But we won't reach our destination until tomorrow. Why not get some rest?'

'If this doesn't work,' Kea said, 'I'll have a lot of time for that.
Permanent rest.'

'You can still call this off,' Imbrociano said. 'Really. I urge you
to.'

'I've made up my mind,' Kea said. 'There's no need for you to feel guilt.'

Imbrociano grew silent. Picked at her sleeve. Then she said, 'If it eases your mind any, there will be no pain tomorrow. No sensation. I'll inject you with trancs first. So there will be no fear. The lethal dose will come next. You'll inhale . . . and by the time you fully exhale, you'll be . . . dead.'

'Reborn, actually,' Kea said with forced lightness. 'Or, as some might say, exchanging one vessel for another.'

'But it can't be really *you*!' she exploded. 'Perhaps by casual definition, yes. It will talk, walk, and think like you in all matters. But it still can't be you. The essence in each of us. That makes us individual. The soul.'

'You sound like a preacher,' Kea said. 'I'm an engineer. A pragmatist. If it walks like a duck . . . talks like a duck . . . it must be Kea Richards.'

Imbrociano put her head back. Tired. Defeated. Then she patted his arm. Rose. And returned to her seat.

Kea felt genuinely sorry about what had to happen next. He fished out the travel case. Peeled away a small panel of material to reveal a depression. A heat-sensitive switch. He *liked* Imbrociano. Despite her stiff manner, she was genuinely human: afflicted with the curse of empathy.

His affection for her was the second reason he had chosen to alter the plan. The first reason was pragmatic. It was best to begin with maximum impact. A suspicious accident. Triggering finger pointing and political purges. Government in disarray. The cheers at his miraculous return would drown out many questions. Some of those he would get around with obscure hints of enemies in hiding. The rest he would erase by simply rewriting history.

He would have a long time to do it.

The second reason was pity. For Imbrociano. He could not bear to think how hurt she would be that he had lied to her. It was a terrible emotion for a person to be confronted with at the moment of his death. Even worse than the betrayal itself.

He trusted her.

But he couldn't take the chance.

Trust no one, an old king had once advised another. Not even me, your friend . . . *Especially* me!

Ah, well. The decision had been difficult. But deadly necessity had won the hand. But he knew he would always mourn

Imbrociano. Just as he would mourn others. It was a king's burden. One he would have to bear.

He moved his finger to the depression in the case. When he touched it, the bomb would destroy the ship. Everyone would die. Instantly. Except for . . .

. . . Him?

He was suddenly sweat-soaked. His heart bruising his ribs with its hammering.

What if Imbrociano was right?

About what?

My soul?

Yes . . . Your soul. Goddamned y—

Kea shuddered in a long breath. Blew it out. Drew another. He closed his eyes. And thought of the gentle curtain of fire billowing in the cosmic winds. He was floating through it now. Saw the particles leaping about as if they were alive.

Now? Should he do it now?

No.

One more moment.

One more thought.

Kea sucked in stale cabin air. It tasted sweet.

I will be the forever king, he thought.

The Eternal Emperor.

He pressed the switch.

Chapter Twenty-Eight

N-Space – Year One

The man sat quietly in his seat, watching the color/noncolor through what appeared to be the ship's port. He was dark and muscular with startling blue eyes. He wore a white form-fitting tunic and soft white slippers. He'd been watching dazzling lights for many . . . days . . . weeks . . . months? The terms made only vague sense.

He never tired of the view, even though it hurt his eyes. It was always the same. But different. Shifting shapes and patterns. Bursting bits of color. It had always been so soothing. But not today. It made him tense. Yearning. The cabin's womblike coziness felt smothering.

A thought came to him. He peered through the port. The Voice said it was the place where two universes touched. A gateway. Yes, he knew that. But, what was it called? An answer crawled into his brain: . . . Discontinuity.

Fazlur's Discontinuity.

He snapped up. Felt the hair on his arms prickle up. Where did that come from? The Voice? No. It came from . . .

Within!

The man rose and padded to the far end of the cabin. There was a mirror on that wall. He peered into it. Saw the face. For the first time, it seemed . . . familiar. As if it didn't belong to . . . someone else? Yes. That was it. He rusked a hand across the cheek. Again . . . the sensation was so . . . deeply . . . familiar. He looked into the eyes. Saw the sardonic creases at the edges. The blue that could turn so quickly gray and cold. He laughed. Heard the echo of that laugh collide around the room.

God. The sound of it was so wonderful.

He touched the surface of the mirror, trembling fingers outlining the reflection.

He nearly wept to find himself there.

Then he pulled himself together. He stood back from the mirror. Put his hands on his hips . . . posing for his own benefit. He looked long and hard at the image of himself. Measuring for any sign of weakness. Finding none. He nodded. Satisfied.

A thought jumped up: The forever king.

He frowned. What was the rest? Back there, when . . .

He remembered.

'I am the Emperor,' he said aloud.

He grinned at his image in the mirror.

'The Eternal Emperor.'

BOOK FOUR

KING IN DANGER

Chapter Twenty-Nine

Blurry. Very blurry. Worse . . . then better as the rangefinder autoadjusted.

A rolling mountain meadow. A series of hillocks around it. The hillocks pocked with cave mouths. Adjustment, Sten's mind told him. You are in the middle of a city. The meadow's turf was artificial. As were the hillocks. The cave mouths were doorways leading down into huge caverns.

Near the end of the meadow, the ruins of what had been a low building with arched openings. Deliberately smashed when a huge Imperial battleship smashed in for a landing atop it.

In front of the building, a platform.

Correction. A scaffold.

Standing on it, a man dressed in black and half-hooded. Holding a pistol.

In front of him, two Imperial soldiers in battledress. Between them, held firmly, a large golden-furred being.

Blur-around: the 'meadow' packed with other golden ones. Between them and the scaffold, more Imperial troops in the mottled-brown combat uniform of the Guards. Their weapons were leveled at the crowd.

A furred out-of-focus head blurred across his vision.

Movement, and Sten was looking again at the scaffold.

Sounds: drumroll.

Sounds: earshattering whistles.

'Th' lad thae's aboot t' gie hieself lopped is Sr Tangeri,' Alex's voice explained. 'I' y' ken th' Cal'gata hae a whistlin't frae speech, y' perhaps sense thae dinnae be fond ae th' notion thae leader's aboot f'r th' high jump. We're i' th' place th' Cal'gata

call their Gatherhome. I's th' equivalent ae Parliament. Or was,
at any rate.'

A hailer voice boomed and echoed from the battleship.

'Y' noo c'n make oot th' words. Th' lad wi' th' pickup hae
antique gear. But th' Cal'gata're being tol' thae this i' th' penalty
frae high treason, an' thae'll be more penalties t' follow.'

The echoes stopped, and Tangeri was turned to face the crowd.
Instantly the executioner's hand came up, and the pistol fired.
The front of Tangeri's skull exploded, and the body slumped.

The soldiers heaved the corpse forward, off the scaffold.

'An' noo,' Kilgour's voice went on, 'i' gie's interestin'.'

Whistles louder, louder, damped by the pickup's controls.
Blackness.

'Th' lad wearin' th' 'corder's movin't closer.'

Blur motion. Running. Moving with the crowd. Guns firing.
Screams. Human screams. Running forward. A squealing Tangeri,
fur blood-soaked, waving an Imperial willygun.

Perspective jolting. Moving over something. Something soft. A
body. A torn-apart Imperial soldier.

Dragonroar.

Blackness.

'Th' battlewagon opened up wi' a chaingun.'

Vision. The sky. A dot an object a diving hawk explosion
SOUNDBLANK . . . groundjar . . . blackness.

'Ev'dently,' Kilgour's voice explained, 'thae wae a wee Cal'gata
who got airborne wi' some sort ae spitkit, an' the' Emp's destroyer
screen didnae stop him. An' he calc'lated a fair trade wae a
battleship frae his life.

'Ah reck th' lad wae right.'

Vision. Flames gouting from the Imperial battleship, from a
great hole just behind the bridge.

Blurmotion again. Running. More shots. Then sky, and Sten
gasped as pain racked him. Blackblank.

He could see. Somebody else could see.

Now he was a long way away from Gatherhome. It was far
below him. The battleship was walled in flames, and the square
appeared deserted. A mill of Imperial destroyers filled the air
above the wreckage. Suddenly one destroyer was a ball of greasy
flame, and again the pickup blanked.

Sten lifted the livie helmet away.

'What happened to the first Cal'gata? The one who started
recording?'

A grim-faced Alex shrugged.

'Thae, Ah dinnae know. Killed, Ah reck. Else why w'd another pick up th' gear? But frae y'r info, th' battlewagon wae th' *Odessa*, an' the Imperials lost twa battalions ae th' Second Guards. Th' rumble Ah heard frae th' smuggler wi' Wild who brought th' tape wae that near ten thousan' Cal'gata went doon ae well. Needless t'say, th' Offic'l Emp News dinnae hae ought ae th' matter.'

'So that's what they're calling a drum patrol,' Cind snarled. 'I guess murderers like the Guard look hard for some kind of label that doesn't say what they're really doing.'

'The Guard may be bad, following orders like they are. What's worse,' Otho rumbled, 'is that's what the Emperor is calling justice.'

Sten got up, walked to a screen, and stared out, thinking. The *Victory* and her escorts hung in deep interstellar space, far from the haunts of man.

'So I'm dead,' he mused aloud, 'but the rebellion continues.'

'Like a summer fire in an ice oasis, one that's been knocked down but not extinguished and can flare up at any time,' Otho confirmed. 'Burning down here, flickering up there. Here they'll chance a battle, there they'll peg an Imperial sentry at his post with a rock.'

'An',' Alex added, 'th' Cal'gata, ae y' saw, are holdin' firm. As are th' Zaginows. Eventually, th' Emp'll hae th' forces t' move in an' level 'em. But nae frae ae least three, four E-years is m' prog.

'While thae's some ae y'r allies thae hae sued frae peace, thae's others that hae gone oot t' th' barricades or are just practicin' noncoop'ration frae reasons ae their own.

'Plus thae's purges i' Prime, i' the Guard, across th' armed forces, i' th' rubberstamp Parliament, e'en.

'Th' Emp hae biggish problems, puir lad.'

The Eternal Emperor did. He may have killed Sten, but the price had been far greater than he'd calculated. The obliteration of the peaceful Manabi, a race respected and admired if only as an ideal, sent a low boil of anger through civilization.

None of the propaganda played, all of which centered around the story that Sten had set a trap for the Eternal Emperor, who had barely escaped after killing the rebel leader in hand-to-hand combat.

Sten was dead, the Emperor lived, was the comeback. Peddle y'r p'raties i' another town.

And it was clear to many beings that the Emperor's offer of a truce and powersharing was exactly what it had been – bait for the Emperor's own trap.

Rebellion roared, died down, rose again, flickered on, stretching the already-strained forces and assets of the Empire.

Sten had wasted no time mourning the Manabi, nor cursing himself for not allowing that final battle to be fought, damn the consequences. He couldn't. He had been betrayed. What of it? The war had just begun.

He didn't realize he'd spoken aloud, until he heard Otho's rumble of approval. He turned.

'It does,' Otho said. 'Now is the time for you to reveal yourself. You did not die. Now is the time for your forces to rally and strike again.'

Both Alex and Cind were shaking their heads. Alex started to say something, then deferred to Cind.

'If we do,' she asked, 'and we get the battlefleets to reassemble, those that haven't been destroyed by the Imperial forces or fled into unknown parts of the universe, what's to say we won't end up where we were? Facing another Asculum, where everybody dies and nobody wins?

'That's the way my ancestors the Jann used to fight. And there's great tales and ballads of how we stood to the last man or woman.

'Very impressive,' she said, her voice oozing sarcasm, 'and inspirational for young heroes. But it didn't play very well for me later, when I grew up, and also when I found out that not only did we lose those battles – but pretty often the war, as well.

'Like Alex might say, clot that for a lark.'

Kilgour nodded.

'Th' lass put i' better'n Ah c'd. Ah'll but mention Culloden, which'll gie wee Otho some'at t' look up a'ter th' meet.'

Sten nodded agreement with Alex and Cind, remembering something his first drill sergeant, a combat veteran named Lanzotta, had told the assembled formation of recruits on their first day of training:

'Some general or other said a soldier's job is not to fight, but to die. If any of you fungus scrapings live to graduate, you'll be ready to help the soldier on the other side die for his country . . . We build killers, not losers . . .'

'Rykor,' Sten said. 'Logic check.'

The psychologist waved a flipper from her tank. She mourned the Manabi, especially Sr Ecu, more than any of the others. Or perhaps, she thought, trying to lift herself from the grief that sent a constant well of tears down her leathery cheeks, these others have lost more friends and loved ones, being experienced soldiers, than I have.

All these years, all these decades, she thought on. Doing the Emperor's frequently bloody work, and because there was seldom a body in front of me – flash-remembering a small-time criminal's body flopping into death on the brainscan – I thought I knew how to deal with loss.

Learn from this, Rykor. Learn that all that you preach may be logical and practical. But the next patient who seems unable to accept the truth of your comforting or logic – don't think them to be thick or obstinate.

'Go ahead, Sten,' she said, forcing attention.

'If I suddenly rise from the dead, I assume I could attract a fair number of allies – old ones, new ones – to my flag. Ignore that. Now, if I stay dead, will the Emperor's persecution of my ex-friends be any worse – will any more beings die – than if I rolled away the stone?'

Rykor thought hard.

'No,' she said finally. 'Your logic is acceptable. Persecution . . . irrational revenge such as the Emperor is practicing right now . . . is terrible. But open war kills far more, including the innocent.'

'As I thought,' Sten said.

'Okay, troops. Here's the plan,' he said. 'We tried the wide-open frontal-charge approach, and it didn't work real well. Maybe it's my fault – I never was the kind of warrior who liked the noonday sun. Reflections off the armor are a pain in the butt, if nothing else.'

Sten was surprised at his mild joke. All right. He was relearning the harsh lesson of war – mourn for your casualties overlong and you will certainly join them.

'This time, we'll do it right. In the dark, in the fog, from behind with a stiletto. And I think staying dead will be part of that.

'No more battles unless we have to, people. Now we're going after the Emperor. And this time we'll take him or we'll kill him. Any way we can.'

He looked around. Rykor was silent. Otho frowned, then grudged agreement. Cind and Alex nodded, as did Captain Freston.

'Ah'm glad t'hear thae, lad. Long live Mantis an' thae,' Alex said. 'I' fits right in wi' m' own plans. Ah'd like permission t' run a wee solo shot ae m' own. Ah wan' Poyndex.'

Alex explained. He had been analyzing these new purges. Some of them were public or secret allies of Sten. Others had obviously offended the Eternal Emperor. But other deaths or imprisonment had no obvious explanation.

'Ah tried runnin' th' basic ineptness ae any tyrant,' Alex continued. 'But th' computer upchucked on m' thinkin't an' sayit try again, goon.'

He did. An answer was Poyndex. The man was clever, Kilgour conceded. Again, he had first thought that Poyndex was adding to the purge list to take care of his own enemies – the head of a secret police normally did that every time his ruler needed some heads rolled. But Poyndex was far brighter than that – he had no problems disposing of his enemies as he encountered them. The Emperor had given him a great deal of authority – and the sanction to kill his own snakes without need to use the Emperor as a cover.

The eventual explanation was simpler. Alex believed that Poyndex was trying to make himself the one indispensable man.

'Wi'oot,' Alex added, 'gie'in' th' Emp thoughts thae Poyndex harbors gran' ambitions ae th' throne f'r himself, although thae'll come, thae'll come.'

The Gurkhas had been discharged, Alex learned. At one time he thought it was out of Imperial irk because a platoon or so of them had volunteered to serve under Sten, before he declared the rebellion. Then he thought they'd been removed to allow Poyndex's own creation, Internal Security, to move in. That was part of the explanation, which also accounted for Poyndex's replacement of Mercury Corps and Mantis Section with IS.

But there was more to Poyndex's maneuvering than just that, Alex believed. Poyndex intended to be the only conduit the Emperor had to anyone – his officers, his military, his Parliament, his people.

'A course, th' mon's dinkydow,' Alex said. 'Afore he gies t' be th' only channel t' th' Emperor on his throne, th' Emp'll roll his wee head. Consider some lads ae th' past. Bismarck. Yezov. Himmler. Kissinger. Johnes.

'Th' only one gray em'nence whae dinnae fall i' Rich'lieu. Poyndex i' a cap'ble lad, but he's noo a Rich'lieu.'

But all that would lie in the future. At present, he'd been fairly effective in isolating the Eternal Emperor. Now, considering that Poyndex was already a turncoat, having headed Mercury Corps during the Interregnum and then lifted to the privy council by the conspirators before he double-crossed them to the Emperor . . .

'Ah hae plans,' Alex finished, 't' mess wi' th' heads ae both Poyndex an' m' frien', th' Emp.

'I' th' lines ae th' poem, "They hunted till darkness coom on, but thae foun'/Nae a button, or feather, or mark,/By which thae c'd tell that thae stood i' th' groun'/Whae th' Baker had met wi' th' Snark."'

Sten eyed his friend. He knew that Alex would only get more specific if directly ordered to. Let Kilgour run his own mission.

'How'll you get to him?' Sten said. 'As far as I know, the bastard barely budges out of Arundel, unless he's traveling with the Emperor.'

Alex grinned.

'Ah hae made tight frien's wi' wee Marr an' Senn. E'en though they're retired, an' on th' oots wi' th' Emp, thae still hae been t' Arundel a bit. Th' *new* Arundel. Which they say, knowin' th' architect i' charge, was built *exact* like th' old one. An' they knew e'ery crook an' nanny ae th' braw stonepile long afore you wandered i' th' scene wi' y'r wee maps an' overlays.'

Sten frowned. Arundel was the Emperor's citadel on Prime, styled like a triple-scale copy of the Earth castle, and with extensive works and gardens added around it and command bunkers and living quarters tunneled far underneath. It had been destroyed as one of the opening shots of the Tahn war, in a futile attempt to kill the Emperor. After the Emperor's return, it had been rebuilt.

Then he got it, remembering that layered map and his own term as conscientious head of the Imperial bodyguard. And he remembered a certain prison break some months afterward, a prison break from Arundel's dungeons.

Sten nodded.

'Take it away, Alex,' he said. 'What kind of backup do you need?'

'Ah dinnae need but whae Ah hae. M' ship thae Wild's loaned me. M' pilot. Ah'll hae transport waitin' ae Prime. Frae there, it'll be one in, twa oot i' th' motto.'

Alex saluted, quite precisely, as if he and Sten were back in the service. Sten puzzled, stood, came to attention, and returned it. It was a very crisp, very military farewell.

And Kilgour was gone.

*

Alex was telling only some of the truth. He had considered that his scheme against Poyndex could succeed best as a solo run. But there was more to it than that.

The back of his neck still crawled.

He savored each day, each minute, because he had the feeling it could well be the last. He had put his house – his huge estates and castles on Edinburgh, assuming they were yet unburnt by the Emperor's revenge – in order.

Now he was ready.

At least, he thought, i' Ah'm answerin't m' weird, Ah'll noo take wee Sten wi' me.

He shut the mood and the thought off.

Dinnae be gloomin't aroun' ae i' y'r some braw Norsemen. Back on Earth, aeons gone, we listen't t' their keenin' an' slipped behind 'em an' slit their weasands.

Go oot wi' a smile, lad.

He was at the door to his own compartments. As he palmed the doorswitch and it slid open, he heard a giggle.

The first woman he saw was Marl.

Oh dear, he thought. Ah'd recked th' lass was gie'in' me th' look back whae Ah wae trainin' her, an' th' Laird knows she's a fine woman, haein' strength i' her bones an' a brain i' her skull. M' type, exactly, an' Ah did hae plans f'r th' twa ae us.

But wee Hotsco made her moves first, and Alex, kind-hearted thug that he was, hadn't quite known what, if anything, to say to Marl, assuming he'd been right about the mutual attraction, not egotistical, and so he'd sort of stayed clear of the Counterintelligence Division he'd set up.

Marl, he noted, as the door slid shut behind him, was looking especially gorgeous, in a sleek wrap of a skirt, a frothed blouse, and a wrap laid to one side.

As was Hotsco, who was wearing one of Alex's shirts and a dab of perfume behind each ear.

Oh dear, he thought. This'll noo be splendifer'us.

'Ladies,' he managed.

Marl and Hotsco looked at each other and laughed. Alex noted an empty bottle in an ice bucket nearby.

'I would guess,' Hotsco said, 'that our hero there is wondering what he should be doing.'

'Ah'm thinkint,' Alex managed, 'Ah'll be needin't a wee drink.'

Hotsco got up and got him a drink from the compartment's bar. Stregg. Iced.

'Your friend Marl showed up a couple of hours ago. She's been telling me stories about spying and that. And we've been . . . talking.'

Hotsco's tongue came out . . . moistened her lips.

'It turns out . . . that we have some common interests,' she said. 'Besides you, I mean.'

'Oh dear.'

It was Marl's turn to laugh.

'With Sten dead,' she said, 'there's not much in the way of CI to do. The Bhor have everything well in hand. And since I'm Head of Section, I gave myself a talking-to. Told myself I was working too hard, and deserved a break.'

Alex shot back the stregg and, while his esophagus returned from hyperspace, poured himself another.

'Marl came here,' Hotsco said. 'And I invited her in. She's quite a woman, you know.'

'Ah ken,' Alex said, now with a note of suspicion.

'Her world has some . . . interesting social customs. Very interesting,' Hotsco purred. 'Ones that *both* of us would be intrigued with.'

'Oh dear.'

'You're repeating yourself, Alex.'

Marl and Hotsco were both trying – with little success – to keep straight faces.

'I thought that she might want to come with us to Prime,' Hotsco said. 'It's a very long passage, you know. She thought that was a wonderful idea. So I helped her pack. She's ready to travel. Isn't that exciting?'

Alex recovered.

'Aye. Aye. Y're welcome t' go, wee Marl. Ah think y're daft, thinkin' goin' int' th' belly ae th' beast is a holiday, but y're welcome.'

Marl walked up, and sedately kissed him on the cheek, in thanks.

'When's the ETD?'

'Ah thought,' Alex said, 'we'll lift ae once. Hotsco's ship's fueled an' ready.'

'Do we have to leave now?' Hotsco wondered. 'I talked to Marr and Senn . . . and they're sending in a wonderful farewell meal. Perhaps in the morning shift?'

'Why then?' Alex asked.

Hotsco walked to the huge, circular bed and sprawled across

it. It had been originally built, it was surmised, for one of the Emperor's favorite's pleasure. She stretched and rolled, a smooth, lithe kitten.

'Why,' she purred, 'there's so much more *room* here. A lot more than on my ship. Even if we put the bunks together in my cabin. Isn't there, Marl?'

And all Alex could manage was yet another 'Oh dear.'

Chapter Thirty

'Down with the Emperor!' the woman screamed, her mouth ragged with hate.

'Death to the slayer of the Manabi!' another being shouted – its display organ swollen to bursting.

'Kill the great blasphemer!' a huge bear of a man bellowed. 'Kill him.'

The three were among fifty agitators working the crowd to a fever pitch. Not that it needed it. Some twenty thousand angry beings were spread out in front of the Parliament building.

They were being held back by a wavering line of black-uniformed Internal Security storm troops.

Banners the size of small buildings jutted from the crowd of demonstrators. The largest one – in the center – was a huge blowup of the Emperor's face. Splashed in blood-red paint across the face was the word MURDERER.

The crowd started chanting in unison: '*Down with the Emperor! Down with the Emperor!*'

Poyndex's gravcar swooped over the crowd. He keyed his mike: 'Move in the tracks,' he said, calm. 'Then activate Alpha and Delta companies.'

'Yessir,' crackled the voice of his aide.

Poyndex watched with professional interest as nine enormous

personnel carriers burst into view. They struck from three sides, boxing the crowd against the front of the Parliament building. Thick clouds of pepper gas spewed from their turrets. As the crowd screamed and pulled back in shock, hundreds of IS troops exploded out of hiding and attacked with clubs and stun rods.

A com shrilled at Poyndex's belt. He glanced down. Irritated. Then he saw the winking red light. It was the Emperor.

Poyndex sighed. Even in the middle of a riot, the Emperor came first.

He patched into his aide and turned over command. Then swung the gravcar around and headed for Arundel.

Poyndex was definitely not looking forward to the meeting. With a full-blown riot in his own backyard, the Emperor was not likely to be the happiest of supreme rulers.

He braced for the worst.

'I'm sick of this nonsense,' the Eternal Emperor roared. 'Don't they know they've lost? Sten is dead. The head has been cut off. There is nothing left for them to do but bleed to death and die, dammit.'

He pointed an accusing finger at Poyndex. 'You're not keeping the pressure on. You're just sitting back and resting on *my* laurels. *My* victory.'

'The rebels can't persist much longer, Your Highness,' Poyndex said. 'It's only a matter of time.'

The Emperor's first slammed down on the desk. A mass of reports spilled to the floor. 'Time? Don't speak to me about time!

'My fleets are still spread out over two-thirds of the Empire. A day doesn't go by that the Zaginows or the Honjo or the Bhor – or some such group of malcontents – find a new and interesting way to embarrass me.

'What's more . . . this madness is costing me. I'm bleeding cash like a pricked pig. And every week these fools oppose me adds at least a year to our eventual recovery.'

The Emperor glared at Poyndex – as if he were the source of all his woes. 'They think we're weak, Poyndex,' he said. 'Even after the Manabi, they don't think we have the nerve to hold the course.'

'A few more victories, Your Majesty,' Poyndex said, 'and the opposition will collapse. All the progs will bear this out.'

'Drakh on the progs,' the Emperor said. 'My gut says different. My gut says this has taken on a life of its own. That bloody mess outside the Parliament building is just one example. No one would have ever dared it, before. And how the hell did they get into the palace grounds, anyway?'

Poyndex grimaced. 'We should have that mopped up shortly, Your Majesty,' he said. 'And the ringleaders brought to justice.'

'Be damned to justice,' the Emperor said. 'I'm the judge. I'm the jury.'

He grew silent a moment. Lost in thought. Then he looked up at Poyndex. He spoke. So soft Poyndex had to strain to hear.

'Why do they make me angry?' he said. 'I can be kind. Generous. Ask any of my friends.' The Emperor looked around the empty room as if to seek them out. Unconsciously his hand moved forward – reaching for the com unit. Then stopped. There was no one to call. The hand snatched back.

Poyndex remained quite still. It was no time to draw notice. He watched emotion play across the Emperor's features. Then they became stone.

He turned to Poyndex. 'I must secure my godhead now,' he said. 'Crush this thing once and for all.'

'Yes, Your Majesty,' Poyndex said, ready for orders.

'They shall go the way of the Manabi,' the Emperor said. 'I want their home worlds destroyed. So when their ships and troops return, they find nothing but dust.'

'Yes, Your Highness,' Poyndex said, already thinking of how to put the order into motion. Choosing the ships, the teams, and the trusted officers who would lead.

'It is not necessary for the explosions to go off simultaneously,' the Emperor said. 'There should be just enough delay – a few hours at most – between each planet buster for the reality to sink in.

'And by God, when I'm done, they'll know what terror is. They'll know my wrath. They want a better life? Fine. Let them look for it in the hereafter.'

He glared at Poyndex. 'Why are you still here?' he snarled. 'You heard what I want. Do it.'

'Immediately, Your Highness,' Poyndex said. He came quickly to his feet, saluted, and moved to the door.

'One more thing, Poyndex,' the Eternal Emperor said.

'Yes, Your Majesty.'

'Next time there's a riot . . . Clot the gas. Use guns. You hear me?'

'Absolutely, Your Highness,' Poyndex said.

The Emperor stared at the door as it hissed closed behind Poyndex. Perhaps he had given the man too much leeway. Lately he'd begun to notice all the Internal Security forces around him. Forces Poyndex commanded.

He realized that he had become isolated. Cut off from all opinion. And everyone about him was a stranger. This was not healthy.

Why had he allowed this to happen? The answer came to him, grudgingly. Fear. Of dying. Clot the duplicate who would replace him. It really wouldn't be *him*, would it? Freedom from the judgment machine came with a curse. The curse of mortality.

So he needed Poyndex and his guards to keep him safe. He required a ring of security so tight, no one could possibly penetrate it.

Yes. But what if Poyndex turns on you? Like he turned on the privy council.

The Emperor didn't think this would happen. Poyndex was ambitious. Supremely so. But he wasn't the kind who desired the spotlight. He'd prefer to rule from the shadows. From behind the throne.

Still . . . his goal *is* to rule, isn't it? To make the Emperor his helpless puppet?

The Emperor decided then what Poyndex's fate would be. But he would wait just a little longer.

A great deal more blood needed to be shed. And when it was done, he would need a fall guy.

To the Eternal Emperor, Poyndex looked like the perfect Judas goat.

Chapter Thirty-One

'Each time I pick up a new trail,' Cind said, 'I think, This is it. Now I've finally got the SOB.'

Cind picked up beach sand and then let it fall in a gentle

stream. 'But then I hit a dead end and that bastard wins again. I can almost hear him laughing at me.'

'You're not alone,' Haines said. 'I've fine-toothed Mahoney's files and come up with a lot of great leads. But they all peter out before I'm barely started. Makes me feel like a clottin' rookie.'

'I still think this is the right way to go,' Sten insisted. 'I'm convinced this is the quickest – and least bloody – way to defeat him. Once we learn where the Emperor gets his AM2, then we can go for his throat.'

'No one's ever done it before,' Cind said. 'Imperial history's littered with failures. Look what happened to Kyes.'

Silence overcame the small group. They were sprawled on one of Nebta's gentle beaches. The day was cozy. The waves lapped softly at the shore. Flying creatures soared above the water, crying their lonely cries.

But the beauty of the day was lost to the conspirators.

Except for one. The gentle giant who was Haines's husband – Sam'l. He was listening to their talk with interest, but a part of his mind kept free. To soar with the flying creatures.

'Discovery is a remarkable thing,' he said, a little dreamily. 'There are stirring tales of beings who have dared and suffered much to succeed in their quest. I read those tales when I was a boy. It's probably why I became an archaeologist. So I could have adventures of my own.'

Sten smiled. He quite liked this big, shambling man. And he had learned to listen with patience. Because Sam'l always had a point.

'And did you?' Sten asked.

'Oh, yes. Many. I shall bore you with them some night over more wine than is good for me. Because that's all they are good for . . . polite conversation.

'In fact, some of the greatest discoveries are found in museum basements. Incredible things. Astounding thoughts. Dumped in a heap to wait for several centuries until some bored student happens to paw through the mess.'

'You're saying the answer is probably right in front of us,' Sten said.

'Something like that,' Sam'l answered. 'Perhaps we just have to hold up what we already know. Turn it this way and that. Until we find the proper light to view it in.'

'Where should we start?' Cind asked.

'Why not start with the element itself?' Sam'l said. 'Anti-Matter Two.'

'If it were gold, or iron, or even Imperium X,' Cind said, 'we'd have a pretty good idea where to look. We'd have the laws of planetary geology and three or four other sciences to go by.'

'That's interesting all by itself,' Haines said. 'In other words – Anti-Matter Two has no counterpart in nature.'

'Possibility one,' Cind said, 'is that AM2 comes from someplace in the universe that has yet to be found. By anyone except for the Emperor, that is. But that's sort of the assumption I've been going on. And that hasn't gotten me anywhere except very old, very cold trails.'

'What about another universe?' Sam'l the dreamer suggested. 'An alternate universe? That would explain why its structure has no counterparts in nature as we know it.'

'I don't mean to be a wet blanket,' Sten said, 'but it was my impression that everyone who's dabbled in alternate-universe theory was pretty much of a strange-o. And that modern science agrees no such thing exists.'

Haines stirred. 'Mahoney had something in his files about that,' she said. 'I didn't pay much attention at the time.'

'What did he have to say?' Sten asked.

'Nothing specific,' Haines said. 'Except he thought it was pretty interesting that the Emperor has always seemed to go out of his way to quash any research on alternate-universe theory. According to Mahoney, some very prominent scientists had their wings clipped for venturing into that area.'

'Maybe I'd better wake up,' Sten said, 'and start paying more attention to some of Ian's weirder ideas.'

'Like the immortality business?' Haines laughed.

'Yeah. Exactly like that. Maybe one has something to do with the other.'

'I like it,' Sam'l said. 'One answer for two. That always makes for an elegant solution.'

'That's what Kyes was after,' Cind said. 'And he came pretty close.'

'I don't know what hat the Emperor pulls his rabbit out of,' Sten said. 'He dies. He comes back. I'll ignore Haines's bit of intelligence that this time around maybe we're not dealing with exactly the same person. Just for a time, we'll put that aside, and stick to what we know.

'One . . . Each time he disappears, according to Mahoney, he's gone for about three years. It was six this last time, but I think we should put that aside as a one-time break in the record.

'Anyway, for three years no one hears or sees anything of him. Which means he must have a hideout. A hideout so secure that no one has found it for – I hate to say this – a couple of thousand years.

'Two . . . Anti-Matter Two comes from a place equally secure. Equally hidden. The privy council found out how well hidden it was, to their extreme bad luck.'

'It would be stupid to use two different places to accomplish pretty much the same thing,' Cind said.

'One thing the Emperor isn't,' Haines said, 'is stupid.'

'So if we find one,' Sten said, 'then that should give us the other.'

'Are we still considering the possibility of an alternate universe?' Sam'l asked.

Sten shrugged. 'Good as anything else.'

'Actually, for our purposes it's far better than most things,' Sam'l said. 'The Emperor would need an entrance and an egress. A door, so to speak. A gateway between universes.'

'Yeah?' Sten looked at him. Blank.

'If I recall my undergraduate physics,' Sam'l said, 'the kind of gateway we are discussing would cause a disturbance in the cosmic background. A discontinuity, I believe it is called.'

Sten got it. He said, 'Finally, we're talking about something you can measure. Instead of never-never lands and spooky supposition. If there's a blip in the cosmic background, we have a chance of finding it.'

'Except, we don't know which way to look,' Haines pointed out. 'It's a big sky. We could spend a lot of forevers checking it out, bit by bit.'

'I'm not so sure about that,' Cind said.

They all looked at her. Praying for a break.

'There were several places Kyes was interested in he hadn't checked out yet,' she said. 'They were areas Kyes suspected might be safehouses on the path the Emperor takes when he returns. All my own progs confirm he was correct to suspect them. They fit the profile.'

'I think we should correlate your stuff with Mahoney's,' Haines told Cind. 'Ian was working a lot of the same angles.'

'Good idea,' Cind said. She smiled at Haines. She quite liked her. And as Sten's former lover, Haines reflected well on Cind's own good taste.

'If this were a homicide case,' Haines continued, 'which this is, in an awful sort of way – once I figured out where the crime was plotted, I'd tie into the com lines. Bug the clot out of the place. And wait for the suspect to call. When he did, all I'd have to do is trace it.'

'Sticking to your analogy, my love,' Sam'l said, stroking his wife's hand, 'I'd guess you wouldn't have to wait. The line would be continuously open, assuming that everyone's theories dovetail. The Emperor would need to maintain communication with his hideout . . . and, Darling, have you ever noticed you've now got me talking like some kind of livie cop? Also, wouldn't there be some kind of open link to a relay station, like the one Kyes evidently came to grief at? There must be more than one of those – the Emperor doesn't depend on chance any more than, say, Schliemann did.'

Sten forced calm. He didn't want to jinx the moment. 'It's at least worth checking out,' he said.

'It's better than that,' Cind said. 'All my instincts are ringing bells that this is the way to go.'

'Go with them, then,' Haines said. 'Instinct is what separates the rookies from the pros.'

Sam'l broke into the flow in his hazy, dreamy way. 'I keep wondering,' he said, 'what our lives would be like if AM2 could be copied and manufactured – like many of the common elements. How different things might have turned out, if you could brew it up as easily as our hosts, the Bhor, brew stregg.'

His lips curved into irony. 'But I suppose it's highly unlikely such a thing is possible. To actually synthesize AM2, I mean. My college text, if I recall correctly, said even if this were a possibility, the expense would make the whole thing an exercise in futility.'

'Mahoney didn't think so,' Haines said.

Sten jumped. 'What?'

'I said, Mahoney didn't think so. He had a lot of stuff in his files on synthetic AM2. Under the heading of Disinformation. I've only just started to go through them.'

She tapped her head, shaking her memory. 'There was something in particular in one of the files. Something Mahoney wanted to bring to your attention.'

Sten nodded. She had shown him several items already that Mahoney had marked with an *S* so Sten would pay particular mind.

Haines smiled, remembering. 'Oh, yeah. Something about a "Bravo Project."' She looked at Sten. 'Do you know what that means?'

Cind saw Sten draw back in shock. Saw his face drain of color.

What was wrong? She reached over to touch his hand. It was cold.

'Yes,' Sten said. Grim. 'I know what Bravo Project means.'

Then he saw the worry on Cind's face. And Haines's. Even the unflappable Sam'l's brow was furrowed.

He forced cheer into his voice. 'But I'll have to do some double-checking on my memory,' he said. 'With Rykor.'

His insides were far from casual – Yeah, he had to see Rykor, all right.

About a nightmare.

He was back on Vulcan.

Karl Sten. A Mig kid turned Delinq with only hours to live before Thoresen's exterminators tracked him down.

Bet was with him. So lovely. So young. And Oron. That odd, brainburned genius who knew only the present.

Mahoney loomed up at him. A much younger Mahoney. Strong and confident. But the adolescent Sten wasn't sure he was to be trusted.

'I must have confirmation of Thoresen's plan,' Mahoney said. 'I've blue-boxed into the exec and central computers, and there was nothing on Bravo Project except inquiry-warning triggers.'

Bravo Project! There it was again. Sten felt a wrenching at his chest. A sob bubbled up, and broke.

Easy, Sten, came Rykor's voice . . . It's past. It's over. It's all been mourned . . . He felt a faint sting. Then calmness as the tranquil took affect. He heard faint scratching sounds. Rykor manipulating the keyboard. Coaxing up images. And Mahoney's big, cheerful face was torn away . . .

One of Thoresen's guards paced along his beat. Sten floated in behind him. His hand circled the man's throat. His knife lunged forward. And he heard the gasp and felt life draining away. There was no remorse in him. Only an odd flicker of joy.

. . . Self-disgust welled. And then flooded over . . . So many deaths by his hand. Murders. Rykor's soothing voice crept in: Let it go, my friend. Let it go.

But he couldn't. The man was dead. Snuffed out. No better than an insect. Sten moaned – God, forgive me . . . and there was another sting . . . and the tranquil lies spread through his veins . . . And the image flipped to—

They were inside the Eye. Thoresen's hidden safe revealed. Sten sprayed the touch lock. Liquid at Kelvin-Zero crystallized the steel. Bet stepped forward with a hammer and tapped. The metal shattered. The door came open. They were in! Sten felt the long-ago thrill. Looked up at Bet and Oron. Grinning like maniacs for beating Thoresen at his own game.

. . . Again, the sting of tranquil. Sten struggled against the terror that would follow. Shouted away the bat wings rustling in his darkest memories. The hammering of his heart eased. He took comfort in the sensation of the hard table under his body. The electrodes attached to his head, arms, and legs. He heard the splash of liquid. It was Rykor, shifting in her tank. No. There was nothing to fear. Trust Rykor. With Rykor operating the brainscan, he was safe. Sten let the images move on . . .

Flip. Flip.

Sten reached into Thoresen's safe. Found the file amid the jumble of paper and bundles of Imperial credits. The folder. Thick and red. Titled: Bravo Project.

The images came slower now. Flip. Flip. Flip . . . Oron taking the folder. Flip! The papers spilling to the floor. Flip! And Sten was scrabbling for the papers. Stuffing them into the folder. No particular order . . . And he saw . . . Flip! Oh, Jesus, one of the Delinqs was falling . . . chest blasted away . . . And . . .

The image froze. Sten felt vomit rise. Heard Rykor mutter, Too far . . . reverse . . . Sten shuddered at the sting of the tranquil and . . .

Flip!

Back to the papers . . . scrabbling for them . . . slower . . . Flip! Slower . . . And he could see them, now. A page at a time. Flip! A title leaping up – RECREATIONAL AREA 26: A SUMMARY OF ACTIONS . . . Flip!

. . . Wait. Have to stop. Have to see. Go back . . . And Rykor's voice called to him, It's no good, Sten. Put it behind you. Go on . . . Sten refused. He fought the voice. The kind coaxing voice. A stinging sensation. And now there was the tranquil to fight.

Sten pushed the veil away. Forced the image forward. *He* was in control, dammit!

And the agony of Recreational Area 26 came tumbling back. The Row.

Riotous voices. Barkers and shills plying their trade. Joyboys and joygirls out in force, emptying Mig pockets for Thoresen's coffers. And there was more. Gambling machines hooting entice-ments. Drunks brawling. Sociopatrolmen charging into the melee, clubs swinging.

There were 1,385 beings on the Row that day.

Among them—

Sten felt a cry of joy burst from his lips. There was his father, Amos. His mother, Freed. And his brother and sister, Johs and Ahd. He shouted. But they didn't hear him.

Stop this, Sten, Rykor hissed. But he wouldn't listen. Couldn't listen . . . because he knew what was going to happen next . . .

Sten tried to shout for his family again. Fear clutched hard as his voice feathered into a whisper. He saw them enter the Row. Saw the big lobby doors shut tight behind them.

He stood there. Frozen. Waiting.

More voices.

'Then dump Twenty-six,' Thoresen said.

The tech protested, 'But we've got almost fourteen hundred people—'

'You have your orders.'

Explosive bolts fired around the dome panels.

In sympathetic reaction, Sten's body flailed against the operating table. At the brainscan's controls, Rykor watched, helpless. If she interfered now, the damage would be so severe Sten would be fortunate to merely die.

Sten jumped again as he heard the typhoon roar of air blasting into space. And he was a forced witness – trapped by his own fool self – as . . .

Almost in slow motion, the escaping hurricane caught the shanty cubicles of the Row – and the people in them – and spat them through the holes into blackness.

He heard a tech's voice: 'Come on. They were only Migs.'

Then the chief tech: 'Yeah. You're right. That's all they were.'

Sten wept.

Rykor worked over him for hours, using all her psychiatric skills as well as her vast pharmacopoeia to bring him back into something vaguely approaching normalcy.

Then she took him back. Past the nightmare of the Row. Back to Bravo Project.

And the secret Thoresen himself later died for.

The secret of synthetic AM2.

Sten huddled in a blanket. Sweat streamed from him, but he was cold. He felt as if he had been pried open, emptied out and discarded.

He took the mug Rykor offered, and sipped at thick, hot, nourishing broth. Rykor's flipper brushed a control panel and soft music swelled. Cleansing music. He closed his eyes and let it wash over him for a long time.

Then he opened his eyes and took another drink. He saw Rykor's large, empathetic eyes studying him.

Sten made a face. 'Never again,' he croaked.

'I am very sorry, my dear friend,' Rykor said. Her rich voice gave meaning to empty words.

'Me, too,' Sten said. 'At least . . . now we know. Not only is it possible to make AM2 . . . but, we have the formula and procedure. I'm not a chemist, and it sounds like the process is a pain, and expensive as hell. But so what? Production cuts prices.'

He stopped, thinking.

'And this just turns the whole clotting universe around and around, doesn't it? Or does it?'

'What do you intend to do with the knowledge?' Rykor asked.

'I'm not sure,' Sten said. 'This changes a great many things.'

He lifted weary eyes to plead with Rykor. 'Don't say anything,' he said. 'I need time to think.'

Rykor studied him. Thinking, He's my friend. A trusted friend. But some secrets are worms that probe and spoil all goodness.

'If something happens to me,' Sten said, 'you've got all the information. Do with it as you please.'

'Very well,' Rykor said. 'I'll wait.'

'Thanks,' Sten said, weak. Then his head slumped. Rykor's flipper came out and lifted the mug away before it spilled.

He slept for many hours. It was a dreamless sleep.

Chapter Thirty-Two

Hotsco let her number two run her ship and the surreptitious movements toward Prime World. She had smuggled things on and off Prime so many times it wasn't a challenge anymore. And her exec had already been making noises about getting her own ship, once this absurd commitment Jon Wild had made to social justice and drakh like that was over.

The third reason was, Hotsco had better things to do. As did Marl. As did Alex. He was most glad, by the time they closed on the Empire's capital, that he stayed in something near shape, and that he was a heavy-worlder.

Hotsco had been right – Marl's culture had some *very*, sometimes even excessively, interesting customs. She was a beaut, he thought fondly. As was Hotsco. He wondered what his wee mum would think if he brought them home and introduced them to her. Hmm. That might require some preparation.

Besides, he was going to die on Prime, he reminded himself.

When Hotsco's ship, the *Rum Row*, closed on the first of Prime's elaborate screens, Hotsco took the bridge.

Sten may have needed an elaborate diversion to slither the *Victory* onto Prime to rescue Haines and the others. Hotsco did not. She ghosted down, past mechanicals that seemed rusted solid, past patrol patterns that seemed loose-weave, even once past a patrolling Imperial destroyer within visual range.

She brought the ship down in atmosphere, and slipped toward a midnight landing, in one of the deepest spots of the River Wye that ran through the center of the green, protected Valley Wye. If the landing had been witnessed by one of the fanatic fishermen who considered the River Wye as their Mecca, Sten and his minions would have been considered fiends incarnate, and the worst punishment the Eternal Emperor could wreak on them considered corporal. Kilgour – who'd been known to cast a bit of feather and fur to assuage the savage salmon gods without ever landing one of the three-meter monsters – felt a little ashamed. But only a little.

He slid out of the ship's airlock in a spacesuit and swam to the bank. The *Rum Row* was under about seven meters of water, resting on the bottom. Not very much, but the dark anodizing would hopefully camouflage the ship against the river's bottom. Of course, if the Wye was overflown by a patrolcraft with sensors, the quality of the camouflage or the depth of the water wouldn't matter.

But why think about trouble?

He buried the suit under a layer of turf for quick retrieval, and headed directly for Ashley-on-Wye, the small town in the valley's center, where he hoped to set up his RV/safehouse. The town appeared abandoned. Quiet, deserted cobbled streets. There was a sign of life in one bar, where, long past closing, songs were being sung, barmaids being pinched and pints poured. Kilgour ignored his thirst and moved on.

The Blue Bhor was dark.

Kilgour settled down to wait for dawn, unobtrusively, under a bush. Either his friend was gone, bankrupt, or conceivably arrested for past sins by IS or the gamekeepers; was out poaching; or else would be out . . .

Just at dawn Chris Frye, ex-Mantis, proprietor of the Blue Bhor Inn, fanatic fisherman and skilled cook and drinker, came out the side door of his inn carrying a rod and creel.

He strolled past a bush, and stiffened. He stopped. Puzzled a bit, then dug into his creel as if to make sure he had not forgotten something.

'Y' c'n drop th' charade,' Alex advised. 'Ah wonder'd i' y' still hae y'r moves, an w'd spot m' marker.'

Frye took the tiny colored metal clip that could've been a flower from a twig and pocketed it as Alex stepped out.

'Sod off, Kilgour. I had those reflexes as a poacher long before I took the clottin' Emp's shilling. What're you doing on Prime? You and your traitorous friend're supposed to be dead, according to the lies I've heard from the drakh-for-brains propaganda mill.'

'Rumors ae m' passin' bein't overrated an' thae. Din't figure you'd put up wi' the drakh comin't doon ae late. How bad is it?'

'Clottin' clotted,' Frye said quietly. 'Anybody who had anything to do with Mercury or Mantis, even way back then, isn't exactly thought of as the best citizen. Nobody's gotten boxed yet, but you're watched pretty close.

'Or so I've heard from friends who drop by. Most folks here in the valley don't remember what kind of sojering I did, and wouldn't cough if they did. Gotta tell you, Alex, I don't know what the hell happened to the Emperor, when he wasn't around – but something sure as hell did.

'Tell you the truth, when they shot Mahoney, and then Sten ran up the black flag, I clotting near nailed the door shut and took off to join you clowns. Only thing that stopped me was a strong feeling of cowardice and old age.'

The two eyed each other. It had been a lot of years, indeed, since Mantis, and almost as many since Frye's Blue Bhor had been used as a safehouse when Sten was investigating the attempted murder of the Eternal Emperor.

'You look a bit older, a bit fatter, and a bit grayer,' Frye observed.

'Dinnae we all, mate,' Alex said. 'An' how's th' life ae a publican?'

'The doors stay open,' Frey's business, offering meals, beds, packed lunches, ghillie-ing, and alk to the dedicated rod-wranglers who came to the Blue Bhor, brought credits in – and Frye's love of good food, drink, and not letting friends pay for anything poured them out just as rapidly.

'I assume you want something?'

'Not much. Just a place for some friends of mine to stay.'

'How many?'

'Twelve.'

'About the crew size of a small spaceship,' Frye said. 'I thought I heard something around midnight. Well, welcome to the king's enemies and all that. Clottin' Emperor. Just one question, so I can shriek quietly and wake up the whole clotting town. Is Sten one of them?'

'No. Ah'm th' hottest ae th' lot, an' Ah'll noo be stayin't.'

'Well, bring 'em in, then. I knew there was something lacking in my life lately. Listenin' for the tread of the hangman, the knock on the door, and the clap on the shoulder. Damn, but I love getting back into harness, particularly if it's something that sounds a lot like high treason. I can't say how *nice* it is to see you, Sergeant Kilgour.'

Since the citizens of Ashley-on-Wye slept late as a habit, there was no problem moving Marl, Hotsco, and the rest of the smugglers into the inn without notice.

Then they waited until nightfall. Frye fed them sumptuously and kept asking if there wasn't something he could help with. Transport? Credits? Frye had some interesting things that went bang buried around somewhere. Phony ID? Hell, did Alex need backup?

No to all of them. What Alex didn't have, he could steal.

He kissed Hotsco and Marl good-bye.

'Y' hae th' orders, noo? I' y' dinnae hear frae me wi'in th' week, or i' y' hae reason to suss thae Ah'm blown or y're under s'picion, y' promise t' haul oot like y' hae a Campbell a'ter y'r skirts?'

The two women promised.

They watched Alex disappear into the darkness, just another

casual laborer headed for towncenter and transport to somewhere on Prime.

They looked at each other.

'How long?' Marl asked.

'We'll wait till there's frost on Sheol,' Hotsco said.

'Good. And if Alex gets nailed?'

'We'll go in after him,' Hotsco said softly. 'If we have to take him out of Arundel itself.'

They touched palms. The compact was made.

Chapter Thirty-Three

This is another fine fix you've gotten me into, Sten. Here I was, Cind thought, a nice, innocent young sniper. All I ever needed was a bit of adrenaline every now and then when a bullet came too close, a chance to prove I could outsneak whoever sent that bullet in my general direction, and perhaps a small medal and a bonus for encouraging that being on to the next metensomatosis.

But no. Sten had to come along and encourage me to larger endeavors. Shouting charge, and letting *other* people go out there and find out if the enemy believes in reincarnation. Sneak down dark alleys that have an absence of the rules of land warfare but a strong presence of thuggery. Declare intent of treason to history's most powerful ruler. Spy, cheat, steal, and assassinate, down in the muck and the mire.

Tsk, she thought.

All because you looked at that reputed demigod of a war chief and thought he looked lonely and had a nice butt.

However, there were, she realized, preening slightly in the mirror, *some* compensatory factors in irregular warfare.

Such as the way she looked at the moment. Nose to toes, she oozed wealth from every centimeter. All her clothes and accessories had been custom-made after her surreptitious landing in a city halfway across the world of Prestonpas.

Kilgour had told her, when you're playing a role, become it, from the mind out. So I settled for the skin out, she thought. Four months' pay for what Sten would, being a man, probably admire as a nice, simple little outfit and pay little real attention to. And as far as the skin? She'd indulged herself with a complete derm treatment, massage, and hairstyling. She noted with amusement that even though her military close-crop didn't give the stylist much room to create, it hadn't affected the size of his bill. But that was one of the prices of being a richbitch.

Cind lifted her rented Stewart/Henry sporter from where it'd been parked out of the mansion's line of sight, and headed for the entrance to the gates.

This being rich, she thought – smelling the sporter's creature-hide seats and admiring the hand-rubbed interior of what appeared to be real wood – could become addictive.

Although there were drawbacks, she admitted. Such as the tiny purse beside her. Once you put in your com, some necessary tools, a recorder, and a handgun, there wasn't room for anything else, really. She guessed one reason the very rich surrounded themselves with retainers was to have someone carry the makeup kit and the gravcar keys.

She grounded the gravcar in front of the mansion's closed gates. Heavy steel, with stone portals. The annunciator on the post beside it lit.

'May we be of assistance?'

'Brett of Mowatt,' she said. 'Plath Architectural Society. I am expected.'

'We welcome you,' the voice smoothed. 'Please proceed directly to the main entrance. Someone will be waiting.'

The gates opened, and she sent the gravcar down the long, winding gravelled road, past the freshly polished sign that read SHAHRYAR, past manicured lawns, past perfect topiary, past stone fountains, to the great rearing mansion in the middle of the estate.

She marveled.

Not the least of her marvel was the knowledge that this was one of the Eternal Emperor's connecting points. Kyes's computer data, and Mahoney's limited information, said this mansion, and others like it, were dotted around the universe, to serve one purpose and only one:

When the Eternal Emperor 'rose from the dead' – and she

shivered slightly, not believing in but still remembering Bhor legends of those who'd passed beyond life – this mansion would be his first stop. Here, assuming Kyes's analysis was correct, he would be brought current with whatever had happened in the Empire during the years since his death/assassination.

A further marvel to her, and this one in anger, was that once the Emperor felt himself properly briefed, he would leave the mansion – and it would be razed to the ground. What a bastard, she thought. So what if the grounds would be donated to the locals as a park? Sarla, it's just like what Sten told me the clot's done to the province of Oregon on Earth. Okay, everybody away from the river. Abandon your homes, your businesses, your lives. Here. Take money, and don't bother the Emperor. He wants to go fishing.

She turned her mind back to the task at hand.

Finding this station, given the initial data, had not been that difficult. Profile: a constantly staffed mansion or its equivalent that purportedly belonged to a family/someone who seldom used it. Yet the mansion would be equipped with a state-of-the-art library computer and personnel, and would receive almost every techno/military/scientific publication.

Interesting, Cind thought, and the basic thinking is worth study. This is an almost-totally-secure path he's designed. Secure because, just as Alex has said, no one looks at the rich too closely. He said that Ian Mahoney had put it best: 'You want to run a safehouse, run a drop, have a team on standby – or anything else nefarious? You don't find a warehouse in the slum, unless you're an amateur or a criminal. Find yourself a nice, rich, bohemian, if possible, neighborhood, where nobody knows or cares who's coming or going . . .'

That gave total security. It was totally secure because, to consider the possibility of something like this mansion even existing, you have to accept the premise that a dead man can come back.

This was only the third mansion that had come close to Cind's profile, and, whereas the first two had a prob of less than 50 percent, this one touched 93 percent. The cover story was – and it was a curiosa item every now and then on the Prestonpas livies – the Shahryar family were ex-traders, who were eccentrically devoted to wandering ways. They would buy an estate on some world they had only heard about, fully equip it, and maybe not visit it for a generation or even longer. And when – or if – they visited it, they would demand complete secrecy.

A woman was waiting for Cind outside the huge entrance to the central house. Either the portal was counterbalanced or else the woman had a Bhor or a heavy-worlder on standby just to open and shut the clotting thing, Cind thought. The woman, Ms Analiza Ochio, as expected from Kyes's analysis, was the estate's librarian. She would be an innocent, absolutely believing the Shahryar cover story, and had been recruited for her technical skills, her liking for a semisolitary life, and probably a certain naïveté.

She was familiar with the Plath Institute and its fiches. Would, umm, what is the correct way to refer to you, m'lady?

'Just Brett.' Cind smiled. 'Titles are something that get you a better table at an overpriced restaurant, and that's it. Sometimes.'

Ms Ochio asked her in. Refreshments? Of course. We have almost everything. It may be a solitary life, but it's a very comfortable one. Perhaps some caff. No, I had lunch before I left my hotel. They chatted for a while, then:

Now, if you'll give me the details, Brett? I'm very curious as to what your interest is in this estate.

Cind explained. The newest series Plath was publishing was to be on the residences of the fabulously wealthy. Not just the flash and filigree of how large the dining hall is, or how many worlds the crystalline chandelier came from, or what rare mineral the swimming pool is surfaced with – although that will be in them, and probably what will make the hoi polloi buy the fiches – but how practical are these grand palaces? Each fiche would contain not only a full floor plan, but livie-portrayals of each room. On a B-track, the occupants or staff of the mansion would discuss how well planned and laid out the mansion was, and on a C-track, one of Plath's resident architects would provide an analysis.

Ms Ochio's smile had vanished.

'*Every* room?'

'Well,' Cind said, 'I don't think we would be interested in all the bathrooms, unless they're something unique.'

'Sorrow,' the woman said. 'That just won't be possible. The grounds . . . some of the outbuildings . . . the first and most of the second floor, and the library are quite open. We had one of the local garden societies tour a portion of the house just three weeks gone. You would be welcome to record them.

'But the rest of the building, particularly the residential areas upstairs? No. The Shahryar family is very protective of their privacy, I was told when I accepted my contract, and was given quite explicit instructions. So . . . if those are your plans, I fear you may have wasted your trip.'

'Could you communicate with the family? To make sure?' Cind asked. 'Oh yes. I forgot. Most reclusive. Oh well. Thank the powers I'm not working on piece rates.'

She stood.

'Might I refresh myself? Then, perhaps, you'll show me, just for my own personal curiosity, the parts of the house that the public is allowed to see?'

'Pleasure. The facilities are just beyond the library doors,' Ms Ochio said.

Cind opened the door and stepped through. As she did, she flicked a small object back, onto the table, in front of the librarian, closed her eyes, and ducked, shielding her face against the blue-flash.

Ochio had time to puzzle at the tiny ovoid – and then the bester grenade went off. She slumped. Two E-hours would pass before she came back to the world, completely unaware of the time loss.

Cind patted the woman down. No vital-signs indicator that would set off an alarm – she had bumped Ochio a couple of times entering the room and had been pretty sure she was clean. No com, no panic button, no nothing. Cind dragged her behind one of the sitting room's small couches.

Two hours . . .

Gun out, but half-concealed, she slipped out the door into the great house.

She looked at the library's doors. Maybe. According to the input on Kyes's computer, gotten from the debriefing of another of the Emperor's librarians, there'd be two sysop stations for it. One would be the central station for the library, the other was code-sealed and could access certain unknown files. Files privy to the Emperor-to-be.

If she had time, and wasn't blown by then, she would take a stab at a little intrusion. But that wasn't the intent of her mission.

She went up the stairs, ignoring a gravlift for fear it'd alert someone there was an interloper loose in the house, and headed for the top floor. From what Ochio had said, that would be the most likely place for what she wanted.

There had been nothing on the roof her preliminary overflight suggested might be a 'cast antenna. so it would either be in a room or – she grimaced – tucked away somewhere under the mansion's eaves. Oh well. It would not be the first set of creepy attic critters she'd crawled through. If she still struck out, she would have to chance combing through the outbuildings. Which would mean a good shot at encountering security – in her over-flight she'd seen uniformed guards walking the grounds.

She went through the mansion's top floor in a blur – checking/cover/checking in the blur of a highly trained security specialist. Clear . . . clear . . . clear . . .

All the rooms appeared quite innocent – furnished as if expecting the momentary arrival of the obviously extended Shahryar family and their equally huge staff of retainers.

Clean. Bright. Sparkling.

Cind went in a door, next to a stairwell curve, glanced around – Kholeric, this bedroom's got to be for the third-ranking appren-tice scullery maid, and she'd have to be a little person, nothing interesting – and back out . . .

She stopped before the door could close.

Looked up and down the hall. At the stairs. Either whoever had laid this floor out was drunk, or else incompetent. Or else I did even worse at geometry than I thought. Back inside. No – the room was still too tiny for the amount of space it evidently occupied. Or maybe, she thought, this room's intended for some-body with a *major* anal fixation, because nobody needs a fresher that big.

The bathroom door was locked. Cind took two of the 'neces-sary tools' from her purse. With the first, she swept the door and jamb. The little 'bugeater' told her there appeared to be no secu-rity monitors on the other side. The second tool went against the pore-pattern 'lock' – odd thing to lock the *outside* of a bathroom. The slimjim hummed, analyzed, and the lock clicked open. Cind pushed the door open. Y-reka.

The com station was elaborate, and automated. Cind ran through the checklist Freston had dummied up for her and, recorder humming, set to work. Not being a commo specialist, she wasn't sure she was getting what she came for – but the registry/control/tracker for the antenna array, evidently secreted in another part of the house or estate, surely looked as if the com was 'aimed' to receive a tightbeam signal from somewhere.

A somewhere that might be the Emperor's sanctuary.

She checked the transmitter nearby. It was completely auto-mated, and she was afraid to mess with it. Most likely the transmitter was intended to send out a 'Don't come here' to the Emperor-in-transit if the mansion's purpose was exposed.

She had – she hoped – what she came after. And she'd left no trace, having plas-coated her fingertips and palms so that any dusting would produce no identifiable prints on the few things that she'd actually touched. She relocked the door behind her.

Now for some cake icing.

She still had just under an hour, and so far had heard no alarums and excursions from downstairs. If necessary, she could always drop back into the sitting room and blank Ochio for another two hours.

The antechamber was still deserted. Cind cracked the library doors. The huge gallery rose to an arched, clear skylight/ceiling. Fiches/reels/files and even books were stacked on the shelves that ran from the floor up ten meters to the ceiling. Now this, she thought, is the kind of library Sten would like to have. When this is all over. If this is ever over.

She looked for life. Nothing.

Cind went in. Near the door was one sysop station. Ochio's. Now where was the other? The one with all those interesting eyes-only files.

She spotted cables – cables, which meant someone was very worried about transmission security – that ran out through one wall.

Cind exited the library and found another unobtrusive room, this one with its wall in common with the library. She popped the door and went in.

Joy, joy, joy, she thought, looking at the computer station. I don't know what I am doing. *When in question/Or in doubt/Run in circles/Hack and shout*, and she sat down at the keyboard. A keyboard, for heaven's sakes. And the computer will be coal-fired, and the screen will be monochromatic. They laughed when I . . .

She touched a blank key. The screen lit.

RECEIVING. ENTER CURRENT DATE AND STATION.

Cind guessed as to the last, and hit keys.

The date, and SHAHRYAR.

SYSOP LOGGED ON. ENTER CLEARANCE.

Oh clot.

Uh . . . Emperor. No. Empire. No. Oh. Wait a minute.

ENTER CLEARANCE. you have thirty seconds before alarm.

The name bubbled up in her mind. Saying a small prayer, she keyed . . . RASCHID.

CLEAR. SYSTEM PRIVILEGE GRANTED.

No way. It could not be this easy. But:

REQUEST COORDS, TRANSMITTER TO SHAHRYAR RECEIVER. PLEASE WAIT.

A light began blinking.

I'm in, she exulted, then, hearing the scuffle of feet outside, rolled out of the chair, and the two security techs burst through the door. They wore gas masks and body armor, and it mattered little as Cind snap-shot them both below their faceplates, and sent two rounds into the lying computer screen, and then dived out the door, bellyfirst.

She hit, skidded, rolled, and dropped the covering guard beside the door, and shot twice at another one coming down a stairway – dammit, I missed, but I sure whitened your hair, woman.

Cind, wanting heavier artillery, shoved her pistol in her suit's waistband, grabbed the dead guards' rifle – an Imperial-issue willygun, she noted, and shame on breaking your cover – thumbed the safety down to autofire, and sent a burst shattering the doors into the library.

And now the alarms were howlingroaringscreaming, and there were shouts, and Cind saw a face peering around a corner. She sent a burst in its general direction, another burst blowing out a huge window, grating, alarm wires and glass and all, and dived through her newly created exit.

Hell, just like a clotting infil course, she thought, turfing down across a bush, feeling that ultraexpensive suit rip and tear, side-rolling down to the ground, burst . . . burst . . . burst . . .

There, that's got them pinned down or at least thinking for a minute; after all, they may be Imperial-trained, but their reflexes are a little slow, and why the clot can't I find the car key.

She found it, as she slid behind the controls of the Stewart/Henry . . . POWER ON . . . GENERATOR TO SPEED . . . WAITING COOLANT FLOW . . . Come on, I really don't give a damn if your luxury handbuilt engine cooks off like a teakettle . . . READY . . . READY . . .

Full lift, full drive, and the passenger door and some of that hand-rubbed dashboard exploded, and the gravcar was airborne, straight ahead, screw the twisty path, for those gates, and she rolled out of the gravcar, three meters in the air, hit turf at twenty kph, rolled a PLF, and was behind some stupid bush carved to look like some clotting animal, and then running, scuttling low, unseen, using every bit of cover.

The Stewart/Henry flamed, ten meters short of the gate, and about fifteen in the air – bastards must've had some kind of antiaircraft capability in that goddammed gate – and plowed into the manicured lawn.

The fence . . . not yet . . . wait a second, woman . . .

Come on, you stupid gravcar . . .

The demo charges she had thoughtfully left in the sporter's trunk blew up, sending the stone portals and metal gates pinwheeling up, around, and then down in a ball of fire.

Cind blasted the fence's alarm system and the jagged glass it was topped with in an obvious distrust of anything electronic. They'll think it's part of the general defunct-o as everything's hemorrhaging.

I hope. Up, up, and away.

Exactly like an infil course, she thought, rifle across the walltop, slither on side, roll down, hit in firing position.

Nothing to shoot at.

She doubled away, into the surrounding brushland, grateful that the Emperor not only secured his mansions with a lot of grounds, but had them built way out in the country.

It would be a three-klick cross-country run to where she had her backup hidden – a bottom-of-the-line utility gravsled bought on the local graymarket.

She surveyed damage – mission, not costume or scrapes. Negligible, she decided. Since the Emperor and his people were operating on the basis that Sten was dead, and she herself wasn't a known entity to the Empire, or so rebel intelligence indicated, the most logical interpretation was that some high-credit computer criminal had tried a speculative B&Eing. And if someone in Internal Security added things together, and got a worst-case explanation – well, she'd asked Sten about that, and he said it was all to the good if the Eternal Emperor got the idea that some unknown hellhound is on his trail.

At least I got to try flashin' and prancin', Cind thought. For an amateur, I didn't do badly, richbitching.

And I think I'm one step closer to the Emperor.

Chapter Thirty-Four

The Eternal Emperor would not have been pleased to see the use Sten and Cind were putting to his former suite aboard the *Victory*. The luxurious sleeping area – with its athletic-field-sized bed – was littered with fiches and printouts and wads of scrawled notes.

Sten and Cind were perched on the bed itself, plotting the Emperor's demise.

They went over all the information Cind had gleaned. And then checked it again. Finally they were done. There was only one more piece missing.

'I don't see any other way to look at it,' Sten said. 'That tightbeam antenna has to be the key.'

'Which gives us one directional leg,' Cind said.

Sten grimaced. 'Yeah. But to get a fix we're still going to have to come up with another. A second leg. Right now all we know is that the Emperor's hideout is somewhere between Point A and infinity.'

Cind nodded, gave a weary sigh, and lay back on the bed. As one side of Sten's mind worried at the problem, the other noted the slender form of his lover. She was gloved into a black skintight jumpsuit that covered her from neck to heel. It had been a long time since they'd had many hours together.

A small part of him wished the impossible. That their existence could be different. That he and Cind could be normal beings with normal problems. Instead, the course he was on required him to continually risk the life of the person who was closest to him.

'Well, I'll be a beardless mother,' the woman of his dreams suddenly exclaimed. She sat up in the bed. Abrupt. 'Wait just a clottin' minute, here!'

'What do you have?'

Cind shook her head, impatient. Started burrowing through notes. 'I'm not sure . . . but if you will button your lip for a second, my love, I'll . . .'

Her voice trailed off as she grabbed a handheld and began punching in data. Sten did as he was told, watching with growing interest as she muttered to herself and pawed about for more bits of information.

She finally looked up at him, eyes bright with excitement. 'I think I've got it,' she said. 'The other leg, I mean. Or how to find it.'

Cind scooted closer to Sten, so he could see the handheld's small screen. 'See . . . That little factor that kept messing us up before. We thought it might be static. Or, maybe even a screwy secondary from all that security apparatus. But look. That wasn't the explanation at all.'

She watched anxiously as Sten weighed the information on the screen. 'Maybe I'm full of it,' she said, beginning to doubt herself. 'Maybe my brain has turned to something like one of Kilgour's pet haggises.'

'No,' Sten said, hastily running a recheck program. 'I'm pretty sure your mind is functioning perfectly.'

A grin split his face from ear to ear. 'It's a second beam, all right. It's gotta be. On a different freq and aimed in a completely different direction!'

Sten quickly patched into the *Victory*'s main logic banks and ran the data. In a few moments the answer came back. 'That's it,' he said. 'There's no other possibility.'

Cind chortled in triumph. 'Now all we have to do is track that bearded wonder down . . . and locate Point B. Which should be . . . I'm hoping . . . one of the relay stations like Kyes found. Except that it hopefully won't have done a meltdown. Run a fix from there, and that should give us the other leg – straight into the Emp's scrotum.'

She knelt on the bed. Hoisted a lovely hand to give Sten a salute. Looking sexier than hell. 'Sir! I respectfully request permission to investigate.'

Sten hated what he had to say next. He would have to tell her no. His rejection would take a great deal of explanation. None of which Cind would buy.

This time, he would be the one to go. Alone.

Not out of love. Or fear of losing her. Well . . . not really, he rationalized, steering to the cold facts of the matter.

When Kyes had confronted the Emperor on that burned-out AM2 station, he had come supported by an entire team of former Mantis operatives. Yet there'd been some kind of mistake made – and the station had self-destructed.

As skilled a soldier as Cind was, she was certainly not as experienced as any member of that grizzled team of stealth warriors. And he assumed the relay station had far more devices for self-protection than just autodestruct.

Sten had spent a small lifetime in Mantis. It was not ego that told him he was the best of the very best. His built-in Mantis calculator delivered this up as solid truth.

He was the only logical choice for the mission.

But how could he say all this to Cind and get her to understand? To see the situation clearly, and unemotionally. With no rationalizations of her own to spare her lover from danger?

He saw the flushed excitement on her face. The dancing lights in her eyes. He hated to kill that look.

Sten told her. She raged at him. She reasoned with him. She pleaded with him. But he held his ground.

Finally the matter was settled. Or at least they'd declared a truce and had agreed not to discuss it for a while.

On the shaky theory that one couldn't eat and be angry at the same time, he rang the mess to serve dinner in the suite.

They spent the first half of the meal in near silence. The second in light chatter. By the time they got to the snifters of crusty old port, the chatter had turned to serious talk.

Sten told her about Rykor and the brainscan and Bravo Project.

'I still don't know what to do about it,' he said.

'Some people would wrap it in suit-proof patents,' Cind said, 'and then sit back and rake in several large fortunes.'

'I know I won't do that,' Sten said.

'I figured as much,' Cind said, with a small smile.

'Besides,' Sten said, 'the ability to manufacture AM2 really doesn't have much to do with the problem we have right now. I suppose one reason I've put off a decision is because I'm not sure how this is going to turn out.'

'I've thought of that, as well,' Cind said. 'I wake up with the cold sweats sometimes, wondering . . . What if the Emperor wins?'

Sten said nothing. He refilled the snifters.

'But that sort of thinking is pointless,' Cind said. 'He either will or he won't. Sometimes Bhor fatalism can save a lot of agonizing.'

She swirled the port in her glass. Thinking. Sten could see she was hesitating to ask a question. Then she spoke, without lifting her eyes.

'What happens if *we* win?' she asked. 'Who – or what – is going to replace the Emperor?'

Sten shook his head. 'It isn't up to me,' he said. 'As far as I'm concerned, this is a revolution. Not a coup. Other beings are going to have to make those kinds of decisions. It's their future. Their choice.'

'I think you're being a little romantic,' Cind said, 'if you think it's going to be that simple. You'll be the man of the hour. The rescuer. More to the point, there's the AM2. Whether it's natural or synthetic. From an alternate universe or a processing plant. You'll be the one holding the keys . . . the keys to the Emperor's kingdom.'

'I'm not much enamored of that thought,' Sten said. Flat.

Cind put a hand on his. 'I know,' she said. 'And that's why I love you. It's also why I want you to think about it. Because when the moment comes, there won't be much time to decide.'

'I notice you didn't offer your opinion on what I ought to do,' Sten said.

'I'm the last person who should say,' Cind answered. 'Do I think you'd make a good ruler? Clot, yes. Would I rather have you to myself? Double clot, yes.'

She squeezed his hand. 'I'm prejudiced, remember?'

Sten flushed, embarrassed. Cind giggled. 'How cute,' she said. 'You're blushing. Now, I've got something on you. The great rebel leader, blushing like a boy.'

'Blackmail,' Sten said.

'Absolutely,' Cind replied.

She slid out of her seat and slipped into his lap. Sten found his arms full of a wriggling, willing woman. Kissing at his neck. Nipping at his earlobes.

'What'll you give me if I don't tell?' she whispered. Naughty.

Sten's hands were busy moving over the form-fitting jumpsuit. Outlining curves. Exploring hollows.

'I'll tell you in a minute,' he said. 'But first, you tell me. How the hell do you get this thing off?'

She took his hand . . . and showed him.

The whisper came hot in his ear: 'There,' she said. 'Press . . . right . . . there!'

Chapter Thirty-Five

The guards' bootheels crashed louder and closer. Alex hung like a spider in his web just above the great blast doors that led from the huge parade-ground/bailey into Arundel Castle. Waited patiently, eye on his timer, trying to ignore the skincrawl.

It had grown worse the closer he got to the Emperor's castle. Not that he had encountered any concrete reasons for this death-tick. Kilgour's self-insertion had been a piece of cake. Thus far. And by his own self-deprecating definition.

He had ridden public trans from Ashley-on-Wye to the nearest decent-sized city. Then he had checked to make sure there had been no recent changes to the ID required on Prime World, and that his own fake cards were correct. Then he found a bad section of town, and bought a currently-in-register gravcar at one of the town's graymarket hurleyburleys. None of the unpleasant questions such as Place of Residence, Place of Work, Reason for Cash Purchase, References, or the rest that might have concerned a conventional dealer were asked.

The sled may have been registered, but its drive was in unspeakable shape – the McLean generator would only lift the gravcar three meters, at max, and held the car at a 15-degree angle to the side. Top speed was no more than 55 kph.

Alex dropped another hundred credits to the seller's purported brother, to get it running right. He knew the 'brother' would jury-rig the repairs, and probably fill the lubricant reserve chambers with something on the specific gravity of molasses – frozen. But what of it? The craft was intended for only a one-way trip.

Twenty klicks outside Fowler, the city closest to the Imperial grounds, Alex found a litter-filled field just beyond one of Prime's omnipresent parks. Clottin' gorgeous, he thought. Put i' a park, w' penalties f'r trash, an' thae'll still be clots thae'll dump their slok ten meters beyon' the gate. Exact whae Ah been seekin', however. He lifted the gravsled into the middle of the lot, grounded it, smashed the ignition and choice parts of the drive, stripped its registry off and buried it, and abandoned the wreck.

He hitched into the city and disappeared into its high-rise slums.

Step One, Two, and Three were accomplished successfully – getting onto Prime, setting up a secure base, and infiltrating into Fowler. Now for a cooling-off period. There was just a possibility he'd been tracked from his arrival, and the Emperor's Internal Security was giving him rope, to see what mischief he had in mind. I' dinnae be likely, he thought. But why chance m' neck i' th' noose? I's th' only one Ah hae.

He had rented the room because it had two separate 'back doors' – one out onto a rusty, abandoned fire ladder that Alex had secretly reinforced, and the second from the other side of the corner room onto some rooftops just made for a rapid departure. Plus it had a half-arsed kitchen, so he wouldn't be forced out into public view.

After a week of lying low and eating packaged food not much better than military rats, he concluded he had dragged no tail with him. On to the next part.

He treated himself to a bottle of expensive brandy, remembering he would have to dump the flask somewhere else to avoid suspicion, since people in the district he had taken lodgings in seemed addicted to simpler pleasures, such as filtered industrial alk or home brew. And he plotted.

Stage Four would be getting himself as close as possible to Arundel. Stage Five would be getting into the Emperor's castle. Stage Six would be out and gone for home, hopefully in one flat-out run.

Alex's plan – one in, twa oot – was that he'd have a partner when he left.

Poyndex. He was fairly sure the man might have some objections to being snatched, and might become violent, or at the very least vocal.

Neither of which was in Kilgour's scheme, especially since a brouhaha would produce an uncomfortable feeling for him, such as death. And for his overall plan to work, Poyndex would have to vanish silently and completely. The Snark would have to be a

Boojum. But he didn't want the distinction to be made positively until it suited Alex, Sten, and the rebellion's plans.

Alex's ambitious plan was to vanish Poyndex straight to the brig of the *Victory*. There he would be offered the same choice his agent on Vi, Hohne, had been given: double or be brain-scanned.

Alex cynically figured that Poyndex, being a purported professional, and having turned his coat once, wouldn't even hesitate as long as Hohne had.

All of Alex's sources on Prime said Poyndex was the Emperor's cat's-paw in everything. His knowledge of the Emperor's closely held secrets would help in the final days.

At that point, Alex planned to have Poyndex surface, publicly. *That* would be yet another blow to the Empire.

All he had to do was bell his pussycat . . .

He forced himself to pay no attention to that little backbrain chant saying, 'And lang lang may the maidens sit/Wi' their goud kaims in their hair, A'waiting for their ain dear love/For him they'll see nae mair . . .'

Maybe he *would* be killed this time. He felt it likely. Maybe this was his last run – but what of it? He had never had the idea he was either immortal or that he would die in a silken bed of old age. But he was determined that at the least, his run on Poyndex would succeed before he would consider taking the journey to the Isle of the Blessed.

He muttered as he finished the bottle. He was going on like a creaking seer, mewling around a cauldron on a blasted heath, thinking naught but wrack and ruin. Stick to bus'ness, lad. But if he *was* a seer, and his plan held up in the sober morn, Alex foresaw a minor crime wave in Fowler's future. At that point, he shut off the single light in the shabby room and rolled over to sleep.

He slept. If he dreamed, he did not remember them when he awoke. He ignored the hangover and reconsidered his drunken plans of the night before. They still made sense. Alex went out for one beer and a plate of greasy eggs and settled down for a nap until night.

The first theft was from an ambulance, parked at the back of an emergency ward. Kilgour, cross-trained as a medic in Mantis, knew just what he needed to clip from the gravsled's kit. He got what he needed, muttered at one object's unwieldiness, and left, relocking the ambulance's door behind him.

He stashed his loot, and checked the time. Ver' good, he thought. Ah still hae time, i' Ah hurry. Th' bistros'll nae be closin't frae another three hours. Back out into the night he went, headed crosstown to another part of Fowler, where an ungrated window didn't immediately suggest a brick and an eyeball-calculated trajectory.

The joint wae jumpin', he thought, looking through the mesh fence at the luxury gravcars parked behind the exclusive boîte. One . . . two security bein's, a couple of carparks. Nae problem.

He used a small laser to cut a Kilgour-sized hole in the fence and went into the lot. He stole the registration plates from six gravcars – and put five of them back. On different craft than the ones they had been taken from. He replaced the fence grating and, with the sixth plate, went back to his tenement. Clean and simple. Kilgour rewarded himself with a couple of beers in an after-hours dive. He bought some rounds, and made some friends.

The next day, he lazed around, after doing minor stretch exercises, only going out for a meal and a shopping expedition. He bought three days' worth of dried rations, a pack, a canteen, a flash, a set of camouflaged coveralls, and a cammie groundsheet. He wished the Mantis phototropic camouflage was available on the open market, which it of course was not. He couldn't have brought a set with him, since he had carried nothing that would even lift an eyebrow in the event of a stripsearch. The bird-watcher's gear would have to do. His final purchase was a small but heavy-bladed 'survival' knife. His next stop was at an electronic hobbyist's center, where he bought some innocuous devices and the tools and circuitry necessary to modify them.

Then he allowed himself one of the two indulgences he had promised himself for the mission. He found a grocer's and bought three kilos of inexpensive, thin-sliced lean beef, salt, fresh parsley, and a collection of dried spices. Back at his tenement, he strip-cut the beef, about three centimeters wide. The strips went into a marinade of soy sauce, water, some cheap red wine, some hot sauce, and spices – garlic, a handful of juniper berries, summer savory, pepper. The garlic, berries, and spices were sautéed a bit, and then dumped, hissing hot, into the rest of the marinade. The strips of beef went in to soak for a day.

About midnight, he went back to the dive he had scouted the night before. One of his new friends was waiting. He had secured what Kilgour had expressed interest in. Actually, he had an assortment. Kilgour sneered audibly at the miniwillygun, although that was the weapon he would have preferred. But, as he told the fence, 'I' Ah gie nabbed, wi' one ae th' Eternal Emperor's owene pieces ae AM2 artillery, Ah'm f'r th' high jump, an' Ah dinnae wan' t' revisit m' old haunts, f'r a while yet.' Also that'd keep the fence from thinking Kilgour had major mayhem in mind, and possibly keep him from singing to the local constabulary about the gun-buying stranger to whom he owed nothing in the way of a buttoned lip.

For similar reasons he rejected a large-caliber handgun, and a folding-stock carbine, even though they were conventional projectile weapons. He chose – and then bargained for half an hour over the price of – a smallbore targetshooter. 'Ah dinnae wan' t' be doin't more'n bluffin',' he lied.

Happy he had convinced the fence he was no more than a lightweight mugger, he trundled home and to bed.

Early the next day he finished off the first indulgence. The strips of beef were drained and laid on the counter. Over them Alex sprinkled salt – at least a pinch per slice. After that, chopped parsley. Then *very* generous pinches of a potpourri of the spices he'd bought. Thyme. More savory. Sweet basil. Pepper. Garlic pepper. Herb pepper. Marjoram. Some cumin, just for the hell of it. He pressed the spices into the meat with the flat of his knife, then flipped the slices over and repeated the seasoning. The meat went into the tenement's dilapidated oven, set at its absolute lowest, and with a cork holding the oven door open a centimeter or two.

While the beef dried, he went to work on the electronic devices, turning them from innocent gimmicks into proper burglar's tools.

He took a long nap, storing energy for the future. When he awoke, just before dusk, the slices of beef were dry, twisted, black, thoroughly nasty, and no more than a kilo in total weight. He admired his jerky. Ah'm noo th' cook th' Emp, Marr, Senn, or e'en m' wee Sten is. But this'll chew easy, i' th' woods i' th' rain. He sealed the jerky in a water-resistant pack. Then he packed and cleaned house. If Security was able to find the tenement, all of their most clever sweeps would yield them nothing, except that the slum had been rented by someone who was compulsively neat.

He went looking for his second indulgence. Taking all of his debris, from that brandy bottle to the electronics tools he'd purchased with him, and leaving them in an industrial dumper.

He found a restaurant big enough so he wouldn't be remembered, and savory-smelling from the outside. And he ate. First he protein-packed, even though he knew that wasn't the best way to prep himself for the run, but clot th' nutritionists, he thought. Ah'll hae someat t' think aboot, eatin' bushes an' pap. Three seafood cocktails. Two very large steaks, ultrarare. A side of sautéed fungi. A large salad, with a simple dressing. A half bottle of wine, to help digestion. The waitress lifted an eyebrow when he finished, sighed, and announced he was now ready for part two of his meal, but said nothing. Part two was carbpacking. He stuffed pasta, in as many permutations as the menu offered, until even he could detect outward movement in his rotund belly. He drank heavily. Water. Pitcher after pitcher of it. Water-packing.

By the time he finished gourmandizing and rolled out, tipping well as Laird Kilgour ought, considering this might be his last *real* meal, it was getting on.

Now he was operational. The plan was running.

In an exclusive residential enclave he had cased several days earlier, he stole an expensive gravcar, easily subverting its alarm and ignition cutouts. He put the registration plate lifted from the bar's parking lot on the car, and that craft's legal plates on the gravcar just in front of it. Confusion shall *noo* be m' epitaph, he thought, and lifted the gravcar away toward his slum. That was a bit of a risk, as he left the out-of-place gravcar down the street long enough to grab his gear and bid a long, last farewell to the slum. Ah'd say thae's naught humbler, but Ah know, i' an hour or so, Ah'll be thinkin't ae aught havin' a roof wi' infin'te fondness.

Into the car, and away. He headed for his jumping-off point – the ultraluxury part of Fowler, the grand estates of the wealthy who sucked around the Emperor and his palace as closely as they could.

Now was when his registration switchy-swappy of a few nights before would pay off, if it had even been noticed yet. If it had been narked, and a copper bleeped him, they would be expecting a prankster, not a criminal. A pity for them, he thought, making sure the pistol in his lap was loaded and locked.

The Imperial Grounds around Arundel were walled and given every imaginable security device. Alex parked his stolen gravsled on the closest street to the wall, and shouldered his gear. Again, another justification for the swapped plates. When the gravcar was reported stolen, it'd be on every rozzer's hotsheet, since it belonged to a richie. Or, at any rate, its registration plate would be. And *that* plate was sitting on another vehicle entirely, back at the theft sight, adding more confusion to the situation.

Kilgour needed this expensive sporter of his to sit where he had parked it without being noticed for at least three days – and he knew that any money district, especially one as close to Arundel as this, would be patrolled. He also planned to use the gravcar for his slither-stage-left, with Poyndex, back to Ashley-on-Wye.

Confusion to m' enemies, he thought, sitting across the street from the wall, meter-metering the security precautions. In two hours, he had the Emperor's system nailed. A walking guard every hour/hour and a half, one well-trained enough to vary his appearances. One sensor just before the wall. One atop it. The coiled razor wire on the wall itself would be tagged. He thought he saw a tree-mounted sweep in a treetop on the other side. An aerial about every hour. A vehicle patrol in between on the street.

Amateurs, Kilgour sneered. A' th' rankest sort. A standard Mantis test was to break in – or out – of a max-security prison within one E-day. The test wasn't regarded as one of the section's more stringent.

It's time, lad. And he went across the street, through the security, over the wall, and was on the far side of that tree-mounted pickup in less than ten minutes.

Tsk, he thought. Th' Emp's noo only gaga, but he's hirin' brainburns t' boot.

Now it would get sticky.

There were twenty-seven kilometers of unpopulated forest and glade between him and Arundel Castle.

What would be a morning's jog took him three days and nearly cost him his life on four occasions. Dogs. More autosensors, of every possible configuration, from seismic to UV to motion to anything the Imperial Household's Head of Security could come up with. Set in unlikely locations. Irregular patrols. Aircraft. It could have been worse, however. A weak point was that the Emperor had insisted his security *must* be as unobtrusive as possible. So this meant dead zones, killing fields, checkboard light-searches, and the like had been forbidden by His Eternalship.

Alex remembered a boast he had once made to Sten, saying he could do something, i' his sleep, draggin' a wee canoe. He felt as if he was doing just that, lugging the McLean-powered stretcher he had stolen from the ambulance that he planned to stick the unconscious Poyndex into, which would give Alex only a few kilos of weight to lug all the way back to the wall.

He moved a few meters at a time, checking his backtrail, sanitizing it when necessary. He never slept, but huddled under the camouflaged groundsheet now and again for a necessary breather and a return to full alertness. He defecated in streams and carried his empty ratpacks with him. Once he hid in a pond, trying to find the promised pleasure in gnawed jerky as a pack of hounds quartered the shores.

At last he saw Arundel, standing black against a blazing hot sky. Its cannonports appeared eyes, staring straight at him. And the crenellations of its battlements . . . he turned off his imagination.

Alex stashed the stretcher in an impenetrable thicket. He was right on schedule – it was midmorning of the first day of the weekend. By tonight, he would have to be inside its walls, or else go to ground for another week.

He would, if necessary. But he would rather not.

There was nothing between him and the 200-meter-tall, 50-degree-sloped walls of the castle's bailey, walls that actually enclosed offices and storerooms for Arundel's vast staff. In the late afternoon there came a clamor, and he imagined the palace employees who had been stuck working on a rec day hurrying toward the pneumosubway that'd whoosh them back to Fowler.

Among them, he knew, would also be the lucky sods of the palace security who had been given passes.

All that would be left in Arundel would be the skeleton weekend shift, plus whatever personnel had pressing tasks that couldn't be put off for two days, the workaholics, and a full staff of palace functionaries, from cooks to bakers to laundry people to butlers.

Big clottin' deal, Kilgour thought. There wae a time whae th' staff'd be taken t' consid'ration, bein' ex-Guard, -Merc, or -Mantis. But wee Poyndex hae all ae *those* dismissed. An' replaced, so Senn an' Marr said, wi' other people, whose qual'fications dinnae be greater'n a droolin' adoration ae th' Emp.

Plus security.

Not Gurkhas – they were long-gone. Nor the Praetorians – they'd never been reformed after their colonel had converted them to a private army in a plot to overthrow the Emperor. Thae wae th' prob' lad, he thought to the memory of the deceased Colonel Fohlee. Y' were whae thae call a preemie antifascist. An f'r y'r pains y' got fed int' a meatslicer.

Now the guards were Internal Security. Poyndex's own. Which no one from Mantis or Mercury who'd encountered Internal Security was very impressed with.

Come night, we'll find oot, Kilgour thought, if the rankin's pure jealousy, or wi' grounds.

There were two other beings who would be in the castle.

Poyndex. Sten had been correct – he seldom left his quarters/ offices in the castle.

And one other.

The Eternal Emperor.

Kilgour considered that, while he waited. W'd thae be the simplest solution, an' avoid all of Sten's moils, toils, an' machinations? An' c'd he e'en get wi'in striking distance? Most likely not. Gettin' ambitious, he reminded himself, most oft means y' bollix up th' whole clottin' mess, i'stead ae endin' wi' th' girl, th' gold haggis, an' all.

Poyndex i' th' lad, an' th' on'y lad.

Come night, after he had timed the overhead aerial patrols, he moved out, slithering up the 50-degree slope of the bailey's walls to just below its crest – to what's known as the military crest, just below the peak. He followed the line as it veed back and forth, to dead-end against Arundel's great wall that climbed 700 meters above him to the leering fangs of the battlements. Alex took off his boots, and tucked them into his pack.

An' noo f'r m' spidger act, he thought, and slid sideways, onto the wall. Notches between stone blocks . . . fingerjam . . . toehold . . . moving sideways, toward where huge blast doors closed off the main entrance into the castle.

'Twould be easier, he thought, wi' climbin' thread an' jumars. But he hadn't been willing to chance buying climbing gear in Fowler. And this wall was not exactly a jo-block fitting . . . He swallowed a gasp, a bit of stone coming away under his fingers, his toe sloppily crooked, coming off, hanging by two clawed fingers and his other leg, god *damn* it, hearing that tiny piece of stone land on the parade ground thirty meters below him, crashing, smashing, its echo ringing around the bailey, louder than an avalanche, louder than a cannonshot, almost as loud as Alex's hard breathing.

Back on the wall. Y' should'a done a few practice climbs afore y' left, lad. Where? Oop an' doon th' main hangar deck wall ae th' *Victory*? Keep on keepin' on.

He stopped just above and to one side of the blast doors. Noo, t' find m'self a home. He found a good one. He drove the thick blade of his knife into a crack for a place to stand. And a nice secure handhold, one that let all four fingers cling to the stone.

Ah c'd dance.

He checked his watch. Bare minutes, he thought, m' timin's perfectamente, till th' first changin' ae th' guard.

The blast doors crashed open just at 1950 hours, and the changing of the guard commenced. Alex watched closely, as a professional.

It was as much a ceremony as a security process. The entire watch paraded out, with the officer of the guard and the watch commander at its head. The formation stopped at each guard's post, the guard challenged the watch – nice touch, thae, Alex thought. Thae's clottin' *clans* ae strange troopies clatterin' through Arundel ae an' evenin' an y' dinnae wan' t' be truckin' wi' strangers – the challenge was answered, and the guard relieved. He came to port arms, doubled to the rear of the formation, and his relief, at the formation's front, took the post. Then, with much crashing and bashing, the formation moved on to the next post and the next relief.

Alex hung happily overhead – he knew that no one in a military formation ever looks up, down, or to either side, in fear of Instant Disembowelment from a noncom or officer – and itemized Internal Security's stupidities.

Since this was a ceremony, IS's black uniforms – nice, functional, and unobtrusive at night – had been prettied up with a white Sam Browne belt, helmet, epaulettes, and gloves, plus white slings on their willyguns. At least, Alex thought, they'd junked the stupid parade-ground rifles, f'r chrissakes, the Praetorians used to parade with.

They were, he concluded, *most* inconspicuous. Especially when he listened, and realized someone had ordered pony and heel taps nailed on their bootsoles. It sounded spectacular against the stone, Alex thought contentedly. Y' c'n hear the clots comin' frae a country mile. Whaee'er a mile is.

Eventually the crashing of bootheels and -toes, the thudding of rifle butts against the ground, and the slap of gloved hands on riflestocks ended, and the old watch disappeared back into Arundel.

Noo, Alex thought, his amusement gone for a total focus, w'll see i' thae parade ground's a sham. I's noo, i's noo, i's noo, he thought in glee, damned near falling off his perch. Thae're ceremonial beings, throo an' throo . . .

Be sick, braw greatness, he thought, a memory from his days in school, an' bid thy ceremony gie thee cure.

Twa hours frae noo. 2200, an' Ah move.

The best time to mount an attack – or a snoop and poop – is either in the wee hours of the morning or else just before dawn, when energies are low and everyone's half-asleep. Normally.

But Kilgour was cagier than that. Which was why he had chosen a weekend as the perfect time to assault an essentially peacetime fortification. Everyone who's not got a pass is either broke, on a striper's drakh-list, lonely with nobody to go see, a lifer, or generally irked at it being their turn in the barrel. Plus supervisors normally take weekends off whenever *they* aren't on the duty roster.

Combine these two facts, and you end up with people going through the motions, generally just a little gruntled about things.

Kilgour, being a sophisticate, also chose the hour carefully. First shift is 1800–2000. These are guards who've been recently fed, but are fairly alert, if for no other reason than the officer of the guard will likely make his rounds on their watch. 2000–2200. Second watch. Not bad, but still a bit early. People are still out and about. 2200. Third watch's first shift. They're fed, had time to stir around the guardroom in boredom, or visit the canteen if the base has one – Arundel did, and it served beer and wine – for a consoling pint, or begin a card game. And then it's time to walk the post in a military manner, all the while realizing at midnight you will be relieved, you will go back to the guardhouse rather than being permitted to return to your own comfortable quarters and personal sack, and will be rousted out at 0400 for yet another tour before dawn. Perfect.

Kilgour's biggest worry was that IS was as subtle as the Gurkhas. They, too, had worked the same patterns when they guarded the castle, and had crashed and bashed with almost as much ceremony, even though they had worn parade-ground gear just on ceremonial occasions. And they had taken their duty very seriously, confining their on-duty canteen purchases to tea and a sweet. But the Gurkhas had their own, uniquely nasty touch, characteristic of the brown men from Nepal. They'd anticipated that some nefarious type, such as Kilgour, might have figured a parade formation is really easy to anticipate, evade, or avoid. So, behind the flashing panoply of the watch change swept a full platoon, in combat gear, weapons ready, at the bloodthirsty lurk.

Evidently IS hadn't gotten word of the twist. The troopies Alex had seen were all there were.

And so, at 2150, as the guards' bootheels crashed louder and closer, Kilgour kept himself from chortling aloud. The third watch came out – Alex heard a few out-of-step marchers who had hit the canteen – and moved through its roundelay. The formation came back, the relieved second-watch guards yawning, looking for a bit of a headdown.

Kilgour slid out of his web, dropped to the parade ground, and went through the blast doors behind the guard, just as the doors crashed closed.

He was inside Arundel Castle.

Now was the moment of maximum danger. Moment, quite literally, since he planned to be visible for not much more than that.

He eeled forward, behind the guard. Ahead was the guardhouse, and the stairs leading down, into the largely ceremonial dungeon far below. Alex *hoped* ceremonial – i.e. deserted. He had once been imprisoned there, as part of the twisting moils of the Hakone plot, with most of the Gurkhas.

The dungeon was his goal. A gaol f'r a goal, he thought merrily, and was suddenly surprised at his cheer. The feeling of doom was just as powerful. More so, really. And he was in greater and greater jeopardy, yet felt strong. Strong and even cheery. N' wonder, he thought with a bit of disgust, we Scots hae taken it i' th' kilt frae th' Brits. We hae songs an' merr'ment, an' they soljer on, grim-arsed, an' tread us int' th' dirt.

Och well. Roll on, death.

The guardhouse. Guard . . . halt. Order . . . harms. Carry . . . harms. Column of files from the left . . . for'rd, harch. The watch went inside, followed by the officer of the guard and the watch commander. Shortly thereafter, Kilgour slunk into the guardhouse as well.

Clatter, shouts, the fresher flushing, rifles clattered into racks, mattresses being unrolled, noisy chatter of young men and women after two hours of walking froo and toe in a military manner.

Nobody even noticed the coverall-clad man who flashed past the open door and down the hall. The hall dead-ended at a thick door, dripping with elaborate locks. Elaborate and old-fashioned. It took less than a minute to pick the three that were locked, another minute to jimmy them so they looked to be still secure, and Alex was inside, at the head of the stairs leading down into the slammer.

He shut the door behind him, wedging it closed. He put his

boots on and started down. The stone steps were worn – as if generations of prisoners and guards had trudged the *via dolorosa*.

Kilgour's flash illuminated the chamber at the base of the steps. Just as he remembered it, although memory was a traitor. But Marr and Senn had sworn Arundel had been rebuilt *exactly* as before. The door to the huge holding cell hung open – a lock he wouldn't have to pick.

Now, Ah rec'lect wee Sten came through th' wall aboot here . . . and he pressed.

Soundlessly, the wall slid away.

Alex moved inside.

This was the 'secret' of Arundel, although not that much of a secret. Sten had discovered it years earlier, when he had been commander of the Guard. Arundel was honeycombed with secret passages. They ran from the Imperial chambers to bedrooms to the dungeon to seemingly pointless openings in main hallways. The tunnels had charmed both of them, in another time, with another Emperor. A proper castle had to have secret passageways, and they were impressed with an Emperor who so indulged his romantic impulses.

Now, the passages would be – if Marr and Senn had been right and they had been built exactly as in the old Arundel – one more step toward the Emperor's destruction.

Alex moved up the winding step and the bending low-ceiling passages, always keeping his carefully memorized picture of the castle's outside interior in mind. He wanted the passageway that led to the row of bedrooms.

Kilgour's mood had changed again. Now, and it might have been claustrophobia from the kilotons of stone and the darkness and the close air around him, he felt as if someone was waiting for him.

Up there. Up above.

Three times he discovered sensors and disarmed them. But this was easy going, moving invisibly, like a rat in the walls, past whatever security was patrolling the interior of Arundel. A rat that stuck *close* to the walls, as any experienced snoop did when climbing stairs and walking down corridors. Not just for cover, but because boards creak, and . . .

Stale air?

No. Suddenly fresh.

Alex looked for a ventilating duct. Nothing but gray stone, or some synthetic cast to look like it. Although Alex suspected the wallmarks, suggesting the passage had been hand-hewn by an ax, might well be genuine.

Definitely fresh air. Alex knelt, holding his palm flat. There. Around this one great flagstone. The stone was a trapdoor. Pressure-activated, most likely. He dug a millcredit coin from his pocket, and slipped it through a crack, and let go. *Ting . . . tiny . . . ting . . .*

a long way down.

An oubliette?

Alex thought of tripping the door, but decided against it. It might be hooked to an alarm. Or . . .

. . . it might be occupied.

Kilgour moved on, hastily, reading his mind the riot act. Ah'm i' th' catacombs, y' clot, an' y're comin' oop wi' dungeons wi' rats an' blind prisoners whae been cast doon i' the dark frae decades. It's nae but a garbage pit. Or a 'spection hatch. Or th' Emp put i' in frae authenticity.

Oh aye. The lad's such a stickler he puts holes i' th' cave no one'll e'er see, except f'r him, whae he hae t' fish one ae his fancy lassies or lads oot of.

Oh aye. Y' lyin' clot.

The long ramp came to an end, and a corridor, wider than the others he'd mazed through, opened.

This, Ah s'spect, i' th' floor Ah wan'. But Alex wanted to make sure. And, again, something was niggling at him. One floor above would be the Emperor's private chambers. And the Emperor would be in them.

Unless he was now hiding like th' ferret he's become, doon i' th' bunker, i' th' catacombs thae run doon t' th' gates ae hell below.

P'raps a wee check, his mind suggested innocently.

Somewhere around here, his mental chart said, should be a braw arch, an' marble steps leadin' oop t' th' mon himself.

There was no arch.

Just solid wall.

Alex touched it in several places, making sure it wasn't another secret doorway. It wasn't.

Aye, he thought. So th' lad dinnae built *ever'thing* ae i' was. Mad, paranoid bastard, he thought, but with relief. It kept him from indulging that wild urge to solve all, with one mad charge into the heart of the enemy.

So he went for the target he'd intended from the beginning.

Alex found one of the panels – intended for observation, perhaps – that swung out into the main outer passageway. He swung it open a trifle . . . and looked.

Ah. Two Internal Security sorts, standing in front of a double set of doors. Marr and Senn told him the entire floor had been ripped apart and rebuilt. Only Poyndex occupied the floor. Only Poyndex was entitled to be this close to the chamber.

Alex smiled.

A very different smile than before, when he hung above the castle's entrance.

Now, the smile was truly on the face of the tiger.

Poyndex swore, but to himself. His frustration didn't show on his face, any more than any other emotion would be allowed to. He kicked out of the program he was running and cut back to the top of the fiche.

He had a dull headache. His eyes felt as if they had been sandblasted.

By rights he should have shut down and gone to bed. It wasn't that late, but he had been putting in twenty-hour days, between normal tasks of Internal Security, the Emperor's constant calls, and then this new mission of planetbusting all of the rebel worlds' capitals.

He had considered and reconsidered the Eternal Emperor's terror program.

At first, it seemed absurd. Not absurd, his mind corrected. Wagnerian, in the sense of Götterdämerung. Like that Earth tyrant, whatever was his name? Oh yes. Adolph the Paretic. But that was impossible. The Eternal Emperor *couldn't* be insane. Of course not.

He vaguely remembered one of his instructors in his youth telling him about some dictator of the past, who had overthrown the old boss and was having his flunkies write a new constitution, legitimizing his powergrab. The dictator had rejected one draft, telling his subordinates the new constitution must not, in any way, interfere with the state's use of terror as a legitimate ruling tool. Terror from above, it had been termed. So there was precedent to the policy.

The problem was, he could not remember either the dictator's name, nor whether his reign had been long and lethal, or brief and bloody . . . and he certainly did not have time to do any idle research.

On further consideration, Poyndex thought the Emperor's plan meritorious. Might this flickering nonsense of a rebellion, which now, with its 'liberator' dead, should properly be called anarchic, be quelled by a huge, nearly instantaneous application of force? Machiavelli, after all, had instructed his prince to ax all of his enemies at one time as soon as he'd seized power.

Not that Poyndex had ever entertained disobeying, or even questioning, this new Imperial policy. He served loyally. Perhaps not the Emperor, but the new fascination he had that it was possible to live forever. To live forever, and . . . and to rule?

The list was drawn up. The Cal'gata's capital world. The Honjo's six canton worlds. The seventeen area centers of the Zaginow. The Bhor capital of Vi. And on and on. The death roster ordered 118 worlds obliterated.

It could be done – the Empire still had far more battleships and completely loyal crews who'd murder an entire planet because it was so ordered.

The problem was the Eternal Emperor wanted the planet-bustings done nearly simultaneously.

On which clock, Poyndex thought, and whose calendar? Local? Zulu? Prime? By rights, he should have been able to rout out Admiral Anders and his planning staff. The navy might be a bit less than stupendous, but it would seem anyone with logistical training would know how to arrange things so that ships would arrive in the target system in time, but not early enough to arouse suspicion. But the Emperor had insisted this would be a totally secure operation, which meant only Poyndex and his own personal IS staff were even aware of the bloodbath to come.

Poyndex got up from his multileveled metal desk. It, and the rest of the technical apparatus he required, clashed with the ornate wood and silk wallpaper of the suite. But what of it? Perhaps, one day, when this was over, he would have it redone. This time with some of his own ideas, rather than what he had done before, letting some imbecile who thought the old ways were the prettiest handle things. When there was time, when there was time.

But there never was enough time.

Perhaps a drink, to get a little sugar in the bloodstream.

Poyndex walked to the small bar, and eyed the bottles. The Scotch the Emperor loved, and Poyndex couldn't stomach. That awful substance called 'shine,' and its even-worse companion, the ET beverage stregg, which the Emperor had reportedly once liked. Poyndex had tasted it once, and shuddered. No one but a soak or an ET could possibly drink that. He lifted the cut-glass decanter that held the multi-fruit brandy of his home world, which was about the only liquor Poyndex enjoyed the taste of, once a month or so.

No. That wasn't it, either.

He turned toward the doorway to his bedroom. *That* was what he really wanted. To lie down. To sleep. For a day, for a week, forever.

It took a moment to realize there was a man crouched in the doorway. A man wearing strange, camouflaged fatigues. His face was blackened. And he held a long-barreled pistol leveled at the center of Poyndex's chest.

'Y'll freeze,' Alex said quietly. Normally he would've used a petrifying shout – but there were two sentries posted outside.

'Y'll noo breathe, 'cept on command,' he went on, coming to his feet and moving forward, neither eyes nor gunbarrel moving from Poyndex.

'You're Kilgour,' Poyndex said, trying, and hoping he succeeded, to keep shock from his voice. A flicker of pride – he didn't feel any fear.

'Aye.'

'You know, killing me won't stop the Empire.'

'Aye?' Kilgour asked, in polite disinterest. 'Thae's noo m' plan. Y'r noo f'r th' big sleep, unless y' do someat daft, like cryin' oot.

'First, y'all step awa' frae th' bar, turn wi' y'r back t' me, kneel, an' clasp y'r hands behin' y'r head. Move!'

Poyndex turned. Started down, then stopped.

'The thought just struck me,' he said. 'If you're not on a personal vendetta . . . is Sten still alive? Did he order this operation?'

'Ah said,' Kilgour repeated, still in a near whisper, 'Ah wan' y' doon ae y'r knees, mate. Noo—'

Poyndex began to kneel . . . and lifted his arms, toward the back of his head. Alex's free hand came forward, the tiny bee sting of the narcdispenser ready. Poyndex's right hand shot out toward the bar.

Kilgour's reflexes cut in.

The heavy-worlder's left hand dropped the syringe, curled to hammerstrike, flashed out.

And struck. Just to the right side of Poyndex's neck. The snap was loud. Poyndex's head dropped to an impossible angle . . . and his body fell forward. Alex caught him by the collar before he could crash into the bar, and eased him down to the carpet.

Knowing he was wasting his time, he checked pulse. Rolled Poyndex over and peeled an eyelid back. Even, stupidly, held his ear to Poyndex's mouth, hoping for the slightest breath.

Nothing.

Y' clot, his mind savaged. Y' *know* bettern' thae! Are y' sarkers? Cannae y' control y'self? I' dinnae matter i' this i' th' lad whae killed Mahoney, or helped th' Emp slaughter who knows how many?

Y'r noo a professional, he thought in disgust. And started to get up.

Then his eye caught the button, mounted in the base of the bar. He looked closer. Nothing in the bar front. There. Above him. A snapaway panel, just like they showed him in training. Behind it would be what? A gun? A gas dispenser? An electrified net? Linked to a panic siren? Whatever it was, it would've been disaster.

Noo, did Ah *really* o'erreact . . . or did th' corner a' m' eye spot the switch? Balls, he thought. Kilgour resolutely refused to believe in any sense beyond the common. Then he realized, for the first time since that sleepless night on the battlements of Otho's castle, the night so long ago when Cind had been named to speak for the Bhor, that feeling of doom was gone.

By th' Stuarts, he thought. Ah been carryin't this death-sense wi me f'rever, stumblin' like a 'cruit i' th' Selection March ae Mantis. An' it's vanished, wi' Poyndex's dirty soul.

Are y' suggestin' his mind snickered, thae y' *sensed* thae wae a death owed? An' thae either you, or Poyndex, wh'd hae t' pay the price? Clot off, he thought. Ah hae noo time f'r Highland devils an' goblins.

Th' *real* question i' whae d' th' milkmaid do, whae she's kick'd o'er th' bucket, an' th' missus a' th' house dinnae hae a cat?

He had it.

He shouldered Poyndex's body and went into the bedroom, back through the panel into the secret passageway.

Feeling bulletproof, he trotted rapidly down it, to where that huge flagstone was. Noo, i' it's nae boobytrapp'd or alarm'd, he thought, Ah'm home free. He dropped Poyndex's corpse on the stone.

It fell away, and the body dropped into darkness.

No sirenscreech. No scurry of guards, if there'd been a silent alarm.

Just a thud. Silence. Another thud. Another silence, even longer. A splash, finally, as the late Poyndex hit bottom. Kilgour wondered, once again, just *what* was at the bottom of the shaft? He shone his tiny flash down into blackness. Nothing.

He touched the flagstone, and it smoothly swung back into place, waiting for the next weight to land on it.

Was it a garbage disposal? A sewer?

Alex shook his head.

He would never know.

He considered what had just happened and, after some reflection, nodded thoughtfully.

Assuming Poyndex's body wasn't discovered, at least for a while, what would the effect be? On Internal Security and, most importantly, the Emperor himself?

A wee bit scary, Kilgour concluded. I' fact, all thae's been sacrificed by giein' Poyndex a braw clout i' y'r original dream-scheme wi' th' brainscan.

Nae a bad night's work, he thought. Ah'm noo th' gowk Ah thought, a few min ago.

He allowed he deserved a pint and a dram. And perhaps a wee walk in the moonlight with Marl and Hotsco.

Feeling romantic – and thirsty – Kilgour headed for home.

Chapter Thirty-Six

The creature eyed Sten through its enormous compound eyes for a very long moment. Sten remained motionless, lying on his belly on the ocean's floor. Three meters above him, waves crested and crashed against a rocky island.

The animal had a three-segmented body, with hard jointed segments extending off in all directions. It looked hostile, but then, anything over a meter long with pincer-jaws usually was logged as unfriendly by Sten. Especially when it was about twenty centimeters from his face.

Eventually, some sort of sitrep was achieved by what passed for the creature's brain: You are the biggest thing in this ocean. No, you are not. There is something that is bigger than you. It is sitting just in front of you. You are a predator. You can devour anything that is in this ocean, No, you cannot. You tried to snag a morsel off this creature. Your pincers did not snag a morsel. This is not a familiar situation. You are in trouble. You should go somewhere, somewhere this creature is not.

The huge 'trilobite,' or so Sten had labeled him, flurried its 'legs,' and was gone, vanished into a floating drift of algae.

Very good. Sten resumed his final mental briefing before he charged wildly off in all directions. It wasn't that the arthopod was any danger to Sten – especially since Sten was wearing a spacesuit. But those clotting pincers snapping on his faceplate made it hard to think.

That transmission beam that had almost been missed, 'casting from the mansion, had led the *Victory* farther out into the back of beyond, into barely explored space. It intersected no system or object for light-centuries.

But then there was a solar system. Three worlds, one moon, and a sun. Not a dead system, like the relay station Kyes had discovered, the relay station that had self-destructed on him. Life was just creating itself here.

Sten had kept the *Victory* on the solar system's fringes, terrified that one mistake would snap the thin lead, like so many others had before. Then, they would have to find another one of the luxury safehouses/way stations, and attempt to duplicate Cind's success. Or else follow that other beam far out into the unknown. It would probably take no more than a lifetime or two to find whatever pot of gold was at the end of that nearly infinite straight-line rainbow.

Freston again returned to his first skill, the com board. He had absolutely guaranteed Sten that the com beam from the mansion impacted on the second world from the sun.

Sten transferred Freston, Freston's com specialists, Hannelore La Ciotat, and himself to the *Aoife*, and again remoraed La Ciotat's tacship to the destroyer.

Very slowly, the *Aoife* closed on the world. Very young, indeed. Continents slowly sinking, seas shallowing and spreading across the world. Cambrian was the description, or so Cind informed him, suggesting that he might wish to take some basic geology courses one of these centuries, in his spare time.

They looked hard. Visually, electronically, actively, passively. It took an E-week before Freston had something. He had picked up some odd indicators from the coast of one of the small subcontinents in the southern hemisphere. Something was down there, something that appeared artificial. But every surface scan, from IR to scope, said the area was just one more rocky outcropping on the still-sterile land.

Freston chanced simulcasting a beam from the *Aoife* on the same freq as the continuous beam from the mansion, 'cast for less than a second. He picked up some bounced radiation. It was his theory that an antenna, or more likely several of them, had been inletted into the planet's surface in that area. Capable of receiving, transmitting, or retransmitting.

Sten thought about it. The moonlet Cind had visited had been hollowed out as it was equipped with antenna, a buried shelter, power, and supplies. The Emperor was smart enough to not choose the same sort of world for each relay station – but it seemed he would be using a similar construct for all of these stations, and, for safety's sake, putting most of the station underground.

Or underwater.

Freston sneered at that – why would you bother adding the additional interference of liquid, not to mention building sediment, crustaceans with claws, and all the rest? Sten nodded – right. The station – if this is where it was – would be just at the shore.

Freston then triumphantly produced his second piece of information. He had put a tight scan on the area, a few hours after nightfall. That really gave him something. Something a searcher would have to be specifically looking for, and looking in a very small area.

The rocks held their warmth for a long time. Far longer than air. That gave Freston some interesting images, particularly when they had been computer-enhanced by an operator with imagination. Here . . . the lines of the buried antenna, where the material the antenna had been made of held its heat even longer than the rocks. Over here, an oblong outline, invisible without enhancement. Big. Freston thought that outline was a hangar door – the outline provided by cool air seeping through the door's edges. Over here – Freston's smile threatened to pass his ears and meet at the medulla oblongata – the door. People type.

All Sten had to do was get to that entrance, figure out how to pick the lock, and voilà.

Voilà, Sten said cynically. And then worry about how big a bomb is located inside. Freston *tsk*ed. He couldn't be expected to do everything, could he? Being just an underpaid captain, and all.

Sten laughed and threw him out. Then he sat down to figure out the rest of the insertion plan. Thinking about underwater gave him the rest of the scheme. He sent for La Ciotat, kissed Cind, and moved out.

The tacship entered atmosphere in a trajectory exactly like that of a meteorite. A big one, but that couldn't be helped. It splashed down just beyond the horizon, but short of the bounce-reflection of any sensor on the subcontinent. La Ciotat sent her ship toward land below the surface, muttering if she'd wanted to run a submarine, she would have been incarnated as a dolphin. Or a Rykor.

About a kilometer offshore, a reef rose to just below the surface. Sten ordered La Ciotat to bottom the tacship behind the reef.

He went out the airlock and began the long trudge toward shore. In the livies, the suit's little reaction jets would have worked splendidly in water and gravity, as they did in space, and sent him zooming like a speedboat toward his rendezvous with whatever. But even with the suit's McLean pack on full, mass was still mass. Sten chugged toward shore at the stately speed of a ferryboat, giving him plenty of time to tourist.

If the land above was barren, the sea was not. Algae in sheets. Ribbonweed thickets. Some things that looked like small crabs. Nautilus-coiled snails. And trilobites, from barely visible to . . . to large enough to make Sten think of big centipedes intermarried with scorpions.

As the bottom shelved, he cut power, and took her down. At three meters, he considered his situation and, until it wove away, the universe's biggest trilobite.

So far, there hadn't been any loud bangs that would indicate he had set off any of the booby traps he knew the relay station was equipped with. Very well. So they were still waiting for him. He wished he could figure out what those booby traps or booby trap could be. None could be that sensitive – the Emperor would hardly want his return slowed because a relay turned the fire on unexpectedly, and a heat sensor blew. Or a motion detector went crackers at an earth tremor. Trick stuff sometimes went off from its own cleverness. Nor, Sten thought, would the Emperor want to spend his time elaborately defusing some really sophisticated diabolism – he had heard the Emperor curse at puzzles and hurl them across rooms minutes after he had picked them up, back when . . .

Just back when, Sten. Stick to the subject at hand.

What the booby trap would most likely be, he concluded, was something the Emperor wouldn't have to worry about, but something that would send any intruder airborne in very small pieces. A retina-coded lock? A pore-pattern lock? Hardly, considering the device's reliability had to be conceivably measured in centuries.

Sten went ashore, wading through the surf, onto dry land. Dry rock. Nothing but rock, of various shades of gray and black. Dark sand at the water's edge. A beach, almost half a meter wide. Sten spotted something and knelt, his mission forgotten for a brief moment. There, just in the surfwash, was a bit of green. Life. Some kind of plant, he thought. Algae? He didn't know. Go on back to the sea, he thought. You don't know what you're starting.

He rose and trudged up toward the shelf where the station would be located. His suit's sensors said the air was breathable, although oxygen poor. But he stayed in the suit. Again, part of his caution. He didn't think that an infrared sensor would be used to set off the self-destruct mechanism – but the spacesuit would sure keep such a device from starting the Big Bang.

The ground flattened. Sten crouched behind a large boulder, and turned on the helmet display. He consulted the map projected above his faceplate.

Over there would be the door. A slant of solid rock. Sten moved as surreptitiously as the bulky suit would allow to the closest cover. He was thirty meters away. He dropped binocs down over his faceplate and minutely examined the rock. Twice he stopped, eyes starting to see things that were or weren't there.

At full magnification, his field of vision was less than a third of a meter on a side. Back and forth, back and forth his eyes moved, just like a photointerpreter scanning a mosaic, looking for the camouflaged enemy.

Ah. Perfectly round. Which rarely exists in nature.

A keyhole.

Punched in the rock about where a keyhole should be . . . for an Emperor-sized being.

All Sten needed was the key.

He went across the open ground like a trundling armadillo. Expecting the shatterblast. Nothing.

He knelt next to the keyhole and unsealed a pouch. After some thought, back aboard *Victory*, he had realized the key would be the simplest part of this operation. The Emperor couldn't wander around carrying some elaborate hex-pattern-coded special key in his return to the throne. Or, anyway, Sten wouldn't plan things that way, if he had been setting this whole paranoiac rigmarole up. So the key would have to be something that the Emperor could procure or have made at the appropriate time. Also, the key wouldn't be part of an exotic locking system that might be unobtainable or superseded by the time he returned.

Sten took out a standard, Mercury-issue electronic lock-pick. Round, eh? He found a pickup of the correct size. He fitted it to the analyzer and inserted the pickup in the hole, wanting to put his fingers in his ears against the blast, even though the pickup was made of completely neutral Imperium X. The analyzer buzzed, and told him what code would open the door. Sten detached the pickup, and plugged it into the sender. He touched the TRANSMIT button . . .

. . . and the door lifted up, Sten tumbling back out of pure fear reaction, seeing a ramp leading down into blackness.

Sten waited until his heart began beating again. He took a flash from the pouch and, lying flat against the ground in the event *this* was the trigger, sent the beam around the inside of the passage. Nothing. He looked down. Just a ramp.

Sten set the flash's beam on full diffuse and started down, a centimeter at a time, a step taking a lifetime, moving forward as he had back on Vulcan so very, very long ago . . .

. . . and then he had it.

Or he thought he did.

All this slok about IR detectors, prox detectors, motion sensors, sensor sensors . . . that wasn't it. The Eternal Emperor had been an engineer. A good one. So his protection would have been conceived using one principle: Keep It Stupid, Simple.

Sten's foot came down more confidently, and he took another step. Another. Another.

The door dropped closed behind him. Sten flinched, but not much – he was increasingly sure he was right. An overhead light went on. There was a standard monitor panel against the wall. It showed an environmental system had gone on, and was bringing the shelter up to an E-normal condition. There was a counter display on the panel. The counter showed 0. Sten started past it, then saw, from the corner of his eye, the counter change to 1.

That *was* it.

There was a door in front of him. With a palmswitch. Sten touched it, and the door opened.

Living quarters inside. Small, but well-equipped.

Beyond them, a doorway.

Sten, trying not to hurry, went through it.

The room was huge. Instrument-filled. Coms and controls.

He'd done it! He was alive . . . and inside the relay station.

Unless something went bang in the next few seconds, Sten's dazzling perception had been correct:

What was the one thing the Emperor would do, but no one else would dare?

To show up solo. No one else would. Anyone smart enough and brave enough to get this close to the heart of power would have allies or subordinates. He didn't know where the sensor was – overhead, in the floor, or in the walls. There could be one, there could be many of them.

Christ, Sten thought with a chill. If Kilgour wasn't off on his run against Poyndex . . . he might have taken him along. Even Mantis killers like someone guarding their back, and Sten and Alex had been friends too long.

Count one . . . count two . . .

And this gleaming room would have been melted-down shambles.

He looked around at the keys to the kingdom. There were four secondary boards in the room. Reporting stations, Sten theorized. Three of them showed identical readouts, the fourth was zero/zero. That would be the station Kyes or Kyes's men had discovered, and, in the discovery, destroyed.

In the center of the room was a great circular control panel. Readouts and controls.

Sten touched nothing as he examined that carefully. Most of them were unlabeled – that wouldn't be necessary for one operator, the operator who'd designed the entire system. But there were enough marked so he could tell what the panel was intended for.

This *was* the secret of the universe. Sten felt a chill.

From here, the Eternal Emperor could turn the 'power' on or off. Direct those great robot convoys to deliver the AM2 to the depot he directed. Increase the amount of AM2 for each depot. His decisions would be repeated at the three surviving relay stations.

And from here his commands would be transmitted out. Out toward another universe. Somewhere out there, somewhere beyond, was the discontinuity. All that was necessary was for Sten to plot the transmission coordinates of the beam from this station and send them up to Freston on the *Victory*. Simple triangulation with the beam from the mansion would locate the discontinuity.

'All right,' Sten whispered, not aware that he spoke aloud. 'All right, you bastard. It's all over now.'

Chapter Thirty-Seven

The Eternal Emperor stormed down the corridor to his office. The long, broad hallway bristled with guards. On one side were the Internal Security thugs. On the other, a grizzled detachment of veteran Imperial Guardsmen.

He had a pistol at his belt and he kept a ready hand on the butt as he rushed by them. His eyes swept their ranks as he moved. At the slightest hint of a threat he was braced to draw and fire.

But not a being's eyes met his as he hurried to the relative safety of his quarters. They were all too busy watching one another. The atmosphere was so thick with suspicion, a sneeze would have set off a full-scale battle.

His chamberlain was waiting by the door. 'What are you doing here, Bleick?' the Emperor snarled. 'I didn't send for you.'

Bleick's weasel eyes took on a startled cast. 'I was only here to report—'

The Emperor chopped in. 'Search him!'

Bleick gave a bleat of fear as four guards – two IS men and two troopers – hurled him to the floor and put him through a humiliating body search. They followed this up with a thorough scanning, to make sure no assassination devices had been surgically implanted.

When they were done, Bleick scrambled to his feet. 'I am so deeply sorry, Your Highness,' he whined, 'if my presence gave you even the slightest cause to worry.'

'Shut up, Bleick,' the Emperor said. 'My orders were clear. No one is to come near me unannounced.'

'But I thought—'

'Did I say you had permission to speak?'

'No, Your Highness.'

'That's your problem, Bleick. You attempt to mimic the thought process. Instead of following orders.'

The Emperor turned slightly to the side, so he could keep both Bleick and the corridor in view.

'All right,' he said. 'As long as you're here, you might as well tell me what you had to say.'

'It's only about Poyndex, Your Majesty.'

'Only? Only? What the clot's wrong with you, man? My chief of security disappears from the face of Prime World, and *you* call that only? For crying out loud, don't you—' He broke off, disgusted. 'What a load of drakh. Okay. Speak up. I'm tired of making like a target in my own damned hallway.'

'Yessir. I only came to report, sir, that I've just finished an exhaustive study of . . .' Bleick saw the Emperor was about to explode again, and dropped a few self-serving modifiers. 'Uh . . . No one on the staff has seen him for some time, sir. I double-checked every room log in the castle. And personally supervised the follow-up interrogation of the staff.'

'Who interrogated *you*?'

Again, that startled look. 'Uh . . . Me, sir? Why . . . No one, Your Majesty.'

The Emperor motioned to two of the guards. Since Poyndex's disappearance he had ordered them paired at all times, so there was always an IS man watching an Imperial Guardsman – and vice versa.

'Take him down to interrogation. Put the screws to him real good. I want to make sure he and Poyndex didn't do a little deal together.'

Bleick squealed in alarm. 'But, Your Majesty. I have certainly proved my loyalty over the—'

A beefy hand slapped over his mush, cutting off the rest of his nonsense, and he was hauled away.

The Emperor turned back to his door. Submitted himself to a thumb- and iris-print check. Then he tapped in the code that only he knew. The door slid open. He glanced around once more to make sure he wasn't threatened, then drew his pistol and stepped inside.

The door hissed shut behind him. He was alone. The Emperor carefully checked the new sensors he'd had installed. A little of the tension eased. His security was intact. No one had breached his office while he'd been gone. The Emperor holstered his weapon.

He crossed to his desk and pulled out some Scotch. He poured a glass. But before he drank, he slipped a small rodlike device from his pocket. Inserted it in the liquid. The pea light at the top of the rod beamed green.

The drink was safe.

He shuddered it down, then sagged into his chair. The Emperor was at the edge of exhaustion. He got out a syrette and pressed it against his arm. There was a slight stinging sensation, a tingling in his vein, then his heart gave a sudden jolt. And he was filled with drug-induced energy.

His hand shook as he reached for the bottle to refill his glass. The Emperor grimaced. It was one of the many downsides of amphets.

Another, he realized, was paranoia. A small laugh burst from his lips. There was a slight hysterical tinge to it that annoyed him. He'd have to watch it. Be very careful. Make sure his reasoning process was his own and not something out of a pharmacy.

On the other hand, as the man once said, even paranoiacs have enemies.

The Eternal Emperor settled back to take stock of his situation.

He had just returned from a personal tour of the interrogation rooms. His lips curled in disgust at the memory of the smells of blood, fear, puke, and body wastes. Only the loud screams of pain had given him any real sense of satisfaction. Not that he enjoyed that sort of thing. Not really. After all, that would be a symptom of madness.

The satisfaction came from seeing for himself that real effort was being put into solving the mystery of Poyndex's disappearance. He had also stressed to his interrogators it was equally important to uncover any conspiracy connected to the disappearance.

There had been a score or more confessions already. A few might even turn out to be true.

They had played a tape of Baseeker's hysterical babblings. She had admitted her disbelief in the Emperor's godhood. Confessed her motivations were only from greed. And then further revealed that Poyndex had suborned her. That she was directly working for him.

There were sure to be others. He would soon learn the extent of Poyndex's game playing.

He doubted Bleick was involved. But the Emperor was not willing to chance it. Of course, the man would be useless for any kind of position when the interrogators were through with him. He would have to find a new chamberlain. Ah, well. It was a price the Emperor was willing to pay.

The Emperor emptied his glass. He pushed the bottle aside. He would wait before having another.

It was time to put the crisis into perspective.

Poyndex's disappearance posed several possibilities – all of them nasty:

1. *Poyndex was dead. Slain by the enemy.*
2. *He'd been kidnapped.*

In either case, it was possible that he had been tortured and had spilled his guts to an agent, or agents, of the rebel forces. Which meant some of the Emperor's deepest secrets might have been revealed. Literally, considering it was Poyndex who'd supervised the removal of the bomb in the Emperor's gut. And that little secret could eventually lead to Alva Sector.

3. *Poyndex had suddenly decided to defect to the other side.*
4. *Poyndex had been in league with the Emperor's enemies for some time, and fled because he feared his treachery was about to be uncovered.*
5. *If numbers three and four were true, it was likely Poyndex had co-conspirators within Arundel itself.*

Internal Security certainly couldn't be trusted. And since Poyndex had crept into so many other areas, neither could any other branch of the Imperial Service. Once again, the Emperor's secrets were in jeopardy.

The most glaring fact – not possibility – of all was that:

6. *Arundel, the most secure facility in the Empire, had been breached.*

On that general topic, there was another item gnawing at him. And might not belong on the list. Although he would put it down anyway.

7. One of his safehouses had also been violated. The Shahryar mansion.

The full report on the incident had only just reached him. The enemy agent had obviously been supremely professional. This was one of the few times any of his sanctuaries had been invaded, by a burglar or otherwise. The agent was also professional enough to escape unscathed after wiping out his security force.

However, the report had assured him the woman had been unsuccessful in getting any useful information.

But, wait! What about the code word she'd attempted to penetrate the computer?

Raschid!

How did she know that name? The Emperor's secret persona? Poyndex?

Possible. But, only if he had secretly joined the enemy some time before. Besides, how would Poyndex have known that name?

No. Highly unlikely. Just as it was unlikely that Poyndex was a longtime traitor. A mole. Nothing in the man's profile fit this. He'd been running his own, complex power game, but the Emperor was just as certain now as before that Poyndex's power yearnings were satisfied by being the most important member of the Emperor's staff.

Could the rebels sweeten that kitty?

Not a chance, the Emperor thought. Besides, Poyndex was the type to take the cash and let the credit go. Promises for the future by a rebel force had to be the rottenest credit in town.

There was one further item that argued against betrayal by Poyndex: the planet busting program the Emperor had ordered. One hundred and eighteen planets and all their inhabitants had been targeted for destruction.

If Poyndex was in league with rebels, those planets would have been warned and their security jumped to the nth degree.

Intelligence assured him this had not happened. All transmissions and traffic from those systems were absolutely normal.

Good.

So, Poyndex was not a traitor.

Was he willing to bet his life on it?

Yes, he was.

This line of logic also erased the possibility Poyndex had been kidnapped. Or that he had revealed anything under torture. Because, once again, the intended victims would have been warned.

Very, *very*, good!

The Emperor rewarded himself with a drink.

As he was pouring, another possibility hit him. The trembling hand shook harder, spilling Scotch. He slammed the bottle down with such force that it shattered. Scotch pooled on his desk.

He didn't notice. Just as he didn't notice the sliver of glass in his palm.

The Shahryar mansion!

His safehouse!

What would be the worst-case scenario if the agent's mission had actually been successful? Even if the woman hadn't actually penetrated the computer, what could she have learned?

There was the tightbeam transmitter. Alone, it meant little. But there was a second clue the enemy might have uncovered. And that clue could lead to one of his AM2 relay stations.

From that point, it would be simple to get a fix on Alva Sector!

Oh, come on, he scoffed. That's foolishness. That's assuming an awful lot. That's seeing a level of professionalism rare in the history of his Empire. Who could possibly have—

Another gut-wrenching thought.

Sten could have accomplished it!

Yes. By himself, or he could have planned a mission to be carried out by one of his supremely efficient comrades. Alex Kilgour, for instance. Or that Bhor woman – what was her name? His warrior lover.

Could she have been the woman at the mansion?

No. That was ridiculous.

Wasn't it?

But . . .

Sten had been the very best he had ever had in his service. He had surpassed even that old warrior and spy master, Ian Mahoney. As an enemy, he had proven his deadly efficiency many times over.

Sten would have also been able to penetrate Arundel at will.

True.

But Sten was dead.

Wasn't he?

It was insanity to believe otherwise.

Wasn't it?

Another wrench of the gut. Bile rose. What was the proof of his death? There was no body. No witnesses.

Yes. But given the circumstances, escape had been impossible.

Hadn't it?

He felt a sudden chill. Hackles prickling like desert thorn.

The Emperor had a sudden certainly that it had all been a sham.

Sten was alive.

The Emperor drew a long breath. What should he do about it?

For the first time in his long reign, the Eternal Emperor was unsure what he ought to do next.

BOOK FIVE

ENDGAME

Chapter Thirty-Eight

'All systems green. Entry to be effected in twenty seconds . . .'

There is a moment that confronts every sentient being. When moral imperative collides with survival in the shadow world that lies between decision and action.

The moment can be as simple as a choice between a lie and a self-destructive truth.

It can be as complex as a choice between the suffering of many or a moral and legal obligation to the few.

Theologians call it 'free will.'

There is no scientific term for this moment, although medical techs can trace with precision the effects of the inward struggle on the organism.

In humans, hormone and adrenal glands spurt their powerful mix into the system. Organs such as the heart and lungs speed up their actions. Fluid pressure and body temperature rise. Blood oxygen levels soar, especially in the muscles and the brain. Infection-fighting cells ready their chemical weapons to stave off attack. In extreme reactions, waste organs spasm empty – to lessen the chances of infection if the body is violently penetrated. The skin tightens to present a harder and smoother surface against a weapon. Sweat glands gape to pour out perspiration as the body's cooling system jumps to full readiness. The perspiration also acts as a lubricant between the limbs and the trunk of the body. In a man, the scrotum tightens and the testes rise to present a smaller, tougher target.

That's what science says.

Sten would have it said it was nothing more than plain animal fear.

He crouched alone on the small bridge of the tacship staring at the ship's monitor. Watching space rain fire. Sten had never seen or experienced anything like Alva Sector.

The tacship's voice rasped over the speaker: '*Entry will be effected in ten seconds . . .*'

His mathematical mind – the side that also contains poetry and music – acknowledged beauty. Saw wonder in the ultimate disharmony at play in the forces unleashed where two universes touched.

But his soul saw nothing but a hole into hell.

'*Entry will be effected in nine seconds,*' came the speaker voice.

Sten watched a small comet streak toward the discontinuity. Tendrils ablaze with scintillants snaked out for it. Enveloped it. The comet shattered with such violence, the pixels on the monitor screen exploded into white glare.

He steadied himself. Reached deep within and got a grip on the fear. He turned it this way and that, studying it by the light of his rational mind.

'*Entry will be effected in eight seconds,*' the voice continued.

Sten wasn't afraid of sharing the fate of the comet. Well . . . to be honest . . . only a little afraid. The tacship – as well as every item that might be exposed to the raw anti-particles of the other universe – had been plated with Imperium X in a lightning stop on Vi – huge deposits of the substance lay just beyond the Wolf Worlds.

In theory, he should be able to slip through the discontinuity into the other universe unscathed. He'd already sent a probe through and it had returned unharmed.

Therefore . . . what was there to fear? The Emperor's security? The dogs he would have set to watch over his treasure? No. Sten imagined whatever he might encounter would be clever and fierce. But, he'd overcome those two dogs before, and trusted enough in himself to overcome them again.

'. . . *seven seconds* . . .'

What then? Sten sent his mind after that probe. Attempting to imagine himself on the other side. In an entirely different reality. An angry thing with a dripping red maw rose at him. He wasn't wanted. He didn't belong. Every thing . . . every minuscule particle . . . would be his enemy in that place. Even in his imagination, the hate was intense.

And he would be . . . absolutely . . . alone.

More than any other human had ever been. With one exception.
The Eternal Emperor.

'. . . *six seconds* . . .'

What made the fear burn hotter was that this was a choice
he could reject. The crawling coward in him was weeping in its
pit. Begging him not to go. Why must it be his responsibility?
Let someone else do it. And if no one would, then clot them all.
He could run and hide where the Emperor could not find him.
And if he tracked him down, Sten could face him on braver
ground. So what if the cause was lost? So what if everyone could
be doomed?

They might die.

He might die.

But at least he wouldn't have to go into that place.

All he had to do was hit the switch and the mission would be
aborted.

'. . . *five seconds* . . .'

His hand lay just to the side of it. Sweating and cold.

'. . . *four seconds* . . .'

A twitch would shut that damned voice off.

'. . . *three seconds* . . .'

The coward in his gut shrilled, 'It isn't too late!'

His fingers curled.

'. . . *two seconds* . . .'

Mahoney's voice floated up to him from the grave: 'Make the
devil into a fist, lad. And strike a blow!'

'. . . *one second* . . .'

Sten's fingers knotted down. Bloodless with effort. Fighting
panic.

'*Entry will now begin,*' the voice said.

Sten kept his eyes glued to the monitor as the tacship shot
forward and closed on the gates of hell.

so small . . .
piteous and small . . .
and they all want to . . .
kill me.
i don't want to die here . . .
please.
no one knows me . . .
here.
no one . . .

cares.
my eyes are . . .
bitter.
and i taste colors on . . .
my tongue.
someone . . .
someone is watching.
where?
i'm afraid.
where is he?
out there.
who is he?
i'm afraid.
who is he?
i don't know.
he's watching . . . and . . . i'm . . .
so small.

Sten vomited into the bucket he had put beside his seat. He
snapped open a freshpac and swabbed his face and neck with a
cool astringent. He rinsed his mouth with stregg and spit into
the bucket.

Then he raised the bottle to his lips and drank. Deeply.

The stregg shuddered and boiled in his belly. But he kept it
down. He took another drink. Felt the fire build. It was warm
and comfortable and familiar. Like a hearth.

Sten rose from his chair and went through stretching motions.
He felt the knots unsnarl and blood sing in his veins. Then he
went through the complete Mantis warm-up. A half hour of
blinding motion and violent ballet.

He went into the small sanitary facility and took a shower
just below blistering temperature. He followed it with an icy blast
that sent his heart racing and brought the blood up stinging just
below the surface of his skin.

He put on a clean shipsuit, made caff, and padded back to
the bridge, with a steaming black cup in his hand. He calmly
eyed the data streaming in from the ship's sensors. The mainframe's
control module winked and gurgled as the computer fed on the
data. Once in a while it gave a red-light hiccup as it digested a
more complicated bit.

Sten nodded. Good. He sipped on his caff.

Feeling quite normal.

In a few moments the computer survey would be completed. The basic laws of this universe would be deciphered. The ship's computer would redefine its own reality.

And Sten and the ship would no longer be blind.

He settled into his seat to wait, sipping at the caff, his mind clear, but settled on nothing, his eyes on the rushing stream of data as if he could actually decipher and make sense of anything moving at such speed.

Sten was carving out a place for himself in this new universe the only way he knew how. Which was – routine. It was an old soldier's trick. Someone experienced in constant changes of post. No matter how distant from home, or bizarre the inhabitants, strangeness can be overcome by establishing a routine. Little things. Familiar things. Selfish things. Like washing and grooming. The first hot, bitter cup of caff at the shift start. And the cool, uninvolved appraisal of the mission to be accomplished.

Then you rolled up your sleeves and plunged in, secure in the knowledge it was only necessary to do this job well. Greater and more complex responsibilities were on the able shoulders of your superiors. Just do your job, and keep your nose clean.

Sten eased back, relaxing. He had found his center now. It was time to populate this place.

He smiled, thinking of Cind. And the warm arms he would go home to when this job was done. Comfort in those arms. Yes, and in that sharp mind as well. The way she had of always finding a way around a problem that was vexing him.

And Kilgour. His brawny, near-lifetime friend and comrade-in-arms. There was a man to have at your back. Any problem that stumped Cind would never get past his cunning Scot's brain.

After them, Sten invited Otho and the Bhor. Applauded as the Gurkhas marched on. Then Marr and Senn. Haines and Sam'l. And his other friends and loyal crew members.

Soon, they were all trooping about in his imagination. Cracking jokes. Slapping him on the back. Kissing him or shaking his hand.

The computer chirped and went silent. Sten looked over and saw the 'Ready' sign blinking.

He took another sip of his caff and set the cup down. His fingers flew over the control board. Then he sent the command.

Sten looked up at the monitor screen. Light began to fill the blankness.

He leaned forward, eager to get his first look at this new universe.

He had no fear of it now.

Because he was no longer alone.

He had found it!

The Emperor's glory hole!

The size of the operation seemed larger . . . but somehow also smaller . . . than he'd imagined.

Big AM2 tanker ships moved in and out of the rubble of an old, destroyed system. On the rubble itself – broken planetoids, or moonlets – his probes showed huge mining machines, harvesting the basic stuff of this universe. Smaller shuttles laden with ore moved back and forth between the tankers. Once full, the tankers moved off – for the long voyage into another universe and back.

It was a vast, complex system – all operating automatically – to accomplish the Emperor's far-off purpose.

Part of him was disappointed in the size, comparing it to the gigantic mining operations he'd seen in his travels. This place would fit in a small corner of one such complex and still have room to rattle around.

He thought it incredible that something this small had such a profound impact on civilization for so many hundreds of years. But a whole empire had been founded on one small particle from an alien universe.

The second thing that amazed him was the age of the ships and machinery. They all functioned perfectly, going about their business as if they were just off the line. But their designs were straight out of a technology museum.

They were all big, clunky things, with sharp edges and many moving parts.

The final thing that startled him – and *this* most of all – was that so far not one shot, not one missile, had been fired at him.

Sten smoothed the tacship past a tanker, moving deeper into the mining complex.

As soon as he had spotted it, Sten had gone into extreme stealth mode. He had cut all extraneous power, maxed his shielding on all freqs, held sensors on passive, and dropped internal operations to the barest hum. Then, using a tortuous, grab-every-speck-of-dust-for-cover route, he had 'crept' in. Not one enemy sensor appeared to have sought him out. Nor did he find a single trip wire to sound the alarm at his approach.

When he was more certain, he had dropped the shields and begun an active search. Still, no reaction. Then he had emerged

in plain view – every gun port of his own open and bristling for
the attack. But the mining colony had gone about its robotic
drudgery without paying him the slightest notice. This was very
strange. Why would the Emperor leave his treasure unguarded?

Perhaps because he felt quite certain it would never be discovered. After all, it did lie in another universe. A universe that
everyone until a short time ago had been led to believe did not
exist. *Could not exist.*

Sten frowned as he ran this through, half his mind occupied
with the moonlet whooshing past him on the monitor screen . . .
Okay. He'd buy that logic.

Although, if it had been Sten's hidey-hole – no matter how
impossible to find – he'd have filled it with wall-to-wall trip wires
and booby traps. His paranoia had been ground in by his Mantis
trainers. Trust nothing to chance.

Sten thought of the Emperor's quirky mind, and felt easier
still. This was simple. The Emperor *liked* simple. Simple meant
it was harder for things to go wrong.

His mind clicked one large step forward. A simple system
would also have a single control. Which meant it was likely the
whole mining operation was run from one command center. Next
step . . . The Emperor would most likely set up his living facilities at the command center. It wouldn't take much space. Sten
was sure the Emperor would always be alone. There was no living
being he could trust with this secret.

Very, very good. Because this meant all Sten had to do to stop
the AM2 flow to the Empire was to hunt that command center
down and blow it in place.

And goddamn the Emperor's eyes!

The big white ship loomed large on the screen. It was older than
his father's ghost stories. Space dust cobwebbed its archaic lines.
He saw sensor banks and antenna pods he had only a dim memory
of from his flight-school history fiches. He saw other apparatus
whose purpose escaped him entirely.

But there was no escaping the purpose of the weapon ports.
Archaic or not, they were instantly recognizable. The Eternal
Emperor was not entirely unarmed.

The puzzling thing was, the ports were sealed.

Sten kept a ready hand on the button that would send two
Goblins hurling toward the ship. A hint of menace and he'd blast
it to whatever hell existed in this universe.

Was this the place? Was this the command center? The Emperor's ultimate safehouse?

He probed it. The ship was alive, but running on a very dim intelligence. There was atmosphere. There was function. But there was no sign of life.

Sten sighed, wishing for the thousandth time that it had been possible to sail in here with the *Victory* and a full crew. With their skill and the *Victory*'s sophisticated sensor system, he would have been able to pick the white ship apart atom by atom.

He *thought* this was the right target. But he wasn't sure.

Sten would have to go on board to investigate.

He studied the white ship, looking for a point of entry. He dismissed the idea of docking with the ship. Or of using any of the main entry ports.

The Emperor liked simple. Booby traps are simple. Which equaled booby-trapped entrances and docking area.

He almost missed the hole back near the engine area. Sten zoomed in on it until its raw edges filled the monitor screen. A meteor impact point. It looked fairly fresh. No more than a few years old. Evidently the AM2 debris had impacted, then detonated on or near the outer skin.

Sten wondered how much damage it had caused. Was this the explanation for the closed weapon ports? The dimmed nature of the ship's operation?

Luck was still running with him. And clot Otho and his 'there's only three' kinds: dumb, blind, and bad. For Sten, the first one was working just fine.

He studied the hole. Then felt luckier still when he realized it was large enough to give him his own private door into the ship.

Getting to it would be no problem. Alex and Otho had sheathed a complete spacesuit and accessories with Imperium X.

So if he encountered a stray particle of AM2 on the way over and back, he would not go bang.

Sten started gathering what he would need. Mentally figuring the size of the charge it would take to blow the ship, if it was indeed the Emperor's command center.

He would have to rig some kind of demo pack. With a one-or two-hour timer. No problem. Except – what to put the unit in. How would he get it there? Clutch it in his damned arms like a baby?

Then he remembered the pack Alex had put through the

Imperium X plating. They hadn't much time, and Sten was impatient.

'What the clot's that for?' Sten had asked. 'Am I supposed to pull it over my head when the shooting starts?'

'Y' noo ken, young Sten,' Alex had answered, 'when y'll hae need t' tote sum'at.'

Sten had let it go rather than argue.

And now, thanks to Alex, he had something to put the demo unit in.

Pure blind luck.

The second on Otho's list.

He'd take it. No problem at all.

He floated out into that mad universe, ignoring the colordazzle he saw through the faceplate and navigating on the suit's own inertial system.

His luck stayed with him and he reached the white ship without incident. It took less than twenty minutes to widen the hole enough to get him and his gear inside.

Once inside, however, confusion was his temporary enemy. The ship's design was too ancient, too unfamiliar, for him to find his bearings. He locked his boots on a work platform – in a cavity just beneath the ship's skin – and swung this way and that. Poking his pinspot into the mouths of the shafts that emptied onto the platform.

Finally, he got a sense of direction. Odd, how that term sounds in another reality. Another universe. Sten shook off this mindbuzzing notion. Direction was the shaft he chose. The one he believed led to the engine room. This was all the definition he needed. He'd save the other for long, philosophical nights when he was deep in his cups with his friends.

He made his choice and kicked off. Floating upward into blackness, moving gracefully, despite the bulk of the demo pack on his back.

The engine room was a shambles. Twisted metal and cable were evidence of just how much damage the meteor impact had caused.

There was no atmosphere. But the ship's gravity was on – he was standing firmly on his feet, with his boots' mag units turned off. Readings on his helmet screen indicated signs of mechanical life just beyond. There was no danger indicated. No sign of a defense system sniffing for Sten.

Sten guessed the meteor's impact – and the resulting explosive reaction of AM2 exposed to alien particles – had only wounded the ship. It had reacted by reducing its functions to the barest minimum. That minimum most probably included the AM2 mining operation, and transport. Assuming this was the Emperor's command ship. Which he still was.

It was still probably capable of effecting repair, but had reserved the power necessary for this to maintain those all-important minimum functions.

In other words, Sten thought, it was too clottin' busy.

It suddenly occurred to him the damage he was looking at might have something to do with what was so wrong about the Emperor.

What was it Haines had said? The Emperor was the same. But, not the same. Same, but different.

Maybe the meteorite had upset some sort of plan. Some sort of . . . He shook his head. This was pointless speculation.

To be saved for that far-off night with his friends.

He moved onward.

Sten slipped down the corridor, in increasing awe at the complexity of the white ship. Now that he was two damage-control locks beyond the damage zone, the atmosphere and temperature were E-normal. His helmet and gloves were off and snapped to his harness. He was breathing deeply, washing out the stale suit air from his lungs.

The air smelled fresh, with a faint sharpness to it. Pine? Yes, or something close to it.

This was the Emperor's place, all right. He was a great lover of nature in the raw.

Sten was following the main corridor. He assumed this from its large size, and the blue line painted down the center. Everywhere he looked were more corridors – smaller corridors – angling into this one. And there were doors. Many doors.

Some led into nothing more than masses of wiring and electronic gear. Some led into storage rooms crammed with equipment and parts. There was even a working repair bay for all the robots scurrying about the ship.

Sten stepped aside as one chugged past, waving a welding wand, intent on its small purpose.

The corridor suddenly opened into a high-vaulting atrium. And he entered a vast hydroponic farm. Filled with exotic plants and fruits and vegetables.

Things the Emperor would find delicious.

Sten kept to the blue line until the path became corridor again.

And that gave way to a large room. Smelling of antiseptics and medical purity. There was a long row of vats, filled with an unfamiliar liquid. The light in the room was oddly bright . . . and warm. He saw steel tables and surgical snap-ons for medical 'bots. The room made him feel quite uneasy. He moved on.

He came to the ship's control center. It was jammed with archaic equipment, all operating as smoothly as if this were the ship's maiden run.

Sten was absolutely sure, now.

This was the Emperor's command center. His safehouse. Blow this ship, and the AM2 would stop.

He unslung the demo pack and put it on the floor, next to an air-fresher vent.

This was as good a place as any.

He looked about, curious. Amazed at what the Emperor had accomplished. Actually, Sten knew he could only have a glimmering of the sophistication.

How had he done it?

Hell! How had he even gotten started?

Sten saw a door just down the corridor. It was marked Library. Maybe there was some kind of an answer in there. A clue to the mystery of the Emperor.

He walked along the corridor to the door. It hissed open and he stepped inside.

As the door shut behind him, he noted with some surprise that there were no banks of fiches. No shelves of books. Just a few tables and chairs.

Was this really a library?

The voice came from behind him.

'Checkmate,' the Eternal Emperor said.

Chapter Thirty-Nine

'You know the drill,' the Eternal Emperor said. 'Don't make a move. Sudden or otherwise.'

His tone was light. Confident. Sten did not make the mistake, however, of thinking he was *over*confident. He stayed quite still.

'Now . . . Shed the spacesuit. Very slowly, please.'

Sten's hands crept to the fastenings. A moment later the spacesuit was heaped at his feet. Now he was wearing only the overall-like shipsuit.

'Kick it away,' the Emperor ordered. 'A good sturdy kick, if you please.'

Sten kicked, and the spacesuit went flying into a corner.

'Walk forward to the far end of the room,' the Emperor ordered.

Sten walked. He stopped when his nose touched the wall.

'You can turn around now,' the Emperor said.

Sten turned. His old boss had a haunch perched on a table. A pleased smile on his face. The gun in his hand was pointed steadily at Sten.

'It's good to see you,' the Emperor said. 'For a while I was afraid you weren't coming.'

His free hand went to a bottle of Scotch sitting on a drink tray. Without moving his eyes from Sten, the Emperor poured himself a drink.

'Sorry I can't offer you any,' the Emperor said. 'But I'm sure you can understand my rudeness.' He sipped from the glass.

Sten understood. Given a chance, he would turn anything handed to him into a weapon. A piece of paper would do just fine. A glass would be even better.

His Mantis senses had taken over the moment he had heard

the Emperor's voice. Respiration and heartbeat calm and steady. Muscles at ease, but set on a hair trigger. Mind working clearly, taking in every object in the room.

Eyes measuring the distance between himself and the Emperor. It was a little far. But doable.

Why he was still alive, he didn't know. Or much care. He was completely focused, however, on remaining in that condition.

'You realize, I suppose,' the Emperor said, 'that you're going to have to tell me who else knows about this. And the disposition of their forces.'

Sten shrugged, but said nothing.

'I won't bother with torture,' the Emperor said. 'Out of respect for our past relationship. Besides, I have a perfectly adequate brainscanner. A little elderly. A little careless with vital cells, sometimes.'

He took another drink. 'Nothing to worry about, however,' he said. 'If it turns you into a vegetable . . . at least you'll be a dead vegetable.'

'Congratulations,' Sten said. 'It looks like you thought of everything.'

The Emperor grinned. 'Tsk. Tsk. No, "Your Majesty" anymore? Or, "Your Highness"? No respectful terms at all for your old boss?'

'It was an easy habit to lose,' Sten said. 'Once the respect was gone.'

'No need for cheap insults,' the Emperor said.

'No insult intended,' Sten said. 'Just a fact. Candidly admitted.'

The Emperor chortled. 'You won't believe this,' he said, 'but I've actually missed you. You can't imagine how dull and incompetent the people I have around me are.'

'So I've heard,' Sten said. 'Especially that character you had – what was his name? – the one who runs the boys in the storm-trooper getups?'

'Poyndex,' the Emperor answered. 'His name *was* Poyndex. Thanks for helping me out, by the way. I hadn't quite decided how to get rid of him.'

'You're welcome,' Sten said. 'I'll be sure to give Kilgour a "well done."'

'Right now,' the Emperor said, 'I imagine you're thinking to play along. Spin it out. Delay the inevitable, until you get your chance.'

Sten did not answer.

'If these thoughts amuse you,' the Emperor said, 'then, please . . . go ahead. Be my guest. Meanwhile . . . aren't you going to compliment me on my digs?' He gestured with his free hand, indicating the white ship . . . everything. 'After all, I put a lot of thought and years into it.'

'It's real nice,' Sten said, dry. 'Too bad about the meteorite.'

The Emperor frowned. 'A one-in-a-trillion happenstance,' he said. 'I'll soon get it fixed.' There was a harsh edge to his voice. Indicating a vulnerability.

'Is that what fouled things up?' Sten prodded.

'Not really,' the Emperor said. 'There have been some difficulties, to be sure. But, on the whole, I think there's been an improvement.'

'You're a lot happier with yourself, now?' Sten guessed.

'Yes. Yes, I am. Certain . . . weaknesses . . . have been shed.'

'Like the bomb in your gut?' Sten hurled another missile.

The Emperor reacted, startled. Then he laughed. 'So, you're on to that as well?'

'It wasn't that difficult,' Sten said. 'You can thank Kilgour again.' He fixed the Emperor with a hard look. 'Just like it wasn't hard to figure out the rest. Of course, Mahoney gave us a big leg up. Ian had just about everything figured.'

'I miss him,' the Emperor said, voice very low.

'I'll bet you miss a lot of people,' Sten said sarcastically.

The Emperor surprised Sten. 'Yes,' he said. 'Yes, I do. Mahoney, especially. He was my friend.' He gave Sten an odd look. 'And once . . . I thought you were, as well.'

Sten barked laughter. 'Is that how you tote up your friends?' he scoffed. 'Put them on a death list and then number them from one to finish?'

The Emperor sighed. 'It's harder being me than you think,' he said. 'The rules are different.'

'Yeah, I know,' Sten said. 'The Big Picture. The Long View. The funny thing is, where you were concerned, I used to believe that stuff. Or at least didn't question it.'

'There really is no other way to run things,' the Emperor said. 'I've done this for the good of all. There's been suffering. True. But life is suffering. Mostly, if you average it all out over a few thousand years, there's been a great many more good times than bad.'

He reached for his Scotch, took a drink, and set the glass down again. 'You should have seen what it was like before I . . . got started.'

'Before you found the AM2?' Sten asked.

'Yes. Before then. You should have seen the inbred braindead clots who ran things. Hell, if it wasn't for me, civilization would still consist of a few stars and planetary systems.'

'I'll take your word for it,' Sten said.

The Emperor stopped, staring at him. 'You think I'm crazy, don't you? Go ahead. I won't be offended.'

Sten answered, not caring whether he was offended or not. 'I don't think – I *know* it!'

'Perhaps I was . . . once,' the Emperor said. 'But, no more. Not since that meteor blessed this ship. As soon as I was . . . aware . . . I knew something was . . . different. Much different! And vastly superior.'

'Superior to the *old* model?' Sten guessed, remembering the room with the biological vats and surgical equipment.

'I suppose you could put it that way,' the Emperor said. 'The chain was broken. It was time to begin anew. With fresh ideas. To build a new order. Of course, there are sacrifices to be made. Nothing good ever comes without sacrifice.'

'As long as it's not your own,' Sten said.

'Do you really think that? Do you really think . . . I don't suffer as well?'

'The guy pulling the trigger,' Sten said, indicating the gun, 'never suffers as much as the person on the receiving end.'

'You're too cynical.' The Emperor laughed. 'You were around me too long. But facts are facts. My . . . predecessor . . . had let things go into the drakh-house.

'Letting the Tahn get out of hand, for a start. And the privy council! How the clot did . . . he . . . allow those fools so much power? It was weakness, I tell you.

'The Empire was allowed to get too fat. Too sloppy. It was time to pare things to the bone. Put things back on the right footing. An Empire is no different than any business. The rules of capitalism require a periodic shakeout.'

'Business leaders don't usually declare themselves God,' Sten said.

The Emperor snorted. 'Don't be stupid,' he said. 'The image was getting rusty. It wanted brightening up. Besides, there's a long tradition in rule by divine right.'

'Then, you don't actually believe you are a god?'

The Emperor shrugged. 'Maybe I do. Maybe I don't. However, last time I checked, immortality fits the definition.'

'Gods don't climb out of vats,' Sten said.

'Oh, really? Perhaps I was misinformed. But, since you've obviously met so many gods, I bow to your wide experience.'

The Emperor took another drink, then replaced the glass on the tray. 'You won't live to see it,' he said, 'but I do promise you things *will* be better. You can take comfort in that.'

'Better than what?' Sten growled. 'You're just a new wrinkle on an old, ugly face. I've led too many kids to their graves for that face. Hell, I've *filled* whole fields of graves, myself. For what? Twenty or thirty centuries of lies?

'You like to think of yourself as unique. The greatest Emperor of the greatest Empire in all history. Well, from where I stand – poor mortal that I am, with only a few years to spend – you're no better . . . or worse than any other tyrant.'

'This is a very stimulating conversation,' the Eternal Emperor said. 'It's been a long time since I've had such an enjoyable exchange. I wish there were some other way. I really do.'

He raised the pistol. Sten's mind shrilled alarms. Wait! What about the brainscan? There was supposed to be more time.

'I've decided,' the Emperor said, 'that it would be too risky for me to move you from this room. So, to be absolutely safe, I'll have to make one of those sacrifices I was mentioning . . . by killing you now.'

His trigger finger tightened.

At that moment a voice blared out, 'The two organisms aboard this ship are ordered to stand in place.'

Sten gaped. What the clot was going on? He saw the Emperor's face. Bewildered . . . and frightened. But the gun remained steady.

'An analysis of the intentions and makeup of these organisms is now complete,' the voice continued. It had to be the ship's command center talking.

The Emperor's judgment machine.

'The Prime Organism's directive to permit the intruder organism's presence has been found in error and has been overridden. The alien organism is an enemy. And shall be killed.'

Big clottin' deal, Sten thought, a little wild. Dead by the gun. Or dead by the ship. What's the difference?

'The Prime Organism has also been found wanting,' the ship's voice said. 'It has been declared flawed. And it, too, shall be killed.'

Sten saw the Emperor jump in even greater surprise. The gun drooped.

It was Sten's first and only break.
He dove for the Emperor.

Chapter Forty

Sten tucked in middive, shoulder scraping the deck, sending him
in a backflip to one side as the Emperor fired and the AM2 round
blew a jagged hole in the deck and metal shrapneled. Feet first,
he slammed into the Eternal Emperor and sent him tumbling.
The Emperor took the fall, pistol aiming. Sten scissor-kicked and
the gun spun away. The Emperor double-rolled and was on his
feet, wrists instinctively up in a V-block as Sten's knife came out
of his arm and slashed. The block caught Sten's knife-hand and
he lost balance, recovering his stance by dropping into a momentary crouch.

Sten lunged . . . and the Emperor threw himself back, across
the tabletop, whirling, and was on his feet.

Feint . . . bob . . .

The Emperor doublefist-smashed the table and the plas shattered. Sten's knife flicked out . . . and first blood ran down the
Emperor's forearm.

The Emperor backed away, hand scooping up a razor fragment
of the tabletop, nearly forty centimeters long. He held it low,
close to his right side. Sten chanced a look away from the
Emperor's eyes. Noted the Emperor held the shard in the relaxed
thumb-forefinger fencing grip of a trained knife-fighter.

Ship hum. Feet shuffle as each of them moved, circling toward
his opponent's offside.

Sten realized he was being maneuvered . . . and caught the
Emperor's goal. The pistol. The Emperor sliced at Sten, and Sten
back-leaned . . . away from the cut . . . chanced a riposte of his
own, missed, recovered.

The Emperor's eyes flickered, giving away his next strike, and Sten's arm wasn't where it'd been a moment earlier. Too long, Sten thought. You haven't been in a real brawl in too long.

But neither have you, Sten.

Sten chanced a bravo's flip, tossing his blade from right to left hand – and the Emperor attacked. Sten damned near lost the knife, reeled back, cursing himself for even thinking of a grandstand play. Again he slashed at the Emperor's wrist, recovered, slashed, blade slicing off a long curl of the plas, and Sten's hand flashed to the deck, came up with the pistol, and the Emperor underhand-cast the plas, and it cut into Sten's shoulder, muscle spasm on the trigger, round going somewhere, missing, pistol flipping out of his hand from recoil and . . .

Darkness.

The voice was calm. 'I have determined that the intruding organism is more dangerous to my assigned duties than the aberrant one that was created. His termination will be given priority.'

Jesus. It hurt. Sten put his knife between his teeth, clenched on the machined crystal, and pulled the long shard from his shoulder. Waves of pain. Put the plas down. Wipe blood from your fingers. Feel the wound. Bleeding? Some. Badly? Not to worry about. For a while. Pain?

Sten mumbled the mantra he had been conditioned with years before, back when he had been a Guards trainee, and his body forgot the pain. He went prone on the deck. Slowly let his fingers move across the deck, looking for that pistol. It could not be far.

Across the chamber, a clatter.

Laser aircrackle *blast* as the round hit somewhere. High, and left.

Sten's fingers touched something.

The pistol butt.

Clot. So the Emperor had a backup gun.

'Stand by,' the voice announced. 'I have the intruding organism located. Prepare to fire.'

Twin lights flashed on, glareblind, and Sten shot twice, explosion, dying into darkness, the Emperor shooting a little late, the bullet smashing down where Sten had been a few seconds earlier.

All right, you bastard, Sten thought, and, concentrating on where those lights had been, sent five rounds rapid into the general area, rolling and spinning as he fired.

If the Emperor shot back, Sten didn't know it, as thunder rocked the room and alarms screamed. Sten thought he heard a shout. The strange voice that had to be the ship itself? The Emperor? He didn't know. Smoke boiled, fire flashed, lights strobed. A panel was sliding closed; Sten snapped a shot through it, buckling the door.

Sten started after the Emperor, trying to stop him before he got to whatever nasty surprise he was heading for in this, his ship. Stopped, damned himself for a fool, and headed for his spacesuit. He tugged it on, but left helmet and gauntlets clipped to the belt. Before he sealed the suit's chest opening he touched his medkit to his arm, and the box clicked, clicked, feeding painkillers and disinfectants into the wound. He sprayed a dressing across it, then buttoned up.

Take your time, he thought. Better to let him get a bit of a lead rather than stumble into something.

'Ship,' he panted, feeling very much a damned fool.

The voice did not respond.

Sten blew two more rounds into the biggest wallcrater. More alarms, and the flicker of flames, and the hiss of extinguishers.

'Ship! I will not harm you,' Sten lied. 'You can continue your mission.'

Toneless: 'Does not compute. Organisms other than the created organism are hostile and to be destroyed. Basic program applies.'

Okay, try to kill me then, Sten thought. If you can.

He went to the buckled doorpanel and started to kick it open. Stopped, cursing himself for still not having his head on correct, picked up a chair and hurled it through the plas. Gunslam, and an AM2 round blew the panel away. Remember, that could have been you.

He sent a doubletap down the corridor for confusion's sake and went through. He was about to go after the Emperor when a thought struck him.

He aimed back into the ruined compartment and blew five carefully aimed shells into the deepening hole in the wall. He flashed metal peel/girder strips/smoke boiling into another chamber and then the smoke and fire closed in as a new alarm *DEE*daw*DEE*daw*DEE*dawed . . .

This one he knew. This one was standard – *Ship holed/ Atmosphere being lost.*

His ears popped as the ship lost air. Sten scrabbled for his helmet. He had it on and was ready to slam the faceplate when pressure returned to normal. The ship was self-repairing. Having given the ship something to busy itself with, Sten ran down the corridor after the Emperor.

He understood none of the rooms he searched, any more than he had the first time through. Some were tiny, yet packed with consoles and equipment. Others were huge and completely bare.

It was in the first of those that the ship tried to kill him, as the McLean generator went off, and Sten floated up toward the ceiling, and then gravity slammed back on, but you didn't wait enough to let the fall kill me, as Sten dropped back, landing cat-quick on his feet. He put two rounds, out of spite, straight down, into the deck. One worry he did not have was ammo – the ammo tube contained five hundred of the 1mm-diameter AM2 rounds in their Imperium X shield.

The blast tincanned the decking, and Sten looked down, into another level. He quickly ran a three-D prog in his head. The Emperor would probably be farther along this deck I'm on, so if I can get down there and circle up behind . . .

Sten dropped through the hole.

'The intruding organism is now on Golf Deck,' the voice narked. 'Proceeding toward medical station.'

Clot. He looked around, to see if he could spot a telltale eye to shoot out. Nothing.

Okay. Bad idea. He would just as soon be back where he had come from. Idea. He stepped into the middle of the passage, the rent in the decking just above him, and the ship took its lead and spun the gravity yet again, sending Sten falling 'up' toward the hole he had come down through. But as he fell he thumbed a bester grenade out. Heard it *tink* against the passageway's upper deck. He fell through the hole toward the overhead deck now twenty meters above/below him, locking a bootheel under a curl of debris, and gravity went back to normal as the grenade went off.

Sten waited – but the voice said nothing about his return. Did the time-loss grenades operate against it? Improbable.

Now what? The Emperor could be anywhere in this great polygon of a ship/station. He would have a spacecraft decked somewhere – probably in the same place that ships would be parked for the Emperor to use to begin his return journey.

This is his turf, not yours. Exactly. And it is his to defend.

Therefore:

Return to your first plan. Except you don't just want to turn off the AM2 now.

The control room is . . . Sten reoriented himself . . . one deck up. And back a short distance. We'll do it the easy way. Don't worry about the ship – just don't let it get you into wide open spaces, and it can play up with down all day long. If that's the worst it can manage, it wasn't that great a danger. Sten wondered why it hadn't been built with some sort of robot gun-cars or something – and then he realized the ship would have to be suicidal to allow shooting in its own 'body.' But he still worried – this last bastion wasn't well defended at all.

A few seconds later, the ship made its first real attack.

The corridor was long. Closed hatches led off to unknown compartments at periodic intervals. Somewhere down near its end, Sten thought he would find a stairwell leading up to the control deck. He heard a sound, like a hundred locks banging closed. Then he saw the far wall of the corridor was coming toward him. As was the near one, he saw, glancing behind him. We'll just divert through this hatch . . . which is bolted. As were the next two he tried. Sten knelt, held a two-handed firing stance, and sent four rounds slamming into the four corners of the oncoming wall.

Blast, smoke, fire . . . but nothing else. The 'piston' kept closing in the cylinder.

Imperium X. Used as armor-plating. Why not? If you had enough of it . . .

The moving walls, he guessed, weren't a livie nightmare impossibility – they were most likely intended to help the ship repair itself. Close off an injured section, and send in repair robots.

So the ship was improvising and learning how to modify its resources into weapons.

Sten shot a door panel apart, as the moving walls were only a few meters away, and darted into the compartment. It was bare. Outside, in the corridor, the two walls stopped on either side of the doorway.

Stalemate. The ship would likely let Sten sit here for the rest of his life. The air was thick, he noticed. The ship must've shut off the corridor's air circulation. He could close his suit's faceplate, which would give him another, what, six E-hours before he ran out of air?

Fine. So get out as you got in. He went to the doorway, made himself into a smallish target for ricochets, and fired once at the far wall.

A smashing explosion, and shards of metalloid sang around the room. A crater. Not a hole. And the blast had eaten even more of the oxygen. Sten coughed in the smoke. How long would it take him to shoot through the wall, even if he buttoned up the suit? Unknown, but certainly longer than it would take pieces of shrapnel to finish him.

Could he use his knife to cut his way through? Possibly, given enough time, and enough leverage. Not probable.

Up there. A vent duct.

Too small.

But as he thought it, his knife was in his hand, slicing the grille away.

The duct was tiny. Sten would never fit. He looked into it – his forehead touching the top, his chin the bottom. Not only was it not much more than a forearm wide, but it turned through 90 degrees about an equal distance in.

Sten's palms were sweat-drenched.

He told his mind to shut up, and stripped naked. He kept the pistol ready. Hell, you can always shoot yourself.

Head turned to the side, he forced himself into the vent. One shoulder cocked forward, palms finding a hold on the smooth metal, pulling, pulling, legs flailing in the room behind him. He pulled himself three centimeters forward. Then another three. And another.

Then he stuck.

His chest and mind swelled in panic. Stop that, he told himself. You can't be stuck. You can always go back in the room and start over. You can always crawl out of anything you can crawl into.

That was a physiological lie.

Don't flail. Don't hyperventilate. Exhale. Wriggle. Exhale again. The lungs are empty. Goddamn it, no they aren't! Lose here and the Emperor wins . . . *clot* the Emperor, and with a great squirm he was in the vent, around the bend, and writhing, writhing down the tight passage not thinking, just moving, pushing his clothes and suit ahead of him, and then it opened down into a wider duct, and he could bring up a knee, and lift his head, and then it widened again, and again, and he was up, feet and hands sending him forward, bearwalking, and hell, now he could move upright, standing, this was just like the ducts you used as a private throughway back on Vulcan, when you were a Delinq and it wasn't so bad back there, was it? You've been through tighter squeezes, you lying clot, and isn't this about right? You *do* want the control room, don't you?

Sten unconfused his mental map. And agreed. He found a grille with an empty room on the other side, cut the grille away, and dropped inside.

A messroom. Tables. Cooking gear over there.

Then he heard it.

It sounded like a voice.

Sten quickly dressed, and moved silently toward the voice.

It was the Eternal Emperor.

He stood in the center of a large, bare compartment. Just in front of him was a shallow pool, now dry. There was a bare stand beside it.

The far wall was a monster screen, sensesmashing with the colors/not colors of N-space.

His back was to Sten. His arms hung empty.

Who had he been talking to? Himself? The ship?

Sten lifted his pistol, then hesitated. It was not any misguided sense of fair play – he'd shot many an enemy from behind without warning in his life.

But . . .

'In my end,' the Emperor said, 'is my beginning.'

Sten jolted. The Emperor laughed, but did not turn.

'Of course, would there even be another beginning is the question?' the Emperor said, in a near monotone. 'Or would the next refute beelzy, and return to that long line of milksops it took to breed me?

'And even if the ship bred true again, what would the path be? Would he . . . would my . . . perhaps you might call him my son . . . find his way, alone, back? Would he be able to cut out the telltale inside as I did, without it detonating?

'But,' and the Emperor's voice slowed, 'it's a question that'll never be answered, will it?

'Either way' – and as he spoke, he whirled, dropping into a gunfighter's crouch, Sten realizing here was the trap, the Emperor's right hand flashing for his belt, gun coming up, reflexpoint aim . . .

Sten fired, and the projection flickered, holograph flashing off, and then the real Emperor came around the corner, close, too

close, real pistol about to fire, Sten's foot up, leg blocking, the
Emperor's arm thudding against the bulkhead, painshout and
somehow his own pistol was gone, knife coming out of armsheath,
into hand, and it was very slow:

Sten's right foot slid forward, just clear of the ground. It found
a firm stance, half a meter in front of his left, as that foot precisely
turned toe outward, and slid backward on its instep.

His knife-hand came up and forward, just as Sten's left hand
caught his right, just at the wrist, clamped for a brace, as his hips
swiveled, shock-impact and he full-stretch lunged, needlepoint
attack lancing out, going home.

His knife buried itself in the Eternal Emperor's throat.
Mouthgape. Bloodgush.

Sten recovered as the Emperor stumbled backward, backward,
then fell, fell through all time and space, and his body struck the
deck with the limp thud of a corpse.

Sten took two steps forward.

The Emperor's face held a look of vast bewilderment.

It softened, toward blankness.

And then the mouth that had ordered too many deaths twisted.
Deathrictus – but Sten thought it to be a smile. The eyes that
had seen too many years and too much evil saw nothing, looking
straight up at the chamber's overhead.

Or perhaps they saw everything.

Time ran free again, and Sten was moving, diving for his pistol,
and in a crouch. He was firing, firing like a madman. Into that
empty pool, into that wallscreen, and, in now-realized carefully
spaced shots, around the room.

An end . . .

. . . there would never be another beginning for the
Emperor.

Fire gouted from the walls, and multicolored smokes whirled.

The ship screamed.

Emergency alarms . . . distorted metal . . . self-destructing
cybernetics and electronics . . .

Perhaps.

But the ship screamed.

And Sten ran for the control room.

Sten swung the targeting indicators across the bulk of the ship.
One here . . . two here . . . three here . . . four here . . . five here
. . . six here . . . seven targeted here.

One reserve.

Fire when . . .

. . . the first charge blew, the screen told him, the demo pack in the control room that Sten had set for a fifteen-E-minute delay as he fled toward the meteor hole and his ship.

One blast, and the robot mining ships brainlessly processing AM2 somewhere in the distance would be stopping. But they could be reprogrammed and recontrolled, if anyone wished. Later.

Sten slammed fingers down onto firing keys, a dissonant chord of hellfire.

Seven nuclear-headed Goblin XII missiles spat from the tacship's launch tubes, and, ignoring the jumble of N-space input their sensors shouted to them, homed as ordered on the Emperor's birth/death ship.

Sten's ship was too close when they impacted.

All his screens blanked, went to secondary, blanked again, and then, probably because they were jury-rigged to give computer enhancements of N-space, stayed dead for long seconds.

Finally, one imaging radar came to life, and adjusted its input to the enhancement program.

Colors/not colors.

Nothing else.

It was as if the great decahedron had never existed.

The Eternal Emperor was gone.

Sten stared for a long, long time at that emptiness, perhaps wishing many things had never been, perhaps making sure the void would not take form.

Finally, he turned to his controls.

He fed in his return course, and went at full drive, for the discontinuity.

And home.

It was over.

Chapter Forty-One

Four screens yammered highest priority – immediate attention. Three others flashed with CRITICAL – PERSONAL messages for Sten, using his private access code that supposedly only Cind, Alex, and Sr Ecu had ever been given.

All of them – and other coms outside Sten's suite in Otho's castle – wanted one thing, in various categories: Sten. Sten's appearance, Sten's advice, Sten's prognostications, Sten's orders, Sten's suggestions, Sten's emissaries.

'Doesn't anybody want to do anything for themselves?' Sten wondered. 'I mean, the Emperor is dead. Go for it, people.'

'Th' Zaginows're feelin' frisky,' Alex said. 'Ah hae logged a un'lateral declaration ae independence an' non-alliance frae th' lads. T' be present'd ae th' Imperial Parl'ment, if i' e'er sits again. Th' copy thae sen' you, f'r inf'rmation on'y, has a wee pers'nal note. Sayin' thanks, an' i' y' e'er hap by their part ae' th' universe, *i' an un'fficial capac'ty*, their emph'sis nae mine, drop by f'r a dram.'

'It's like an infected tusk,' Otho said. 'It hurts, and it hurts, and then it falls out. And your tongue keeps seeking the gap, wondering where the tusk went, and maybe even missing it a trace.'

There were only two other beings in the chamber – Cind and Rykor.

But there should have been more:

The dead: Mahoney. Sr Ecu. Others, stretching back into the dimness of Sten's memory, soldiers, civilians, even bandits and criminals, who had died for the mask of freedom that they never knew concealed the skullface of tyranny.

The living: Haines. Her husband. Marr. Senn. Ida. Jemedar Mankajiri Gurung and the other Gurkhas. A woman, long ago, named Bet.

And just as there had been invisible beings with Sten before he entered the discontinuity, all these were now in this chamber.

Waiting.

'Cind,' Sten wondered. 'What will the Bhor do?'

'I will no longer be speaking for them,' Cind said. 'I'll be traveling. With a friend.' She smiled at Sten, a promising smile.

'The Bhor will accept my retirement. Even if I have to grow a beard to cut.'

She nodded across the room. 'I rather imagine Otho will be the speaker once more, even if he has to be drafted.'

Otho growled. 'Perhaps. But only for the moment. I have seen as much of the slow dry death of politics as any being could wish for his worst enemy.

'Perhaps I shall outfit a ship, as I did when young. There will be great chances for a trader now, with freedom instead of Empire.

'Perhaps I shall go looking for those strange human friends of yours. The Rom, I believe they called themselves? You know that none of them remain on Vi? They departed before your return from that other place . . . leaving no word as to their intent.'

Sten was silent, surprised. Ida, gone? Evidently without even a farewell. She didn't even stick around to see that the good guys won. He remembered words of hers, said over her shoulder: 'Freedom cannot be served by making laws and fences . . .'

Otho got up. 'Or perhaps I shall take up sewing,' he said. 'But enough of this, by Kholeric. I am thirsty and hungry, and a bit angry. I shall butcher out your incompetent staff, Sr Sten, and inform them when you wish privacy, there are no alternative choices.'

Otho banged out, and a few seconds later, Sten heard loud growls. All of the screens blanked.

But in his mind he still saw their pleas.

He was suddenly, irrationally, angry.

'What the hell,' he near-snarled, 'do they want? Me to declare myself the new Eternal Emperor? What, the tyrant is dead, now put your necks down for the iron boot again?'

'Some of them wish exactly that,' Cind said softly. 'Muscles get lazy when they aren't worked. And it's always easier to let somebody else make the decisions, isn't it?

'I know. All that my forebears had to do was obey

– absolutely – the Jannissar general. He would tell them when
to eat, when to sleep, who to kill, and when to die. If they
obeyed – absolutely – they were rewarded, and had a place
after death guaranteed.

'Right,' she said. 'That was all.'

'Both a y' appear a wee bit hard ae our allies,' Alex said, his
face carefully composed. 'Thae'll hae t' be somebody ae th' top,
aye? T' oversee th' changes an' th' transition. There cannae be
an empty throne, e'en i' thae's but a caretaker gov'mint. Can
there?

'F'r beginnin's, who's t' divvy th' AM2?'

Again, Anti-Matter Two, hell and heaven, riches and death.

There was a splash from Rykor's tank. She was watching Sten,
her great compassionate eyes wide. But she said nothing of the
common secret they held.

'A caretaker,' Sten mused, his anger gone. 'What? You think I
should soldier on? At least until somebody figures out who should
run things? Maybe until we put together some kind of coalition
like Ecu would have overseen?'

'To most beings,' Cind said, 'that'd be the most comfortable.
The hero slays the dragon . . . and helps the people begin their
lives anew.'

'Just like in the livies,' Sten said cynically.

Cind shrugged. 'Why do you think they're so popular?'

'How does that play, Rykor?' Sten asked.

Rykor considered, whiskers fluffing. 'Logical. Psychologically
welcome, as Cind said. Certainly you have the experience
for it. How many times did your ambassadorial duties in fact
mean you were the entire government in a cluster? I know you
hardly bothered getting the Emperor's approval for every
decision.'

No, Sten thought. He hadn't. And he had run things with, he
thought pridefully, a certain measure of success, assuming
clotheads hadn't gotten in the way, clotheads who just didn't
understand what was supposed to happen, and that their best
interests would be eventually served.

Christ. With no one second-guessing his decisions after the
fact from afar. Not a section commander. Not a general. Not
even an Eternal Emperor.

Not anyone.

A chance to correct a lot of those wrongs he'd seen across the
years, wrongs too big or too distant to confront. And there would

be the time – Sten could easily train a diplomatic equivalent of a general staff that would be able to carry out Sten's policies.

All those dictators some mythical thing called Policy or Expediency said should be supported. All those crimes that Pragmatism told him to ignore. All the beings who stole and murdered from their lessers, beings that Sten had never had the opportunity to confront and destroy.

Call it caretaking.

If you wished.

Now, that would not be a bad way to *really* serve the universe, would it? Especially after all those decades of blood and slaughter.

It would also be an example for those who came later, that someone could rule for a while, and then, when his charges reached maturity, step aside. Pass the reins along.

'Say I agreed,' Sten said. 'Sorry, that's the wrong way to put it. Say that when the smoke cleared that a lot of worlds wanted me to act as some kind of, what? "Regent" isn't the proper word. "Manager"? I guess that'd be it.'

'There would be few if any systems that would object,' Rykor said firmly.

'Right. Now. If I did this, agreed to serve for a few more years, until the time was right and everybody realized that they had to rule themselves . . . would you stay with me?'

Rykor wallowed in the tank without answering. Then: 'You would be welcome to my advice, such as it is, for as long as I am able to offer it.'

Sten noted her answer.

'Alex?'

The tubby man looked at him for a very long moment.

'Y' hae m' word, boss,' he said finally. 'Ah'll sign on agin, ae y'r strong right bower. But thae'll be a time whae Ah'll be retirin't, Ah'll hae t' warn you.'

Twice.

'Cind?'

'I'll stay,' she said, without a hesitation. 'As long as you're caretaker. As long as you're Sten.'

Three times.

There it was.

Sten saw, once more, the smile on the Emperor's corpse, and icy fingers moved down his spine as he wondered if this moment explained the Gioconda smile.

'I just wonder,' Sten said, 'if anybody ever knows when that time is? Or,' he said, being as honest as he knew how, 'if every time somebody gets offered a crown, he always thinks that he's taking it just for universal good?'

The chamber was silent, very silent, as silent as the icy, frozen night outside.

'Ah dinnae knoo aboot thae,' Alex said, finally. 'Thae's Phliposophy, an' thae's noo Scots sol'jer permitted t' think ae that, 'r thae toss him oot ae th' pub an' make him' drink piss wi' th' Brits.

'But Ah hae a wee tale. Call i' a par'ble, i' y' wish.

'Thae wae a mon. Always wanted t' prove himself, aye? An' he hears thae' th' mos' fearsome sort ae huntin' i' on Earth. Ae a wee island, i' a north' ae froze ae Vi.

'Huntin' th' bear. Cind, thae's a—'

'I know what a bear is. You've called Otho one enough times. GA,' she said.

'A'right. So, he goes oot i' th' forest, wi' a rifle, an' a sharp eye. An' sooner come later, he spots th' bear. Binga-banga-bonga he shoots, an' th' bear goes't doon.

'An' he bounds o'er, an' to his vast sur'prise an' dismay, thae's noo bear.

'Tap tap on th' shoulder, an' thae's th' bear! An' th' bear growls, an' says, "I' y' wan' t' live, y'll be giein' doon ae y'r han's an' knees an' committin' a disgustin' sexual act ae m' bod'.

'An' th' hunter goes eech an' ech an' och, but th' bear's fangs are braw, an' his claws are great. An' he goes doon ae his knees . . .

'Noo, when he gies back t' his camp, he's fill't wi' disgust. Wi' loathin'. He's aboot t' suicide. But first, he thinks, Ah'll hae th' skin ae thae bear!

'An' next mornin, he goes oot t' th' forest agin, an' pret' quick, he spots th' bear. An' its bompa-bompa-bompa, an' agin' th' bear goes doon.

'An' th' hunter goes clip-cloppin' t' th' site, knowin' he hae th' revenge . . . but thae's no bear.

'Tap tap on th' shoulder . . . an' thae's th' bear! Loomin't o'er him!

'An' th' bear says, "I' y' be wantin' y'r life, y'll be disrobin't, an' turnin't aroun', an' Ah'll be performin't a revoltin' sexual act wi' y'!'

'An' yeesh an' bleah an' yargh, but th' bear's claws are braw, an' his teeth are great. An' so th' hunter drops hi' trews . . .

'Thae's it. Thae's all. Th' hunter slink't back t' camp. He feels worsen' a Campbell. H's th' lowest ae th' low. Killin' himself i' th' best fate he c'd dream of.

'But firs' . . . th' bear mus' die! Wi' oot fail, wi'oot question.

'An' so, th' next morn, just ae dawn, th' hunter's oot i' the woods. An' *agin* he sees th' bear. An' again he raises his rifle. An *agin* i's blastawayblastawayblastaway all. An' agin' th' bear goes doon.

'An' agin' th' hunter rushes oop.

'An' agin', thae's noo clottin' bear!

'But agin, thae's a tap tap on th' shoulder.

'An', knowin't whae he's aboot t' see, th' hunter turns aroun'. An' thae's th' bear!

'An' th' bear eyes him, an' says, "Lad, y' dinnae coom f'r th' huntin' noo did y'?"'

Sten stared at Kilgour, who, after a space, smiled a gently benevolent smile.

'Right,' Sten said.

He turned around.

'Rykor. From the abstract of my brainscan, could you help some engineers put together a synth on Project Bravo? A how-to-do-it on AM2?'

'I could.'

'That's my first request. We'll bring in some hotshot – maybe that woman reporter, Ranett, who used to give the Emperor the kolrobbies – and let her disseminate the information.

'I want that to go out on every livie, vid, and broadsheet possible.

'Second. Ask Otho to get the voyage tapes from my tacship. That should give a fair triangulation to the discontinuity and the Emperor's treasure.

'Put that out, too. Let anyone who wants AM2 know where to find it.'

Rykor thrashed in her tank.

'Intellectually, I approve,' she said. 'And personally, caring for a single being named Sten, this is good. But considering its effect on the masses—'

'I can't think for them,' Sten said. 'I can barely take care of myself.

'All I can do is say . . . Here. Here's the AM2. Here's the keys to the kingdom. Every being can make himself a king, or a bloody despot. Let them make the universe as they like it. A paradise or a desert.

'That's not for me. I'm not going to play God. Not now. Not ever.'

Sten thought he heard a murmur from all those beings, dead and alive, who had been in the chamber. Of agreement? Disappointment?

But they were gone. Gone forever.

Sten looked back at Alex.

'Do you think anybody'll grudge me the *Victory*?'

'Ah dinnae think so, lad. An' thae'll be clots like Otho'll be glad t' serve. Y'll hae t' beat 'em awa' wi' a blackthorn.'

'Good. Now. I'll ask you again. About staying with me.'

'Ah'll hae need ae a few weeks, boss. T' intr'duce twa lassies t' m' mum. An' t' hae th' banns posted, assumin't Ah'll be able t' coerce a wee pulpitbanger. C'n Ah hae a' month?'

Sten nodded.

Alex beamed. He went to the door where Rykor waited.

'Ah, lad. It'll be braw. It'll be braw. Thae's entire *galaxies* thae dinnae ken aboot spotted snakes.'

And he and Rykor were gone.

'You left me for last,' Cind said.

'I did.'

'Are you going to ask?'

'Surely. You got any conflicting plans for the next couple of centuries?'

Cind didn't answer.

She kissed him.

Then she took him by the hand . . . and they walked across the chamber to the door to the balcony. She opened it and they went out, into the clear, frost-chiming night.

Neither of them felt the cold.

They looked up and out, far and beyond, at the unknown stars that stretched on forever.

An Explanation of Sorts

The idea for Sten came to us a few years back. It was encouraged by the fact that, at the time, very few people were writing the kind of science fiction we grew up reading and appreciating – a situation that's changed for the better of late, we're delighted to observe.

But the main reason was out of general pissoff.

Science fiction, for some unknown reason, has always been overly enamored of social and political fascism, primarily because of ignorance, we suspect.

Our irk was best expressed by Damon Knight, in his classic collection of essays, *In Search Of Wonder*, when he was busily ripping the lips off of A.E. van Vogt, Scientologist/confusionaire extraordinary:

'It strikes me as singular that, in van Vogt's stories, nearly all of which deal with the future, the form of government which occurs most often is the absolute monarchy; and further, that the monarchs in these stories are invariably depicted sympathetically, (one of his heroes being) a "benevolent dictator" if you please.

'. . . I shall not say what I think of a man who loves monarchies . . . neither do I think it relevant that these stories were written and published during a time when both van Vogt's country (Canada) and ours were at war with dictatorships . . .'

'. . . The absolute monarchy was a form of government which evolved to meet feudal economic conditions everywhere, and which has died everywhere with feudalism . . . Modern attempts to impose a similar system on higher cultures have just been proven, very decisively, to be failures . . . It is no crime for van

Vogt as a private citizen to wish this were not so; but ignorance, for an author, is a crime . . .'

Just so.

The second quote is far better known:

John Emerich Edward Dalberg, Lord Acton, in a letter to Bishop Mandell Creighton, 1887:

'Power tends to corrupt; absolute power corrupts absolutely.'

Equally true.

And so it was absurd for us that science fiction, in spite of its loud bannering of thinking of the future, in fact spends all too much of its substance sucking the empty husk of a false past.

Therefore . . . *Sten*.

We used all of the hard, cynical knowledge that we'd gained in fourteen years *each* in mainstream journalism of just how politics and raw power works.

We would create an empire, we decided, that would be big enough and old enough to contain all our bizarre notions of that great, dark, comic figure, the Human Race. We would see this empire through the eyes of an ordinary, working-class man who is overtaken by extraordinary events.

He would be just smart enough, swift enough, and – this was most important – have enough of a sense of humor to survive. And grow into a bona fide hero. Or, at least, our idea of a hero – someone with enormous clumps of clay for feet.

It would be a long story, we both agreed. It would take eight books to tell it all. One novel – in eight parts.

We guessed it would take about a million words.

Today we passed that mark.

And the story is done.

About the Authors

Chris Bunch is the author of the Sten series, the Dragonmaster series, the Seer King series and many other acclaimed SF and fantasy novels. A notable journalist and bestselling writer for many years, he died in 2005.

Allan Cole is a bestselling author, screenwriter and former prize-winning newsman. The son of a CIA operative, Cole was raised in the Middle East, Europe and the Far East. He currently lives in Boca Raton, Fl. with his wife, Kathryn. For details see Allan's website at www.acole.com

Find out more about Chris Bunch and Allan Cole and other Orbit authors by registering for the free monthly newsletter at www.orbitbooks.net